Silhouette® is proud to present three marvellous
linked novels by award-winning author

LINDA HOWARD

all featuring

The Mackenzie Family

Wolf, Joe and Zane are all dangerous, sexy,
Mackenzie men, who find love in the most
surprising situations!

Separately these books were terrific,
but together they're an irresistible collection.

LINDA HOWARD

Whether she is reading them or writing them, books have long played a profound role in Linda Howard's life. She cut her teeth on Margaret Mitchell and from then on read widely and eagerly, although she's easily bored by murder, mayhem and politics.'

After twenty-one years of penning stories for her own enjoyment, Linda finally worked up the courage to submit a novel for publication—and met with success! To date she has more than ten million books in print around the world and has written more than twenty-five titles, some of them *New York Times* bestsellers.

LINDA HOWARD

The Collection

First published as a collection in Great Britain 1999 Silhouette Books, Eton House, 18-24 Paradise Road, Richmond, Surrey TW9 1SR

Linda Howard: The Collection © Harlequin Books S.A. 1999

The publisher acknowledges the copyright holder of the individual work as follows:

Mackenzie's Mountain © Linda Howington 1989
Mackenzie's Mission © Linda Howington 1992
Mackenzie's Pleasure © Linda Howington 1996

ISBN 0 373 59693 6

47-9911

Printed and bound in Spain by Litografia Rosés S.A., Barcelona

Contents

Dear Reader,

Ah, the Mackenzies. They're tough, sexy and bigger than life. They'll dare anything and they're willing to fight for what they believe in. When they love, they love forever.

From the time *Mackenzie's Mountain* hit the stands nine years ago (good heavens, has it been that long?) I've felt as if I had a tiger by the tail and there was no way to turn loose. I never intended this to be a continuing series, but in the first book I fell in love with Wolf's son, Joe, and just *had* to write his story, *Mackenzie's Mission*. In that book I fell in love with one of his younger siblings, Zane, so of course I had to write his story, too.

In *Mackenzie's Pleasure*, Zane, a SEAL team commander, is called upon to rescue an ambassador's kidnapped daughter. The rescue doesn't go according to plan; Barrie Lovejoy is much more than he expected, and rescuing her doesn't end the danger. But during their short time together Barrie becomes *his* woman, and Zane is the most dangerous of the Mackenzies, a man who will stop at nothing to protect those he loves.

I hope you enjoy these instalments of the Mackenzies saga. Happy reading!

MACKENZIE'S MOUNTAIN

To the Fayrene Principle,
otherwise known as
the effect of water dripping on stone:
the stone loses.

Chapter 1

He needed a woman. Bad.

Wolf Mackenzie spent a restless night, with the bright full moon throwing its silver light on the empty pillow beside him. His body ached with need, the sexual need of a healthy man, and the passing hours only intensified his frustration. Finally he got out of bed and walked naked to the window, his big body moving with fluid power. The wooden floor was icy beneath his bare feet but he welcomed the discomfort, for it cooled the undirected desire that heated his blood.

The colorless moonlight starkly etched the angles and planes of his face, living testimony to his heritage. Even more than the thick black hair worn long to touch his shoulders, even more than the heavy-lidded black eyes, his face proclaimed him Indian. It was in his high, prominent cheekbones and broad forehead, his thin lips and high-bridged nose. Less obvious, but just as fierce, was the Celtic heritage from his father, only one generation

removed from the Scottish Highlands. It had refined the
Indian features inherited from his mother into a face like
a blade, as clean and sharply cut as it was strong. In his
veins ran the blood of two of the most warlike peoples
in the history of the world, Comanche and Celt. He had
been a natural warrior, a fact soon discovered by the
military when he had enlisted.

He was also a sensualist. He knew his own nature well,
and though he controlled it, there were times when he
needed a woman. He usually visited Julie Oakes at those
times. She was a divorced woman, several years older,
who lived in a small town fifty miles distant. Their ar-
rangement had lasted five years; neither Wolf nor Julie
was interested in marriage, but both had needs, and they
liked each other. Wolf tried not to visit Julie too often,
and he took care that he was never seen entering her
house; he accepted the fact, unemotionally, that her
neighbors would be outraged if they knew she slept with
an Indian. And not just any Indian; a rape charge stuck
to a man forever.

The next day was a Saturday. There would be the normal chores, and he had to pick up a load of fencing
materials in Ruth, the small town just at the base of his
mountain, but Saturday nights were traditionally for
howling. He wouldn't howl, but he'd visit Julie and burn
off his sexual tension in her bed.

The night was turning colder, and low heavy clouds
were moving in. He watched until they obscured the
moon, knowing they meant new snow. He didn't want
to return to his empty bed. His face was impassive, but
his loins ached. He needed a woman.

Mary Elizabeth Potter had numerous small chores to
occupy her time that Saturday morning, but her conscience wouldn't let her rest until she had talked to Joe

Mackenzie. The boy had dropped out of school two months before, a month before she had arrived to take the place of a teacher who had abruptly quit. No one had mentioned the boy to Mary, but she'd run across his school record, and curiosity had led her to read it. In the small town of Ruth, Wyoming, there weren't that many students in school, and she had thought she'd met them all. In fact, there were less than sixty students, but the graduation rate was almost one hundred percent, so any dropout was unusual. When she had read Joe Mackenzie's record, she'd been stunned. The boy had been at the *top* of his class, with straight A's in all subjects. Students who did poorly would get discouraged and drop out, but every teaching instinct she had was outraged that such an outstanding student would just quit. She had to talk to him, try to make him understand how important it was to his future that he continue his education. Sixteen was so young to make a mistake that would haunt him the rest of his life. She wouldn't be able to sleep at night until she had done her best to talk him into returning.

It had snowed again during the night and had turned bitterly cold. The cat meowed plaintively as it wound around her ankles, as if complaining about the weather. "I know, Woodrow," she consoled the animal. "The floor must be cold to your feet." She could sympathize. She didn't think her feet had been warm since she had moved to Wyoming.

Before another winter came, she promised herself, she would own a pair of warm, sturdy boots, fur-lined and waterproof, and she would stomp about in the snow as if she'd been doing it all her life, like a native. Actually she needed the boots now, but the expenses of moving had wiped out her cash reserves, and the teachings of her thrifty aunt prevented her from buying the boots on credit.

Woodrow meowed again as she put on the warmest, most sensible shoes she owned, the ones she privately called her "old maid schoolteacher shoes." Mary paused to scratch behind his ears, and his back arched in ecstasy. She had inherited him with the house, which the school board had arranged for her to live in; the cat, like the house, wasn't much. She had no idea how old Woodrow was, but both he and the house looked a little run-down. Mary had always resisted owning a cat—it seemed the crowning touch to an old maid's life—but finally her fate had caught up with her. She *was* an old maid. Now she owned a cat. And wore old maid shoes. The picture was complete.

"Water seeks its own level," she told the cat, who looked back at her with his unconcerned Egyptian gaze. "But what do you care? It doesn't hurt *you* that my personal water level seems to stop at sensible shoes and cats."

But as she looked in the mirror to make certain her hair was tidy, she sighed. Sensible shoes and cats were just her style, along with being pale, slight and nondescript. "Mousy" was a good word. Mary Elizabeth Potter had been born to be an old maid.

She was dressed as warmly as she could manage, unless she put on socks to wear with her sensible shoes, but she drew the line at that. Dainty white anklets with long ruffled skirts were one thing, but knee socks with a wool dress were something else entirely. She was willing to be dowdy for the sake of warmth; she was not willing to be tacky.

Well, there was no point in putting it off; it wasn't going to get any warmer until spring. Mary braced herself for the shock of cold air on a system that still expected the warmth of Savannah. She had left her tidy little nest in Georgia for the challenge of a tiny school in Wyoming, for the excitement of a different way of life; she even admitted to a small yearning for adventure, though of course she never allowed it to surface. But somehow, she hadn't taken the weather into account. She had been prepared for the snow, but not the bitter temperatures. No wonder there were so few students, she thought as she opened the door and gasped as the wind whipped at her. It was too cold for the adults to undress enough to do anything that might result in children!

She got snow in her sensible shoes when she walked to her car, a sensible two-door, midsize Chevrolet sedan, on which she had sensibly put a new set of snow tires when she had moved to Wyoming. According to the weather report on the radio that morning, the high would be seven degrees below zero. Mary sighed again for the weather she had left behind in Savannah; it was March now, and spring would be in full swing, with flowers blooming in a riot of colors.

But Wyoming was beautiful, in a wild, majestic way. The soaring mountains dwarfed the puny man-made dwellings, and she had been told that, come spring, the meadows would be carpeted in wildflowers, and the crystal-clear creeks would sing their own special song. Wyoming was a different world from Savannah, and she was just a transplanted magnolia who was having trouble getting acclimated.

She had gotten instructions on how to get to the Mackenzie residence, though the information had been reluctantly given. It puzzled her that no one seemed interested in the boy, because the people in the little town had been friendly and helpful to her. The most direct comment she had gotten had been from Mr. Hearst, the grocery-store owner, who had muttered that "the Mackenzies aren't worth your trouble." But Mary considered any child worth her trouble. She was a teacher, and she meant to teach.

As she got into her sensible car, she could see the mountain called Mackenzie's Mountain, as well as the narrow road that wound up its side like a ribbon, and she quailed inside. New snow tires notwithstanding, she wasn't a confident driver in this strange environment. Snow was…well, snow was *alien*, not that she'd let it stop her from doing what she had set her mind on doing.

She was already shivering so hard that she could barely fit the key into the ignition. It was so cold! It actually hurt her nose and lungs to inhale. Perhaps she should wait for better weather before attempting the drive. She looked at the mountain again. Maybe in June all of the snow would have melted…but Joe Mackenzie had already been out of school for two months. Maybe in June the gap would seem insurmountable to him, and he wouldn't make the effort. It might already be too late. She had to try, and she didn't dare let even another week go by.

It was her habit to give herself pep talks whenever she was pushing herself to do something she found difficult, so she muttered under her breath as she began the drive. "It won't seem so steep once I'm actually on the road. All uphill roads look vertical from a distance. It's a perfectly negotiable road, otherwise the Mackenzies wouldn't be able to get up and down, and if they can do it, I can do it." Well, perhaps she could do it. Driving on snow was an acquired skill, one she hadn't as yet mastered.

Determination kept her going. When she finally reached the mountain and the road tilted upward, her hands clenched on the steering wheel as she deliberately refrained from looking over the side at the increasing distance to the valley floor. Knowing how far it was possible for her to fall if she drove off the edge wouldn't help her at all; in Mary's opinion, that would be in the category of useless knowledge, of which she already had quite enough.

"I won't slide," she muttered. "I won't go fast enough to lose control. This is like the Ferris wheel. I was certain I was going to fall out, but I didn't." She had ridden the Ferris wheel once, when she'd been nine years old, and no one had ever been able to talk her into trying it again. Carousels were more her style.

"The Mackenzies won't mind if I talk to Joe," she reassured herself in an attempt to get her mind off the drive. "Maybe he had trouble with a girlfriend, and that's why he doesn't want to go to school. At his age, it's probably all blown over by now."

Actually the drive wasn't as bad as she'd feared. She began to breathe a little easier. The incline was more gradual than it had appeared, and she didn't think she had too much farther to go. The mountain wasn't as enormous as it had looked from the valley.

She was so intent on her driving that she didn't notice the red light appear on the dash. She had no warning of overheating until steam suddenly erupted from beneath the hood, the frigid air instantly converting the mist into ice crystals on the windshield. Mary instinctively hit the brakes, then uttered a discreet oath when the wheels began sliding. Quickly she lifted her foot from the brake pedal, and the tires found traction again, but she couldn't see. Closing her eyes, she prayed that she was still going in the right direction and let the car's weight slow it to a stop.

The engine was hissing and bellowing like a dragon. Shaking in reaction, she turned off the ignition and got out of the car, gasping as the wind lashed her like an icy whip. The hood release mechanism was stiff from the

bitter cold, but finally yielded, and she raised the hood
to see what had happened, on the grounds that it would
be nice to know what was wrong with the car even if
she couldn't fix it. It didn't take a mechanic to see the
problem: one of the water hoses had split, and hot water
was spitting fitfully from the break.

Instantly she recognized the precariousness of her position. She couldn't stay in the car, because she couldn't
let the motor run to keep her warm. The road was a
private one, and the Mackenzies might not leave their
ranch at all that day, or that entire weekend. It was too
far, and too cold, for her to walk back to her own house.
Her only option was to walk to the Mackenzie ranch and
pray it wasn't very far. Her feet were already numb.

She didn't let herself dwell on the thought that she
might not make it to the Mackenzie ranch, either. Instead
she began to walk steadily up the road and tried to ignore
the snow that got inside her shoes with each step.

She rounded a curve and lost sight of her car, but when
she looked ahead there was still no sign of a house, or
even a barn. She felt alone, as if she had been dropped
into the middle of a wilderness. There was only the
mountain and the snow, the vast sky and herself. The
silence was absolute. It hurt to walk, and she found that
she was sliding her feet instead of picking them up. She
had gone fewer than two hundred yards.

Her lips trembled as she hugged herself in an effort to
retain her body's heat. Painful or not, she would just have
to keep walking.

Then she heard the low growl of a powerful engine,
and she stopped, relief welling in her so painfully that
tears burned her eyes. She had a horror of crying in public and blinked them back. There was no sense in crying;
she had been walking less than fifteen minutes and hadn't
been in any real danger at all. It was just her overactive

imagination, as usual. She shuffled through the snow to the side of the road, to get out of the way, and waited for the approaching vehicle.

It came into view, a big black pickup with enormous tires. She could feel the driver's eyes lock on her, and in spite of herself she ducked her head in embarrassment. Old maid schoolteachers weren't accustomed to being the center of attention, and on top of that she felt a perfect fool. It must look as if she had gone for a stroll in the snow.

The truck slowed to a stop opposite her, and a man got out. He was big, and she instinctively disliked that. She disliked the way big men looked down at her, and she disliked being forced by sheer physical size to look up at them. Well, big or not, he was her rescuer. She wound her gloved fingers together and wondered what she should say. How did a person ask to be rescued? She had never hitched a ride before; it didn't seem proper for a settled, respectable schoolteacher.

Wolf stared at the woman, astounded that anyone would be out in the cold while dressed so stupidly. What in hell was she doing on his mountain, anyway? How had she gotten here?

Suddenly he knew who she was; he'd overheard talk in the feed store about the new schoolteacher from someplace down South. He'd never seen anyone who looked more like a schoolteacher than this woman, and she was definitely dressed wrong for a Wyoming winter. Her blue dress and brown coat were so frumpy that she was almost a cliché; he could see wisps of light brown hair straggling out from under her scarf, and oversize horn-rimmed glasses dwarfed her small face. No makeup, not even lip gloss to protect her lips.

And no boots. Snow was caked almost to her knees.

He had surveyed her completely in two seconds and

didn't wait to hear what explanation she had for being
on his mountain, if she intended to say anything at all.
So far she hadn't uttered a word, but continued to stare
at him with a faintly outraged look on her face. He wondered if she considered it beneath her to speak to an
Indian, even to ask for help. Mentally he shrugged. What
the hell, he couldn't leave her out here.

Since she hadn't spoken, he didn't, either. He simply
bent down and passed one arm behind her knees and the
other behind her back, and lifted her as he would a child,
ignoring her gasp. As he carried her to the truck, he reflected that she didn't weigh much more than a child. He
saw a flash of startled blue eyes behind the lenses of her
glasses; then her arm passed around his neck and she
was holding him in a convulsive grip, as if she were
afraid he'd drop her.

He shifted her weight so he could open the passenger
door and deposited her on the seat, then briskly wiped
the snow from her feet and legs as well as he could. He
heard her gasp again, but didn't look up. When he had
finished, he dusted the snow from his gloves and went
around to climb behind the wheel.

"How long have you been walking?" he muttered reluctantly.

Mary started. She hadn't expected his voice to be so
deep that it almost reverberated. Her glasses had fogged
from the truck's heat, and she snatched them off, feeling
her cold cheeks prickle as blood rushed to them. "I…not
long," she stammered. "About fifteen minutes. I blew a
water hose. That is, my car did."

Wolf glanced at her in time to see her hastily lower
her eyes again and noticed her pinkened cheeks. Good,
she was getting warm. She was flustered; he could see it
in the way she kept twisting her fingers together. Did she
think he was going to throw her down on the seat and

rape her? After all, he was a renegade Indian, and capable of anything. Then again, the way she looked, maybe this was the most excitement she'd ever had.

They hadn't been far from the ranch house and reached it in a few minutes. Wolf parked close to the kitchen door and got out; he circled the truck and reached the passenger door just as she opened it and began to slid down. "Forget it," he said, and lifted her again. Her sliding motion had made her skirt ride halfway up her thighs. She hastily pushed the fabric down, but not before his black eyes had examined her slim legs, and the color deepened in her cheeks.

The warmth of the house enfolded her, and she inhaled with relief, hardly noticing as he turned a wooden chair away from the table and placed her on it. Without speaking he turned on the hot water tap and let it run, then filled a dishpan, frequently checking the water and adjusting the temperature.

Well, she had reached her destination, and though she hadn't accomplished her arrival in quite the manner she had intended, she might as well get to the purpose of her visit. "I'm Mary Potter, the new schoolteacher."

"I know," he said briefly.

Her eyes widened as she stared at his broad back. "You know?"

"Not many strangers around."

She realized that he hadn't introduced himself and was suddenly unsure. Was she even at the right place? "Are…are you Mr. Mackenzie?"

He glanced over his shoulder at her, and she noticed that his eyes were as black as night. "I'm Wolf Mackenzie."

She was instantly diverted. "I suppose you know your name is uncommon. It's Old English—"

"No," he said, turning around with the dishpan in his

hands. He placed it on the floor beside her feet. "It's Indian."

She blinked. "Indian?" She felt incredibly stupid. She should have guessed, given the blackness of his hair and eyes, and the bronze of his skin, but she hadn't. Most of the men in Ruth had weathered skin, and she had simply thought him darker than the others. Then she frowned at him and said in a positive tone, "Mackenzie isn't an Indian name."

He frowned back at her. "Scottish."

"Oh. Are you a half-breed?"

She asked the question with the same unconsciousness as if she had been asking directions, silky brows lifted inquiringly over her blue eyes. It set his teeth on edge. "Yeah," he grunted. There was something so irritating about the primness of her expression that he wanted to shock her out of her prissiness. Then he noticed the shivers shaking her body, and he pushed his irritation aside, at least until he could get her warm. The clumsy way she had been walking when he'd first seen her had told him that she was in the first stages of hypothermia. He shrugged out of his heavy coat and tossed it aside, then put on a pot of coffee.

Mary sat silently as he made coffee; he wasn't a very talkative person, though that wasn't going to make her give up. She was truly cold; she would wait until she had a cup of that coffee, then begin again. She looked up at him as he turned back to her, but his expression was unreadable. Without a word he took the scarf from her head and began unbuttoning her coat. Startled, she said, "I can do that," but her fingers were so cold that any movement was agony. He stepped back and let her try for a moment, then brushed her hands aside and finished the job himself.

"Why are you taking my coat off when I'm so cold?"

she asked in bewilderment as he peeled the coat down her arms.

"So I can rub your arms and legs." Then he proceeded to remove her shoes.

The idea was as alien to her as snow. She wasn't accustomed to anyone touching her, and didn't intend to become accustomed. She started to tell him so, but the words vanished unsaid when he abruptly thrust his hands under her skirt, all the way to her waist. Mary gave a startled shriek and jerked back, almost oversetting the chair. He glared at her, his eyes like black ice.

"You don't have to worry," he snapped. "This is Saturday. I only rape on Tuesdays and Thursdays." He thought about throwing her back out into the snow, but he couldn't let a woman freeze to death, not even a white woman who obviously thought his touch would contaminate her.

Mary's eyes grew so wide they eclipsed the rest of her face. "What's wrong with Saturdays?" she blurted, then realized that she had almost issued him an invitation, for pity's sake! She clapped her gloved hands to her face as a tide of red surged to her cheeks. Her brain must have frozen; it was the only possible explanation.

Wolf jerked his head up, not believing she had actually said that. Wide, horrified blue eyes stared at him from over black leather gloves, which covered the rest of her face but couldn't quite hide the hot color. It had been so long since he'd seen anyone blush that it took him a minute to realize she was acutely embarrassed. Why, she was a prude! It was the final cliché to add to the dowdy, old maid schoolteacher image she presented. Amusement softened his irritation. This was probably the highlight of her life. "I'm going to pull your panty hose off so you can put your feet in the water," he explained in a gruff voice.

"Oh." The word was muffled because her hands were still over her mouth.

His arms were still under her skirt, his hands clasped on her hips. Almost unconsciously he felt the narrowness of her, and the softness. Dowdy or not, she still had the softness of a woman, the sweet scent of a woman, and his heartbeat increased as his body began to respond to her nearness. Damn, he needed a woman worse than he'd thought if this frumpy little schoolteacher could turn him on.

Mary sat very still as one powerful arm closed around her and lifted her so he could strip the panty hose down her hips and legs; the position put his head close to her breasts and stomach, and she stared down at his thick, shiny black hair. He had only to turn his head and his mouth would brush against her breasts. She had read in books that a man took a woman's nipples into his mouth and sucked them as a nursing infant would, and she had always wondered why. Now the thought made her feel breathless, and her nipples tingled. His roughly callused hands brushed against her bare legs; how would *they* feel on her breasts? She began to feel oddly warm, and a little dizzy.

Wolf didn't glance at her as he tossed the insubstantial panty hose to the floor. He lifted her feet onto his thigh and slid the dishpan into place, then slowly lowered her feet into the water. He had made certain the water was only warm, but he knew her feet were so cold even that would be painful. She sucked in her breath but didn't protest, though he saw the gleam of tears in her eyes when he looked up at her.

"It won't hurt for long," he murmured reassuringly, moving so that his legs were on each side of hers, clasping them warmly. Then he carefully removed her gloves, struck by the delicacy of her white, cold hands. He held

them between his warm palms for a moment, then made
a decision and unbuttoned his shirt as he crowded closer
to her.

"This will get them warm," he said, and tucked her
hands into the hollows of his armpits.

Mary was dumbstruck. She couldn't believe that her
hands were nestled in his armpits like birds. His warmth
seared her cold fingers. She wasn't actually touching
skin; he wore a T-shirt, but it was still the most intimate
she had ever been with another person. Armpits...well,
everyone had them, but she certainly wasn't accustomed
to touching them. She had never before been this *surrounded* by anyone, least of all a man. His hard legs were
on each side of hers, clasping them; she was bent forward
a little, her hands neatly tucked beneath his arms, while
he briskly rubbed his hands over her arms and shoulders,
then down to her thighs. She made a little sound of surprise; she simply couldn't believe this was happening,
not to Mary Elizabeth Potter, old maid schoolteacher *or-
dinaire*.

Wolf had been concentrating on his task but he looked
up at the sound she made, into her wide blue eyes. They
were an odd blue, he thought, not cornflower or that pure
dark blue. There was just a hint of gray in the shade.
Slate blue, that was it. Distantly he noticed that her hair
was straggling down from the ungodly knot she'd twisted
it into, framing her face in silky, pale brown wisps. She
was very close, her face just inches from his. She had
the most delicate skin he'd ever seen, as fine-grained as
an infant's, so pale and translucent he could see the fragile tracery of blue veins at her temples. Only the very
young should have skin like that. As he watched, another
blush began to stain her cheeks, and unwillingly he felt
himself become entranced by the sight. He wondered if
her skin was that silky and delicate all over—her breasts,

her stomach, her thighs, between her legs. The thought was like an electrical jolt to his system, overloading his nerves. Damn, she smelled sweet! And she would probably jump straight out of that chair if he lifted her skirt the way he wanted to and buried his face against her silky thighs.

Mary licked her lips, oblivious to the way his eyes followed the movement. She had to say something, but she didn't know what. His physical nearness seemed to have paralyzed her thought processes. My goodness, he was warm! And close. She should remember why she had come here in the first place, instead of acting like a ninny because a very good-looking, in a rough sort of way, very masculine person was too close to her. She licked her lips again, cleared her throat, and said, "Ah...I came to speak to Joe, if I may."

His expression changed very little, yet she had the impression that he was instantly aloof. "Joe isn't here. He's doing chores."

"I see. When will he be back?"

"In an hour, maybe two."

She looked at him a little disbelievingly. "Are you Joe's father?"

"Yes."

"His mother is...?"

"Dead."

The flat, solitary word jarred her, yet at the same time she was aware of a faint, shocking sense of relief. She looked away from him again. "How did you feel about Joe quitting school?"

"It was his decision."

"But he's only sixteen! He's just a boy—"

"He's Indian," Wolf interrupted. "He's a man."

Indignation mingled with exasperation to act as a spur. She jerked her hands from his armpits and planted them on her hips. "What does that have to do with anything? He's sixteen years old and he needs to get an education!"

"He can read, write and do math. He also knows everything there is to know about training horses and running a ranch. He chose to quit school and work here fulltime. This is my ranch, and my mountain. One day it will be his. He decided what to do with his life, and it's train horses." He didn't like explaining his and Joe's personal business to anyone, but there was something about this huffy, dowdy little teacher that made him answer. She didn't seem to realize he was Indian; intellectually she knew it, but she obviously had no idea what it *meant* to be Indian, and to be Wolf Mackenzie in particular, to have people turn aside to avoid speaking to him.

"I'd like to talk to him anyway," Mary said stubbornly.

"That's up to him. He may not want to talk to you."

"You won't try to influence him at all?"

"No."

"Why not? You should at least have tried to keep him in school!"

Wolf leaned very close, so close that his nose was almost touching hers. She stared into his black eyes, her own eyes widening. "He's Indian, lady. Maybe you don't know what that means. Hell, how could you? You're an Anglo. Indians aren't welcome. What education he has, he got on his own, without any help from the Anglo teachers. When he wasn't being ignored, he was being insulted. Why would he want to go back?"

She swallowed, alarmed by his aggression. She wasn't accustomed to men getting right in her face and swearing at her. Truthfully, Mary admitted that she wasn't accustomed to men at all. When she had been young, the boys had ignored the mousy, bookish girl, and when she had gotten older the men had done the same. She paled a little, but she felt so strongly about the benefits of a good education that she refused to let him intimidate her. Big people often did that to smaller people, probably without even thinking about it, but she wasn't going to give in simply because he was bigger than she. "He was at the head of his class," she said briskly. "If he managed that on his own, think of what he could accomplish with help!"

He straightened to his full height, towering over her. "Like I said, it's up to him." The coffee had long since finished brewing, so he turned to pour a cup and hand it to her. Silence fell between them. He leaned against the cabinets and watched her sip daintily, like a cat. Dainty, yeah, that was a good word for her. She wasn't *tiny*, maybe five three, but she was slightly built. His eyes dropped to her breasts beneath that dowdy blue dress; they weren't big, but they looked nice and round. He wondered if her nipples would be a delicate shell pink, or rosy beige. He wondered if she would be able to take him comfortably, if she would be so tight he'd go wild—

Sharply he brought his erotic thoughts to a halt. Damn it, that particular lesson should have been etched into his soul! Anglo women might flirt with him and twitch themselves around him, but few of them really wanted to get down and dirty with an Indian. This prissy little frump wasn't even flirting, so why was he getting so turned on? Maybe it was because she *was* a frump. He kept imagining how the dainty body beneath that awful dress would look, stripped bare and stretched out on the sheets.

Mary set the cup aside. "I'm much warmer now. Thank you, the coffee did the trick." That, and the way he'd run his hands all over her, but she wasn't about to tell him that. She looked up at him and hesitated, suddenly uncertain when she saw the look in his black eyes.

She didn't know what it was, but there was something about him that made her pulse rate increase, made her feel faintly uneasy. Was he actually looking at her *breasts*?

"I think some of Joe's old clothes will fit you," he said, face and voice expressionless.

"Oh, I don't need any clothes. I mean, what I have on is perfectly—"

"Idiotic," he interrupted. "This is Wyoming, lady, not New Orleans, or wherever you're from."

"Savannah," she supplied.

He grunted, which seemed to be one of his basic means of communication, and took a towel from a drawer. Going down on one knee, he lifted her feet from the water and wrapped them in a towel, rubbing them dry with a touch so gentle it was at odds with the thinly veiled hostility of his manner. Then, standing, he said, "Come with me."

"Where are we going?"

"To the bedroom."

Mary stopped, blinking at him, and a bitter smile twisted his mouth. "Don't worry," he said harshly. "I'll control my savage appetites, and after you get dressed, you can get the hell off my mountain."

Chapter 2

Mary drew herself up to her full height and lifted her chin, her mouth setting itself in a prim line. "It isn't necessary to make fun of me, Mr. Mackenzie," she said calmly, but her even tone was hard won. She knew she fell short in the come-hither department; she didn't need sarcasm to remind her. Usually she wasn't disturbed by her mousiness, having accepted it as an unchangeable fact, much like having the sun rise in the east. But Mr. Mackenzie made her feel strangely vulnerable, and it was oddly painful that he should have pointed out how unappealing she was.

Wolf's straight black brows drew together over his high-bridged nose. "I wasn't making fun of you," he snapped. "I was dead serious, lady. I want you off of my mountain."

"Then I'll leave, of course," she replied steadily. "But it was still unnecessary to make fun of me."

He put his hands on his hips. "Make fun of you? How?"

A flush tinged her exquisite skin, but her gray-blue eyes never wavered. "I know I'm not an attractive woman, certainly not the type to stir a man's—er, savage appetites."

She was serious. Ten minutes ago he'd have agreed with her that she was plain, and God knew she was no fashion plate, but what astounded him was that she honestly didn't seem to realize what it meant that he was Indian, or what he'd meant by his sarcasm, or even that he had been strongly aroused by her closeness. A lingering throbbing in his loins reminded him that his reaction hadn't completely subsided. He gave a harsh laugh, the sound devoid of amusement. Why not put a little more excitement in her life? When she heard the flat truth, she wouldn't be able to get off his mountain fast enough.

"I wasn't joking or making fun," he said. His black eyes glittered at her. "Touching you like that, being so close to you that I could smell the sweetness, turned me on."

Astonished, she stared at him. "Turned you on?" she asked blankly.

"Yeah." She still stared at him as if he were speaking a different language, and impatiently he added, "Got me hot, however you want to describe it."

She pushed at a silky strand that had escaped from her hairpins. "You're making fun of me again," she accused. It was impossible. She had never made a man... aroused a man in her life.

He was already irritated, already aroused. He had learned to use iron control when dealing with Anglos, but something about this prim little woman got under his skin. Frustration filled him until he thought he might explode. He hadn't intended to touch her, but suddenly he had his hands on her waist, pulling her toward him.

''Maybe you need a demonstration,'' he said in a rough undertone, and bent to cover her mouth with his.

Mary trembled in profound shock, her eyes enormous as he moved his lips over hers. His eyes were closed. She could see the individual lashes, and for a moment marveled at how thick they were. Then his hands, still clasped on her waist, drew her into firm contact with his muscled body, and she gasped. He took instant advantage of her opened mouth, probing inside with his tongue. She quivered again, and her eyes slowly closed as a strange heat began to warm her inside. The pleasure was unfamiliar, and so intense that it frightened her. A host of new sensations assailed her, making her dizzy. There was the firmness of his lips, his heady taste, the startling intimacy of his tongue stroking hers as if enticing it to play. She felt the heat of his body, smelled the warm muskiness of his skin. Her soft breasts were pressed against the muscular planes of his chest, and her nipples began to tingle in that strange, embarrassing way again.

Suddenly he lifted his mouth from hers, and sharp disappointment made her eyes fly open. His black gaze burned her. ''Kiss me back,'' he muttered.

''I don't know how,'' Mary blurted, still unable to believe this was happening.

His voice was almost guttural. ''Like this.'' He took her mouth again, and this time she parted her lips immediately, eager to accept his tongue and feel that odd, surging pleasure once more. He moved his mouth over hers, molding her lips with fierce pleasure, teaching her how to return the pressure. His tongue touched hers again, and this time she responded shyly in kind, welcoming his small invasion with gentle touches of her own. She was too inexperienced to realize the symbolism of her acceptance, but he began to breathe harder and faster, and his kiss deepened, demanding even more of her.

A frightening excitement exploded through her body, going beyond mere pleasure and becoming a hungry need. She was no longer cold at all, but burning inside as her heartbeat increased until her heart was banging against her ribs. So this was what he meant when he'd said she got him hot. He got her hot, too, and it stunned her to think he had felt this same restless yearning, this incredible wanting. She made a soft, unconscious sound and moved closer to him, not knowing how to control the sensations his experienced kisses had aroused.

His hands tightened painfully on her waist, and a low, rough sound rumbled in his throat. Then he lifted her, pulled her closer, adjusted her hips against his and graphically demonstrated his response to her.

She hadn't known it could be like that. She hadn't known that desire could burn so hot, could make her forget Aunt Ardith's warnings about men and the nasty things they liked to do to women. Mary had quite sensibly decided that those things couldn't be too nasty, or women wouldn't put up with them, but at the same time she had never flirted or tried to attract a boyfriend. The men she had met at college and on the job had seemed normal, not slavering sex fiends; she was comfortable with men, and even considered some to be friends. It was just that she wasn't sexy herself; no man had ever beaten down doors to go out with her, or even managed to accomplish the dialing of her telephone number, so her exposure to men hadn't prepared her for the tightness of Wolf Mackenzie's arms, the hunger of his kisses, or the hardness of his manhood pushing against the juncture of her thighs. Nor had she known that she could want more.

Unconsciously she locked her arms around his neck and squirmed against him, tormented by increasing frus-

tration. Her body was on fire, empty and aching and
wanting all at once, and she didn't have the experience
to control it. The new sensations were a tidal wave,
swamping her mind beneath the overload from her nerve
endings.

Wolf jerked his head back, his teeth locked as he re-
lentlessly brought himself back under control. Black fire
burned in his eyes as he looked down at her. His kisses
had made her soft lips red and pouty, and delicate pink
colored her translucent porcelain skin. Her eyes were
heavy-lidded as she opened them and slowly met his
gaze. Her pale brown hair had slipped completely out of
its knot and tumbled silkily around her face and over her
shoulders. Desire was on her face; she already looked
tousled, as if he had done more than kiss her, and in his
mind he had. She was light and delicate in his arms, but
she had twisted against him with a hunger that matched
his own.

He could take her to bed now; she was that far gone,
and he knew it. But when he did, it would be because
she had consciously made the decision, not because she
was so hot she didn't know what she was doing. Her
inexperience was obvious; he'd even had to teach her
how to kiss—the thought stopped as abruptly as if he'd
hit a mental wall, as he realized the full extent of her
inexperience. Damn it, she was a *virgin*!

The thought staggered him. She was looking at him
now with those grayish blue eyes both innocent and
questioning, languid with desire, as she waited for him
to make the next move. She didn't know what to do. Her
arms were locked around his neck, her body pressed
tightly to his, her legs opened slightly to allow him to
nestle against her, and she was waiting for him because
she didn't have a clue how to proceed. She hadn't even
been kissed before. No man had touched those soft

breasts, or taken her nipples in his mouth. No man had loved her at all before.

He swallowed the lump that threatened to choke him, his eyes still locked with hers. "God Almighty, lady, that nearly got out of hand."

She blinked. "Did it?" Her tone was prim, the words clear, but the dazed, sleepy look was still in her eyes.

Slowly, because he didn't want to let her go, and gently, because he knew he had to, he let her body slip down his until she was standing on her feet again. She was innocent of the ramifications, but he wasn't. He was Wolf Mackenzie, half-breed, and she was the schoolteacher. The good citizens of Ruth wouldn't want her associating with him; she was in charge of their young people, with untold influence on their forming morals. No parents would want their impressionable daughter being taught by a woman who was having a wild fling with an Indian ex-con. Why, she might even entice their sons! His prison record could be accepted, but his Indian blood would never go away.

So he had to let her go, no matter how much he wanted to take her to his bedroom and teach her all the things that went on between a man and a woman.

Her arms were still around his neck, her fingers buried in the hair at his nape. She seemed incapable of movement. He reached up to take her wrists and draw her hands away from him.

"I think I'll come back later."

A new voice intruded in Mary's dreamworld of newly discovered sensuality, and she jerked away, color burning her cheeks as she whirled to face the newcomer. A tall, dark-haired boy stood just inside the kitchen door, his hat in his hand. "Sorry, Dad. I didn't mean to barge in."

Wolf stepped away from her. "Stay. She came to see you, anyway."

The boy looked at her quizzically. "You could have fooled me."

Wolf merely shrugged. "This is Miss Mary Potter, the new schoolteacher. Miss Potter, my son, Joe."

Even through her embarrassment, Mary was jolted that he would call her "Miss Potter" after the intimacy they had just shared. But he seemed so calm and controlled, as if it hadn't affected him at all, while every nerve in her body was still jangling. She wanted to fling herself against him and give herself up to that encompassing fire.

Instead she stood there, her arms stiffly at her sides while her face burned, and forced herself to look at Joe Mackenzie. He was the reason she was here, and she wouldn't allow herself to forget it again. As her embarrassment faded, she saw that he was very like his father. Though he was only sixteen, he was already six feet tall and would likely match his father's height, just as his broad young shoulders showed the promise of being as powerful. His face was a younger version of Wolf's, as strong-boned and proud, the features precisely chiseled. He was calm and controlled, far too controlled for a sixteen-year-old, and his eyes, oddly, were pale, glittering blue. Those eyes held something in them, something untamed, as well as a sort of bitter acceptance and knowledge that made him old beyond his years. He was his father's son.

There was no way she could give up on him.

She held out her hand to him. "I'd really like to talk to you, Joe."

His expression remained aloof, but he crossed the kitchen to shake her hand. "I don't know why."

"You dropped out of school."

The statement hardly needed verification, but he nodded. Mary drew a deep breath. "May I ask why?"

"There was nothing for me there."

She felt frustrated by the calm, flat statement, because she couldn't sense any uncertainty in this unusual boy. As Wolf had said, Joe had made up his own mind and didn't intend to change it. She tried to think of another way to approach him, but Wolf's quiet, deep voice interrupted.

"Miss Potter, you can finish talking after you get into some sensible clothes. Joe, don't you have some old jeans that might be small enough to fit her?"

To her astonishment, the boy looked her over with an experienced eye. "I think so. Maybe the ones I wore when I was ten." For a moment amusement sparkled in his blue-diamond eyes, and Mary primmed her mouth. What did these Mackenzie men get out of needlessly pointing out her lack of attractiveness?

"Socks, shirt, boots and coat," Wolf added to the list. "The boots will be too big, but two pairs of socks will hold them on."

"Mr. Mackenzie, I really don't need extra clothes. What I have on will do until I get home."

"No, it won't. The high temperature today is about ten below zero. You aren't walking out of this house with bare legs and those stupid shoes."

Her sensible shoes were suddenly stupid? She felt like flying to their defense, but suddenly remembered the snow that had gotten inside them and frozen her toes. What was sensible in Savannah was woefully inadequate in a Wyoming winter.

"Very well," she assented, but only because it was, after all, the sensible thing to do. She still felt uncomfortable about taking Joe's clothes, even temporarily. She had never worn anyone else's clothes before, never swapped sweaters or blouses with chums as an adolescent. Aunt Ardith had thought such familiarity ill-bred.

"I'll see about your car while you change." Without even glancing at her again, he put on his coat and hat and walked out the door.

"This way," Joe said, indicating that she should follow him. She did so, and he looked over his shoulder. "What happened to your car?"

"A water hose blew."

"Where is it?"

She stopped. "It's on the road. Didn't you see it when you drove up?" An awful thought struck her. Had her car somehow slid off the mountain?

"I came up the front side of the mountain. It's not as steep." He looked amused again. "You actually tried driving up the back road in a car, when you're not used to driving in snow?"

"I didn't know that was the back road. I thought it was the only road. Couldn't I have made it? I have snow tires."

"Maybe."

She noticed that he didn't sound very confident in her ability, but she didn't protest, because she wasn't very confident herself. He led the way through a rustic but comfortable living room and down a short hallway to an open door. "My old clothes are boxed up in the storage room, but it won't take long for me to dig them out. You can change in here. It's my bedroom."

"Thank you," she murmured, stepping inside the room. Like the living room, it was rustic, with exposed beams and thick wooden walls. There was nothing in it to indicate it was inhabited by a teenage boy: no sports apparatus of any kind, no clothes on the floor. The full-size bed was neatly made, a homemade quilt smoothed on top. A straight chair stood in one corner. Next to his bed, bookshelves stretched from floor to ceiling; the shelves were obviously handmade, but weren't crude. They had been finished, sanded and varnished. They were crammed with books, and curiosity led her to examine the titles.

It took her a moment to realize that every book had to do with flight, from da Vinci's experiments through *Kitty Hawk* and space exploration. There were books on bombers, fighters, helicopters, radar planes, jets and prop planes, books on air battles fought in each war since pilots first shot at each other with pistols in World War I. There were books on experimental aircraft, on fighter tactics, on wing design and engine capability.

"Here are the clothes." Joe had entered silently and placed the clothes on the bed. Mary looked at him, but his face was impassive.

"You like planes," she said, then winced at her own banality.

"I like planes," he admitted without inflection.

"Have you thought about taking flying lessons?"

"Yes." He didn't add anything to that stark answer, however; he merely left the room and closed the door behind him.

She was thoughtful as she slowly removed her dress and pulled on the things Joe had brought. The collection of books indicated not merely an interest in flying, but an obsession. Obsessions were funny things; unhealthy ones could ruin lives, but some obsessions lifted people to higher planes of life, made them shine with a brighter light, burn with a hotter fire, and if those obsessions weren't fed, then the person withered, a life blighted by starvation of the soul. If she were right, she had a way to reach Joe and get him back in school.

The jeans fit. Disgusted at this further proof that she had the figure of a ten-year-old boy, she pulled on the too-big flannel shirt and buttoned it, then rolled the sleeves up over her hands. As Wolf had predicted, the worn boots were too big, but the two pairs of thick socks padded her feet enough that the boots didn't slip up and down on her heels too much. The warmth was heavenly, and she decided she would pinch pennies any way she could until she could afford a pair of boots.

Joe was adding wood to the fire in the enormous rock fireplace when she entered, and a little grin tugged at his mouth when he saw her. "You sure don't look like Mrs. Langdale, or any other teacher I've ever seen."

She folded her hands. "Looks have nothing to do with ability. I'm a very good teacher—even if I do look like a ten-year-old boy."

"Twelve. I wore those jeans when I was twelve."

"What a consolation."

He laughed aloud, and she felt pleased, because she had the feeling neither he nor his father laughed much.

"Why did you quit school?"

She had learned that if you kept asking the same question, you would often get different answers, and eventually the evasions would cease and the real answer would emerge. But Joe looked at her steadily and gave the same answer as before. "There was nothing for me there."

"Nothing more for you to learn?"

"I'm Indian, Miss Potter. A mixed-breed. What I learned, I learned on my own."

Mary paused. "Mrs. Langdale didn't—" She stopped, unsure of how to phrase her question.

"I was invisible." His young voice was harsh. "From the time I started school. No one took the time to explain anything to me, ask me questions, or include me in anything. I'm surprised my papers were even graded."

"But you were number one in your class."

He shrugged. "I like books."

"Don't you miss school, miss learning?"

"I can read without going to school, and I can help Dad a lot more if I'm here all day. I know horses, ma'am, maybe better than anyone else around here except for Dad, and I didn't learn about them in school. This ranch will be mine someday. This is my life. Why should I waste time in school?"

Mary took a deep breath and played her ace. "To learn how to fly."

He couldn't prevent the avid gleam that shone briefly in his eyes, but it was quickly extinguished. "I can't learn how to fly in Ruth High School. Maybe someday I'll take lessons."

"I wasn't talking about flying lessons. I was talking about the Air Force Academy."

His bronze skin whitened. This time she didn't see a gleam of eagerness, but a deep, anguished need so powerful it shook her, as if he'd been shown a glimpse of heaven. Then he turned his head, and abruptly he looked older. "Don't try to make a fool of me. There's no way."

"Why isn't there a way? From what I saw in your school records, your grade average will be high enough."

"I dropped out."

"You can go back."

"As far behind as I am? I'd have to repeat this grade, and I won't sit still while those jerks call me a stupid Indian."

"You aren't that far behind. I could tutor you, bring you up fast enough that you could start your senior year in the fall. I'm a licensed teacher, Joe, and for your information, my credentials are very good. I'm qualified to tutor you in the classes you need."

He took a poker and jabbed at a log, sending a shower of sparks flying. "What if I do it?" he muttered. "The

Academy isn't a college where you take an entrance exam, pay your money and walk in.''

"No. The usual way is to be recommended by your congressman."

"Yeah, well, I don't think my congressman is going to recommend an Indian. We're way down on the list of people it's fashionable to help. Dead last, as a matter of fact."

"I think you're making too much of your heritage," Mary said calmly. "You can keep blaming everything on being Indian, or you can get on with your life. You can't do anything about other people's reactions to you, but you *can* do something about your own. You don't know what your congressman will do, so why give up when you haven't even tried yet? Are you a quitter?"

He straightened, his pale eyes fierce. "I don't reckon."

"Then it's time to find out, isn't it? Do you want to fly bad enough that you'll fight for the privilege? Or do you want to die without ever knowing what it's like to sit in the cockpit of a jet doing Mach 1?"

"You hit hard, lady," he whispered.

"Sometimes it takes a knock on the head to get someone's attention. Do you have the guts to try?"

"What about you? The folks in Ruth won't like it if you spend so much time with me. It would be bad enough if I were alone, but with Dad, it's twice as bad."

"If anyone objects to my tutoring you, I'll certainly set him straight," she said firmly. "It's an honor to be accepted into the Academy, and that's our goal. If you'll agree to being tutored, I'll write to your congressman immediately. I think this time your heritage will work in your favor."

It was amazing how proud that strong young face could be. "I don't want it if they give it to me just because I'm Indian."

"Don't be ridiculous," she scoffed. "Of course you won't be accepted into the Academy just because you're half Indian. But if that fact catches the congressman's interest, I say, good. It would only make him remember your name. It'll be up to you to make the grade."

He raked his hand through his black hair, then restlessly walked to the window to look out at the white landscape. "Do you really think it's possible?"

"Of course it's possible. It isn't guaranteed, but it's possible. Can you live with yourself if you don't try? If *we* don't try?" She didn't know how to go about bringing someone to a congressman's attention for consideration for recommendation to the Academy, but she was certainly willing to write to every senator and representative Wyoming had seated in Congress, a letter a week, until she found out.

"If I agreed, it would have to be at night. I have chores around here that have to be done."

"Night is fine with me. Midnight would be fine with me, if it would get you back in school."

He gave her a quick look. "You really mean it, don't you? You actually care that I dropped out of school."

"Of course I care."

"There's no 'of course' about it. I told you, no other teacher cared if I showed up in class. They probably wished I hadn't."

"Well," she said in her briskest voice, "I care. Teaching is what I do, so if I can't teach and feel I'm doing some good, then I lose part of myself. Isn't that how you feel about flying? That you *have* to, or you'll die?"

"I want it so bad it hurts," he admitted, his voice raw.

"I read somewhere that flying is like throwing your soul into the heavens and racing to catch it as it falls."

"I don't think mine would ever fall," he murmured, looking at the clear cold sky. He stared, entranced, as if paradise beckoned, as if he could see forever. He was probably imagining himself up there, free and wild, with a powerful machine screaming beneath him and taking him higher. Then he shook himself, visibly fighting off the dream, and turned to her. "Okay, Miss Teacher, when do we start?"

"Tonight. You've already wasted enough time."

"How long will it take for me to catch up?"

She gave him a withering look. "Catch up? You're going to leave them in the dust. How long it takes depends on how much work you can do."

"Yes, ma'am," he said, grinning a little.

She thought that already he looked younger, more like a boy, than he had before. He was, in all ways, far more mature than the other boys his age in her classes, but he looked as if a burden had been lifted from him. If flying meant that much to him, how had it felt to set himself a course that would deny him what he wanted most?

"Can you be at my house at six? Or would you rather I come here?" She thought of that drive, in the dark and snow, and wondered if she'd make it if he wanted her to come here.

"I'll come to your house, since you aren't used to driving in snow. Where do you live?"

"Go down the back road and take a left. It's the first house on the left." She thought a minute. "I believe it's the first house, period."

"It is. There isn't another house for five miles. That's the old Witcher house."

"So I've been told. It was kind of the school board to arrange living quarters for me."

Joe looked dubious. "More like it was the only way they had of getting another teacher in the middle of the year."

"Well, I appreciated it anyway," she said firmly. She

looked out the window. "Shouldn't your father be back by now?"

"Depends on what he found. If it was something he could fix right then, he'd do it. Look, here he comes now."

The black pickup roared to a stop in front of the house, and Wolf got out. Coming up on the porch, he stomped his feet to rid his boots of the snow caked on them and opened the door. His cool black gaze flickered over his son, then to Mary. His eyes widened fractionally as he examined every slim curve exhibited by Joe's old jeans, but he didn't comment.

"Get your things together," he instructed. "I have a spare hose that will fit your car. We'll put it on, then take you home."

"I can drive," she replied. "But thank you for your trouble. How much is the hose? I'll pay you for that."

"Consider it neighborly assistance to a greenhorn. And we'll still take you home. I'd rather you practiced driving in the snow somewhere other than on this mountain."

His dark face was expressionless, as usual, but she sensed that he'd made up his mind and wouldn't budge. She got her dress from Joe's room and the rest of her things from the kitchen. When she returned to the living room, Wolf held a thick coat for her to wear. She slipped into it; since it reached almost to her knees and the sleeves totally obscured her hands, she knew it had to be his.

Joe had on his coat and hat again. "Ready."

Wolf looked at his son. "Have you two had your talk?"

The boy nodded. "Yes." He met his father's eyes squarely. "She's going to tutor me. I'm going to try to get into the Air Force Academy."

"It's your decision. Just make sure you know what you're getting into."

"I have to try."

Wolf nodded once, and that was the end of the discussion. With her sandwiched between them, they left the warmth of the house, and once again Mary was struck by the bitter, merciless cold. She scrambled gratefully into the truck, which had been left running, and the blast of hot air from the heater vents felt like heaven.

Wolf got behind the wheel, and Joe got in beside her, trapping her between their two much bigger bodies. She sat with her hands primly folded and her booted feet placed neatly side-by-side as they drove down to an enormous barn with long stables extending off each side of it like arms. Wolf got out and entered the barn, then returned thirty seconds later with a length of thick black hose.

When they reached her car, both Mackenzies got out and poked their heads under the raised hood, but Wolf told her, in that tone of voice she already recognized as meaning business, to stay in the truck. He was certainly autocratic, but she liked his relationship with Joe. There was a strong sense of respect between them.

She wondered if the townspeople were truly so hostile simply because the Mackenzies were half Indian. Something Joe had said tugged at her memory, something about it would be bad enough if it were just him involved, but it would be twice as bad because of Wolf. What about Wolf? He'd rescued her from an unpleasant, even dangerous, situation, he'd seen to her comfort, and now he was repairing her car.

He'd also kissed her silly.

She could feel her cheeks heat as she remembered those fierce kisses. No, the kisses, and remembering them, begot a different kind of heat. Her cheeks were hot because her own behavior was so appalling she could barely bring herself to think about it. She had never—never!—been so forward with a man. It was totally out of character for her.

Aunt Ardith would have had a conniption fit at the thought of her mousy, sedate niece letting a strange man put his tongue in her mouth. It had to be unsanitary, though it was also, to be honest, exciting in a primitive way.

Her face still felt hot when Wolf got back into the truck, but he didn't even look at her. "It's fixed. Joe will follow us."

"But doesn't it need more water and antifreeze?"

He cast her a disbelieving look. "I had a can of anti-freeze in the back of the truck. Weren't you paying attention when I got it out?"

She blushed again. She hadn't been paying attention; she'd been lost in reliving those kisses he'd given her, her heart thundering and her blood racing. It was an ex-traordinary reaction, and she wasn't certain how to han-dle it. Ignoring it seemed the wisest course, but was it possible to ignore something like that?

His powerful leg moved against hers as he shifted gears, and abruptly she realized she was still sitting in the middle of the seat. "I'll get out of your way," she said hastily, and slid over by the window.

Wolf had liked the feel of her sitting next to him, so close that his arm and leg brushed her whenever he changed gears, but he didn't tell her that. Things had gotten way out of hand at the house, but he didn't have to let them go any further. This deal with Joe worried him, and Joe was more important to him than the way a soft woman felt in his arms.

"I don't want Joe hurt because your do-gooder in-stincts won't leave well enough alone." He spoke in a

low, silky tone that made her jump, and he knew she
sensed the menace in it. "The Air Force Academy!
That's climbing high for an Indian kid, with a lot of
people waiting to step on his fingers."

If he'd thought to intimidate her, he'd failed. She
turned toward him with fire sparking in her eyes, her chin
up. "Mr. Mackenzie, I didn't promise Joe he would be
accepted into the Academy. He understands that. His
grades were high enough to qualify him for recommendation, but he dropped out of school. He has no chance
at all unless he gets back into school and gets the credits
he needs. That's what I offered him: a chance."

"And if he doesn't make it?"

"He wants to try. Even if he isn't accepted, at least
he'll know he tried, and at least he'll have a diploma."

"So he can do exactly what he would have done without the diploma."

"Perhaps. But I'm going to begin checking into the
procedure and qualifications on Monday, and writing to
people. The competition to get into the Academy is really
fierce."

"The people in town won't like you tutoring him."

"That's what Joe said." Her face took on that prim,
obstinate look. "But I'll have something to say to anyone
who kicks up about it. Just let me handle them, Mr. Mackenzie."

They were already down the mountain that had taken
her so long to drive up. Wolf was silent for the rest of
the drive, so Mary was, too. But when he pulled up to
the old house where she was living, he rested his gloved
hands on the steering wheel and said, "It isn't just Joe.
For your sake, don't let on that you're doing it. It's better
for you if no one knows you've ever even spoken to
me."

"Why ever not?"

His smile was wintry. "I'm an ex-con. I did time for
rape."

Chapter 3

Afterward, Mary kicked herself for simply getting out of the truck without saying a word in response to his bald statement, but at the time she had been shocked to the core and incapable of a response. Rape! The crime was repulsive. It was unbelievable. She had actually kissed him! She'd been so stunned that she'd merely nodded goodbye to him and told Joe that she'd see him that night, then gone in the house without thanking them for all their help and trouble.

Now reality set in. Standing alone in the old-fashioned kitchen, she watched Woodrow hungrily lapping milk from his saucer while she considered the man and his statement. She abruptly snorted. "Hogwash! If that man's a rapist, I'll boil you for supper, Woodrow."

Woodrow looked remarkably unconcerned, which to Mary indicated that the cat agreed with her judgment, and she had a high opinion of Woodrow's ability to know what was best for himself.

After all, Wolf hadn't said that he'd committed rape. He'd said that he had served time in prison for rape. When Mary thought of the way both Mackenzies automatically and bitterly accepted that they would be shunned because of their Indian blood, she wondered if perhaps the fact that Wolf was part Indian figured in his conviction. But he hadn't done it. She knew that as well as she knew her own face. The man who had helped her out of a bad situation, warmed her cold hands against his own body and kissed her with burning male hunger, simply wasn't the type of man who could hurt a woman like that. *He* was the one who had halted before those kisses had gone too far; she had already been putty in his hands.

It was ridiculous. There was no way he was a rapist.

Oh, perhaps it hadn't been any great hardship for him to stop kissing her; after all, she was mousy and inexperienced and would never be voluptuous, but... Her thoughts trailed off as remembered sensations intruded. She was inexperienced, but she wasn't stupid. He had been—well, hard. She had distinctly felt *it*. Perhaps he hadn't had an outlet for his physical appetites lately and she had been handy, but still he hadn't taken advantage of her. He hadn't treated her with a sailor's attitude that any port in a storm would suffice. What was that awful term she had heard one of her students use once? Oh, yes—horny. She could accept that Wolf Mackenzie had been in that condition and she had accidentally stirred his fire in some way that still remained a mystery to her, but the bottom line was that he hadn't pushed his advantage.

What if he had?

Her heart started a strong, heavy beat, and heat crept through her, while an achy, restless feeling settled low inside. Her breasts tightened and began throbbing, and automatically she pressed her palms over them before she realized what she was doing and jerked her hands down. But what if he had touched them? What if he had put his mouth on her? She felt as if she would melt now, just thinking about him. Fantasizing. She pressed her thighs together, trying to ease the hollow ache, and a whimper escaped her lips. The sound was low, but seemed inordinately loud in the silent house, and the cat looked up from his saucer, gave a questioning meow, then returned to the milk.

Would she have been able to stop him? Would she even have tried to stop him? Or would she now be standing here remembering making love instead of trying to imagine how it would be? Her body tingled, but from barely awakened instincts and needs rather than true knowledge.

She had never before known passion, other than the passion for knowledge and teaching. To find her body capable of such strong sensations was frightening, because she had thought she knew herself well. Suddenly her own flesh was alien to her, and her thoughts and emotions were abruptly unruly. It was almost like a betrayal.

Why, this was lust! She, Mary Elizabeth Potter, actually *lusted* after a man! Not just any man, either. Wolf Mackenzie.

It was both amazing and embarrassing.

Joe proved a quick, able student, as Mary had known he would be. He was prompt, arriving right on time, and thankfully alone. After stewing over the morning's events for the entire afternoon, she didn't think she could ever face Wolf Mackenzie again. What must he think of her? To her mind, she had practically attacked the man.

But Joe was alone, and in the three hours that followed, Mary found herself liking him more and more.

He was hungry for knowledge and absorbed it like a dry sponge. While he worked on the assignments she had set out for him, she prepared a set of records in which to keep the time he spent on each subject, the matter covered and his test scores. The goal they had set for themselves was much higher than just a high school diploma. Though she hadn't promised it, she knew she wouldn't be satisfied unless Joe was accepted into the Air Force Academy. There had been something in his eyes that told her he would never be complete unless he could fly; he was like a grounded eagle, his soul yearning for the sky.

At nine o'clock she called a halt and noted the time in her records. Joe yawned as he rocked the chair onto its back legs. "How often do we do this?"

"Every night, if you can," she replied. "At least until you catch up with the rest of your class."

His pale, blue-diamond eyes glittered at her, and again she was struck by how old those eyes were. "Do I have to go back to regular classrooms next year?"

"It would help if you did. You'd be able to get much more work done, and we could do your advanced studies here."

"I'll think about it. I don't want to leave Dad in the lurch. We're expanding the ranch now, and it means a lot more work. We have more horses now than we've ever had before."

"Do you raise horses?"

"Quarter horses. Good ranch horses, trained to handle cattle. We not only breed them, but people bring their own horses to the ranch for Dad to train. He's not just good, he's the best. Folks don't mind that he's an Indian when it comes to training their horses."

Again the bitterness was apparent. Mary propped her elbows on the table and leaned her chin on her upraised, folded hands. "And you?"

"I'm Indian, too, Miss Potter. Half Indian, and that's more than enough for most people. It wasn't as bad when I was younger, but an Indian kid isn't much of a threat to anyone. It's when that kid grows up and starts looking at the white Anglo daughters that all hell breaks loose."

So a girl had been part of the reason Joe had quit school. Mary raised her eyebrows at him. "I imagine the white Anglo daughters looked back, too," she said mildly. "You're very good-looking."

He almost grinned at her. "Yeah. That and two bits will get me a cup of coffee."

"So they looked back?"

"And flirted. One acted like she really cared something about me. But when I asked her to a dance, the door was slammed in my face right quick. I guess it's okay to flirt with me, sort of like waving a red flag at a bull from a safe distance, but there was no way she was actually going to go out with an Indian."

"I'm sorry." Without thinking, Mary reached out and covered his strong young hand with her own. "Is that when you quit school?"

"There didn't seem to be any point in going. Don't think I was serious about her, or anything like that, because it hadn't gotten that far. I was just interested in her. But the whole thing made it plain that I was never going to fit in, that none of those girls would ever go out with me."

"So what did you plan on doing? Working on the ranch for the rest of your life and never dating, never getting married?"

"I'm sure not thinking of getting married!" he said strongly. "As for the rest of it, there are other towns, bigger towns. The ranch is doing pretty good now, and we have a little extra money." He didn't add that he'd lost his virginity two years before, on a trip to one of those bigger towns. He didn't want to shock her, and he was certain she would be shocked if she had any idea of his experience. The new teacher wasn't just prim, she was innocent. It made him feel oddly protective. That, and the fact that she was different from the other teachers he'd known. When she looked at him she saw *him*, Joe Mackenzie, not the bronzed skin and black hair of a half-breed. She had looked into his eyes and seen the dream, the obsession he'd always had with planes and flying.

After Joe had left, Mary locked the house and got ready for bed. It had been a tumultuous day for her, but it was a long time before she slept, and then she overslept the next morning. She deliberately kept herself busy that day, not giving herself time to moon over Wolf Mackenzie, or fantasize about things that hadn't happened. She mopped and waxed until the old house was shiny, then dragged out the boxes of books she had brought from Savannah. Books always gave a house a lived-in look. To her frustration, however, there was no place to put them. What she needed was some of that portable shelving; if all it required for assembly was a screwdriver, she should be able to put it up herself. With her customary decisiveness, she made plans to check at the general store the next afternoon. If they didn't have what she needed, she would buy some lumber and hire someone to build some shelves.

At lunch on Monday she made a call to the state board of education to find out what she had to do to make certain Joe's studies would be accepted toward his diploma. She knew she had the qualifications, but there was also a good deal of paperwork to be done before he could earn the necessary credits by private tutoring. She made the call on the pay phone in the tiny teacher's lounge, which was never used because there were only three teachers, each teaching four grades, and there was never any time for a break. Nevertheless it had three chairs and a table, a tiny, dented refrigerator, an automatic coffee maker and the pay phone. It was so unusual for any of the teachers to use the lounge that Mary was surprised when the door opened and Sharon Wycliffe, who taught grades one through four, poked her head in.

"Mary, are you feeling sick or anything?"

"No, I'm fine." Mary stood and dusted off her hands. The receiver had carried a gray coating, evidence of how often it was used. "I was making a call."

"Oh. I just wondered. You'd been in here a long time, and I thought you might not be feeling well. Who were you calling?"

The question was asked without any hesitancy. Sharon had been born in Ruth, had gone to school here, had married a local boy. Everyone in Ruth knew every one of the other one hundred and eighty inhabitants; they all knew each other's business and saw nothing unusual about it. Small towns were merely large extended families. Mary wasn't taken aback by Sharon's open curiosity, having already experienced it.

"The state board. I needed some information on teaching requirements."

Sharon looked alarmed. "Do you think you aren't properly certified? If there's any trouble, the school board will likely commit mass suicide. You don't know how hard it is to find a teacher with the proper qualifications willing to come to a town as small as Ruth. They were almost at the panic stage when you were located. The kids were going to have to start going to school over sixty miles away."

"No, it isn't that. I thought I might begin private tutoring, if any of the kids need it." She didn't mention Joe Mackenzie, because she couldn't forget the warnings both he and his father had given her.

"Thank goodness it isn't bad news," Sharon exclaimed. "I'd better get back to the kids before they get into trouble." With a wave and a smile she withdrew her head, her curiosity satisfied.

Mary hoped Sharon didn't mention it to Dottie Lancaster, the teacher who taught grades five through eight, but she knew it was a futile hope. Eventually, everything in Ruth became common knowledge. Sharon was warm and full of good humor with her young charges, and Mary's teaching style was rather relaxed, too, but Dottie was strict and abrupt with the students. It made Mary uncomfortable, because she sensed Dottie regarded her job as merely a job, something that was necessary but not enjoyed. She had even heard that Dottie, who was fifty-five, was thinking about an early retirement. For all Dottie's shortcomings, that would certainly upset the local school board, because as Sharon had pointed out, it was almost impossible to get a teacher to relocate to Ruth. The town was just too small and too far away from everything.

As she taught the last classes of the day, Mary found herself studying the young girls and wondering which one had daringly flirted with Joe Mackenzie, then retreated when he had actually asked her out. Several of the girls were very attractive and flirtatious, and though they had the shallowness typical of teenagers, they all seemed likable. But which one would have attracted Joe, who wasn't shallow, whose eyes were far too old for a sixteen-year-old boy? Natalie Ulrich, who was tall and graceful? Pamela Hearst, who had the sort of blond good looks that belonged on a California beach? Or maybe it was Jackie Baugh, with her dark, sultry eyes. It could be any of the eight girls in her classes, she realized. They were used to being pursued, having had the stupendous good luck to be outnumbered, nine to eight, by the boys. They were all flirts. So which one was it?

She wondered why it mattered, but it did. One of these girls, though she hadn't broken Joe's heart, had nevertheless dealt him what could have been a life-destroying blow. Joe had taken it as the final proof that he'd never have a place in the white man's world, and he'd withdrawn. He still might never re-enter this school, but at least he'd agreed to be tutored. If only he didn't lose hope.

When school was out, she swiftly gathered all the materials she would need that night, as well as the papers she had to grade, and hurried to her car. It was only a short drive to Hearst's General Store, and when she asked, Mr. Hearst kindly directed her to the stacks of shelving in a corner.

A few minutes later the door opened to admit another customer. Mary saw Wolf as soon as he entered the store; she had been examining the shelving, but it was as if her skin was an alarm system, signaling his nearness. Her nerves tingled, the hair at the nape of her neck bristled, she looked up, and there he was. Instantly she shivered, and her nipples tightened. Distress at that uncontrollable response sent blood rushing to her face.

With her peripheral vision she saw Mr. Hearst stiffen, and for the first time she truly believed the things Wolf had told her about the way he was regarded in town. He hadn't done anything, hadn't said anything, but it was obvious Mr. Hearst wasn't happy to have him in the store.

Quickly she turned back to the shelving. She couldn't look him in the eye. Her face heated even more when she thought of the way she'd acted, throwing herself at him like a sex-starved old maid. It didn't help her feelings that he probably thought she *was* a sex-starved old maid; she couldn't argue with the old maid part, but she had never paid much attention to the other until Wolf had taken her in his arms. When she thought of the things she had done...

Her face was on fire. Her body was on fire. There was no way she could talk to him. What must he think of her? With fierce concentration, she read the instructions on the box of shelving and pretended she hadn't seen him enter the store.

She had read the instructions three times before she realized she was acting just like the people he had described: too good to speak to him, disdaining to acknowledge knowing him. Mary was normally even-tempered, but suddenly rage filled her, and it was rage at herself. What sort of person was she?

She jerked the box of shelving toward her and nearly staggered under the unexpected weight. Just as she turned, Wolf laid a box of nails on the checkout counter and reached in his pocket for his wallet.

Mr. Hearst glanced briefly at Wolf; then his eyes cut to where Mary was struggling with the box. "Here, Miss Potter, let me get that," he said, rushing from behind the counter to grab the box. He grunted as he hefted it in his arms. "Can't have you wrestling with something this heavy. Why, you might hurt yourself."

Mary wondered how he thought she would get it from her car into her house if she didn't handle it herself, but refrained from pointing that out. She followed him back to the counter, squared her shoulders, took a deep breath, looked up at Wolf and said clearly, "Hello, Mr. Mackenzie. How are you?"

His night-dark eyes glittered, perhaps in warning. "Miss Potter," he said in brief acknowledgment, touching the brim of his hat with his fingers, but he refused to respond to her polite inquiry.

Mr. Hearst looked sharply at Mary. "You know him, Miss Potter?"

"Indeed I do. He rescued me Saturday when my car broke down and I was stranded in the snow." She kept her voice clear and strong.

Mr. Hearst darted a suspicious look at Wolf. "Hmmph," he said, then reached for the box of shelving to ring it up.

"Excuse me," Mary said. "Mr. Mackenzie was here first."

She heard Wolf mutter a curse under his breath, or at least she thought it was a curse. Mr. Hearst turned red.

"I don't mind waiting," Wolf said tightly.

"I wouldn't dream of cutting in front of you." She folded her hands at her waist and pursed her lips. "I couldn't be that rude."

"Ladies first," Mr. Hearst said, trying for a smile.

Mary gave him a stern look. "Ladies shouldn't take advantage of their gender, Mr. Hearst. This is an age of equal treatment and fairness. Mr. Mackenzie was here first, and he should be waited on first."

Wolf shook his head and gave her a disbelieving look. "Are you one of those women's libbers?"

Mr. Hearst glared at him. "Don't take that tone with her, Indian."

"Now, just a minute." Controlling her outrage, she shook her finger at him. "That was rude and entirely uncalled for. Why, your mother would be ashamed of you, Mr. Hearst. Didn't she teach you better than that?"

He turned even redder. "She taught me just fine," he mumbled, staring at her finger.

There was something about a schoolteacher's finger; it had an amazing, mystical power. It made grown men quail before it. She had noticed the effect before and decided that a schoolteacher's finger was an extension of

Mother's finger, and as such it wielded unknown authority. Women grew out of the feeling of guilt and helplessness brought on by that accusing finger, perhaps because most of them became mothers and developed their own powerful finger, but men never did. Mr. Hearst was no exception. He looked as if he wanted to crawl under his own counter.

"Then I'm certain you'll want to make her proud of you," she said in her most austere voice. "After you, Mr. Mackenzie."

Wolf made a sound that was almost a growl, but Mary stared at him until he jerked the money from his wallet and threw it on the counter. Without another word, Mr. Hearst rang up the nails and made change. Equally silent, Wolf grabbed the box of nails, spun on his heel and left the store.

"Thank you," Mary said, finally relenting and bestowing a forgiving smile on Mr. Hearst. "I knew you would understand how important it is to me that I be treated fairly. I don't wish to take advantage of my position as a teacher here." She made it sound as if being a teacher was at least as important as being queen, but Mr. Hearst only nodded, too relieved to pursue the matter. He took her money and dutifully carried the box of shelving out to her car, where he stored it in the trunk for her.

"Thank you," she said again. "By the way, Pamela—she *is* your daughter, isn't she?"

Mr. Hearst looked worried. "Yes, she is." Pam was his youngest, and the apple of his eye.

"She's a lovely girl and a good student. I just wanted you to know that she's doing well in school."

His face was wreathed in smiles as she drove away.

Wolf pulled over at the corner and watched his rearview mirror, waiting for Mary to exit the store. He was so angry he wanted to shake her until her teeth rattled, and that made him even angrier, because he knew he wouldn't do it.

Damn her! He'd warned her, but she hadn't listened. Not only had she made it plain they were acquainted, she had outlined the circumstances of their meeting and then championed him in a way that wouldn't go unnoticed.

Hadn't she understood when he'd told her he was an ex-con, and why? Did she think he'd been joking?

His hands clenched around the steering wheel. She'd had her hair twisted up in a knot again, and those big glasses perched on her nose, hiding the soft slate-blue of her eyes, but he remembered how she had looked with her hair down, wearing Joe's old jeans that had clung tightly to her slender legs and hips. He remembered the way passion had glazed her eyes when he'd kissed her. He remembered the softness of her lips, though she had had them pressed together in a ridiculously prim expression.

If he had any sense he'd just drive away. If he stayed completely away from her, there wouldn't be anything for people to talk about other than the fact that she was tutoring Joe, and that would be bad enough in their eyes.

But how would she get that box out of the car and into the house when she got home? It probably weighed as much as she did. He would just carry the box in for her, and at the same time peel a strip off her hide for not listening to him.

Oh, hell, who was he fooling? He'd had a taste of her, and he wanted more. She was a frumpy old maid, but her skin was as pale and translucent as a baby's, and her slender body would be soft, gently curving under his hands. He wanted to touch her. After kissing her, holding her, he hadn't gone to see Julie Oakes because he hadn't been able to get the feel of Miss Mary Potter out of his mind, off of his body. He still ached. His physical frustration was painful, and it was going to get worse, because if he'd ever known anything, it was that Miss Mary Potter wasn't for him.

Her car pulled out from in front of the store and passed him. Smothering another curse, he put the truck in gear and slowly followed her. She maintained a sedate pace, following the two-lane highway out of town, then turning off on the narrow secondary road that led to her house. She had to see his truck behind her, but she didn't give any indication that she knew she was being followed. Instead she drove straight to her house, carefully turned in at the snow-packed driveway and guided the car around to her customary parking spot behind the house.

Wolf shook his head as he pulled in behind her and got out of the truck. She was already out of her car, and she smiled at him as she fished the house key out of her purse. Didn't she remember what he'd told her? He couldn't believe that he'd told her he'd served time for rape and still she greeted him as calmly as if he were a priest, though they were the only two people for miles around.

"Damn it all, lady!" he barked at her, his long legs carrying him to her in a few strides. "Didn't you listen to anything I said Saturday?"

"Yes, of course I listened. That doesn't mean I agreed." She unlocked the trunk and smiled at him. "While you're here, would you please carry this box in for me? I'd really appreciate it."

"That's why I stopped," he snapped. "I knew you couldn't handle it."

His ill temper didn't seem to faze her. She merely smiled at him again as he lifted the box onto his shoulder, then led the way to the back door and opened it.

The first thing he noticed was that the house had a fresh, sweet smell to it, instead of the musty smell of an old house that had stood empty for a long time. His head lifted, and against his will he inhaled the faint scent. "What's that smell?"

She stopped and sniffed delicately. "What smell?"

"That sweet smell. Like flowers."

"Flowers? Oh, that must be the lilac sachet I put in all the drawers to freshen them. So many of the sachets are overpowering, but the lilacs are just right, don't you think?"

He didn't know anything about sachets, whatever they were, but if she put them in all the drawers, then her underwear must smell like lilacs, too. Her sheets would smell like lilacs and the warm scent of her body. His body responded strongly to the thought, and he cursed, then set the box down with a thud. Though the house was chilly, he felt sweat break out on his forehead.

"Let me turn up the heat," she said, ignoring his cursing. "The furnace is old and noisy, but I don't have any wood for the fireplace, so it'll have to do." As she talked, she left the kitchen and turned down a hallway, her voice growing fainter. Then she was back, and she smiled at him again. "It'll be warm in just a minute. Would you like a cup of tea?" After giving him a measuring look she said, "Make that coffee. You don't look like a tea-drinking man."

He was already warm. He was burning up. He pulled off his gloves and tossed them on the kitchen table. "Don't you know everybody in that town will be talking about you now? Lady, I'm Indian, and I'm an ex-con—"

"Mary," she interrupted briskly.

"What?"

"My name is Mary, not 'lady.' Mary Elizabeth." She added the second name out of habit because Aunt Ardith

had always called her by both names. "Are you certain
you don't want coffee? I need something to warm up my
insides."

His hat joined the gloves, and he raked an impatient
hand through his hair. "All right. Coffee."

Mary turned to run the water and measure the coffee,
using the activity to hide the sudden color in her face.
His hair. She felt stupid, but she'd hardly noticed his hair
before. Maybe she'd been too upset, then too bemused,
or maybe it was just that his midnight-black eyes had
taken her attention, but she hadn't noticed before how
long his hair was. It was thick and black and shiny, and
touched his broad shoulders. He looked magnificently pagan; she had immediately pictured him with his powerful
chest and legs bare, his body covered only by a breech-
clout or loincloth, and her pulse rate had gone wild.

He didn't sit down, but propped his long body against
the cabinet beside her. Mary kept her head down, hoping
her blush would subside. What was it about the man that
the mere sight of him triggered erotic fantasies? She had
certainly never had any fantasies before, erotic or otherwise. She had never before looked at a man and wondered what he looked like nude, but the thought of Wolf
nude made her ache inside, made her hands itch to touch
him.

"What the hell are you doing letting me even come
in your house, let alone inviting me to have coffee?" he
asked in a low, rough voice.

She blinked at him, her expression startled. "Why
shouldn't I?"

He thought he might explode with frustration.
"Lady—"

"Mary."

His big fists clenched. "*Mary.* Don't you have any
better sense than to let an ex-con into your house?"

"Oh, that." She dismissed it with a wave of her hand. "It would be wise to follow your advice if you were truly a criminal, but since you didn't do it, I don't think that applies in this instance. Besides, if you *were* a criminal, you wouldn't give me that advice."

He couldn't believe the casual way she disregarded any possibility of his guilt. "How do you know I didn't do it?"

"You just didn't."

"Do you have any reason for your deduction, Sherlock, or are you going on good old feminine intuition?"

She jerked around and glared at him. "I don't believe a rapist would have handled a woman as tenderly as you—as you handled me," she said, her voice tapering off into a whisper, and the color surged back into her face. Mortified by the stupid way she continued to blush, she slapped her palms to her face in an effort to hide the betraying color.

Wolf clenched his teeth, partly because she was white and therefore not for him, partly because she was so damned innocent, and partly because he wanted so fiercely to touch her that his entire body ached. "Don't build any dreams because I kissed you Saturday," he said harshly. "I've been too long without a woman, and I'm—"

"Horny?" she supplied.

He was staggered by the incongruity of that word coming from her prim mouth. "What?"

"Horny," she said again. "I've heard some of my students say it. It means—"

"I know what it means!"

"Oh. Well, is that what you were? Still are, for all I know."

He wanted to laugh. The urge almost overpowered

him, but he changed the sound into a cough. "Yeah, I still am."

She looked sympathetic. "I understand that can be quite a problem."

"It's hard on a guy."

It took a moment, but then her eyes widened, and before she could stop herself, her gaze had slid down his body. Instantly she jerked her head back up. "Oh. I see. I mean—I understand."

The need to touch her was suddenly so strong that he had to give in to it, had to touch her in even the smallest way. He put his hands on her shoulders, savoring her softness, the delicacy of her joints under his palms. "I don't think you do understand. You can't associate with me and still work in this town. At best, you'd be treated like a leper, or a slut. You would probably lose your job."

At that, she pressed her lips together, and a militant light came into her eyes. "I'd like to see someone try to fire me for associating with a law-abiding, tax-paying citizen. I refuse to pretend I don't know you."

"There's knowing, and there's knowing. It would be bad enough for you to be friends with me. Sleeping with me would make your life here impossible."

He felt her stiffen under his hands. "I don't believe I've asked to sleep with you," she said, but the color rose in her face again. She hadn't actually said the words, but he knew she certainly had thought about what it would be like.

"You asked, all right, but you're so damned innocent you didn't realize what you were doing," he muttered. "I could crawl on top of you right now, sweetheart, and I'd do it if you had any real idea of what you're asking for. But the last thing I want is to have some prissy little

Anglo screaming 'rape' at me. Believe me, an Indian doesn't get the benefit of the doubt.''

"I wouldn't do anything like that!''

He smiled grimly. "Yeah, I've heard that before. I'm probably the only man who has ever kissed you, and you think you'd like more, don't you? But sex isn't pretty and romantic, it's hot and sweaty, and you probably wouldn't like the first time at all. So do me a favor and find some other guinea pig. I have enough troubles without adding you to the list.''

Mary jerked away from him, pressing her lips firmly together and blinking her eyes as fast as she could to keep the tears from falling. Not for anything would she let him make her cry.

"I'm sorry I gave you that impression,'' she said, her voice stifled but even. "It's true I've never been kissed before, but I'm sure you aren't surprised by that. I'm obviously not Miss America material. If my—my response was out of line, I apologize. It won't happen again.'' She turned briskly to the cabinet. "The coffee is ready. How do you take yours?''

A muscle jerked in his jaw, and he grabbed his hat. "Forget the coffee,'' he muttered as he jammed the hat on his head and reached for his gloves.

She didn't look at him. "Very well. Goodbye, Mr. Mackenzie.''

Wolf slammed out the door, and Mary stood there with an empty coffee cup in her hand. If it really was goodbye, she didn't know how she would be able to stand it.

Chapter 4

Mary wasn't weak-willed, and she refused to give in to the desolation that filled her every time she thought of that horrible day. During the days she prodded, cajoled and enticed her students toward knowledge; at night she watched Joe devour the facts she spread before him. His thirst for knowledge was insatiable, and he not only caught up with the students in her regular classes, he passed them.

She had written her letters to the Wyoming members of Congress, and had also written to a friend for all the information she could find on the Air Force Academy. When the package came, she gave it to Joe and watched his eyes take on that fiercely intent, enthralled look he got whenever he thought of flying. Working with Joe was a joy; her only problem was that he reminded her so strongly of his father.

It wasn't that she missed Wolf; how could she miss someone she had seen only twice? He hadn't imbedded himself in her daily routine so that her life seemed empty without him. But while she had been with him, she had felt more vividly alive than she ever had before. With Wolf, she hadn't been Mary Potter, old maid, she had been Mary Potter, woman. His intense masculinity had reached parts of her that she hadn't known existed, bringing to life dormant yearnings and emotions. She argued with herself that what she felt was plain old garden-variety lust, but that didn't stop the ache she felt whenever she thought of him. Even worse was her humiliation because her inexperience had been so obvious, and now she *knew* he thought of her as a sex-starved old maid.

It was April before the inevitable happened and word got out that Joe Mackenzie was spending a lot of time at the new teacher's house. At first Mary wasn't aware of the rumor flying through the town, though the kids in her classes had been watching her strangely, and there had been a lot of whispering. Sharon Wycliffe and Dottie Lancaster, the other two teachers, also took to giving her odd looks and whispering to each other. It didn't take Mary long to decide that the secret was no longer secret, but she went about her business with a serene smile. She had already received a favorable letter from a senator, signaling his interest in Joe, and despite her own arguments for caution, her spirits were high.

The school board's regular meeting was scheduled for the third week in April. The afternoon of the meeting, Sharon, with elaborate casualness, asked Mary if she planned to attend. Mary looked at her in surprise. "Of course. I thought all of us were expected to attend on a regular basis."

"Well, yes. It's just that—I thought—"

"You thought I would avoid the meeting now that everyone knows I've been teaching Joe Mackenzie?" Mary asked directly.

Sharon's mouth fell open. "What?" Her voice was weak.

"You didn't know? Well, it isn't an earth-shattering secret." She shrugged. "Joe thought people would be upset if I tutored him, so I haven't said anything. From the way everyone has been acting, I thought the cat was out of the bag."

"I think it was the wrong cat," Sharon admitted sheepishly. "His truck was seen at your house at night and people—um—got the wrong idea."

Mary felt blank. "What wrong idea?"

"Well, he's big for his age and all."

Still Mary didn't understand, until Sharon blushed hotly. Then comprehension burst on her brain like a flash, and horror filled her, followed swiftly by anger. "They think I'm having an affair with a *sixteen-year-old boy*?" Her voice rose with each word.

"It was late at night when his truck was seen," Sharon added, looking miserable.

"Joe leaves promptly at nine o'clock. Someone's idea of 'late' differs from mine." Mary stood and began shoving papers into her tote, her nostrils flaring, her cheeks white. The awful thing was that she had to simmer until seven o'clock that night, but she didn't think waiting would cool her temper. If anything, pressure would build. She felt savage, not only because her reputation had been impugned, but because Joe had also been attacked. He was trying desperately to make his dreams come true, and people were trying to tear him down. She wasn't a hen fussing with one chick; she was a tigress with one cub, and that cub had been threatened. It didn't matter that the cub was seven inches taller than she and outweighed her by almost eighty pounds; Joe, for all his unusual maturity, was still young and vulnerable. The father had disdained her protection, but there was no power on earth that could stop her from defending the son.

Evidently word had spread, because the school board meeting was unusually crowded that night. There were six members of the board: Mr. Hearst, who owned the general store; Francie Beecham, an eighty-one-year-old former teacher; Walton Isby, the bank president; Harlon Keschel, who owned the combination drugstore/hamburger joint; Eli Baugh, a local rancher whose daughter, Jackie, was in Mary's class; and Cicely Karr, who owned the service station. All of the board members were solid members of the small community, all of them property owners, and all of them except Francie Beecham had stony faces.

The board meeting was held in Dottie's classroom, and extra desks were brought from Mary's classroom so there would be enough seats for everyone, an indication of how many people felt it necessary to attend. Mary was certain that at least one parent of each of her students was present. As she entered the room, every eye turned toward her. The women looked indignant; the men looked both hostile and speculative, and that made Mary even angrier. What right did they have to look down on her for her supposed sins, while at the same time they were wondering about the details?

Leaning against the wall was a tall man in a khaki deputy sheriff's uniform, watching her with narrowed eyes, and she wondered if they meant to have her arrested for sexual misconduct. It was ridiculous! If she had looked anything other than exactly what she was, a slight, mousy old maid, their suspicions would at least have made more sense. She poked an errant strand of hair back into the knot at the back of her head, sat down and folded her arms, intending to let them make the first move.

Walton Isby cleared his throat and called the meeting to order, no doubt feeling the importance of his position with so many people present to watch the proceedings. Mary drummed her fingers on her arm. The board went through the routine of its normal business, and suddenly she decided she wasn't going to wait. The best defense, she'd read, was an attack.

When the normal business was finished, Mr. Isby cleared his throat again, and Mary took it as a signal that they were about to get down to the real purpose of the meeting. She rose to her feet and said clearly, "Mr. Isby, before you continue, I have an announcement to make."

He looked startled, and his florid face turned even redder. "This is—uh, well, irregular, Miss Potter."

"It's also important." She kept her voice at the level she used when lecturing and turned so she could see the entire room. The deputy straightened from his position against the wall as everyone's attention locked on her like a magnet to a steel bar. "I'm certified to tutor pupils privately, and the credits they earn in private lessons are as legitimate as those earned in a public classroom. For the past month, I've been tutoring Joe Mackenzie in my home—"

"I'll just bet you have," someone muttered, and Mary's eyes flashed.

"Who said that?" she demanded crisply. "It was incredibly vulgar."

The room fell silent.

"When I saw Joe Mackenzie's school records, I was outraged that a student of his intelligence had quit school. Perhaps none of you know it, but he was at the top of his class. I contacted him and persuaded him to take lessons to catch up to his classmates, and in one month he has not only caught them, he has surpassed them. I have also been in contact with Senator Allard, who has expressed an interest in Joe. Joe's strong academic standing has made him a candidate for recommendation to the Air Force Academy. He's an honor to the community, and I know all of you will give him your support.''

She was gratified to see the stunned looks in the room and sat down with the cool poise Aunt Ardith had tirelessly drummed into her. Only rabble got into brawls, Aunt Ardith had said; a lady could make her point in other ways.

Whispers rustled through the room as people put their heads together, and Mr. Isby shuffled the three sheets of paper in front of him as he searched for something to say. The other members of the board put their heads together, too.

She looked around the room, and a shadow in the hall beyond the open door caught her attention. It was only a slight movement; if she hadn't looked at precisely that second, she would have missed it. As it was, it took her a moment to make out the outline of a tall man, and her skin tingled. Wolf. He was out in the hall, listening. It was the first time she had seen him since the day he'd come to her house, and even though all she could see was a darker outline against the shadows, her heart began to pound.

Mr. Isby cleared his throat, and the murmuring in the room settled down. "That is good news, Miss Potter," he began. "However, we don't think you've given the best appearance as an example to our young people—"

"Speak for yourself, Walton," Francie Beecham said testily, her voice cracking with old age.

Mary stood again. "In precisely what way have I given the wrong appearance?"

"It doesn't look right to have that boy in your house all hours of the night!" Mr. Hearst snapped.

"Joe leaves my home at exactly nine o'clock, after

three hours of lessons. What is your definition of 'all hours of the night'? However, if the board doesn't approve of the location, I take it all are agreed that the schoolhouse will be used for night classes? I have no objection to moving the lessons here.''

Mr. Isby, who was at heart a good-natured soul, looked harassed. The board members put their heads together again.

After a minute of heated consultation, they looked up again. Harlon Keschel wiped his perspiring face with a handkerchief. Francie Beecham looked outraged. This time it was Cicely Karr who spoke. ''Miss Potter, this is a difficult situation. The odds against Joe Mackenzie being accepted into the Air Force Academy are high, I'm sure you'll admit, and the truth is that we don't approve of your spending so much time alone with him.''

Mary's chin lifted. ''Why is that?''

''Because you're a newcomer to this area, I'm sure you don't understand the way things are around here. The Mackenzies have a bad reputation, and we fear for your safety if you continue to associate with the boy.''

''Mrs. Karr, that's hogwash,'' Mary replied with inelegant candor. Aunt Ardith wouldn't have approved. She thought of Wolf standing out in the hallway listening to these people slandering both him and his son, and she could almost feel the heat of his temper. He wouldn't let it hurt him, but it hurt her to know he was hearing it.

''Wolf Mackenzie helped me out of a dangerous situation when my car broke down and I was stranded in the snow. He was kind and considerate, and refused payment for repairing my car. Joe Mackenzie is an outstanding student who works hard on their ranch, doesn't drink or carouse—'' she hoped that was true ''—and has never been anything but respectful. I consider both of them my friends.''

In the hallway, the man standing in the shadows knotted his fists. Damn the little fool, didn't she know this would probably cost her her job? He knew that if he stepped into that room all the hostility would instantly be focused on him, and he started to move, to draw their attention away from her, when he heard her speaking again. Didn't she know when to shut up?

"I would be as concerned if any of your children dropped out of school. I can't bear to see a young person give up on the future. Ladies and gentlemen, I was hired to teach. I intend to do that to the best of my ability. All of you are good people. Would any of you want me to give up if it were *your* child?"

Several people looked away and cleared their throats. Cicely Karr merely raised her chin. "You're sidestepping the point, Miss Potter. This isn't one of our children. This is Joe Mackenzie. He's…he's—"

"Half Indian?" Mary supplied, lifting her brow in question.

"Well, yes. That's part of it. The other part is his father—"

"What about his father?"

Wolf had to stifle a curse, and he started to step forward again when Mary asked scornfully, "Are you concerned because of his prison sentence?"

"That's cause enough, I should think!"

"Should you? Why?"

"Cicely, sit down and hush," Francie Beecham snapped. "The girl has a point, and I agree. If you start trying to think at this stage of your life, it could bring on hot flashes."

Just for a moment there was stunned silence in the room; then it exploded in thunderous laughter. Rough ranchers and their hard-working wives held their stomachs as they bent double, tears running down their faces.

Mr. Isby turned so red his face was almost purple; then he burst into a great whooping laugh that sounded like a hysterical crane laying eggs, or so Cicely Karr told him. Her face was red, too, from anger. Big Eli Baugh actually rolled out of his chair, he was laughing so hard. Cicely grabbed his hat from the back of his chair and hit him over the head with it. He continued to howl with laughter as he protected his head with his arms.

"You can buy your motor oil from some other place from now on!" Cicely roared at Mr. Baugh, continuing to bash him with his hat. "And your gas! Don't you or any of your hands set foot on my property again!"

"Now, Cicely," Eli choked as he tried to dodge his hat.

"Folks, let's have some order in here," Harlon Keschel pleaded, though he looked as if he were enjoying the spectacle of Cicely bashing Eli with his own hat. Certainly everyone else in the room was. Almost everyone, Mary thought, as she spotted Dottie Lancaster's cold face. Suddenly she realized that the other teacher would have been glad to see her fired, and she wondered why. She'd always tried to be friendly with Dottie, but the older woman had rebuffed all overtures. Had *Dottie* seen Joe's truck at Mary's house and started the gossip? Would Dottie have been out driving around at night? There were no other houses on Mary's road, so no one would have been driving past to visit a neighbor.

The uproar had died down, though there was still an occasional chuckle heard around the room. Mrs. Karr continued to glare at Eli Baugh, having for some reason made him the focal point of her embarrassed anger rather than turning it on Francie Beecham, who had started it all.

Even Mr. Isby was still grinning as he raised his voice. "Let's see if we can get back to business here, folks."

Francie Beecham piped up again. "I think we've handled enough business for the night. Miss Potter is giving the Mackenzie boy private school lessons so he can go to the Air Force Academy, and that's that. I'd do the same thing if I were still teaching."

Mr. Hearst said, "It still don't look right—"

"Then she can use the classroom. Everyone agreed?" Francie looked at the other board members, her wrinkled face triumphant. She winked at Mary.

"It's okay by me," Eli Baugh said as he tried to reshape his hat. "The Air Force Academy—well, that's something. I don't reckon anyone from this county has ever been to any of the academies."

Mr. Hearst and Mrs. Karr disagreed, but Mr. Isby and Harlon Keschel sided with Francie and Eli. Mary stared hard at the shadowed hallway, but couldn't see anything now. Had he left? The deputy turned his head to see what she was looking at, but he didn't see anything, either, because he gave a slight shrug and looked back at her, then winked. Mary was startled. More people had winked at her that night than in the rest of her life total. What was the proper way to handle a wink? Were they ignored? Should she wink back? Aunt Ardith's lectures on proper behavior hadn't covered winking.

The meeting broke up with a good deal of teasing and laughter, and more than a few of the parents took a moment to shake Mary's hand and tell her she was doing a good job. It was half an hour before she was able to get her coat and make it to the door, and when she did, she found the deputy waiting for her.

"I'll walk you to your car," he said in an easy tone. "I'm Clay Armstrong, the local deputy."

"How do you do? Mary Potter," she replied, holding out her hand.

He took it, and her small hand disappeared in his big

one. He set his hat on top of dark brown curly hair, but
his blue eyes still twinkled, even in the shadow of the
brim. She liked him on sight. He was one of those strong,
quiet men who were rock steady, but who had a good
sense of humor. He'd been delighted by the uproar.

"Everyone in town knows who you are. We don't often have a stranger move in, especially a young single
woman from the South. The first day you were here, the
whole county heard about your accent. Haven't you noticed that all the girls in school are trying to drawl?"

"Are they?" she asked in surprise.

"They sure are." He slowed his walk to keep pace
with her as they walked to her car. The cold air rushed
at her, chilling her legs, but the night sky was crystal
clear, and a thousand stars winked overhead in compen-
sation.

They reached her car. "Would you tell me something,
Mr. Armstrong?"

"Anything. And call me Clay."

"Why did Mrs. Karr get so angry at Mr. Baugh, instead of at Miss Beecham? It was Miss Beecham who
started the whole thing."

"Cicely and Eli are first cousins. Cicely's folks died
when she was young, and Eli's parents took her to raise.
Well, Cicely and Eli are the same age, so they grew up
together and fought like wildcats the whole time. Still
do, I guess, but some families are like that. They're still
pretty close."

That kind of family was strange to Mary, but it
sounded warm and secure, too, to be able to fight with
someone and know he still loved you.

"So she hit him for laughing at her?"

"And because he was convenient. No one is going to
get too angry with Miss Beecham. She taught all the

adults in this county, and we all still think a lot of that old lady.''

"That sounds so nice," Mary said, smiling. "I hope I'm still here when I'm that old.''

"Are you planning to raise cain at school board meetings, too?''

"I hope so," she repeated.

He leaned down to open the car door for her. "I hope so, too. Be careful driving home." After she got in, he closed the door and touched his fingers to his hat brim, then strode away.

He was a nice man. Most of the people in Ruth were nice. They were blind where Wolf Mackenzie was concerned, but basically they weren't vicious people.

Wolf. Where had he gone?

She hoped Joe wouldn't decide to stop his lessons because of this. Though she knew it was foolish to count her chickens prematurely, she felt a growing certainty that he would be accepted into the Academy and was inordinately proud that she could be part of getting him there. Aunt Ardith would have said that pride goeth before a fall, but Mary had often thought that a person would never fall if he didn't first try to stand. On more than one occasion she had countered Aunt Ardith's cliché of choice with her own "nothing ventured, nothing gained." It had always made Aunt Ardith huffy when her favorite weapon was turned against her. Mary sighed. She missed her acerbic aunt so much. Her supply of clichés might wither from lack of use without Aunt Ardith to sharpen her wits against.

When she turned into her driveway, she was tired, hungry and anxious, afraid that Joe would try to be noble and stop his lessons so she wouldn't have any more trouble because of him. "I'll teach him," she muttered aloud as she stepped out of the car, "if I have to follow him around on horseback."

"Who are you following around?" Wolf demanded irritably, and she jumped so violently that she banged her knee against the car door.

"Where did you come from?" she demanded just as irritably. "Darn it, you scared me!"

"Probably not enough. I parked in the barn, out of sight."

She stared up at him, drinking in the sight of his proud, chiseled face and closed expression. The starlight was colorless, revealing his features in stark angles and shadows, but it was enough for her. She hadn't realized how starved she had been for the sight of him, the heart-pounding nearness of him. She couldn't even feel the cold now, the way blood was racing through her veins. This was probably what "being in heat" meant. It was breathtaking and a little scary, but she decided she liked it.

"Let's go in," he said when she made no effort to move, and Mary silently led the way to the back door. She'd left it unlocked so she wouldn't have to fumble with a key in the dark, and Wolf's black brows drew together when she turned the knob and pushed the door open.

They entered, and Mary closed the door behind them, then turned on the light. Wolf stared down at her, at the silky brown hair escaping from its knot, and he had to clench his fists to keep from grabbing her. "Don't leave your door unlocked again," he ordered.

"I don't think I'll be burgled," she countered, then admitted honestly, "I don't have anything a self-respecting burglar would want."

He'd sworn he wouldn't touch her, but even though he'd known it would be difficult to keep his hands to

himself, he hadn't realized quite *how* difficult. He wanted
to grab her and shake some sense into her, but he knew
if he touched her in any way at all, he wouldn't want to
stop. Her female scent teased his nostrils, beckoning him
closer; she smelled warm and delicately fragrant, so feminine it made his entire body ache with longing. He
moved away from her, knowing it was safer for them
both if he put some distance between them.

"I wasn't thinking about a burglar."

"No?" She considered that, then realized what he'd
meant and what she'd said in response. She cleared her
throat and marched to the stove, hoping he wouldn't see
her red face. "If I make a pot of coffee, will you drink
a cup this time or storm out like you did before as soon
as it's made?"

The tart reproach in her voice amused him, and he
wondered how he had ever thought her mousy. Her
clothes were dowdy, but her personality was anything but
timid. She said exactly what she thought and didn't hesitate to take someone to task. Less than an hour before
she had taken on the entire county on his behalf. The
memory of it sobered him.

"I'll drink the coffee if you insist on making it, but
I'd rather you just sat down and listened to me."

Turning, Mary slid into a chair and primly folded her
hands on the table. "I'm listening."

He pulled the chair next to her away from the table
and turned it to the side, facing her, before he sat down.
She turned an unsmiling gaze on him. "I saw you in the
hall tonight."

He looked grim. "Damn. Did anyone else notice me?"
He wondered how she had seen him, because he'd been
very careful, and he was good at not being seen when
he didn't want to be.

"I don't think so." She paused. "I'm sorry they said those things."

"I'm not worried about what the good people of Ruth think about me," he said in a hard tone. "I can handle them, and so can Joe. We don't depend on them for our living, but you do. Don't go to bat for us again, unless you don't like your job very much and you're trying to lose it, because that's damn sure what will happen if you keep on."

"I won't lose my job for teaching Joe."

"Maybe not. Maybe they'll have some tolerance for Joe, especially since you threw the Academy at them, but I'm another story."

"Nor will I lose my job for being friendly with you. I have a contract," she explained serenely. "An ironclad contract. It isn't easy to get a teacher in a place as small and isolated as Ruth, especially in the middle of winter. I can lose my job only if I'm judged incompetent, or break the law, and I defy anyone to prove me incompetent."

He wondered if that meant she didn't rule out breaking the law, but didn't ask her. The kitchen light was shining directly down on her head, turning her hair to a silvery halo and distracting him with its glitter. He knew her hair was brown, but it was such a pale, ash brown that it had no red tones, and when light struck it the strands actually looked silver. She looked like an angel, with her soft blue eyes and translucent skin, and her silky hair slipping from its confining knot to curl around her face. His insides knotted painfully. He wanted to touch her. He wanted her naked beneath him. He wanted to be inside her, to gently ride her until she was all soft and wet, and her nails were clawing at his back—

Mary reached out and put her slim hand on his much larger one, and just that small touch burned him. "Tell me what happened,'' she invited softly. ''Why were you sent to prison? I know you didn't do it.''

Wolf was a hard man, by nature as well as necessity, but her simple, unquestioning faith in him shook him to the bone. He had always stood alone, isolated by his Indian blood from Anglos and by his Anglo blood from Indians. Not even his parents had been close to him, though they had loved him and he had loved them in return. They had simply never truly known him, never been admitted into his private thoughts. Nor had he been close to his wife, Joe's mother. They had slept together, he'd been fond of her, but she, too, had been kept at a distance. Only with Joe had his reserve been breached, and Joe knew him as no other person on earth did. They were part of each other, and he fiercely loved the boy. Only the thought of Joe had gotten him through the years in prison alive.

It was more than alarming that this slight Anglo woman had a knack for touching nerves he'd thought completely insulated; he didn't want her close to him, not in any emotional way. He wanted to have sex with her, but he didn't want her to matter to him. Angrily he realized that she already mattered to him, and he didn't like it at all.

He stared at her fragile hand on his, her touch light and soft. She didn't shrink from touching him, as if he were dirty; nor was she grasping at him as some women did, rapaciously, wanting to use him, to see if the savage could satisfy their shallow, greedy appetites. She had simply reached out to touch him because she cared.

Ever so slowly he watched his hand turn and engulf hers, enfolding the pale, slim fingers within his callused palm as if to protect them.

''It was nine years ago.'' His voice was low, harsh; she had to lean forward to hear him. ''No—almost ten

years. Ten years this June. Joe and I had just moved here.
I was working for the Half Moon Ranch. A girl from the
next county was raped and killed, and her body dumped
just within the far boundary of Half Moon. I was picked
up and questioned, but hell, I'd been expecting it from
the minute I heard about the girl. I was new to the area,
and Indian. But there was no evidence against me, so
they had to let me go.

"Three weeks later, another girl was raped. This one
was from the Rocking L Ranch, just to the west of town.
She was stabbed, like the other girl, but she lived. She'd
seen the rapist." He paused for a minute, the expression
in his black eyes shuttered as he looked back at those
long-ago years. "She said he looked like an Indian. He
was dark, with black hair, and he was tall. Not many tall
Indians around. I was picked up again before I even
knew another girl had been raped. They put me in a
lineup with six dark-haired Anglos. The girl identified
me, and I was charged. Joe and I lived on Half Moon,
but somehow no one remembered seeing me at home the
night that girl was raped, except Joe, and a six-year-old
Indian kid's word didn't carry much weight."

Her chest hurt when she thought of how it had been
for him, and for Joe, who had been only a small child.
How much worse had it been for Wolf because of Joe,
worrying what would happen to his son? She didn't
know of anything she could say now to lessen that ten-
year-old outrage, so she didn't try; she just tightened her
fingers around his, letting him know he wasn't alone.

"I was put on trial and found guilty. I'm lucky they
weren't able to tie me to the first rape, the girl who'd
been murdered, or I'd have been lynched. As it was,
everyone thought I'd done it."

"You went to prison." It was so hard to believe, even
though she knew it was true. "What happened to Joe?"

''He was made a ward of the state. I survived prison. It wasn't easy. A rapist is considered fair game. I had to be the roughest son of a bitch in there just to live from one night to the next.''

She had heard tales about what happened to men in prison, and her pain increased. He had been locked up, away from the sun and the mountains, the clear fresh air, and she knew it had been like caging a wild animal. He was innocent, but his freedom and his son had been taken from him, and he'd been thrown in with the dregs of humanity. Had he slept soundly even once the entire time he'd been in prison, or had he merely dozed, his senses attuned to attack?

Her throat was tight and dry. All she could manage was a whisper. ''How long were you in?''

''Two years.'' His face was hard, his eyes full of menace as he stared at her, but she knew the menace was directed inward, at his bitter memories. ''Then a series of rapes and murders from Casper to Cheyenne were tied together and the guy was caught. He confessed, seemed proud of his accomplishments, but a little put out that they hadn't given him complete credit. He admitted to the two rapes in this area, and gave them details no one but the rapist could have known.''

''Was he Indian?''

His smile was flinty. ''Italian. Olive-skinned, curly haired.''

''So you were released?''

''Yeah. My name was cleared, and they said 'Sorry about that,' and turned me loose. I'd lost my son, my job, everything I'd owned. I found out where they'd put Joe and hitched there to get him. Then I rodeoed for a while to get some money and lucked out. I did pretty well. I won enough to come back here with something in my pocket. The old guy who had owned Half Moon had died with no heirs, and the land was about to be sold for taxes. It wiped me out, but I bought the land. Joe and I settled here, and I began training horses and building up the ranch.''

''Why did you come back?'' She couldn't understand it. Why return to the place where he'd been so mistreated?

''Because I was tired of always moving on, never having a place of my own. Damn tired of being looked down on as a trashy, shiftless Indian. Tired of my son not having a home. And because there was no way in hell I was going to let the bastards get the best of me.''

The aching in her intensified. She wished she could ease the anger and bitterness in him, wished she dared take him in her arms and soothe him, wished he could become a part of the community instead of a thorn in its side.

''They're not all illegitimate,'' she said, and wondered why his mouth suddenly twitched as if he might smile. ''Any more than all Indians are trashy or shiftless. People are just people, good and bad.''

''You need a keeper,'' he replied. ''That Pollyanna attitude is going to get you in trouble. Teach Joe, do what you can for him, but stay the hell away from me, for your own sake. These people didn't change their minds about me just because I was released.''

''You haven't tried to change their minds. You've just kept rubbing their noses in their guilt,'' she pointed out, her tone acerbic.

''Am I supposed to forget what they did?'' he asked just as sharply. ''Forget that their 'justice' consisted of putting me in a lineup with six Anglos and telling that girl to 'pick out the Indian'? I spent two years in hell. I still don't know what happened to Joe, but it was almost three months after I got him back before he spoke a word. Forget that? Like hell.''

"So, they won't change their minds, you won't change your mind, and I won't change mine. I believe we have a stalemate.''

His dark eyes burned with frustration as he glared at her, and suddenly he seemed to realize he was still holding her hand. He released her abruptly and stood. "Look, you can't be my friend. *We* can't be friends.''

Now that her hand was free, Mary felt abandoned and cold. She clasped her hands in her lap and looked up at him. "Why? Of course, if you simply don't like me...'' Her voice trailed off, and she bent her head to examine her hands as if she'd never seen them before.

Not like her? He couldn't sleep, his temper was frayed, he got hard whenever he thought about her, and he thought about her too damn much. He was so physically frustrated that he thought he might go mad, but he couldn't even ease himself with Julie Oakes or any other woman now, because all he could think about was baby-fine brown hair, slate-blue eyes and skin like translucent rose petals. It was all he could do to keep from taking her, and only the knowledge of how the good townspeople of Ruth would turn on her if he made her his woman kept him from grabbing her. Her stubborn principles hadn't prepared her for the pain and trouble she would face.

Suddenly his frustration boiled over, and he was filled with rage at having to walk away from the one woman he wanted to the point of madness. Before he could stop himself, he reached down and grasped her wrists, hauling her to her feet. "No, damn it, we can't be friends! Do you want to know why? Because I can't be around you without thinking of stripping you naked and taking you, wherever we happen to be. Hell, I don't know if I'd take

the time to strip you! I want your breasts in my hands,
your nipples in my mouth. I want your legs around my
waist, or your ankles on my shoulders, or any position
at all if I can just get inside you.'' He'd pulled her so
close that his warm breath brushed her cheeks as he
rasped the low, harsh words at her. ''So, sweetheart,
there's no way we can be *friends*.''

Mary shivered as her body responded to his words.
Though they'd been spoken in anger, they told her that
he felt the same way she did, and described actions she
could only half imagine. She was too inexperienced and
honest to hide her feelings from him, so she didn't even
try. Her eyes were filled with painful longing. ''Wolf?''

Just that, but the way she said his name, with an aching little inflection at the end, made his grip on her wrists
tighten. ''No.''

''I—I want you.''

Her whispered, trembly confession left her completely
vulnerable to him, and he knew it. He groaned inwardly.
Damn it, didn't she have any sense of self-protection at
all? Didn't she know what it did to a man to have the
woman he wanted offer herself like that, with no qualifications or holding back? His control was stretched hair-
thin, but he grimly held on to it because the hard truth
was that she truly didn't know. She was a virgin. She
was old-fashioned, strictly raised, and had only the vagu-
est idea of what she was inviting.

''Don't say that,'' he finally muttered. ''I've told you
before—''

''I know,'' she interrupted. ''I'm too inexperienced to
be interesting, and you…you don't want to be used as a
guinea pig. I remember.'' She seldom cried, but she felt
the salty wetness burning her eyes, and he winced at the
hurt he saw there.

''I lied. God, how I lied.''

Then his control broke. He had to hold her, feel her in his arms just for a little while, have her taste on his mouth again. He drew her wrists up and placed her hands around his neck, then bent his head even as he locked his arms around her and drew her up tight against him. His mouth covered hers, and her eager response seared him. She knew what to do now; her lips parted, allowing his tongue entrance, where she met him with soft, welcoming touches from her own tongue. He had taught her that, just as he'd taught her to melt against him, and the knowledge drove him almost as crazy as the feel of her soft breasts flattening against his chest.

Mary drowned in the sheer ecstasy of being in his arms again, and the tears that she'd held back spilled past her lashes. This was too painful, and too wonderful, to be mere lust. If this was love, she didn't know if she could bear it.

His mouth was hungry and hard, taking long, deep kisses that left her clinging to him mindlessly. His hand moved surely up her stomach and closed over her breast, and all she could do was make a soft sound of pleasure low in her throat. Her nipples burned and throbbed; his touch both assuaged the pain and intensified it, making her want more. She wanted it the way he had described it, with his mouth on her breasts, and she twisted feverishly against him. She was empty and needed to be filled. She needed to be his woman.

He jerked his head up and pressed her face against his shoulder. "I have to stop. Now." He groaned the words. He was shaking, as hot as any teenage stud in the back seat of his daddy's car.

Mary briefly weighed all of Aunt Ardith's strictures against the way she felt and accepted that she was in love, because this mingled glory and torment could be nothing else. "I don't want to stop," she said raggedly. "I want you to love me."

"No. I'm Indian. You're white. The people in this town would destroy you. Tonight was just a taste of what you'd have to go through."

"I'm willing to risk it!" she cried desperately.

"I'm not. I can take it, but you—you hang on to your Pollyanna principles, sweetheart. I can't offer you anything in return." If he'd thought there was even a fifty-fifty chance of living here in peace, Wolf would have taken the risk, but he knew there wasn't, not the way things were. Other than Joe, she was the only human being in the world he'd ever wanted to protect, and it was the hardest thing he'd ever done.

Mary lifted her head from his shoulder, revealing her wet cheeks. "All I want is you."

"I'm the one thing you can't have. They'd tear you apart." Very gently he pulled her arms down and turned to leave.

Her voice came behind him, low and strained as she fought against tears. "I'll risk it."

He stopped, his hand on the doorknob. "I won't."

For the second time she watched him walk away, and this time was far worse than the first.

Chapter 5

Joe was unusually distracted; he was normally the most attentive of students, applying himself to the subject at hand with almost phenomenal concentration, but tonight he had something else on his mind. He'd accepted without comment their move to the school for lessons and never even hinted that he'd learned the subject of the school board meeting that had resulted in the change of locations. As it was the beginning of May, and the day had been unseasonably warm, Mary was half inclined to put his restlessness down to spring fever. It had been a long winter, and she was restless herself.

Finally she closed the book before her. "Why don't we go home early tonight?" she suggested. "We're not getting much done."

Joe closed his own book and pushed his fingers through his thick black hair, identical to his father's. Mary had to look away. "Sorry," he said on a long exhalation. It was typical that he didn't offer an explanation. Joe didn't often feel the need to justify himself.

But in the weeks she'd been tutoring him, they had had a lot of personal conversations between the prepared lessons, and Mary never hesitated when she thought one of her students might be troubled. If it were only spring fever gnawing at him, then she wanted him to say so. "Is something bothering you?"

He gave her a wry smile, one that was too adult to belong to a sixteen-year-old boy. "You could say that."

"Ah." That smile relieved her, because now she thought she knew the cause of his restlessness. It was indeed spring fever, after a fashion. As Aunt Ardith had often lectured her niece, "When a young man's sap rises, a girl should look out. I declare, they seem to run mad." Evidently Joe's sap was rising. Mary wondered if women had sap, too.

He picked up his pen and fiddled with it for a moment before tossing it aside as he made up his mind to say more. "Pam Hearst asked me to take her to a movie."

"Pam?" This was a surprise, and possible trouble. Ralph Hearst was one of the townspeople most adamantly opposed to the Mackenzies.

Joe's ice-blue eyes were hooded as he glanced at her. "Pam is the girl I told you about before."

So, it *was* Pam Hearst. She was pretty and bright, and her slim young body had a form guaranteed to affect a young man's sap. Mary wondered if Pam's father knew she had been flirting with Joe and that was one reason for his hostility.

"Are you going to go?"

"No," he said flatly, surprising her.

"Why?"

"There aren't any movie houses in Ruth."

"So?"

"That's the whole point. We'd have to go to another town. No one we know would be likely to see us. She wanted me to pick her up behind the school, after it got dark.'' He leaned back in his chair and looped his hands behind his head. ''She was too ashamed to go to the dance with me, but I'm good enough for her to sneak around and see. Maybe she thought that even if we were seen, the idea that I might go to the Academy would keep her from getting in too much trouble. Folks seem taken with the idea.'' His tone was ironic. ''I guess it makes a difference when the Indian wears a uniform.''

Suddenly her impulsive announcement at the school board meeting didn't seem like such a good idea. ''Do you wish I hadn't told them?''

''You had to, considering,'' he replied, and by that she knew he was aware of the subject of that meeting. ''It puts extra pressure on me to get into the Academy, because if I don't they'll all say that the Indian just couldn't cut it, but that's not a bad thing. If it will push me to do more, then I'm that much closer to getting in.''

Privately, Mary didn't think Joe needed any added incentive; he wanted it so badly now that the need burned in him. She returned the conversation to Pam. ''Does it bother you, that she asked now?''

''It made me mad. And it *really* made me mad having to turn her down, because I sure would like to get my hands on her.'' He stopped abruptly and gave Mary another of those too-adult looks before a little grin tugged at his lips. ''Sorry. I didn't mean to get too personal. Let's just say that I'm attracted to her physically, but that's all it is, and I can't afford to fool with that kind of situation. Pam's a nice girl, but she doesn't figure in my plans.''

Mary understood what he meant. No woman figured in his plans, other than to provide physical release, for a long time, if ever. There was something solitary about him, as there was about Wolf, and in addition, Joe was so possessed by the specter of flight that part of him was already gone. Pam Hearst would marry some local boy, settle down in Ruth or nearby, and raise her own family in the same calm setting where she'd grown up; she wasn't meant for the brief attention Joe Mackenzie could give her before he moved on.

"Do you have any idea who started the gossip?" Joe asked, his pale eyes hard. He didn't like the idea of anyone hurting this woman.

"No. I haven't tried to find out. It could have been anyone who drove by and saw your truck at my house. But most people seemed to have forgotten about it now, except for—" She stopped, her eyes troubled.

"Who?" Joe demanded flatly.

"I don't mean that I think she started the gossip," Mary said hastily. "I just feel uneasy around her. She dislikes me, and I don't know why. Maybe she's this way with everyone. Has Dottie Lancaster—"

"Dottie Lancaster!" He gave a harsh laugh. "Now there's a thought. Yeah, she could have started the gossip. She's had a rough life, and I kind of feel sorry for her, but she did her best to make my life hell when I was in her classes."

"Rough? How?"

"Her husband was a truck driver, and he was killed years ago when her son was just a baby. He was on a run in Colorado, and a drunk driver ran him off the side of a cliff. The drunk was an Indian. She never got over it and blames all Indians, I guess."

"That's irrational."

He shrugged, as if to say a lot of things were irrational. "Anyway, she was left alone with her kid, and she had a hard time. Not much money. She started teaching, but she had to pay someone to take care of the kid, and he needed special training when he was old enough to start school, which took even more money.''

''I didn't know Dottie had any children,'' Mary said, surprised.

''Just Robert—Bobby. He's about twenty-three or four, I guess. He still lives with Mrs. Lancaster, but he doesn't go around other people much.''

''What's wrong with him? Does he have Down's syndrome, or a learning disability?''

''He's not retarded. Bobby's just different. He likes people, but not in groups. A lot of people together make him nervous, so he pretty much stays to himself. He reads a lot, and listens to music. But once he had a summer job at the building supply store, and Mr. Watkins told Bobby to fill a wheelbarrow full of sand. Instead of pushing the wheelbarrow to the sandpile and shoveling the sand in, Bobby would get a shovelful of sand and carry it back to the wheelbarrow. It's things like that. He'd have trouble getting dressed, because he'd put his shoes on first, and then he couldn't get his jeans on.''

Mary had seen people like Bobby, who had trouble with practical problem-solving. It was a learning disability, and took a lot of patient, specialized training to handle. She felt sorry for him, and for Dottie, who couldn't have had a happy life.

Joe pushed his chair back and stood up, stretching his cramped muscles. ''Do you ride?'' he asked suddenly.

''No. I've never even been on a horse.'' Mary chuckled. ''Will that get me thrown out of Wyoming?''

His tone was grave. ''It could. Why don't you come up on the mountain some Saturday and I'll give you riding lessons? School will be out for the summer soon, and you'll have a lot of time to practice.''

He couldn't know how appealing the idea was, not only to ride but to see Wolf again. The only thing was, it would hurt just as much to see him as it did not to see him, because he was still out of her reach. "I'll think about it," she promised, but she doubted she would ever take him up on the offer.

Joe didn't push it, but he didn't intend to let it drop, either. He'd get Mary up on the mountain one way or another. He figured Wolf had about reached the limits of his restraint. Parading her right under his nose would be like leading a mare in heat in front of a stallion. His pretty, tart-tongued little teacher would be lucky if his dad didn't have her flat on her back before she had the hello out of her mouth. Joe had to hide his smile. He'd never seen anyone get to Wolf the way Miss Mary Elizabeth Potter had. She had Wolf so tied in knots he was as dangerous as a wounded cougar.

He mentally hummed a few bars of "Matchmaker."

When Mary got home the next Friday afternoon, there was a letter in the mailbox from Senator Allard, and her fingers trembled as she tore it open. If it was bad news for Joe, if Senator Allard had declined to recommend him to the Academy, she didn't know what she would do. Senator Allard wasn't their only possibility, but he had seemed the most receptive, and a turndown from him would really be discouraging.

The senator's letter to her was brief, thanking her for her efforts in bringing Joe to his attention. He had decided to recommend Joe for admittance to the Academy, for the freshman class beginning after Joe's graduation from high school. From there on, it would be up to Joe to pass the rigorous academic and physical examinations.

Enclosed was a private letter of congratulations to Joe.

Mary hugged the letters to her breast, and tears welled in her eyes. They had done it, and it hadn't even been that difficult! She had been prepared to petition every congressman every week until Joe was given his chance, but it hadn't been necessary. Joe's grades and credits had done it for him.

It was news too good to wait, so she got back into her car and drove up Mackenzie's Mountain. The drive was much different now; the snow had melted, and wildflowers bloomed beside the road. After the harsh winter cold, the spring warmth felt like a blessing on her skin, though it still wasn't nearly as warm as the springs she had known in Savannah. She was so excited and happy that she didn't even notice the steep drop on the side of the road as it wound higher, but she did notice the wild grandeur of the mountains, stretching magnificently toward the dark blue heavens. She drew a deep breath and realized that the spring did make up for the winter. It felt like home, a new home, a place dear and familiar.

The tires threw out a spray of gravel as she slid to a stop at the kitchen door of Wolf's one-story frame house, and before the vehicle had rocked back on its springs she was bounding up the steps to pound on the door. "Wolf! Joe!" She knew she was yelling in a very unladylike manner, but she was too happy to care. Some situations just called for yelling.

"Mary!"

The call came from behind her, and she whirled. Wolf was coming from the barn at a dead run, his powerful body surging fluidly. Mary yelped in excitement and launched herself from the steps, her skirt flying up as she bolted down the graveled drive toward the barn. "He got it!" she screamed, waving the letters. "He got it!"

Wolf skidded to a halt and watched the sedate teacher literally skipping and leaping toward him, her skirt kicking up around her thighs with each step. He just had time to realize there was nothing wrong, that she was laughing, when, three steps away, she went airborne. He braced himself and caught her weight against his chest, his brawny arms wrapping around her.

"He got it!" she shrieked again, and threw her arms around his neck.

Wolf could think of only one thing, and it made his mouth go dry. "He got it?"

She waved the letters under his nose. "He got it! Senator Allard—the letter was in my mailbox—I couldn't wait—where's Joe?" She knew she was almost incoherent and made an effort to compose herself, but she just couldn't stop grinning.

"He's in town picking up a load of fencing. Damn it, are you sure that's what it says? He still has a year of school—"

"Not a year, not at the rate he's going. But he'll have to be seventeen, anyway. The senator has recommended him for the freshman class starting after he graduates. Less than a year and a half!"

Fierce pride filled Wolf's face, the warrior's pride he'd inherited from both Comanche and Celt. His eyes glittered with black fire, and exultantly he lifted her high, his hands under her armpits, and twirled around with her. She threw back her head, shrieking with laughter, and suddenly Wolf felt his entire body clench with desire. It was as powerful as a blow to the gut, knocking the wind out of him. She was soft and warm in his arms, her laughter was as fresh as the spring, and he wanted her out of the prim little shirtwaist she wore.

Slowly his face changed to a harder, more primitive cast. She was still laughing as he lowered her, her hands braced on his shoulders, but he stopped when her breasts were level with his face. The laughter died in Mary's throat as he deliberately brought her closer to him and buried his face between her breasts. His grip shifted, one arm locking around her buttocks and the other around her back, and his hot mouth searched for her nipple. He found it, his mouth clamping down on it through the barriers of her dress and bra, but the sensation was still so exquisite that her breath caught on a moan and her back arched, pushing her breast against him.

It wasn't enough. She burrowed her fingers through his hair, digging into his skull to push him harder against her, but it wasn't enough. She wanted him with sudden, fierce desperation. The layers of cloth that kept him from her drove her mad, and she squirmed against him, low whimpers coming from her throat. "Please," she begged. "Wolf—"

He lifted his head, his eyes savage with need. His blood was thundering through his veins, and he was breathing hard. "Do you want more?" The words were guttural, a normal tone beyond him.

She squirmed against him again, her hands clutching desperately. "Yes."

Very gently he let her slide down his body, deliberately rubbing her over the hardened bulge in his jeans, and both of them shuddered. Wolf was beyond thinking of all his reasons for not becoming involved with her, beyond anything but the urge to mate. To hell with what anyone thought.

He looked around, gauging the distance to both house and barn. The barn was closer. Clamping his hand around her wrist, he strode toward the big open double doors that revealed the dim interior.

Mary could barely get her breath as she was all but dragged in his wake. Her senses bewildered by the sudden cessation of pleasure, she was confused by his actions and wanted to ask what he was doing, but she didn't have enough oxygen in her lungs to form the question. Then they were inside the barn, and she was swamped by the perceptions of dim light, animal warmth and the

earthy smells of dust, hay, leather and horses. She heard
soft nickers and the muffled stamping of hooves on
straw. Wolf led her into an empty stall and dragged her
down onto the fresh hay. She sprawled on her back, and
he came down on top of her, his muscled weight pressing
her even deeper into the hay.

"Kiss me," she whispered, reaching up to thrust her
fingers into his long hair and pull him down to her.

"I'll kiss you all over before I'm through with you,"
he muttered, and bent his head. Her mouth opened under
the force of his, and his tongue moved into her in a deep
rhythm that she instinctively recognized and accepted,
responded to eagerly. He was heavy, but it was so natural
that she bear his weight that she rejoiced in the pressure
of his body. She wrapped her arms around his thickly
muscled shoulders and hugged him even tighter to her;
she wanted to be as close as she could to him, and to
that end her hips undulated slightly, adjusting to the car-
nal pressure of his loins.

The slow movements of her hips beneath him made
him feel as if his head would explode from the rush of
blood through his body. He made a low, rough sound in
his throat and reached for the zipper at the back of her
dress. He thought he would die if he didn't feel her silky
skin under his hands, if he didn't sheathe his throbbing
flesh inside her.

It was startlingly new to her, bringing a delicate flush
to her cheeks, but it was still so *right* that she didn't even
think of protesting. She didn't want to protest. She
wanted Wolf. She was female to his male, warm and
sexual, intensely aware of being a woman and offering
herself to the man she loved. She wanted to be naked for
him, so she helped him by pulling her arms free of the
sleeves as he tugged the dress from her shoulders and let
it fall to her waist. She had felt racy, daring to buy a bra

with a single front clasp, but as he looked down at her breasts, barely covered by the thin, flesh-colored material, she was so glad she had done it. He deftly opened the clasp with one hand, a trick she hadn't learned yet, and watched the edges pull back to bare her soft curves, stopping before her nipples were revealed.

He made that rough sound again, almost like a growl, and bent to nuzzle the bra aside. His mouth, warm and wet, slid across her breast and clamped on the tightly beaded nipple. She jumped, her entire body reacting to a pleasure so intense it bordered on pain, as he sucked strongly at her. Mary's eyes closed, and she moaned. She couldn't bear it; it felt *too* good, a hot river of pleasure-pain impulses running from breast to loin, where an empty ache made her press her legs together and arch beneath him, silently begging for the release her body had never known, but sensed with ancient wisdom.

Wolf felt her move beneath him again, and the last shred of control he'd retained, vanished. Roughly he jerked her skirt to her waist and kneed her thighs apart, settling himself between the vulnerable V of her legs. She opened her eyes, a little shocked by what she could feel down there, but eager to know more. "Take off your clothes," she whispered frantically, and tore at the buttons on his shirt.

He reared back on his knees and tore his shirt open, then off. His naked skin glistened with a fine patina of sweat; in the dim light, filled with floating dust motes, the overlay of sleek bronze skin on powerful muscles gave him the look of live art sculpted by a master's hand. Mary's gaze moved hungrily, feverishly, over him. He was perfect, strong and male, the scent of his body hot and faintly musky. She reached out for him, her hands sliding over his broad chest, lightly haired in a diamond pattern stretching from nipple to nipple. She touched those tight little buds, and he froze, a massive shiver of pleasure rippling through his muscles.

He groaned aloud and dropped his hands to his belt. He unbuckled the wide band of leather, then unsnapped his jeans and jerked the zipper down, the hissing of the metal teeth blending with their harsh breathing. With some last desperate fragment of willpower, he kept himself from lowering his pants. She was a virgin; he couldn't allow himself to forget that, even in his urgency. Damn it, he had to regain some control, or he'd both scare and hurt her, and he would die before he turned her first time into a nightmare.

Mary's slim fingers curled in the hair on his chest and tugged lightly. "Wolf," she said. Just his name, just that one word, but her voice was warm and low and drugged sounding, and it beckoned him more powerfully than anything he'd known before.

"Yes," he said in response. "Now." He leaned forward to cover her again, then froze as a distant sound came to his ears.

He swore quietly and sank back on his heels, battling desperately to control his body and his frustration.

"Wolf?" Now her tone was hesitant, consternation and self-consciousness creeping into it. That inflection made him feel murderous, because she hadn't been self-conscious before. She had been warm and loving, willing to give herself without reserve.

"Joe will be here in a few minutes," he said flatly. "I can hear his truck coming up the mountain."

She was still so far out of it that she merely looked confused. "Joe?"

"Yes, Joe. Remember him? My son, the reason you're up here in the first place."

Her cheeks flooded with color, and she jerked into an upright position, as far as she could, because her thighs were still draped over his. "Oh my God," she said. "Oh my God. I'm naked. You're naked. Oh my God."

"We're not naked," Wolf muttered, wiping his sweaty face. "Damn it."

"Almost!"

"Not enough." Even her breasts were rosy with embarrassment now. He looked at them with regret, remembering her sweet taste and the way her velvety little nipple had bloomed in his mouth. But the sound of the truck was much closer now, and with a low, obscene comment on his son's rotten timing, he got to his feet and effortlessly lifted Mary to hers.

Tears blurred her vision as she turned her back to fumble with that blasted space-age clasp on her bra. Whatever had possessed her to buy such a contraption? Aunt Ardith would have been outraged. Aunt Ardith would have fallen on the ground in a hissy fit if she'd even thought of her niece *rolling naked in the hay* with a man. And, darn it, she hadn't even been able to finish her rolling!

"Here, I'll do it," Wolf said in a far gentler tone than she'd ever before heard from him. He turned her around and deftly handled the diabolical clasp. Mary kept her head down, unable to look him in the eye, but the contrast of his sun-bronzed hands against her pale breasts made her feel hot again. She swallowed and looked at his belt buckle. He'd zipped his jeans back up and buckled his belt, but the visible swell of his loins told her he wasn't completely unaffected by this interruption. That made her feel better, and she blinked the tears from her eyes as he helped her back into her dress and turned her around to zip it.

"You have hay in your hair," he teased, and picked the straw from the tangled tresses, then brushed it from her dress.

Mary put up both hands to discern the state of her hair and found it had come completely down. "Leave it," Wolf said. "I like it down. It looks like silk."

Nervously she combed her fingers through the strands and watched as he leaned down to pick up his shirt from the hay. "What will Joe think?" she blurted as the truck pulled to a stop outside the barn.

"That he's lucky he's my son, or I'd have killed him," Wolf muttered grimly, and Mary wasn't certain he was teasing. He put his shirt on but didn't bother buttoning it before stepping into the open door. Taking a deep breath, Mary braced herself to get through the embarrassment and followed him.

Joe had just gotten out of the truck, and now he stood beside the door, his ice-blue eyes moving from his father to Mary and back, taking in Wolf's stone face and open shirt, and Mary's tousled hair. "Damn it!" he swore and slammed the door shut. "If it had just taken me fifteen minutes longer—"

"My feelings exactly," Wolf concurred.

"Hey, I'll leave—"

Wolf sighed. "No. She came to see you anyway."

"That's what you said the first time." Joe grinned hugely.

"And I just said it again." He turned to Mary, and some of the enjoyment of her stunning news returned to his eyes. "Tell him."

She couldn't think. "Tell him?'"

"Yeah. Tell him."

Slowly her dazed mind registered what he was saying. She looked in bewilderment at her empty hands. What had happened to the letters? Had they lost them in the hay? How mortifying it would be to have to search through the hay for them! Not knowing what else to do, she spread her hands and said simply, "You're in. I got the letter today."

Blood drained from Joe's face as he stared at her, and he reached out blindly to rest his hand on the truck as if to steady himself. "I got in? The Academy? I got into the Academy?" he asked hoarsely.

"You got the recommendation. It's up to you to pass the exams."

He threw back his head and screamed, an exultant, spine-chilling sound like that of a hunting panther, then leaped at Wolf. The two of them pounded each other's backs, laughing and yelling, then finally just hugging each other in a way two weaker men couldn't have done. Mary folded her hands and watched them, smiling, so happy her heart swelled to the point of pain. Then suddenly an arm reached out and snagged her, and she found herself sandwiched between the two Mackenzies, almost smashed flat by their celebration.

"You're smothering me!" she protested in a gasping voice, wedging her hands against two broad chests and pushing. One of those chests was bare, exposed by an unbuttoned shirt, and the touch of his warm skin made her go weak in the knees. Both of them laughed at her protest, but both of them immediately gentled their embrace.

Mary patted her hair down and smoothed her dress. "The letters are here somewhere. I must have dropped them."

Wolf gave her a wicked look. "You must have."

His teasing made her happy deep inside, and she smiled at him. It was a quietly intimate smile, the sort that a woman gives the man she loves after she has been in his arms, and it warmed him. To cover his reaction, he turned to look for the dropped letters and spotted one on the drive, while the other had fallen close to the barn door. He retrieved both of them, and gave Joe the one addressed to him.

The boy's hands shook as he read the letter, even though he already knew the contents. He couldn't believe it. It had happened so fast. A dream come true should have been harder to attain; he should have had to sweat blood to get it. Oh, he wasn't driving one of those twenty-million dollar babies yet, but he would. He had to, because he would be only half alive without wings.

Mary was watching him with proud indulgence when she felt Wolf stiffen beside her. She looked at him inquiringly. His head was lifted as if he scented danger, and his face was suddenly as impassive as stone. Then she heard the sound of an engine and turned as a deputy sheriff's car rolled to a stop behind Joe's truck.

Joe turned, and his face took on the same stony look as Wolf's as Clay Armstrong got out of the county car.

"Ma'am." Clay spoke to her first, tipping his hat.

"Deputy Armstrong." Two hundred years of strict training on social behavior were in her voice. Aunt Ardith would have been proud. But she sensed some threat to Wolf, and it was all she could do not to put herself between him and the deputy. Only the knowledge that he wouldn't appreciate the action kept her standing at his side.

Clay's friendly blue eyes weren't friendly at all now. "Why are you up here, Miss Potter?"

"Why are you asking?" she shot back, putting her hands on her hips.

"Just skip to the good part, Armstrong," Wolf snapped.

"Fine," Clay snapped back. "You're wanted for questioning. You can come with me now, the easy way, or I can get a warrant for your arrest."

Joe stood frozen, fury and hell in his eyes. This had

happened before, and he'd lost his father for two nightmarish years. It seemed even more terrible this time, because just moments before they had been celebrating, and he'd been on top of the world.

Wolf began buttoning his shirt. In a voice like gravel he asked, "What happened this time?"

"We'll talk about that at the sheriff's office."

"We'll talk about it now."

Black eyes met blue, and abruptly Clay realized this man wouldn't move a foot unless he had some answers. "A girl was raped this morning."

Sulfuric rage burned in those night-dark eyes. "So naturally you thought of the Indian." He spat the words like bullets from between clenched teeth. God, this couldn't be happening again. Not twice in one lifetime. The first time had almost killed him, and he knew he'd never go back to that hellhole, no matter what he had to do.

"We're just questioning some people. If you have an alibi, there's no problem. You'll be free to go."

"I suppose you picked up every rancher in this area? Do you have Eli Baugh at the sheriff's office answering questions?"

Clay's face darkened with anger. "No."

"Just the Indian, huh?"

"You have priors." But Clay looked uncomfortable.

"I don't have…one…single…prior conviction," Wolf snarled. "I was *cleared*."

"Damn it, man, I know that!" Clay suddenly yelled. "I was told to pick you up, and I'm going to do my job."

"Well, why didn't you just say so? I wouldn't want to stop a man from doing his job." After that sarcastic jab, Wolf strode to his truck. "I'll follow you."

"You can ride in the car. I'll bring you back."

"No, thanks. I'd rather have my own wheels, just in case the sheriff decides a walk would do me good."

Swearing under his breath, Clay went to the car and got in. Dust and gravel flew from his tires as he headed back down the mountain, with Wolf behind him slinging even more dust and gravel.

Mary began shaking. At first it was just a tremor, but it swiftly escalated into shudders that rattled her entire body. Joe was standing as if turned to stone, his fists clenched. Suddenly he whirled and slammed his fist into the hood of his truck. "By God, they won't do it to him again," he whispered. *"Not again."*

"No, they certainly won't." She was still shaking, but she squared her shoulders. "If I have to get every judge and court in this country involved, I will. I'll call newspapers, I'll call television networks, I'll call—oh, they don't have any idea of who all I can call." The network of Old Family contacts she had left behind in Savannah was still there, and more favors would be called in than the sheriff of this county could count. She'd hang him out to dry!

"Why don't you go home?" Joe suggested in a flat tone.

"I want to stay."

He'd expected her to quietly walk to her car, but at her words he looked at her for the first time. Deep inside, part of him had thought she wouldn't be able to leave fast enough, that he and Wolf would be alone again, as they had always been. They were used to being alone. But Mary stood her ground as if she had no intention of budging off this mountain, her slate-blue eyes full of fire and her fragile chin lifted in the way that he'd learned meant others could just get out of her path.

The boy, forced by circumstance to grow up hard and fast, put his strong arms around the woman and held her, desperately absorbing some of her strength, because he was deathly afraid he'd need it. And Mary held him. He was Wolf's son, and she'd protect him with every ounce of fight she had.

Chapter 6

It was after nine when they heard Wolf's truck, and both of them froze with mingled tension and relief: tension because they dreaded to hear what had happened, and relief because he was home instead of locked in jail. Mary couldn't imagine Wolf in jail, even though he'd spent two years in prison. He was too wild, like a lobo that could never be tamed. Imprisoning him had been an act so cruel as to be obscene.

He came in the back door and stood there staring at her, his dark face expressionless. She and Joe sat at the kitchen table, nursing cups of coffee. "Why are you still here? Go home."

She ignored the flatness of his tone. He was so angry she could almost feel the heat from across the room, but she knew it wasn't directed against her. Getting up, she dumped her lukewarm coffee into the sink and got another cup from the cabinet, then poured fresh coffee into both cups. "Sit down, drink your coffee and tell us what happened," she said in her best schoolteacher voice.

He did reach for the coffee, but he didn't sit down. He was too angry to sit. The rage boiled in him, robbing his movements of their usual fluidity. It was starting all over again, and he'd be damned if he'd go to prison again for something he hadn't done. He'd fight any way he could and with any weapon he could, but he'd die before he'd go back to prison.

"They let you go," Joe said.

"They had to. The girl was raped around noon. At noon I was delivering two horses to the Bar W R. Wally Rasco verified it, and the sheriff couldn't figure out a way I could have been in two different places, sixty miles apart, at the same time, so he had to let me go."

"Where did it happen?"

Wolf rubbed his forehead, then pinched his nose between his eyes as if he had a headache, or maybe he was just tired. "She was grabbed from behind when she got in her car, parked in her own driveway. He made her drive almost an hour before telling her to pull off on the side of the road. She never saw his face. He wore a ski mask. But she could tell he was tall, and that was enough of a description for the sheriff."

"The side of the road?" Mary blurted. "That's... weird. It doesn't make sense. I know there's not much traffic, but still, someone could have come by at any time."

"Yeah. Not to mention that he was waiting for her in her driveway. The whole thing is strange."

Joe drummed his fingers on the table. "It could have been someone passing through."

"How many people 'pass through' Ruth?" Wolf asked dryly. "Would a drifter have known whose car it was, or when she was likely to come out of the house? What if the car belonged to a man? That's a big chance to take, especially when rape seems to have been the only thing on his mind, because he didn't rob her, even though she had money.''

''Are they keeping her identity secret?'' Mary asked.

He looked at her. ''It won't stay a secret, because her father was in the sheriff's office waving a rifle and threatening to blow my guts out. He attracted a lot of attention, and people talk.''

His face was still expressionless, but Mary sensed the bitter rage that filled him. His fierce pride had been dragged in the dust—again. How had he endured being forced to sit there and listen to insults and threats? Because she knew he'd been insulted, by vile words describing his mixed heritage as well as by the very fact he'd been picked up for questioning. He was holding it all in, controlling it, but the rage was there.

''What happened?''

''Armstrong stopped it. Then Wally Rasco got there and cleared me, and the sheriff let me go with a friendly warning.''

''A *warning*?'' Mary jumped to her feet, her eyes flashing. ''For what?''

He pinched her chin and gave her a coldly ferocious smile. ''He warned me to stay away from white women, sweetcake. And that's just what I'm going to do. So you go on home now, and stay there. I don't want you on my mountain again.''

''You didn't feel that way in the barn,'' she shot back, then darted a look at Joe and blushed. Joe just quirked an eyebrow and looked strangely self-satisfied. She decided to ignore him and turned back to Wolf. ''I can't believe you're letting that mush-brain sheriff tell you who you can see.''

He narrowed his eyes at her. ''Maybe it hasn't dawned on you yet, but it's all starting again. It doesn't matter that Wally Rasco cleared me. Everyone is going to remember what happened ten years ago, and the way they felt.''

''You were cleared of that, too, or doesn't that count?''

''With some people,'' he finally admitted. ''Not with most. They're already afraid of me, already distrust and dislike me. Until this bastard is caught, I probably won't be able to buy anything in that town, not groceries, gas or feed. And any white woman who has anything to do with me could be in real danger of being tarred and feathered.''

So that was it. He was still trying to protect her. She stared at him in exasperation. ''Wolf, I refuse to live my life according to someone else's prejudices. I appreciate that you're trying to protect me—''

She could hear an audible click as his teeth snapped together. ''Do you?'' he asked with heavy sarcasm. ''Then go home. Stay home, and I'll stay here.''

''For how long?''

Instead of answering her question, he made an oblique statement. ''I'll always be a half-breed.''

''And I'll always be what *I* am, too. I haven't asked you to change,'' she pointed out, pain creeping into her voice. She looked at him with longing plain in her eyes, as no woman had ever looked at him before, and the rage in him intensified because he couldn't simply reach out and take her in his arms, proclaim to the world that she was his woman. The sheriff's warning had been clear enough, and Wolf knew well that the hostility toward him would rapidly swell to explosive proportions. It could easily spill over onto Mary, and now he wasn't just worried that she would lose her job. A job was nothing compared to the physical danger she could suffer. She could be terrorized in her own home, her property vandalized; she could be cursed and spat upon; she could be physically attacked. For all her sheer determination, she was still just a rather slight woman, and she would be helpless against anyone who wanted to hurt her.

"I know," he finally said, and despite himself, he reached out to touch her hair. "Go home, Mary. When this is over—" He stopped, because he didn't want to make promises he might not be able to keep, but what he'd said was enough to put a glowing light in her eyes.

"All right," she murmured, putting her hand on his. "By the way, I want you to get a haircut."

He looked startled. "A haircut?"

"Yes. You want me to wear my hair down, and I want you to get a haircut."

"Why?"

She gave him a shrewd look. "You don't wear it long because you're Indian. You wear it long just to upset people, so they'll never forget your Indian blood. So get it cut."

"Short hair won't make me less Indian."

"Long hair won't make you more Indian."

She looked as if she would stand there until doomsday unless he agreed to get a haircut. He gave in abruptly, muttering, "All right, I'll get a haircut."

"Good." She smiled at him and went on tiptoe to kiss the corner of his mouth. "Good night. Good night, Joe."

"Goodnight, Mary."

When she was gone, Wolf wearily ran his hand through his hair, then frowned as he realized he'd just agreed to cut it off. He looked up to find Joe watching him steadily.

"What are we going to do?" the boy asked.

"Whatever we have to," Wolf replied, his expression flinty.

When Mary bought groceries the next morning, she found everyone in the store huddling together in small groups of two or three and whispering about the rape. The girl's identity was quickly revealed; it was Cathy Teele, whose younger sister, Christa, was in Mary's class. The entire Teele family was devastated, according to the whispers Mary heard as she gathered her groceries.

Next to the flour and cornmeal, she encountered Dottie Lancaster, who was flanked by a young man Mary assumed was Dottie's son. "Hello, Dottie." Mary greeted the woman pleasantly, even though it was possible Dottie had started the rumor about her and Joe.

"Hello." Dottie wore a distressed expression, rather than her habitual sour one. "Have you heard about that poor Teele girl?"

"I haven't heard anything else since I entered the store."

"They arrested that Indian, but the sheriff had to let him go. I hope now you'll be more careful about the company you keep."

"Wolf wasn't arrested." Mary managed to keep her voice calm. "He was questioned, but he was at Wally Rasco's ranch when the attack occurred, and Mr. Rasco backed him up. Wolf Mackenzie isn't a rapist."

"A court of law said he was and sentenced him to prison."

"He was also cleared when the true rapist was caught and confessed to the crime for which Wolf had been convicted."

Dottie drew back, her face livid. "That's what that Indian said, but as far as we know, he just got out on parole. It's easy to see whose side you're on, but then, you've been running with those Indians since the day you came to Ruth. Well, miss, there's an old saying that if you sleep with dogs, you're bound to get fleas. The Mackenzies are dirty Indian trash—"

"Don't you say another word," Mary interrupted, color high in her cheeks as she took a step toward Dottie. She was furious; her hand itched to slap the woman's self-righteous face. Aunt Ardith had said that a lady never brawled, but Mary was ready to forever relinquish any claim she had to the title. "Wolf is a decent, hardworking man, and I won't let you or anyone else say he isn't."

Dottie's color was mottled, but something in Mary's eyes made her refrain from saying anything else about Wolf. Instead she leaned closer and hissed, "You'd better watch yourself, Miss Goody-Goody, or you'll find yourself in a lot of trouble."

Mary leaned closer, too, her jaw set. "Are you threatening me?" she demanded fiercely.

"Mama, please," the young man behind her whispered in a frantic tone, and tugged at Dottie's arm.

Dottie looked around at him, and her face changed. She drew back, but told Mary contemptuously, "You just mark my words," and stalked away.

Her son, Bobby, was so distressed he was wringing his hands as he hurried after Dottie. Immediately, Mary was sorry she had let the horrid little scene develop; from what Joe had told her, Bobby had a hard enough time handling everyday problems without adding more.

She took a few deep breaths to regain her composure, but almost lost it again when she turned and found several people standing in the aisle, staring at her. They had all obviously heard every word, and looked both shocked and avid. She had no doubt the tale would be all over town within the hour: two of the schoolteachers brawling over Wolf Mackenzie. She groaned inwardly as she picked up a bag of flour. Another scandal was just what Wolf needed.

In the next aisle, she met Cicely Karr. Remembering the woman's comments during the school board meeting, Mary couldn't stop herself from saying, "I've received a letter from Senator Allard, Mrs. Karr. He's recommending Joe Mackenzie for admission to the Academy." She sounded challenging even to her own ears.

To her surprise, Mrs. Karr looked excited. "He is? Why, I never would've believed it. Until Eli explained it to me, I didn't quite realize what an honor it is." Then she sobered. "But now this terrible thing has happened. It's awful. I—I couldn't help overhearing you and Dottie Lancaster. Miss Potter, you can't imagine what it was like ten years ago. People were frightened and angry, and now the same nightmare has started again."

"It's a nightmare for Wolf Mackenzie, too," Mary said hotly. "He was sent to prison for a rape he didn't commit. His record was cleared, but still he was the first person the sheriff picked up for questioning. How do you think he feels? He'll never get back the two years he spent in prison, and now it looks as if everyone is trying to send him there again."

Mrs. Karr looked troubled. "We were all wrong before. The justice system was wrong, too. But even though Mackenzie proved he didn't rape Cathy Teele, don't you see why the sheriff wanted to question him?"

"No, I don't."

"Because Mackenzie had reason to want revenge."

Mary was aghast. "So you thought he'd take revenge by attacking a young woman who was just a child when he was sent to prison? What sort of man do you think he is?" She was horrified by both the idea and the feeling that everyone in Ruth would agree with Mrs. Karr.

"I think he's a man who hates," Mrs. Karr said firmly. Yes, she believed Wolf capable of such horrible, obscene revenge; it was in her eyes.

Mary felt sick; she began shaking her head. "No," she said. "No. Wolf is bitter about the way he was treated, but he doesn't hate. And he would never hurt a woman like that." If she knew anything in this world, she knew that. She had felt urgency in his touch, but never brutality.

But Mrs. Karr was shaking her head, too. "Don't tell me he doesn't hate! It's in those black-as-hell eyes every time he looks at us, any of us. The sheriff found out he'd been in Vietnam, in some special assassination group, or something. God only knows how it warped him! Maybe he didn't rape Cathy Teele, but this would be a perfect opportunity for him to get revenge and have it blamed on whoever *did* rape her!"

"If Wolf wanted revenge, he wouldn't sneak around to get it," Mary said scornfully. "You don't know anything about the kind of man he is, do you? He's lived here for years, and none of you *know* him."

"And I suppose you do?" Mrs. Karr was getting red in the face. "Maybe we're talking about a different kind of 'knowing.' Maybe that rumor about you carrying on with Joe Mackenzie was half right, after all. You've been carrying on with *Wolf* Mackenzie, haven't you?"

The scorn in the woman's voice enraged Mary. "Yes!" she half shouted, and honesty impelled her to add, "But not as much as I'd like."

A chorus of gasps made her look around, and she stared into the faces of the townspeople who had stopped in the aisle to listen. Well, she'd really done it now; Wolf had wanted her to distance herself from him, and instead she'd all but shouted from the rooftops that she'd been "carrying on" with him. But she couldn't feel even the tiniest bit of shame. She felt proud. With Wolf Mackenzie she was a woman, not a dowdy, old maid school-teacher who even owned a cat, for heaven's sake. She didn't feel dowdy when she was with Wolf; she felt warm, wanted. If she had any regrets, it was that Joe hadn't been fifteen minutes later returning the day before, or even five minutes, because more than anything she wanted to be Wolf's woman in every way, to lie beneath his thrusting body, eagerly accepting the force of his passion and giving him her own. If for that, for loving him, she was ostracized, then she counted society well lost.

Mrs. Karr said icily, ''I believe we'll have to have another school board meeting.''

''When you do, consider that I have an ironclad contract,'' Mary shot back, and turned on her heel. She hadn't gathered all of the groceries she needed, but she was too angry to continue. When she plunked the items down on the counter, the clerk looked as if she wanted to refuse to ring them up, but she changed her mind under Mary's glare.

She stormed home and was gratified when the weather seemed to agree with her, if the gray clouds forming overhead were any indication. After storing her groceries, she checked on the cat, who had been acting strange lately. A horrid thought intruded: surely no one would have poisoned the cat? But Woodrow was sunning himself peacefully on the rug, so she dismissed the idea with relief.

When this is over...

The phrase echoed in her memory, tantalizing her and stirring an ache deep inside. She longed for him so intensely that she felt as if she were somehow incomplete. She loved him, and though she understood why he thought it better for her to stay away from him right now, she didn't agree. After what had happened that morning with Dottie Lancaster and Cicely Karr, there was no point in allowing this exile. She might as well have stood in the middle of the street and shouted it: she was Wolf Mackenzie's woman.

Whatever he wanted from her, she was willing to give. Aunt Ardith had raised her to believe that intimacy belonged only in marriage, if a woman for some reason felt she simply *couldn't* live without a man, though Aunt Ardith had made it plain she couldn't imagine what such a reason would be. While Mary had accepted that people obviously were intimate outside of marriage, she had never been tempted to it herself—until she'd met Wolf. If he wanted her for only a short time, she counted that as better than nothing. Even one day with him would be a bright and shining memory to treasure during the long, dreary years without him, a small bit of warmth to comfort her. Her dream was to spend a lifetime with him, but she didn't allow herself to expect it. He was too bitter, too wary; it was unlikely he would permit an Anglo to get that close to him. He would give her his body, perhaps even his affection, but not his heart or his commitment.

Because she loved him, she knew she wouldn't demand more. She didn't want anger or guilt between them. For as long as she could, in whatever way, she wanted to make Wolf happy.

He had asked her to wear her hair down, and the silky weight of it lay around her shoulders. She had been surprised, looking in the mirror that morning, how the relaxed hairstyle softened her face. Her eyes had glowed, because leaving her hair down was something she could do for him. She looked feminine, the way he made her feel.

There was no point in trying to make people think her neutral now, not after those arguments she'd gotten into. When she told him what had happened, he'd see the uselessness of trying to maintain the sham. She even felt relieved, because her heart hadn't been in it.

She had started to change into one of her shapeless housedresses when she caught sight of herself in the mirror and paused. In her mind she relived that moment the day she'd first met Wolf, when he'd seen her in Joe's old jeans and his eyes had momentarily widened with a look so hot and male it had the power, even now, to make her shake. She wanted him to look at her like that again, but he wasn't likely to as long as she kept wearing these—these *feed sacks*!

Suddenly she was dissatisfied with all her clothing. Her dresses were, without exception, sturdy and modest, but they were also too drab and loose-fitting. Her slight build would be better displayed in delicate cottons and light, cheerful colors, or even hip-hugging jeans. She turned and looked at her bottom in the mirror; it was slim and curvy. She could see no reason why she should be ashamed of it. It was a very nice bottom, as bottoms went.

Muttering to herself, she zipped herself back into her serviceable "good" dress and grabbed her purse. Ruth wouldn't offer much in the way of new clothes, but she could certainly buy some jeans and sassy little tops, as well as some neat skirts and blouses that, above all, actually fit her.

And she never wanted to see another "sensible" shoe in her life.

The gray clouds lived up to their promise, and it began to rain as she made the drive into town. It was a steady rain, just the sort ranchers and farmers everywhere loved, rather than a downpour that simply ran off instead of soaking into the ground. Aunt Ardith wouldn't have set foot out of the house during a rain, but Mary ignored it. She stopped first at the one store in Ruth that dealt exclusively in women's clothing, though by necessity the clothes weren't hot from a fashion show in Paris. She bought three pairs of jeans, size six, two lightweight cotton sweaters, and a blue chambray shirt that made her feel like a pioneer. A snazzy denim skirt, paired with a ruby-red sweater, flattered her so much she spun on her heel in delight, just like a child. She also chose a brown skirt, which fit so well she couldn't turn it down despite the color, and teamed a crisp pink blouse with it. Her final choice was a pale lavender cotton skirt and matching top, which sported a delicate lace collar. Still in a fit of defiance and delight, she picked out a pair of dressy white sandals as well as a pair of track shoes. When the saleswoman rang them up and called out the total, Mary didn't even blink an eye. This had been too long in coming.

Nor was she finished. She locked her packages in the car and dashed through the rain to Hearst's general store, where everyone bought boots. Since Mary planned to be spending most of her time on Wolf's mountain, she figured she'd need a pair.

Mr. Hearst was almost rude to her, but she stared him down and briefly thought of shaking her schoolteacher's finger at him. She discarded the idea because the finger lost its power if used too often, and she might really need it sometime in the future. So she ignored him and tried on boots until she finally found a pair that felt comfortable on her feet.

She couldn't wait to get home and put on her jeans and chambray shirt; she might even wear her boots around the house to get them broken in, she thought. Woodrow wouldn't know her. She thought of that look in Wolf's eyes and began to shiver.

Her car was parked up the street, a block away, and it was raining hard enough now that she made a disgusted noise at herself for not driving from the clothing store to Hearst's. Ruth didn't have sidewalks, and already huge puddles were standing on the pavement. Well, she had on her sensible shoes; let them earn their keep!

Putting her head down and holding the box containing her boots up in an effort to ward off part of the rain, she darted from the sheltering overhang of the roof and immediately got wet to the ankles when she stepped into a puddle. She was still grumbling to herself about that when she passed the small alley that ran between the general store and the next building, which had formerly been a barbershop but now stood empty.

She didn't hear anything or see a flurry of movement; she had no warning at all. A big hand, wet with rain, clamped over her mouth, and an arm wrapped around the front of her body, effectively holding her arms down as her attacker began hauling her down the alley, away from the street. Mary fought instinctively, wriggling and kicking while she made muffled sounds behind the man's palm. His hand was so tight on her face that his fingers dug painfully into her cheek.

The tall, wet weeds in the alley stung her legs, and the pounding rain stung her eyes. Terrified, she kicked harder. This couldn't be happening! He couldn't just carry her off in broad daylight! But he could; he had done it to Cathy Teele.

She got one arm free and reached back, clawing for his face. Her desperate fingers found only wet, woolly cloth. He cursed, his voice low and raspy, and hit her on the side of the head with his fist.

Her senses blurred as her head was rocked with pain, and her struggles grew aimless. Vaguely she was aware when they reached the end of the alley and he dragged her behind the abandoned building.

His breathing was fast and harsh in her ear as he forced

her down on her stomach in the gravel and mud. She managed to get her arm free again and put her hand out to break her fall; the gravel scraped her palm, but she barely felt it. His hand was still over her mouth, suffocating her; he ground her face into the wet dirt and held her down with his heavy weight on her back.

He scrabbled with his other hand for her skirt, pulling it up. Wildly she clawed at his hand, trying to pull it free so she could scream, and he hit her again. She was terrified and kept clawing. Cursing, he forced her legs apart and thrust himself against her. She could feel him through his pants and her undergarments, pushing at her, and began gagging. *God, no!*

She heard her clothing tear, and overpowering revulsion gave her strength. She bit savagely at his hand and reached back for his eyes, her nails digging for flesh.

There was a roaring in her ears, but she heard a shout. The man on top of her stiffened, then braced his hand beside her head and used it to balance himself as he leaped to his feet. Her vision blurred by rain and mud, she saw only a blue sleeve and a pale, freckled hand before he was gone. From above and behind her came a loud boom, and vaguely she wondered if now she would be struck by lightning. No, lightning came before the thunder.

Running footsteps pounded the ground, going past her. Mary lay still, her body limp and her eyes closed.

She heard low cursing, and the footsteps returned. ''Mary,'' a commanding voice said. ''Are you all right?''

She managed to open her eyes and looked up at Clay Armstrong. He was soaked to the skin, his blue eyes furious, but his hands were gentle as he turned her onto her back and lifted her in his arms.

''Are you all right?'' The words were sharper now.

The rain stung her face. "Yes," she managed, and turned her head into his shoulder.

"I'll get him," Clay promised. "I swear to you, I'll get the bastard."

There was no doctor in town, but Bessie Pylant was a registered nurse, and Clay carried Mary to Bessie's house. Bessie called the private practitioner for whom she worked and got him to drive over from the next town. In the meantime she carefully cleaned Mary's scrapes and put ice on the bruises, and began pouring hot, too-sweet tea down her.

Clay had disappeared. Bessie's house was suddenly full of women; Sharon Wycliffe came and assured Mary that she and Dottie could handle things on Monday if Mary didn't feel like working; Francie Beecham told tales of her own teaching days, her purpose obvious, and the other women took their cues from her. Mary sat quietly, clutching so tightly at the blanket Bessie had wrapped around her that her knuckles were white. She knew the women were trying to divert her, and was grateful to them; with rigid control she concentrated on their commonplace chatter. Even Cicely Karr came and patted Mary's hand, despite the argument they'd had only a few hours before.

Then the doctor arrived, and Bessie led Mary into a bedroom for privacy while the doctor examined her. She answered his questions in a subdued voice, though she winced when he probed the sore place on the side of her head where the man had struck her with his fist. He checked her pupil response and her blood pressure, and gave her a mild sedative.

"You'll be all right," he finally said, patting her knee. "There's no concussion, so your headache should go away soon. A good night's sleep will do more for you than anything I can prescribe.''

"Thank you for driving out here," Mary said politely.

Desperation was growing in her. Everyone had been wonderful, but she could feel a fine wire inside her being coiled tighter and tighter. She felt dirty and exposed. She needed privacy and a shower, and more than anything she needed Wolf.

She left the bedroom and found that Clay had returned. He came to her immediately and took her hand. "How are you feeling?"

"I'm all right." If she had to say that one more time, she thought she would scream.

"I need a statement from you, if you think you can do it now."

"Yes, all right." The sedative was taking effect; she could feel the spreading sensation of remoteness as the drug numbed her emotions. She let Clay lead her to a chair and pulled the blanket tight around her once more. She felt chilled.

"You don't have to be afraid," Clay soothed. "He's been picked up. He's in custody now."

That aroused her interest, and she stared at him. "Picked up? You know who it is?"

"I saw him." The iron was back in Clay's voice.

"But he was wearing a ski mask." She remembered that, remembered feeling the woolly fabric under her fingers.

"Yeah, but his hair was hanging out from under the mask in back."

Mary stared up at him, the numbness in her changing into a kind of horror. His hair was long enough to hang out from under the mask? Surely Clay didn't think— surely not! She felt sick. "Wolf?" she whispered.

"Don't worry. I told you he's in custody."

She clenched her fists so tightly that her nails dug crescents in her palms. "Then let him go."

Clay looked stunned, then angry. "Let him go! Damn, Mary, can't you get it through your head that he attacked you?"

Slowly she shook her head, her face white. "No, he didn't."

"I saw him," Clay said, spacing out each word. "He was tall and had long black hair. Damn it, who else could it have been?"

"I don't know, but it wasn't Wolf."

The women were silent, sitting frozen as they listened to the argument. Cicely Karr spoke up. "We did try to warn you, Mary."

"Then you warned me about the wrong man!" Her eyes burning, Mary stared around the room, then turned her gaze back to Clay. "I saw his hands! He was a white man, an *Anglo*. He had freckled hands. *It wasn't Wolf Mackenzie!*"

Clay's brow creased in a frown. "Are you certain about that?"

"Positive. He put his hand on the ground right in front of my eyes." She reached out and grabbed his sleeve. "Get Wolf out of jail, right now. Right now, do you hear me! And he'd better not have a bruise on him!"

Clay got up and went to the telephone, and once again Mary looked at the women in the room. They were all pale and worried. Mary could guess why. As long as they had suspected Wolf, they had had a safe target for their fear and anger. Now they had to look at themselves, at someone who was one of them. A lot of men in the area had freckled hands, but Wolf didn't. His hands were lean and dark, bronzed by the sun, callused from years of hard manual work and riding. She had felt them on her bare skin. She wanted to shout that Wolf had no reason to attack her, because he could have her any time he wanted, but she didn't. The numbness was returning. She just wanted to wait for Wolf, if he came at all.

An hour later he walked into Bessie's house as if he owned it, without knocking. An audible gasp rose when he appeared in the doorway, his broad shoulders reaching almost from beam to beam. He didn't even glance at the other people in the room. His eyes were on Mary, huddled in her blanket, her face colorless.

His boots rang on the floor as he crossed to her and hunkered down. His black eyes raked her from head to toe; then he touched her chin, turning her head toward the light so he could see the scrape on her cheek and the bruises where hard fingers had bitten into her soft flesh. He lifted her hands and examined her raw palms. His jaw was like granite.

Mary wanted to cry, but instead she managed a wobbly smile. "You got a haircut," she said softly, and linked her fingers together to keep from running them through the thick, silky strands that lay perfectly against his well-shaped head.

"First thing this morning," he murmured. "Are you all right?"

"Yes. He—he didn't manage to…you know."

"I know." He stood. "I'll be back later. I'm going to get him. I promise you, I'll get him."

Clay said sharply, "That's a matter for the law."

Wolf's eyes were cold black fire. "The law isn't doing a very good job." He walked out without another word, and Mary felt chilled again. While he had been there, life had begun tingling in her numb body, but now it was gone. He had said he would be back, but she thought she should go home. Everyone was very kind, too kind; she felt as if she would scream. She couldn't handle any more.

Chapter 7

Though he was stunned by Wolf's changed appearance, it took Clay only a moment to follow him. As he had suspected, Wolf stopped his truck at the alley where Mary had been attacked. By the time Clay parked the county car and entered the alley, Wolf was down on one knee, examining the muddy ground. He didn't even glance up when Clay approached. Instead he continued his concentrated examination of every weed and bit of gravel, every scuff mark, every indentation.

Clay said, "When did you get a haircut?"

"This morning. At the barbershop in Harpston."

"Why?"

"Because Mary asked me to," Wolf said flatly, and returned his attention to the ground.

Slowly he moved down the alley and to the back of the buildings, pausing at the spot where Mary's attacker had thrust her to the ground. Then he moved on, following exactly the path the attacker had taken, and it was in the next alley that he gave a grunt of satisfaction and knelt beside a blurred footprint.

Clay had been over the ground himself, and so had many other people. He said as much to Wolf. "That print could belong to anyone."

"No. It's made by a soft-soled shoe, not a boot." After examining the print awhile longer, he said, "He toes in slightly when he walks. I'd guess he weighs about one seventy-five, maybe one eighty. He isn't in very good shape. He was already tired when he got this far."

Clay felt uneasy. Some people would have simply passed off that kind of tracking ability as part of Wolf's Indian heritage, but they would have been wrong. There were excellent trackers of wildlife who could follow a man's footsteps in the wilderness as easily as if he had wet paint on the bottoms of his boots, but the details Wolf had discerned would have been noted only by someone who had been trained to hunt other men. Nor did he doubt what Wolf had told him, because he had seen other men, though not many, who could track like that.

"You were in Nam." He already knew that, but suddenly it seemed far more significant.

Wolf was still examining the footprint. "Yes. You?"

"Twenty-first Infantry. What outfit were you with?"

Wolf looked up, and a very slight, unholy smile touched his lips. "I was a LRRP."

Clay's uneasy feeling became a chill. The LRRPs, pronounced "lurp," were men on long-range reconnaissance patrol. Unlike the regular grunts, the LRRPs spent weeks in the jungles and hill country, living off the land, hunting and being hunted. They survived only by their wits and ability to fight, or to fade away into the shadows, whichever the situation demanded. Clay had seen them come in from the bush, lean and filthy, smelling like the wild animals they essentially were, with death in their eyes and their nerves so raw, so wary, that it was dangerous to touch them unexpectedly, or walk up to their backs. Sometimes they hadn't been able to bear the touch of another human being until their nerves settled down. A smart man walked lightly around a LRRP fresh in from the field.

What was in Wolf's eyes now was cold and deadly, an anger so great Clay could only guess at its force, though he understood it. Wolf smiled again, and in the calmest tone imaginable, one almost gentle, he said, "He made a mistake."

"What was that?"

"He hurt *my* woman."

"It's not your place to hunt him. It's a matter for the law."

"Then the law had better stay close to my heels," Wolf said, and walked away.

Clay stared after him, not even surprised by the blunt words claiming Mary as his woman. The chill ran down his back again and he shivered. The town of Ruth had made a mistake in judging this man, but the rapist had made an even bigger one, one that might prove fatal.

Mary stoically ignored all the protests and pleas when she announced her intention of driving home. They meant well, and she appreciated their concern, but she couldn't stay another moment. She was physically unharmed, and the doctor had said her headache would fade in the next few hours. She simply had to go home.

So she drove alone in the misting rain, her movements automatic. Afterward, she could never recall a moment of the drive. All she was aware of when she let herself into the creaky old house was a feeling of intense relief, and it so frightened her that she pushed it away. She

couldn't afford to let herself relax, not now. Maybe later.
Right now she had to hold herself together very tightly.

Woodrow looped around her ankles several times, me-
owing plaintively. Mary stirred herself to feed him,
though he was as fat as a butterball already, then found
herself exhausted by that brief effort. She sat down at
the table and folded her hands in her lap, holding herself
motionless.

That was how Wolf found her half an hour later, just
as the gray daylight began to fade. "Why didn't you wait
for me?" he asked from the doorway, his tone a low,
gentle growl.

"I had to come home," Mary explained.

"I would have brought you."

"I know."

He sat down at the table beside her and took her cold,
tightly clasped hands in his. She looked at him steadily,
and his heart clenched like a fist in his chest.

He would have given anything never to have seen that
look in her eyes.

She had always been so indomitable, with her "damn
the torpedoes" spirit. She was slight and delicately made,
but in her own eyes she had been invincible. Because
the very idea of defeat was foreign to her, she had
blithely moved through life arranging it to suit herself
and accepted it as only natural that shopkeepers quaked
before her wagging finger. That attitude had sometimes
irritated, but more often entranced, him. The kitten
thought herself a tiger, and because she acted like a tiger,
other people had given way.

She was no longer indomitable. A horrible vulnerability was in her eyes, and he knew she would never forget
the moments when she had been helpless. That scum had
hurt her, humiliated her, literally ground her into the dirt.

"Do you know what really horrified me?" she asked after a long silence.

"What?"

"That I wanted the first time to be with you, and he was going to—" She stopped abruptly, unable to finish.

"But he didn't."

"No. He pulled up my skirt and pushed against me, and he was tearing my clothes when Clay—I think Clay shouted. He might have fired a shot. I remember hearing a roaring sound, but I thought it was thunder."

Her flat little monotone bothered him, and he realized she was still in shock. "I won't let him get near you again. I give you my word."

She nodded, then closed her eyes.

"You're going to take a shower," Wolf said, urging her to her feet. "A long, warm shower, and while you're taking it, I'll fix something for you to eat. What would you like?"

She tried to think of something, but even the thought of food was repugnant. "Just tea."

He walked upstairs with her; she was steady, but the steadiness seemed fragile, as if she were barely holding herself under control. He wished that she would cry, or yell, anything that would break the tension encasing her.

"I'll just get my nightgown. You don't mind if I get my nightgown, do you?" She looked anxious, as if afraid she was being too troublesome.

"No." He started to reach out and touch her, to slide his arm around her waist, but dropped his hand before contact was made. She might not want anyone to touch her. A sick feeling grew in him as he realized she might find his, and any other man's, touch disgusting now.

Mary got her nightgown and stood docilely in the old-fashioned bathroom while Wolf adjusted the water. "I'll be downstairs,'' he said as he straightened and stepped back. ''Leave the door unlocked.''

''Why?'' Her eyes were big and solemn.

''In case you faint, or need me.''

''I won't faint.''

He smiled a little. No, Miss Mary Elizabeth Potter wouldn't faint; she wouldn't allow herself to be so weak. Maybe it wasn't tension holding her so straight; it might be the iron in her backbone.

He knew he wouldn't be able to coax her to eat much, if anything, but he heated a can of soup anyway. His timing was perfect; the soup had just boiled and the tea finished steeping when Mary entered the kitchen.

She hadn't thought to put on a robe; she wore only the nightgown, a plain white cotton eyelet garment. Wolf felt himself begin to sweat, because as demure as the nightgown was, he could still see the darkness of her nipples through the fabric. He swore silently as she sat down at the table like an obedient child; now wasn't the time for lust. But telling himself that didn't stop it; he wanted her, under any circumstances.

She ate the soup mechanically, without protest, and drank the tea, then thanked him for making it. Wolf cleared the table and washed up the few dishes; when he turned, Mary was still sitting at the table, her hands folded and her eyes staring at nothing. He froze briefly and muttered a curse. He couldn't bear it another minute. Swiftly he lifted her out of the chair and sat down in it, then settled her on his lap.

She was stiff in his arms for a moment; then a sigh filtered between her lips as she relaxed against his chest. ''I was so frightened,'' she whispered.

''I know, honey.''

''How can you know? You're a man.'' She sounded faintly truculent.

"Yeah, but I was in prison, remember?" He wondered if she would know what he was talking about, and he saw her brow furrow as she thought.

Then she said, "Oh." She began scowling fiercely. "If anyone hurt you—" she began.

"Hold it! No, I wasn't attacked. I'm good at fighting, and everyone knew it." He didn't tell her how he'd established a reputation for himself. "But it happened to other prisoners, and I knew it could happen to me, so I was always on guard." He'd slept only in light naps, with a knife made from a sharpened spoon always in his hand; his cell had hidden a variety of weapons, a lot of which the guards had seen and not recognized for what they were. It would have taken another LRRP to have seen some of the things he'd done and the weapons he'd carried. Yeah, he'd been on guard.

"I'm glad," she said, then suddenly bent her head against his throat and began to cry. Wolf held her tightly, his fingers laced through her hair to press against her skull and hold her to him. Her soft, slender body shook with sobs as she wound her arms around his neck. She didn't say anything else, and neither did he, but they didn't need words.

He cradled her until finally she sniffed and observed dazedly, "I need to blow my nose."

He stretched to reach the napkin holder and plucked a napkin from it to place in her hands. Mary blew her nose in a very ladylike manner, then sat still, searching in her depths for the best way to handle what had happened. She knew it could have been much worse, but it had been bad enough. Only one thought surfaced: she didn't want to be alone tonight. She hadn't been able to tolerate the women fussing around her, but if Wolf would just stay with her, she'd be all right.

She looked up at him. "Will you stay with me to-night?"

Every muscle in his big body tensed, but there was no way he could deny her. "You know I will. I'll sleep on the—"

"No. I mean—if you could sleep with me tonight, and hold me so I won't be alone, just for tonight, I think I'll be all right tomorrow."

He hoped it would be that easy for her, but he doubted it. The memories would linger on, springing out from dark corners to catch her when she least expected it. Until the day she died, she would never entirely forget, and for that he wanted to catch her assailant and break the guy's neck. Literally.

"I'll call Joe and let him know where I am," he said, and lifted her from his lap.

It was still early, but her eyelids were drooping, and after he called Joe he decided there was no point in put-ting it off. She needed to be in bed.

He turned out the lights and put his arm around her as they climbed the narrow stairs together. Her flesh was warm and resilient beneath the thin cotton, and the feel of her made his heart begin a slow, heavy beat. His jaw clenched as blood throbbed through his body, pooling in his groin. He was in for a miserable night, and he knew it.

Her bedroom was so old-fashioned it looked turn-of-the-century, but he hadn't expected anything else. The delicate lilac smell he associated with Mary was stronger up here. The ache in his loins intensified.

"I hope the bed is big enough for you," she said, worrying as she eyed the double bed.

"It'll do." It wasn't big enough, but it would do. He'd have to spend the night curled around her. Her bottom would be nestled against him, and he would quietly go insane. Suddenly he didn't know if he could do it, if he could lie with her all night and not take her. No matter what his mind said, his body knew exactly what it wanted; he was already so hard it was all he could do to keep from groaning.

"Which side do you want?"

What did it matter? Torment was torment, no matter what side he was on. "The left."

Mary nodded and turned back the covers. Wolf wanted to look away as she climbed into bed, but his eyes wouldn't obey. He saw the curve of her buttocks as the nightgown was momentarily pulled tight. He saw her pale, slim legs and immediately pictured them clasped around his waist. He saw the outline of her pretty breasts with their rosy nipples, and he remembered the feel of her breasts in his hands, her nipples in his mouth, her smell and taste.

Abruptly he bent down and pulled the sheet up over her. "I have to take a shower."

He saw the brief dart of fear at being alone in her eyes, but then she conquered it and said, "The towels are in the closet next to the bathroom door."

He was swearing savagely to himself as he stood in the bathroom, jerking his clothes off. A cold shower wouldn't help; he'd had a lot of them lately, and the effect was remarkably short-lived. He needed Mary—naked, beneath him, sheathing his swollen and throbbing flesh. She would be so tight that he wouldn't last a minute—

Damn. He couldn't leave her, not tonight. No matter what it cost him.

His entire body was aching as he stood under the warm, beating water. He couldn't crawl into bed with her like this. The last thing she needed right now was to have him poking at her all night. She needed comfort, not lust. Not only that, he wasn't entirely certain of his control. He'd been too long without a woman, had wanted *her* for too long.

He couldn't leave her, but he couldn't go to her like this. He knew what he had to do, and his soapy hand slid down his body. At least this would give him some modicum of control, because he would rather slit his own throat than see that fear and vulnerability in Mary's eyes again.

She was lying very still when he rejoined her, and she didn't move as he turned out the light. It wasn't until his weight depressed the mattress that she shifted to lie on her side. He positioned himself on his side, too, and hooked an arm around her waist to pull her firmly back into the cradle of his body. She sighed, and he felt the tension slowly ebb from her body as she relaxed against him.

"This is nice," she whispered.

"You aren't afraid?"

"Of you? No. Never of you." Her tone was liquid with tenderness. She lifted her hand to reach back and cup his jaw in her palm. "I'll be all right in the morning, wait and see. I'm just too tired right now to deal with it. Will you hold me all night?"

"If you want me to."

"Please."

He brushed her hair to one side and pressed a kiss into the nape of her neck, delighting in the delicate little shiver that rippled through her body when he did so. "My pleasure," he said gently. "Good night, sweetheart."

It was the storm that woke her. It was barely dawn, the light still dim, though the black clouds contributed to the grayness. The storm was fierce, reminding her of the ferocious thunderstorms in the South. Lightning ripped the dark sky apart, and the booming thunder made the very air vibrate. She lazily counted the seconds between the lightning flashes and the thunder to see how far away the storm was: seven miles. But it was pouring rain, the sound loud on the old tin roof. It was wonderful.

She felt both acutely alive and deeply calm, as if she were waiting for something. Yesterday was, by its very definition, in the past. It could no longer hurt her. Today was the present, and the present was Wolf.

He wasn't in the bed, but she knew he had been there during the night. Even in sleep she had sensed him, felt his strong arms holding her. Sleeping together was a joy so deep she couldn't express it, as if it had been meant to be. Perhaps it had been. She couldn't stop herself from hoping.

Where was he? She thought she smelled coffee and got out of bed. She visited the bathroom, brushed her hair and teeth, and returned to the bedroom to dress. Oddly she felt suddenly constrained by the bra she put on and discarded it. A subtle pulsating sensation had enveloped her entire body, and the sense of waiting increased. Even underpants were too much. She simply pulled on a loose cotton housedress over her nude body and went downstairs in her bare feet.

He wasn't in the parlor, or the kitchen, though the empty coffeepot and the cup in the sink explained the lingering scent. The kitchen door was open, the screen door no barrier to the cool damp air, and the fresh smell of rain mingled with that of the coffee. His truck was still parked at the back porch steps.

It took only a few minutes to boil water and steep a tea bag, and she drank the tea while sitting at the kitchen table, watching the rain sheet down the window. It was cool enough that she should have been chilled, wearing only the thin dress, but she wasn't, even though she could feel how her nipples had tightened. Once that would have embarrassed her. Now she thought only of Wolf.

She was halfway between the table and the sink, empty cup in hand, when suddenly he was there, standing on the other side of the screen door, watching her through the wire mesh. His clothing was plastered to his skin, rainwater dripping off of his face. Mary froze, her head turned to stare at him.

He looked wild, primitive, his eyes narrow and glittering, his feet braced apart. She could see every breath that swelled his chest, see the pulse that throbbed at the base of his throat. Though he was very still, she could feel his entire body pulsating with tension. In that moment she knew he was going to take her, and she knew that was why she had waited.

"I'll always be a half-breed," he said in a low, harsh voice, barely audible over the drumming rain. "There will always be people who look down on me because of it. Think long and hard before you agree to be my woman, because there's no going back."

Softly, clearly, she said, "I don't want to go back."

He opened the screen door and entered the kitchen, his movements slow and deliberate. Mary's hand shook as she reached out to place her cup on the cabinet; then she turned to face him.

He put his hands on her waist and gently drew her up against him; his clothes were wet, and immediately the front of her dress absorbed the moisture until the damp fabric was molded to her body. Mary slid her hands up his shoulders to join at the back of his neck and lifted her mouth to his. His kiss was slow and deep, making her toes curl as hot excitement began to dart through her. She knew how to kiss now and welcomed his tongue while she teased him with her own. His chest lifted with a deep, sharp intake of breath, and his grip on her tightened. Suddenly the kiss was no longer slow, but hungry and urgent, and the pressure of his mouth was almost painful.

She felt him gathering her skirt in his hand to lift it; then his callused palm was sliding up her thigh. He reached her hip and paused, shuddering with violent arousal as he realized she was naked under the dress; then his hand moved to her bare buttocks and caressed them. It was surprisingly pleasurable, and she moved her bottom against his hand. He had opened up an entire new world for her, the world of sensual pleasure, and he was constantly expanding the limits.

He couldn't wait much longer, and he lifted her in his arms. His face was hard and intent as he looked down at her. "Unless the house catches on fire, I won't stop this time," he said quietly. "I don't care if the phone rings, or if anyone drives up, or even knocks on the bedroom door. This time, we finish it."

She didn't reply, but gave him a slow, sweet smile that made him burn to take her right there. His arms tightened as he carried her up the narrow, creaky stairs and into her bedroom, where he carefully placed her on the bed.

He stood looking down at her for a moment, then walked to the window and raised it. "Let's let the storm in," he said, and then it was with them, filling the half-dark room with sound and vibration. The rain-chilled air washed over her, cool and fresh on her heated skin. She sighed, the small sound drowned out by the din of thunder and rain.

There by the window, with the dim gray light outlining the bulge and plane of powerful muscle, Wolf removed his wet clothing. Mary lay quietly on the bed, her head turned to watch him. The shirt went first, revealing his sleek, heavy shoulders and washboard stomach. She knew from touching him that he was unbelievably hard, with no give beneath his smooth skin. He bent down to tug off his boots and socks, then straightened and unbuckled his belt. The noise of the storm made his movements a pantomime, but she imagined the small pop as he unsnapped his jeans, then the hissing of the zipper as metal teeth pulled apart. Without hesitation he pushed down his jeans and underwear and stepped free of them.

He was naked. Her heart jerked painfully in her chest as she stared at him, for the first time feeling remarkably small and helpless beside him. He was big, he was strong, and he was undeniably male. She couldn't look away from his hard manhood. She was going to take him inside her, accept his heavy weight as they joined in the act of mating, and she was a little frightened.

He saw it in her eyes as he eased down beside her. "Don't be afraid," he whispered, brushing her hair away from her face. His hands were gentle as he reached under her and unzipped her dress.

"I know what's going to happen," she murmured, turning her face against his shoulder. "The mechanics of it, anyway. But I just don't see how it's possible."

"It is. I'll take it slow and easy."

"All right." She whispered her acquiescence and let him lift her so he could pull the dress off of her shoulders. Her breasts were bare, and she could feel them tightening, swelling, her nipples puckering. He bent to kiss both nipples, wetting them with his tongue, and her back arched as heat spread through her. He quickly stripped the dress down her hips and legs, the need to have her bare under his hands too urgent for him to ignore it any longer.

Mary quivered, then lay still. It was the first time since

babyhood that anyone but herself had seen her completely nude; her cheeks heated, and she closed her eyes as she struggled with the sensations of embarrassment and painful exposure. He touched her breasts, gently squeezing them; then his rough palm slowly moved down her stomach until his fingers touched her silky triangle of curls. She made a small sound, and her eyes flew open to find him watching her with such a fierce, heated expression that she forgot her embarrassment. She was suddenly proud that he wanted her so intensely, that her body aroused him. Her legs relaxed, and one finger delved between her soft folds, lightly stroking the ultra-sensitive flesh he found. Mary's entire body tensed again, and she moaned. She hadn't known anything could feel like that, but she sensed there was more, and she didn't know if she could survive it. This was pleasure too intense to be borne.

"Do you like that?" Wolf murmured.

She gasped, her slender body beginning to writhe slowly on the sheets in a rhythm as old as the ages. He opened her legs farther with his hand, then returned to his sensual exploration, and at the same time bent to hungrily cover her mouth with his own. Mary's head spun, and her nails dug into his shoulders as she clung to him. She couldn't believe how he was touching her, how it made her feel, but she never wanted it to stop. He was causing a fever inside her, one that spread and intensified until she was aware of nothing but her own body and his. His stroking fingers raised her to delirium while his mouth muffled the small moans she made.

She tore her mouth away from his. "Wolf, please," she begged, frantic with need.

"Just a minute longer, sweetheart. Look at me. Let me see your face when I—ahh."

She whimpered. He was touching her even more intimately, finding her damp and swollen. His black gaze was locked with hers as he slowly slid his finger inside her, and they both shuddered convulsively.

Wolf knew he couldn't wait any longer. His entire body was throbbing. She was soft and wet and incredibly tight, and she was writhing on the verge of ecstasy. Her pale, translucent skin intoxicated him, enthralled him; just touching her made him wild. The textures of her body excited him more than anything he'd ever known before. Everything about her was soft and silky. Her hair was baby-fine, her skin delicate and satiny; even the curls between her legs were soft, rather than springy. He wanted her more than he wanted his next breath.

He moved between her legs, spreading them to make room for his hips to nestle against her. She inhaled sharply as she felt him, hard and burning. Their eyes met again as he reached down between their bodies and guided himself into position, then began entering her.

The storm was right over them now. The lightning cracked, and the almost simultaneous thunder boomed, rattling the old house. The sharply gusting wind blew the curtains straight out into the room, spattering rain on the floor in front of the open window and carrying a fine mist over their bodies. Mary cried, her tears mingling with the mist on her face, as she accepted his slow penetration.

He was braced over her on his forearms, his face just an inch from hers. He licked the tears away, then kissed her mouth, and she tasted salt. She could feel burning pain as her body stretched to admit him, and enormous pressure. More tears seeped from the corners of her eyes. He deepened the kiss as his buttocks flexed, exerting more pressure, and suddenly her body's barrier gave way. He pushed deep into her, burying himself to the hilt with a deep, almost tortured groan of pleasure.

There was pain, but there was also a lot more. He'd told her that making love was hot and sweaty, and that she probably wouldn't like it, and he was both right and wrong. It *was* hot and sweaty, and raw, and primitive. It was so powerful that it swept her along with its rhythms. Despite the pain, she felt exalted by his possession. She could feel the tension and savage excitement in his powerful body as she cradled him with her legs and arms, her soft depths filled with him. She loved him, and he needed her. She had never really lived before, until this moment when she gave herself to the man she loved.

She couldn't keep it back, not that it mattered. He had to know already. Mary had never worn an emotional mask. Her hands moved over his sleek, wet shoulders and into his thick hair. "I love you," she said, her soft voice barely audible over another booming roll of thunder.

If he replied, she didn't hear him. He reached down between their bodies again, but this time his hand was on her, and he began moving. Heat shimmered through her again, making the discomfort fade; her body arched, hips lifting in an effort to take him even deeper, and she told him again that she loved him. Sweat beaded his taut face as he tried to control his thrusts, but the storm was in the room, in their bodies. Her hips undulated, rolling, driving him mad. They strained together, their movements punctuated by the thunder, by the thudding of the headboard against the wall, and by the creaking of the bedsprings beneath them. Low groans and soft cries; wet flesh and trembling muscles; hands clutching frantically; harsh, rapid breathing and urgent thrusts—she knew all of that, felt it, heard it, and felt herself being consumed by the fever.

"Wolf?" Her questioning cry was thin, frantic. Her nails dug into the flexing muscles of his back.

"Don't fight it, baby. Let it go." He was groaning, feeling his own completion approaching, and he had no more control left. He removed his hand from between them and gripped her hips, lifting them, fitting himself more solidly to her and rocking against her loins.

Mary felt the tension and fever increase to unbearable levels, and then her senses exploded. She cried out, her entire body shuddering and clenching. It was the sweetest madness imaginable, a pleasure beyond description, and it continued until she thought she might die of it. He held her until she quietened, then began thrusting hard and fast. His guttural cries blended with the thunder as he crushed her against the mattress, his body convulsing as the powerful jetting of completion emptied him.

They were silent afterward, as if words would be an intrusion between them. Their mating had been so compelling and urgent that nothing else had existed. Even the storm, as violent as it was, had been only an accompaniment. Slowly, reluctantly, Mary felt reality return, but she was content to lie beneath him and do nothing more than stroke his hair.

Their breathing had long since steadied and the storm moved away when he disengaged their bodies and shifted onto his side. He cradled her for a time, but now that their skin had cooled, the mist-dampened bed was distinctly uncomfortable. When she began to shiver, he got out of bed and crossed to the window to close it. She watched as his muscles alternately bunched and relaxed with each movement of his nude body. Then he turned, and she was instantly, helplessly, fascinated. She wished for the nerve to run her hands all over him, especially his loins. She wanted to inspect him, like an exploration, going over uncharted territory.

"Like what you see?" His voice was low and filled with amusement.

Things had gone too far between them for her to be embarrassed now. She looked up at him and smiled. "Very much. I imagined you once in a loincloth, but this is much better."

He reached down and plucked her from the bed as easily as if she were a feather. "We'd better get dressed before you get cold, and before I forget my good intentions."

"What good intentions?"

"Not to keep at you until you're so sore you can't walk."

She looked gravely at him. "You made it wonderful for me. Thank you."

"It was pretty damn wonderful for me, too." One side of his mouth quirked upward, and he slid his hands into her silvery brown hair. "No bad moments?"

She understood what he meant and leaned her head against his chest. "No. That was an entirely different thing."

But she hadn't forgotten, either, and he knew it. She was still shaky and vulnerable inside, though she kept her chin proudly lifted. He intended for someone to pay for the damage done to her indomitable spirit.

He'd spent years living quietly on the fringes, maintaining the sort of armed truce that had existed between him and the citizens of Ruth, but no more. For Mary, he would find the creep who had attacked her, and if the townspeople didn't like it, that was just too bad.

Chapter 8

She threw Wolf's wet clothes into the dryer, then prepared a late breakfast. Neither of them talked much. Despite her determination to overcome her shock, she couldn't quite forget those horrifying moments when she had been helpless at the hands of a madman, for he certainly was mad. No matter what she was doing or thinking, a lightning flash of memory would catapult her back to the attack, just for a minute, until she could regain control and put it from her again.

Wolf watched her, knowing what she was experiencing by the way her slight body would tense, then slowly relax. He'd lived through flashbacks, of Vietnam, of prison, and he knew how they worked, as well as the toll they took. He wanted to take her to bed again, to keep the shadows at bay for her, but knew from the occasional gingerness of her movements that she was too new to lovemaking for another bout right now to be anything other than abusive. When she was used to him… A very slight smile curved his lips as he thought of the hours of pleasure and all the different ways he would take her.

But first he had to find the man who had attacked her.

When his clothes were dry, he dressed and pulled Mary out to the back porch with him. The rain had diminished to a drizzle, so he figured they wouldn't get too wet. "Come out to the barn with me," he said, taking her hand.

"Why?"

"I want to show you something."

"I've been in the barn. There's nothing interesting in there."

"There is today. You'll like it."

"All right." They hurried through the drizzle to the old barn, which was dark and musty, without the warmth and rich, animal smells of his barn. Dust tickled her nose. "It's too dark to see anything."

"There's enough light. Come on." Still holding her hand, he led her into a stall where a couple of boards were missing from the wall, letting in the dreary light. After the darkness of the inner barn, she could see fairly well.

"What is it?"

"Look under the feed trough."

She bent down and looked. Curled up, in a nest of dusty straw and an old towel she recognized, was Woodrow. Curled against Woodrow's belly were four little rat-looking things.

She straightened abruptly. "Woodrow's a father!"

"Nope. Woodrow's a mother."

"A mother!" She stared at the cat, who stared back at her enigmatically before beginning to lick the kittens. "I was specifically told that Woodrow is male."

"Well, Woodrow is female. Didn't you look?"

Mary gave him a severe look. "I don't make a habit of looking at an animal's private parts."

"Just mine, right?"

She blushed, but couldn't deny the charge. "Right."

He slipped his arms around her waist and pulled her close for a slow, warm kiss. She sighed and softened against him, reaching up to clasp the back of his neck as his mouth moved over hers. The strength of his big body reassured her, made her feel safe. When his hard arms were around her, nothing could harm her.

"I have to go home," he murmured when he lifted his mouth from hers. "Joe will do as much as he can, but it takes both of us to get everything done."

She had thought she could handle it, but panic seized her at the thought of being alone. Quickly she controlled herself and let her arms drop from around his neck. "Okay." She started to ask if she'd see him later, but kept the words unsaid. Oddly, now that their relationship was so intimate, she felt far less sure of herself than she had before. Letting him get that close, letting him enter her body, had exposed a vulnerability she hadn't known was there. That kind of intimacy was a little scary.

"Get a jacket," he said as they left the barn.

"I already have a jacket."

"I meant, get one now. You're going with me."

She gave him a quick look, then dropped her gaze away from the awareness in his. "I have to be alone sometime," she said quietly.

"But not today. Go on, get that jacket."

She got the jacket and climbed up into his truck, feeling as if she had been reprieved from execution. Maybe by the time night came she would have her fears under control.

Joe came out of the barn as they drove up and walked to the passenger side of the truck. When Mary opened the door, he reached in and lifted her from the truck, then hugged her tightly. "Are you all right?" His young voice was gruff.

She hugged him in return. "He didn't hurt me. I was just scared."

Over her head Joe looked at his father and saw the cold, controlled rage in those black eyes as they lingered on the slight woman in his son's arms. Someone had dared to hurt her, and whoever it was would pay. Joe felt a deep primitive anger, and knew it was only a fraction of what Wolf felt. Their eyes met, and Wolf gave a slight shake of his head, indicating that he didn't want Joe to pursue the subject. Mary was here to relax, not relive the attack.

Wolf approached and looped his arm over her shoulder, using the pressure to turn her toward the stable. "Feel up to helping with the chores?"

Her eyes lit. "Of course. I've always wanted to see how a ranch works."

He automatically shortened his long stride to match hers as the three of them walked toward the stable. "This isn't a ranch, exactly. I run a small herd, but more for training and our personal beef than any other reason."

"What sort of training?"

"Training the horses to work a herd. That's what I do. I break and train horses. Quarter horses mostly, for ranchers, but sometimes I handle the odd show horse or Thoroughbred, or a fractious pleasure mount."

"Don't Thoroughbred owners have their own trainers?"

He shrugged. "Some horses are harder to train than others. An expensive horse isn't worth a damn if no one can get near him." He didn't elaborate, but Mary knew that he got the horses no one else was able to handle.

The long stable jutted out to the right of the barn.

When they entered, Mary inhaled the rich earth scents of horses, leather, manure, grain and hay. Long satiny necks poked over the stall doors, and inquisitive whickers filled the air. She had never been around horses much, but she wasn't afraid of them. She moved down the line, patting and stroking, murmuring to the animals. "Are these all quarter horses?"

"No. That one in the next stall is a Canadian cutting horse—that's a type, not a breed. He belongs to a rancher in the next county north. Down in the last stall is a saddle-bred, for some big rancher's wife in Montana. He's going to give her the horse for her birthday in July. The rest of them are quarter horses."

They were all young horses, and as playful as children. Wolf treated them as such, talking to them in a low, crooning tone, gentling them like overgrown babies. Mary spent the entire afternoon in the stables with Wolf and Joe, watching them attend to the endless chores of cleaning and feeding, checking shoes, grooming. The drizzle finally stopped in the late afternoon, and Wolf worked with a couple of the young quarter horses in the pen behind the stable, slowly and gently getting them accustomed to bits and saddles. He didn't rush them, or lose his patience when a fractious young horse shied away from him whenever Wolf tried to lift a saddle onto his back. He just soothed the colt and reassured him before trying again. Before the afternoon was over, the colt was ambling around the pen as if he'd been wearing a saddle for years.

Mary was enthralled, partly by his low, velvety voice, and partly by the way his strong hands moved over the young animals, teaching and soothing all at once. He had done that with her, but his hands had also excited her. She shivered as memories washed over her, and her breasts tightened.

"I've never seen anyone like him," Joe said beside her, keeping his tone low. "I'm good, but not near as good as he is. I've never seen a horse he couldn't settle down. We had a stallion brought to us a couple of years ago. He'd been put out to stud, but he was so damn vicious the handlers couldn't control him. Dad just put him in a stall and left him alone, but every so often he'd leave sugar cubes, apples or carrots on the top of the stall door and stand there until the stallion got a good look at him. Then he'd walk off, and the stallion would get whatever he'd left on the door.

"The stallion started watching for him and snorting at him if Dad was taking his time about getting the food over there. Then Dad stopped moving away, and the stallion, Ringer, had to come up to the door while Dad was there if he wanted the food. The first few times, he tried to tear the stall apart, but finally he gave in and got the food. Next he had to eat out of Dad's hand if he wanted his treat. Dad switched completely to carrots then, to make sure he didn't lose any fingers. Finally Ringer was hanging his head over the stall, and he'd nuzzle Dad's shirt like a kid hunting candy. Dad petted him and groomed him—Ringer loved being brushed—and gradually broke him to the saddle and started riding him. I worked with him, too, after Dad had him settled down, and I guess he finally decided he didn't have to fight all the time.

"We had a mare come in heat, and Dad called Ringer's owner to ask if he wanted us to try Ringer on our mare. The guy gave his okay, Ringer performed like a real gentleman, and everybody was happy. The owner got his expensive stud civilized, and we got a hefty fee, as well as a hell of a colt out of the mare Ringer covered."

Mary blinked at all this talk of being "in heat" and

"covered," and cleared her throat. "He's wonderful," she agreed, and cleared her throat again. Her skin felt hot and sensitive. She couldn't take her eyes off Wolf, tall and lean and broad-shouldered, the weak sunlight glinting off his black hair.

"When we get through here, maybe we could do a few lessons tonight, since I missed Friday night," Joe said, interrupting her thoughts.

She didn't like thinking about why he had missed Friday night, about the long hours spent waiting to hear if Wolf had been jailed. This afternoon had been a small oasis of calm, with the semblance of normality, but it would be a long time before things were back to normal in the county. A young girl had been raped, and Mary had been attacked the very next day. People would be enraged and wary, looking at their neighbors and wondering. God help any stranger who happened to wander through, at least until the man was caught.

Tires crunched on the gravel, and Joe left his post to see who had ventured up on Mackenzie's Mountain. He was back in a moment, with Clay Armstrong behind him. It was a replay of Friday afternoon, and Mary felt her heart lurch; surely Clay wasn't going to arrest Wolf now?

"Mary." Clay nodded at her and touched the brim of his hat. "You doing okay?"

"Yes." She said it firmly.

"I thought I'd find you up here. Do you feel like going over it again with me?"

Wolf pulled off his gloves as he approached. His eyes were flinty. "She went over it with you yesterday."

"Sometimes people remember little things after the shock has passed."

Because she sensed Wolf was about to throw Clay off his property, she turned and put her hand on his arm. "It's okay. *I'm* okay."

She was lying, and he knew it, but her mouth had taken on that stubborn set that meant she wouldn't back down. He felt a tinge of amusement; his kitten was getting back some of her confidence, after all. But no way was he going to let Clay question her alone. He looked at Joe. ''Put the horse up. I'm going with Mary.''

''That isn't necessary,'' Clay said.

''It is to me.''

Mary felt dwarfed between the two big men as they walked up to the house; she thought she might soon find such protectiveness smothering. A smile touched her lips. Clay probably felt he had to protect her from Wolf as well as from another attack, while Wolf was determined to protect her, period. She wondered what Clay would think if he knew that she didn't want to be protected from Wolf. Aunt Ardith would say Wolf had taken advantage of her, and Mary earnestly hoped he would do so again. Soon.

Wolf caught her sidelong glance and stiffened as he felt her interest and warmth. Damn it, didn't she know how he'd react, and that it could get embarrassing? Already he could feel the tension in his loins. But, no, she didn't know. Despite their early morning lovemaking, she was still too innocent about sex in general, and the effect she had on him in particular, to know what that look did to him. He hurried his step. He needed to sit down.

When they entered the kitchen, Mary moved around making coffee as naturally as she would have in her own house, emphasizing to Clay that she and Wolf were a couple. Folks in the county were just going to have to get used to it.

''Let's go through it from the beginning,'' Clay said.

Mary paused fractionally, then resumed her steady movements as she measured coffee into the percolator.

"I'd just bought new boots at Hearst's store and was walking back to my car—my boots! I dropped them! Did you see them? Did anyone pick them up?"

"I saw them, but I don't know what happened to them. I'll ask around."

"He must have been standing against the side of Hearst's store, because I'd have seen him if he had been on the other side of the alley. He just grabbed me and put his hand over my mouth. He held my head arched back, so I couldn't move it at all, and started dragging me down the alley. I got one hand free and reached back, trying to scratch his face, but he had on a ski mask. He hit me in the head with his fist and I—I really don't remember much after that until he pushed me down. I kept scratching him, and I think I clawed his hand, because he hit me again. Then I bit him on the hand, but I don't know if I drew blood.

"Someone yelled, and he got up and ran. He put his hand on the ground right in front of my face when he got up. His sleeve was blue, and he had freckles on his hand. A lot of freckles. Then...you were there."

She fell silent and moved to look out the kitchen window, her back to the men sitting at the table, so she didn't see the murderous look in Wolf's eyes, or the way his big fists clenched, but Clay did, and it worried him.

"I was the one who yelled. I saw the package lying on the ground and went over to see what it was, and then I heard scuffling from the back of the building. When I saw him, I yelled and pulled my revolver, and fired over his head to try to stop him."

Wolf looked savage. "You should have shot the son of a bitch. That would have stopped him."

In retrospect Clay wished he'd shot the guy, too. At least then they wouldn't be racking their brains trying to put an ID to him, and the townspeople wouldn't be so jittery. Women were carrying an assortment of weapons with them wherever they went, even outside to hang the wash to dry. The mood people were in, it would be dangerous for a stranger to stop in the county.

That was what bothered him, and he said as much. "It looks like someone would have noticed a stranger. Ruth is a small town, and people pretty well know everyone in the county. A stranger would have been noticed right off, especially one with long black hair."

Wolf gave a wintry smile. "Everyone would have thought it was me."

At the window, Mary stiffened. She had been trying not to listen, trying to push away the memories that had been called up by her recounting of what had happened. She didn't turn around, but suddenly all her attention was focused on the conversation behind her. What Wolf had said was true. On seeing her attacker's long black hair, Clay had immediately had Wolf arrested.

But that long black hair, so distinctive, didn't fit with the wealth of rust-colored freckles she'd seen on the man's hand. And his skin had been pale. Fair people freckled. The black hair didn't fit.

Unless it was a disguise. Unless the object had been to frame Wolf.

Her spine prickled, and she felt both hot and cold. Whoever had done it hadn't known that Wolf had had his hair cut. But the choice of victim was puzzling; it didn't make sense. Why attack her? Surely no one would think Wolf would attack the one person in town who'd championed him, and she'd made it plain how she felt. Unless she had been a random choice, *it just didn't make sense*. After all, there was no link between herself and Cathy Teele, no common ground. It could all be chance.

Still without turning around, she asked, "Wolf, do you know Cathy Teele? Have you ever spoken to her?"

"I know her by sight. I don't speak to little Anglo girls." His tone was ironic. "Their parents wouldn't like it."

"You're right about that," Clay said wearily. "A few months back Cathy told her mother you were the best-looking man around, and that she wouldn't mind dating Joe if he weren't younger than she was. The whole town heard about it. Mrs. Teele pitched a fit."

That chill ran down Mary's spine again. There was a link, after all: Wolf. Nor could she dismiss it as coincidence, though something about the whole thing was skewed.

She twisted her hands together, and turned to face them. "What if someone is deliberately trying to frame Wolf?"

Wolf's face went hard and blank, but Clay looked startled. "Damn," he muttered. "Why did you think of that?"

"The long black hair. It could have been a wig. The man had freckles on his hand, a lot of freckles, and his skin was pale."

Wolf got to his feet, and though Mary knew she never had anything to fear from him, she fell back a step at the expression in his eyes. He didn't say anything; he didn't have to. She had seen him angry before, but this was different. He was enraged, but it was an icy rage, and he was in perfect control of himself. Perhaps that was what alarmed her.

Then Clay said, "Sorry, but I don't think it'll wash. Once we had all thought about it, it didn't make sense that Wolf would have attacked you, of all people. You've stood up for him right from the beginning, when the rest of the people in town—"

"Wouldn't spit on me if I were on fire," Wolf finished.

Clay couldn't deny it. "Exactly."

The coffee had finished brewing, and Mary poured three cups. They were silent and thoughtful as they sipped, all of them turning things around in their minds, trying to make the pieces fit. The truth was that no matter how things were arranged, something was always off, unless they went with the idea that a criminal had chosen Mary and Cathy at random, and had perhaps used a long black wig for disguise by pure coincidence.

Everything in Mary rejected the idea of coincidence. So that meant someone was deliberately trying to implicate Wolf. But why choose *her* as a victim?

To punish Wolf by hurting the people who had championed him?

It was all supposition, without a shred of evidence. Wolf had lived here for years without anything like this happening, even though his presence was like salt on the wound of the town's conscience. They didn't like him, and he didn't let them forget. Still, they had all existed under a silent truce.

So what had triggered the violence?

She rubbed her temples as a sudden twinge of pain threatened to become a full-scale headache. Since she seldom had headaches, she supposed the tension was getting to her, and determined not to let it. She'd never been a Nervous Nellie and didn't intend to start now.

Clay sighed and pushed his empty cup back. "Thanks for the coffee. I'll get the report finished tomorrow. I'll bring the papers by the school for you to sign—uh, are you planning to go to work, or stay home?"

"Why, work, of course."

"Of course," Wolf muttered, and scowled at her. Mary lifted her chin at him. She saw no reason why she should suddenly become an invalid.

Clay left soon afterward, and Joe came up from the

stables to join in the dinner preparations. It felt right, the
three of them together, working together as comfortably
as if they had done so for years. Joe winked at her once,
and she blushed, because it was fairly easy to read the
expression in his young-old eyes. Awareness, amusement
and approval were all there. Was he simply assuming she
and Wolf had become intimate because Wolf had spent
the night at her house, which she supposed was the com-
monsense thing to assume, or was there something different about her? What if everyone in town could just
look at her and know?

Wolf curved his hand around her waist. She had been
standing motionless for several minutes, the pan in her
hand forgotten, as she both frowned and blushed. The
blush told him what she was thinking, and the familiar
tension in his body made his fingers tighten until they
dug into her ribs. She looked up at him, her gray-blue
eyes wide and startled; then awareness shot into them,
and her eyelids dropped to half veil the desire she
couldn't disguise.

Joe reached to take the pan from her nerveless fingers.
"I think I'll go see a movie somewhere," he announced.

Mary jerked her head around, tearing herself from the
sensual spell Wolf spun about her so easily. "No! Your
lessons, remember?"

"Another night won't hurt."

"Another night will hurt," she insisted. "The Academy isn't something you can take for granted just because Senator Allard is going to recommend you. You
can't afford to let up for a minute."

Wolf released her. "She's right, son. You can't let
your grades slip." He could wait. Barely.

It was after nine when Mary closed the books she and
Joe had been using and stretched her arms over her head.

"Could you take me home now?" she asked Wolf, barely suppressing a yawn. It had been an eventful day.

His face was impassive. "Why don't you stay here." It was more of a command than a suggestion.

"I can't do that!"

"Why not?"

"It isn't proper."

"I stayed with you last night."

"That's different."

"How?"

"I was upset."

"Your bed's too small. Mine's bigger."

"I'm getting out of here," Joe said, and suited the action to the words.

Mary got huffy. "Did you have to say that in front of him?"

"He knew anyway. Remember what I said about no going back?"

She stilled and said, "Yes." That warm look entered her eyes again. "I don't want to go back. But I can't stay here tonight. I have to go to work in the morning."

"No one would think any less of you if you didn't."

"*I* would." She had that look again, the stubborn, determined expression of a fierce will.

Wolf got to his feet. "All right. I'll take you home." He went into his bedroom and several minutes later reappeared with a small shaving kit in his hand and a change of clothes slung over his shoulder. He knocked briefly on Joe's door as he passed it. "I'll be home in the morning."

The door opened. Joe was barefoot and shirtless, having been preparing to take a shower. "Okay. Are you going to take her to school, or do you want me to?"

"I don't need anyone to take me to work," Mary interrupted.

"That's tough." Wolf turned back to his son. "Baugh is bringing a couple of horses up in the morning, so I'll have to be here. You take her to school, and I'll get her in the afternoon."

"I'm driving my own car, and you can't stop me!"

"That's okay. You'll just have an escort." Wolf crossed the floor to her and took her arm. "Ready?"

Realizing that he'd made up his mind and there wasn't anything she could do about it, Mary walked with him out to the truck. The night air was growing cold, but his big body radiated heat, and she moved closer to him. As soon as they were in the truck, he roughly took her in his arms and bent his head to hers. She opened her mouth beneath his onslaught and thrust her fingers into his thick hair. The warm taste of his mouth filled her; the pressure of his arms around her rib cage, of his hard-muscled chest on her breasts, drugged her more surely than any sedative. If he had pulled her down onto the seat and taken her right then, she wouldn't have objected.

As it was, when he put her from him, her entire body was throbbing. She sat silently on the drive down the mountain, thinking of their lovemaking that morning, aching for it to be repeated. A thought echoed in her mind: so this was what it meant to be a woman.

Woodrow was waiting patiently on the back doorstep. Mary fed him—her!—while Wolf showered and shaved. He didn't have a heavy beard, but two days' growth had darkened his jaw, and her face burned a little from contact with his when they had kissed. She felt that deep, almost painful sense of waiting again as she climbed the stairs to her bedroom.

He silently entered and stood for a moment watching her before she sensed his presence and turned. "The shower's yours."

He was naked, and slightly damp from the humidity

in the bathroom. His black hair glistened under the light, and glittering droplets of water were caught in the dark curls of hair on his chest. He was already aroused. The throbbing in her body became acute.

She showered, and afterward, for the first time, sprayed perfume on her pulse points. She had never bought perfume in her life, but luckily one of her students in Savannah had given her the bottle for Christmas. The scent was sweetly exotic.

She opened the bathroom door, then gasped and fell back. Wolf was waiting for her in the doorway, his eyes narrow and fierce as they raked her. She had boldly left off her nightgown, and under his perusal the deep throbbing intensified. He put his big hands on her breasts and lifted them slightly so that they were plumped in his palms. Her nipples tightened even before he began rubbing them with his thumbs. Mary stood very still, her breath quick and shallow, her eyes half closed as she tried to deal with the pleasure his hands brought.

Wolf's own eyes were narrow black slits. "I wanted to do this the day I found you on the road," he murmured. "Such a pretty little body inside that ugly dress. I wanted to take it off of you and see you naked."

The heat in his eyes, in his voice, made her shiver and sway toward him. He pulled her out of the doorway and into the dark hall, then put his hands on her waist and lifted her. She remembered when he had done that before and moaned even before his mouth closed over her nipple. He sucked it so strongly that her back arched, and she cried out as her legs parted and wrapped around his hips for balance. He groaned, unable to wait a minute longer. He had to get inside her or go mad. He shifted her, guided himself and entered her.

Mary shuddered, then went very still as he slowly pushed into her. It was even better than before. Her inner muscles gently clasped and relaxed as she accommodated him, sending waves of pleasure radiating out through her body. She clung to him, gasping. Desire worked its magic on her body, tightening some muscles, loosening others, so that she was both taut and pliable as she lifted herself, then sank back down. The effect of that small movement had both of them gasping, and Wolf shifted to brace his back against the wall. She did it again, then again. He put his hands on her buttocks to take control of the motion and began driving into her. Her skin felt on fire. She radiated heat, making her skin feel tight and smooth and so extraordinarily sensitive that she could feel each of his fingers on her bottom, the rasp of his chest hair on her breasts, the tiny nubs of his nipples, the muscled wall of his belly, the coarse hair at his groin. She could feel him deep inside her.

Her back arched, and her nerves convulsed. Wolf fought his own response, not wanting it to end so quickly, and held her until she quietened. Then he carried her into the bedroom, her legs still locked around him, and eased her down on the bed.

She swallowed and relaxed her hold on him. "You haven't—?"

"Not yet," he murmured, and began moving strongly into her.

She didn't want it to end. She took his thrusts, cradled him when a harsh groan tore from his throat and the powerful shudders of completion shook him, and afterward held him as he rested on her body. She didn't want him to withdraw, to leave her empty again. She had existed in a sort of genteel limbo all her life until she had met him and begun to live. In just a few short months he had so completely taken over the focus of her life that the years before were hazy.

He gathered himself and tried to move off her. Mary tightened her legs around him, and he grunted.

"Let me up, sweetheart. I'm too heavy for you."

"No you aren't," she whispered, and kissed his throat.

"I weigh twice what you do. Do you even weigh a hundred pounds?"

"Yes," she said indignantly. She weighed a hundred and five.

"Not much more than that. I weigh two hundred, and I'm a foot taller than you. If I go to sleep on you, you'll smother."

He did sound drowsy. She ran her hand down the muscled ridges of his side. "I want to stay like this."

He thrust gently against her. "Like this?"

"Yes." She breathed the word.

He settled onto her, but shifted part of his weight to the side. "Is this okay?"

It was wonderful. She could breathe, but he was still close to her, still inside her. He quickly dozed off, as content as she with the position, and Mary smiled in the darkness as she held him.

The dark thoughts slowly intruded. Someone had deliberately tried to frame him, to put him back in prison. The thought of Wolf without his freedom was obscene and scary, because she knew enough about him to know he would never let himself be sent to prison again.

She wanted to keep him safe, to shield him in her arms, putting her own body between him and danger. Dear God, what had started it all? Things had been so quiet! What had been the trigger?

Then she knew, and horror almost stopped her breath. *She* had been the trigger.

While Wolf and Joe had been outcasts, punished for their heritage and Wolf's past, everything had been calm. Then she had come to town, an Anglo woman, but in-

stead of aligning herself with the townspeople, she had
championed the Mackenzies. With her help, Joe had
achieved an honor offered to very few. Other people had
begun saying what a nice thing it was that the Mackenzie
boy was going to the Academy. Cathy Teele had said
that Wolf was the best-looking man in the county. The
boundaries between the town and the Mackenzies had
begun blurring. Someone, with a maggot of hate festering
deep inside, had been unable to stand it.

And she had been the cause of it all. If anything happened to Wolf, it would be her fault.

Chapter 9

She didn't know what to do. The thought that she was the cause of all that had happened tormented her, disturbing her sleep. She moved restlessly, waking Wolf, and he sensed her distress though he attributed it to the wrong cause. He soothed her with whispers and pulled her more completely beneath him. She felt him harden inside her. His lovemaking was gentle this time, and when it was over she slept as effortlessly as a child until he awoke her again in the total darkness before dawn. She turned to him without question.

Joe drove up just as she and Wolf were preparing breakfast, and without a word Wolf broke more eggs into a bowl to be scrambled. Mary smiled at him, even though she was placing more bacon in the frying pan. "How do you know he's hungry?"

"He's awake, isn't he? My kid eats like a horse."

Joe came in the back door and headed for the coffee, which had already finished brewing. "Morning."

"Good morning. Breakfast will be ready in about ten minutes."

He grinned at her, and Mary smiled back. Wolf watched her, his gaze sharp. She looked frail this morning, her skin pale and even more translucent than usual, with faint mauve shadows under her eyes. She smiled readily, but he wondered what had made her look so delicate. Had he tired her with his lovemaking, or were memories of the attack disturbing her? He thought it must be the latter, because she had responded eagerly every time he'd reached for her. Knowing that she was still frightened made him even more determined to find whoever had attacked her. After Eli Baugh had delivered the horses and left, Wolf planned to do some tracking.

Joe was right behind Mary's car on the way to the school, and he didn't leave immediately, as she had expected. It was still too early for the students to begin arriving, so he walked with her into the empty building and even inspected the rooms. Then he leaned against the doorjamb and waited.

Mary sighed. "I'm perfectly safe here."

"I'll just wait until some other people show up."

"Did Wolf tell you to do this?"

"Nope. He knew he didn't have to."

How did they communicate? By telepathy? Each seemed to know what the other was thinking. It was disconcerting. She just hoped they couldn't read her thoughts, because she'd had some decidedly erotic ones lately.

What would everyone think of Joe's presence? He was so obviously a watchdog. She wondered if it would trigger another act of violence, and she felt sick, because she knew it might. Instinct, sharpened by her fierce protectiveness for both Mackenzies, told her that her theory was correct. Just the possibility that they could become accepted had driven someone over the edge. It revealed so much hate that she shivered.

Sharon and Dottie entered the building and halted briefly when Joe turned his head and looked at them as they passed the open door. "Mrs. Wycliffe. Mrs. Lancaster," he said in acknowledgment as he touched his fingertips to the brim of his hat in a brief salute.

"Joe," Sharon murmured. "How are you?"

Dottie gave him a brief, almost frightened look and hurried to her classroom. Joe shrugged. "I've been doing a bit of studying," he allowed.

"Just a bit?" Sharon asked wryly. She stepped past him to greet Mary, then said, "If you don't feel like working today, Dottie and I can handle your classes. I never dreamed you'd be here today, anyway."

"I was merely frightened," Mary said firmly. "Clay prevented anything else from happening. Cathy is the one who needs sympathy, not I."

"The whole town is in an uproar. Anyone who has freckles on his hands is getting the third degree."

Mary didn't want to talk about it. The image of that freckled hand made her feel nauseated, and she swallowed convulsively. Joe frowned and stepped forward. Mary put up her hand to keep him from throwing Sharon out of the classroom, but at that moment several students entered, and their chatter distracted everyone. The kids said, "Hi, Joe, howya been?" as they clustered around him. They all wanted to know about his plans for the Academy and how he'd gotten interested.

Sharon left to attend to her own classes, and Mary watched Joe with the kids. He was only sixteen, but he seemed older than even the seniors. Joe was young, but he wasn't a kid, and that was the difference. She noticed that Pam Hearst was in the group. She wasn't saying much, but she never took her eyes off Joe, looking at him with both longing and pain, though she tried to hide it. Several times Joe gave the girl a long look that made her fidget uncomfortably.

Then he checked his watch and left his former classmates to say to Mary, "Dad will be here to follow you home. Don't go anywhere alone."

She started to protest, then thought of the man out there who hated them enough to do what he'd done. She wasn't the only one at risk. She reached out and caught his arm. "You and Wolf be careful. You could be the next targets."

He frowned, as if that hadn't occurred to him. The attacker was a rapist, so men wouldn't consider themselves in danger. She wouldn't have thought of it, either, if she hadn't been convinced that the whole thing was intended to punish the Mackenzies. What greater punishment could there be than to kill them? At some point the madman might decide to take a rifle and dispense his own twisted brand of justice.

Clay showed up at lunch with the papers for her to read and sign. Aware of the kids watching them with acute interest, she walked with him out to the car. "I'm worried," she admitted.

He propped his arm on top of the open door. "You'd be foolish if you weren't worried."

"Not for myself. I think Wolf and Joe are the real targets."

He gave her a quick, sharp look. "How do you figure that?"

Heartened that he hadn't immediately dismissed the idea, but was watching her with a troubled expression in his eyes, Mary told him her theory. "I think Cathy and I were specifically chosen as targets to punish Wolf. Don't you see the link? She said she thought Wolf was handsome, and that she'd like to date Joe. Everyone knows I've been friends with them from the first. So we were chosen.''

''And you think he'll attack again?''

''I'm certain he will, but I'm afraid he'll go after one of them this time. I doubt he'd try to manhandle either of them, but what chance would they have against a bullet? How many men in this county have a rifle?''

''Every last mother's son,'' Clay replied grimly. ''But what set this guy off?''

She paused, her face miserable. ''I did.''

''What?''

''I did. Before I came here, Wolf was an outcast. Everyone was comfortable with that. Then I made friends with him and worked with Joe to get him into the Academy. A lot of people were a little proud of that and were friendlier. It was a crack in the wall, and whoever is doing this just couldn't stand it.''

''You're talking about a lot of hate, and it's hard for me to see. People around here don't get along with Wolf, but a lot of it is fear instead of hate. Fear and guilt. The people in this county sent him to prison for something he didn't do, and his presence constantly reminds them of it. He isn't a very forgiving person, is he?''

''Something like that would be a little hard to forgive,'' Mary pointed out.

He had to agree with that and sighed wearily. ''Still, I can't think of anyone who seems to hate him to the point of attacking two women just because they were friendly to him. Hell, Cathy wasn't even friendly. She just made a chance remark.''

''So you agree with me? That all of this is because of Wolf?''

''I don't like it, but I guess I do. Nothing else makes sense, because there may be a few coincidences in life, but none in crime. Everything has a motive.''

"So what can we do?"

"*We* won't do anything," he said pointedly. "*I* will talk to the sheriff about it, but the fact is we can't arrest anyone without evidence, and all we have is a theory. We don't even have a suspect."

Her jaw set in firm lines. "Then you're passing up a marvelous chance."

He looked suspicious. "To do what?"

"Set a trap, of course."

"I don't like this. I don't know what you're thinking, but I don't like it."

"It's common sense. He failed in his—er, objective with me. Perhaps I could—"

"No. And before you get on your high horse, just think of what Wolf would say if you told him you were setting yourself up as bait. You might—*might*—be allowed out of his house by Christmas."

That was true enough, but she saw a way around it. "Then I just won't tell him."

"There's no way to keep it from him, unless it didn't work. If it did work—I sure as hell wouldn't want to be around when he found out, and something like that couldn't be kept quiet."

Mary considered all of Wolf's possible reactions and didn't like any of them. On the other hand, she was terrified that something might happen to him. "I'll take the chance," she said, making her decision.

"Not with my help, you won't."

Her chin lifted. "Then I'll do it without your help."

"If you get in the way of our investigations, I'll put you in the pokey so fast your head will spin," he threatened. When she didn't appear impressed, he swore under his breath. "Hell, I'll just tell Wolf and let him ride herd on you."

She frowned and considered shaking her schoolteacher's finger in his face. "You listen to me, Clay Armstrong. I'm the best chance you have of luring this guy out into the open. You don't have any suspects now. What are you going to do, wait until he attacks some other woman and maybe kills her? Is that how you want to work it?"

"No, that isn't how I want to work it! I want you and every other woman to stay alert and not go anywhere alone. I don't want to risk you or anyone else. Have you thought that sometimes traps don't work, that the animal gets the bait and still gets away? Do you really want to face the possibility of that?"

The thought made her sick to her stomach, and she swallowed to control the sudden rise of nausea. "No, but I'd do it anyway," she said steadily.

"For the last time, no. I understand that you want to help, but I don't like the idea. This guy is too unstable. He grabbed Cathy in her own driveway, and took you off of the town's main street. The chances he took are crazy, and *he* probably is, too."

With a sigh, Mary decided that Clay was simply too protective for him to be able to agree to use a woman as bait; it was totally against his basic nature. That didn't mean, however, that she needed his agreement. All she needed was someone who could act as a guard. She hadn't thought of any real plan yet, but obviously there had to be two people to make even the simplest trap work: the bait, and the one who kept the bait from being harmed.

Clay got in the car and closed the door, then leaned out the open window. "I don't want to hear any more about it," he warned.

"You won't," she promised. Not talking to him about it wasn't the same as not doing it.

He gave her a suspicious look, but started the car and

drove away. Mary returned to her classroom, her thoughts darting around as she tried to think of a solid plan for luring a rapist with a minimum of danger to herself.

Wolf arrived at the school ten minutes before classes were over. He propped his shoulder against the wall just outside her classroom door and listened to her clear voice instructing her students on how geography and history had combined to produce the current state of Middle East politics. He was certain that wasn't in any of the text-books, but Mary had a knack for giving her students a way of relating the present to their studies. It made the subjects both more interesting and more understandable. He had heard her doing the same thing with Joe, not that Joe needed encouragement to read. Her students responded easily to her; in such a small class, there was very little formality. They called her "Miss Potter," but weren't shy about asking questions, offering answers, even teasing.

Then she looked at her watch and released them, just as the doors to the other two classrooms opened. Wolf straightened from the wall and walked into her room, aware of how the kids' chatter halted abruptly when they became aware of his presence. Mary looked up and smiled, a private smile meant only for him, and it made his pulse accelerate that she was so open about how she felt.

He removed his hat and shoved his fingers through his hair. "Your escort service has arrived, ma'am," he said.

One of the girls giggled nervously, and Wolf slowly turned his head to look at the motionless teenagers. "Are you girls going home in pairs? Any of you boys making sure they get home all right?"

Christa Teele, Cathy's younger sister, murmured that she and Pam Hearst were walking together. The other four girls said nothing. Wolf looked at the seven boys. "Go with them." It was an order, one that the boys obeyed instantly. The kids left the room, automatically separating so that each girl had at least one male escort.

Mary nodded. "Very nicely done."

"You'll notice that they all had enough sense not to argue that they didn't need an escort."

She frowned at him, because she felt it hadn't been necessary for him to make that point. "Wolf, really, I'm perfectly safe on the drive from my house to here. How could anything happen to me if I don't stop?"

"What if you had a flat? What if a radiator hose blew again?"

It was obvious there was no way she could set her trap if Wolf or Joe was hovering over her every second. It was also obvious from the narrow look Wolf was giving her that he had no intention of changing his mind. Not that it mattered at the moment, as she hadn't come up with a plan yet. But when she did, she would also have to come up with some scheme for slipping away from her watchdogs.

Wolf draped her sweater over her shoulders and picked up her purse and keys, then ushered her out the door. Dottie looked up from where she was locking her own classroom door and stood transfixed while Wolf locked Mary's door, rattled the knob to make certain the lock held, then put his arm around her waist. He saw Dottie and touched the brim of his hat. "Mrs. Lancaster."

Dottie ducked her head and pretended to be having trouble with her key. Her face was flushed. It was the first time Wolf Mackenzie had ever spoken to her, and her hands shook as she dropped the key into her purse. Almost uncontrollable fear made her break out in a sweat. She didn't know what she was going to do.

Wolf's arm was solid around Mary's waist as they

walked to her car. Its weight made her heartbeat quicken. All he had to do was put his hands on her and her body began to ready itself for him. An exquisite shudder began deep inside, spreading outward in a warm tide.

He felt the sudden tension in her slender body as he opened the car door. She was breathing faster, too. He looked down at her, and his entire body tightened, because she was watching him with desire plain in her soft, slate-blue eyes. Her cheeks were flushed, her lips parted.

He stepped back. "I'll be right behind you." The words were guttural.

She drove sedately home, though her blood was thundering through her veins and pounding in her ears. Never had the isolated, bedraggled old house looked better. Woodrow was sunning on the steps, and Mary stepped over her to unlock the back door. Wolf was out of his truck and right behind her, just as he had promised, by the time she had the door open.

Without a word she took off her sweater, deposited her purse on a chair and walked up the stairs, acutely aware of the heavy tread of Wolf's boots as he followed. They stepped into her bedroom.

He had her naked before she could gather her wits, though she wouldn't have wanted to protest even if he'd given her time. He bore her down on the bed, his big body overwhelming her, his brawny arms cradling her. The hair on his chest rasped her sensitive nipples into hardened peaks, and with a low moan of excitement she rubbed her breasts against him to increase the sensation. He opened her thighs and settled himself between them. His voice was low and rough as he murmured in her ear an explicit explanation of what he was going to do.

Mary drew back a little, her blue eyes slightly shocked, feeling slightly excited, and also slightly embarrassed *because* she was excited. How was it possible

to feel both scandalized and excited? "Wolf Mackenzie!" she said, her eyes going even larger. "You said...
that word!"

His hard face looked both tender and amused. "So I
did."

She swallowed. "I've never heard anyone say it before. I mean, not in real life. In movies—but of course
that isn't real life, and in movies it almost never means
what it really means. They use it as an adjective instead
of a verb." She looked perplexed at such an inexplicable
grammatical oversight.

He was smiling as he entered her, his black eyes shining. "This," he said, "is the verb."

He loved the way she looked when he made love to
her, her eyes languorous, her cheeks flushed. She sucked
in her breath and moved beneath him, taking him completely into her and enveloping him in her sweet heat.
Her hands moved up to the back of his neck. "Yes,"
she agreed seriously. "This is the verb."

If their first lovemaking had been fierce, since then he
had been teaching her how sweet it was when the pleasure was protracted, when the caresses and kisses lingered while tension slowly coiled within until it was so
hot and powerful that it exploded out of control. His
hunger for her was so strong that he tried to put off his
climax for as long as possible, so he could stay inside
her and feed that hunger. It wasn't a hunger for sex, per
se, though it had a strong sexual base. He didn't simply
want to make love, he wanted—*needed*—to make love
to her specifically, to Mary Elizabeth Potter. He had to
feel her silky, fragile skin under his hands, feel her soft
body sheathing him, smell her unique scent of womanhood, forge ancient bonds with each slow thrust and acceptance of their bodies. He was a half-breed; his spirit
was strong and uncomplicated, his instincts close to those

of his ancestors of both races. With other women, he had had sex; with Mary, he mated.

He wrapped his arms around her and rolled onto his back. Startled, Mary sat up, accidently assuming the exact position he'd wanted her in. She gasped as the motion forced him deep inside her. "What are you doing?"

"Nothing," he murmured, reaching up to place his hands over her breasts. "I'm letting you do the doing."

He watched her face as she considered the situation and was aware of the exact second that her excitement and arousal overcame her discomfort with the unfamiliar position. Her eyelids dropped again, and she bit her lower lip as she moved gently on him. "Like this?"

He almost groaned aloud. That slow movement was exquisite torture, and she quickly got into the rhythm of it. He had thought to prolong their lovemaking by changing positions, but now he was afraid he'd outsmarted himself. As old-fashioned as she was, she was also astonishingly sensuous. After a few minutes he desperately rolled again and put her under him.

Mary linked her arms behind his neck. "I was having fun."

"So was I." He kissed her briefly, then again, their lips lingering together. "Too much."

She smiled, that secret, womanly little smile she used only with him, and the sight of it made him burn. He forgot about control, forgot about everything but the pleasure that awaited them. Afterward, sated and exhausted, they both dozed.

At the sound of a vehicle, Wolf rolled out of bed, instantly alert. Mary stirred sleepily. "What is it?"

"You have company."

"Company?" She sat up and pushed her hair out of her face. "What time is it?"

"Almost six. We must have gone to sleep."

"Six! It's time for Joe's lesson!"

Wolf swore as he began jerking on his clothes. "This situation's getting out of hand. Damn it, every time I make love to you my own son interrupts us. Once was bad enough, but he's making a habit of it."

Mary was scrambling into her own clothes, wishing that the circumstances weren't so embarrassing. It was hard to face Joe when it was so obvious that she and his father had just been in bed together. Aunt Ardith would have disowned her for so forgetting her morals and sense of proper behavior. Then she looked at Wolf as he stamped his feet into his boots, and her heart felt as if it had expanded until it filled her entire chest. She loved him, and there was nothing more moral than love. As for proper behavior—she shrugged, mentally kissing propriety goodbye. One couldn't have everything.

Joe had deposited his books on the table and was making a pot of coffee when they entered the kitchen. He looked up and frowned. "Look, Dad, this situation is getting out of hand. You're cutting into my lesson time." Only the twinkle in his ice-blue eyes kept Wolf from getting angry; after a moment, he tousled his son's hair.

"Son, I've said it before, but you've got lousy timing."

Joe's lesson time was even more limited because they had to take time to eat. They were all starving, so they decided on sandwiches, which were quick, and had just finished when another car drove up.

"My goodness, this house is getting popular," Mary muttered as she got up to open the door.

Clay took his hat off as he entered. He paused and sniffed. "Is that coffee fresh?"

"Yep." Wolf stretched to reach the pot while Mary got a cup from the cabinet for Clay.

He sprawled in one of the chairs and gave a weary sigh, which turned to one of appreciation as he inhaled the fragrant steam rising from the coffee as Wolf poured it. "Thanks. I thought I'd find you two here."

"Has anything come up?" Wolf drawled.

"Nothing except a few complaints. You made some people a little nervous."

"Doing what?" Mary interjected.

"Just looking around," Wolf said in a casual tone that didn't fool her at all, nor did it fool Clay.

"Leave it alone. You're not a one-man vigilante committee. I'm warning you for the last time."

"I don't reckon I've done anything illegal, just walking around and looking. I haven't interfered with any law officers, I haven't questioned anyone, I haven't destroyed or hidden any evidence. All I've done is look." Wolf's eyes gleamed. "If you're smart, you'll use me. I'm the best tracker you're going to find."

"And if you're smart, you'll spend your time looking out after what's yours." Clay looked at Mary, and she primmed her mouth. Darn him, he was going to tell!

"That's what I'm doing."

"Maybe not as well as you think. Mary told me about a plan she's got to use herself as bait to bring this guy out in the open."

Wolf's head snapped around, and his brows lowered over narrowed black eyes as he pinned her with a gaze so furious it was all she could do to keep her own gaze steady. "I'll be damned," he said softly, and it was an expression of determination rather than surprise.

"Yeah, that's what I said. I heard you and Joe are escorting her to and from the school, but what about the time in between? And school will be out in a couple of weeks. What about then?"

Mary drew her slender shoulders up. "I won't be

talked around as if I'm invisible. This is my house, and let me remind all of you that I'm well over twenty-one. I'll go where I want, when I want." Let them make of that what they would! She hadn't lived with Aunt Ardith for nothing; Aunt Ardith would have died, just on principle, before she would have let a man tell her what to do.

Wolf's eyes hadn't wavered from her. "You'll do what you're damn well told."

"If I were you," Clay suggested, "I'd take her up on the mountain and keep her there. Like I said, school will be out in a couple of weeks, and this old house is pretty isolated. No one has to know where she is. It'll be safer that way."

Enraged, Mary reached out and whisked the cup of coffee away from Clay, then dumped the contents in the sink. "You're not drinking *my* coffee, you tattletale!"

He looked astounded. "I'm just trying to protect you!"

"And I'm just trying to protect him!" she shouted.

"Protect who?" Wolf snapped.

"You!"

"Why do I need protecting?"

"Because whoever is doing this is trying to harm you! First by trying to frame you for the attacks, and second by attacking people who don't hate you as he does!"

Wolf froze. When Mary had first advanced the beginnings of her theory the night before, he and Clay hadn't believed it because it simply hadn't made sense that anyone trying to frame Wolf would try to make anyone believe he would attack Mary. But when Mary put it the way she just had, that the attacks were a sort of twisted punishment, it began to make horrible sense. A rapist was warped, so his logic would be warped.

Mary had been attacked because of him. Because he

had been so attracted to her that he hadn't been able to control it, some madman had attacked her, terrified and humiliated her, tried to rape her. His lust had brought attention to her.

His expression was cold and blank as he looked at Clay, who shrugged. "I have to buy it," Clay said. "It's the only thing that even halfway makes sense. When she made friends with you and got Joe into the Academy, folks began to look at you differently. Someone couldn't stand it."

Mary twisted her hands. "Since it's my fault, the least I can do is—"

"No!" Wolf roared, surging to his feet and turning over his chair with a clatter. He lowered his voice with a visible effort. "Go upstairs and get your clothes. You're going with us."

Joe slapped his hand on the table. "About damn time." He got up and began clearing the table. "I'll do this while you pack."

Mary pursed her lips. She was torn between wanting the freedom to put her plan into action—when she thought of it—and the powerful temptation of living with Wolf. It wasn't proper. It was a terrible example to her students. The townspeople would be outraged. *He'd watch her like a hawk!* On the other hand, she loved him to distraction and wasn't the least ashamed of their relationship. Embarrassed, sometimes, because she wasn't accustomed to such intimacy and didn't know how to handle it, but never ashamed.

Also on the other hand, if she dug in her heels and remained here, Wolf would simply stay here with her, where they would be far more visible and far more likely to outrage the town's sensibilities. That was what decided her, because she didn't want even more animosity directed at Wolf because of her. That could be all that was needed to goad the rapist into attacking him directly, or going after Joe.

He put his hands on her shoulders and gave her a little push. "Go," he said gently, and she went.

When she was safely upstairs and out of hearing, Clay looked at Wolf with a troubled, angry expression. "For what it's worth, she thinks you and Joe are in danger, that this maniac may just start shooting at you. I kind of agree with her, damn it."

"Let him try," Wolf said, his face and voice expressionless. "She's most vulnerable on the way to and from school, and I don't think this guy is going to wait patiently. He hit two days in a row, but he got scared when you nearly got him. It'll take a while for him to settle down, then he'll be looking for another hit to make. In the meantime, I'll be looking for him."

Clay didn't want to ask, but the question was burning his tongue. "Did you find anything today?"

"I eliminated some people from my list."

"Scared some of them, too."

Wolf shrugged. "Folks had better get used to seeing me around. If they don't like it, tough."

"I also heard that you made the boys escort the girls home from school. The girls' parents were mighty relieved and grateful."

"They should have taken care of it themselves."

"It's a quiet little town. They aren't used to things like this."

"That's no excuse for being stupid." And it *had* been stupid to overlook their daughters' safety. If he'd been that careless in Nam, he would have been dead.

Clay grunted. "I still want to make my point. I agree with Mary that you and Joe are the primary targets. You may be good, but nobody's better than a bullet, and the same goes for Joe. You don't just have to look after

Mary, you have to look after yourselves, too. I'd like it if you could keep her from even finishing out the year at school, so the three of you could stay up on your mountain until we catch this guy.''

It went against Wolf's grain to hide from anyone, and that was in the look he gave Clay. Wolf had been trained to hunt; more than that, it was in his nature, in the genes passed down from Comanche and Highland warriors that had mingled in his body, in the formation of his character.

''We'll keep Mary safe,'' was all he said, and Clay knew he'd failed to convince Wolf to stay out of it.

Joe was leaning against the cabinets, listening. ''The people in town are going to raise hell if they find out Mary's staying with us,'' he put in.

''Yeah, they will.'' Clay stood up and positioned his hat on his head.

''Let them.'' Wolf's voice was flat. He'd given Mary the chance to play it safe, but she hadn't taken it. She was his now, by God. Let them squawk.

Clay sauntered to the door. ''If anyone asks me, I've arranged for her to live in a safer place until this is over. Don't reckon it's anyone's business where that place is, do you? Though of course, knowing Mary, she'll probably tell everyone right out, just like she did Saturday in Hearst's store.''

Wolf groaned. ''Hell! What did she do? I haven't heard about it.''

''Didn't reckon you would have, what with all that happened that afternoon. Seems she got into it with both Dottie Lancaster and Mrs. Karr, and all but told both of them she was yours for the taking.'' A slow grin shaped Clay's mouth. ''From what I heard, she laced into them good.''

When Clay had left, Wolf and Joe looked at each other. "It could get interesting around here."

"It could," Joe agreed.

"Keep an eye out, son. If Mary and Armstrong are right, we're the ones this bastard is really after. Don't go anywhere without your rifle, and stay alert."

Joe nodded. Wolf wasn't worried about hand-to-hand fighting, not even if the other guy was armed with a knife, because he'd taught Joe how to fight the way he'd learned in the military. Not karate, kung fu, tae kwon do, or even judo, but a mixture of many, including good old street fighting. The object of a fight wasn't fairness, but winning, in any way possible, with any weapon handy. It was what had kept him alive and relatively unscathed in prison. A rifle was something else, though. They would have to be doubly alert.

Mary returned and plunked two suitcases on the floor. "I have to have my books, too," she announced. "And someone has to get Woodrow and her kittens."

Chapter 10

Mary tried to tell herself that she couldn't sleep because she was in a strange bed, because she was too excited, because she was too worried, because—she ran out of excuses and couldn't think of anything else. Though she was pleasantly tired from Wolf's lovemaking, she felt too uneasy to sleep and finally knew why. She turned in his arms and put her hand on his jaw, loving the feel of his facial structure and the slight rasp of his beard beneath her fingers. "Are you awake?" she whispered.

"I wasn't," he said in a low rumble. "But I am now."

She apologized and lay very still. After a moment he squeezed her and pushed her hair away from her face. "Can't you sleep?"

"No. I just feel—strange, I think."

"In what way?"

"Your wife—Joe's mother. I was thinking of her in this bed."

His arms tightened. "She was never in this bed."

"I know. But Joe's in the other room, and I thought this was how it must have been when he was little, before she died."

"Not usually. We were apart a lot, and she died when Joe was two. That was when I got out of the military."

"Tell me about it," she invited, still in a whisper. She needed to know more about this man she loved. "You must have been very young."

"I was seventeen when I enlisted. Even though I knew I'd probably have to do a tour in Vietnam, it was my only way out. My folks were dead, and my grandfather, Mother's father, never really accepted me because I was half Anglo. All I knew was that I had to get off the reservation. It was almost as bad as prison. It *is* prison, in a different way. There was nothing to do, nothing to hope for.

"I met Billie when I was eighteen. She was a Crow half-breed, and I guess she married me because she knew I'd never go back to the reservation. She wanted more. She wanted bright lights and city life. Maybe she thought a soldier had it good, transferring from base to base, partying when he was off duty. But she didn't look down on me because I was a half-breed, and we decided to get married. A month later I was in Nam. I got her a ticket to Hawaii when I had R and R, and she went back pregnant. Joe was born when I was nineteen, but I was home from my first tour and got to see him being born. God, I was so excited. He was screaming his head off. Then they put him in my hands, and it was like taking a heart punch. I loved him so much I would have died for him."

He was silent for a moment, thinking. Then he gave a low laugh. "So there I was, with a newborn son and a wife who didn't think she'd gotten such a good deal, and my enlistment was almost up. I had no prospects of a job, no way of supporting my baby. So I re-upped, and things got so bad between Billie and me that I volunteered for another tour. She died right before my third tour ended. I got out and came home to take care of Joe.''

''What did you do?''

''Worked ranches. Rodeoed. It was all I knew. Except for the time I spent in service, I can't remember not working with horses. I was horse crazy when I was a kid, and I guess I still am. Joe and I drifted around until it was time for him to start school, and we landed in Ruth. You know the rest of it.''

She lay quietly in his arms, thinking of his life. He hadn't had it easy. But the life he'd led had shaped him into the man he was, a man of strength and iron determination. He had endured war and hell and come out even stronger than before. The thought that someone would want to harm him made her so angry she could barely contain it. Somehow she had to find some way to protect him.

He escorted her to school the next morning, and again Mary was aware of how everyone stared at him. But it wasn't fear or hatred she saw in the kids' eyes; rather, they watched him with intense curiosity, and even awe. After years of tales, he was a larger-than-life figure to them, someone glimpsed only briefly. Their fathers had dealt with him, the boys had watched him at work, and his expertise with horses only added to tales about him. It was said that he could ''whisper'' a horse, that even the wildest one would respond to a special crooning tone in his voice.

Now he was hunting the rapist. The story was all over the county.

Dottie wouldn't even talk to Mary that day; she walked away whenever she approached and even ate lunch by herself. Sharon sighed and shrugged. ''Don't pay any attention to her. She's always had a burr under her blanket about the Mackenzies.''

Mary shrugged, too. There didn't seem to be any way she could reach Dottie.

Joe drove into town that afternoon to follow her home. As they walked out to their respective vehicles, she told him, ''I need to stop at Hearst's for a few things.''

''I'll be right behind you.''

He was on her heels when she entered the store, and everyone turned to look at them. Joe gave them a smile that could have come straight from his father, and several people hastily looked away. Sighing, Mary led her six-foot watchdog down the aisle.

Joe paused fractionally when his gaze met that of Pam Hearst. She was standing as if rooted, staring at him. He tipped his hat and followed Mary.

A moment later he felt a light touch on his arm and turned to see Pam standing behind him. ''Could I talk to you?'' she asked in a low voice. ''I—it's important. Please?''

Mary had moved on. Joe shifted his position so he could keep her in sight and said, ''Well?''

Pam drew a deep breath. ''I thought…maybe…would you go with me to the town dance this Saturday night?'' she finished in a rush.

Joe's head jerked. ''What?''

''I said—will you go with me to the dance?''

He thumbed his hat back and gave a low whistle under his breath. ''You know you're asking for trouble, don't you? Your dad just might lock you in the cellar for a year.''

''We don't have a cellar.'' She gave him a small smile, one that had an immediate reaction on his sixteen-year-old hormones. ''And I don't care, anyway. He's wrong, wrong about you and your dad. I've felt horrible about how I acted before. I—I like you, Joe, and I want to go out with you.''

He was cynical enough to say, ''Yeah. A lot of people started liking me when they found out I had a shot at the Academy. Sure funny how that worked out, isn't it?''

Hot spots of color appeared on her cheeks. ''That's not why I'm asking you out!''

''Are you sure? It seems I wasn't good enough to be seen in public with you before. You didn't want people to say Pam Hearst was going out with a 'breed. It's different when they can say you're going out with a candidate for the Air Force Academy.''

''That's not true!'' Pam was truly angry now, and her voice rose. Several people glanced their way.

''It looks that way to me.''

''Well, you're wrong! You're just as wrong as my dad is!''

As if he'd been cued, Mr. Hearst, alerted by Pam's raised voice, started down the aisle toward them. ''What's going on back here? Pam, is this br—boy bothering you?''

Joe noticed how quickly ''breed'' had been changed to ''boy'' and lifted his eyebrows at Pam. She flushed even redder and whirled to face her father.

''No, he isn't bothering me! Wait. Yes. Yes, he is! He's bothering me because I asked him to go out with me and he refused!''

Everyone in the store heard her. Joe sighed. The fat was in the fire now.

Ralph Hearst turned purplish red, and he halted in his tracks as abruptly as if he'd hit a wall. ''What did you say?'' he gasped, evidently not believing his ears.

Pam didn't back down, even though her father looked apoplectic. ''I said he refused to go out with me! I asked him to the Saturday night dance.''

Mr. Hearst's eyes were bulging out of their sockets. "You get on to the house. We'll talk about this later!"

"I don't want to talk about it later, I want to talk about it right now!"

"I said get on to the house!" Hearst roared. He turned his infuriated gaze on Joe. "And you stay away from my daughter, you—"

"He's *been* staying away from me!" Pam yelled. "It's the other way around! I won't stay away from him! This isn't the first time I've asked him out. You and everyone else in this town are wrong for the way you've treated the Mackenzies, and I'm tired of it. Miss Potter is the only one of us who's had the guts to stand up for what she thinks is right!"

"This is all her fault, that do-gooding—"

"Stop right there." Joe spoke for the first time, but there was something in his cool voice, in his pale blue eyes, that stopped the man. Joe was only sixteen, but he was tall and muscular, and there was a sudden alertness to his stance that made the older man pause.

Pam jumped in. She was bright and cheery-natured, but as headstrong as her father. "Don't start on Miss Potter," she warned. "She's the best teacher we've ever had here in Ruth, and if you do anything to get rid of her, I swear I'll drop out of school."

"You'll do no such thing!"

"I swear I will! I love you, Dad, but you're wrong! All of us talked about it at school today, about how we'd seen the teachers treat Joe over the years, and how wrong it was, because he's obviously the smartest of us all! And we talked about how Wolf Mackenzie was the one who made sure all of us girls got home all right yesterday. No one else thought of it! Or don't you care?"

"Of course he cares," Mary said briskly, having walked up without anyone except Joe noticing. "It's just that Wolf, with his military experience, knew what to do.'' She'd made that up, but it sounded good. She put her hand on Mr. Hearst's arm. ''Why don't you take care of your customers and just let them fight it out? You know how teenagers are.''

Somehow Ralph Hearst found himself at the front of the store again before he realized it. He stopped and looked down at Mary. ''I don't want my girl dating a half-breed!'' he said fiercely.

''She'll be safer with that half-breed than with any other boy around,'' Mary replied. ''For one thing, he's steady as a rock. He won't drink or drive fast, and for another, he has no intention of getting involved with any girl around here. He'll be going away, and he knows it.''

''I don't want my daughter dating an Indian!''

''Are you saying that character doesn't mean anything? That you'd rather have Pam go out with a drunk Anglo, who might get her killed in a car accident, than with a sober Indian, who would protect her with his life?''

He looked stricken and rubbed his head in agitation. ''No, damn it, that isn't what I mean,'' he muttered.

Mary sighed. ''My Aunt Ardith remembered every old chestnut she ever heard, and one of the ones she brought out most often was 'pretty is as pretty does.' You go by how people act, don't you, Mr. Hearst. You've voted according to how the candidates have stood on issues in the past, haven't you?''

''Of course.'' He looked uncomfortable.

''And?'' she prompted.

''All right, all right! It's just—some things are hard to forget, you know? Not things that Joe has done, but just…things. And that father of his is—''

''As proud as you are,'' she cut in. ''All he ever wanted was a place to raise his motherless son.'' She was laying it on so thick she expected to hear violins in the background any moment now, but it was about time these people realized some things about Wolf. Maybe he was more controlled than civilized, but his control was very good, and they would never know the difference.

Deciding it was time to give him some breathing room, she said, "Why not talk it over with your wife?"

He looked relieved at the suggestion. "I'll do that."

Joe was walking up the aisle; Pam, who had turned her back, was busily neatening a stack of paint thinner in an obvious effort to act casual. Mary paid for the items she'd gathered, and Joe lifted the sack. Silently they walked out together.

"Well?" she asked as soon as they were outside.

"Well, what?"

"Are you taking her to the dance?"

"It looks like it. She won't take no for an answer, like someone else I know."

She gave him a prim look and didn't respond to his teasing. Then, as he opened the car door for her, a thought struck, and she looked at him in horror. "Oh, no," she said softly. "Joe, that man is attacking women who are friendly to you and Wolf."

His whole body jerked, and his mouth tightened. "Damn," he swore. He thought a minute, then shook his head. "I'll tell her tomorrow that I can't go."

"That won't do any good. How many people heard her say what she did? It will be all over the county by tomorrow, whether you take her to the dance or not."

He didn't reply, merely closed the door after she'd gotten into the car. He looked grim, far too grim for a boy his age.

Joe felt grim, too, but an idea was taking form. He'd watch out for Pam and warn her so she'd be on guard, but maybe this would draw the rapist out. He'd use

Mary's plan, but with different bait: himself. He'd make certain Pam was safe, but leave himself open at times when he was alone. Maybe, when the guy realized he couldn't get at a helpless woman, he'd get so frustrated he'd go after one of his real targets. Joe knew the chance he was taking, but unless Wolf could find the track he was looking for, he didn't see any other option.

Mary looked around for Wolf when they got home, but she couldn't find him. She changed into jeans and walked outside. She found Joe in the barn, grooming a horse. "Is Wolf out here?"

He shook his head and continued brushing the horse's gleaming hide. "His horse is gone. He's probably checking fences." Or hunting for a certain track, but he didn't say that to Mary.

She got him to show her how to brush the horse and took over for him until her arm began to hurt. The horse snorted when she stopped, so she went back to brushing. "This is harder than it looks," she panted.

Joe grinned at her over the back of another horse. "It'll give you a few muscles. But you've finished with him, so don't spoil him. He'll stand there all day if someone will keep brushing him."

She stopped and stepped back. "Well, why didn't you say so?" He put the horse in his stall, and Mary walked back to the house. She had almost reached the porch when she heard the rhythmic thudding of a horse's hooves and turned to see Wolf riding up. She caught her breath. Even though she was ignorant about horses, she knew that not many people looked the way he did on a horse. There was no bouncing or jiggling; he sat so easily in the saddle, and moved so fluidly with the animal, that he looked motionless. The Comanche had arguably been the world's best horsemen, better even than the Berber or Bedouin, and Wolf had learned well from his mother's people. His powerful legs controlled the big bay stallion he was riding, so that the reins were lightly held and no harm done to the horse's tender mouth.

He slowed the horse to a walk as he approached her. "Any trouble today?"

She decided not to tell him about Pam Hearst. That was Joe's business, if he wanted it known. She knew he'd tell Wolf, but in his own time. "No. We didn't see anyone suspicious, and no one followed us."

He reined in and leaned down to brace his forearm on the saddle horn. His dark eyes drifted over her slim figure. "Do you know how to ride?"

"No. I've never been on a horse."

"Well, that situation is about to be remedied." He kicked his boot free of the stirrup and held his hand out to her. "Put your left foot in the stirrup and lift yourself as I swing you up."

She was willing. She tried. But the horse was too tall, and she couldn't reach the stirrup with her foot. She was staring at the bay with an aggravated expression when Wolf laughed and shifted back in the saddle. "Here, I'll pick you up."

He leaned out of the saddle and caught her under the arms. Mary gasped and grabbed at his biceps as she felt her feet leave the ground; then he straightened and set her firmly on the saddle in front of him. She grabbed the saddle horn as he lifted the reins, and the horse moved forward.

"This is a long way up," she said, bouncing so hard her teeth rattled.

He chuckled and wrapped his left arm around her, pulling her back against him. "Relax and let yourself go with the horse's rhythm. Feel how I'm moving and move with me."

She did as he said and felt the rhythm as soon as she

relaxed. Her body automatically seemed to sink deeper into the saddle, and her torso moved with Wolf's. The bouncing stopped. Unfortunately by that time they had reached the barn and her first ride was over. Wolf lifted her down and dismounted.

"I liked that," she announced.

"You did? Good. We'll start you on riding lessons tomorrow."

Joe's voice came to them from a stall farther down. "I started her on grooming lessons today."

"You'll be as comfortable with horses as if you'd been around them all of your life," Wolf said, and leaned down to kiss her. She went on tiptoe, her lips parting. It was a long moment before he lifted his head, and when he did, his breathing was faster. His eyes were hooded and narrow. Damn, she got to him so fast he reacted like a teenager when he was around her.

When Mary had gone back to the house, Joe came out of the stall and looked at his father. "Find anything today?"

Wolf began unsaddling the bay. "No. I've had a good look around the ranches, but none of the prints match. It has to be someone from town."

Joe frowned. "That makes sense. Both of the attacks were in town. But I can't think of anyone it could be. I guess I've never noticed before if someone has freckled hands."

"I'm not looking for freckles, I'm looking for that print. I know how he walks, toeing in a little and putting his weight on the outside of his feet."

"What if you find him? Do you think the sheriff will arrest him just because he has freckles on his hands and walks a certain way?"

Wolf smiled, a movement of his lips that was totally without mirth. His eyes were cold. "When I find him," he said softly, "if he's smart, he'll confess. I'll give the law a chance, but there's no way he'll walk free. He'll be a lot safer in jail than out on the streets, and I'll make certain he knows it."

It was an hour before they finished with the horses. Joe lingered to look over his tack, and Wolf walked up to the house alone. Mary was absorbed in cooking, humming as she stirred the big pot of beef stew, and she didn't hear him come in the back door. He walked up behind her and put his hand on her shoulder.

Blind terror shot through her. She screamed and threw herself sideways, to press her back against the wall. She held the dripping spoon in her hand like a knife. Her face was utterly white as she stared at him.

His face was hard. In silence they stared at each other, time stretching out between them. Then she dropped the spoon on the floor with a clatter. "Oh God, I'm sorry," she said in a thin voice, and covered her face with her hands.

He drew her to him, his hand in her hair, holding her head to his chest. "You thought it was him again, didn't you?"

She clung to him, trying to drive away the terror. It had come out of nowhere, taking her by surprise and shattering the control she'd managed to gain over her memory and emotions. When Wolf's hand had touched her shoulder, for a brief, horrifying moment it had been happening all over again. She felt cold; she wanted to sink into his warmth, to let the reality of his touch overcome the hideous memory of another touch.

"You don't have to be afraid," he murmured into her hair. "You're safe here." But he knew her memory was still there, that a touch from behind meant a nightmare to her. Somehow he had to take away that fear, so she could be free of it.

She regained control and eased herself away from him, and he let her, because he knew it was important to her. She appeared almost normal through dinner and Joe's lesson; the only sign of strain was an occasional haunted expression in her eyes, as if she hadn't completely succeeded in pushing the memory away.

But when they went to bed and her silky body was under his hands, she turned to him as eagerly as ever. Wolf's lovemaking left her no room for anything else, no lingering memories or vestiges of terror. Her entire body and mind were occupied with him. Afterward she curled against him and slept undisturbed, at least until the graying dawn, when he woke her and pulled her beneath him again.

Mary was fully aware of the tenuousness of both her relationship with Wolf and her presence in his house. He often told her explicitly how much he wanted her, but in terms of lust, not love. He never spoke a word about loving, not even during lovemaking, when she was unable to keep from telling him over and over that she loved him. When the fever of lust passed, he might well cut her out of his life, and she tried to prepare herself for that possibility even while she absorbed the maximum pleasure from the present situation.

She knew that living with him was for her protection, and only temporary. She also knew that it was nothing short of scandalous for a small-town schoolteacher to shack up with the local black sheep, and that was exactly how the townspeople would view the situation if they knew about it. She knew the risk she was taking with her career, and decided that the days and nights with Wolf were worth it. If she lost her job, there were other jobs, but she knew there would be no other loves for her. She was twenty-nine and had never even felt a twinge of interest or excitement over any other man. Some people loved only once, and it appeared she was one of them.

The only time she allowed herself to worry over the future was on the drives to and from school, when she was alone in the car. When she was with Wolf she didn't want to waste even a single second on regrets. With him, she was totally alive, totally female.

She worried about Wolf and Joe, too. She knew Wolf was actively hunting the man who had attacked her, and she was terrified he would be hurt. She couldn't let herself even think that he might be killed. And Joe was up to something; she knew it. He was too much like Wolf for her not to recognize the signs. He was preoccupied, and far too sober, as if faced with making a choice when neither of the alternatives was very attractive. But she couldn't get him to open up to her, and that alone frightened her, for Joe had talked to her from the beginning.

Joe was on edge. He'd told Pam to be more cautious than usual, and he tried to make certain she never walked home alone, but there was always a chance she'd be careless. He'd also made a point of letting himself be seen alone, and evidently unaware of the need for caution, but nothing happened. The town was quiet, if edgy. He was forced to the same awareness that Wolf already had, that with so few clues, all they could do was stay alert and wait until the man made a mistake.

When Joe told his father that he was going to the dance with Pam, Wolf looked piercingly at the boy. "Do you know what you're doing?"

"I hope so."

"Watch your back."

The terse advice brought a thin smile to Joe's mouth. He knew he could be making a big mistake by going to that dance, that the scene could turn ugly, but he'd told Pam he'd take her, and that was that. He'd have to be doubly alert, but damn, he wanted to hold her in his arms while they shuffled slowly across the sawdust floor. Even though he knew he was going away and they'd never have anything permanent between them, he was strongly attracted to her. He couldn't explain it and knew it wouldn't last, but he felt it *now*, and it was now that he had to deal with it.

Pam was edgy, too, when he picked her up. She tried to hide it by talking too fast and too brightly, until he put his hand over her mouth. "I know," he muttered. "It worries me, too."

She tossed her head, freeing her mouth. "I'm not worried. It'll be all right, you'll see. I told you, all of us have talked about it."

"Then why are you so nervous?"

She looked away from him and cleared her throat. "Well, this *is* the first time I've been out with you. I just felt—I don't know—nervous and scared and excited all at once."

He thought about that for a few minutes, and silence filled the cab of the truck. Then he said, "I guess I can understand being nervous and excited, but why scared?"

Now it was Pam's turn to be silent, and she flushed a little when she finally said, "Because you're not like the rest of us."

That grim look settled around Joe's mouth. "Yeah, I know. I'm a 'breed."

"It isn't that," she snapped. "It's—you're *older* than the rest of us, somehow. I know we're the same age, but inside you're all grown up. We're ordinary people. We'll stay right here and ranch the way our folks have. We'll marry people from the same background and stay in the county, or move to another county just like it, and have kids and be content. But you're not like that. You're going to the Academy, and you won't be back, at least not to stay. You may come back for a visit, but that's all it'll be.''

It surprised him that she had it so neatly pegged. He did feel old inside, and always had, especially in comparison to other kids his age. And he knew he wouldn't be back here to ranch. He belonged in the sky doing Mach 2, marking his place in the universe with a vapor trail.

They were quiet the rest of the way to the dance. When Joe parked his truck with the collection of other trucks and a few cars, he braced himself for whatever could happen.

He was prepared for almost anything, but not for what actually took place. When he and Pam walked into the rundown old building used for the dances, for a moment there was a certain stillness, a strange silence; then in the next heartbeat the noise picked back up and everyone returned to his own conversation. Pam put her hand in his and squeezed it.

A few minutes later the live band started up, and couples drifted onto the sawdust-covered planks of the dance floor. Pam led him to the middle of the floor and smiled at him.

He smiled back, wryly admitting and admiring her courage. Then he took her in his arms to enter the slow rhythm of the dance.

They didn't talk. After wanting for so long just to touch her, he was content to hold her and move with her. He could smell her perfume, feel the softness of her hair, the resilient mounds of her breasts, the movement of her legs against his. As young people have done from the beginning of time, they swayed together in their own private world, reality suspended.

Reality intruded, however, when he heard an angry

mutter of "dirty Indian" and automatically stiffened as he looked around for the speaker.

Pam said, "Please," and drew him back into the dance.

When the song ended, a boy stood on his chair and yelled, "Hey, Joe! Pam! Over here!"

They looked in the direction of the yell, and Joe couldn't help grinning. Every student in the three classes Mary taught was grouped at the table, with two empty chairs waiting for him and Pam. They were waving and calling.

The kids saved the evening. They enveloped him and Pam in a circle of laughter and dancing. Joe danced with every girl in the group; the boys talked horses, cattle, ranching and rodeoing, and between them made certain none of the girls had a chance to sit down much. The kids also talked to the other people at the dance, and soon everyone knew that the half-breed was going to the Air Force Academy. Ranchers are generally hard-working, conservative and firmly patriotic, and before too long, anyone who had a hard word to say about the half-breed found himself hushed and told to mind his manners.

Joe and Pam left before the dance was over, because he didn't want to keep her out too late. As they walked to his truck, he shook his head. "I never would have believed it," he said softly. "Did you know they would all be here?"

Pam denied it. "But they knew I'd asked you. I guess the whole town knew I'd asked you. It was fun, wasn't it?"

"It was fun," he agreed. "But it could have gotten rough. You know that, don't you? If it hadn't been for the guys—"

"And girls!" she interrupted.

"Them, too. If it hadn't been for them, I'd have been thrown out."

"It didn't happen. And next time it will be even better."

"Is there going to be a next time?"

She looked suddenly unsure of herself. "You—you can still come to the dances, even if you don't want to come with me."

Joe laughed as he opened the truck door. He turned and put his hands on her waist, then lifted her onto the seat. "I like being with you."

About halfway back to Ruth, Pam put her hand on his arm. "Joe?"

"Yeah?"

"Do you want to—uh, that is, do you know any place to stop?" She faltered on the words.

He knew he should resist the temptation, but he couldn't. He turned off on the next side road they came to, then left the road to bounce across a meadow for about a mile before he parked beneath a stand of trees.

The mild May night wrapped around them. The moonlight couldn't penetrate the shelter of the trees, and the dark cab of the truck was a warm, safe cave. Pam was a pale, indistinct figure as he reached for her.

She was pliant and eager, yielding to his hands, pressing against him to take more of his kisses. Her firm young body made him feel as if he would explode. Barely aware of what he was doing, Joe shifted and twisted until they were lying on the seat with Pam half beneath him. Soon her breasts were bare, and he heard her strangled intake of breath as he took a nipple into his mouth. Then her nails were digging into his shoulders, and her hips arched.

It was quickly getting out of control. Clothing was opened and pushed aside. Bare skin touched bare skin.

Somehow, Pam's jeans were off. But when he slid his hands inside her panties, she whispered, "I've never done this before. Will it hurt?"

Joe groaned aloud, but forced himself to stillness. It took every ounce of willpower he possessed, but he stopped his hands. His body throbbed painfully, and he savagely controlled it. After a long minute he sat up and pulled Pam to a sitting position astride his lap.

"Joe?"

He leaned his forehead against hers. "We can't do it," he murmured regretfully.

"But why?" She moved against him, her body still empty and aching with a need she didn't understand.

"*Because* it would be your first time."

"But I want you!"

"I want you, too." He managed a wry grin. "I guess it's pretty obvious. But your first time—baby, it should be with someone you love. And you don't love me."

"I could," she whispered. "Oh, Joe, I truly could."

He was so frustrated that he could barely control his voice enough to speak, but he managed. "I hope you don't. I'm leaving. I have a chance waiting for me that I'd die before I'd give up."

"And no girl is going to change your mind?"

Joe knew the truth inside him, and he knew Pam wouldn't like it, but he had to be honest with her. "No girl *could* change my mind. I want to go to the Academy so much that nothing can keep me here."

She caught his hands and shyly brought them up to her breasts. "We could still, you know, do it. No one would know."

"You'd know. And when you fall in love with some guy, you'd regret that your first time wasn't with him. God, Pam, don't make this so hard for me! Slap my face or something." The way her firm young breasts filled his hands made him wonder if he wasn't crazy for passing this up.

She leaned forward and rested her head on his shoulder. He felt the way her body shook as she began to cry, and he folded his arms around her.

"You've always been special to me," she said in a stifled tone. "Do you have to be so darn conscientious?"

"Do you want to take a chance on getting pregnant at sixteen?"

That stopped her tears. She sat up. "Oh. I thought you'd have a—don't all boys carry them?"

"I guess not. And it wouldn't matter if I did have one. I don't want to get involved—not this kind of involved— with you or anyone else, because no matter what, I'm going to the Academy. Besides, you're too young."

She couldn't stop the giggle that burst out. "I'm as old as you are."

"Then *we're* too young."

"You're not." She sobered and cupped his face in her hands. "You're not young at all, and I guess that's why you stopped. Every other boy I know would have had his jeans off so fast he'd have fabric burns on his legs. But let's make a bargain, okay?"

"What kind of bargain?"

"We'll still be friends, won't we?"

"You know it."

"Then we'll go around together and keep things light. No more messing around like this, because it hurts too much when you stop. You go away to Colorado like you've planned, and I'll take things as they come. I may get married. But if I don't, you come on back here one summer and we'll *both* be old enough then. Will you be my first lover?"

"It won't keep me in Ruth," he said steadily.

"I don't expect it to. But is it a bargain?"

He accepted that the years could make a difference, and he knew she'd most likely be married. If not— maybe.

"If you still want to then, yeah, it's a bargain."

She held out her hand, and they solemnly shook to seal the deal. Then she kissed him and began putting on her clothes.

Mary was waiting up for him when he got home, an anxious look in her eyes. She got to her feet and tightened the belt of her robe. "Are you okay?" she asked. "Did anything happen?"

"I'm fine. Everything went okay."

Then he saw that the anxious look was really fear. She touched his arm. "You didn't see anyone who—" She stopped, then started again. "No one shot at your truck, or tried to run you off the road?"

"No, it was quiet." They looked at each other for a moment, and Joe realized that Mary had feared the same thing that had occurred to him. More than that, she knew he had decided to take the chance in an effort to draw the rapist out.

He cleared his throat. "Is Dad in bed?"

"No," Wolf said quietly from the doorway. He wore only a pair of jeans. His black eyes were steady. "I wanted to make certain you were okay. This was like watching Daniel walk into the lion's den."

"Well, Daniel made it out okay, didn't he? So did I. It was even fun. The whole class was there."

Mary smiled, the dread lifting from her mind. She knew now what had happened. Knowing that the situation could get ugly if Joe had gone to the dance without backup, the kids had taken it on themselves to make him a part of their group and let everyone at the dance know he was accepted.

Wolf held out his hand, and Mary went to him. She could sleep now. They were safe for another night, these two men whom she loved.

Chapter 11

School was out. Mary was intensely proud of her students. The seniors had all graduated, and all of the undergraduates had passed. All of them intended to finish high school, and a couple of them wanted to go to college. It was a record to thrill any teacher's heart.

Joe didn't get a respite. Mary decided he needed more advanced classes in math than she was qualified to teach and began a search for a teacher who was qualified. She found one in a town seventy miles distant, and three times a week Joe made the trip for a two-hour accelerated course. She continued to teach him at night.

The days passed in a haze of happiness for Mary. She seldom left the mountain, seldom saw anyone except Wolf and Joe. Even when they were both gone, she felt safe. It had been only a little over two weeks since the attack, but it seemed as if it had happened a long time ago. Whenever a sliver of memory surfaced to unsettle her emotions, she scolded herself for letting it bother her.

Nothing had happened, except she had been terrified. If anyone needed care and consideration, it was Cathy Teele. So Mary pushed the memories away and concentrated on the present. The present, inevitably, was Wolf.

He dominated her life, waking and sleeping. He began teaching her how to ride and how to help him with the horses, and she suspected he used the same method with her that he used with the young colts and fillies that were brought to him. He was firm and demanding, but utterly clear in his instructions and what he wanted out of both her and the horses. When they obeyed, he rewarded them with approval and affection. In fact, Mary mused, he was easier on the horses than he was on her! When *they* disobeyed, he was unfailingly patient. When *she* didn't do something exactly as he'd told her, he let her know about it in unmistakable terms.

But he was always affectionate. Actually, she decided, "lusty" was a better description. He made love to her every night, sometimes twice. He made love to her in the empty stall where Joe had interrupted them. He made love to her in the shower. She knew she wasn't even close to voluptuous, but he seemed enthralled with her body. When they lay in bed at night he would turn on the lamp and lean on his elbow, watching as he stroked his hand over her from shoulders to knees, seemingly fascinated by the difference between her pale, delicate skin and his dark, powerful, work-callused hand.

Wyoming weather in the summer was generally cool and dry, at least compared to Savannah, but the summer vacation from school had scarcely begun when a heat wave sent the temperatures into the nineties, even edging into the low hundreds by late afternoon. For the first time in her life, Mary wished she had some shorts to wear, but Aunt Ardith had never allowed them. She did find, however, that her plain cotton skirts were cooler than the new jeans she was so proud of, allowing for the circulation of whatever breeze happened to wander by. Not that Aunt Ardith would have approved of Mary's attire even then, for Mary declined to wear a slip or hosiery. Aunt Ardith had donned both articles of clothing every day of her life and would have considered anyone who dared to go without a slip an out-and-out hussy.

One morning just after Joe had left to drive to his class, Mary walked out to the barn and reflected on her state of hussiness. All in all, she was satisfied with it. Being a hussy had its advantages.

She could hear some horses snorting and stamping around in the small corral behind the barn, though Wolf usually used the larger one adjacent to the stables for training. The sound of activity, however, told her where she could find him, and that was all she wanted to know.

But when she rounded the corner of the barn, she stopped in her tracks. Wolf's big bay stallion was mounting the mare she had been riding during her lessons. The mare's front hooves were hobbled, and protective boots covered her rear hooves. The stallion was snorting and grunting, and the mare squealed as he entered her. Wolf moved to her head to steady her, and then she stood quietly. "There, sweetheart," he crooned. "You can handle this big old guy, can't you?"

The mare shivered under the impact of the stallion's thrusts, but she stood still for the service and it was over in only a couple of minutes. The stallion snorted and dropped off her, his head down low as he snuffled and blew.

Wolf continued talking in that low, soothing voice to the mare as he bent down to remove the hobble. As he started to remove the boots, Mary stepped forward and caught his attention. "You—you *tied* her!" she said accusingly.

He grinned as he finished unbuckling the protective boots. Miss Mary Elizabeth Potter stood before him in full form, her back ramrod-straight, chin lifted. "I didn't tie her," he said with amused patience. "I hobbled her."

"So she couldn't get away from him!"

"She didn't want to get away from him."

"How do you know?"

"Because she would have kicked him if she hadn't been ready for him to cover her," he explained as he led the mare back into the barn. Mary followed, her face still filled with indignation.

"A lot of good it would have done if she'd kicked him—you put those boots on her so she wouldn't hurt him!"

"Well, I didn't want my stallion damaged. On the other hand, if she had resisted service, I would have gotten her out of there. When a mare resists, it means I've misjudged the time, or something is wrong with her. But she took him nicely, didn't you girl?" he finished, patting the mare's neck.

Mary watched, fidgeting, as he washed the mare. She still didn't like the idea of the mare being unable to run away from the stallion, even though this particular mare was now standing as placidly as if nothing had happened a few minutes ago. It disturbed her on a deep emotional level that didn't respond to logic, and she felt uneasy.

Wolf led the mare to her stall, fed her and gave her fresh water. Then he squatted in front of the faucet to wash his hands and arms. When he looked up, Mary was still standing there, a troubled, almost frightened look in her eyes. He straightened. "What's wrong?"

Desperately she tried to shrug her uneasiness aside, but it didn't work. It was plain in her face and voice. "It looked—it looked...." Her voice trailed off, but suddenly he understood.

He moved slowly toward her and wasn't surprised when she backed up a step. "Horses aren't people," he said gently. "They're big, and they snort and squeal. It looks rough, but that's just how horses mate. It would be even rougher if they were allowed to run free, because they'd kick and bite."

She looked at the mare. "I know. It's just—" She stopped, because she really couldn't say what was bothering her.

Wolf reached her and put his hands on her waist, holding her lightly so she wouldn't be alarmed and wouldn't know that she couldn't break free unless he let her. "It's just that the roughness reminded you of being attacked?" he finished for her.

She gave him a quick, disturbed look, then just as quickly looked away.

"I know the memory is still there, baby." He slowly tightened his hands, bringing her close against him and just holding her. After a moment she began to relax, and her silky head rested against his chest. Only then did he put his arms around her, because he didn't want her to feel restrained.

"I want to kiss you," he murmured.

She lifted her head and smiled at him. "That's why I came out here: to tempt you into a kiss. I've become a shameless hussy. Aunt Ardith would have disowned me."

"Aunt Ardith sounds like a pain in the—"

"She was wonderful," Mary said firmly. "It's just that she was very old-fashioned and had strict notions of what was proper and what wasn't. For instance, only shameless hussies would wear a skirt without a proper petticoat underneath." She lifted her skirt a little to show him.

"Then let's hear it for shameless hussies." He bent

his head and kissed her, and felt the familiar hot excitement begin building in his body. Ruthlessly he controlled it, because control was critical right now. He had to show Mary something, and he couldn't do it if his libido overcame his common sense. He had to do something to banish that ever-present fear from the back of her mind.

He raised his head and hugged her for a minute before letting his arms drop. Instead he took her hands and held them, and the expression on his face made the smile leave her eyes. He said slowly, "Are you willing to try something that might get you over being frightened?"

She looked cautious. "Such as?"

"We could reenact parts of the attack."

Mary stared at him. She was curious, but also wary. Part of her didn't want to do anything that would remind her of that day, but on the other hand, she didn't like being afraid. She said, "Which parts?"

"I could chase you."

"He didn't chase me. He grabbed me from behind."

"So will I, when I catch you."

She considered it. "It won't work. I'll know it's you."

"We could try."

She stared at him for a long time, then stiffened as a thought came to her. "He threw me facedown on the ground," she whispered. "He was on top of me, rubbing himself against me."

Wolf's face was strained. "Do you want me to do that, too?"

She shuddered. "Want you to? No. But I think you're going to have to. I don't want to be afraid any longer. Make love to me like that—please."

"What if you get really scared?"

"Don't—" She swallowed. "Don't stop."

He looked at her for a long minute, as if measuring

her resolve; then his mouth began to quirk up on one side. "All right. Run."

She didn't. She stared at him. "What?"

"Run. I can't chase you if you don't run."

All of a sudden she felt silly at the thought of running about the yard like a child. "Just like that?"

"Yeah, just like that. Think of it this way: when I catch you, I'm going to pull your clothes off and make love to you, so why are you waiting?"

He removed his hat to hook it on a post. Mary took a step backward, then, despite her dignity, whirled and ran. She heard the thudding of his boots as he came after her, and laughed with excitement despite herself. She knew she didn't have a prayer of reaching the house; his legs were much longer than hers. Instead she relied on agility and dodged around his truck, then a tree.

"I'm going to get you," he growled, his voice right behind her, and his hand closed briefly on her shoulder before she sprinted away from him.

She sought refuge behind his truck again, with him on the other side. They feinted, but neither gained an advantage. Panting, her face alight with both excitement and triumph, Mary taunted him, "Can't catch me, can't catch me."

A slow, unholy smile touched his mouth as he looked at her. She was almost glowing with her success, her silky brown hair tumbling around her face, and he wanted her so much it hurt. He wanted to take her in his arms and make love to her, and he swore to himself because he couldn't, not right now. First he had to play this through, and, despite her brave words, he hoped she could bear it.

They had been staring at each other, and suddenly it struck her how savage he looked. He was aroused. She knew that look on his face as well as she knew her own, and her breath caught. He wasn't playing; he was deadly earnest. For the first time, fear began to creep in on her. She tried to tamp it down, because she knew Wolf would never hurt her. It was just—oh, damn, something about it *did* remind her of the attack, no matter how she tried to push the thought away. The playfulness drained out of her, and an unreasonable panic took its place. "Wolf? Let's stop now."

His chest rose and fell with his breathing, and a bleak look entered his eyes, but his voice was guttural. "No. I'm going to catch you."

She ran blindly, leaving the dubious safety of the truck. His running steps behind her sounded like thunder, obscuring every other sound, even that of her rasping breath. It was like being in that alley again, even though a part of her clung to the knowledge that this was Wolf, and she wanted him to do this. She hadn't had a chance to run from her attacker, but he had been behind her; she had heard his breathing just as she now heard Wolf's. She screamed, a high, terrified sound, just before Wolf caught her and bore her down, on her stomach, to the ground, his heavy weight coming down on top of her.

He supported himself on his arms to keep from crushing her, and nuzzled her ear. "Ha, I caught you." He forced himself to say the words lightly, but his chest was tight with pain at what she was going through. He could feel the terror that held her in its grip, and he began trying to loosen its bonds, speaking softly to her, reminding her of the heated, sensuous pleasures they had shared. Tears stung his eyes at the sounds she made, those of a trapped and terrified animal. God, he didn't know if he could do it. The lust had died in him at her first scream.

At first she struggled like a wild thing, kicking and bucking, trying to free her arms, but he held them clamped down. She was maddened with fear, so much so that despite the difference in their sizes and strength, she might have hurt him if not for his training. As it was, all he could do was hold her and try to break through the black mist of fear that enveloped her.

"Calm down, sweetheart, calm down. You know I won't hurt you, and I won't let anyone else hurt you. You know who I am." He repeated it over and over, until exhaustion claimed her, and her struggles became weak and aimless. Only then could she begin to listen; only then could his crooning words penetrate the barrier of fear. Suddenly she collapsed on the ground with her face buried in the hot, sweet grass and began to cry.

Wolf lay on top of her with his arms still locked securely around her and soothed her while she cried. He petted her and kissed her hair, her shoulder, her delicate nape, until at last she lay limply on the grass, both tears and energy exhausted. The endless caresses affected him, too, now that she was calmer; he felt a return of the desire that was never far away from him since he'd met her.

He nuzzled her neck again. "Are you still frightened?" he murmured.

Bruised, swollen eyelids were closed over her eyes. "No," she whispered. "I'm sorry I keep putting you through this. I love you."

"I know, sweetheart. Hold on to that thought." Then he lifted himself back on his knees and pushed her skirt to her waist.

Mary's eyes flared open when she felt him pulling down her underpants, and her voice was sharp. "Wolf! No!"

He stripped the garment down her legs, and Mary trembled in reaction. It was so much like before, in the alley. She was on her stomach on the ground, with a man's weight on top of her, and she couldn't bear it. She tried to scramble forward, but he locked one arm around her waist and held her while he unfastened his jeans with the other hand. He kneed her thighs farther apart and eased himself against her, then let his weight down on her again.

"This reminds you of it, doesn't it?" he asked in a low, gentle voice. "Being on the ground, on your stomach, with me behind you. But you know I won't hurt you, that you don't have to be afraid, don't you?"

"I don't care. I don't like this! Let me up, I want up!"

"I know, baby. Come on now, relax. Think of how many times I've made love to you and how much you've enjoyed it. Trust me."

The smell of the hot earth was in her nostrils. "I don't want you to make love to me now," she managed to say, albeit raggedly. "Not like this."

"Then I won't. Don't be afraid, baby. I won't go any further unless you want me to. Just relax, and let's feel each other. I don't want you to be afraid when I come up behind you. I admit, your pretty little rear end turns me on. I like to look at it and touch it, and when you cuddle it against me in bed it drives me crazy. I guess you've noticed, though, haven't you?"

Dazedly, she tried to gather her scattered senses. He'd never hurt her before, and now that the haze of fear was fading, she knew he never would. This was Wolf, the man she loved, not her attacker. She was in his strong arms, where she was safe.

She relaxed, her tired muscles going limp. Yes, he was definitely aroused. She could feel him, nestled between her spread legs, but true to his word he was making no move to enter her.

He stroked her sides and kissed her neck. "Are you all right now?"

She sighed, a barely audible release of breath. "Yes," she whispered.

He shifted to his knees again and sat back on his heels. Before she could guess what he was about, his steely hands lifted her up and back, so she was sitting astride his thighs, but facing away from him. Their naked loins were pressed together, but still he didn't enter her.

The first twinge of excitement sang along her nerves. The moment was doubly erotic because they were out in the open, crouched on the grass with the hot, bright sun blazing down on them. If anyone happened to drive up, they would be caught. The sudden sense of danger sharply heightened her arousal. Actually, from the front they were covered, because her skirt was draped over his thighs.

Then that protective cover was whisked away as he pulled her skirt up and to the side. He held her to him with one hand on her stomach, and the other hand slid down between her legs. The intimate contact brought a sharp little cry to her lips.

"Do you like that?" he murmured against her ear and gently nipped the lobe.

Mary made some incoherent answer. His rough fingertips were rasping over her most sensitive flesh, creating and building such pleasure that she could barely speak. He knew exactly how to touch her, how to build her to readiness and take her to ecstasy. Mindlessly she arched back against him; the movement brought his manhood more solidly against her, and she groaned aloud.

"Wolf—please!"

He groaned, too, from between clenched teeth. "I'll please you any way you want, baby. Just tell me how."

She could barely speak for the powerful coil of sensation tightening inside her. "I want you."

"Now?"

"Yes."

"Like this?"

She moved against him and this time had to choke back a cry. "Yes!"

He eased her forward until she was on her stomach again and covered her. His entry was slow and gentle, and fever enveloped her. Eagerly she met the impact of his thrusts, her body on fire, all thoughts suspended before such all-consuming need. This wasn't a nightmare; this was another part of the sensual delights he'd been teaching her. She writhed against him and felt the coil tighten unbearably. Then it sprang free, and she convulsed in his arms. He clamped his hands on her hips and loosed his own responses, driving into her hard and fast until his pulsing release freed him.

They lay together on the grass for a long time, halfdozing, too exhausted to move. Only when Mary felt her legs begin to tingle from too much sun did she find the strength to push her skirt down. Wolf murmured a protest and slid his hand up her thigh.

She opened her eyes. The sky was bright blue, cloudless, and the sweet scent of fresh grass filled her lungs, radiated through her body. The earth was hot beneath her, the man she loved dozed beside her, and every inch of her still held the remnants of sensation from their lovemaking. The memory of it, so fresh and powerful, began to warm her body to desire again, and suddenly she realized that his plan had worked. He had recreated the scenario that had so terrified her, but substituted himself for the attacker. Instead of fear, pain and humiliation, he had given her desire and, ultimately, an ecstasy so strong it had taken her out of herself. He had replaced a terrible memory with a wonderful one.

His hand was lying low on her abdomen now, and the simple intimacy of his touch stunned her. She could be carrying his child. She had been aware of the probable consequences of making love without protection, but it was what she wanted, and he had made no mention of birth control. Even if their relationship didn't last, she wanted his baby, a child with his strength and fire. If it could be a duplicate of him, nothing would make her happier.

She stirred, and the pressure of his hand on her abdomen increased. "The sun is too hot," she murmured. "I'm getting burned."

He groaned, but fastened his jeans and sat up. Then he picked up her underpants, put them in his pocket and lifted her in his arms in the same motion he used to get to his feet.

"I can walk," she informed him, though she wound her arms around his neck.

"I know." He grinned down at her. "It's just that it's more romantic to carry you into the house to make love."

"But we just made love."

There was fire in his black eyes. "So?"

Wolf was just about to enter the feed store when a tingle touched the back of his neck like a cool wind. He didn't stop, which would have signaled an alarm to anyone watching, but, using his peripheral vision, he took a quick look around. The sense of danger was like a touch. Someone was watching him. His sixth sense was highly developed from hard training and years of application, and further enhanced by the strong mysticism of his heritage.

It wasn't just that he was being watched; he could feel the hatred directed toward him. He strode into the feed store and immediately stepped to the side, flattening himself against the wall as he looked out the door. Conversation in the store halted as if the words had hit a stone wall, but he ignored the thick silence. Adrenaline pumped through his body; he didn't notice that his gloved hand automatically slid over his chest to touch the knife that had been securely attached to the webbing he'd worn sixteen years before, in a steamy, hauntingly beautiful little country that reeked of blood and death. Only when his hand encountered nothing but his shirt did he realize that old habits had come to the fore.

Suddenly he realized that it was the man he'd been hunting, standing somewhere out there and staring at him with hatred, and rage surged through him. He didn't need a knife. Without a word he removed his hat and boots, the hat because it increased his silhouette, the boots because they were too noisy. In his sock feet he ran lightly past the stunned and silent little knot of men who had been standing around chewing the fat. Only one voiced a hesitant, "What's going on?"

Wolf didn't take time to answer, but slipped out the back door of the feed store. His movements were silent, deliberate, as he used every available bit of cover while moving from building to building, working his way around so he would come out behind where he had estimated the man to be. It was hard to pinpoint his position, but Wolf had automatically picked out the best locations for concealment. If he kept looking long enough, he'd find another of the tracks he'd been searching for; the guy would get careless, and Wolf would get him.

He slid around the back of the drugstore, feeling the heat of the sun-warmed boards against his back. He was more cautious than before, not wanting the wood to rasp against his shirt. It was gravelly here, too, and he placed his feet with care to keep the little rocks from making a telltale grinding.

He heard the heavy, thudding sound of someone running, as if he had bolted in panic. Wolf ran around the front of the building and knelt briefly to inspect a faint print in the dust, only a part of a print, but his blood surged. It was the same print, same shoe, same toeing-in stride. He sprinted like the big timber wolf he'd been named for, no longer caring about noise, racing up the street, looking left and right for anyone in the street.

Nothing. No one. The street was empty. He stopped to listen. He heard birds, the rustle of a fitful breeze in the trees, the far-off sound of an engine climbing the slight rise on the north side of the town. Nothing else. No fast breathing, no running footsteps.

Wolf swore to himself. The guy was worse than an amateur, he was clumsy and made stupid moves, as well as being out of shape. If he'd been anywhere close by, Wolf would have been able to hear his labored breathing. Damn it, somehow his quarry had slipped away.

Wolf looked at the quiet houses nestled under the trees. Ruth didn't have residential and commercial zoning; it was too small. The result was that the houses and few businesses were mixed together without order. The man could have gone into any of the houses; the way he'd disappeared so suddenly left no other possibility. It verified Wolf's conviction that the rapist lived in Ruth; after all, both attacks had happened right in town.

He noted who lived in the houses on the street and tried to think of who inside them matched Mary's description of a heavily freckled man. No one came to mind. But someone would. By God, Wolf vowed, someone would. He was slowly eliminating men from his mental list. Eventually, there would be only one left.

From inside a house, a curtain moved fractionally. The sound of his own raspy breathing as he sucked air into his laboring lungs filled the man's ears. Through the tiny crack he'd made, he could see the Indian still standing in the street, staring at first one house, then another. Murderous black eyes moved across the window where the man stood, and he automatically stepped back out of sight.

His own fear sickened and enraged him. He didn't want to be afraid of the Indian, but he was.

"Damn filthy Indian!" He whispered the words, then echoed them in his head. He liked doing that, saying things out loud the first time, then saying them to himself for his private understanding and enjoyment.

The Indian was a murderer. They said he knew more ways of killing people than normal folks could even imagine. The man believed it, because he knew firsthand how Indians could kill.

He'd like to kill the Indian, *and* that boy of his with the strange, pale eyes that looked through him. But he was afraid, because he didn't know how to kill, and he knew he'd wind up getting killed himself. He was too afraid of getting that close to the Indian to even try it.

He'd thought about it, but he couldn't come up with a plan. He'd like to shoot the Indian, because he wouldn't have to get close to do that, but he didn't have a gun, and he didn't want to draw attention to himself by buying one.

But he liked what he'd done to get back at the Indian. It gave him savage satisfaction to know he was punishing the Indian by hurting those stupid women who had taken up for him. Why couldn't they see him for the filthy, murdering trash he was? That stupid Cathy had said the Indian was good-looking! She'd even said she'd go out with the boy, and he knew that meant she'd let the boy touch her, and kiss her. She'd been willing to let the filthy Mackenzies kiss her, but she'd fought and screamed and gagged when *he'd* touched her.

It didn't make sense, but he didn't care. He'd wanted

to punish her and punish the Indian for—for being there, for letting stupid Cathy look at him and think he was good-looking.

And the schoolteacher. He hated her almost as much as he hated the Mackenzies, maybe more. She was so goody-goody, making people think the boy was something special, trying to talk people around so they'd be friendly to the half-breeds. Preaching in the general store!

He'd wanted to spit on her. He'd wanted to hurt her, bad. He'd been so excited he almost hadn't been able to stand it when he'd dragged her down that alley and felt her squirming beneath him. If that stupid deputy hadn't shown up, he'd have done to her what he'd done to Cathy, and he knew he'd have liked it more. He'd wanted to hit her with his fists while he did it to her. That would have shown her. She would never have stuck up for the half-breeds again.

He still wanted to get her, to teach her a lesson, but school was out now, and he'd heard people say that the deputy had made her move to some safe place, and no one knew where she was. He didn't want to wait until school started again, but he thought he might have to.

And that stupid Pam Hearst. She needed a lesson, too. He'd heard that she had gone to a dance with the half-breed boy. He knew what that meant. He'd had his hands on her, and she'd probably let him kiss her and maybe do a lot more, because everyone knew what the Mackenzies were like. As far as he was concerned, that made Pam a slut. She deserved to be taught a lesson just like Cathy, and just like the lesson the schoolteacher still had coming.

He peeked outside again. The Indian was gone. He immediately felt safe, and he began to plan.

When Wolf walked back into the feed store, the same group of men were still there. ''We don't much like you tracking folks around like we're criminals,'' one man snapped.

Wolf grunted and sat down to pull on his boots. He didn't care if they liked it or not.

"Did you hear what I said?"

He looked up. "I heard."

"And?"

"And nothing."

"Now look here, damn it!"

"I'm looking."

The men fidgeted under his cold black stare. Another spoke up. "You're making the women nervous."

"They should be nervous. It might keep them on guard, keep them from getting raped."

"It was some drifter trash who blew in and blew out! Likely the sheriff won't ever find who did it."

"It's trash, all right, but he's still here. I just found his track."

The men fell silent and looked at each other. Stu Kilgore, the foreman on Eli Baugh's spread, cleared his throat. "We're supposed to believe you can tell it was made by the same man?"

"I can tell." Wolf gave them a smile that was closer to a snarl. "Uncle Sam made sure I got the best training available. It's the same man. He lives here. He slipped into one of the houses."

"That's hard to believe. We've lived here all our lives. The only stranger around is the schoolteacher. Why would someone just up and start attacking women?"

"Someone did. That's all I care about, that and catching him."

He left the men murmuring among themselves while he loaded his feed.

* * *

Pam was bored. Since the two attacks, she hadn't even stepped outside the house by herself; she'd been pretty scared at first, but the days had passed without any more attacks, and the shock had worn off. Women were beginning to venture out again, even by themselves.

She was going to another dance with Joe, and she wanted a new dress. She knew he was going away, knew she couldn't hold him, but there was still something about him that made her heart race. She refused to let herself love him, even though she knew any other boyfriend would have a hard time replacing Joe. Hard, but not impossible. She wasn't going to mope after he'd left; she'd get on with her life—but right now he was still *here*, and she savored every moment with him.

She really wanted a new dress, but she'd promised Joe she wouldn't go anywhere alone, and she didn't intend to break her promise. When her mother returned from shopping with a neighbor, she'd ask her about going with her to get a new dress. Not in Ruth, of course; she wanted to go to a real town, with a real dress shop.

Finally she picked up a book and walked out onto the back porch, away from the sun. There were neighbors on both sides, and she felt safe. She read for a while, then became sleepy and lay down on the porch swing, arranging her long legs over the back of the swing. She dozed immediately.

The abrupt jolting of the swing awakened her some time later. She opened her eyes and stared at a ski mask, with narrowed, hate-filled eyes glittering through the slits. He was already on her when she screamed.

He hit her with his fist, but she jerked her head back so that the blow landed on her shoulder. She screamed again and tried to kick him, and the unsteady swing toppled them to the porch. She kicked again, catching him in the stomach, and he grunted, sounding oddly surprised.

She couldn't stop screaming, even as she scrabbled away from him. She was more terrified than she'd ever been before in her life, but also oddly detached, watching the scene from some safe distance. The wooden slats of the porch scraped her hands and arms, but she kept moving backward. He suddenly sprang, and she kicked at him again, but he caught her ankle. She didn't stop. She just kicked, using both legs, trying to catch him in the head or the groin, and she screamed.

Someone next door yelled. The man jerked his head up and dropped her ankle. Blood had seeped through the multicolored ski mask; she'd managed to kick him in the mouth. He said "Indian's dirty whore" in a hate-thickened voice, and jumped from the porch, already running.

Pam lay on the porch, sobbing in dry, painful gasps. The neighbor yelled again, and somehow she garnered enough strength to scream "Help me!" before the terror made her curl into a ball and whimper like a child.

Chapter 12

Wolf wasn't surprised when the deputy's car pulled up and Clay got out. He'd had a tight feeling in his gut since he'd found that footprint in town. Clay's tired face told the story.

Mary saw who their visitor was and automatically got a cup for coffee; Clay always wanted coffee. He took off his hat and sat down, heaving a sigh as he did so.

"Who was it this time?" Wolf asked, his deep voice so rough it was almost a growl.

"Pam Hearst."

Joe's head jerked up, and all the color washed out of his face. He was on his feet before Clay's next words came.

"She fought him off. She isn't hurt, but she's scared. He jumped her on the Hearsts' back porch, for God's sake. Mrs. Winston heard her screaming, and the guy ran. Pam said she kicked him in the mouth. She saw blood on the ski mask he was wearing."

"He lives in town," Wolf said. "I found another print, but it's hard to track in town, with people walking around destroying what few prints there are. I think he ducked into one of the houses along Bay Road, but he might not live there."

"Bay Road." Clay frowned as he mentally reviewed the people living on Bay Road; most of the townspeople lived along it, in close little clusters. There was also another cluster of houses on Broad Street, where the Hearsts lived. "We might have him this time. Any man who has a swollen lip will have to have an airtight alibi."

"If it just split his lip, you won't be able to tell. The swelling will be minimal. She would have to have really done some damage for it to be visible more than a day or so." Wolf had had more than his share of split lips, and delivered his share, too. The mouth healed swiftly. Now if Pam had knocked some teeth out, that would be a different story.

"Any blood on the porch?"

"No."

"Then she didn't do any real damage." There would have been blood sprayed all over the porch if she'd kicked out his teeth.

Clay shoved his hand through his hair. "I don't like to think of the uproar it would cause, but I'm going to talk to the sheriff about making a house-to-house search along Bay Road. Damn it, I just can't think of anyone it could be."

Joe abruptly left the room, and Wolf stared after his son. He knew Joe wanted to go to Pam, and knew that he wouldn't. Some of the barriers had come down, but most of them were still intact.

Clay had watched Joe leave, and he sighed again. "The bastard called Pam an 'Indian's dirty whore.'" His gaze shifted to Mary, who had stood silently the whole time. "You were right."

She didn't reply, because she'd known all along that she was right. It made her sick to hear the name Pam had been called, because it so starkly revealed the hatred behind the attack.

"I suppose all the tracks at Pam's house have been ruined." Wolf said it as a statement, not a question.

"Afraid so." Clay was regretful, but practically everyone in town had been at the Hearsts' house before he'd gotten there, standing around the back porch and tromping around the area.

Wolf muttered something uncomplimentary under his breath about damn idiots. "Do you think the sheriff will go along with a house-to-house search?"

"Depends. You know some folks are going to kick up about it no matter what the reason. They'll take it personally. This is an election year," he said, and they took his point.

Mary listened to them talking, but she didn't join in. Now Pam had been hurt; who was next? Would the man work up enough courage to attack Wolf or Joe? That was her real terror, because she didn't know if she could bear it. She loved them with all the fierceness of her soul. She would gladly put herself between them and danger.

Which was exactly what she would have to do.

It made her sick to even think of that man's hands on her again, but she knew in that moment that she was going to give him the opportunity. Somehow, she was going to lure him out. She wouldn't allow herself the luxury of hiding out on Mackenzie's Mountain any longer.

She would begin driving into town by herself. The only problem would be in getting away from Wolf; she knew he'd never agree if he had any idea what she was doing. Not only that, he was capable of preventing her from leaving at all, either by disabling her car or even locking her in the bedroom. She didn't underestimate him.

Since he had moved her up on the mountain with him, he'd been delivering and picking up horses, rather than letting the owners come up to the ranch, where they might see her. Her whereabouts were a well-kept secret, known only to Wolf, Joe and Clay. But that meant she was left alone several times a week while Wolf and Joe ran errands and delivered horses. Joe also left for his math lessons, and they had to ride fences and work the small herd of cattle, just as every rancher did. She really had a lot of opportunities for slipping away, at least the first time. It would be infinitely more difficult to get away after that, because Wolf would be on his guard.

She quietly excused herself and went in search of Joe. She peeked into his bedroom, but he wasn't there, so she went out on the front porch. He was leaning against one of the posts, his thumbs hooked in his front pockets.

"It isn't your fault."

He didn't move. "I knew it could happen."

"You aren't responsible for someone else's hate."

"No, but I am responsible for Pam. I knew it could happen, and I should have stayed away from her."

Mary made an unladylike sound. "I seem to remember it was the other way around. Pam made her choice when she made that scene in her father's store."

"All she wanted was to go to a dance. She didn't ask for this."

"Of course not, but it still isn't your fault, any more than it would have been your fault if she'd been in a car accident. You can say you could have delayed her so she'd have been a minute later getting to that particular section of road, or hurried her up so she'd have been earlier, but that's ridiculous, and you know it.''

He couldn't prevent a faint smile at the starchiness of her tone. She should be in Congress, cracking her whip and haranguing those senators and representatives into some sort of fiscal responsibility. Instead she'd taken on Ruth, Wyoming, and none of them had been the same since she'd set foot in town.

''All right, so I'm taking too much on myself,'' he finally said. ''But I knew it wasn't smart to go out with her in the first place. It isn't fair. I'll be leaving here when I finish school, and I won't be back. Pam should be dating someone who's going to be around when she needs him.''

''You're still taking too much on yourself. Let Pam make her own decisions about who she wants to date. Do you plan to isolate yourself from women forever?''

''I wouldn't go that far,'' he drawled, and in that moment he sounded so much like his father that it startled her. ''But I don't intend to get involved with anyone.''

''It doesn't always work out the way you want. You were involved with Pam even before I came here.''

That was true, as far as it went. He sighed and leaned his head against the post. ''I don't love her.''

''Of course not. I never thought you did.''

''I like her; I care for her. But not enough to stay, not enough to give up the Academy.'' He looked at the Wyoming night, the almost painful clarity of the sky, the brightly winking stars, and thought of jockeying an F-15 over these mountains, with the dark earth below and the glittering stars above. No, he couldn't give that up.

''Did you tell her that?''

''Yes.''

''Then it was her decision.''

They stood in silence, watching the stars. A few

minutes later Clay left, and neither of them thought it strange that he hadn't said goodbye. Wolf came out on the porch and automatically slid his arm around Mary's waist, hugging her to his side even as he put his hand on his son's shoulder. "You okay?"

"Okay enough, I suppose." But he understood now the total rage he'd seen in Wolf's eyes when Mary had been attacked, the same rage that still burned in a rigidly controlled fire inside his father. God help the man if Wolf Mackenzie ever got his hands on him.

Wolf tightened his arm around Mary and led her inside, knowing it was best to leave Joe alone now. His son was tough; he'd handle it.

The next morning Mary listened as they discussed their day. There were no horses to deliver or pick up, but Joe had a math lesson that afternoon, and they intended to use the morning inoculating cattle. She had no idea how long it would take to treat the whole herd, but imagined they would both be tied up the entire morning. They would be riding a couple of the young quarter horses, to teach them how to cut cattle.

Joe had changed overnight; it was a subtle change, but one that made Mary ache inside. In repose, his young face held a grimness that saddened her, as if the last faint vestiges of boyhood had been driven from his soul. He'd always looked older than his age, but now, despite the smoothness of his skin, he no longer looked young.

She was a grown woman, almost thirty years old, and the attack had left scars she hadn't been able to handle alone. Cathy and Pam were just kids, and Cathy had to handle a nightmare that was far worse than what Mary and Pam had undergone. Joe had lost his youth. No matter what, that man had to be stopped before he damaged anyone else.

When Wolf and Joe left the house, Mary gave them plenty of time to get far enough away so they wouldn't hear her car start, then hurried out of the house. She didn't know what she was going to do, other than parade through Ruth on the off chance that her presence might trigger another attack. And then what? She didn't know. Somehow she had to be prepared; she had to get someone to keep watch so the man could be caught. It should have been easy to catch him; he'd been so careless, attacking out in the open and in broad daylight, making stupid moves, as if he attacked on impulse and without a plan. He hadn't even taken the simplest precautions against getting caught. The whole thing was strange. It didn't make sense.

Her hands were shaking as she drove into town; she was acutely aware that this was the first time since the day she'd been attacked that she was without protection. She felt exposed, as if her clothing had been stripped away.

She had to get someone to watch her, someone she trusted. Who? Sharon? The young teacher was her friend, but Sharon wasn't aggressive, and she thought the situation called for aggressiveness. Francie Beecham was too old; Cicely Karr would be too cautious. She discounted the men, because they would get all protective and refuse to help. Men were such victims to their own hormones. Machismo had killed a lot more people than PMS.

Pam Hearst sprang to mind. Pam would be extremely interested in catching the man, and she'd been aggressive enough to kick him in the mouth, to fight him off. She was young, but she had courage. She'd had the courage to go against her father and date a half-breed.

Conversation ceased when she walked into Hearst's store; it was the first time she'd been seen since the end of school. She ignored the thick silence, for she had what

she suspected was a highly accurate guess as to the subject of the conversation she'd interrupted, and approached the checkout counter where Mr. Hearst stood.

"Is Pam at home?" she asked quietly, not wanting her
question to be heard by the entire store.

He looked as if he'd aged ten years overnight, but
there was no animosity in his face.

He nodded. The same thing had happened to Miss Potter, he thought. If she could talk to Pam, maybe she could
take that haunted look out of his baby girl's eyes. Miss
Potter had a lot of backbone for such a little thing; maybe
he didn't always agree with her, but he'd damn sure
learned to respect her. And Pam thought the world of
her.

"I'd appreciate it if you'd talk to her," he said.

There was an odd, almost militant expression in her
soft bluish eyes. "I'll do that," she promised, and turned
to leave. She almost bumped into Dottie and was startled
into a gasp; the woman had been right behind her.

"Good morning," Mary said pleasantly. Aunt Ardith
had drilled the importance of good manners into her.

Strangely, Dottie seemed to have aged, too. Her face
was haggard. "How are you doing, Mary?"

Mary hesitated, but she could detect none of the hostility she was accustomed to from Dottie. Had the entire
town changed? Had this nightmare brought them to their
senses about the Mackenzies? "I'm fine. Are you enjoying the vacation?"

Dottie smiled, but it was merely a movement of her
facial muscles, not a response of pleasure. "It's been a
relief."

She certainly didn't look relieved; she looked worried
to a frazzle. Of course, everyone *should* be worried.

"How is your son?" Mary couldn't remember the

boy's name, and she felt faintly embarrassed. It wasn't like her to forget names.

To her surprise, Dottie went white. Even her lips were bloodless. "W—why do you ask?" she stammered.

"He seemed upset the last time I saw him," Mary replied. She could hardly say that only good manners had prompted the question. Southerners always asked after family.

"Oh. He—he's all right. He hardly ever leaves the house. He doesn't like going out." Dottie looked around, then blurted "Excuse me," and left the store before Mary could say anything else.

She looked at Mr. Hearst, and he shrugged. He thought Dottie had acted a bit strange, too.

"I'll go see Pam now," she said.

She started to walk to the Hearst house, but the memory of what had happened the last time she'd walked through town made chills run up her spine, and she went to her car. She checked the back seat and floorboard before opening the door. As she started the engine, she saw Dottie walking swiftly up the street, her head down as if she didn't want anyone to speak to her. She hadn't bought anything, Mary realized. Why had she been in Hearst's store, if not to make a purchase? It couldn't be browsing, because everyone knew what every store in town carried. Why had she left so suddenly?

Dottie turned left down the small street where she lived, and abruptly Mary wondered what Dottie was doing walking around alone. Every woman in town should know better. Surely she had enough sense to be cautious.

Mary drove slowly up the street. She craned her neck when she reached the street where Dottie had turned and saw the woman hurrying up the steps of her house. Her eyes fell on the faded sign: Bay Road.

Bay Road was where Wolf thought the rapist had

dodged into a house. It made sense that he wouldn't have entered a house that wasn't his home, unless he was a close friend who came and went just like a family member. That was possible, but even a very close friend would give a yell before just walking into someone else's house, and Wolf would have heard that.

Dottie was certainly acting odd. She'd looked as if she'd been stung by a bee when Mary had asked about her son.... Bobby, that was his name. Mary was pleased that she'd remembered.

Bobby. Bobby wasn't "right." He did things in a skewed way. He was unable to apply logic to the simplest of chores, unable to plan a practical course of action.

Mary broke out in a sweat and had to stop the car. She'd only seen him once, but she could picture him in her mind: big, a little soft-looking, with sandy hair and a fair complexion. A fair, freckled complexion.

Was it *Bobby*? The one person in town who wasn't totally responsible for himself? The one person no one would ever suspect?

Except his mother.

She had to tell Wolf.

As soon as the thought formed, she dismissed it. She couldn't tell Wolf, not yet, because she didn't want to put that burden on him. His instincts would tell him to go after Bobby; his conscience would argue that Bobby wasn't a responsible person. Mary knew him well enough to know that, no matter which decision he made, he would always have regrets. Better for the responsibility to be hers than to push Wolf into such a position.

She'd call Clay. It was his job, after all. He'd be better able to deal with the situation.

Only a few seconds passed as her thoughts rushed through her mind. She was still sitting there staring at

Dottie's house when Bobby came out on the porch. It took him a moment, but suddenly he noticed her car and looked straight at her. A distance of less than seventy-five yards separated them, still too far for her to read his expression, but she didn't need a close-up for sheer terror to spurt through her. She stomped on the gas pedal and the car shot forward, slinging gravel, the tires squealing.

It was only a short distance to the Hearst house. Mary ran to the front door and banged her fist on it. Her heart felt as if it would explode. That brief moment when she had been face-to-face with him was almost more than she could stand. God, she had to call Clay.

Mrs. Hearst opened the door a crack, then recognized Mary and swung it all the way open. "Miss Potter! Is something wrong?"

Mary realized that she must look wild. "Could I use your phone? It's an emergency."

"Why—of course." She stepped back, allowing Mary inside.

Pam appeared in the hallway. "Miss Potter?" She looked young and scared.

"The phone's in the kitchen."

Mary followed Mrs. Hearst and grabbed the receiver. "What's the number of the sheriff's department?"

Pam got a small telephone book from the countertop and began flipping through the pages. Too agitated to wait, Mary dialed the number for Information.

"Sheriff's department, please."

"What city?" the disembodied voice asked.

She drew a blank. For the life of her, she couldn't remember the name of the town.

"Here it is," Pam said.

Mary disconnected the call to Information, then dialed as Pam recited the number. The various computer clicks as the connection was made seemed to take forever.

"Sheriff's office."

"Deputy Armstrong, please. Clay Armstrong."

"One moment."

It was longer than one moment. Pam and her mother stood tensely, not knowing what was going on but reacting to her urgency. Both of them had dark circles under their eyes. It had been a bad night for the Hearst family.

"Sheriff's office," a different voice said.

"Clay?"

"You looking for Armstrong?"

"Yes. It's an emergency!" she insisted.

"Well, I don't know where he is right now. You want to tell me what the trouble is—hey, Armstrong! Some lady wants you in a hurry." To Mary, he said, "He'll be right here."

A few seconds later Clay's voice said, "Armstrong."

"It's Mary. I'm in town."

"What the hell are you doing there?"

Her teeth were chattering. "It's Bobby. Bobby Lancaster. I saw him—"

"Hang up the phone!"

It was a scream, and she jumped, dropping the receiver, which dangled from the end of its cord. She flattened against the wall, for Bobby stood there, inside the kitchen, with a huge butcher knife in his hand. His face was twisted with both hate and fear.

"You told!" He sounded like an outraged child.

"Told—told what?"

"You told him! I heard you!"

Mrs. Hearst had shrunk back against the cabinets, her hand at her throat. Pam stood as if rooted in the middle of the floor, her face colorless, her eyes locked on the young man she'd known all her life. She could see the slight swelling of his lower lip.

Bobby shifted his weight from one foot to the other, as if he didn't know what to do next. His face was red, and he looked almost tearful.

Mary strove to steady her voice. "That's right, I told him. He's on his way now. You'd better run." Maybe that wasn't the best suggestion in the world, but more than anything she wanted to get him out of the Hearsts' house before he hurt someone. She desperately wanted him to run.

"It's all your fault!" He looked hunted, as if he didn't know what to do except cast blame. "You—you came here and changed things. Mama said you're a dirty Indian-lover."

"I beg your pardon. I prefer clean people."

He blinked, confused. Then he shook his head and said again, "It's your fault."

"Clay will be here in a few minutes. You'd better go."

His hand tightened on the knife, and suddenly he reached out and grabbed her arm. He was big and soft, but he was faster than he looked. Mary cried out as he twisted her arm up behind her back, nearly wrenching her shoulder joint loose.

"You'll be my hostage, just like on television," he said and pushed her out the back door.

Mrs. Hearst was motionless, frozen in shock. Pam leaped for the phone, heard the buzzing that signaled a broken connection and held the button down for a new line. When she got a dial tone, she dialed the Mackenzies' number. It rang endlessly, and she cursed, using words her mother had no idea she knew. All the while she leaned to the side, trying to see where Bobby was taking Mary.

She was just about to hang up when the receiver was picked up and a deep, angry voice roared, "Mary?"

She was so startled that she almost dropped the phone. "No," she choked. "It's Pam. He has Mary. It's Bobby Lancaster, and he just dragged her out of the house—"

"I'll be right there."

Pam shivered at the deadly intent in Wolf Mackenzie's voice.

Mary stumbled over a large rock hidden by the tall grass and gagged as the sudden intense pain made nausea twist her stomach.

"Stand up!" Bobby yelled, jerking at her.

"I twisted my ankle!" It was a lie, but it would give her an excuse to slow him down.

He'd dragged her across the small meadow behind the Hearsts', through a thick line of trees, over a stream, and now they were climbing a small rise. At least it had looked small, but now she knew it was deceptively large. It was a big open area, not the smartest place for Bobby to head, but he didn't plan well. That was what had thrown everyone off from the beginning, what had never seemed quite *right*. There had been no logic to his actions; Bobby reacted rather than planned.

He didn't know what to do for a twisted ankle, so he didn't worry about it, just pushed her along at the same speed. She stumbled again, but somehow managed to retain her balance. She wouldn't be able to bear it if she fell on her stomach and he came down on top of her again.

"Why did you have to tell?" he groaned.

"You hurt Cathy."

"She deserved it!"

"How? How did she deserve it?"

"She liked him—the Indian."

Mary was panting. She estimated they'd gone over a mile. Not a great distance, but the gradual uphill climb was telling on her. It didn't help that her arm was twisted up between her shoulder blades. How long had it been? When could she expect Clay to arrive? It had been at least twenty minutes.

Wolf made it off his mountain in record time. His eyes were like flint as he leaped from the truck before it had rocked to a complete stop. He and Joe both carried rifles, but Wolf's was a sniper rifle, a Remington with a powerful scope. He'd never had occasion to try a thousand-yard shot with it, but he'd never missed his target at closer range.

People milled around the back of the house. He and Joe shouldered their way through the crowd. "Everybody freeze, before you destroy any more tracks!" Wolf roared, and everyone stopped dead.

Pam darted to them. Her face was streaked with tears. "He took her into the trees. There," she said and pointed.

A siren announced Clay's arrival, but Wolf didn't wait for him. The trail across the meadow was as plain to him as a neon sign would have been, and he set off at a lope, with Joe on his heels.

Dottie Lancaster was terrified, and nearly hysterical. Bobby was her son, and she loved him desperately no matter what he'd done. She'd been sick when she'd realized he was the one who had attacked Cathy Teele and Mary; she'd almost worried herself into an early grave as she wrestled with her conscience and the sure knowledge that she'd lose her son if she turned him in. But that was nothing compared to the horror she'd felt when she discovered he'd slipped from the house. She'd followed the sounds of a disturbance and found all of her nightmares coming true: he'd taken Mary, and he had a knife. Now the Mackenzies were after him, and she knew they would kill him.

She grabbed Clay's arm as he surged past her. "Stop them," she sobbed. "Don't let them kill my boy."

Clay barely glanced at her. He shook her loose and ran after them. Distraught, Dottie ran, too.

By then some of the other men had gotten their rifles and were joining the hunt. They'd always felt sorry for Bobby Lancaster, but he'd hurt their women, and there was no excuse for it.

Wolf's heartbeat settled down, and he pushed the panic away. His senses heightened, as they always did when he was on the hunt. Every sound was magnified in his ears, instantly recognizable. He saw every blade of grass, every broken twig and overturned rock. He could smell every scent nature had left, and the faint acrid, coppery tang of fear. His body was a machine, moving smoothly, silently.

He could read every sign. Here Mary had stumbled, and his muscles tightened. She had to be terrified. If he hurt her—she was so slight, no match at all for a man. The bastard had a knife. Wolf thought of a blade touching her delicate, translucent skin, and rage consumed him. He had to push it away because he couldn't afford the mistakes rage could cause.

He broke out of the tree line and suddenly saw them, high on the side of the rise. Bobby was dragging Mary along, but at least she was still alive.

Wolf examined the terrain. He didn't have a good angle. He moved east, along the base of the rise.

"Stop!"

It was Bobby's voice, only faintly heard at that distance. They had halted, and Bobby was holding Mary in front of him. "Stop or I'll kill her!"

Slowly, Wolf went down on one knee and raised the

rifle to his shoulder. He sighted through the scope, not for a shot, but to see how he should set it up. The powerful scope plainly revealed the desperation on Bobby's face and the knife at Mary's throat.

"Bobbeee!" Dottie had reached them, and she screamed his name.

"Mama?"

"Bobby, let her go!"

"I can't! She told!"

The men had clustered around. Several of them measured the distance by eye and shook their heads. They couldn't make the shot, not at that range. They were as likely to hit Mary as Bobby, if they hit anything at all.

Clay looked down at Wolf. "Can you make the shot?"

Wolf smiled, and Clay felt that chill run up his spine again at the look in Wolf's eyes. They were cold and murderous. "Yeah."

"No!" Dottie sobbed the word. "Bobby!" she screamed. "Please, come down!"

"I can't! I've got to kill her! She likes him, and he's a dirty Indian! He killed my father!"

Dottie gasped and covered her mouth with her hands. "No," she moaned, then screamed again. "No! He didn't!" Pure hell was living in her eyes.

"He did! You said—an Indian—" Bobby broke off and began dragging Mary backward.

"Do it," Clay said quietly.

Wolf braced the barrel of the rifle in the notch of a sapling. It was small but sturdy enough to be steady. Without a word he sighted in the cross hairs of the scope.

"Wait," Dottie cried, anguish in her voice.

Wolf looked at her.

"Please," she whispered. "Don't kill him. He's all I have."

His black eyes were flat. "I'll try."

He concentrated on the shot, shutting everything out as he always had. It was maybe three hundred yards, but the air was still. The image in the scope was huge and clear and flattened, the depth perception distorted. Mary's face was plain. She looked angry, and she was tugging at the arm around her shoulder, the one that held the knife to her throat.

God, when he got her back safe and sound, he was going to throttle her.

Because she was so small, he had a larger target than would normally have been presented. His instincts were to go for a head shot, to take Bobby Lancaster completely out of life, but he'd promised. Damn, it was going to be a bitch of a shot. They were moving, and he'd limited his own target area by promising not to go for a kill.

The cross hairs settled, and his hands became rock steady. He drew in a breath, let out half of it and gently squeezed the trigger. Almost simultaneously with the sharp thunder in his ear he saw the red stain blossom on Bobby's shoulder and the knife drop from his suddenly useless hand even as he was thrown back by the bullet's impact. Mary staggered to the side and fell, but was instantly on her feet again.

Dottie sagged to her knees, sobbing, her hands over her face.

The men surged up the hill. Mary ran down it and met Wolf halfway. He still had the rifle in his hand, but he caught her up in his arms and held her locked to him, his eyes closed as he absorbed the miracle of her, warm and alive against him, her silky hair against his face, her sweet scent in his lungs. He didn't care who saw them, or what anyone thought. She was his, and he'd just lived through the worst half hour of his existence knowing that at any moment her life could be ended.

Now that it was over, she was crying.

She'd been dragged up the hill, and now Wolf dragged her down it. He was swearing steadily under his breath, ignoring her gasping protests until she stumbled. Then he snatched her up under his arm like a sack and continued down. People stared after them in astonishment, but no one moved to stop him. After today, they all viewed Wolf Mackenzie differently.

Wolf ignored her car and thrust her into his truck. Mary pushed her hair out of her face and decided not to mention the car; they would pick it up later. Wolf was in a rage, his face set and hard.

They had almost reached the road that wound up his mountain before he spoke. "What in hell were you doing in town?" The even tone didn't fool her. The wolf was dangerously angered.

Perhaps she wasn't as cautious as she should have been, but she still wasn't afraid of him, not of the man she loved. She respected his temper, but she didn't fear him. So she said, just as calmly, "I thought seeing me might trigger him into doing something stupid, so we could identify him."

"You *triggered* him, all right. What he did wasn't nearly as stupid as what you did. What did you do, parade up and down the streets until he grabbed you?"

She let the insult pass. "Actually it never came to that. I intended to talk to Pam first. I stopped at the store to ask Mr. Hearst if she was home and bumped into Dottie. She acted so strange and looked so worried that it made me wonder. She almost ran out of the store. Then, when I saw her turn onto Bay Road, I remembered Bobby, what he looked like. He came out on the porch and looked at me, and I knew he was the one."

"So you made a citizen's arrest?" he asked sarcastically.

Mary got huffy. "No. I'm not stupid, and you'd better not make another smart remark, Wolf Mackenzie. I did what I thought I had to do. I'm sorry if you don't like it, but there it is. Enough was enough. I couldn't take the chance someone else could be hurt, or that he might start taking shots at you or Joe.

"I drove to Pam's house and called Clay. I had no intention of confronting Bobby, but it didn't work out that way. He followed me to Pam's and heard me talking on the phone. So he grabbed me. You know what happened then."

She was so matter-of-fact about it that he tightened his hands on the steering wheel to keep from shaking her. If she hadn't been crying just a few minutes ago, he might have lost his tenuous control on his temper.

"Do you know what might have happened if I hadn't come back to the barn for something and noticed your car was missing? It was just chance I was there when Pam called to tell me Bobby had grabbed you!"

"Yes," she said patiently. "I know what could have happened."

"It doesn't bother you that he came close to cutting your throat?"

"Close doesn't count except in horseshoes and hand grenades."

He slammed on the brakes, so enraged he could barely see. He wasn't aware of shutting off the motor, only of closing his hands on her slender shoulders. He was so close to pulling her across his knees that he was shaking, but she didn't seem to realize that she should be frightened. With a faint sound she dived into his arms, clinging to him with surprising strength.

Wolf held her and felt her trembling. The red haze left his vision, and he realized that she *was* frightened, but not of him. With her normal damn-the-torpedoes attitude, she'd done what she'd thought was right and was probably trying to put up a calm front so he wouldn't be alarmed.

As if anything could ever alarm him more than seeing an unbalanced rapist hold a knife to her throat.

Frantically he started the truck. It wasn't far to his house, but he didn't know if he could make it. He had to make love to her, soon, even if it was in the middle of the road. Only then would the fear of losing her begin to fade, when he felt her beneath him once more and she welcomed him into her delicate body.

Mary brooded. It had been four days since Wolf had shot Bobby; the first two days had been filled with statements and police procedures, as well as newspaper interviews and even a request from a television station, which Wolf had refused. The sheriff, not being a fool, had hailed Wolf as a hero and praised the shot he'd made. Wolf's military service record was dug up, and a lot was written about the "much-decorated Vietnam veteran" who had saved a schoolteacher and captured a rapist.

Bobby was recuperating in a hospital in Casper; the bullet had punctured his right lung, but he was lucky to be alive under the circumstances. He was bewildered by everything that had happened and kept asking to go home. Dottie had resigned. She'd have to live the rest of her life knowing that her hatred had taken seed in her son's mind and caused the entire nightmare. She knew Bobby would be taken away from her, at least for a time, and that they would never be able to live in Ruth again, even if he was ever a free man. But wherever Bobby was sent, she intended to be close by. As she'd told Wolf, he was all she had.

It was over, and Mary knew that Wolf would never be

treated as an outcast again. The threat was past, and the town was safe. Just knowing who it was and that he'd been caught made a lot of difference in Cathy Teele's recovery, though what had happened would always mark her life.

So there was no reason why Mary couldn't return to her own house.

That was why she was brooding. In those four days, Wolf hadn't said a word about her remaining with him. He'd never said a word of love, not even during their wild lovemaking after he'd snatched her to safety. He hadn't said anything at all about their personal situation.

It was time to go home. She couldn't stay with him forever, not when there was no fear for her safety now. She knew their affair would probably continue, at least for a while, but still the thought of leaving his house depressed her. She'd loved every minute of her time on Mackenzie's Mountain, loved sharing the little commonplace things with him. Life consisted of the small things, with only scattered moments of intensity.

She calmly packed and refused to let herself cry. She was going to be under control and not make a scene. She loaded her suitcases into her car, then waited for Wolf to return to the house. It would be childish to sneak off, and she wouldn't do it; she'd tell him she was returning to her home, thank him for his protection and leave. It would be immensely civilized.

As it happened, it was late afternoon when Wolf got back. He was sweaty and coated with dust, and limping a little, because a cow had stepped on his foot. He wasn't in a good mood.

Mary smiled at him. "I've decided to get out of your hair, since there's no reason to be afraid of staying by myself now. I've already packed and loaded everything in the car, but I wanted to stay until you got home to thank you for everything you've done.''

Wolf paused in the act of gulping cool, fresh water down his parched throat. Joe froze on the step, not wanting them to see him. He couldn't believe Wolf would let her leave.

Slowly, Wolf turned his head to look at her. There was a savage expression in his eyes, but she was concentrating too hard on maintaining control to see it. She gave him another smile, but this one was harder, because he hadn't said a word, not even, ''I'll call you.''

''Well,'' she said brightly, ''I'll see you around. Tell Joe not to forget his lessons.''

She marched out the front door and down the steps. She'd gotten halfway to her car when a hard hand clamped down on her shoulder and spun her around.

''I'll be damned if you're setting foot off this mountain,'' he said in a harsh tone.

He towered over her. For the first time Mary felt it was a disadvantage that she only reached his shoulder. She had to tilt her head back to talk to him, he was so close. The heat from his body enveloped her like steam. ''I can't stay here forever,'' she replied reasonably, but now she could see the look in his eyes and she shivered. ''I'm a small-town schoolteacher. I can't just cohabit with you—''

''Shut up,'' he said.

''Now see here—''

''I said shut up. You aren't going anywhere, and you're damn well going to cohabit with me for the rest of your life. It's too late today, but first thing in the morning we're going into town for our blood tests and license. We're going to be married within a week, so get your little butt back in that house and stay there. I'll bring your suitcases in.''

His expression would have made most men back up a few steps, but Mary crossed her arms. "I'm not marrying someone who doesn't love me."

"Hellfire!" he roared and jerked her up against him. "Not love you? Damn, woman, you've been wrapping me around your little finger since the first time I set eyes on you! I'd have killed Bobby Lancaster in a heartbeat for you, so don't you ever say I don't love you!"

As a declaration of love cum marriage proposal, it wasn't exactly romantic, but it was certainly exciting. Mary smiled up at him and went on tiptoe to loop her arms around his neck. "I love you, too."

He glared down at her, but noticed how pretty she looked with her soft pink sweater bringing out the delicate roses in her cheeks, and her slate-blue eyes twinkling at him. A breeze flirted with her silky, silvery-brown hair, and suddenly he buried his face in the baby-fine strands at her temple.

"God, I love you," he whispered. He'd never thought he would love any woman, least of all an Anglo, but that was before this slight, delicate creature had bulldozed her way into his life and completely changed it. He could no more live without her now than he could live without air.

"I want children," she stated.

He smiled against her temple. "I'm willing."

She thought about it some more. "I think I'd like four."

A slight frown creased his brow as he held her tighter. "We'll see." She was too small and delicate for that many pregnancies; two would be better. He lifted her in his arms and started for the house, where she belonged.

Joe watched from the window and turned away with a grin as his father lifted Mary against his chest.

Epilogue

Joe opened the letter from Mary and began grinning as he read. His roommate looked at him with interest. "Good news from home?"

"Yeah," Joe said without looking up. "My stepmother is pregnant again."

"I thought she just had a baby."

"Two years ago. This is their third."

His roommate, Bill Stolsky, watched Joe finish the letter. Privately he was a little awed by the calm, remote half-breed. Even when they'd been doolies, first-year cadets, and normally regarded as lower than the low, there had been something about Joe Mackenzie that had kept the upperclassmen from dealing him too much misery. He'd been at the top of his class from the beginning, and it was already known that he was moving on to flight training after graduation. Mackenzie was on the fast track to the top, and even his instructors knew it.

"How old is your stepmother?" Stolsky asked in curiosity. He knew Mackenzie was twenty-one, a year younger than himself, though they were both seniors in the Academy.

Joe shrugged and reached for a picture he kept in his locker. "Young enough. My dad's pretty young, too. He was just a kid when I was born."

Stolsky took the picture and looked at the four people in it. It wasn't a posed photograph, which made it more intimate. Three adults were playing with a baby. The woman was small and delicate, and was looking up from the baby in her lap to smile at a big, dark, eagle-featured man. The man was one tough-looking dude. Stolsky wouldn't want to meet him in an alley, dark or otherwise. He glanced quickly at Joe and saw the strong resemblance.

But the baby was clinging to the big man's finger with a dimpled fist and laughing while Joe tickled his neck. It was a revealing and strangely disturbing look into Mackenzie's private life, into his tightly knit family.

Stolsky cleared his throat. "Is that the newest baby?"

"No, that picture was made when I was a senior in high school. That's Michael. He's four years old now, and Joshua is two." Joe couldn't help grinning and feeling worried at the same time when he thought of Mary's letter. Both his little brothers had been delivered by cesarean, because Mary was simply too slender to have them. After Joshua's birth, Wolf had said there would be no more babies, because Mary had had such a hard time carrying Josh. But Mary had won, as usual. He'd have to make a point of getting off on leave when this baby was due.

"Your stepmother isn't—uh—"

"Indian? No."

"Do you like her?"

Joe smiled. "I love her. I wouldn't be here without her." He stood and walked to the window. Six years of hard work, and he was on the verge of getting what he'd lived for: fighter jets. First there was flight training, then Fighter Training School. More years of hard work loomed before him, but he was eager for them. Only a small percentage made it to fighters, but he was going to be one of them.

The cadets in his class who were going on to flight training had already been thinking of fighter call signs, picking theirs out even though they knew some of them would wash out of flight training, and an even greater number would never make it to fighters. But they never thought it would be them; it was always the other guy who washed out, the other guy who didn't have the stuff.

They'd had a lot of fun thinking up those signs, and Joe had sat quietly, a little apart as he always was. Then Richards had pointed at him and said, "You'll be Chief."

Joe had looked up, his face calm and remote. "I'm not a chief." His tone had been even, but Richards had felt a chill.

"All right," he'd agreed. "What do you want to be called?"

Joe had shrugged. "Call me 'Breed.' It's what I am."

Already, though they hadn't even graduated yet, people were calling him Breed Mackenzie. The name would be painted on his helmet, and a lot of people would forget his real name.

Mary had given him this. She'd pushed and prodded, fought for him, taught him. She'd given him his life, up in the blue.

Mary turned into Wolf's arms. She was nude, and his big hand kept stroking down her pale body as if searching out signs of her as-yet-invisible pregnancy. She knew he was worried, but she felt wonderful and tried to reassure him. "I've never felt better. Face it, pregnancy agrees with me."

He chuckled and stroked her breasts, lifting each one in turn in his palm. They were fuller now, and more sensitive. He could almost bring her to satisfaction just with his mouth on her nipples.

"But this is the last one," he said.

"What if it's another boy? Wouldn't you like to try for a girl just once more?"

He groaned, because that was the argument she'd used to talk him into getting her pregnant this time. She was determined to have her four children.

"Let's make a deal. If this one is a girl, there won't be any more. If it's a boy, we'll have one more baby, but that's the limit, regardless of its sex."

"It's a deal," she agreed. She paused. "Have you thought that it's possible you could father a hundred children and they'd all be boys? You may not have any female sperm. Look at your track record, three boys in a row—"

He put his hand on her mouth. "No more. Four is the absolute limit."

She laughed at him and arched her slender body against him. His response was immediate, even after five years of marriage. Later, when he slept, Mary smiled into the darkness and stroked his strong back. This baby was a boy, too, she felt. But the next one—ah, the next one would be the daughter he craved. She was certain of it.

*   *   *   *   *

MACKENZIE'S MISSION

Leslie Wainger, my friend and editor for over a decade, through deaths, hotel fires, hurricanes, hotel fires, stuck elevators, hotel fires, missed deadlines, hotel fires…I think we set a record. We've gone through Sonny and McMurphy together, now we're on Joel and Maurice and Maggie and Ed, may they be exposed forever. So for all the good times, this Joe's for you.

Prologue

"Man must be trained for war, and woman for the relaxation of the warriors; all else is folly."
                                    —Friedrich Nietsche

"Hogwash."   —Linda Howard

He was a legend even before he graduated from the Academy, at least among his own classmates and the underclassmen. As first in his graduating class he had his pick of assignments, and to no one's surprise, he chose fighter jets. The politically savvy all knew that the fastest way to promotion in the Air Force was as an aviator, and fighter wings, with their inherent glamour, had always been the most visible. But those who knew Joe Mackenzie, newly commissioned officer in the United States Air Force, knew he didn't give a damn about promotion, only about flying.

His superiors had doubts about his suitability for fighters, but that was the training he had chosen, and they decided to give him the opportunity. He was six foot three, almost too tall for a fighter jockey. He'd be okay as a bomber pilot, but the dimensions of the cockpit in a fighter meant it would be a tight fit for him, and the physical demands of G forces were generally better met by men who were less than six feet tall, and of stockier build. Of course, there were exceptions to every rule, and the statistics for the physical build of the best fighter pilots were general profiles, not hard-and-fast rules. So Joe Mackenzie was given his chance at fighter training.

His training instructors found that, despite his height, he was better than competent: he was superb. He was that once-in-a-lifetime jet jockey, the one who set the standards for everyone who came after him. He was peculiarly suited, both physically and mentally, for the job he had chosen. His eyesight was better than twenty-twenty, his reflexes were phenomenal and his cardiovascular condition was so good that he was able to withstand greater G forces than his shorter fellow trainees. He remained at the top in his classes on physics and aerodynamics. He had a light touch with the controls and was willing to spend extra hours in the flight simulator perfecting his skills. Most of all, he had the unteachable quality of "situation awareness," the ability to be aware of everything going on around him in a fluid situation and adjust his actions accordingly. All aviators had to have it to some degree, but only in the best of them was it highly developed. He had an amazing degree of it. By the time Joe Mackenzie earned his wings, he was already known as a "hot stick," one of those with the magic touch.

As a very young captain in the first Gulf War, he downed three enemy aircraft in *one day,* an achievement that, to his relief, wasn't publicized. The reasons for it were political: to ensure better public relations with their allies, the United States Air Force was willing to let pilots from the other countries get the glory. Captain Mackenzie was more than willing to go along with policy. It had been mere chance, on the second day of the war, that had put him in the middle of the toughest resistance the enemy put up during the short length of the hostilities. He hadn't been impressed with the enemy pilots' skills. Nevertheless, for about three minutes it had been a real fur ball, when he and his wingman had been jumped by six enemy fighters.

The end result was an almost indecently fast promotion to Major, and Joe Mackenzie, tactical call sign "Breed," was recognized as the fastest of the fast trackers, a fast-burner on his way to a general's star.

During the second Gulf War, Major Mackenzie scored two more official kills in air-to-air combat and was designated an ace. This time there was no way to keep his achievements out of the media, not that the Pentagon wanted to; it recognized that it had a public-relations gold mine in the handsome half-breed

American Indian, who exemplified all of the qualities
they most wanted to project. He was given the choice
assignments and made lieutenant colonel at the age of
thirty-two. It was generally recognized that for Breed
Mackenzie, there was nowhere to go but up.

Chapter 1

She was the most beautiful bitch he'd ever seen, fast and sleek and deadly. Just looking at her made his heart beat faster. Even parked in the hangar, her engines cold and wheels chocked, she gave the impression of pure speed.

Colonel Joe Mackenzie reached out and touched the fuselage, his long fingers caressing her with the light touch of a lover. The dark metallic skin of her airframe had a slick feel to it that was different from every other fighter he'd flown, and the difference entranced him. He knew it was because her airframe was a revolutionary new composite of thermoplastics, graphite and industrial spider silk, which was far stronger and more flexible than steel, meaning she could withstand far greater force without breaking

apart than any aircraft ever before built. Intellectually
he knew that, but emotionally he felt that it was because she was so alive. She didn't feel quite like
metal; maybe it was the spider silk, but she wasn't as
cold to the touch as any other airplane.

Developmental programs were usually given code
names that didn't reflect the program's nature, which
was why the earlier SR-71 Blackbird had been code
named "Oxcart." This particular bird, a second-
generation advanced tactical fighter, bore the unusually descriptive code name of Night Wing, and when
it went into production it would receive some suitably
macho designation like the F-15 Eagle or the F-16
Fighting Falcon, but to Colonel Mackenzie she was
"Baby." There were actually five prototypes, and he
called them all Baby. The test pilots assigned to the
program under his command complained that she—
whichever "she" it was—always acted up with them
because he had spoiled her for other pilots. Colonel
Mackenzie had given them his legendary ice-blue
stare and replied, "That's what all my women say."
His face had remained perfectly expressionless, leaving his men uncertain if that was the truth or a joke.
They suspected it to be the truth.

Joe Mackenzie had flown a lot of hot planes, but
Baby was special, not just in her construction and
power, but her weapons system. She was truly revolutionary, and she was his; as program manager, it
was his responsibility to get the kinks worked out of
her so she could go into full production. That was
assuming Congress came through with the funding,

but General Ramey was confident that there wouldn't be any problem there. For one thing, the manufacturer had brought her in on budget, unlike the overrun fiasco that had killed the A-12 in the last decade.

For a long time stealth technology had detracted from a fighter plane's agility and power, until the advent of supercruise had alleviated some of the power problems. Baby was both stealthy and agile, with vectored thrust that let her turn tighter than any fighter had ever turned before, and at higher speeds. She supercruised at Mach 2, and broke Mach 3 in afterburner. And her weapons system used adjustable laser firing, ALF, a mild little acronym for what would someday revolutionize warfare. Mackenzie knew he was involved in the making of history. Lasers had been used for targeting for some time, the beam guiding missiles to the selected location, but for the first time lasers were being used as the weapons themselves. Scientists had finally solved the difficulty of a manageable energy source for X-ray lasers and teamed it with sophisticated optics. Sensors in the pilot's helmet allowed him to spot a missile, target or enemy plane *in any direction,* and the adjustable targeting system followed the direction of the sensors in the helmet. No matter how an enemy plane turned and juked it couldn't escape; a target would have to go faster than the speed of light to escape the laser beam, something not likely to happen.

Baby was so complex that only the best of the best had been assigned to this phase of her development, and the security surrounding her was so tight that an ant would have had a hard time getting into the hangar without proper clearance.

"Anything you need, sir?"

Joe turned, shifting his attention to Staff Sergeant Dennis Whiteside, known as "Whitey," who possessed fiery red hair, a multitude of freckles and a mechanical genius that bordered on miraculous where airplanes were concerned. Whitey considered Baby *his* plane and suffered the pilots touching her only because he couldn't figure out a way to prevent it.

"Just checking her over before I turn in," Joe replied. "Weren't you supposed to go off duty hours ago?"

Whitey took a rag from his back pocket and gently polished the spot where Joe's fingers had touched the plane. "There were some things I wanted to make sure were done right," he replied. "You're taking her up in the morning, aren't you, sir?"

"Yes."

Whitey grunted. "At least you don't jerk her around the way some of those guys do," he said grouchily.

"If you notice any of my guys treating any of the birds rough, let me know."

"Well, it ain't rough, exactly. It's just that they don't have your touch."

"All the same, I mean what I said."

"Yes, sir."

Joe clapped Whitey on the shoulder and headed for his quarters. The sergeant stared after him for a long minute. He had no doubt that the colonel would indeed make any pilot pray he would die and go to hell just to escape his wrath if any of them were caught being careless or stupid with any of the Night Wing prototypes. Colonel Mackenzie was notorious for accepting nothing less than perfection from his pilots, but at the same time they all knew that he valued his men's lives above all else, and maintenance on the birds had to be top-notch, which was why Whitey was still in the hangar long after he should have been off duty. Mackenzie demanded the best from everyone in this program, with no exceptions. A mistake in maintenance on the ground could lead to the loss of one of these eighty-million-dollar aircraft, or even the death of a pilot. It wasn't a job for anyone with a casual attitude.

As Joe walked through the desert night he saw a light on in one of the offices and turned his steps toward the metal building. He didn't object to people working late, but he wanted everyone to be awake and alert the next day, too. There were some workaholics assigned to the Night Wing project who would work eighteen hours a day if he didn't ride herd on them.

His steps were silent, not because he was trying to sneak up on anyone but because that was how he'd been taught to walk from the time he'd taken his first step. Not that anyone in the offices would have heard him approaching anyway; the air conditioners were humming, trying to offset the late July heat and never quite succeeding. The metal Quonset huts seemed to absorb the blistering sun.

The building was dark except for the light in a cubicle on the left. It was one of the offices used by the civilian laser-targeting team, working on-site to troubleshoot the glitches that inevitably showed up when a new system was put into operation. Joe remembered that a new technician had been scheduled to arrive that day, to replace one of the original team who had had a slight heart attack a week before. The guy who'd had the attack was doing okay, but his doctor didn't want him working in the hundred-degree-plus heat, so the company had flown in a replacement.

Joe was curious about the replacement, a woman named Caroline Evans. He'd heard the other three members of the team grousing about her, calling her "the Beauty Queen," and their tone hadn't been admiring. The team might be civilian, but he couldn't allow friction within the group to affect their work. If everyone couldn't get along, he would have to tell the laser-systems people to replace their replacement. He wanted to talk to whichever of the team was working late, find out if Ms. Evans had arrived without incident and exactly what the problem was that they didn't want to work with her.

He walked silently up to the open doorway and stood in it for a minute, watching. The woman in the office had to be the Beauty Queen herself, because she sure as hell wasn't anyone he'd ever met before. He would have remembered if he had.

It wasn't any hardship to watch her, that was for certain. His erect posture slowly stiffened as every muscle in his body surged to alert status. He'd been tired, but suddenly adrenaline was humming through his system and all of his senses became acute, just the way they did when he kicked in the afterburners and went ballistic.

She wore a straight red skirt that ended well above her knees. Her shoes were off, and she was leaning back in her chair, her bare feet propped on the desk. Joe leaned his shoulder against the door frame, leisurely surveying the smooth, curved legs that had been exposed. No stockings; the heat made them impractical. Nice legs. Better than nice. Verging on stupendous.

A sheaf of computer printouts were on her lap, and she was checking each item, referring occasionally to a textbook beside her. A cup of pale green tea was gently steaming within easy reach of her often blindly reaching hand. Her hair was a pale, bell-shaped curve, combed straight back from her face in the classic style and just long enough to bounce on her shoulders. He could see only part of her face, enough to note her high cheekbones and full lips.

Suddenly he wanted her to face him. He wanted to see her eyes, hear her voice.

''Time to shut it down for the night,'' he said.

She shot up from the chair with a stifled shriek, tea spilling in one direction and the computer printout in another, long legs flying as she brought them down to the floor, the chair sent spinning across the room to crash into the filing cabinets. She whirled to face him, one hand pressed to her breast as if she could physically calm her heartbeat. A very shapely breast, he noticed, for her hand had pulled the fabric of her cotton blouse tight across her flesh.

Anger flashed like lightning across her face, then was just as suddenly gone as her eyes widened. "Oh my God," she said in a hushed tone. "It's G.I. Joe."

He caught the subtle undertone of sarcasm, and his black eyebrows lifted. "*Colonel* G.I. Joe."

"So I see," she said admiringly. "A full bird colonel. And a ring-knocker," she added, pointing to his academy ring and using the less than complimentary term for an academy graduate. "Either you mugged a colonel and stole his insignia, had a fantastic face-lift and dyed your hair black, or you have a sponsor with some heavy-duty juice who's rushing you through the grades."

He kept his expression bland. "Maybe I'm damn good at what I do."

"Promotion on merit?" she asked, as if it were a concept so impossible it was beyond consideration. "Naahh."

He was accustomed to women reacting to him in varying ways, ranging from fascination to a certain intimidation that bordered on fear, always based on a very physical awareness of him. He was also used to commanding respect, if not liking. None of that was in Caroline Evans' expression. She hadn't taken her eyes off him for a second, her gaze as steady and piercing as a gunslinger's. Yeah, that was it; she was facing him like an adversary.

He straightened away from the door frame and held out his hand, abruptly deciding to put the situation on a professional standing and let her know who she was dealing with. "Colonel Joe Mackenzie, project manager." Service protocol stated that shaking hands was a woman's choice, that a male officer should never extend his hand to a woman first, but he wanted to feel her hand in his and sensed that if he gave her the option, even that touch wouldn't be allowed.

She didn't hesitate but firmly clasped his hand. "Caroline Evans, replacement for Boyce Walton on the laser team." Two quick up and down pumps, then she withdrew her hand.

Since she was barefoot, he could accurately estimate her height as around five-four; the top of her head was even with his collarbone. The difference in their sizes didn't intimidate her, even though she had to look up to meet his gaze. Her eyes were a dark green, he saw, framed by dark lashes and brows that suggested the gold of her hair was chemically achieved.

He nodded toward the printout on the floor. "Why are you working so late, especially on your first day on the job? Is anything wrong that I need to know about?"

"Not that I know of," she replied, stooping down to pick up the accordion of paper. "I was just double-checking some items."

"Why? What made you think of it?"

She gave him an impatient look. "I'm a chronic double-checker. I always double-check that the oven is off, the iron unplugged, the door locked. I look both ways *twice* before I cross a road."

"You haven't found anything wrong?"

"No, of course not. I've already said so."

He relaxed once he was assured that nothing was wrong with the targeting system and resumed his leisurely and enjoyable survey of Caroline Evans as she took a roll of paper towels from a desk drawer and used a couple of sheets to blot up the spilled tea. She bent and twisted with a fluid ease that struck him as sexy. Everything she had done so far, even the barely veiled challenge of her gaze, had struck him as sexy. His loins tightened in response.

She tossed the wet paper towels in the trash and slipped her feet into her shoes. "Nice meeting you, Colonel," she said without looking at him. "See you tomorrow."

"I'll walk you to your quarters."

"No thanks."

The immediate, casual dismissal of his offer irritated him. "It's late, and you're alone. I'm walking you to your quarters."

She did look at him then, turning to face him and putting her hands on her hips. "I appreciate the offer, Colonel, but I don't need those kinds of favors."

"*Those kinds* of favors? What kind are we talking about?"

"The kind that do more harm than good. Look, you're the head honcho. If anyone sees you walking me to my quarters, within two days I'll be hearing snide comments about how I wouldn't be on the team if I wasn't playing footsie with you. It's a hassle I can do without."

"Ah," he said as understanding dawned. "You've run into this before, haven't you? No one thinks you can look like that and have a brain, too."

She stared at him belligerently. "What do you mean, 'look like that'? Just how do I look?"

She had the temperament of a hedgehog, but Joe had to fight the urge to put his arms around her and tell her that he would fight her battles for her from now on. She wouldn't appreciate the gesture, and he wasn't certain why he wanted to make it, since she appeared more than capable of waging her own wars. If he were smart, he would play it safe, make some noncommittal comment to keep from treading on her toes any further, but he hadn't become a fighter pilot because he wanted to play it safe. "Fetching," he replied, and his eyes were hard and bright and hungry.

She blinked, as if startled. She took a step back and said, "Oh," in a soft, befuddled tone.

"You have to know you're attractive," he pointed out.

She blinked again. "Looks shouldn't enter into it. You look like a walking recruiting poster, but it hasn't hurt your career, has it?"

"I'm not defending discrimination," he said. "You asked the question, and I answered it. You look fetching."

"Oh." She was watching him warily now as she sidled past.

He put his hand on her arm, stopping her. The feel of her smooth, warm flesh under his palm tempted him to explore, but he resisted. "If anyone here hassles you, Caroline, come to me."

She darted an alarmed look at his hand on her arm. "Uh—yeah, sure."

"Even if it's a member of your own team. You're civilians, but this is my project. I can have anyone replaced if he causes trouble."

His touch was making her visibly jittery, and he studied her for a long minute, his brows drawing together in a slight frown, before he let her go. "I mean it," he said in a gentler tone. "Come to me if you have any trouble. I know you don't want me to walk you to your quarters, but I'm going in that direction anyway, since I'm turning in, too. I'll give you a thirty-second head start, so we won't be walking together. Is that okay?"

"Thirty seconds isn't very long."

He shrugged. "It'll put about thirty yards between us. Take it or leave it." He checked his watch. "Starting now."

She immediately turned and fled. That was the only word for it. She all but hiked up that tight skirt and ran. Joe's eyebrows climbed in silent question. When the thirty seconds were up, he left the building and caught sight of her slim figure, barely visible in the darkness and still moving at a fast clip. All the way to his own quarters, he pondered on what had turned an Amazon into a skittish filly.

Caroline slammed and locked the door to her Spartan quarters and leaned against the wood as she re-

leased her breath in a big whoosh. She felt as if she'd
just had a narrow escape from a wild animal. What
was the Air Force thinking, letting that man run
loose? He should be locked up somewhere in the
bowels of the Pentagon, where they could use him for
their posters but keep the susceptible women of
America safe.

Maybe it was his eyes, as pale blue and piercing
as the lasers she worked on. Maybe it was the way
he towered over her, or the graceful power of his muscular body. Maybe it was his deep voice, the particular note in it when he said she was "fetching," or
the heat of his lean, callused hand when he'd touched
her. Maybe it was all of that, but what had all but
panicked her had been the hungry, predatory gleam
in those eyes when he'd looked at her.

She'd been doing well up until then. She had definitely been at her off-putting best, both arrogant and
dismissive, which had never before failed to keep men
at a safe distance. It was a trade-off; it kept her from
being friends with her co-workers, but it also stopped
any sexual advances before they started. She had bat-
tled her way out of so many clinches during college
and graduate school and her early days on the job,
that she had learned to go on the offensive from the
beginning. With all of that experience, she should
have been able to keep her composure, but one look
from Colonel "Laser-Eye" Mackenzie, one slightly
admiring comment, and she had lost both her composure and her common sense. She had been ignominiously routed.

Well, that was what happened when you had Ph.D.s for parents. They had seen the signs of superior intelligence in their only offspring and taken immediate steps to give her the schooling she deserved. All through elementary and high school she had been the youngest in her class, due to her accelerated progress. She hadn't had one date in high school; she had been too weird, too gangly and awkward as she went through puberty two or three years after her classmates. It hadn't been any better in college. She had started her freshman year right after her sixteenth birthday, and what college man in his right mind would go out with a girl who was legally still jailbait, when there were so many legal lovelies both willing and available?

Isolated and lonely, Caroline had devoted herself to her studies and found herself finishing her senior courses during her eighteenth year. At about the same time the guys in her classes had realized that the Evans girl might be an egghead, but she was easy on the eyes. This time, there was no issue of age to protect her. Having never learned dating skills with anyone her own age, she was totally at a loss on how to handle these…these *octopuses* who suddenly couldn't seem to keep their hands off her. Disconcerted, alarmed, she had withdrawn further into her studies and begun developing a prickly shield for protection.

Her transformation as she reached maturity wasn't drastic enough to equal that of an ugly duckling into a swan; she had simply grown from a gangly adolescent into a woman. Her menses had been late in coming, as if her body had to balance nature by dawdling along while her mind raced ahead. It was all a matter of bad timing. When her classmates were going through puberty, she was still literally playing with dolls. When she went through puberty, they were already settled into the dating game. She never matched them in terms of physical or emotional maturity. When she was ready to begin dating, she found herself being groped by boys accustomed to a much more sophisticated level of intimacy.

In the end, it was just easier to drive them all away.

So here she was, twenty-eight years old, genius IQ, a bona fide specialist in light amplification and optic targeting, possessed of a Ph.D. in physics, reduced to idiocy and panic because a man had said she was "fetching."

It was disgusting.

It was also a bit frightening, because she sensed Colonel Mackenzie hadn't been alienated as she had intended; instead, he'd looked like a man who enjoyed a challenge.

She hit herself on the forehead. How could she have been such an idiot? The colonel was a *jet jockey,* for heaven's sake. He was a member of a different breed, a man who positively thrived on challenge. The way to keep from attracting his attention was to appear meek and mild, with maybe a little simpering thrown in. Problem was, she didn't know how to simper. She should have gone to a finishing school rather than graduate school. She would have taken Simpering 101 over and over until she had it nailed.

Maybe it wasn't too late. Maybe she could act sweet and helpless enough to fool him. No—that would invite attention from the men who *did* like that sort of behavior in a woman. She was caught— damned if she did and damned if she didn't.

The only thing left to do was put up a good fight.

When Joe reached his quarters he stripped out of his uniform, then stood under a cool shower until he began to feel human again. The desert in July was a real bitch, sucking the moisture from his body until even his eyeballs felt dry, but Baby required tight se- curity, and Nellis Air Force Base in Nevada supplied that, in spades. Despite the discomfort and spartan conditions, he was grateful for the security and didn't look forward to taking the wraps off Baby, as would happen when Congress voted on funding. The media would see her then, not that her revolutionary nature was evident in her appearance; her design wasn't rad- ically different from that of the F-22, which was what made it possible for them to do the test flights at Nel- lis instead of Edwards in California, where test flights were traditionally made. Snoops looked for something different at Edwards, but here at Nellis, with so many different types of aircraft taking part in the war games they conducted, she wasn't so obvious.

The other pilots based here had to notice that they were doing test flights with an aircraft that wasn't exactly like the F-22, but no one who wasn't working on the program was allowed a close look at the Night Wing prototypes, and security was a way of life here anyway. Baby's differences were in her skin and in the electronics suite, her weapons system; when she was unveiled, she would galvanize every hostile espionage agency in the world, and security would have to be even tighter, though he didn't see how it could.

He'd been thinking of Baby, but suddenly the image of Caroline Evans filled his mind and he grinned, wondering what it would take to tame the little hedgehog. His skin suddenly felt hot and tight, despite the cool water, so he shut off the shower and stepped out of the cubicle. It he could get her in the shower with him, they would probably turn the water to steam.

He stood in front of the air conditioner, letting the cold air blow over his wet, naked body and enjoying the shivers that rippled over him, but it didn't do much to ease the sense of fullness in his loins. Grimly he pushed thoughts of Ms. Evans out of his mind. When he was dry enough not to drip, he went, still naked, into the tiny kitchen area and slapped a sandwich together. The freedom from clothes let something inside him relax. He had spent almost half his life in the military, surrounded by regulations and wearing uniforms, and he felt comfortable with it at home, but at the same time there was still a primitive part of him that sometimes said, ''That's enough,'' and he had to strip.

He had grown up on a horse ranch in Wyoming and he returned there every chance he got; spending a week or two riding the roughest broncs on the ranch satisfied the same wild restlessness in him, but he was tied up with the Night Wing project and couldn't get any free time, so the clothes had to go. The only garment he ever regretted having to remove was his flightsuit; if he could just spend all his time in the air, he'd be all right.

Damn it, the higher he was promoted, the less he flew. Responsibilities and paperwork took up more and more of his time. He had accepted the position of project manager on Night Wing only because he'd been guaranteed he would be able to fly the babies. The Air Force had wanted its best in the cockpits of the new planes, and the pilots assigned were all top-notch, but more than that, it had wanted the hands-on opinion of the best of the best, and Colonel Joe Mackenzie still stood head and shoulders above all the others.

Joe wasn't vain about his skill with a fighter, because he'd worked too damn hard to attain it. He'd been born with the intellect, eyesight and lightning-fast reflexes, but the rest was the result of countless hours of study, of practice, of drilling himself in the flight simulator until every reaction was automatic and instantaneous. Even at the age of thirty-five his reaction time was still faster than that of the young Turks coming out of flight school, and his eyesight was still better than twenty-twenty. He had a lot of flying time left, if the military would let him have it. He'd shot up through the ranks so fast that he would probably get his first star in another year, and then he'd be lucky if he could wrangle enough flying time to remain qualified.

The alternative was to resign his commission to

take a job with an aircraft manufacturer as a test pilot, throwing away his years in the military. He liked the Air Force, didn't want to leave it, but the idea of being grounded was unbearable. Life would be flat without the challenge of mastering both nature and machine, and knowing his life hung in the balance if he didn't do it right.

Caroline slid into his mind again, a challenge of a different sort plain in her gunslinger's eyes. He could plainly picture the color of those eyes, dark green mostly, mingled with a bit of blue, and gold flecks lighting the depths. The thought of those eyes looking up at him as he moved over her in bed made his heart begin pounding hard and fast, just the way he would take her.

He wanted to make the little hedgehog purr like a kitten.

Chapter 2

Caroline had stringent comfort requirements, which meant it sometimes took her a while to get dressed. If something didn't feel right on a particular day, she took it off and put on something else. Before she left for work each morning she sat, stretched, twisted, moved her arms back and forth, then lifted them over her head to see if her clothes were going to irritate her during the day. She couldn't bear being distracted by an uncomfortable seam or an aggravating fit.

Women's fashions were a sore point with her. Why were most designers men? She thought it should be against the law for a man to design women's clothes. She had decided while still in adolescence that men had no idea how uncomfortable women's fashions usually were and really didn't care, since they themselves weren't called upon to spend hours standing in tendon-shortening high heels, encased in sweltering hosiery, bound either by bras or dresses tight enough to take over the job of lifting and separating, or pushing together to create cleavage, according to the dictates of the occasion.

And why were women's fashions made out of flimsy material, while the temperatures in most offices and restaurants was always set low, so the men in their suits would be comfortable? She found this stupid on two counts: one, why were men required to wear jackets anyway—and was there anything more ridiculous than that remnant of the breastplate, the necktie, that they knotted around their throats like a hangman's noose, interfering with a few basic things like breathing and swallowing—and why weren't women allowed to wear coats, too, if the men felt unable to give theirs up? Fashion, in her mind, consisted of equal parts stupidity and lunacy. In a logical world, people would wear functional clothing, like jeans and loafers and sweatshirts.

She couldn't change the world, but she could control her own small part of it by insisting on her own comfort. Today she chose a full, gathered white skirt that came to midcalf, with an elastic waistband. She topped it with an oversize white T-shirt and twisted two scarves, one melon and one aqua, together to be tied around her waist as a belt. Her shoes were white flats. She was cool, coordinated and comfortable, just the way she wanted to be.

During the night she had tried to analyze just what

it was about Colonel Mackenzie that had so discomfited her; other men had come on to her like gangbusters and she'd managed to handle it, so why had his rather mild remark, coupled with a look that wasn't mild at all, sent her into such panic? It was definitely the look that had done it. She'd never seen eyes like those before, pale blue diamonds glittering in a bronzed face, so piercing it felt as if they were cutting right into her flesh, and she'd sensed that the man behind them wasn't like any man she'd met before, either.

There were several possible reasons, but none that she could pin down as the primary cause of her reaction. She would just have to handle herself as well as possible, keep her guard up and try to make certain there were always other people around whenever she had dealings with the colonel. Why couldn't he have come around earlier the day before, when the rest of the team had still been working? If he had, she would have slept better last night.

She glanced around, making certain that everything was switched off, then patted her skirt pockets to assure herself that her keys were in there. Pockets were required; every outfit she wore had to have pockets, because handbags were another of her pet peeves. Why were women condemned to lug them around their entire lives? Why couldn't women have pockets like men? Because fashion said that it ruined the ''lines'' of their clothes. Because women were thought to be too vain. Because men were continually handing items to women with a casual, ''Put this in your purse,'' meaning, ''So you can carry it and I won't have to.'' For women to be truly liberated, she thought, they should have burned their purses instead of their brassieres. And then thrown their high-heeled shoes onto the bonfire.

To keep from having to carry a bag, she had stocked her desk the day before with the grooming items she was likely to need during any given day. After all, not liking purses was no reason to go without lipstick. She did have personal standards to uphold.

She was normally the first person at work, and that morning was no exception. She liked mornings, and dawn in the desert was something special, with everything so clear and crisply outlined. Later in the day heat waves would blur the edges of the landscape, but right now it was perfect. She hummed as she made coffee. No matter how hot it got, coffee was a necessity in every workplace she'd ever seen.

She tore the wrapper off a honey bun, slapped the pastry into the microwave and zapped it for ten seconds. Breakfast was now ready. She settled into her chair and began rereading a report on the targeting system's last performance as she absently pinched bites from the pastry.

Thirty minutes later Cal Gilchrist came in, looking surprised when he saw her at her desk. ''You're in early,'' he said as he went straight to the coffeepot. ''I didn't see you at chow.''

''I ate a honey bun here.'' Having finished reading, she tossed the report aside. Of the other three members of the team, Cal was the most amiable. To be honest, she admitted, he was more amiable than even herself. He was good-natured, friendly and capable, maybe thirty years old, still single and he enjoyed an active social life. She had met him before, but this was the first time they'd worked on a project together. They actually worked for two different companies, she with Boling-Wahl Optics, which had developed the laser targeting system, and Cal with DataTech, which had teamed with Boling-Wahl on the computer program that ran the system.

"There's another test at 0800," Cal said as he sipped his coffee. "When Adrian and Yates get here, we'll all go to the control room so we can listen in on the flights. Colonel Mackenzie's going up today. He always comes back to the control room after a flight, and I'll introduce you to him."

"We've already met," she replied. "He came by last night before I quit for the day."

"What did you think of him?"

She thought for a moment, trying to come up with a concise answer, and finally settled on "Scary."

Cal laughed. "Yeah, I wouldn't want to cross him. I would have sworn that fighter pilots didn't respect anything, but they sure as hell respect him, in the air and on the ground. One of them said that Mackenzie is the best pilot in the Air Force, period. That's saying a lot, considering none of this group are slouches."

The other two members of the team arrived. Yates Korleski, a short, sturdy, balding man, was the senior member and head of the team. Adrian Pendley was

Caroline's fly in the ointment on this particular assignment. He was tall and good-looking, divorced, and unrelentingly negative about having Caroline on the team. When she had first gone to work for Boling-Wahl he had given her the rush, and he'd never forgiven her for the brush-off she had given him in return. He was good at his job, though, so she was determined to work with him, even if it meant ignoring his incessant little gibes.

He walked past her without speaking, but Yates paused beside her desk. "Did you get settled in okay?"

"Yes, thanks. Met the head honcho last night, too."

Yates grinned. "What did you think of him?"

"Like I told Cal, he's a bit scary."

"Just don't ever make a mistake, or you'll find out *how* scary."

"No allowing for human error, huh?"

"Not with his birds or his men."

Yates wandered off in the direction of the coffee-pot, and Caroline decided that maybe her panic of the night before had been justified. Yates had been working on defense contracts for twenty years, so if he was impressed, the colonel wasn't any ordinary joe. She grimaced at the inadvertent mental play on words.

At the appointed time they all trooped to the airfield, where the flights were being monitored. Their IDs were checked before they were allowed to enter the control room, reminding her of the tight security. The place swarmed with guards, and she knew that the Night Wing project was only one of several going on. There were a lot of civilians working at Nellis, people with both the highest credentials and the highest security rating. Just being here meant that her background had been checked so thoroughly that her file probably even contained the brand of breakfast cereal she'd liked best as a child.

The control room was a busy place, lined with monitors and people manning them. Practically every part of the Night Wing aircraft incorporated some radical change from how aircraft had been designed in the past, so there were a lot of different companies and defense contractors working to make certain everything was operational. A group of pilots had gathered, too, some in flightsuits and some in regular service uniforms. Several whistles filled the air when they caught sight of Caroline, and one grinning pilot clasped his hands over his heart.

"I'm in love," he announced to the group at large.

"Don't pay any attention to him, ma'am," another of the pilots said. "That's the third time this week, and it's only Tuesday. He's fickle, very fickle."

"But good-looking," the first pilot said in defense of himself. "So what about it, beautiful? Want to get married, live in a rose-covered cottage and have beautiful children?"

"I'm allergic to roses," she said.

"And men," Adrian muttered behind her, just loud enough for her to hear. She ignored him.

"Forget the roses," the pilot said grandly. The tag on his shirt said his name was Major Austin Deale.

"I'm adaptable. And fun. Did I mention that we'll have lots of fun?"

A deep voice came over the speaker, and as if a switch had been thrown, the pilots stopped their bantering and turned toward the monitor. It took Caroline a moment to realize that it was an in-cockpit camera, letting them see what the pilot was doing and seeing.

"There are four planes up today," Lieutenant Colonel Eric Picollo said, setting up the situation for them. "Two Night Wings and two F-22s. The F-22 is the only thing in production fast enough to give the prototypes a good test. The Night Wings are doing some stress maneuvers, and then they'll test the targeting system."

The deep voice came from the speakers again, laconic and matter-of-fact, as if the man weren't screaming along faster than the speed of sound high above the desert floor. Caroline shivered, and goose bumps rose on her arms.

"Go to MIL."

"Going to MIL," another voice answered.

"Military power throttle setting," Cal, who was standing just to her right, whispered. "All or more of an engine's rated thrust."

She nodded her understanding, her attention fixed on the monitor. All she could see of Colonel Mackenzie was his gloved hands and long legs, with the throttle between them, but she knew it was him she was watching rather than the other Night Wing pilot. There was just something about the way he moved.

The pilots took the aircraft through a series of maneuvers, and the sensors embedded in the aircraft's skin sent back readings of the stress levels on the airframe.

"Twenty degrees alpha," the deep voice said, confirming what the digital readout on the computer screen was telling them. "Thirty…forty…fifty… sixty."

One of the pilots standing behind her muttered, "Damn," in a nervous tone.

"Alpha is angle of attack," Major Deale whispered, noticing Caroline's puzzled look. His own expression was tense. "Most high-performance aircraft can only do about twenty degrees before they stall out. We've taken Baby to fifty degrees, because her vectored thrust gives better control, but even the X-29 wasn't controllable above seventy degrees."

"Seventy," said the calm voice. "Seventy-five."

The major had turned pale. He was staring at the changing numbers on the computer screen as if he could control them by willpower alone.

"Seventy-seven…seventy-nine…eighty…controls feel a little spongy. That's enough for now, leveling out."

"How'd Mad Cat do?" someone asked.

"Sixty-five," another someone replied, and the group chuckled.

"Was that his alpha, or his pucker factor?"

"I was sweating at fifty."

"We'll have to haul Mad Cat out of the cockpit. He won't have any starch left in his legs at all."

''Bet Breed's heart rate didn't even go up. He bleeds ice water, man, pure ice water.''

Next, the aircraft pulled both negative and positive Gs, provoking more comments as the speakers carried the sounds of the grunts the pilots made to force more oxygen into their brains and keep from blacking out. A trained pilot could normally withstand up to six positive Gs before gray-out began, but with specialized breathing techniques tolerance could be raised to about nine Gs for short periods of time.

The colonel was pulling ten Gs.

''Level out, level out,'' a captain said under his breath.

Major Deale was sweating. ''Don't do this to me,'' he muttered. ''Come on, Breed. Don't push it any further.''

''Levelling out,'' a calm voice said over the radio, and she heard the quiet release of air from several pairs of lungs.

''That son of a bitch is a genetic freak,'' the captain said, shaking his head. ''*Nobody* is supposed to be able to tolerate that. How long?''

''Not long,'' the second lieutenant at the monitor replied. ''He actually hit ten for about four-tenths of a second. He's done it before.''

''I can only tolerate nine for that long. And he was making sense when he talked! I'm telling you, he's a genetic freak.''

''Gawdamighty, think what he must've been like ten years ago.''

''About the same as now,'' Major Deale said.

The next series of tests involved the laser targeting, and Caroline edged her way closer to the monitors. She felt oddly shaky inside, and she tried to gather her thoughts. When she had been chosen to replace Walton on the test site, she had done some quick research on jet aircraft, and that, coupled with her general technical knowledge, told her exactly how dangerous those maneuvers had been. He could have lost control of the aircraft at such extreme angles of attack, or he could have blacked out pulling so many Gs and not regained consciousness in time to keep from drilling the aircraft nose-first into the desert floor. The reactions of the other pilots told their own tale.

Adrian slipped in front of her, effectively blocking her view, since he was so much taller. Caroline brought her mind back to the current situation. She had no doubt he had done it deliberately, and if she let him get away with it he would only do something worse the next time. "Excuse me, Adrian," she said politely. "Since you're so tall, let me stand in front of you so we both can see."

Yates looked up and smiled, either not seeing or choosing to ignore the sour expression on Adrian's face. "Good idea. Step up in front, Caroline."

The targeting test went well. They were currently sighting in on stationary targets, and all of the components performed within the acceptable range. The data streamed across the screen, each item swiftly checked and noted against the hard-copy lists they all carried.

The four aircraft landed safely, and the atmosphere

in the control room suddenly lightened to an almost giddy buzz. The laser team stood around Lieutenant Colonel Picollo and went over the rest results with him. Caroline was initially surprised at his knowledge of the subject, then realized that she shouldn't be. After all, he and the other pilots had been working on this project for some time; they would have had to be brain-dead not to absorb some of the information. "The colonel may have more questions," he finally said, "but it looks like we can start testing how well it targets and tracks a moving object now."

An arm slipped around her waist, and Caroline went rigid. Her head whipped around. Major Deale grinned at her as his arm tightened. Behind him, she could see the other pilots watching and grinning, too. They all looked like posters for a dental convention. Dismay filled her. Damn, it was starting already.

"So, beautiful, where do you want to go for dinner tonight?" the major asked.

"Hands off, Daffy," came a deceptively mild voice behind them. "Dr. Evans will be with me tonight."

There was no mistaking the speaker's identity. Even if she hadn't recognized those smooth, deep tones, she would have known by the way her heart began pulsing wildly and her lungs suddenly constricted, making it difficult to breathe.

They all turned around at once. Mackenzie was still in his flightsuit, helmet under his arm. His black hair was drenched with sweat and plastered to his skull, and his eyes were bloodshot from pulling Gs. His expression was calm and remote as he looked at them.

"I saw her first," Major Deale protested, but he dropped his arm from around her waist. "Damn it, Breed, you can't just take one look and decide—"

"Yes I can," Mackenzie said, then turned to Picollo and began firing questions at him.

The major turned and gave Caroline a slow, considering look, as if he were really seeing her for the first time, and maybe he was. Until then she had been just a reasonably pretty face, a lark, but now he had to look at her as a person. "I've never seen Breed do that before, and I've known him for fifteen years," he said thoughtfully.

"I don't know him at all," Caroline replied in a tart voice. "I mean, I met him last night. Is he always that autocratic?"

"Breed? Autocratic?" The major pursed his lips.

"Despotic," Caroline elaborated helpfully. "Dictatorial. Peremptory."

"Oh, *that* kind of autocratic. You mean, does he make a habit of commandeering a woman's company for dinner?"

"That narrows it down nicely."

"Nope. First time. He usually has to beat women off with a stick. They love him to death. It's the glamour of his profession, you know, the lure of the wild. Women *looove* uniforms, but underneath he's really dull and boring."

"Daffy…" The calm voice was both patient and warning.

The major looked over Caroline's shoulder and broke into a smile. "I was just singing your praises."

"I heard."

Mackenzie was right at her elbow, but she didn't dare glance at him. She had specifically asked him the night before not to single her out in any way, but the very next time she met him he had all but hung a sign around her neck that said "Mackenzie's Woman." She struggled to subdue the impulse to sink her fist into his belly. For one thing, violence was seldom the answer to anything. For another, he was the project manager, and it would be a very stupid career move. For yet another, he looked like he was made of tempered steel and it would probably break her hand.

So she did the prudent thing and concentrated on Major Deale. "Daffy? As in duck?"

"No," Mackenzie said with grim relish. "As in petunia."

"As in flower child," added the captain, who had been in the group watching the monitors.

"As in...*blooming idiot,*" several others said in unison.

"Petunia," Caroline repeated. "Flowers. Daffy Deale. Daffydeale. *Daffodil!*" she finished with a peal of laughter.

The major gave Mackenzie a dirty look. "I used to have a good, macho nickname. Concise. Thought provoking. Provocative. 'Big.' That's a good nickname, isn't it? Big Deale. It made women think. Was it just a play on my name, or was there a deeper meaning there? Then this...this spoilsport started calling me Daffy, and Petunia, and I got stuck with it."

Mackenzie smiled. Caroline glimpsed it from the

corner of her eye, and the reaction she had been trying
to ignore was back in full force. She felt simultaneously hot and cold. Shivers ran up her back, but her
skin felt flushed.

"Could you see me in my office in half an hour,
Dr. Evans?" the colonel asked now. She hated the
way he phrased something as a question when the
underlying tone made it an order.

She turned and smiled brightly at him. "If you insist, Colonel."

His eyes gleamed with recognition of the way she
had forced him to make it an outright order, but he
didn't hesitate. "I do."

"Half an hour, then."

As she and the others walked back to their own
offices, Adrian paused beside her. "Smart move," he
said, his hostility plain. "Snuggle up to the head man
and it doesn't matter if you screw up on the job."

She kept her eyes straight ahead. "I don't screw up
on the job." There wasn't any point in denying that
she had any sort of relationship with Mackenzie, so
she didn't waste the effort.

Cal glanced back, saw Adrian walking beside her,
and slowed his steps to allow them to come even with
him. "The complicated stuff starts with the moving
targets, but so far there haven't been many problems
with the program. It's almost scary how well the tests
have gone."

Adrian walked on ahead without speaking, and Cal
whistled softly through his teeth. "He's not the president of your fan club, is he? When we heard you

were going to be the replacement he made some snide remarks, but I didn't figure it was open warfare. What's the deal?''

''Personality conflict,'' Caroline replied. Trying to place the blame was another pointless exercise.

He looked worried. ''We have to function well as a team, or Colonel Mackenzie will have us all replaced, and that won't look good on our records. They're under a deadline with these tests. They want something good to show Congress and the media when the vote for funding comes up, and that's in a few weeks, I think.''

''I can ignore Adrian,'' she assured him.

''I hope so. I'll try to be a buffer when I can, but at some point the two of you will have to work together.''

''When it comes to work, I think both of us are professional enough to put our differences aside. But thanks for the thought.''

Cal nodded, then grinned at her. ''So, the good colonel's interested. He made it pretty plain, didn't he?''

''Without reason,'' she said grimly.

''Maybe from your way of thinking, but not from his.''

It was foolish of her, but she began to look forward to meeting Colonel Mackenzie in the privacy of his office. Project manager be damned, she was going to tell him a few things. At the appointed time, she got directions to the appropriate Quonset hut and marched across the tarmac with anger propelling every stride.

The outer desk was occupied by Sergeant Vrska, a burly young man who looked better suited to a pro-football team than a desk, but he greeted Caroline pleasantly and ushered her into the colonel's private office.

Mackenzie had showered and changed into his summer service uniform; the blue of the material only intensified the pale blue of his irises. He leaned back in his chair and watched her calmly, as if waiting for her explosion.

Caroline considered exploding, even though he was obviously expecting it. For one thing, it would release a great deal of tension. Losing her temper, however, would only give the advantage to him. There was no invitation to take a seat, but she did so anyway, then crossed her legs and leaned back, her manner making it plain that the opening gambit was his.

"I read your file," he said. "Impressive credentials. You were always ahead of your age group in school, began college at sixteen, B.S. degree at eighteen, master's at nineteen, got your doctorate at twenty-one. Boling-Wahl considers you one of the most brilliant physicists in the country, if not the world."

She didn't know what she had expected, but a listing of her accomplishments wasn't it. She gave him a wary look.

"You've never dated," he continued. Alarm shot through her, and she sat up straight, her thoughts darting around as she tried to anticipate where he was going with that line. "Not in high school, which is halfway understandable, considering your age and study load, but not in college or graduate school, either. You've never had a boyfriend, period. In short, Dr. Evans, you don't have any experience at all in handling a rowdy bunch like my men. It upset you when Major Deale put his arm around your waist."

She didn't speak, but continued to watch him.

"We all have to work together, because we have a lot to do and not much time left to do it in. I don't want morale wrecked by hostility, and I don't want you to suffer behavior from my men that makes you uncomfortable. They're men, and they live their lives flying on the edge of disaster. They're wild and arrogant, and they need to blow off steam, typically with booze and women and dumb stunts. One way to keep them from hitting on you is to turn this base into a war zone, with everybody disliking you and not cooperating with you, which won't get the work done. The other way is to let them think you're mine."

She didn't like his phrasing. "That's so Neanderthal, it has hair all over it."

"They won't bother you then," he continued, ignoring her comment. "In fact, they'll be downright protective."

She stood up and began pacing his office. "I just want to be left alone so I can work. Is that such a big thing to ask? Why should I have to hide behind a false relationship?"

"For one thing, they all assume that you've had the normal experiences of a woman your age."

She scowled at him, not liking the way he'd

phrased the sentence. Her "age" indeed! He'd made
it sound as if she were almost ready to file for Social
Security.

"It won't occur to them that their actions could
actually be frightening to you," he continued.
"There's also the possibility that some of their teasing
won't be so lighthearted, that a couple of them might
make some serious moves on you and could turn ugly
when you slap them down. I can't afford the disrup-
tion to the program if I had to bring disciplinary
charges against any of my men. I need them, and I
need you. Even if they knew you're so inexperienced,
it wouldn't keep them from trying to get in your
pants. If anything, knowing that you're a virgin would
make it worse. The best thing is to mark you out of
bounds for them by pretending you're involved with
someone else, and the only man on the base they
wouldn't consider poaching on is me. So from now
on, as far as they're concerned, you're mine. All you
have to do is act halfway friendly to me in front of
them, rather than glaring at me as if you'd like to have
my head on a platter."

"With an apple stuffed in your mouth," she muttered. Then the details of what he'd just said hit her
and she stared at him in mortification, her eyes widening and color burning in her cheeks. Damn it, why
hadn't she hooted with laughter when he'd talked
about her being a virgin? Now it was too late to deny
it.

Joe was still watching her with that calm, remote

expression, but his eyes were narrowed and strangely intense.

She couldn't meet that penetrating gaze. Her embarrassment was almost unbearable. She summoned her last dregs of composure and said, "All right." Then, for the second time in less than twenty-four hours, she succumbed to the powerful urge to run from him.

Chapter 3

For several minutes after she had literally run from his office, Joe remained leaning back in his chair, his hands clasped behind his head and a small, satisfied smile curving the corners of his firm mouth.

So she was a virgin. He had only been guessing, but it had been a good guess. An experienced woman wouldn't have been so embarrassed or at such total loss about what to say or do. Poor little darling. For all her intelligence, she was a babe in the woods when it came to men and sex, and the reaction she had learned in her youth, when some idiot had probably scared the hell out of her by grabbing at her, had become her standard way of dealing with a man's attention.

He had been in the office before dawn, his mind

on her rather than the coming flight and on impulse he had requested her file. It had been interesting reading. From the time she had started school, she had been separated from her own age group, and she had responded to the inevitable social alienation by devoting herself to her studies, thereby widening the gulf as she outpaced her schoolmates. That wasn't exactly what had been in her file, of course; the impersonal papers had listed only numbers and accomplishments, except for the detailed security check, which had noted the lack of a personal relationship with a man—ever—but neither her psychological profile nor a detailed investigation had revealed any hint of homosexuality. Her work record did reveal a few instances when Dr. Evans hadn't gotten along with a co-worker, always male, but as the field of physics was dominated by men that wasn't in itself meaningful.

Remembering her reaction to him the night before, Joe had begun thinking. Was she so bristly because she had always been the odd man out, socially, emotionally and physically, during her childhood and adolescence? Her own age group would have shunned her, and her classmates wouldn't have been interested in socializing with someone who, compared to them, was a child. By the time she was physically mature and old enough for it not to matter, the pattern was set and she had so many defenses in place that no one could get past all the thorns.

The only way for a man to get close to her was for her to open the gate herself, something that wasn't likely to happen. But then he had seen the way she tensed when Daffy had put his arm around her waist, and the answer had flashed into his mind. A second later he had put his plan into action.

Her work was important to her. For that, she would tolerate the fiction of having a relationship with him, even though she had made it plain the night before that she didn't want to be gossiped about. He knew she was going to be gossiped about under any circumstances, because she just wasn't the type of woman who faded into the woodwork. Given the choice of having to pretend to be involved with him and putting up with the gossip, or possibly not being able to work on the Night Wing project at all, she had chosen the former. He had counted on that very reaction while he had been forming his argument.

Now the other men would leave her alone, giving him an unobstructed field, and he meant to use his advantage to the fullest. She would have to spend time with him, get to know him, learn to relax with him.

Her seduction would be the sweetest mission he'd ever undertaken. Taming that little hedgehog in bed would be more exciting than breaking Mach 3.

Caroline didn't dare return to work; she knew her discomfort would be written plainly on her face for everyone to see, and Adrian would make some snide comments about taking care of her love life on her own time. She darted into the nearest ladies' room and sought privacy in a stall.

She was trembling all over and felt strangely close

to tears. She seldom cried, because it didn't accomplish anything except making her nose stuffy. Even more strangely, she had been ignominiously routed again, and it was time she faced the facts.

It wasn't anything Colonel Mackenzie had done that frightened her so; it was her own reactions to him that were terrifying. Intelligence wasn't worth anything if she hid her head in the sand and didn't admit the truth to herself. She had let herself grow too cocky about her ability to keep men at a distance by using her sharp tongue; not only was the colonel not intimidated by it—damn the man, he seemed to enjoy it!— but maybe she had been able to hold off those other men only because she hadn't been attracted to any of them. The shortness of breath, the panic attacks, the pounding of her heart and cowardly behavior, could all mean only one thing: sexual attraction. As an intelligent female, her instinctive impulse was to run for her life.

She excused herself for not having recognized it immediately, because after all, it was the first time she had ever experienced the phenomenon. She hadn't known how to drive a car the first time she had gotten behind the steering wheel, either. She had always been slightly puzzled by both genders' sometimes feverish antics when trying to attract someone of the opposite sex, but now she knew what was at the bottom of it all. Gonads. It was disconcerting to have one's glands turn traitor.

And now there was this situation she had somehow become mired in. She felt certain that if she only applied herself to it, she would be able to come up with some other solution, but her brain didn't seem to want to work. It was probably a side effect of overactive gonads. After all, thinking wasn't conducive to mating.

She tried to organize her thoughts. As the situation stood, she had agreed to pretend to be having a relationship with Colonel Mackenzie so the men would leave her alone and she would be able to work, and also so the men wouldn't be distracted by her. Did the colonel pretend to have a relationship with every woman on base? Why her? What was it about her that was so disruptive that she had to be *neutralized?* She knew she was a reasonably attractive woman, but she certainly wasn't a femme fatale.

And just what would pretending to be involved with him entail? Small talk and smiling? She thought she could handle that. She had never cooed like a lovesick bird the way she had seen some women do, but it couldn't be that difficult. But if he thought this pseudorelationship involved any hugging and kissing, she would have to call it off immediately, because her heart just couldn't stand the strain. All that adrenaline rushing around couldn't be healthy.

But the situation wasn't unmanageable. If she just kept her head and remembered not to trust him no matter how reasonable he seemed, she should be all right.

With that thought firmly in mind, she squared her shoulders and left her refuge. As she crossed the tarmac, the desert heat scorched the top of her head and made her arms burn. Everything shimmered around her, and her ears were assaulted by the constant roar of jet engines as planes took off and landed. Airmen swarmed everywhere, attending to the business of the huge base. The activity was exhilarating, and even more exciting was the knowledge that she was working on the most advanced jet fighter ever designed.

Work had always been her panacea. She enjoyed it, embraced it, because it was the one part of her life where she excelled, where she fit in. It was comforting and familiar, even though Adrian Pendley was certain to do his best to ruin it for her. Well, if she could ignore Mackenzie, she could easily ignore Adrian.

The colonel's darkly tanned, hawkish face swam before her eyes, forming amid the heat waves, and she stumbled on the edge of the tarmac before quickly regaining her balance. So she wasn't ignoring Mackenzie that well; she would get better at it. For her own sake, she had to.

Sure enough, when she walked back to the office, with her clothing damp with sweat and wisps of hair sticking to her face, Adrian looked at her and sneered. "Didn't you know it's too hot for a quick tussle? You'll learn to save it for a weekend in Vegas."

Yates looked up and frowned. Caroline caught his eye and shrugged to show that it didn't matter.

The laser program was fully developed; they were there as a trouble-shooting team, and since the day's tests had gone well, there was little more to do than recap what they'd seen. Then they went over the next planned test, the first one using a moving target. The aircraft that would be used in the next tests weren't the two that had flown that day, and their targeting systems had already been checked as part of the regularly implemented maintenance schedule. All of that had been done before Caroline's arrival on the base. They did have to check the systems on the aircraft that had flown that day, and she, Yates and Adrian changed into coveralls for the job. Cal remained behind, rechecking the computer data.

"All the different systems people working on the Night Wing project have gotten along well," Yates said as they walked to the hangar. "It's been one of the smoothest operations I've been involved in."

"So don't go screwing it up by insulting any of them," Adrian said.

Yates stopped and swung around to confront Adrian. "That's enough," he said evenly.

"It's only the truth. You know she has a reputation for being hard to work with."

"I know what I'm hearing, and Caroline isn't the one who's being an ass. I hope I don't have to tell you that Colonel Mackenzie can have anyone on this team replaced with one phone call, and he'd do it in a heartbeat if he thought friction between any of us was hindering the work. If that happens, your career at Boling-Wahl would effectively be over, and that goes for both of you."

Caroline stuffed her hands deep in the pockets of her coveralls. Though Yates had been directing his ire toward Adrian, she knew that her position at Boling-Wahl was a bit tenuous, due to her past difficulties

on a couple of jobs. One of those incidents had been
with Adrian. Perhaps she had been assigned to work
with him as a sort of test and her job depended on
passing it.

Adrian turned to glare at her. "I'll stay out of her
way," he finally muttered, "if she stays out of mine."
Then he strode on ahead of them.

Yates sighed, and he and Caroline resumed walking, but at a more leisurely pace. "Ignore him as
much as you can," he advised. "I didn't realize the
situation between the two of you was so hostile."

"I'm not hostile," Caroline said in surprise.

He gave her a thoughtful look. "No, I don't guess
you are. But *he* is. Is it just a case of mutual dislike,
or did something happen that I need to know about?"

She shrugged. "I don't suppose it's any big secret.
He came on to me when I first started work for Boling-Wahl, and I turned him down."

"Ahh. A hurt ego."

"It would make more sense if we'd been involved
and then broken up, but it was never that personal. I
guess he doesn't take rejection well."

"That's all it was? You turned him down for a
date?" Yates asked skeptically.

"Not exactly. He made a pass at me."

"And you…?"

She stared straight ahead, but she could feel her
cheeks heating again. "He was…well, it was a pretty
strong pass, if you know what I mean, and I couldn't
seem to make him understand that I wasn't interested.
I tried being polite, but it wasn't getting through and

he wouldn't let me go. So I told him I'd have gone to work at a zoo if I'd wanted to be grabbed by an ape.''

Yates chuckled. "Not very tactful, but effective."

That wasn't all she'd told Adrian, but she thought she had admitted to enough. "He took it personally."

"The two of you will have to get along for the duration."

"I understand. I won't snipe back. But if he grabs me again," she warned, "I won't be nice."

Yates patted her arm. "If he grabs you, knock him on the head with something."

She fully intended to.

They spent the rest of the day checking the targeting systems on the two aircraft, and everything looked good. As maintenance crews crawled in, under, over and around the sleek black aircraft, the scene reminded Caroline of Gulliver being swarmed over by the Lilliputians. Lines and hoses snaked everywhere, crisscrossing the hangar floor.

Adrian didn't speak to her except about work, and that suited her fine. He was good at what he did, and as long as he restricted himself to that, she had no problem with him. Maybe Yates' lecture had made an impression on him.

It was late afternoon before they had the two systems thoroughly checked, and Caroline was glad to call it a day. Thoughts of a long, cool shower filled her head. She returned to the office and didn't bother changing out of the coveralls, simply collecting her dress and checking to make certain everything was locked up. Security demanded that nothing be left out on their desks.

When she reached her quarters she turned the air conditioning on high and stood in front of the cold air for a minute, sighing with relief. There was a benefit to having small rooms: they cooled off quickly. She counted herself lucky to have two rooms, period. The first room was a combination living room, dining room and kitchen, meaning that a nondescript couch and matching nondescript chair, with a scratched fake-wood coffee table, occupied one half of the room and the other half was taken up by a galley-size kitchen and a battered Formica table with two chairs. The predominant color seemed to be institutional green. The room was about twelve feet square and opened directly into the bedroom. The bedroom and bath combined were the same size as the front room. She had a bed that was supposed to be double-sized but didn't quite make it, but since she slept alone it didn't matter. There was a scarred chest of drawers, a cramped closet and a cramped bathroom with barely enough room for the essential plumbing, and then only because there was a small shower stall rather than a bathtub. It was livable, but she couldn't see herself ever growing fond of it.

On the bright side, one of the first things she had done had been to replace the light bulbs in the bathroom with new ones of sufficient wattage for the application of makeup. She probably had the brightest bathroom on base. She rather liked the idea.

She took the long, cool shower she had promised

herself, gradually turning the hot water off as she became accustomed to the chill, until the spray was satisfyingly cold. She felt herself revive as her overheated skin drank in the moisture. She didn't turn the water off until she was shivering, then dried herself briskly and dressed in loose, cotton knit pants and a big T-shirt, which perfectly suited her notions of comfort.

Now for food. She had decided from the outset to eat in her quarters as much as possible, so she had stocked the tiny kitchen with a few staples. She was standing in front of an open cabinet door studying the contents and trying to decide on her meal when someone knocked on the door.

"Who is it?" she called.

"Mackenzie."

He didn't have to identify himself by name, she thought irritably as she strode to the door and opened it. All he had to do was rumble something in that deep voice.

She braced herself in the opening and felt the heat settle over her like a suffocating blanket. "What do you want?" she demanded. He wasn't wearing a uniform, but the glove-soft jeans, scuffed boots and white T-shirt were oddly disturbing, while the inevitable dark sunglasses every pilot wore hid his eyes. She didn't like it; she didn't want to know what he was like when he was off duty.

Joe noted her challenging stance and the fierceness of her glare. Evidently she had decided that her best course of action was to simply carry on as usual. He was glad; being around her might not be comfortable, but it was sure as hell exciting, and he didn't want that to change.

"Supper," he said.

She crossed her arms. "I'm not feeding you."

"No, I'm feeding you," he said mildly. "Remember? I told Daffy you'd be with me tonight, and everyone will know about it tomorrow if you aren't." It was an effort to keep his voice mild and his eyes on her face, because she was obviously braless. The thin T-shirt she was wearing plainly revealed the shape of her high breasts and the darker circles of her nipples. Every muscle in his big body tensed with growing arousal.

"Just a cheeseburger," he cajoled in the soft voice he'd often used to calm nervous mares. "You don't even have to change. Just slip on your shoes and we'll go off base and find a hamburger joint."

Caroline hesitated. The thought of a cheeseburger was enticing, since she had been about to choose between two brands of cold cereal.

"All right," she decided abruptly. "Give me a minute." She dashed into the bedroom and put on a pair of sandals, then raked a comb through her hair. Her freshly washed face stared back at her from the mirror, and she contemplated putting on makeup, then shrugged. A cheeseburger was waiting.

Just before she left the room she remembered that she wasn't wearing a bra and hurriedly put one on. She didn't think he would have noticed, but it was better to play it safe.

He hadn't entered her quarters but was still standing just outside the open door. Caroline turned the lock on the door and stepped out, closed the door firmly, then tried the knob to make certain the lock had caught. Satisfied, she dropped her keys into her pocket.

He was driving a muscular black pickup truck. Caroline looked at him in surprise as he opened the door and she climbed up into the seat. "I never would have figured you for a truck person," she said as he slid his long legs under the steering wheel.

"I grew up on a horse ranch in Wyoming," he said. "I've driven pickups all my life. What did you think I'd drive?"

"Something low and red and flashy."

"I save my speeding for the air." His ice-blue eyes flicked at her. "What do you drive? I know what you're driving now is a rental car, since you flew in, so that doesn't count."

Caroline settled back in the seat. She decided that she rather liked sitting up high so she could see, and she was feeling more comfortable by the minute. Maybe it was the truck that did it; it was such a no-nonsense kind of vehicle. "What do you think I drive?"

"Something safe and dependable."

"Oh."

The one syllable was a little disgruntled. Joe controlled a smile. "Am I wrong?"

"A tad."

"So what *do* you drive?"

She turned her head to the side and stared out the window. "Something low and red and flashy." She had absolutely rebelled against buying anything sedate and conservative. She had wanted power and speed and handling, and had paid a small fortune to get it.

"How flashy?" he asked.

"A Corvette," she said, and suddenly chuckled at the contrast between them.

Joe looked at her again. He couldn't keep from it. She had lived the life of a total egghead, reclusive and socially awkward, but the fire in her couldn't be hidden. It was revealed in the unconscious sex appeal with which she moved and dressed, the fierceness of her temper, the adventurous car she drove. She sat so decorously on the passenger side, but her face was lifted to the hot wind blowing in through the lowered windows. There was a streak of wildness in her that intrigued him, and he shifted restlessly to ease the constriction of his jeans.

They were checked through the gate, and he turned the truck toward the sunset, blazing red and gold in front of them. She didn't seem to feel any need to carry on a conversation; Joe was comfortable with silence, too, so he let it continue.

Caroline couldn't stop herself from glancing at him every few minutes, though she would then jerk her gaze back to the sunset. The T-shirt bared his powerful arms, darkly tanned by the desert sun. He had so many muscles, it was unnerving. She knew that fighter pilots regularly worked out, because a dense muscle mass seemed to help them resist the effects of pulling Gs, but his muscularity was somehow different. He was powerful—the way a panther or a wolf is powerful—from a lifetime of work and using his body. The sun outlined his profile in gold, mercilessly revealing the bladelike bone structure, as clean and fierce as an ancient warrior's face cast on a coin.

She stared at the thin, high-bridged nose, the wide forehead and high, chiseled cheekbones. His mouth was almost brutally clear-cut. The hot wind was sifting through his thick black hair, disarranging the short military cut and her vision blurred as a disturbing vision filled it of this man with his hair long and flying around his broad, bare shoulders. Her heart thumped in a sort of painful panic, and she jerked her gaze away yet again, but it didn't do any good. She could still see him in her mind. It took her only a minute to decide that if out of sight wasn't going to be out of mind, she might as well give in and let her eyes feast.

She turned her head toward him, and her hungry gaze slipped down over his wide, powerful chest to his flat belly. She just couldn't stop it, though neither was she brave enough to let her eyes rest on the fly of his jeans, instead hurriedly skimming on to those long, muscled legs.

She blurted out, ''Aren't you almost too big to get into a cockpit?''

He briefly took his eyes off the road to look at her, though the dark lenses kept her from reading his expression. She wished he would take them off. ''It's a tight fit,'' he replied, his voice low and slow and growling. ''But I always manage to squeeze in.''

The underlying sexuality of his words hit her like a sledgehammer. She was woefully inexperienced but not naive, and there was no mistaking his meaning. Now she was glad he had those dark glasses on, because she didn't *want* to read his expression. She wanted to hide her face in her hands. She wanted to jump out of the truck and run all the way back to the base and the safety of her quarters. Had she been *mad?* She had actually climbed in the truck with this man, and now here they were, alone in the Nevada desert with the sunset rapidly darkening to purple.

Then she remembered that it was her own reaction to him that frightened her, not anything he had done, and she wondered miserably if she should tell him to bail out now while he still could. The way she had been ogling him, he was probably wondering if he would make it back to the base with his pants on, though considering the notorious libido of pilots in general and military pilots in particular, he might not fight very hard. Maybe it was the contrast he presented that got to her the way no man had before, the sense of an intense, smoldering sexuality beneath that cool remoteness. And maybe, if she was lucky, he had no idea of the tumult going on inside her.

Joe was glad of the dark lenses that protected his eyes from the sun, because they allowed him to study her without her being aware of it. She had put on a bra, damn it, but the thin restricting material couldn't quite disguise the pebbled hardness of her nipples.

The little darling was aroused—and upset by it; he could feel her tension, see it in the faint trembling of her body that her still posture couldn't control. His eyes went back to her distended nipples, and his hands tightened on the steering wheel as he inevitably began thinking about taking those hard buds into his mouth. She was so beautifully responsive, and she didn't even know it. If she could be so aroused by a naughty comment, what would she be like when he was actually making love to her?

She wasn't the only one who was aroused. If he looked at her nipples one more time, he might have to stop the truck on the side of the road, and she was far from ready for that. To keep himself from making a big mistake, he didn't look at her again until they had reached his favorite drive-in hamburger joint, which was just seedy enough to be interesting.

He parked beside one of the speakers and turned off the ignition, then removed his sunglasses and put them on the dash. "What do you want?"

She wished he had phrased it differently. She leaned down so she could read the menu posted above the speaker and scowled as she forced herself to concentrate on food. The heavenly aroma of frying hamburgers, onions and French fries filled the air; why did the most unhealthy food always smell the best? "A cheeseburger basket and large soft drink."

He punched the button on the speaker, and when a tinny voice answered, he ordered two cheeseburger baskets. Then he half turned toward Caroline, his wide shoulders wedged into the corner of the truck, and casually said, "I'm going to kiss you when we get back to the base."

Caroline stared wide-eyed at him, her heart going into its crazy thumping rhythm again. "I want onions on my cheeseburger. Lots of onions."

"You don't have to be afraid I'm going to grab you," he continued as if she hadn't spoken. "It'll just be a kiss, outside your door where anyone walking by can see us, and someone probably will. I won't even put my arms around you if you don't want me to."

"I don't want you to kiss me," she said, withdrawing to her own corner of the truck and glaring at him across the expanse of the front seat.

"I'm going to anyway. It's expected."

"I don't care what's expected. I agreed to come out with you tonight because it does seem to be a good way to keep all the others in line, but I never agreed to any kissing."

"Don't you like kissing?"

She glared sullenly at him. The perfect answer would be that yes, she liked kissing, but she didn't want to kiss *him*. The perfect answer, however, was a bald-faced lie, and from the way her heart was fluttering like a Victorian maiden's at the prospect of kissing him, she wouldn't be able to carry it off. Lying, she found, seemed to work better when performed with a certain amount of detachment.

On the other hand, the truth was the worst answer she could give him. No, she hadn't liked any of the sloppy kisses that had been forced on her in a hit-or-

miss fashion because she'd been fighting like a wild-
cat to avoid them, but the thought of kissing him
made her light-headed, and she was afraid she would
like it *too* much.

When she didn't reply he said calmly, ''When we
get back to your quarters, unlock your door, then turn
and hold out your hand to me. I'll take it, lean over
and kiss you. It won't be a long kiss, but it can't be
a quick peck, either. Does three seconds sound long
enough to you? Then I'll let go of your hand and say
good-night. On a busy base, any number of people
will see us, and the word will spread that we don't
seem to be having a flaming affair, but we're definitely involved.''

She cleared her throat. ''Three seconds?'' That
didn't sound like very long. Surely she could manage
not to disgrace herself for three seconds.

''Just three seconds,'' he reassured her.

Chapter 4

The cheeseburger—without onions—and fries were delicious, reminding her of those few precious times during her childhood when she had been allowed to stay over with her mother's brother and his wife, both of them about ten years younger than her parents, and Uncle Lee had invariably treated her to the biggest, juiciest hamburger she could eat, followed by ice cream, another forbidden food. Her parents had allowed her to eat sorbet or frozen yogurt, but never ice cream. If it hadn't been for Uncle Lee, Caroline thought she might have reached the age of majority without knowing the joys of junk food. She still always felt as if she were having a special treat when she indulged.

After the cheeseburgers, he gave her a slow smile and asked, "Ever played the slots?"

"No. I've never been to a casino."

"That's about to change." He started the truck, and soon they were tooling down Las Vegas Boulevard, an endless array of flashing neon lights in every color of the rainbow. They blinked, they arrowed, they cascaded, they exploded in endless neon showers, inviting one and all to sample whatever it was they were advertising. The big casinos drew the largest crowds, of course, but a goodly number of people were just strolling, tourists determined to see everything in this town geared toward attracting them. People were dressed in clothing that ran the gamut from shorts to formal gowns.

"Do you like to gamble?" she asked.

"I never gamble."

She snorted. "Except with your life. I was in the control room today, remember? Hitting eighty degrees alpha and pulling 10 Gs isn't what I'd call safe living."

"That isn't gambling. Baby was built to give us an unlimited angle of attack, but her capability doesn't do us any good if we don't know how to fly her. My job is to make certain she does what she's supposed to do, get her fully tested out and operational and find out her limitations. I can't do that if I don't exceed what we're already doing in the F-22."

"None of the other pilots are pushing the envelope like that."

His eyes were utterly calm when he looked at her. "They will now. Now that they know Baby will operate under those conditions."

"You did it just to show them it could be done?"

"No. I did it because it's my job."

And because he loved it. The thought echoed in her mind. She had seen it that day when he had entered the control room after his flight, tired and sweaty, his eyes bloodshot, his expression as remote as ever. But his eyes had given him away. They had been fierce and...exalted, the fires of life burning white hot in him.

He parked the truck, and they strolled down the sidewalk. "Do you feel lucky?" he asked.

She shrugged. "How does lucky feel?"

"Want to try it?"

She paused before the entrance to one of the casinos, feeling the cool air gush out through the opened doors. Rows and rows of slot machines stretched before her and even spread out on the sidewalk. Most of them were manned by people automatically feeding in their tokens of worship and pulling the levers. Occasionally there were cries of delight as coins in varying numbers came tumbling out to reward their persistence, but mostly the machines took rather than gave.

"It isn't cost-effective," she said after studying the procedure for a few minutes.

He laughed softly. "That isn't the point. Never gamble if you can't afford to lose, that's rule number one. Rule number two is to have fun."

"They don't look like they're having fun," she said doubtfully.

"That's because they've forgotten rule number

two, and maybe even number one. C'mon, I'll stake you.''

But she waited another few minutes, until she saw someone abandon a machine that hadn't paid anything in quite a while. The law of averages said it was more likely to pay out than one that had just disgorged a few coins would be to do so again. She sat down in front of it and fed in the quarters, feeling like an idiot as she did so. Joe stood behind her, softly laughing when the mechanical bandit gave her nothing in return. After she had fed in about five dollars without winning anything, Caroline began to take it personally. She muttered warnings and threats as she went through the procedure again—and lost again.

''Remember rule number two,'' Joe cautioned, amusement in his voice.

She told him what he could do with rule number two, and he chuckled.

She hitched her stool closer to the machine and shoved a quarter into the slot. She pulled the lever and the pictures began whirring, then one by one clicked into place. Bells began ringing and quarters began flooding out of the bottom slot, spilling out onto the floor. Caroline jumped up and stared at the silver coins as other slot players crowded around, offering congratulations, and a smiling casino employee came over. Then she gave Joe a look of consternation. ''All those quarters won't fit in my pocket.''

He threw back his head and began laughing. She stared at his strong brown throat and felt suddenly dizzy as that damn light-headed feeling swept over her again.

The casino employee, still smiling, said, "We'll be glad to change the coins into bills."

They did, and to her relief Caroline found that the flood of quarters wasn't a great fortune after all, only a little over seventy dollars. She returned Joe's stake to him and stuffed the remaining bills into her pocket.

"Did you have fun?" he asked as they left the casino.

She thought about it. "I suppose so, but I was beginning to feel a little vindictive toward that machine. I don't think I have the temperament to be a gambler."

"Probably not," he agreed, and took her hand in his to gently pull her out of the path of a man who wasn't looking where he was going. But then he didn't release her as she had expected.

She looked down at their clasped hands. His hand was big and hard, the fingers lean, his palm tough with calluses, but his grip was careful, as if he were very aware of his strength. She had never held hands before, and the touch of palm against palm was surprisingly intimate. She was beginning to realize that fear had kept her from doing a lot of pleasurable things before, but then, she had never before been even tempted to explore them. Her reactions to other men who had tried to venture into a physical relationship with her had varied from bored and disinterested to absolute revulsion.

She could tug her hand free. That was the safest

course of action, but somehow she couldn't do it. So
she ignored the situation, acted as if her hand wasn't
nestled in his much more powerful one like a bird
taking shelter, and inwardly she savored every moment of it.

Finally they walked back to the truck, and she realized she was reluctant for the night to come to an
end. It was her first date, if she cared to categorize it
as such, and it was almost over.

They were both silent on the drive back to the base,
and inevitably her mind turned to the coming kiss.
She felt both panicked and excited. Another first for
her, the first kiss she had actually agreed to and welcomed. It was a toss-up whether she would bolt in
fear or hurl herself into his arms.

The moment of truth came all too soon. He parked
in front of her quarters and got out to walk around
the truck and open the door for her. There were a
number of personnel going about their business,
glancing at them with idle curiosity, and she knew he
had perfectly gauged the situation.

She took out her keys and unlocked the door, then
turned and faced him in the colorless glow of the vapor lights overhead. Her eyes were solemn and de-
fenseless as she stared at him, his eyes glittering like
ice.

"Hold out your hand," he commanded softly, and
she obeyed.

His hard, warm hand enclosed her fingers, and he
pulled her closer even as he bent. His mouth lightly
touched hers, lifted, settled again. He turned his head

slightly to adjust the pressure, and somehow the motion parted her own lips, so that they yielded to the molding of his.

His taste was warm and pleasant and…male. The scent of him enveloped her, and she shivered in response. His mouth was still on hers, moving gently. She felt the tip of his tongue touch and tease, making her stiffen at the jumbled memory of some uninvited, intrusive kiss, but this was nothing like that. She felt enticed rather than coerced, and his taste was filling her senses. Warm pleasure shuddered up from her depths; with a little whimper she opened her mouth, and slowly he took her.

The carnality of it was staggering, and so was her reaction to it. She heard herself whimper again, and then somehow she was pressed hard against him, her head tilted up and back to give him deeper access, an access he took with a hard male dominance that stunned her. She felt weak and hot, and her breasts tightened with an ache that contact with his hard chest both soothed and intensified. Her loins felt hot, too, as coils of pleasure tightened deep inside. She was clinging to his hand like a lifeline.

Slowly he lifted his mouth, and it was all he could force himself to do to break the contact. He gave in to the temptation to take several more quick kisses from the soft, innocent mouth that had so quickly warmed to awareness, then he *had* to release her hand and step back. He had promised her. He wanted nothing more than to shove her inside her dark quarters and carry her down to the floor, mounting her with quick, hard urgency, but restraint now would bring him much sweeter rewards in the future. So he controlled his rough, quick breathing and tried to control the fierce rush of blood through his veins.

"Three seconds," he said.

Her eyes were glazed as she stared at him, and she was weaving slightly. "Yes," she whispered. "Three seconds."

She didn't move. He put his hands on her shoulders and turned her around. "Go inside, Caroline." His voice was low and calm. "Good night."

"Good night." She moved jerkily to obey, and as she reached the threshold she paused to look at him over her shoulder. Her eyes were huge and dark with some indefinable emotion. "That was much longer than three seconds."

She switched on the light, then closed and carefully locked the door. Even as she turned the bolt, she heard him drive away, telling her that he hadn't been tempted to linger for even a second, or hadn't considered the idea of knocking on her door. He had accomplished his mission, which was to establish their "relationship," so as far as he was concerned, there was no reason to hang around.

She sat down on the couch and remained there, motionless, for quite some time. She had some thinking to do, and she always concentrated better if she could just sit still and totally lock herself inside her brain, or perhaps it was more a matter of locking everything else *out,* and that included physical stimuli.

It hadn't taken any psychoanalysis for her to understand years ago how her upbringing and accelerated progress through school had combined with her own nature to make her the odd man out, but she hadn't minded. Why should she worry that she had never learned how to associate with the opposite sex on a social and emotional level, when there hadn't been anyone of the opposite sex she was interested in associating with anyway? So she had never regretted her out-of-sync relationship with the rest of the world—until now.

Now, for the first time, she was strongly attracted to a man and wanted him to be attracted to her, but how did she go about accomplishing that feat? When other girls had been learning how, she had been studying physics. She was an expert in laser optics, but she didn't know a damn thing about flirting.

Why couldn't she have gotten her feet wet with someone less challenging, say a fellow physicist who had also spent more time with books than people and was a little awkward socially, too? But, no, instead she had fallen head over heels in *attraction* with a hotshot fighter pilot, a man who could make women go weak in the knees with one look from those diamond-blue eyes. She didn't have to be an expert at kissing to be able to tell that *he* was, and she had a sneaking suspicion that she had made a fool out of herself. All he had done was hold her hand, as he'd promised, and she had practically been all over him. She had a distinct memory of pushing hard against him and rubbing her front against his like a cat, and thinking that she was going to fall in a heap at his feet.

He'd been nice to her this evening. He'd treated her as a friend, had let her relax, and she had had fun. She couldn't remember the last time she had done something so totally useless and enjoyed it. Simple playing hadn't been part of her childhood; her parents had carefully monitored her activities to make certain they were geared toward her educational progress. No ABC blocks for her; she had used flash cards. In defense of her parents, though, she had been an impatient child, irascible when the pace had lagged behind the speed of her inquisitive, hungry intellect. Her childhood hadn't been unhappy, just different, and she had made her own choices in life.

She was groping her way through unfamiliar territory, but Caroline's approach to any problem was to tackle it head-on. She didn't really know how to use the weapons nature had given her, but Joe Mackenzie was about to find them all brought to bear on him.

The first step in solving any problem was to research the subject. It was early enough that a lot of people were still awake, and there were plenty of female Air Force personnel who turned out to be willing to lend her magazines with articles that she thought addressed the problem, and she was even able to come up with quite a bit of research on fighter pilots in general. She was an accomplished speed reader and sat up for several hours plowing her way through magazines offering such intriguing articles as ''He's Bad, Bad, Bad— So Why Do You Love Him Anyway?'' and ''Finding The Gold in The Dross— When Not To Give Up.'' Double titles seemed to abound, as well as hundreds of glossy photos of women five feet nine inches tall who weighed a hundred and fifteen pounds, most of which was evidently hair and breasts. She learned how to tell when he was cheating, and how to get revenge. She learned how to break into real estate or start her own company, how to win at blackjack—she committed that to memory—and where to stay on vacation in Europe. Interesting stuff. She just might subscribe.

The material on fighter pilots was even more interesting.

She was in the office before dawn, dressed in a loose, lightweight jumpsuit. When she had been making her selection that morning, seduction had collided with comfort, and seduction had lost without even a whimper. The temperature hit a hundred and ten during the day, for heaven's sake.

She hauled out the specs for the day's tests and began rechecking them, making a mental note to ask Cal a few questions about the computer program. She had taken a second major in computer programming, which had seemed to be a good complement to physics, and it had in fact come in very handy on several occasions. She logged onto the computer and began running the tests through it, rechecking once again that everything was as perfect as they could get it.

''How long have you been in—''

She shrieked at the voice right behind her and came

up swinging, overturning her chair in the process. Joe's hand shot up and caught her right fist before it could connect with his face, and a split second later he caught the left one in his other hand, the twin movements like lightning.

"Don't do that again!" she yelled, going up on tiptoe to glare at him, thrusting her jaw up to his. Her eyes were still dilated from fright. "What are you trying to do, give me a heart attack? From now on, *whistle* before you get to the door!"

With a deft motion he twisted her arms behind her back, still holding her fists clasped in his palms. The action brought her breasts firmly against him and encased her within his arms. "I didn't mean to scare you," he said softly. "But if your first reaction is always to attack, you should learn how to do it right, so you won't wind up in the sort of predicament you're in now." He saw interest sharpen the dark bluish-green of her eyes and knew that he had successfully deflected her attention from the fact that he was holding her captive.

Caroline considered the situation. She tugged briefly on her arms, but he held her firmly, and there was no way she could free herself from those iron hands. He was too tall for her to hit him in the face with her head. "I still have the option of stomping your instep and kicking your ankle or knee."

"Yes, but you're too close to put much power behind it. You can hurt me, but not enough to make me let you go. If I were an attacker, sweetheart, right now you'd be in some serious trouble."

She wiggled experimentally again, testing her limits of movement. His arms were locked around her, and she was pressed fully against his muscled body. She shivered a little at the unexpected pleasure of it, so surrounded by his warmth and scent. He smelled delicious; she had never noticed any other man smelling the way Joe did, and it wasn't just the fresh scent of soap lingering on his skin. It was a hot, musky scent, subtle and powerful, making her want to bury her nose against him and drink it in. The effects were strong and immediate; her breasts began to tingle and ache as her nipples peaked, and hot tension tightened her loins.

She cleared her throat and tried to take her mind off her body's reaction; they were in the office, for heaven's sake. Just because she had changed her mind about wanting to experience more of this man/woman thing didn't mean she wanted to do it *here.* "Umm… so what should I do when I want to attack?"

"You should learn how to fight first," he replied, and pressed a quick, hard kiss on her mouth as he released her.

Her lips tingled from the kiss, and she licked them. His gaze slid to her mouth and darkened. She tried for nonchalance to hide the fact that she was shaking all over. "So, what do you recommend?" she asked as she set the chair upright and briskly backed out of the computer program, just to give herself something to do. She switched the machine off and faced him with a bright smile. "Martial arts?"

"Dirty street fighting would be better. It teaches

you how to win any way you can, and to hell with
fighting fair. It's the only way you should ever go
into a fight.''

''You mean like throwing dirt in the guy's eyes and
stuff like that?''

''Whatever works. The idea is to win, and stay
alive.''

''Is that the way you fight?'' she asked. She desperately needed to sit down, her legs were shaking so
much, but he would tower over her if she did, and the
thought of that made her nervous, too. She compromised by propping herself on the edge of the desk.
''Is that what the Air Force teaches its pilots now?''

''No, that's the way I was taught to fight when I
was a kid.''

''Who taught you?''

''My father.''

She supposed it was a masculine bonding thing.
Her father had taught her calculus, but that wasn't
quite the same.

''I've been researching the typical fighter pilot,''
she said. ''It's interesting reading. In some ways,
you're the perfect stereotype.''

''Is that so?'' He showed his teeth in a very white
smile, though maybe it wasn't a smile at all.

''Well, in some ways you're atypical. You're unusually tall, more suited to a bomber than a fighter.
But fighter pilots are typically intelligent, aggressive,
arrogant and as determined—maybe *stubborn* is a better word—as a bulldog. They want to be in control at
all times.''

He crossed his arms over his chest, dark lashes shadowing his glittering eyes.

"Fighter pilots have keen eyesight and fast reactions. Most of you have blue or light-colored eyes, so you're certainly typical on that. And here's an interesting little tidbit…fighter pilots usually have more female children than male."

"Finding out will be fun," he drawled.

She cleared her throat. "Actually, I thought you might already know."

He lifted his eyebrows. "Why's that?"

"I *did* notice that they called you Breed. I assumed it's because you do it so well."

One corner of his mouth moved in a slow smile. "My breeding productivity doesn't have anything to do with it. They call me Breed because I'm a half-breed Indian."

Caroline was so startled that she could only stare at him. "A Native American?"

He shrugged. "That's what you can call it if you want, but I've always called myself an Indian. Changing labels doesn't change anything else." His voice was casual, but he was watching her closely.

She studied him just as closely. His skin was certainly dark enough, with a deep bronze hue that she had assumed was a dark tan. His hair was thick and black and straight, those sculpted cheekbones high and prominent, his nose thin and high-bridged, and his mouth was typically clean-cut and sensual. His eyes, however, were an oddity. She frowned and said

accusingly, "Then how can you have blue eyes? Blue
is a recessive gene. You should have dark eyes."

He had been alert to how she would receive his
heritage, but at her reply something in him relaxed.
How else would Caroline respond to something but
with a demand for more information? She wasn't
shocked or repelled, as some people still were by his
mixed heritage, or even titillated, as sometimes happened—though he had become accustomed to that because women were often excited by his profession,
too. Nope, she honed right in on the genetic question
of why he had blue eyes.

"My parents were both half-breeds," he explained.
"Genetically I'm still half Indian and half white, but
I got the recessive blue-eyed gene from both my parents. I'm one-quarter Comanche, one-quarter Kiowa
and half white."

She nodded in satisfaction, the mystery of his eye
color having been explained. She pursued the subject
with interest. "Do you have any brothers or sisters?
What color are their eyes?"

"Three brothers and one sister. Half brothers and
sister, to be precise. My mother died when I was a
baby. My stepmother is white, and she has blue eyes.
So do my three brothers. Dad was wondering if he
was ever going to have a black-eyed baby until my
sister was born."

She was fascinated by this glimpse of family life.
"I'm an only child. I always wanted a brother or sister
when I was little," she said, unaware of the faint wist-
ful note in her voice. "Was it fun?"

He chuckled and hooked his foot in the chair, turning it around so he could drop his tall frame into it. Caroline remained propped against the edge of the desk, still effectively pinned there, because he was in the way, but she wasn't paying attention to that any longer.

"I was sixteen when Dad married Mary, so I didn't grow up with them, but it was fun in a different way. I was old enough to appreciate babies, to take care of them. The best times were when I would go home on leave and they would swarm all over me like little monkeys. Dad and Mary always take off for one night alone while I'm there, and I have the kids to myself. They aren't little anymore, but we all still like it."

She tried to imagine this big, dangerous-looking man relaxed and surrounded by kids. Even just talking about them had softened his face. It wasn't until she saw him that way that she realized what a barrier he kept between himself and everyone else, because there was no barrier between him and his family. With them he would relax the iron control that characterized his every move, lose the remoteness that lay over his expression and in his eyes. The relationship he had with his men was different. It was the camaraderie that is established with a group whose members work together and depend on each other for a long time. That wasn't personal, and in a way it *required* him to retain his control. Suddenly she felt cold and a little lost, because she wasn't inside his intimate little circle. She wanted him to relax that guard with her, let her see the inner man and get close to him. With her

recent feminine awakening came another insight, one
that hurt even more: she wanted him to want her
enough to lose that frightening control. It hurt because
he didn't, and she knew it. What was frightening was
that she knew it wouldn't matter to her unless she was
already far more involved emotionally than she had
thought.

She became aware that she had been staring silently
at him for several long minutes, and he had been just
as quietly watching her, one eyebrow slightly quirked
as he waited for her to say something. She blushed
without knowing why. He came lithely to his feet,
stepping forward, so close that his legs were touching
hers. "What's on your mind, sweetheart?"

"You," she blurted out. Why was he standing so
close? Her pulse was beginning to race again. What
was it about him that being close to him put her brain
into neutral and her body into overdrive?

"What about me?"

She tried to think of something clever and casual,
but she had never learned how to prevaricate or hide
her feelings. "I don't know anything about men. I
don't know how to act around them or how to attract
them."

His expression was wry. "You're doing okay."

What did he mean by that? She was being her usual
blunt self, which had always sent men running. This
was more difficult than she'd imagined it would be.
She found that she was wringing her hands and was
vaguely astonished at herself, because she'd never
thought she was the hand-wringing type. "Am I?

Good. I've never seen anyone I wanted to attract before, so I'm at something of a loss. I know you said we'd just pretend to have a relationship so your men wouldn't bother me, but would it be too much of a bother for you if I wanted to make it more real?''

''Just how 'real' did you have in mind?'' he asked, amused.

Again she was at a loss. ''Well, how would I know? I just know that I'm attracted to you, and I'd like for you to be attracted to me, but I've never done this before, so you're asking me to play a game without knowing the rules. Would you hand a football to some guy who'd never heard of the game before and say 'Here you go, buddy. Play ball'?''

His eyes danced at the astringency of her tone, but his voice was calm and grave when he replied, ''I see your point.''

''So?'' She spread her hands inquiringly. ''What are the rules? That is, if you don't mind playing.''

''Oh, I like a little game now and then.''

He was drawling again. She gave him an uncertain glance, wondering if he was making fun of her.

He put his hands on her hips and moved her a little farther back on the desk. Caroline grabbed his upper arms, her nails digging into his biceps. No one had ever touched her hips before, except for one eager beaver who had pinched her bottom and gotten shoved over a wastebasket for his effort. The steely muscles under her fingers made her doubt she would be able to shove Joe anywhere.

He moved even closer and somehow used his hard

thighs to spread her legs. She looked down in shock.
He was between her legs. Her head jerked back up,
but before she could say anything he brushed a light,
gentle kiss across her mouth. The contrast between
that nonthreatening kiss and his very threatening position between her legs disoriented her.

He cupped her face with one hand, slowly caressing
her cheek, his fingertips moving lightly over the
smooth, velvet texture of her skin. His other hand
slipped around over her bottom and firmly pulled her
forward until he was nestled intimately in the notch
of her thighs. Caroline's heart thumped violently, and
she lost her breath, as well as her ability to sit upright.
Her bones turned liquid and she sank against him,
unintentionally deepening the embrace. The hard
bulge of his sex throbbed against the soft yielding of
her loins, and she felt an answering throbbing begin
deep inside her.

He kissed her again, this time with a slowly increasing demand. Helplessly she opened her mouth to
the probing of his tongue. His hips moved against her,
between her spread thighs, in the same rhythm as his
tongue moved in her mouth. The hard bulge in his
trousers was even harder, even bigger.

Her senses were swimming, just as they had been
the night before. His tongue probed deep into her
mouth, stroking her own tongue and demanding a response. His taste was hot and heady, his skin smelling
of soap and man. Her breasts were throbbing, and
again the only relief seemed to be contact with his
hard, muscled chest. It was all almost too much to

bear, but the only alternative was to tear herself out of his arms, and she couldn't make herself do that.

She couldn't, but he could. Somehow she found herself being gently freed and set away from him. She swayed, and he steadied her, his hard hands clasping her arms. She stared up at him a little wildly. Damn his control! Why couldn't he feel even a little of the turmoil that enveloped her? He had gotten aroused, no doubt about *that,* but it hadn't affected his control at all, while she was about to go up in flames.

"The rules are simple," he said calmly. "We have to let you get accustomed to touching and being touched, and find out what you like. We'll take it slow, go a little bit further each time. I'll pick you up at seven tonight."

He kissed her again and left as silently as he had entered the room. Caroline sat on the desk, trying to get control of her heart and lungs, trying to deal with the empty ache of her body. She was in trouble. She was in big trouble. She had started something she couldn't handle, but she wouldn't have called it off even if she thought she could, and she strongly suspected it was beyond her control anyway.

Unless she was very much mistaken, Joe Mackenzie intended to have an affair with her. A full-fledged, get-naked, lovemaking affair. And she was willing; she was going into this with her eyes open, knowing full well that for him it was likely to be only an affair, while it would be much more to her. He would always be in control, the strong core of him always guarded and remote and uninvolved, while she was well on her way to losing her heart.

Chapter 5

The tests went well that day, which was a good thing, because Caroline was in a daze. Adrian made a snide remark to her when they were alone and she confounded him by giving him a vague smile. She was alarmed at her own lack of concentration. That had never been a problem before; her ability to concentrate was so strong that one professor in college had made the comment that she would be able to read during an earthquake, and he hadn't been far off the mark.

She would never have believed that a man could totally disrupt her thought processes, especially since he wasn't paying her any particular attention. He didn't have to, she realized. He had made his intention plain the day before, and he'd been seen kissing her good-night; as far as everyone on base was concerned, she was Colonel Mackenzie's woman. He was the alpha male, and none of the other men would challenge him for his chosen mate. She was a little appalled at this demonstration of how little things had changed since prehistoric times, even though she had done her part by going along with him. Now there was food for thought. Had she gone along with him because his suggestion had made sense, or because he was the alpha male and she had felt subconsciously compelled to obey him?

Nah. She had never felt compelled, subconsciously or otherwise, to obey anyone. She had gone along with him because he made her heartbeat go crazy, pure and simple, and it was useless to keep looking for extenuating circumstances with which to excuse herself.

When they were back in the office going over the day's test results and preparing for the next day's flights, Cal rolled his chair over to hers. "So, how'd it go on the date with the boss man?"

Despite herself, her hands immediately started trembling and she laid down the paper she had been trying to read. "Very casual, low-key. Why do you ask?"

To her surprise, his friendly eyes were full of concern. "Well, I've never known you to date before, and I guess I just wanted to make sure he wasn't twisting your arm. He *is* the head man on this project, and he has a lot of influence, not just with the base commander and the men here, but all the way to the Pentagon.''

She was touched. ''And you thought I might feel I had to go out with him to stay on the team?''

''Something like that, yeah.''

She patted his hand, smiling. ''Thanks, but everything's okay.''

''Good. Adrian isn't bothering you too much, is he?''

''I haven't paid any attention to him, so I guess he isn't.''

Cal smiled and rolled back to his own desk.

Caroline checked the time. Three and a half hours until seven o'clock. She had always found her work engrossing, but along with her loss of concentration she had evidently become a clock-watcher, too. No one had ever warned her that associating with men was efficiency-destroying.

For almost the first time in her life she stopped work when everyone else did. She hurried to her quarters, turned the air conditioner on high and jumped into the shower. It was only as she was stepping out of the stall that she realized she didn't know where they were going or how she should dress.

She stared at the telephone. She could call him. She didn't know his number, but that wasn't any problem, because the base operator would. It was the sensible thing to do. She was a big believer in being sensible, so she sat down on the bed and placed the call before she talked herself out of her own common sense. He answered on the first ring. ''Mackenzie.''

God, his voice sounded even deeper on the phone. She took a deep breath. "This is Caroline. Where are we going tonight?" There, that was just right. To the point, no silliness, a simple request for information.

"Wear a skirt," he replied maddeningly, cutting through her no-nonsense question to the reason behind it. "Something I can get my hands under."

The receiver clicked in her ear, and she stared at it. The damn man had hung up on her! And her heart was racing again. Damn him, damn him, *damn* him. It wasn't fair. She was all but in a panic with anticipation and fear and wanting, and his heartbeat was probably as steady as a rock.

A skirt? After that comment, he was lucky she wasn't running for the hills. There was no way she could get in that truck with him expecting at any moment to feel those hot, callused hands sliding up her thighs. If he'd kept his mouth shut she would probably have worn a skirt because it was cooler, but if she wore one now, she would automatically be giving him permission to put his hand up it, and God knows what else. And it wasn't that she didn't want him to, just that he'd said they would go slow and that didn't sound slow at all to her, and even if it was, she would like to have a little control over the situation. What she would really like was to destroy *his* control, to have him as hot and bothered and on the verge of madness as she was.

She sat down on the bed and took several deep breaths. Maybe nuns had the right idea. Men were obviously detrimental to a woman's mental health.

She put on khaki fatigue pants and a tailored white shirt. That was as close as she was going to get to a skirt…not very close at all.

He knocked on the door at seven o'clock precisely, and when she opened it he burst out laughing. "What have you been thinking?" he asked, still chuckling. "That I'm a big bad wolf all set to gobble you up?"

"The thought crossed my mind."

He watched as she double-checked the appliances in the small quarters, then locked and double-checked the door. She was a cautious woman indeed. He put his hand on her waist as he walked her to the truck. "You don't have anything to worry about," he said soothingly. "I'm not going to eat you." Three seconds ticked by before he murmured, "Yet."

He felt her jump. Her peculiar blend of inexperience and sexuality was slowly driving him mad. When he kissed her, she responded with a heat and intensity that brought him to the brink of violence, but at the same time he sensed that she was ready to bolt at any time. She reminded him of nothing so much as a filly when a stallion is brought to her for the first time, nervous and apt to bite or kick, while at the same time her scent was telling the stallion she was more than ready for his mounting and he was going wild trying to accomplish it. Well, he'd calmed many a mare for both riding and servicing, and he knew just how to go about it.

He lifted her into the truck before she could change her mind and went around to the driver's side. The proposition she had put to him that morning had been in his mind all day, as had the blunt, forthright way she had done it. Caroline didn't know how to be flirtatious or sweetly cajoling; she had just laid it on the line, and her ego with it. He had wanted to take her in his arms and hold her, tell her that she needed to learn how to protect herself better than that. She had no defenses and didn't even realize it. Everything about her was straight ahead, no detours or subterfuges. He'd never had a woman ask for him like that before, ask him to teach her about men and sex. He'd been half-aroused all day, silently cursing the constrictions of his uniform.

Now he was in his customary off-duty jeans and boots, but the jeans were even more restrictive. He shifted position uncomfortably, trying to stretch his leg out to give himself more room. Damn it, he either needed to get out of his pants or get rid of his hard-on—preferably both, and in that order.

"Where are we going this time?" she asked, pushing her wind-blown hair out of her face.

"Do you like Mexican?"

Her eyes lit up. "Tacos," she purred. "Enchiladas. Sopapillas."

He laughed. "Got it." As she pushed her hair back once more, he said, "Would you rather I put up the windows and turned on the air conditioning?"

"No, I like it." She paused before admitting, "My 'vette is a convertible."

He was smiling as he returned his attention to the road. Her name should have been Paradox, because she was one conflicting characteristic after another.

They went to his favorite Mexican restaurant in Vegas, where the best enchiladas she'd ever eaten, coupled with a frozen Margarita, relaxed her and made her forget that she was nervous. Joe drank water with his dinner, something she found curious. "I thought pilots were supposed to be hard drinkers," she said.

"Most of us put away our share of pilot juice," he said lazily.

"But not you?"

"Nope. There's a time limit within which you aren't supposed to drink if you're going to be flying the next day, but I think it's too close. I want perfect control of myself and my machine. The laws of physics and aerodynamics aren't very forgiving at Mach 2." He lifted his glass of water in a little toast. "Not only that, I'm a half-breed. I don't drink. Period."

She gave a brief nod as if admitting the wisdom of that. "If it's so dangerous, why do any pilots drink?"

"To wind down. You're so tense for so long, with the adrenaline burning up your veins, that you can't come down from the high. Our lives are on the line every minute up there, even on routine flights. Hell, there's no such thing as a routine flight."

She started to ask a question about Night Wing, but remembered where they were and left it for another time. Security wasn't something she took lightly.

After dinner she said, "What now?" then wished she hadn't. She also wished she hadn't had that Margarita. She saw his point about needing perfect control.

"Now, sweetheart, we play."

When he said play, he meant play. Ten minutes later they were on a miniature golf course.

She hefted the putter experimentally. "I've never done this before."

"Looks like I'm going to be first with you at a lot of things," he replied with that maddening calm of his.

She scowled and lifted the putter like a bat. "Maybe not."

He kissed her even as he relieved her of the putter with a move so fast she saw only a blur. Disgruntled, she thought that if he'd lived in the Old West he would have been a gunfighter.

"Your first lesson," he said, turning her so her back was to him and putting his arms around her. He folded her hands around the handle in the correct manner and showed her how to swing, smooth and level, hitting the ball with carefully restrained power. Strength wasn't a factor in miniature golf; the game required judgment and coordination.

He made a hole in one on the first green. "You've done this before," she accused.

"Among other things."

"New rule. Each innuendo will add a stroke to your score."

"Good. Added strokes means it'll last longer."

She wanted to throw her ball at him and stomp off the green, but instead she shouted with laughter and firmly added another stroke to his score. Rules were rules.

To her surprise, she seemed to have the needed judgment of distance, force and direction, and challenged him even though she had never played before. He was too aggressive by nature to give her the game and set himself to the task of beating her, displaying intense concentration and superb hand-eye coordination. Caroline was just as determined, and the game was largely played in silence, to a tie. He pointed out that it was a draw only because of the penalty stroke she'd added to his score.

"So let's play another," she challenged. "Throw this one out, and the best two out of three wins."

"Deal."

They had to play five more games, because two others ended in draws. He won the first game, she won the second, and the next two were the ties; he finally ended it by winning the fifth game by one stroke.

She was scowling as they turned in their putters, and Joe was reminded of the look on her face the night before, when the slot machine had kept taking her quarters without making a payoff. He had had the idle thought that she was on the verge of dismantling the machine when it had finally paid out. No doubt about it, Caroline made no pretense of being good-natured about losing. She didn't like it. He understood that, because he didn't like it, either.

On the drive back to the base he slowed and pulled off the road, then drove about a quarter of a mile into the desert before stopping. He killed the lights and motor, and the night silence poured in through the open windows.

"Are you ready for another first?"

Caroline tensed. "What kind of first?"

"Parking."

"Thanks, but I had to pass a test on that when I got my driver's license."

He chuckled at the testy comment but sensed the nervousness behind it. "Here are our rules on making out. Number one, I'm not going to make love to you. Your first time is going to be on a bed, not in the front seat of a truck. Number two, we're going to keep most of our clothes on, because if we don't, your first time *will* be in the front seat of a truck."

She cleared her throat. "It sounds pretty frustrating."

"It is. That's the whole point of parking and making out." He laughed and slid out from behind the steering wheel, then scooped her onto his lap. A little more shifting and he was sitting with his back propped against the passenger door, his long legs stretched out on the seat, while she was lying pressed against his right side, half on the seat and half on him, her head on his shoulder with her face tilted up, and he was leisurely kissing her.

If the windows had been up they would have fogged over. His mouth was slow and hot and demanding, making her forget about time. The slow beat of pleasure began to pound in her veins, and her arms wound about his neck.

His palm covered her breast and the shock jolted

her, making her tear her mouth from his. He ruthlessly took it again, stifling her instinctive protest, so she could only whimper into his mouth. As the shock faded, she began to whimper from the pleasure of it, and her nipple beaded tightly beneath the layers of cloth.

"Do you like it?" he murmured. "Or do you want me to stop?"

She liked it, maybe too much, but she didn't want him to stop. Her breast was tingling and throbbing, the heat from it spreading down to her loins. His strong fingers were slowly kneading, taking care not to hurt her; then he found the turgid nipple and rubbed it through her shirt. She moaned and arched against him.

"Caroline?" he prompted. "Do you want me to stop? Or do you want more?"

"Don't stop," she said, her voice hoarse with strain. "Please, don't stop."

He kissed her reassuringly. "I won't. I'm going to unbutton your shirt and slip my hand inside. All right?"

How was she supposed to stand that when she felt as if she were flying into a thousand pieces right now? But as soon as he said it, she knew that she wanted his hand on her naked breast, that the barriers of cloth between them were too maddening to tolerate. "All right," she whispered, and somehow her hand was busy with the buttons of his shirt as he unfastened hers. She wanted to feel his bare skin as much as she wanted his touch on hers.

His long fingers dipped inside her open shirt and trailed lightly along the edges of her bra, pausing at the front center fastening. "Umm, good," he said, and deftly unfastened the garment. She felt suddenly vulnerable as it loosened; then he slid his hand inside, and all her nerve endings rioted. His palm was hot and rough, the callused skin rasping over her swollen nipples as he rubbed and lightly pinched. She heard herself moan and buried her face against his shoulder to stifle the sound.

He shifted on the seat so he was more on his side and she was lying flatter. She felt like a doll, helpless to prevent him from moving her as he willed. He spread her open shirt wide, exposing her breasts to the bright starlight shining through the windshield. She had seen men do it to women in movies, but still she was unprepared when he bent his head and closed his mouth over her nipple, drawing it in with a curling motion of his tongue. Caroline arched wildly under the lash of a sensation so exquisite and unbearable that her entire body quivered. He controlled her with those incredibly strong hands of his and the pressure of his iron-muscled legs, pressing her down into the seat, and somehow he was on top of her.

Her heart was beating so hard it hurt, and her blood was pounding through her veins. She clung to him, barely able to breathe as her body adjusted to his weight and unyielding hardness. The jarring unfamiliarity of it was matched by a deeper, more primitive sense of rightness. He moved his thighs, spreading her legs and settling himself between them, pushing the hard ridge of his manhood against her soft folds. "This is how we'll be when we make love," he whispered, pressing slow kisses on her neck and collarbone, then moving down to suckle deeply on both her breasts, leaving her nipples tight and wet and painfully sensitive to the night air when he lifted his head. He eased the coolness with the hot pressure of his chest.

His voice was a low, almost soundless rustle in her ear. "I'll move like this, slow and easy, until we're both ready to climax." His hips rocked leisurely, rhythmically pressing his sex against hers. Caroline's whole body lifted into the contact, her slender hips straining and reaching. She wanted to speak, to beg him to do something to ease this unbearable tension inside her, but all she could do was gasp for air and dig her nails into his shoulders in an effort to communicate her need to him.

"Then, when it's time, when we can't stand it any longer, I'll start moving harder and faster, going deeper and deeper into you."

She made a high, wild, pleading sound, spreading her thighs wider and lifting them to clasp his hips. Her ankle banged the steering wheel, a welcome distraction, because the slight pain eased her body's primal attention, but it wasn't enough. She twisted under him, frantic with heat and need and a deep, empty ache.

Joe caught his breath at her wild beauty, fierce and demanding, with only the starlight shining across her face. Her body was hot and tense and untamed, de-

manding a satisfaction she hadn't yet known, but the
lure of which was compelling her ever closer and
closer to the edge. He wanted to unfasten her pants
and drag them down, then bare his own loins and
drive into her, hard and fast, just as he'd told her. He
wanted her naked, lying stretched out before him on
a bed to cushion her from the force of his thrusts. He
wanted to take her with swift, rough lust, plunging
into her hot womanhood from behind so her buttocks
slapped against his belly with the raw sound of sex.
The blood of his ancestors ran hot and thick through
his veins, the blood of warriors, uncomplicated, as
forceful as the elements. He saw himself taking her
with the sun burning down on their naked skin and
nothing beneath them but the hard, hot earth. And she
was clinging to him, a warrior's woman, as fierce and
demanding as he was. He had known she was wild
the first time he'd seen her, a wildness that had been
stifled and controlled, but it was there, just waiting to
break out.

He hadn't intended to go this far, but she was pure
flame in his arms, her response immediate and strong.
His hardness stretched painfully beneath his jeans, demanding his own release, and grimly he knew it
wouldn't take much. But the seat of his truck wasn't
the place to take her virginity; it was too cramped,
too awkward, too inconvenient, and he had also promised her that he wouldn't make love to her tonight.
Caroline needed to know that she could trust him, so
he grimly fought for control. It wasn't easy; he was
close to climax himself, racked with frustration, but

his iron will slowly won out, and he eased himself from the clinging embrace of her arms and legs.

"We have to stop," he said, making his voice even. It took more effort than he liked. "If we don't, you'll lose your cherry right here."

"Yes," she whispered, reaching for him again. She didn't care if her first time was in a pickup truck. Her body burned and ached, and she needed the surcease of his possession.

He caught her hands and firmly held them down. "No. Not here and not now."

She stared at him, her eyes wild with frustration; then anger exploded hotly through her veins. She shoved at him, fighting to sit up in a flurry of tangled arms and legs, and scrambled away from him. "Then why did you let it go that far if you didn't intend to finish it?" she shouted. "You...you *tease!*"

Frustration frayed his own temper. Damn it, did she think it had been easy for him to stop? "Because I got carried away, too!" he snapped.

"Yes, I can tell," she said with a sneer. "It really shows. Your breathing speeded up a little bit there."

Furious, he grabbed her hand and carried it to the front of his jeans, pressing her palm hard against the rigid length of his manhood. "Maybe this feels unaffected to you, but you came damn close to finding out just how involved I am." His voice was guttural with rage, and that made him even angrier, because it was evidence of just how far his control had eroded.

She jerked her hand away, even though the feel of that thick ridge was fascinating. She was too angry to be diverted. "I didn't say no, did I?" she demanded hotly. "Just what was wrong with here and now?"

He ground his teeth together, savagely fighting both his anger and a violent resurgence of sexual need. It had been a mistake to force her hand down on his groin. "*Here* isn't a bed, and *now* isn't enough time. When I get in you, I'm not going to get up for a long time. A cramped quickie isn't what you need or what I want."

She crossed her arms and stared furiously out the windshield.

He was silent, too, as he mastered his temper and his voice, reaching deep down to find the icy control for which he was famous. He was astonished at how quickly she had made him lose his temper, something he couldn't remember doing since childhood. He had been angry, but losing control was something he didn't permit himself to do. It seemed Caroline had an astonishing knack for breaking through to his primitive impulses, and, even more disturbingly, she wasn't even trying. He had always controlled the relationships he had with women, letting them get only as intimate as *he* wanted, ending things when *he* wanted. The first night he had met Caroline he had coolly decided to have an affair with her, but on his terms and his timetable. It was disconcerting to realize she could not only tempt him to break his own rules but could actually make him fight to control himself.

"My quarters are in the BOQ," he finally said evenly. "I can't take you there. It would be just as inappropriate to use your quarters. Tomorrow is Friday, and I'm off duty this weekend. We'll check into a hotel in Vegas and spend the weekend there.''

He assumed she was still willing, she thought angrily, and was disgusted with herself because she was. But he'd made it plain that it had to be his way or not at all. He was the man in control.

''All right,'' she said through clenched teeth.

The drive back to the base was completed in an atmosphere more like that between adversaries rather than two people who had just decided to begin an affair. When they reached her quarters, she opened the door and jumped down without waiting for him.

He left the engine running and caught her just as she reached the door, catching her arm and whirling her around. ''My good-night kiss,'' he reminded her, and hauled her into his arms.

There was no way anyone watching could have mistaken that kiss as polite or friendly or in the getting-to-know-you stage. He held her plastered to him from knees to breast, her head bent back under the pressure of his kiss. His mouth was hot and angry and overwhelming, forcing her to acknowledge his dominance. For a few seconds she tried to push him away; then she yielded abruptly to the penetration of his tongue and pressed herself even closer to his hard frame, accepting his aggression and meeting it with her own.

He released her abruptly and stepped away, his eyes glittering. ''You won't need to pack a nightgown,'' he said.

She stood silently glaring as he walked to the truck and got in. ''I hadn't planned to,'' she muttered as he drove off.

Chapter 6

Caroline couldn't find her ID tag the next morning. She searched the dresser top where she usually put it, the kitchen table, the cabinet tops, under the furniture, in the dirty laundry where she had thrown the clothes she had worn the day before, even the trash cans, but it wasn't to be found. She sat down and tried to think what she had done with the thing, since she knew she had worn it the day before, but she drew a complete blank. Joe had had her so distracted that she might have eaten it for all she knew.

She couldn't get into the buildings without that tag; they were coded and electronically scanned at the entrances, and anyone entering a classified area without the proper ID set off an alarm that had the security police swarming with weapons drawn. She was mortified that she had so carelessly misplaced it. Security was so tight that cards couldn't be duplicated; the lost or damaged one had to be voided out of the computer system, a new one issued with a new code and that information fed into the computers. Also because of the security, a jillion forms had to be filled out in quadruplicate to authorize and verify the change. Probably even the base commander, Major General Tuell, would have to sign off on it.

She had had it the day before; she couldn't have gotten into the buildings without it. She distinctly remembered it snagging on a file folder. The tag had just been clipped on, so could it have been tugged loose without her noticing it? Probably. Joe's kisses had turned her brain into mush, and she hadn't been able to concentrate on anything but seeing him that night.

If the tag was lying somewhere in the office, why hadn't the alarm been set off when she had *left* without the proper identification? Or was the scan positioned so that it only read the tags of those entering the building, on the theory that if no one without identification got in, they didn't have to worry about who got out. It was a logical theory; she had no problem with it. Her problem was how to find out if her tag was in the office.

She considered her options. If she called the security police to have them check, it would mean reports and explanations, the very thing she wanted to avoid. So she called Cal to get him to search the office for her. If he didn't find the tag, she would report it lost and face the hassle.

It took him several rings to answer the phone, and his voice was groggy. "Hullo."

"Cal, this is Caroline. I'm sorry to wake you, but I think I dropped my ID card in the office yesterday, and I need you to look for it before I report that it's gone."

He made a grunting noise. "Wha—?" He sounded bewildered and still half-asleep. "Caroline?"

"Yes, this is Caroline. Are you awake? Did you understand what I said?"

"Yeah. Yeah, I'm awake. I got it." He yawned into the receiver. "Look for your ID card. Lord, Caroline, how'd you misplace something like that?"

"I think I snagged it on a file folder."

"So wear it on a chain around your neck instead of clipping it on."

Since she had roused him from a sound sleep, she allowed him his disgruntled advice. Maybe it was a psychological thing, but she didn't like chains around her neck, even when they were called necklaces. Instead she would make a mental note to add her ID card to the list of things she double-checked.

"How long will it take you to get dressed?" she asked.

"Give me five minutes." He yawned again. "What time is it?"

She looked at the clock. "It's 5:43."

He groaned audibly. "I'm on my way. Actually,

I'm trying to focus my eyes. You owe me one. I wouldn't do this for just anybody.''

"Thanks," she said fervently.

She met him outside the Quonset building five minutes later. He was unshaven, his hair rumpled, his eyes bleary, but he was dressed, and his own ID tag was hanging on a chain around his neck. She stood outside while he shuffled through the door, still yawning. He was back in less than three minutes, carrying her tag, which she took with a stream of thank-you's.

"It was under your desk," he said, blinking owlishly at her. "What are you doing going to work this early?"

"I usually do," she said, surprised. She thought everyone knew her habit of going in early and staying late.

He suddenly broke into his normal, easygoing grin. "I'm going to have to revise my opinion of Colonel Mackenzie downward, since he obviously isn't keeping you up late. I'm disappointed in the man."

She lifted her eyebrows in feigned astonishment. "You thought he would let anything interfere with work? Surely you jest."

"Evidently I do. Well, have fun. I'll mosey on back to shower and shave and mainline some coffee. More moving-target tests today. We need to be on our toes, and I'm barely on my feet."

She gave him a quick kiss on his beard-roughened cheek. "Thanks, Cal. It would have taken forever to get it replaced, not to mention all of the reports."

"Anytime, anytime." Then he snickered. "Or you could have called Adrian to look for it."

"I'd rather face the security police."

"That's what I thought." With a wave, he began trudging back to his own quarters, and Caroline firmly clipped the tag in place with a sigh of relief.

At six-thirty, she was engrossed in running through the tests when a low, melodious whistle caught her attention. She burst out laughing and looked up, and two seconds later Joe silently appeared in the doorway.

"Another first," he observed. "No flying cups, reports or fists."

He was dressed in his flightsuit, though he wasn't in full harness yet. Her heart was suddenly in her throat. None of the other flights or tests had made her nervous, but abruptly she felt stricken, barely able to breathe. She had never *cared* before, and all of a sudden her objectivity was destroyed.

It took a special type of man to be a military aviator, and even more so to qualify as a fighter pilot. The numbers were still overwhelmingly male, though women were now accepted into fighter training. Analysts were finding that the female jet jockey shared some personality characteristics with the male pilots, mostly coolness under pressure and situation awareness, but in other significant ways the female pilots were indubitably different from the males. The men were naturally arrogant and supremely self-confident; it took that kind of man to *be* a fighter pilot, to have

the kind of assurance that would not only allow him
to climb into a machine and streak through the sky at
three times the speed of sound, but to have the bloody
confidence that he could master not only the machine
but anything that might happen, and live to do it
again. Fighter training only reinforced that supreme
self-confidence.

She stared at him, seeing not only the cool confidence in his eyes but the actual eagerness to strap on
that lethal beauty he called Baby. He enjoyed the
speed and power, the risk, the ultimate challenge of
it. He had no doubt in his ability to make the aircraft
perform as he wanted and bring it safely to earth
again. His air of arrogant invincibility was almost
godlike in its fierceness.

But for all his skill and superiority, he was a man,
a human being. And men could be killed.

"You're going up today," she said, barely able to
force the words through her constricted throat. "You
didn't tell me."

One eyebrow rose in a faintly quizzical expression.
"I'm going up today," he replied mildly. "What
about it?"

What was she supposed to tell him, that she was
terrified because his chosen occupation was one of the
most dangerous in the world? She didn't have the
right to impose her fears on him. There was no commitment between them, only an agreement to have an
affair, which officially hadn't even begun yet. It
wasn't his fault that she was falling in love with him,
and even if he returned the sentiment, she wouldn't

tell him she was afraid, because she wouldn't risk the possibility of distracting him when he needed to concentrate wholly on his job.

"So she swallowed her fear and fought for control. "You're too…um, I think *overwhelming* is the word, in a flightsuit. What do you have on under it?"

The diversion worked. The other eyebrow rose to join its twin. "T-shirt and shorts. Did you expect me to be stark naked?"

"I didn't know. I'd never thought about it before." She made a shooing motion with her hand. "Go on, get out of here. You destroy my concentration. I couldn't work all day yesterday after what you did, so I'm not letting you near me this morning."

As soon as the words were out of her mouth she realized she should have known better. The light of battle gleamed coolly in his eyes as he walked toward her. She had inadvertently issued a challenge, and his dominant nature compelled him to call her on it.

She was still sitting down, and he leaned over her, bracing his hands on the arms of the chair and capturing her before she could scramble away. He kissed her, slanting his hard mouth over hers and using his tongue with devastating thoroughness. Her toes curled in her shoes; she surrendered without even the pretense of struggle, accepting his intrusion and welcoming it with unguarded eagerness.

He shuddered and instantly straightened, his face hard with lust. "What are you wearing tonight?"

She struggled to gather her senses, so easily scattered by his touch. "I don't know. Does it matter?"

She had never before seen his eyes so blue and intense. "No. You'll be naked five minutes after we check into the hotel."

The image was shattering. Helplessly she closed her eyes, her mouth going dry. When she opened them again, he was gone.

If she affected him even half as much as he affected her, he wouldn't be able to fly the damn plane. The fear rose nauseatingly in her throat again, surging back at full force. It took all of her willpower to force it away, but she managed it, because she knew that when it came down to it, that cold-blooded control of his would shut out every thought that didn't pertain to flying, the real love of his life. The truth hurt, but she took comfort in it, too, for as unpalatable as it was it would keep him safe, and that was all she asked.

Cal had been making a point of arriving in the mornings before Adrian, but she had disrupted his schedule that morning and was still alone when Adrian came in. He gave her an almost automatic look of dislike, poured a cup of coffee and sat down without speaking. Adrian didn't bother her much, anyway, but that morning she was so on edge that she scarcely even noticed he was there. She sat at her desk, torn between fear and anticipation. Part of her mind persisted in dwelling on the dangers of test flights, while the other part kept sliding away to sensual images of the coming night. She couldn't believe she was actually looking forward to it, but not even the realistic expectation of discomfort, at the least, was enough to quell her fever. She wanted Joe, needed him desperately, with an instinct so primal that the threat of pain was swept aside like a toothpick in a flood.

But first she had to live through the flights today.

"Dreaming about lover boy?" Adrian asked nastily.

She blinked at the interruption. "What? Oh—yes. I was. Sorry. Did you ask me something?"

"Only about your love life. I'm a little surprised, though. I didn't think it was men you liked, or have you decided to try some variety?"

Inexperience was not the same thing at all as ignorance, and she knew exactly what he was hinting at. She gave him a cold look, suddenly relishing the idea of a good, clean battle, free of entangling emotions. "Did you know I was always so much younger than the boys in my class that I was almost through college before I was mature enough for any of them to notice me?"

The question startled him; the puzzlement showed on his good-looking face. "So?"

"So they came after me hot and heavy, expecting me to know the score, but I didn't know anything at all about men and dating. I'd never been around kids my own age. I'd never been kissed, never been to a prom, never learned the things other girls learned at parties and on double dates. When those guys came on so strong it scared the hell out of me, so I said and did whatever it took to run them off. Are you getting the picture?"

He didn't, not at first. His incomprehension was

plain. But then understanding broke through his hostility, and he stared at her in shocked disbelief. "Are you saying you were *afraid* of me?"

"Well, what else could I be?" she flashed. "You were grabbing at me and wouldn't take no for an answer."

"For God's sake, I'm not a rapist!" he snapped.

"How was I supposed to know?" She stood up and shook her fist at him. "If you hadn't been so damn sure of yourself and thought no woman could resist you, you might have noticed that I was scared!"

"You didn't act scared!"

"So I get belligerent when I feel threatened." She was standing over him now, glaring and all but breathing fire. "For your information, Colonel Mackenzie is the first man to notice how uneasy I was, and *he* doesn't attack me like a hungry octopus." No, all he did was make love to her with that infuriating control of his, reducing her to mush while he remained perfectly clearheaded. That, however, wasn't any of Adrian's business. "I'm tired of your snide remarks, do you understand? Put a sock in it, as of right now, or I'll stuff one in for you."

The shock left his face, and he glared back at her with a return of hostility. "Am I supposed to feel guilty because you're a social misfit? You're not the only one with problems, lady. I'd just gone through a god-awful divorce, my wife had dumped me for a weasel who made twice as much money as I did and I needed a little ego building myself. So don't blame

me for not noticing your delicate psyche and pander-
ing to it, because you sure as hell didn't notice mine!''

"Then we're even," she charged. "So get off my
back!''

"With pleasure!''

She stomped back to her chair and flung herself
into it. After glaring at the spec sheet for about thirty
seconds she muttered, "I'm sorry about your wife.''

"Ex-wife.''

"She probably isn't happy.''

Adrian leaned back in his chair, scowling at her.
"I'm sorry I scared you. I didn't mean to.''

It was an effort, but she growled, "That's okay.''

He mumbled something and turned to his own
work.

She had sought relief and distraction in anger, and
it had succeeded while it lasted, but now that the confrontation was over her edginess came creeping back.
Still, it looked like the air might have cleared some
between Adrian and herself, or at least settled down,
so it had been beneficial in that way.

Yates and Cal came trooping in, Cal still looking
rumpled and sleepy, but he gave Caroline a grin and
a wink. Then they all went over to the control room
for the day's flights. The pilots were still there, four
of them suited up in full harness, with straps and
hoses and oxygen masks, and wearing speed jeans.
Joe and Captain Bowie Wade were flying the Night
Wings; Daffy Deale and Mad Cat Myrick were flying
chase in the F-22s. Joe was totally absorbed in the
job at hand, as she had known he would be, and the

knot of fear in her throat relaxed some to actually be able to see it.

She tried not to let herself stare at him but the impulse was irresistible. He was a lodestone to her eyes, and she was fascinated by him. It wasn't just his tall, superbly muscled body or the chiseled perfection of his face, but the aura surrounding him. Joe Mackenzie was a warrior—cool, nerveless, lethal in his controlled savagery. The blood of countless generations of warriors ran in his veins; his instincts were those honed in past wars, in numberless bloody battles. The other pilots had some of the same instincts, the same aura, but in him those things had been condensed and purified, meeting in a perfect combination of body, intellect and ability. The others knew it; it was obvious in the way they looked at him, the respect they automatically gave him. It wasn't just that he was a colonel and in charge of the project, though his rank garnered its own respect, but what they gave him as a man and a pilot they would have given him even had they all outranked him. Some men stood out from the crowd, and Joe Mackenzie was one of them. He could never have been a businessman, a lawyer or a doctor. He was what he was, and he had sought the profession that would let him do what he was so perfectly suited to do.

He was a warrior.

He was the man she loved.

Somehow she had lost the ability to breathe, and it didn't matter. She felt dazed, mired in unreality. There couldn't be any more fooling herself. She had admitted her vulnerability to him, but never the immediacy of it. She had warned herself against the danger of *letting* herself fall in love with him, fretted that she *might* be losing her heart, but it had all been an emotional smoke screen to keep her from admitting that it was already too late. She'd had no more control over it than she had over her own body whenever he touched her, which should have been enough warning by itself. Her only excuse for her own blindness was that she'd never been in love before and simply hadn't recognized it.

She couldn't look at him as he and the three other pilots left the control room. If he'd glanced at her, everything that she was feeling would have been plain on her face, and she didn't want him to see it, to maybe think about it at the wrong time. She felt absurdly naked, stripped of all her emotional protection, every nerve ending exposed and agitated by the merest stirring of air.

All four birds lifted off, and technicians crowded the terminals, intently studying the information already pouring back in from the sensors embedded in the skins of the Night Wings.

Within half an hour they were in position over the test site, where drones would provide them with moving targets at which to aim their lasers. Caroline always anticipated trouble, because in her experience no new system worked in practice exactly the way it worked in theory, but the tests had gone well so far, and she was optimistic that there wouldn't be any major problems. That day, however, seemed to prove her right in her anticipation of trouble and wrong in her hope that it would be minor. The targeting systems refused to lock on the drones, though they had done so the day before. Two different aircraft were up there today, however, and a totally disgusted project manager ordered the day's tests scrapped and the birds back to the base for a thorough check of the targeting systems.

Joe didn't lose his temper, but his displeasure was plain when he strode back into the control room, his hair matted with sweat from the helmet.

"The birds are in the hangar," he said with icy control, including Caroline in his ire as part of the laser team. "The same two are going back up Monday morning. You still have most of today to find the problem and fix it." He turned and strode off, and Cal whistled softly between his teeth.

Yates sighed. "Okay, people, let's get into our coveralls and get out to the hangars. We have work to do."

Caroline was already mentally sorting through the options. Laser targeting wasn't new; just the way they were applying it was. The problem could be the sensors in the pilots' helmets, those in the missile optics, even the switch that activated the targeting. What was disturbing was that it had happened to both aircraft at the same time, possibly indicating a basic problem in manufacturing or even design. She glanced at Cal and saw that he was frowning deeply, for *he* would be thinking that for both aircraft to experience the same difficulty at the same time could indicate trouble with the programming of the on-board computers. They were worrying about the problem from different angles, but both of them had realized the implications.

This had just been a peachy-keen day from the very beginning. If the night with Joe followed the same pattern, she would probably find out she was frigid.

They worked through lunch, running computer analyses of the sensors to try to pinpoint the trouble, but nothing showed up. Everything seemed to be working perfectly. They ran the same tests on the three birds that hadn't had any trouble and compared the results, again coming up with nothing. Everything matched. According to the computer, there was no reason why the lasers shouldn't have locked on to the moving targets.

It was late afternoon, and the heat had built to an uncomfortable level inside the hangar despite the best efforts of the huge air conditioners, when Cal reran the tests on the firing mechanisms of one of the malfunctioning units, and on one that was working. For whatever reason, maybe just the gremlins that invariably plagued every project, this time the computer showed a break in the electrical current in the trigger mechanisms. They were all aggravated because the problem had turned out to be so relatively simple after they had driven themselves crazy for hours and forgone lunch when it was something that could be repaired in less than an hour.

She was in a wonderful mood for a romantic assignation: tired, hungry, hot and ill-tempered. She made a point of scowling down at the ID tag clipped to her pocket before she left the building and headed for her quarters.

A long, cold shower made her feel better, though she was still scowling as she literally threw some clothes and toiletry items into an overnight bag. If *he* wasn't such a martinet, they wouldn't have felt so driven to solve the problem. She could have eaten lunch. She wouldn't now feel so frazzled and out of sorts. It would serve him right if she refused to go.

The only thing was, she wasn't that big a fool. She wanted to be with him more than she wanted to eat, more than she wanted anything.

It was only six o'clock when the knock came on the door. She was dressed, but her hair was still wet, and she was still hungry. She threw the door open. "We worked through lunch," she charged ominously. "We got finished—" she turned to check the clock "—thirty-five minutes ago. It was *nothing*—just a break in the current in the switches—but it took us forever to find it, because we were hungry and couldn't concentrate."

Joe lounged in the open doorway and surveyed her thoughtfully. "Do you always get ill-tempered when you're hungry?"

"Well, of course. Doesn't everyone?"

"Um, no. Most people don't."

"Oh."

He held out his hand to her. "Come on, then, and I'll feed you."

"My hair isn't dry."

"It'll dry fast enough in this heat. Are you packed?"

She fetched the overnight bag and did her quick, automatic tour to make certain everything was turned off. Joe took the bag from her hand and ushered her out, closing the door behind him. She stood there and stared meaningfully at the doorknob until he sighed and tried to turn it, to show her it was locked. Satisfied, she walked to the truck. He stowed the bag, then lifted her onto the seat. She had chosen to wear a halter-top sundress with a full skirt, deciding that it no longer mattered if he could slide his hand under it, since she had given him permission to do much more than that, but she nearly had heart failure when that warm, hard hand slipped up under the material and squeezed her bare thigh.

All thoughts of food fled her mind. She stared at him, hunger of another sort building, her need revealed in her suddenly darkened eyes and quickened breath. Joe lightly stroked her inner thigh with his fingertips, then forced himself to withdraw his hand. *"Maybe* I'll feed you first," he muttered.

Chapter 7

They could have eaten sawdust for all the attention she paid to their meal. All she remembered afterward was that the restaurant was cool and dim, and the dry wine had a crisp, pleasant bite to it. He sat across from her, big and masculine, and with that dangerous glitter in his blue-diamond eyes. He was thinking about the coming night, too, and his sexual intent was plain for her to see. He meant for her to know what he was thinking; he made his possessiveness obvious in the way he looked at her, his gaze lingering on her breasts, his voice low and deep with the gentling, persuasive note of seduction.

They lingered over the meal, and the waiting abraded her nerves like coarsely woven wool. Her clothing irritated her; her breasts ached. She blurted out, "Why are we waiting?"

He had been leisurely studying her erect nipples thrusting against her bodice, and his gaze slowly lifted to her face, scorching her with blue fire. "For you to settle down and relax," he murmured. "For night to fall, so you can have complete darkness, if it would make you feel more secure."

"I don't care." She stood up, her face as fierce and proud as a Valkyrie, her hair as pale as that of those virgin warriors. "You'll have to find some other way to relax me."

Slowly he stood, too, his face hard with the force of his surging lust. Silence strained between them as he paid the bill and they went back out to the truck. The heat was still almost suffocating, the sun a huge red ball low on the horizon, bathing everything with a crimson glow. His fierce, ancient bloodlines were obvious in the primal light falling across the stark lines of his face, giving the lie to the facade of civilization he wore in the form of a white dress shirt and black slacks. He should have been wearing buckskin pants and moccasins, his torso bare, his thick black hair falling free to those wide, powerful shoulders.

She remembered her terror of the morning, that he could be hurt or killed during a flight, and knew she would try never to tell him.

He checked them in at one of the Hilton hotels and, still silently, they rode the elevator upward, with the bellboy carrying their two small bags.

He had taken a one-bedroom suite, and the bellboy performed his customary routine, carrying the bags into the bedroom, showing them how to operate

things they already knew how to operate, busily drawing open the curtains to let in the fierce red light of
sundown. Joe pressed a five-dollar bill into his hand,
and the bellhop took off.

She was still standing in the bedroom, her feet
rooted to the carpet while she very determinedly did
not stare at the king-size bed, and she listened to Joe
lock and chain the door. He walked into the bedroom
and very calmly pulled the curtains again, plunging
the room into a gloom relieved only by what light
spilled through the open doorway. The very air felt
charged with tension. He opened his black leather bag
and took out a box of condoms, placing it on the
bedside table.

"A whole box?" she asked in a husky voice that
didn't sound like her own.

He came to stand behind her and deftly undid her
dress. As it loosened and fell off her shoulders he
said, "I'll go down to the gift shop and buy some
more when we run out."

She was suddenly trembling madly, for she had
worn only her panties under the dress. No bra, no slip,
no hosiery. As the dress pooled around her ankles she
was left standing all but naked in front of him, her
breasts tight, her nipples thrusting forward in aching
need. He lifted her in his arms, and her shoes were
left behind on the floor, caught in the froth of material.

He placed one knee on the bed as he lowered her
to the surface, then remained kneeling that way while
he swiftly, efficiently stripped her panties down her

legs. Until that moment she hadn't realized how desperately she had needed that small scrap of protection, or how exposed and vulnerable she would feel without them. She made an incoherent sound of protest as she tried to sit up, for she was naked while he was still completely dressed, but the glitter in his eyes as he stretched her out on her back made her stop struggling.

Joe paused, taking the time to study her naked form and savor the primal satisfaction of the moment when she finally lay bare before him, her tender body exposed and his for the taking. He could already see the signs of arousal in her, manifested in the way her nipples had flushed darker and tightened into buds, and in the way her slim thighs, instinctively pressed together to guard the exquisitely sensitive flesh between them, quivered and flexed in a subtle message. Pale curls, only a shade or two darker than her hair, decorated her mound; a small, fleeting smile tugged at his mouth for a second as he remembered that he hadn't thought her hair color was natural. According to the evidence of his eyes, it indisputably was her own. Those blond curls were so tempting that suddenly just looking wasn't enough.

He put his hand on her breast, gently kneading, cupping, his rough thumb circling her nipple and making it draw even tighter. She caught her breath, which made her breast swell even more fully into his palm. With the same calm assurance he stroked his other hand down her abdomen to slip it between her legs, pressing his fingers hard against the soft folds of her womanhood. Lightning shimmered through her, lifting her hips from the bed in an automatic seeking of more. If his thumb had felt rough on her nipple, it felt even more so now as it rasped across flesh so sensitive she quivered wildly at the slightest touch.

It was unbearable and she suddenly fought away from him, rising to her knees on the bed, her breasts heaving with the force of her breathing. Joe stood up and began unbuttoning his shirt.

His powerful torso was bared as he stripped out of the garment, his skin bronzed, soft black hair matting his chest in a neat diamond and running in a silky line down the center of his stomach. His own nipples were small, dark and tight. He kicked his shoes off. Lean fingers unbuckled his belt, unzipped his fly, hooked in the waistbands of both trousers and undershorts and pushed them down. His eyes never left her slim, nude body as he bent to remove them. When he straightened, he was as naked as she.

The strength evident in his masculine body was almost frightening. He could overwhelm her without effort if he chose. Iron-hard muscles ridged his flat belly, corded his rib cage and long thighs. His male length rose thick and full from his groin, visibly throbbing with the force of his lust. Despite the responding heat of her own blood, beating through her veins in rhythm with the throbbing in her loins, she began to have serious doubts about the possibility of this. She made a soft, panicked sound.

''Shh, sweetheart,'' he murmured softly. ''Don't be nervous.'' His hard hands closed gently on her shoulders, and somehow she found herself lying on her back again, and he was lying beside her, the heat of his big body searing and enveloping her as he folded her close to him. His nakedness was overwhelming, the strength of his sexuality no longer masked either by clothing or the boundaries enforced by society. He continued to soothe her with low whispers that might not even have been words, while his hands stroked slow fire over her.

Caroline clung to him, unsure of herself in this dramatically intensified situation. She had thought he had led her into sensual territory before, but now she found that she had only been loitering in the doorway. If it hadn't been for the pleasure, she would have bolted. But the pleasure...ah, it was slow and insidious and mind numbing, gently seducing her into relaxing her tight muscles; then, when her resistance was gone, it abruptly turned into a thundering storm that crashed through her nerves and muscles. Her slender body quivered with it, drawing tight as a bowstring again, but this time from a different cause, and he was too instinctive a male animal not to immediately sense that difference. His hands moved over her with a sure and shattering purpose, no longer to calm, but to intensify her arousal.

His mouth drew her nipples into wet beads of sensual torment, punished by sharp little bites and soothed by his tongue. She writhed sinuously in his arms, her hips lifting and rolling in an ancient rhythm that called to him as surely as a drumbeat. Once again his fingers delved between the soft feminine folds and found her moist and swollen, aching for his touch; her thighs opened unconsciously to give him greater freedom, an opportunity he immediately exploited. He carefully penetrated her with one long finger, and a wild little sound burst from her throat as she surged upward against his hand. He lingered over her, drunk with the scent of her warm, aroused body, the silkiness of her skin. He would have crushed her against him if he could have absorbed her into himself, so violent was the urge to meld their two bodies together.

His probing touch taught him both the height of her excitement and the strength of her virginity, and his stomach muscles tightened with almost unbearable anticipation. He couldn't wait much longer, but he wanted her so hot that she would willingly accept the pain of his penetration in order to take the deeper pleasure of their joining. She was so tight he didn't know if he could stand it, but he would go mad if he didn't thrust himself into her sweet depths.

She was arching nearer and nearer to climax as his sensual torment continued, her head thrashing on the bed in a tangle of blond hair, her hands clutching at him with desperate strength. She moaned and sank her nails into his chest. "Now." Her voice was hoarse. "Now now now *now!*"

He couldn't stand it any longer himself. He spread her thighs wide and mounted her, his hard weight pressing her into the mattress as his rigid length pushed against the soft heat of her intimate flesh and felt it begin to yield beneath the pressure. Then the exquisite feel of nakedness brought him to his senses, and he drew back from her, from the maddening closeness of penetration. He reached for the box on the bedside table, extracting one of the small foil packets and tearing it open with his teeth.

"No," Caroline said fiercely, pushing his hand away. "Not this time, not the first time. I want to feel *you*, only you."

Her passion-dark eyes glared up at him; her slim, heated body called to him with a primitive message. She was wild and pagan, even more the Valkyrie now when she lay naked, her thighs open to accept the male intrusion that would end her maidenhood. She challenged his domination, demanded his body and seed in this most ancient celebration of fertility.

Joe braced himself on his arms above her, his face savage as he brought his hips back to hers. He was experienced sexually where she wasn't, knew the wild risk they were taking, but this one time, this first time he, too, wanted her without anything between them.

Caroline went still at the first blunt probing.

Their eyes met and held. A tiny muscle in his cheek twitched as he increased the pressure. Pain threatened for her, became a reality, but she didn't try to push him away. She wanted this, hungered for his possession with a violence that made the pain as nothing. He didn't take it easy with her. His penetration was inexorable: invading, stretching, forcing her soft sheath to accept and hold his turgid length. She arched wildly, unable to take any more, and by her own action found that she could. He gave a harsh sound of pleasure.

"Yes," he muttered tightly. "That's right, sweetheart, you can take me. Come on. More. Do it again." The exquisite feel of her was mind shattering, like hot silk, tight and wet and incredibly soft.

Driven by some frantic need she did, and suddenly he was seated in her to the hilt, the solidness of his possession making hot tears spring to her eyes. The stretched, too-full sensation was unbearable, yet she bore it because the only alternative was to stop, and that was impossible. She was impelled by a need too instinctive for caution, too fierce to slow. The hard planes of his chest crushed her breasts; his hands slid under her and gripped her buttocks with bruising force as he lifted her into his thrusts, and sharp pleasure exploded through her. She clung to him, sobbing and gasping and half screaming.

Grinding his teeth, he fought his own climax and rode her hard, intensifying her spasms of release. Gradually she stopped shaking and the frantic tension eased from her muscles, letting her relax in his arms. A soft, almost purring note sounded in her throat. "Joe," she whispered, just his name, and the lazy pleasure in her voice almost sent him over the edge.

"Now," he said gutturally, rising to his knees. It was his turn, and his need was so savage he could barely control it. He hooked his arms under her legs and leaned forward, bracing himself on his hands with her legs forced high and wide, draped over his arms. She was completely vulnerable to him like that, totally unable to limit the depth of his thrusts, and he took full advantage of it. He drove into her hard and deep,

his powerful shoulders hunched with the effort as he
hammered into her, and the pleasure hit him just as it
had her, without warning, slamming into him like a
runaway train. He jerked convulsively under the force
of it, a harsh cry ripping from his throat. The spasms
went on and on, emptying him into the hot depths of
the woman beneath him. When it finally did end, he
sank heavily onto her, his chest heaving as his tortured lungs fought for air. His heart was thudding
frantically in his chest, and he was so weak he
couldn't roll away from her. He'd never felt like this
even when pulling Gs, and certainly never from having sex.

He dozed. She should have protested his heavy
weight, but instead she cradled him close, loving the
feel of his big body crushing her into the mattress.
She could barely move, barely breathe, and it was
heaven. She ached all over, but especially between her
legs, where his heavy manhood still nestled within
her, yet she was filled with a sense of contentment
that permeated every cell of her body and all but ne-
gated the discomfort. Her eyes drifted shut. She had
wanted it just the way it had been—raw and forceful.
The only thing that could have made it better would
have been if he had lost that damnable control of his.
It had given a little, but still it had held, whereas she
had been helpless in the grip of a wild passion that
had known no limits.

"Caroline." His mouth settled over hers just as he
said her name, and drowsily she realized that she must
have slept, because she hadn't felt him move, but now

he was braced on his elbows, her head cradled in his palms. Without pause she responded, her mouth opening and molding itself to his.

A little while later he forced himself to stop kissing her and gently disengaged their bodies. She remained limply sprawled on the bed while he went into the bathroom and came out a moment later with a wet washcloth. She thought she should be embarrassed at the intimate way he cleaned her, but it was beyond her. She yawned like a sleepy cat and curled onto her side when he had finished. "Did I bleed?" she asked, her voice holding only an absentminded curiosity.

"Only a little." He caressed her buttocks possessively, filled with fierce satisfaction that she had given herself to him so completely. She hadn't held anything back, hadn't let discomfort or fear of the unknown prevent her from hurling herself headlong into the situation. He'd never been wanted like that before, had never wanted anyone like that before, with no reservations or restraints, no boundaries. Any other woman would have been frightened by the savagery of his possession, but Caroline had reveled in it. He'd never *been* so savage before, had never allowed himself to give in to the fierceness of his sexual needs. His rampant sexuality had always been held under ruthless control, yet now he had not only given in to it, he had done so without protection. He might have made her pregnant with that one irresponsible act.

He should have been furious and disgusted with himself, but somehow he wasn't. The utter pleasure of it had been too strong to allow room for regrets. A dangerous image formed in his mind, a picture of Caroline swollen with his child, and to his surprise he began to be aroused again.

She was asleep. He carried the washcloth back to the bathroom and returned to turn back the covers and tuck her between the cool sheets. She murmured softly; then, when he slipped in beside her, she cuddled against him, automatically seeking the comfort of his warmth. He cradled her head on his shoulder, his free arm wrapped possessively around her hips to hold her close. He went to sleep almost as easily as she had.

When he awakened later, his acute sense of time told him that he'd been asleep for about two hours. He was achingly aroused, and by the time he had caressed her awake, she was, too. This time he forced himself to use protection, though for the first time he bitterly resented the thin barrier between their complete intimacy. She gasped a little when he entered her, her tender flesh sore from the first time, but again she wouldn't let him be gentle, even if he had wanted to be. There would be time for gentleness later; for now there was only the flood tide of desire, demanding release. They writhed and surged together in the darkness, the only sound the roughness of their breathing and the creaking of the bed beneath them.

They slept again. He awakened three more times during the night and had her. He wondered when the urgency would lessen.

It was after eight the next morning when he opened his eyes to find the bright morning sun trying valiantly to pierce the heavy curtains. The room was dim, the air conditioning quietly humming, the air pleasantly cool. His body ached from the unbridled activities of the night.

Caroline lay curled on her side, facing away from him, and for a moment he admired the delicate line of her spine. How could such a soft, delicately made body have withstood the demands he had made on it?

The bed was a wreck. The covers were all pulled loose and twisted, and mostly on the floor. At some point during the night Caroline had pulled one corner of the bedspread up to hug to her breasts. Even the fitted bottom sheet had come loose. One pillow was stuffed under the headboard. He had a distinct memory of there having been three pillows, but he had no idea where the other two were. He also had a distinct memory of having placed one under her hips during one of their ravenous encounters. He yawned, wondering if she would want to remake the bed before the hotel maids could see it. He didn't see much point in remaking it at all.

He was hungry and gently shook her awake. "What do you want for breakfast, sweetheart? I'll call room service, then we can take a bath while we're waiting."

She opened one eye. "Coffee," she murmured.

"What else?"

She sighed. "Food." The eye closed.

He chuckled. "Can you narrow it down a little?"

She thought about it. "Nothing green," she finally mumbled into the mattress. "I can't eat green in the mornings."

Stunned by the idea, he shuddered with revulsion. Come to think of it, he couldn't eat anything green in the mornings, either.

He ordered pecan waffles and bacon for both of them, with coffee and orange juice. The impersonal voice on the other end of the line informed him that it would be forty-five minutes to an hour before his order arrived, which was fine with him. He hung up the phone and shook Caroline awake again.

"Do you want a shower or a tub bath?"

"Tub. Can't sit down in a shower."

He went into the bathroom and turned on the faucets of the playground-size bathtub. Despite the size of the thing, the water level rose quickly. He returned to the bedroom and lifted Caroline in his arms. Her own arms curled trustingly around his neck. "Are you very sore?" he asked with concern.

"Not *too* sore, if that's what you're asking." She rubbed her cheek against his shoulder. "It's just that I can't walk."

He stepped into the tub with her still in his arms and carefully lowered himself into the warm water, then reclined against the back of the tub with her between his legs, her back to his chest. She sighed with pleasure as the warm water began soaking the stiffness from her legs and easing the discomfort between them.

She would have expected to be embarrassed by the intimacy that had passed between them during the night, as well as uneasy with their nudity, but she didn't feel any of that. She felt bone-deep contentment, a sense of rightness and completion that she'd never before known existed. He was her man, she was his woman; how could she be embarrassed with him?

He bathed her, lathering his hands with the fragrant soap and gently sliding them over the tender parts of her body, which somehow seemed to need more attention than the other parts. By the time he finished she was feeling very warm and so was he, if the fullness of his hard male length was any indication. She returned the favor and bathed him, but the imminent arrival of their food prevented him from doing anything to relieve his arousal.

There were two thick, hooded terry bathrobes hanging on the back of the bathroom door, and they put them on a scant two minutes before the brisk knock on the door heralded room service. Joe signed the order slip while the cart was immobilized and the covers removed from the dishes.

The delicious scent of coffee brought her drifting in from the bedroom. Joe's eyes sharpened with the quick resurgence of lust. Even with her face bare of makeup, her hair tousled and her body wrapped in a thick bathrobe, she was more alluring than every other woman he'd had or even seen. The men she worked with might call her the Beauty Queen because of her fastidious attention to her appearance, but her attraction didn't rely on it.

She attacked the food with unselfconscious appetite, and he thought that even the way she ate made him hard. When she was finished she leaned back with a sigh of contentment and smiled at him, a lazy smile that made his blood sizzle.

"What are we going to do today?"

He lifted his black eyebrow. His pale eyes looked as hard and brilliant as diamonds, and there was fire in their depths. "I don't plan on leaving the suite this entire weekend," he said evenly. "Unless we run out of condoms."

Slowly she stood up. "Maybe room service will deliver," she said in a voice that was suddenly tight with need, and then she was in his arms.

Chapter 8

She drowned in sensuality that weekend. The two rooms of that impersonal hotel suite became very personal, imbued with the aura and memories of their lovemaking. They didn't leave the suite at all, relying on room service for their food, and never dressing in anything except the bathrobes.

As a lover, he more than matched the strength of her passion. Caroline never did anything in halfway measures; she had been fiercely virgin, and now she was just as fierce in the giving of herself. He had never before given free rein to his appetites, but with Caroline he could. He sated himself with her, and yet never felt as if he had had enough. The hunger would roar back, again and again.

He had no inhibitions. He was earthy and powerful,

sweeping her along with him, introducing her to more variations, techniques and positions than she could have imagined. Sometimes he was on top and sometimes she was; sometimes he was behind her. Sometimes he used his mouth, and he taught her how to use hers to pleasure him. He made love to her in the bathtub, on the couch, on the floor, wherever they happened to be.

He had a beeper on his belt, but the beeper remained silent and the outside world didn't intrude on them. She had never before been so completely, overwhelmingly involved with another human being, to the exclusion of everything else. She didn't think about work, didn't fret for a book to read. She simply experienced.

By Sunday morning the initial frenzied hunger had been fed and their lovemaking had become more leisurely, bringing with it the patience to linger over both arousal and satisfaction. An hour of sensual play had satisfied them for the moment, and Joe ordered a late breakfast; then they lounged in the parlor with their feet up while they watched television and caught up on the news. Caroline curled against his side, heavy-eyed with contentment.

He lifted a pale strand of her hair and let it drift down, the sunlight catching the gold and making it glitter. "Where are your parents?" he asked absently, paying more attention to the play of light than to his own question.

"Usually, or at this exact moment?" Her voice was just as lazy as his.

"Both."

"Usually they're in North Carolina, where they teach. Right this moment, they're in Greece on a summer-long cultural tour. They're supposed to come home the middle of September."

"Were you lonely when you were little?"

"Not that I noticed. I wanted to *learn*," she explained. "I couldn't learn fast enough to keep myself satisfied. I wasn't a comfortable child to be around, I don't think. If I hadn't had them for parents I probably would have been a complete wreck, but they helped me handle the frustration and didn't try to limit what I learned."

"You were probably a holy terror," he said dryly.

"Probably." She felt comfortable with it. "What about you?"

He didn't answer immediately, and a tiny quiver of unease intruded on her massive contentment. He would talk easily about his experiences as a pilot, about work, but he kept his private life very private. He had relaxed his guard a little in telling her that he was a half-breed, and that he had three brothers and one sister, but very little else. He hadn't related any childhood experiences to let the conversation get very close to him. Of course, she reminded herself, she hadn't known him for long at all, actually less than a week. The speed and intensity of their relationship dazed her, made the flow of time seem exaggeratedly long.

"No, I wasn't a holy terror," he finally said. She sensed the remoteness in his answer.

"Are any of your brothers or your sister?"

Because she was so close to him, she could feel the subtle relaxation of his muscles. "Just my sister, and it isn't that she's destructive or bad tempered, just *very* determined to have her own way. She's a little steamroller."

His deep love for his family was evident in his voice. She snuggled closer to him, hoping to keep him talking. "How old are your brothers and sister? What are their names?"

"Michael is eighteen. He's just gotten out of high school and starts college next month. He's interested in cattle ranching and will probably start his own spread when he gets out of college. Joshua is sixteen, and he's the best-natured of the bunch, but he's a jet freak, just like I was at his age. Damn his hide, though, he wants to be a Navy flier. Zane is thirteen, and he's…intense. Silent and dangerous, like Dad. Then there's Maris. She's eleven going on a hundred. Small for her age, so delicate she looks like a breeze would send her airborne, and a will like iron. We're all good with horses, damn good, but Dad is sheer magic with them, and so is Maris."

"What about your stepmother?" Anything to keep him talking.

He gave a quiet laugh. "Mary. She's even smaller than you are."

She sat up. "I'm not small." Her chin jutted out belligerently.

"You're not exactly tall, either. Not quite average, I'd say. I'm almost a foot taller than you." He pulled her back down against his side, her head nestled in the hollow of his shoulder. "Do you want to know about Mary or not?"

"Go ahead," she grumbled, and he kissed her forehead.

"Mary is warm and open and loving, and when she makes up her mind to do something she's unstoppable. She's a teacher. I wouldn't have made it into the Academy without her tutoring."

"So you didn't mind when she and your father married?"

"Mind?" He gave that quiet laugh again. "I did everything I could to throw them together. Not that it was all that difficult. Dad was like a corralled stallion. He was determined to have her, no matter how many fences he had to kick down or go over."

His ease and earthy understanding of his father's sexual nature made her smile. For her part, she simply couldn't imagine her own parents as intensely sexual beings, probably because they weren't. She was proof that they did have sex, but both of them were low-key and concerned more with intellectual matters than those of a physical nature. Their love life was probably warm and affectionate, rather than the raw, raunchy, intense lovemaking Joe had swept her into.

"What about your dad? What's he like?"

"Tough. Dangerous. And the best father in the world. Even when I was a little kid, I always knew he'd fight to the death for me."

That was an odd way to describe one's parent, but looking at Joe she could easily believe that his father was dangerous. They were probably mirror images of each other.

"That's enough about me," he said abruptly, though very little of the conversation had actually told her about *him*. She sensed that wariness in him again as the steel door guarding his inner thoughts clanged shut. He lifted her astride his lap and pushed her robe open, closing his hands over her breasts. "I want to find out about you."

She shivered and looked down at her breasts, at his bronze hands covering the soft, pale mounds. "That's no longer virgin territory to you."

"So it isn't." The blue of his eyes grew darker, more intense. He stroked one of his hands down her belly and into the notch of her legs, lightly probing. "This isn't, either, but it's even more exciting now than it was before. I could only imagine what you'd feel like before, but now I know how tight and hot you are, and how you start getting wet as soon as I touch you." He circled her delicate opening with one rough fingertip, using exquisite care. She shuddered as pleasure rushed through her, hot and sharp, tightening her muscles and giving him the dampness he sought as her body immediately began preparing to receive him. He pushed his finger a little way into her, and her body quickened, her breath sighing in and out of her lungs, a fine quivering seizing her.

Joe pushed his own robe open. He was as ready as a stallion, his thin nostrils flaring at the female scent of her. With his hand on her bottom he urged her forward, positioned her, then reached down to hold himself steady as she sank onto him with a soft, wild cry. She enveloped him, and he moved his hand, using it to urge her closer.

"Now I know how soft you are," he whispered, "and how you shiver around me, how all those sweet little muscles try to grab me tight and start milking me when we're...*damn!*" The last word was low and fierce. Caroline scarcely heard it. She began moving on him, hungry for him, desperate for the release already luring her.

His hands bit into her hips almost as if he would stay her movements, and she whimpered, but then with another muttered curse he grasped her buttocks and moved her in a hard, quick rhythm on his invading length. This wasn't one of the leisurely times; it was fast and ruthless and basic. She grabbed at his shoulders for balance as she began convulsing and only a heartbeat later he joined her, his head arching back, veins and tendons cording in his muscular neck.

Recovery took longer than the act itself. She slumped forward to lie in exhausted silence on his chest. He smoothed her hair away from her face with gentle fingers, then held her close to him. "I haven't been taking very good care of you," he said quietly. "That's twice."

She couldn't think of any way he could take any *better* care of her. "What is?" she murmured.

"That I've taken you without protection."

"But I asked you to." She closed her eyes, savoring in both memory and actuality the intimate feel of him. "I wanted to know everything, feel everything, about you."

"The first time, yes. Even then, I should have had better sense. And there wasn't any excuse for this time."

At the hardness of his tone she sat up and squarely met his gaze. "I'm neither a child nor an idiot, Joe. I know the risk and the consequence, and the responsibility is half mine. I could have said no, but I didn't. The risk isn't that great. One of the benefits of having an inquiring mind is that I'm curious about almost everything, so I read about it. I know all about rhythm and timing, and we're fairly safe. Safe enough that I'm not going to sweat and watch the calendar."

"There's no guarantee on that. All the timing can give us is better than even odds, and I told you, I'm not a gambler."

"Would you mind so very much?" she asked steadily.

"Wouldn't *you?*"

She shook her head. "No." Her voice was quiet and rock solid.

He gave her a piercing look. She waited for him to ask her why, but he didn't. Instead he said, "I want to know if your next period is even a day late."

His tone of command was so obvious that she snapped off a sharp salute and barked, "Yes, sir!" Sometimes he was very much the colonel.

He laughed and swatted her lightly on the bottom as he shifted her off his lap. She stood up and tied the robe around her. "When do we have to leave?"

"I arranged for a late checkout," he said. "By six tonight."

So their remaining time locked in their private little world could now be counted in a dwindling number of hours. It was amazing how quickly she had grown accustomed to room and maid service, to having him all to herself, to the intoxicating delights of the flesh. Probably this seclusion would wear thin if it stretched out for a week, but she would like to have that week. It wasn't to be, however. Tomorrow they would both be back at work, she on the ground and he in the air. Tomorrow she would have to deal with the fear all over again, because the man she loved was doing something dangerous and she couldn't stop it. It would be obscene to even try. Joe was an eagle; only death or age would ground him. She would gladly endure years of quiet terror, if only they would be granted.

For now, she didn't want to waste even one minute before they were forced to face real life again.

She didn't know what this weekend had meant to him, maybe only a prolonged, intense roll in the hay, sufficient for the pleasure it provided, but for her the man and the weekend had been the catalyst that had unlocked the passion of her nature. She felt…changed inside, somehow, freer, more content. It was as if she had been viewing life through a gray veil and it had been ripped aside, letting her see the true, vibrant colors. She no longer felt set aside and isolated, but part of it all. She was no longer alone, as she had essentially been for most of her life, from the time she had first realized that her brain made her different. In giving herself to him, she had gained rather than lost, because she now had a part of Joe that would never leave her. He had given her memories, experience... ecstasy. Under his earthy tutelage, she had bloomed inside herself, learned the rich depths of her own nature.

Abruptly, despite her own common sense and in full recognition of the difficulties it would involve, she hoped that the timing had been wrong for her and she was carrying his child.

"What?" he asked, black brows lifted, and she realized she had been standing in front of him staring intently at him for God only knew how long.

A slow smile broke across her face, lighting her up like dawn. "I was just thinking," she said seriously, "that a lot more women would enlist if you'd just pose for recruiting posters in the nude."

He looked briefly startled, then gave a roar of laughter as he surged to his feet. He grabbed a fistful of robe and hauled her to him. "Do you mean you'd share me with the women of America?"

"Not in this lifetime."

"Not even if my country needed my services? Where's your patriotism?"

She reached into his open robe and firmly cupped him. "One place it isn't," she replied sweetly, "is here."

He began to fill her palm as he responded to her touch, despite their recent lovemaking. "I'll give you two days to stop that, then I'm calling the police."

"We don't have two days," she pointed out. She looked at the clock. "We only have about eight hours."

"Then damn if I'm going to waste a minute of it," he replied, swiftly lifting her into his arms. He preferred the bed for prolonged lovemaking. As he carried her into the other room she clung tightly, wishing that time could stand still.

It didn't, of course. It couldn't, despite her wishes. It felt strange leaving their intimate cocoon, but by six-thirty they were headed back to the base. She sat silently, trying to brace herself for the abrupt end to the intimacy they had shared for the past two days. She would sleep alone that night and every night, until the weekend came again. Perhaps even then. He hadn't said anything about tomorrow night, much less next weekend.

She glanced at him. It was a subtle difference, but the closer they got to the base he became less her lover and more the colonel. His thoughts were already on Night Wing, on those sleek, deadly, beautiful planes and how they responded to his skilled hands. Maybe the change in him was that he became their lover rather than hers. They flew for him; they carried him higher and faster than she ever could. She only hoped they would protect him as fiercely, and bring him back to her.

Long before she was ready, he was depositing her at her door. He stood in front of her, those clear, bottomless eyes lingering over every detail of her appearance. "I'm not going to kiss you good-night," he said. "I won't want to stop. I'm too used to having you."

"Then…good night." She started to hold out her hand, then quickly pulled it back. She couldn't share even a handshake with him. It was too much after the concentrated intimacy of the weekend, too much of a temptation, too sharp a reminder that tonight they would sleep alone.

"Good night." He turned abruptly and strode to his truck. Caroline quickly unlocked the door and stepped inside, not wanting to see him drive away. The tiny quarters, luxurious as they were in comparison with most of the temporary quarters on base, were both desolate and suffocating. She quickly turned the air conditioner on high, but nothing could ease the emptiness. Nothing, that is, except Joe.

She didn't sleep well that night. She kept reaching for him, searching for his warmth, for the big, hard, masculine body she had slept draped over and entangled with for the past two nights. Her own body, abruptly deprived of the sensual orgy it had become accustomed to, ached with frustration.

She was awake well before dawn and finally gave up on sleep. Work had always been a panacea for her, so perhaps it would be again. She *was* assigned to the project to work, after all, not to moon over the project manager.

It did help. She managed to lose herself quite satisfactorily in preparation for the day's tests. Joe didn't stop by, for which she was oddly grateful. She was just now getting her bearings back; if he'd kissed her, she would have been lost again. She would probably also have been stretched out across one of the desks with her legs wrapped around his waist. Typically, he had seen the temptation and resisted it. She wasn't certain she could have.

As usual, Cal was the second to arrive. "Where were you this weekend?" he asked casually. "I tried to call a couple of times to see if you wanted to catch a movie."

"In Vegas," she replied. "I stayed there."

"Wish I'd thought of that. It's a fun town, isn't it? Did you hit the casinos?"

"I'm not much of a gambler. Miniature golf is more my game."

He laughed as he got himself a cup of coffee. "You'd better watch living in the fast lane like that," he advised. "Too much excitement can make you old."

If that were the case, she would have aged at least a hundred years over the weekend. Instead, she felt more alive than she ever had before.

Joe wasn't in the control room when the laser team arrived; the pilots were already in the aircraft, engines screaming. The assignments were the same as they had been on Friday: Joe and Bowie Wade in the Night Wings, Daffy Deale and Mad Cat Myrick in the F-22s. All the project teams gathered around their assigned monitors so they could scan the sensor readouts during the flight.

The birds lifted off.

It went smoothly at first, with the lasers locking on to the drones just the way they were supposed to do. Caroline let out a long sigh of relief. She wasn't naive enough to think there wouldn't be any more problems, but at least that particular one seemed to have been solved. They ran through it time after time, at different speeds and ranges. Yates was smiling.

On their return to base, Mad Cat was on Joe's wing and Daffy was shadowing Bowie Wade, to provide visual verification during the flights. Caroline was still idly watching the monitor when suddenly Bowie's target signal lit up. "Did he hit the switch?" she asked aloud.

Yates and Adrian turned back to the monitor, their brows knit with puzzlement. Cal looked up from his own computer. Almost simultaneously, the computer started flashing the red firing signal and all hell broke loose on the radio and in the control room.

"I'm hit, I'm hit!" Daffy screamed, and Bowie was yelling, "This goddamn thing just went off! What the hell happened?"

"What's the damage?" It was Joe's voice, deep and cool, the authority in it overriding everything else.

"No control, my hydraulics are shot to hell. I can't hold it." Daffy's voice was tight.

"Eject!" Bowie was yelling. "Stop screwing around, Daffy. You can't make it!"

The voices were stepping all over each other, and the control room was in an uproar. The pilots there were turned to stone, their faces frozen masks as they waited to see if one of their own made it back or was going to die right in front of them.

Then Joe's voice again, roaring. "Eject—eject— *eject! Now!*"

The iron authority got through to Daffy as nothing else could have, and the computers registered a pilot ejection.

"I see a chute!" It was Mad Cat. "He's too low, he's too low—"

Then the radio exploded with noise as the F-22 augered into the desert floor.

Chapter 9

Joe was in a rage when he strode into the control room, but his rage was cold, ice-cold. His eyes were blue frost as he fastened them on the laser team. "What the *hell* happened?" he snapped. "The laser cannon isn't even supposed to be activated, much less go off by itself."

They were all at a loss. The systems had checked out perfectly on Friday afternoon.

"Well?" The single word was as sharp as the crack of a rifle. "I nearly lost a man because of it. An eighty-million-dollar aircraft is in tiny pieces all over a square mile of desert. Do any of you have any idea *what the hell you're doing?*"

The control room was dead silent as everyone waited for a reply, any reply. Yates said softly, "We don't know what happened. But we'll find out."

"You're damn right you will. I want a report on this within thirty-six hours, your analysis of the problem and what you've done to fix it. All flights are scrubbed until I know what happened and I'm satisfied it won't happen again." He didn't even glance at Caroline as he turned and walked out, still as furious as he had been when he had entered the room.

Someone whistled softly through their teeth. Yates' face was drawn. "We don't sleep until we know," he said simply.

The loss of the aircraft was bad enough, but it was Daffy's close call that had stretched Joe's control perilously close to the snapping point. Daffy was lost to him anyway: he'd been too low when he ejected for his chute to adequately deploy, and he had landed too hard and too fast. He was hospitalized now with a concussion and a broken left leg.

Bowie, badly shaken, swore he hadn't touched either the lock-on switch or the trigger, and Joe believed him. Bowie was too good, too careful, but the damn laser cannon had somehow locked on and fired by itself, and Daffy had nearly died. The computers would tell them exactly what had happened, but what Joe wanted to know was *why*. The lasers weren't supposed to be activated yet, but the one on Bowie's bird, at least, had been. Had peak energy been used, the F-22 would have been destroyed in the air and Daffy wouldn't have had any chance at all.

Joe's anger was intensified because the misfire was probably linked to the lock-on problem they'd had the

Friday before. Caroline had said the problem was a simple break in the electrical signal and that it had been corrected, but obviously the trouble was much worse than that, and, far from being corrected, it had nearly killed a man. His fury included Caroline; she was part of the laser team, and his relationship with her had nothing to do with her responsibility as a team member. It wouldn't win her any special favors or leniency.

The laser team wouldn't be the only one working late. The loss of an F-22 and the injury of a pilot weren't things the Air Force took lightly. He had to make a report to the base commander and to General Ramey in the Pentagon. Moreover, they couldn't afford this kind of trouble with the Night Wings, not with the vote for funding coming up shortly in Congress. He had to get the tests completed and the kinks worked out; one of the major pluses the project had going for it was that it was coming in on time and under budget, and delays meant money. If the Night Wings were over budget and not working properly when the vote was taken, the project would be in trouble. Funding depended on how well he did his job and demonstrated both the feasibility and dependability of the birds.

His call on a secure line to General Ramey only underlined his concern. "You have to find out what happened with that laser cannon and make damn sure it never happens again," the general said quietly, but those who knew Ramey knew that he meant what he said. "The vote is close, too close for us to afford this kind of snafu. What good is it to have the first feasible X-ray laser cannon if it's uncontrollable? We have to have it, Joe. The Night Wing project is too important.''

''Yes, sir,'' Joe replied. Having flown the birds, he knew exactly how important they were. An aviator going up in a superior aircraft had a much better chance, all other things being equal, of coming back alive. The Night Wing birds gave a huge advantage to American pilots, and to Joe that meant American lives saved as well as wars won. He had already been in two wars and he was only thirty-five, and the world situation was even more volatile now than it had been when he had entered the Academy back during the Cold War. Brushfire wars sprang up overnight, and all of them had the potential of dragging the rest of the world into the maw, while technology was exploding. Within five years the F-22s would merely be equal to other countries' fighters, rather than vastly superior. The Night Wings would get that edge back—in a big way.

''Is there any indication of sabotage?'' the general asked.

''There haven't been any alarms triggered, but I've asked the security police for an analysis of the work patterns to see if there's anything suspicious.''

''What's your gut feeling?'' General Ramey had the utmost respect for Joe's instincts.

Joe paused. ''A catastrophic situation developed without warning. We don't know yet if it involves only that one laser cannon or if it's common to all the aircraft, but it's either a major problem with the system, or someone deliberately caused it. It's fifty-fifty, so I can't ignore the possibility of sabotage. I'll know more after I get the computer analysis.''

"Call me immediately when you know something.''

"Yes, sir, I will.''

Joe sat back in his chair, his eyes thoughtful. Sabotage. No one ever liked to consider it, but he couldn't afford to discount it. Technology constantly created new techniques in spying and sabotage. The security police had gone to great lengths to keep Night Wing under wraps, which was why every entrance into every building, both doors and windows, contained sensors linked to a central computer that kept track or who was in each building at any given time, recording both entrance and exit times. Guards were also posted at the hangars at night and no one had approached the planes without proper clearance, but if the problem was sabotage, that meant only that the saboteur had the required security clearance.

If he were lucky, the laser team would find the problem and it would be something mechanical, something explicable. If not, he wanted to have the security check already in progress.

What a bitch. If they didn't find out what was wrong immediately, it would ensure that he wouldn't see Caroline tonight, and last night without her had been pure torment. It was amazing how quickly his body had become accustomed to frequent gratification, and how strong his sexual hunger for her was.

He'd never wanted a woman that way before, like an incessant fever that refused to be cooled. He'd never enjoyed a woman that way before, without any boundaries or restrictions. She was vital and electric, as straightforward with her loving as her thoughts and personality were.

It had been a mistake to let his thoughts slip to her. His pants had become very uncomfortable. *Down, boy,* he thought wryly. Now was definitely not the time or the place.

No matter how they checked, they couldn't discover how the laser had been activated by accident. Caroline's actual expertise was with the laser itself, not with the triggering mechanism. That was Adrian's field, and he was surly because of it. If the problem was laid at his door, he might be recalled from the project or possibly even fired. Typically, he took out his frustration on Caroline.

"What are you, a jinx?" he muttered, scowling as he painstakingly checked every detail of the firing mechanism. "Everything was going fine, just a few minor kinks now and then, until you showed up. Things started falling apart as soon as you started working on them."

"I haven't worked on that mechanism," she pointed out, refusing to let him anger her or to get embroiled in a finger-pointing episode. She didn't have to say anything else, however, because Adrian took her comment to mean that he *had* been working on it, so therefore it was obviously his fault.

"Let's stop the bickering," Yates ordered. "Cal, is *anything* showing up on the computer?"

Cal looked exhausted, his eyes bloodshot from staring at a monitor screen and stacks of dim printouts for too many hours. He shook his head. "It's all checking out on paper."

They were standing grouped around the laser pod on the belly of the aircraft Bowie had been flying. Caroline stared at the pod, deliberately blotting out what everyone else was saying as she tried to sort things out. The laser seemed to be in perfect working order, as did the firing mechanism. The lock-on was also performing perfectly, but then, they already knew that. After all, it had locked on to Daffy's bird and blown it out of the sky. But what had *told* it to lock on? According to the computer record, Bowie definitely hadn't touched the switch, so the lock-on and firing mechanisms had both operated automatically, something they weren't supposed to do. Nor was the laser supposed to have been activated; actually firing the lasers hadn't been scheduled for another ten days. Three things had gone wrong simultaneously: the laser had activated, the lock-on had targeted Daffy's aircraft and the thing had automatically fired. None of those three things was supposed to have happened at all; for all of them to have happened at the same time went beyond chance or Murphy's Law.

She didn't like the direction her thoughts were taking. If it wasn't logical for those three things to have happened by accident, then they had to have happened by design. The laser couldn't be activated by an accidental bump, and it certainly didn't have an outside switch labeled On and Off. Activating the laser was something the laser team had to do with a precise set of commands to the computer. Because of the security involved, they were the only ones with access to those commands.

Inescapable logic indicated that one of the team had activated the laser.

Caroline didn't believe in leaping to conclusions. Her work habits were orderly and painstakingly precise. Before she let herself begin thinking that one of the three men she worked with was deliberately sabotaging the laser, she had to make certain there was no way anyone outside the team could do it. Everything was computerized now, and though safeguards were built into the programs and elaborate precautions taken, nothing was impossible. There were a lot of things so difficult that no one had done them yet, but that didn't make them impossible. It was feasible that if someone could get the activation commands, he or she could also get into the program and use them. And it would be child's play for anyone that knowledgeable about computers to add commands that would override the pilot's physical keying of the lock-on switch, say if another aircraft came within a certain distance. Maybe Bowie had been flying a ticking timebomb today, just waiting for the right set of circumstances. It had been Daffy's bad luck that he had been assigned to shadow Bowie, but it could as easily have been Mad Cat, or even Joe, who had been shot down.

Yates had been watching her thoughtfully for several minutes. She was standing motionless, her gaze locked on the pod but not seeing it, with all her concentration turned inward. He could almost see that computer brain running down a checklist and inexorably narrowing the possibilities.

"What is it?" he finally asked when he couldn't stand the suspense any longer. "Any ideas?"

She blinked, and her eyes slowly refocused on him. "I think we should check the computer program," she finally said. "If it isn't the equipment, it has to be the program."

Cal looked positively haggard. "Do you know how long it will take to check this entire program?" he asked incredulously. "This thing is huge. It's the most complicated program I've ever worked on."

"Maybe a Cray..." she murmured, looking back at the pod.

"Book time on a Cray supercomputer?" Yates made it a question, but he was already mentally running through the logistics. "Expensive as hell."

"Not as expensive as stopping the program."

"It could take forever to get a booking, unless the Pentagon can line up some priority time."

"Yeah, that's a fine idea," Adrian said impatiently, "but you people are forgetting that the big man gave us thirty-six hours, of which we have already used ten. I don't think he's going to be satisfied with a possibility."

"We've come up with nothing everywhere else. Do

you have a better idea?'' Caroline replied just as impatiently.

He glared at her without answering. The truth was, they had all reached a dead end.

Caroline didn't mention her other conclusion, that if the solution to their problem was in the computer program they still had to discover whether it was a basic error in programming or if someone had deliberately programmed it in, but running everything through a Cray would give them the answer to that. By comparing the working program with the original, the Cray could tell them if the working program had been altered in any way. If it hadn't, then it was back to the drawing board for DataTech; if it had, then they had to find the person responsible for the changes.

''So what do we do?'' Cal asked, rubbing his eyes. ''Stop looking and just assume we're going to find it in the program, or stay up all night looking for something when we don't know what we're looking for?''

Despite herself, Caroline had to grin. ''If you're as groggy as that sentence sounded, I don't think you *can* stay up all night.''

He gave her a bleary look and an equally bleary grin. ''Sad, isn't it? In my younger days I could carouse all night and work all day, then go back out for more carousing. What you see here is a shadow of my former self.''

''I'm glad you two don't find this serious,'' Adrian snapped.

''Knock it off!'' Yates ordered, temper in his usually calm voice. They were all tired and frazzled. He moderated his tone. "I mean it literally as well as figuratively. We aren't accomplishing anything except exhausting ourselves. We're calling it quits for the night, despite what I said earlier. I think we've eliminated everything it could be except the program, so that's our logical next step, and we can't do it here. I'm going to clean up and have a good meal while I think about this, then I'm going to have a talk with Colonel Mackenzie. Let's get some rest."

Captain Ivan Hodge, head of security, said without preamble, "We have a very suspicious pattern here, sir."

Joe's stern face showed no emotion, though he wished the captain hadn't found anything.

Major General Tuell's flinty eyes became even flintier. As base commander, he was ultimately responsible for everything that happened, and he was intensely concerned with whatever had caused the crash of an F-22. "Show us what you've found."

The captain was carrying a thick log. He deposited it on Joe's desk and flipped it open to a premarked page. "Here." He noted an entry he had already highlighted in yellow. "This is the security code number for a member of the laser team, Caroline Evans. She arrived last Tuesday as a replacement for a worker who had a heart attack."

Joe's guts knotted up and his eyes went blank as he waited for Captain Hodge to continue.

"She has a pattern of arriving in the morning before everyone else and being the last to leave," the captain said, and Joe relaxed a little. Caroline was a workaholic; hardly damning circumstances, and he himself had walked in on her unannounced several times, catching her doing nothing suspicious... although she had quickly cleared the computer screen that one time. He had briefly wondered about it, then forgotten it, until now.

"You yourself have that pattern, sir," Captain Hodge said to Joe. "In itself, it doesn't mean anything." He flipped to another premarked page. "But here, on Thursday night, the sensors show Ms. Evans entering the laser work area shortly before 2400 and not leaving until almost 0400. She was alone the entire time. She reentered the building at 0600 for her normal workday. The birds went up that morning and for the first time experienced some malfunction with the lasers, isn't that right?"

The ice was back in Joe's eyes. "Yes."

"She left the area late that afternoon with the other members of the team and didn't return until Sunday night, again shortly before 2400. Again, she was the only person there. She left the building at 0430, returned at her usual time of 0600. This time, Major Deale's aircraft was shot down. Hell of a lot more disruptive than the lasers not working at all. These midnight appearances in the work area, combined with the fact that the trouble didn't start until she arrived, don't look good." The captain hesitated as he looked at Joe. The colonel's expression was enough to make any sane man hesitate, and Captain Hodge considered himself very sane. Nevertheless, it had to be said. "I understand you've taken a...uh, personal interest in Ms. Evans."

"We've gone out together a few times." They'd done a hell of a lot more than that, he thought savagely. She had given herself to him with a completeness that had shattered his memories of other women, reduced them to nothingness. And after they had returned from Vegas Sunday night she had slipped out to the work area and...done what? Secretly activated the laser on Bowie's aircraft? Had the laser on the bird he'd been flying been activated, too? Could he just as easily have been the one who shot down a friend?

Captain Hodge looked uncomfortable. "While you were with her, did she say anything? Ask any questions pertaining to Night Wing?"

"No." He was certain of that. Work had been mentioned in only the most general way. But then again, why should she have to ask him anything? "She has the clearance to find out anything about the project that she wants without having to ask anyone else."

"That's true. But did she say anything that, in retrospect, you could construe as being a reason for wanting the lasers to fail? Or for wanting to scuttle the Night Wing project?"

"No." But she wouldn't; Caroline was too smart for that. Caroline was brilliant. Caroline was perfectly capable of activating the lasers; she was not only an expert, she had access to the codes. "She has the knowledge and she had the opportunity," he heard himself saying. "Do you have anything else? Motive, anything suspicious in her past, any current money problems?''

''Her background is clean as a whistle,'' the captain admitted. ''We're going to do a total recheck to make certain it's correct and none of it has been fabricated, but that's only a precaution. Everyone connected with this project has been verified down to the fillings in their teeth.''

''Clarify this for me,'' Major General Tuell said. ''She could activate the lasers from the work area, without actually being in contact with the lasers themselves? The birds are under twenty-four-hour guard.''

''Yes, sir,'' Captain Hodge said. ''By computer command. And Ms. Evans carried a double major in college. She got her doctorate in physics, but she also has a master's in computer sciences. She knows her way around computers.''

''I see.'' The general sighed. ''What are your recommendations?''

''We won't file formal charges, sir. We can prove opportunity, and the timing is very suspicious, but we haven't as yet proven that the computers have actually been reprogrammed to arm and fire the lasers. There's still a possibility that it's a mechanical snafu.''

''But you don't think so?''

''No sir. The problems began when she arrived, and in both instances they occurred after she had made midnight visits to the work area. She's a civilian. I recommend that the FBI be notified and that she be restricted to base, but not yet taken into custody. As a precaution, I would also restrict the entire laser team from the work area until this is settled.''

''Why is that, Captain?''

''As I said, sir, as a precaution. She may not be the only one involved.''

''The logs don't show anyone else entering the work area at suspicious times.''

''That doesn't mean they didn't know about it. I think Colonel Mackenzie will agree with me that it's less expensive to halt testing for a few days than to lose another F-22, or maybe even one of the prototypes.''

''Yes.'' Joe's voice was hard. ''Are you going to question Ms. Evans?''

''Yes sir.''

''I'd like to be there.''

''Of course, sir.'' Captain Hodge thought wryly that Colonel Mackenzie didn't have to have permission; he had supreme authority on this base with anything concerning the Night Wing project. He would defer to Major General Tuell, but it would be by choice.

''When?''

''I can have my people escort her here now, if you'd like.''

''Then do it.''

Major General Tuell stood. ''Gentlemen, I'm leaving this in your hands. I trust you'll both make certain of our position before charges are filed. However, do whatever has to be done to solve this. The project is too important.''

They both saluted, and he returned it. As he left, Captain Hodge gestured to Joe's telephone and said, "With your permission, sir."

Joe nodded curtly. Captain Hodge lifted the receiver and pressed a code. "Have Ms. Caroline Evans, C12X114, escorted to Colonel Mackenzie's office. Verify."

Whoever had answered the phone repeated the code number. Captain Hodge said, "Correct. Thank you."

He hung up the phone and turned to Joe. "Ten minutes," he said.

Chapter 10

Caroline had never felt so small and exposed and terrified. She sat in a chair in Joe's office and tried to catch his eye, to silently plead with him to believe her, but he wouldn't look at her. Or rather, he was looking at her all right, but it was with a cold, totally impersonal gaze, as if he were observing a bug. He wasn't seeing *her,* Caroline. It was the look on his face more than anything else that frightened her. It was as hard as stone.

"No, I did not reenter the work area on those occasions," she repeated for what seemed like the hundredth time.

"The sensors logged both your entrance and exit times, Ms. Evans." Captain Hodge, the head of base security, was also good at repeating himself.

"Then the sensors are wrong."

"No, the sensors are extremely accurate. State-of-the-art."

"The sensors are *wrong.*" She drew a deep breath, trying to calm herself. She felt almost sick with fear. "I dislodged my ID card somehow during the day Thursday. I discovered it was missing Friday morning when I dressed."

"So you keep saying. We have no record of you filing a report on this so-called missing card, and you realize, of course, how important this would be on a top-security project. Perhaps you would like to explain your reasoning again."

"I remembered snagging it on a file folder Thursday and thought it must have come loose then. I didn't notify security because it seemed like a lot of bother when I was fairly certain it wasn't lost but was still in the office."

"But the sensors record you leaving the building that afternoon with the other members of your team. You had to have had your tag on for that to be possible, and believe me, Ms. Evans, the security works on both entering and exiting. If anyone crosses that threshold from any direction without the proper identification, it triggers an alarm."

"And that's why I'm telling you that the sensors *have* to be malfunctioning. When I discovered that I'd misplaced my tag, I called Cal Gilchrist and got him to check the office for me. He found my tag lying on the floor under my desk. He brought it back out to me and returned to his quarters while I began work. All you have to do is ask him."

"Mr. Gilchrist will be asked the appropriate questions. However, what the logs show is that both you and Mr. Gilchrist entered the building together and left together two minutes later. Then you reentered alone, and it was over an hour before Mr. Gilchrist returned."

"That's impossible. I did *not* go into the building until Mr. Gilchrist returned with my tag. What do your precious sensors tell you when two tags but only one body leave a building?"

The captain ignored her question and instead made a quick notation on the clipboard he carried. "Did you also misplace your tag on Sunday night?"

"No. I didn't enter the building on Sunday night." She couldn't prevent herself from giving Joe another quick, imploring glance. What was he thinking? Surely he didn't suspect her of sabotaging the lasers.

"The sensors say you did. And by your own testimony, your ID tag was with you."

"The tag was exactly where I had left it Friday afternoon when I put it on again this morning."

"You didn't move it at all during the weekend?"

"I spent the weekend in Vegas."

"And left your tag behind."

"Do you wear *your* ID tag off-base, Captain?" she shot back.

He said mildly, "I'd like to remind you that I'm not the one under suspicion."

"Under suspicion of what? Spell it out for me," she challenged.

He refused to be drawn. "You spent all weekend in Vegas, you say. You didn't return to the base either Friday night or Saturday night?"

"No."

"Where were you in Vegas?"

"At the Hilton."

"There's more than one. But of course this can be verified?"

Joe interrupted. "Ms. Evans and I spent the weekend together. I can verify her time from late Friday afternoon until 1900 hours Sunday."

"I see." Captain Hodge kept his voice noncommittal, but Caroline's face burned. This time she didn't glance at Joe. "So the name tag was locked in your quarters the entire time."

She tried another calming breath. They didn't seem to be working very well. "Yes."

"You're certain your quarters were secured."

"Yes. I always double-check my door."

He looked sceptical. "'Always' is a very exact term. It means without fail. Are you saying you've never failed to double-check your door?"

"On this occasion, Colonel Mackenzie himself checked the door while I watched."

The captain glanced at Joe, who nodded. Joe's eyes were hooded, his expression unreadable.

"You verify that the tag was in your possession and no one else's. You were recorded entering the work area at exactly—'' he paused to check the log ''—2347 on Sunday night.''

''I was in bed at that time Sunday night.''

''Alone?'' the captain asked indifferently.

''Yes.''

''No one can verify that. You say you were in bed. The computer log says you were in the work area.''

''Talk to Cal Gilchrist!'' she said fiercely. ''Stop wasting time with this and verify what I've already told you.''

''On Thursday morning, when I walked into your office you cleared the screen and turned the computer off,'' Joe said. His voice was cold and deep. ''What was on the screen that you didn't want me to see?''

She stared at him in silence, completely at a loss. He sounded as certain of her guilt as Captain Hodge was, but surely he knew... She tried to concentrate, to bring the occasion to mind. Thursday morning. He had startled her yet again, she remembered, and when she had reflexively started to slug him he had jerked her into his arms. She remembered fiddling with the computer to give herself something to do while she tried to get a handle on her reaction to him, but she had no idea what she had been working on.

''I don't remember,'' she said weakly.

''Come on,'' he scoffed. ''You remember everything. You have a mind like a steel trap.''

''I don't remember,'' she repeated, staring at him. With a shock she realized that the expression in his eyes was one of disdain...disgust...even rage. Yes, it was mostly rage, but not the normal heat of temper.

Joe Mackenzie's rage was ice-cold, and all the more frightening because of it. He was looking at her as if he could destroy her without regret. *He didn't believe her!*

The enormity of that realization almost choked her. As it was, a huge knot in her chest swelled until she could scarcely breathe, until her heart was beating with slow, painful effort. Had their situations been reversed she would have given him her complete, unqualified trust without hesitation, because, despite the evidence, she knew he would never betray his country. Evidently he believed her capable of doing just that. Her thought processes were orderly and logical, but all of a sudden a staggering instinctive knowledge filled her: she would trust him because she had been fascinated by him, intensely involved with learning about him as a man because she loved him, while for him their time together had been purely physical. He hadn't bothered to learn about her as a person because he didn't care.

In shock, she withdrew. She didn't move physically, but she had been reaching out to him mentally, and now she slammed her mind's door on those thoughts. She pulled all her reactions inward, bolting them inside in an effort to reestablish her emotional safeguards. It was probably too late, but the human animal's instincts were always to survive, and so she obeyed those instincts. Her face went smooth and expressionless, and she stared back at him with eyes as blank as glass. She couldn't afford to give him even a sliver of herself.

"What were you working on?" he repeated.

"I don't remember." Even her voice was flat. She had so desperately clamped down on her emotions that none of them stood a chance of escaping. Just as emotionlessly she said, "I'm going to assume I'm under suspicion of sabotage."

"We haven't said that," Captain Hodge replied.

"Nor have you said that I'm not, and this feels very much like an interrogation." She fastened her gaze on him, because she couldn't bear to look at Joe. She didn't know if she could ever look at Joe again. Later, when she was alone, she would regroup and take stock, do a damage assessment, but for right now she felt as if everything in her would shatter if she had to look at him. The pain was just too great; she couldn't handle it, so she had to ignore it.

"We couldn't find any malfunction at all in the laser on Captain Wade's aircraft," she said, and even managed a little bit of pride in the evenness of her tone. It was as flat as the EEG line of a corpse. "We all talked it over. Yates Korleski, the team leader, was going to talk to Colonel Mackenzie tonight after he'd thought about it a bit longer, but we think the problem is in the computer program."

Captain Hodge looked mildly interested. "What kind of problem are you talking about, Ms. Evans?"

"We don't know. We want to compare the working program with the original to tell us if any changes have been made on the program we're actually using."

"And if there are changes?"

"Then we find out what those changes are."

"Whose idea was it to verify the program?"

"Mine."

"What made you think of it?"

"It was a process of elimination. The computer program is about all that's left that *could* be wrong."

"But the program was working perfectly before you arrived. It would be a major feather in your cap if you solved a problem of this magnitude, wouldn't it, Ms. Evans?"

She didn't flinch, just continued to stonily watch him. "I didn't sabotage the program so I could have the glory of finding the problem."

"I didn't accuse you of doing so. I merely asked if it would be a feather in your cap if you pinpointed a major flaw in a project this large and important."

"I already have a good professional reputation, Captain. That's why I'm on the team."

"But you weren't an original member, so evidently you weren't good enough for that. Did you resent not being picked in the beginning?"

"I didn't know about it, so I couldn't be resentful. I was working on something else. The Night Wing project was already in full swing before I finished my own project. I only became available a month ago. That's verifiable," she added before he could ask.

"Hmmm." He studied the notes he had on his clipboard a moment longer, then looked up with a thin smile that didn't reach his eyes. "I believe that's all I have to ask you for now, Ms. Evans. You may go.

Oh—you're restricted to the base. It wouldn't look good if you were caught trying to leave.''

"Are my telephone calls also restricted?"

"Do you need to call someone?" he asked without answering her question. "An attorney, perhaps?"

"Do I need one?"

He gave her that thin smile again. "We haven't pressed any charges yet."

He just had to put that "yet" in there, she noticed distantly, but it didn't affect her. "You aren't filing charges but I'm restricted to base. Let me remind you that I'm a civilian, Captain Hodge, not a part of the military."

"And let me remind you, Ms. Evans, that you *are* on a military base and this is a military matter. If necessary, we can hold you in the brig for the maximum length of time before charges have to be formally filed. A lot of this can be checked out by then, and you may be exonerated, but if you insist on spending the time behind bars, we can accommodate you."

"You've made your point."

"I thought I had."

Caroline got up and concentrated on her legs. She made certain they didn't wobble, that they moved when she told them to. She didn't look at Joe as she walked out of the office, or at burly Sergeant Vrska on duty in the outer office. Evidently the good sergeant left only when the colonel did.

They would talk to Cal, and he would verify everything she had told them, which would force them to accept that their precious security sensors could and had malfunctioned. Perhaps there had been a major foul-up in security and two ID tags had been issued with the same bar code. Perhaps someone had been entering the work area with a duplicate of her tag and had indeed been sabotaging the computer program, but questioning Cal would force them to admit that it wasn't her.

She wasn't worried about being charged with sabotage, though enduring the captain's questions hadn't been a pleasant experience. But she might never recover from the look in Joe's eyes and the realization that he didn't trust her, that he believed her capable of sabotage.

She had made a monumental, colossal fool of herself. Despite the superior capability of her brain, she had made the fundamental feminine mistake of assuming that making love with a man signaled a commitment from him. No, not making love, having sex. That was another mistake she had made, assigning too much importance to the act. To men it was the simple gratification of a physical appetite, like eating. No emotional baggage was involved. She had made love; he had had sex. She had given herself to him, heart, soul and body, and he had given her pleasure in return but nothing of himself beyond the temporary use of his own body. Magnificent as his body was, she had wanted more. She had thought she was getting more.

Oh, she hadn't gone so far as to think he was in love with her, but she had still thought he *cared,* at least a little. But she had been confusing sexual technique with emotions. He had none, at least none that she could reach. He was always controlled, his inner self firmly locked away from everyone except his immediate family. She was beginning to see the wisdom of that. Right now she would give anything if her own emotions had been that protected, so she wouldn't be about to collapse and curl up in a fetal knot from the pain of it. She would do so if she thought it would ease the pain, but she knew it wouldn't. There was no ease.

Perhaps when he knew the truth he would expect to continue their affair as if nothing had happened. Caroline tried to imagine how she would handle the situation if he did, but she simply couldn't bring anything to mind.

Nor could she imagine continuing to work here, seeing him every day. She had always been right, after all, never to become involved with anyone. The first time she had done so had certainly been a disaster. So now she either had to do the unthinkable and somehow manage to survive working with him, or she had to ruin her professional reputation by asking to be taken off the project.

It looked as if her work would be all she had, so she'd be damned if she would throw that away just because of a man, even if that man was Colonel Joe Mackenzie. If it took every ounce of strength she had, she would finish this damn project. She would talk with him about work. She would even be polite. But there was no way she would ever risk opening her heart to him again. She simply couldn't afford the pain. This was already costing her almost more than she could bear, and the ordeal had just begun.

"Cal Gilchrist categorically denies finding her ID card under her desk," Hodge told Joe later. It was almost midnight, but there was no possibility of sleep in sight. "He says she called him early Friday morning and asked him to walk her to the building because she thought someone had followed her the morning before and it made her nervous. He says he also went inside with her for a quick check of the building, then returned to his quarters to shower and shave."

Joe's face was stony. He hadn't allowed himself to hope that Gilchrist would verify everything she had said. It would have been asking for too much, when the sensors had plainly placed her there when she shouldn't have been.

"Then why use him for an alibi? She must have known he wouldn't cover for her."

"Maybe not. Evidently they're fairly good friends. Certainly Adrian Pendley wouldn't have gone a single step out of his way for her. And maybe she and Gilchrist had something going on in the past, for her to feel confident he would protect her if he could."

"No." At least he was certain about that. Caroline had never been intimate with anyone but him. Before Ivan could question him on his certainty Joe asked, "What about Korleski? Did they discuss the possibility that the problem was with the computer program?"

"Yes. She told the truth right down the line with

that. He verified that she's the one who suggested the program be checked. He was also vehement that she wouldn't sabotage a project so she could have the credit of saving it. Neither did he believe she would do it for money.''

"Did he think anyone else on the laser team *would* do it for either money or prestige?" Joe asked.

Ivan shook his head.

"How do the rest of them check out?"

"It'll take time to reverify everything, but all of them are spotless. I never would have suspected her if it hadn't been for the entrance and exit records.''

Joe could understand that. He never would have suspected her, either, but then, he hadn't been able to see past his own obsession with her. All he'd been able to think about was getting her in bed and burying himself in that sweet body. Now he had to wonder how much of it had been calculated, if she had indeed been so attracted to him that she'd given up her virginity to him with hardly a thought or if she had done it... God, what possible reason *was* there for making love with him the way she had, other than desire? No, she hadn't come on to him in an attempt to find out classified information on Night Wing or to use him for protection if she were caught. She hadn't needed him to find out anything; she had access to all the information she wanted. And it was simply too iffy to assume he would protect her just because he'd slept with her. Caroline had wanted him. Even if he couldn't trust anything else about her, he could trust that.

So what did he do now? He'd never before been
so enraged and...hurt. He might as well admit it. This
had been like taking a roundhouse to the gut. Nobody
had ever gotten to him the way Caroline had, with
her uncomplicated fierceness. She had been forthright
and brutally honest, without any hidden agenda or
stratagems. He wanted to be able to step back from
the situation and look at it without emotion, but he
couldn't.

He'd never felt about any aircraft the way he felt
about Night Wing. It was special. It was more than
special. It was history in the making, pure magic in
the air. He would give his own life unhesitatingly to
protect those planes, because they were necessary to
protect his country. Simple patriotism, pure love for
those birds. They were *his*.

And he'd considered *Caroline* his, too. His woman.

If the choice had been simply between Caroline and
the aircraft, he would have chosen Caroline. He might
despise himself for it, but he couldn't have stood by
and let her be harmed. But between Caroline and his
country... There was no choice. There couldn't be.
He couldn't let there be. No matter how fierce and
gutsy she was, no matter how she challenged him on
a level no one else ever had before and threw herself
without restraint into the battle. She hadn't let him be
gentle when he'd taken her for the first time; she had
insisted on receiving his full strength and had met him
with her own. Caroline met life head-on, without wavering.

He paused in his thoughts, a tiny frown puckering

his eyebrows. Caroline didn't seem the type to sneak around in the dark. Maybe he hadn't known her as well as he'd thought, but he would have sworn there wasn't a devious bone in her body.

He wanted to see her. He wanted to ask her some questions one on one, without anyone else in the room to buffer them. He would get the truth out of her come hell or high water.

Chapter 11

He had intended to go straight to her quarters, but he stopped halfway there and detoured to his own quarters in the BOQ instead. He was too angry to face her now, especially in the temporary civilian housing where there would be too many onlookers who didn't need to know any of what was going on.

He didn't think he'd ever been this angry before, but then, he'd never been betrayed like this before. Damn it, why would she do something like that? It had to be money, but he'd never understood the mentality that could view treason as just another financial opportunity.

Treason. The word reverberated through his consciousness. If she were charged and convicted, she would likely spend the rest of her natural life behind bars, without possibility of parole.

He would never make love to her again. The thought made him erupt with fury, and he restlessly paced the small confines of his quarters. One weekend hadn't been enough. He doubted that a thousand weekends would be enough to get her out of his system. Nor could he let himself forget that he had made love to her twice without protection. Despite her assurances that the timing was wrong, she could be pregnant.

Hell, what a mess! If she was pregnant... There wasn't any use in borrowing trouble; he'd know soon enough. But what would he do if she was carrying his child? There still wasn't any way he could keep her out of prison.

That was assuming she would even tell him. By the time she had left his office that night she had refused to even look at him. He'd been watching her, trying to read her reactions, and all of a sudden she had started withdrawing. He'd seen it happen right in front of his eyes. It was as if a light had been quenched. All the vitality, the responsiveness, the incredible energy of her, had vanished, and all that had been left was a frozen mannequin of a woman who had answered in a monotone and whose eyes were as blank as a doll's.

It had been infuriating to see her that way. He had wanted to jerk her to her feet and shake her, to make that wonderful, uncomplicated anger come rushing upward to meet him. But he hadn't. If he gave in to those urges, he would lose his control once and for all, and he never wanted to do that.

What he did want to do, more than anything else in the world, was storm over to her quarters and make love to her so hard and so long that when it was over she would know she belonged to him. Maybe it wouldn't solve any of this, but it would sure as hell make him feel better. But he couldn't do that, either. Seeing her at all would knock down the last critical brick behind which he had dammed up his temper, releasing a flood of emotion that would sweep him away along with everything else.

Caroline lay on top of the covers on her narrow mattress, too listless to crawl between the sheets and actually go to bed. Such a normal action was beyond her. She had showered and dressed for bed, but she couldn't even go through the motions of pretending to sleep. All she could do was lie there in the silent darkness and stare at the ceiling. She could feel her heart beating, feel the slow, rhythmic expansions of her rib cage as she breathed. Those actions said that she still lived, but she didn't feel alive. She felt numb, dead inside.

By now they would have talked to Cal, who would have verified that she'd been telling the truth. Joe would know that he'd been wrong, but somehow that didn't give her any satisfaction. Still, she had expected at least a phone call from either him or Captain Hodge, to say "Sorry, we made a mistake." Surely they wouldn't be stupid enough to think she was *resting* and would rather they wait until morning to tell her.

Or Cal could have lied.

She couldn't deny the possibility. The thought had slipped into her consciousness not long after she had lain down on the bed. If she hadn't been so upset, it might have occurred to her earlier. It was the natural progression of the line of thought she had been following earlier in the hangar, when she had been staring at the laser pod and sorting out the various ways in which what had happened could have happened.

Cal was a whiz with computers. He was the one who had found that minor glitch on Friday, but only when Caroline had begun nosing around the computer. She hadn't thought anything of it then, but if he had tampered with the commands, he wouldn't have wanted her to really concentrate on the program. He knew she had a degree in computer science, because they had talked shop on several occasions. And on both Friday and today—yesterday, now, since it was past midnight—he had really looked exhausted. From being up all night? Cal was normally as bouncy as a rubber ball.

And Cal was the only other person who had touched her ID tag. Maybe he had picked it up on Thursday when she'd lost it and had left when she had so that the sensors would match the number of warm bodies leaving with the number of ID cards. She hadn't known the sensors monitored those leaving the buildings, too, but maybe Cal had; after all, he'd been working here from the beginning and noticed things like that, while she tended to pay attention only to what directly concerned her job.

Even if he had used her ID tag to regain entrance to the building Thursday night, she knew he hadn't had it on Sunday night.

But how easily could they be duplicated? He would have had to leave the base to get it done, but she was certain it was possible. After all, the sensors had said she had reentered the work area at midnight, which would have given him several hours to have a copy made.

Then she had called him on Friday morning asking him to search the office for her tag, which had given him the perfect opportunity to return it to her and keep security from being notified. Otherwise he wouldn't have been able to use the card again, because security would have removed that particular code from the computers.

She stopped her thoughts and rubbed her forehead, trying to force everything into making sense. If her call for help had been pure chance, then there wouldn't have been any reason for him to have had the card duplicated. Had he played the odds that she *would* call *him?* They were good odds, she had to admit. She wouldn't have called Yates, and she certainly wouldn't have wasted her time calling Adrian. It was also a good bet that she wouldn't have wanted to call security. Not a certainty, but good enough that it wasn't much of a risk, either.

So what had happened then? The sensors showed both her and Cal entering the building, then both leaving. He must have had her card on him where the sensor could read it, thereby establishing proof that he hadn't had the opportunity to tamper with the computer program because he hadn't been in there alone. But why hadn't the sensor noticed that there were two cards but only one body?

Maybe the sensors weren't as good as Captain Hodge obviously liked to believe they were. Maybe they were programmed to catch people without cards, but no one had thought to program it to catch cards without people. Maybe Cal had figured out a way to fool it. There were a lot of maybes, all of them possible. As good as he was with computers, maybe he had somehow gotten into the base computers and logged her both in and out of the building that morning. She didn't know and might never find out.

But what would Cal do now, if he were guilty? If the programs had been tampered with, he would know that analysis would discover it. Would he try to get back into the program and cover his tracks by undoing what he had done, hoping that the analysis wouldn't go any further than a simple comparison? Or would he try to plant more evidence against her?

She had to go with the second option. It was so much more feasible. Why would Cal go to so much trouble only to undo it? No, as long as the finger was pointing toward her, he would be smart to try to make certain it remained pointing in that direction.

Her heart suddenly began thundering in her chest. If Cal were guilty, if he were going to do anything else, he would have to do it *tonight*, while things were still in an upheaval. Given enough time, the security net would settle down so tightly that nothing would be able to escape, but there were still windows of opportunity when things first started happening.

She knew the entire laser team was being restricted from the work area, but had their bar codes already been deleted from the computers? The military worked a lot like big business when it came to office work: most of it was done during the day. Since the restriction order had only been issued that night, had Captain Hodge called in someone to enter it into the computer or left it to be done first thing in the morning? Knowing human nature, she would bet on the latter. After all, she was the only one under suspicion, and she was probably under surveillance in the interim.

On a hunch she rolled out of bed and silently walked to the small, old-fashioned crank-out window set high in the wall in the kitchen area. She had to stand on a chair to see out of it. Sure enough, a security police car was parked on the opposite side of the street. In the glow of the streetlight she could plainly see two men in the front seat. They were making no effort to disguise their purpose, but then, why should they? This wasn't clandestine surveillance, but plain old guard duty.

There was no other door.

There was, however, another high, narrow window in the bedroom. In the almost total darkness she carefully made her way back to the bedroom and stared at the small oblong of light in the wall. A man certainly couldn't get through there, and she had doubts that she could, either. Nevertheless, she stood on the bed and peeped out. That side of the street was empty.

Well, there was no point in putting herself to a lot of trouble if Cal was peacefully sleeping in bed. She mustn't let herself forget that he might be totally innocent, that he had indeed verified her story. Innocent until proven guilty was the law of the land, though Captain Hodge could use a little refresher course in the concept.

She didn't want to turn on any lights, alerting those two out front that she was awake, so she dialed Cal's number by feel. What better way to find out if he was in his quarters than to call him? If he answered, she might even chat awhile.

By the fifth ring she began to have serious doubts that he was there. She let it ring longer, just in case he was sleeping very soundly, but on the twentieth ring she replaced the receiver. Twenty rings, especially since the phones were installed right beside the beds to make certain the occupants would be awakened by any middle-of-the-night phone calls, would wake even the soundest of sleepers. Cal wasn't in his quarters.

She clenched her teeth in anger. Damn him! She had thought he was her friend; she had liked him, trusted him. First Joe, now Cal. Her mind immediately shied away from Joe, because that hurt was too powerful to linger over. It was much safer to focus her anger on Cal.

She stared up at that little window again. Two long, narrow louvered panes that cranked out to let the

built-up heat of the day escape. She would have to
dismantle the entire mechanism in the dark, and even
then, she wasn't certain she would fit through the slot.

Well, she would never know if she didn't try.

Working on lasers and computers had made her familiar with tools, and she never traveled anywhere
without a small pouch containing a selection of screw-
drivers and pliers, because she never knew when she
would need them. She fetched the pouch from the
closet and dumped the tools out on the bed. Problem
was, in the dark she couldn't tell which tool she
needed.

She did have a pencil flashlight and decided she
would have to take the risk of the small beam being
detected through the window, but it wasn't likely to
throw a lighted patch on the ground outside and alert
the guards. She climbed up on the bed and switched
the flashlight on for only the smallest of intervals, just
long enough for her to see that the screws holding the
mechanism in place needed a Phillips head screwdriver. Five minutes later the two window slats and
the cranking mechanism, in pieces, were lying on her
bed.

That had been the easy part. Getting through the
window was something else.

She measured it visually. She could angle her
shoulders through; her head and hips would be the
biggest problem, but her buttocks would compress
and her skull wouldn't. She decided to go headfirst,
so she could find out immediately if her head would
fit through. It would be awful to go out feetfirst, then

be stuck with her head inside and the rest of her body outside. Humiliating, at the very least. That is, if she didn't find herself hanged.

First, she had to change clothes and put on some shoes. She shone the pencil flashlight on the contents of her closet, taking care that no light was visible from the outer rooms. Dark clothes would be practical, but she hadn't brought any dark clothes with her. It was August in the southern Nevada desert; she hadn't anticipated being obliged to sneak around in the dark.

She would stand out like a sore thumb in her light-colored clothes, but there wasn't any help for it. She would just have to make certain no one saw her.

Nevertheless irritated by her lack of preparedness, she quickly pulled on a pair of thin cotton pants and a T-shirt, and defiantly slipped her ID tag into her pocket. If she got caught, they wouldn't be able to say she didn't have proper identification. As an afterthought, she added her keys to her pocket. She could hardly reenter by the window, though if she managed to catch Cal up to no good, she wouldn't have to worry about the guards out front.

She climbed up on the bed again, but a minute's experimentation made it plain that she needed to be higher so she could angle through from a more horizontal position. She got a kitchen chair and balanced it on the bed, then climbed up on the chair. It was a wobbly perch, but she was holding on to the edge of the window and wasn't afraid of falling.

One arm and shoulder went first, then she turned her head to the side and eased it through the slot,

earning nothing more horrendous than a minor scrape.
She wiggled the other shoulder and arm through and
braced her arms on the wall below her as she wriggled
forward. As soon as her hips were through, she suspected, her center of gravity would shift drastically
forward and she would fall on her head, dragging her
legs the rest of the way through the window. It wasn't
a high drop, but she didn't want to break her neck
landing. To prevent it, or at least slow her down, she
hooked her legs backward so her heels were braced
against the inside wall, and inched forward some
more.

The edge of the window cut into her soft bottom
but she ignored the pain and forced herself on
through. Immediately she lurched forward and only
her hooked legs inside kept her from doing exactly as
she had feared. Frantically, she braced her arms again,
forcing herself as far away from a vertical position as
possible, then cast a fearful glance toward the front
of the building where the guards were parked. To her
relief, she couldn't see the car from where she was.

She hung there a minute before she faced the inevitable: there was no graceful way to do it. She was
going to be scraped and bruised. Moreover, there was
no way she could now reverse the process and inch
back inside. Her legs were trembling from the strain.
Without giving herself time to dwell on how much it
was going to hurt, she straightened her legs and gave
a push with her arms at the same time, launching herself the rest of the way out of the window. She tried
to turn in midair so nothing vital was damaged on

landing, like her head, and succeeded in turning mostly to the side. The impact was harder than she ever would have suspected for such a short distance. The loose gravel scraped skin on her temple and cheek, down the side of her left arm and on her left ankle. She had banged both knees somehow, and jarred her shoulder.

But she couldn't just sit there and take stock of her injuries. Her senses were still swimming when she forced herself to move, to scramble against the shadows at the side of the building and walk quickly in the opposite direction. Only when she had gone almost a hundred yards without hearing a warning shout did she relax and take a deep breath. Immediately her pains made themselves felt, and she stopped to lean over and rub both aching knees, then her bottom. She rotated her shoulder to make certain it was in working order and gingerly touched the side of her face. She didn't seem to be bleeding, but the scrapes burned. A scarf threaded through the loops of the pants usually served her as a belt, but she stripped it out and carefully blotted the scrapes to remove the dirt and tiny bits of gravel from her face.

Something else she could lay at Cal's door.

She trudged the long way around, no longer making an effort to avoid being seen on the theory that someone would be more likely to notice her if she was trying not to be noticed. If she acted normally, no one would pay any attention to her.

Joe sat up and threw the sheet off, cursing steadily under his breath even as he got up and began dressing

in jeans and boots. It wasn't military business he had
to attend to, and the long, restless hours in a bed that
was far too empty had steadily eroded his patience
until there was none left. He glanced at his watch,
surprised to see that it was only about 0200 hours.
He'd been in bed less than two hours, but it had felt
more like four or five. It didn't matter. No matter how
long it had been, he wasn't going to be able to sleep
until he'd had it out with Caroline. He wanted to hear
her explanation of why she'd done what she had, and
he wanted her to tell him to his face. He wouldn't let
her ignore him again the way she had earlier in his
office.

He decided to walk rather than take the truck for
the relatively short distance; maybe the walk would
settle him down. He was dangerously close to exploding, and he knew it. He had been six years old
the last time he'd lost his temper, and he'd sworn then
never to do it again, but Caroline tested his control to
the extreme.

He'd walked less than a quarter of a mile when he
first saw the slim figure walking boldly through the
night, and his first thought was that temper was making him hallucinate. He stopped and stepped back out
of sight, going down on one knee next to a trash can.
He hadn't mistaken her identity; the overhead street-
lights gleamed on her pale hair, and he knew that
walk as intimately as he knew his own face. The arrogant set of slim shoulders, the gentle sway of
rounded hips, were burned into his memory.

Was she coming to see him? His heart thumped wildly, but then he wondered how she had gotten past her guards. He knew they had been there, because he had suggested to Hodge that it would be a good idea, and Hodge had agreed. He'd even heard Hodge give the orders. But here she was, walking around the base at two a.m., not a guard in sight.

He waited until she had walked past him before slipping from his cover. As always, he moved soundlessly, dropping back about fifty yards but always keeping her in sight. If she turned toward the BOQ he could rapidly close the distance and approach her. But she didn't even pause at the BOQ, and his anger rose to the boiling point. She was headed straight for the laser work area, damn her treacherous little heart. His palm itched with the almost irresistible impulse to storm up behind her, take her by the nape of the neck and bend her over his knee. By the time he got through walloping that pretty little backside he would feel a lot better and she would have a better appreciation of just how angry he was. Damn it, didn't she know how serious her situation was?

Of course she did. By her own actions, she was proving herself guilty. Probably she intended to finish the traitorous work she had already begun.

He thought of stopping to alert the security police, but decided in favor of keeping her in sight. If she tried anything like setting the place on fire he could subdue her and hold her until security got there. In fact, he would *enjoy* subduing her. He just might get that walloping accomplished while they were waiting.

He saw her stop and get something out of her pocket, then attach it to her shirt. Her ID tag. Why hadn't Hodge relieved her of it? Because he hadn't seen any need to; she had been under guard, and the codes would be deleted from the computer first thing in the morning. Joe was suddenly furious again, but this time at both Hodge and himself. They had been inexcusably lax, especially for a project with security as tight as Night Wing. She couldn't get off the base, but she could still wreak havoc *on* base. They relied too much on technology to do their guarding for them, something he intended to change immediately.

Someone was already inside the building; there was a very dim glow coming from one of the windows, barely noticeable. Caroline saw it, too. He saw her head turn as she stared at the light; then she continued straight up to the door and slipped inside, as silent as a wraith.

Twenty seconds later, he followed. He wasn't wearing his ID tag, so he knew central security would be alerted immediately.

Up ahead, he saw Caroline reach into the office and flip on the light switch, bathing her in the bright light. "What did you do, use my name tag again?" she demanded furiously of someone else inside. "The computers will probably go crazy when they record Caroline Evans entering twice in a row. You sabotaged my project, damn you!"

Realization burst in his brain like a bomb, and shock slammed through him as she stepped completely inside the office, out of sight. Damn the little idiot! She didn't have one iota of caution. She had simply charged straight in without thinking that cornering a traitor could be dangerous. Joe launched himself down the corridor, running silently, desperately praying with every fiber in him that he wouldn't hear a gunshot that would mean the end of that foolhardy courageousness.

He heard a sudden movement, a gasp, a sickening thud, and he burst through the open doorway just as Caroline slid to the floor. Cal Gilchrist was standing in front of a glowing computer monitor, his face utterly white. Too late Joe saw Cal's eyes dart to the side, behind him. He tried to whirl, but he'd been too distracted by his own unreasoning fear. Before he could react, something hard crashed against his temple. It felt as if his head was exploding. Then there was nothing but total blackness.

Chapter 12

Caroline slowly regained consciousness, at first aware only of being jounced uncomfortably. Her head hurt with a deep throbbing that dulled her senses, but gradually she became aware of pain in her shoulder and arms, too. Then she began to realize that she could hear voices, that there was someone else near her, but for a blank, frightening moment she didn't know who or where she was.

Then she recognized one of the voices, and awareness swept through her. She remembered everything. Cal. It was his voice she recognized, and just as she realized that, she also realized that she was in a vehicle of some sort, perhaps a van, and she was tied. Gagged, too, damn it.

Slowly she opened her eyes, quickly closing them

again in pain when a bright light flashed quickly through the windows. She heard a rushing sound and realized some other vehicle had passed them on the road, nothing more. She tried again, this time opening her lids only a slit so she could accustom herself to the discomfort. This must be what a hangover felt like, and she hadn't even indulged. All the misery without any of the fun.

Someone was lying beside her.

This time she closed her eyes in panic, startled by the realization that there was a man right next to her. She was acutely aware of her helplessness. Oh, God, were they going to rape her?

But the man wasn't moving. Cautiously she opened her eyes one more time and found herself staring straight into Joe Mackenzie's pale, furious eyes.

Even if she hadn't been gagged, she couldn't have said a word, she was so astonished. How had he gotten there? She had a good idea how *she* had come to be in such a predicament, because she had foolishly rushed into the office to confront Cal without making certain he was alone. But how had Joe gotten involved? Then fear swelled in her chest, because he was in danger, too.

"I say we forget about it and get out of the country," Cal was saying feverishly. "It's over. I can't take it any further. They're going to check the entire system, and they'll find everything."

"I told the others you didn't have the nerve for this," someone else replied dismissively. Caroline tore her gaze from Joe's and craned her neck so she

could see up front. Another man was sitting beside
Cal, who was driving. She didn't recognize him, but
at the same time he looked vaguely familiar.

"Nothing was said about murder," Cal replied furiously.

"And I suppose if that pilot had died when his
plane was shot down, you wouldn't have been responsible for that?"

"That was different." Despite his words, Cal's
tone was uneasy.

"Yeah, sure."

"That was…chance. But this is cold-blooded murder. I can't do it."

"No one's asking you to do it," the other man said
impatiently. "You don't have the nerve for it. We'll
take care of it. Don't worry, you won't even see it
happen."

If her hands hadn't been tied behind her back, Caroline would have lunged for the man, she was so angry. He was talking about killing them as casually as
he would talk about doing the laundry! Joe silently
nudged her ankle with his boot; actually, it was more
of a kick, and her ankle was already sore. She turned
her glare on him, and he gave a tiny, warning shake
of his head. She kicked him in return, and he blinked
at the pain.

They were in a van, one which was evidently used
for hauling cargo rather than people, for there was no
carpeting on the floor, only bare metal. The vehicle
swayed with every turn, curve and bump, adding to
the discomfort of her position. She was lying on her

sore shoulder anyway, and having her hands tied behind her made it worse.

She tried to discern what they had used to bind her; it felt like nylon cord, while it was probably her own scarf they had tied around her mouth, adding insult to injury. Her keys were still in her pocket. If she could get them out, and if she and Joe turned so their backs were to each other, and if they had enough time, she might be able to use the edge of a key to saw through the nylon. The keys weren't sharp, but they were rough. Joe's pockets had probably been searched for a knife, a common item for men to carry, but women weren't expected to carry anything in their pockets, and evidently Cal and his cohort had totally overlooked hers.

"There's no point in killing them," Cal was saying raggedly. "It's over. We barely got out of there before the security police started swarming all over the place. By now they know I left the base, and they have a record of the van's license plate. When Caroline and the colonel are both reported missing but neither of them is recorded as leaving the base, they'll put two and two together so fast there'll be an APB out for the van within another hour, at most. Right now we're looking at life, but if we kill them, we'll get the death penalty."

To Caroline that sounded like a very convincing argument, but the other man didn't seem impressed. He didn't even bother to respond.

Sometimes she wished she weren't so darn logical. She couldn't turn off her thought processes even when they were telling her something she would rather not know. If the other man disregarded Cal's argument, then it must be because he had some reason to believe he himself wouldn't be tied in to the sabotage. As Cal had pointed out, his own involvement was known, but this other guy must think himself safe…except Cal knew about him and could tie him to everything. Therefore, the man felt safe only if he knew that Cal wasn't going to be alive to make the connection.

Furiously she began rubbing her face against the floor of the van, trying to scrape the gag away from her mouth, pushing against it with her tongue at the same time. Joe glared another warning at her, but she ignored him. Her frantic movements attracted the attention of the man in the passenger seat up front, and he turned around.

His voice was genial. "Welcome back, Ms. Evans. I hope your headache isn't too bad."

Joe had closed his eyes again and was still lying motionless. Caroline made an angry noise, muffled by the scarf, and continued her struggles. She kicked her bound feet and twisted her torso, all the while fighting the gag.

"You might as well stop wasting your time," the man said in a mild, faintly bored tone. "You can't get free, and all you're doing is pulling the cord tighter."

She wasn't concerned about the cord. Her two aims were to get the gag off and somehow dislodge the keys from her pocket. Not an impossible task, since her pants were loose, flimsy cotton, but not an easy one, either, because the pockets were deep. She mumbled a few unintelligible curses at him and continued with her struggle.

She had managed to push the scarf out of her mouth, and on an impulse she scooted over next to Joe and pushed her face hard against his shoulder, using the contact and the friction between his shirt and the scarf to roll the gag downward. Joe didn't move, and his eyes remained closed. She worked her jaw until the gag slipped down to hang around her neck. The man in the front seat was frowning at her, starting to get up on his knees and twist around.

"You dirtbag, you've killed him!" she croaked, forcing as much rage as possible into her voice, even though her tongue and jaw didn't want to work.

The van swayed alarmingly as Cal jerked on the wheel, his head swiveling around to stare into the back. The other man fought for his balance. "Keep your eyes on the road!" he barked at Cal.

"You said he was just unconscious!"

"He isn't dead, damn it. I hit him harder than I did her because I didn't want any trouble with the big bruiser if he woke up before we could get them out of there and tied up."

Caroline yelled, "Cal, he's going to kill you, too! Why else wouldn't he be worried about a murder charge unless he's going to try to blame the whole thing on you?"

The man lunged at her from over the seat, reaching back to grab her around the throat. Quick as a cat she turned her head and sank her teeth into his arm. He howled and tried to jerk back, but she hung on like a limpet, working her jaws to inflict as much damage as possible.

The van was swerving all over the road. Cal was using his right arm to grab at the other man while still driving. Both men were yelling and cursing. Suddenly the other man used his right fist to club her on the side of the head and she saw stars, her jaws going slack as she helplessly sank back. She didn't lose consciousness, but the blow definitely addled her.

They were fighting in the front seat, and the van rose dangerously on two wheels; then Cal jammed on the brakes and it slewed violently to one side, sliding off the pavement. She felt the distinct difference between pavement and dirt; then the van tipped a little to the right as it came to rest, probably in a shallow ditch. The movement threw her against Joe, and she felt his muscles tense as he took her weight, but he didn't so much as even grunt. Instead, there was an almost soundless, barely intelligible whisper against her ear. "There's a knife in my right boot."

Well, of course there was. Didn't all colonels carry knives in their shoes? Furious because he managed to be armed when she couldn't even get her keys out of her pocket, she thought about biting *him,* too. Instead, she hurled herself toward the rear of the van, collecting even more bruises in the process. Cal and the other man were still grappling, and she caught a glimpse of something metallic gleaming in the other man's hand. Instinctively she recognized it as a pistol.

Cal somehow got his door open and leapt out, probably figuring he didn't have very good odds in such close quarters with a pistol. The other man was swearing viciously, steadily, as he shoved open his own door and went in pursuit.

Caroline rolled around so her back was to Joe's feet, searching by feel for his right boot, struggling to push his pants leg up so she could reach the knife. They wouldn't have long, probably less than a minute. Her scrabbling fingers, numbed from the tightness of the nylon cord, finally grasped the knife handle and drew it out.

Joe was already rolling, presenting his bound hands to her. It wasn't easy to position the knife between their backs, unable to see if she was slicing into flesh or nylon, but she figured Joe would let her know when she got to skin. The knife must have been sharp; within five seconds she felt the cord give and he was rolling away from her again and sitting up. The blade was removed from her numb hands. She twisted her head to see him bending forward to quickly slice the cord around his feet; then he whirled toward her. She felt a swift tug at her hands and they came free. Before she could even bring her arms around he had jackknifed to a sitting position and freed her feet. Only then did he remove his own loosened gag, tugging it down so it hung around his neck just the way the scarf hung around hers.

A shot boomed from in front of them.

"Stay back here," Joe ordered as he lithely swung into the front and folded himself behind the steering wheel. The engine was still running; he slammed the

van into gear and stepped on the gas pedal. The
wheels spun uselessly, and he cursed himself even as
he let up on the gas and put the transmission in reverse, this time easing down on the gas. He was used
to his truck, but the van didn't have that kind of traction. The tires clawed for purchase on the loose, shifting dirt, finally caught and reversed out of the rut he'd
dug with the first effort.

In the beam of the headlights he could see the second man running back toward the van. There wasn't
any sign of Cal.

Caroline's head popped up beside him as he shifted
into first, and simultaneously the man stopped and
lifted the pistol. Joe put his hand on Caroline's head
and shoved her sideways as he ducked himself, just
as the pistol boomed again and the windshield shattered, spraying shards of glass all over the interior of
the van. He kept his foot on the gas pedal and his
head down as the van leapt out of the slight depres-
sion and skidded when the tires touched asphalt, slew-
ing sideways again. He fought to keep the vehicle
upright.

More shots, one following immediately after the
other. He could feel the impact of the heavy slugs on
the van. One headlight went out. Briefly he saw the
man pinned in the remaining headlight; then the guy
jumped sideways to safety as the van roared past.

"Caroline!" he shouted, needing to know if she
was okay, but he had his hands full battling the van,
the wind full in his face and blinding him now that
the windshield was gone, and he couldn't turn to see.

"What?" she shouted in reply.

"Stay down, he might shoot—"

Before he could complete the sentence, bullets ripped into the rear of the van, shattering those windows, too. His blood went cold.

"Caroline!"

"What?" she roared, plainly aggravated, and he could have laughed with relief. If Caroline was in a bad mood, she was all right.

The relief didn't last half a minute. A quick glance at the gauges showed the engine's temperature was quickly climbing; one of the shots must have hit the radiator. They were out in the desert somewhere, without a sign of a town, community or even a lone dwelling. The only light was from the stars and their one headlight. They wouldn't be able to get far before the engine locked up, but he intended to put every foot of distance that he could between them and the man with the gun.

The temperature gauge redlined. He kept his foot on the gas pedal.

The engine locked with a harsh, grinding sound. Caroline shot up beside him as they rolled to a stop. "What's going on?"

"Some of those shots hit the radiator. The motor's gone. Come on, out of the van."

She obeyed, pushing the sliding side door open and staggering out into the cool desert night. "Over here," Joe ordered, and she made her way painfully around the van.

"Now what?"

"Now we walk. I hope you're wearing good shoes."

She shrugged. She was wearing loafers, not as good as boots, but better than sandals. She hadn't dressed with an odyssey like this in mind, but what did it matter? She had to walk, even if she'd been barefoot.

"In which direction?"

"Back the way we came."

"*He's* back there."

"Yeah, but we don't know where we are, or how far it is to even a gas station going in the direction we were heading. At least we know that if we go back the way we came, we're going at least roughly toward the base."

Logical. But… "If we're going back the way we came, why didn't you drive in that direction to begin with?"

"Because then he'd *know* what direction we were going in," he explained. "He'll find the van, but he won't know if we continued on ahead or doubled back."

"But obviously we're going to have to pass by him at some point."

"Very possible, but not a dead certainty. He may decide to run rather than try to catch us. Since we don't know, we have to assume he's after us."

She trudged silently beside him as he walked out into the desert. They didn't dare risk walking on the road, so that meant they had to parallel it, far enough from the roadside that they couldn't easily be spotted, but close enough that they wouldn't lose sight of the pavement. She ached in so many places that it didn't seem worth the effort to worry about any of them. They had to walk, so she walked. It was as simple as that.

"Are you wearing a watch?" she asked. "What time is it? It isn't dawn yet, so they couldn't have taken us far."

Joe tilted his wrist to read the luminous dial. "It's four-thirty, so it'll be dawn soon. If they just threw us in the van and left immediately, before the security police could close the base, we're talking at least an hour of driving time. We could be anywhere from thirty to sixty miles away from base."

Walking sixty miles was a daunting thought, but not nearly as daunting as facing that man again. "There are others," she said aloud. "Maybe close by. They could have been taking us to turn over to them. It'll be dawn soon, but we don't dare try to flag anyone down, because we don't know who the others are or what they look like."

"You got it," he said grimly.

"So we have to walk every foot of that blasted sixty miles."

"Unless we see a state trooper. At least when the sun comes up I'll have some idea where we are."

Too far away from anything to suit her. She stopped talking, partly because sound carried so far in the desert and she didn't want to alert anyone to their presence, but mostly because it was taking all her effort just to walk. She had been awake all night—except for when she'd been unconscious, but she was fairly certain that didn't qualify as rest—and she was exhausted. Her head pounded. She supposed Joe's head hurt, too, but he'd only been hit once. First she had tumbled out her window, then she'd been hit on the head, probably with the pistol, then with that guy's fist, and finally she had hit her head against the side of the van when Joe had shoved her. The wonder was that she had any sense left at all. She ached in every muscle of her body, and a good many of the bruises adorning her had come at Joe's hands. She was glad she'd kicked him back and only wished she had gone ahead and bitten him, too. She hoped he had the granddaddy of all headaches.

Twice he drew her down when a noise alerted him. She never did see anything, but he had superior eyesight, so she let him do the work while she seized the opportunity to rest. When he decided it was safe to continue on he would urge her to her feet with an implacable hand under her elbow, and she would walk some more.

Dawn began to turn the sky pearly to their left, giving them the basic information that they had been carried north into the desert and were now headed south, back toward the base. She supposed it was good information to have, in case they had to lose contact with the road.

"We can't go on much longer," Joe murmured in her ear. "Anyone passing will be able to see us from the road, and it'll get too hot to walk, anyway. We need to find shelter for the day."

She didn't like the sound of that. It was safer to

stay hidden and sleep during the day, walking only at night, but it was sure going to take them a long time to get to the base. If she hadn't been so tired she could have argued, but she was beginning to feel incapable of going another foot, and she suddenly realized just how much the night's events had taken out of her. They simply had to rest.

He veered sharply away from the road, deeper into the desert. The light slowly changed to gray, letting them see details but not yet color. A huge rocky outcropping loomed in the distance, and she stared at it in dismay. That was almost surely where he was going, and she wasn't certain she could make it. She ground her teeth to keep from protesting. She either made it or she took a nap in the sun, which would soon be broiling. She was also thirsty, but they had no water, so there wasn't any point in bringing it up. He had to be thirsty, too.

When they finally reached the rocks she leaned thankfully against one huge boulder. "Now what?" she gasped.

"Stay here."

He was already gone, vanished into the rocks. She mumbled, "Sure," and sank down to the ground. Her temples were throbbing. She closed her eyes and leaned her head against the stone behind her.

It felt as if she had no sooner closed her eyes than he was saying, "Come on," as he ruthlessly hauled her to her feet. He pulled her higher up into the rocks and shade enveloped her. Until then, she hadn't realized how quickly the desert had heated. He'd found a niche in the rock deep enough to provide protection for both of them, and he deposited her in the crude shelter.

"I've already checked for snakes," he said as he put a stick in her hand. "But if any show up, knock them away with this. I'm going to wipe out our tracks and find something to drink."

Automatically she closed her fingers around the stick. She knew she should be uneasy at the thought of snakes, not to mention watchful, but she had more important things to do right then, like sleep. She turned over onto her right side, because it hurt the least, and immediately dozed.

Joe stared down at her, his jaw muscles flexing. The left side of her face was bruised and scraped, and so was her left arm. He could plainly see a lump on her temple. She was chalk white with exhaustion and pain, her clothes dirty and sporting a few small tears. The contrast between her normally pristine appearance and now, when she lay bedraggled at his feet, sleeping in the dirt, utterly enraged him. Cal Gilchrist was probably dead, but he wanted the other one dead, too, for what they had put her through. He himself hadn't done a very spectacular job of keeping her safe, and he included himself in his rage.

She looked so small and helpless, curled on her side like that, though he knew she wasn't exactly helpless. He remembered her furious struggle to free her mouth from the gag so she could yell her suspicions at Gilchrist; she had caused the fight between the two men, thereby engineering their own escape. It was up to him now to make certain nothing else happened to her.

His own fatigue pulled at him as he backtracked for quite a distance, then obliterated all sign of their passing on his return to the outcropping. He ignored the weariness of his muscles. They needed water; not desperately, not yet, but they would stay much stronger if they had adequate liquids. Before he let her get dehydrated he would take the chance of flagging down a car, but it hadn't come to that yet, and he didn't want to take unnecessary chances. With an expert eye he noted the stunted plant life dotting the desert floor, studying the growth pattern and picking out the plants that looked slightly more succulent than others growing nearby and indicating more moisture underground. They would be all right.

He climbed back to the niche in the rocks. Caroline hadn't moved; she was breathing with the slow, heavy rhythm of deep sleep. Suddenly it seemed like a lifetime since he had held her, felt her nestling trustingly in his arms, and one moment longer was too long. He lay down beside her and eased her into his arms, cradling her head on his shoulder. She sighed, her soft breath brushing his skin.

Damn her, why hadn't she called him, told him of her suspicions about Gilchrist? It had been obvious that she wasn't surprised to find the man in the work area, had in fact gone there specifically to find him. She had barged straight into danger rather than picking up the telephone and calling him, or even Hodge.

All of this could have been prevented if she'd just made that call instead of trying to do things herself.

That would be the first thing he got straightened out between them when she woke up. Why the hell hadn't she trusted him? If he had to tie her to the bed every time she was out of his sight to keep her from rushing headlong into dangerous situations, he would do it. He remembered the black terror he'd felt, seeing her dart into the office to confront the saboteur, and he wanted to shake her until her teeth rattled.

Instead he held her tighter, smoothing her pale hair back from her face. He could feel her heart beating against his, and right now that was all he required. He slept as easily as she had, simply closing his eyes and letting weariness sweep over him in a tide.

Chapter 13

It was the heat that woke her. She felt rested, her headache having subsided to a distant and far more tolerable ache. Slowly she sat up, staring out at the glaringly hot landscape stretched before her, wavering in the heat: reds in every shade, yellows, browns, sand colors. Small specks of green that testified to the sparse plant life. Beautiful. Basic. Cal was probably dead somewhere out there, and despite what he had done, what he had tried to do, she couldn't help but mourn him. He hadn't wanted to kill them, had argued against harming them. Poor Cal. He'd been a traitor, but not a murderer, though what he'd been doing could easily have led to someone's death. Poor Cal. But if Joe had been harmed because of him, she would have killed him herself.

Sweat stung her eyes, and she dried her face on the arm of her shirt. If it hadn't been for the sheltering rock, the heat would have been intolerable. She reached out and touched the stone, found it cool to the touch. Where the sun kissed it, it would fry eggs.

Joe wasn't there, but she wasn't alarmed. She had a vague impression that he'd been lying beside her, and the imprint in the dirt confirmed that. Probably he had disturbed her when he'd gotten up, and that had allowed the heat to intrude on her consciousness.

She felt incredibly grubby, and looking down at herself, she saw that she *was* incredibly grubby. She didn't think she'd been this dirty since…come to think of it, she'd never been this dirty before. She had been a fastidious child, eschewing the joys of mud puddles for those of computers and books.

Stiffly she climbed to her feet, wincing as her various aches made themselves felt. Aching or not, nature called.

When she returned to the niche, she found Joe leaning propped against the rocks, looking disgustingly capable. His eyes were piercingly alert, and even though his clothes were as dirty as hers, they looked made to be dirty. Jeans and a khaki shirt were far more utilitarian than thin white cotton pants and an oversize white T-shirt. Even his scruffy boots were better suited to the desert than her loafers; she had to be careful how she stepped, to avoid getting the fine silt inside her shoes, where it would promptly rub her feet raw.

After a single encompassing look that avoided

meeting his gaze, she stepped past him and sank down in the shade of the rocks again.

Joe's back teeth ground together. He'd thought he had himself firmly in control once more, but all of a sudden he was right back to where he'd started, dangerously close to the precipice. She was shutting him out, damn it, and he found it intolerable.

Grimly he regulated his breathing, forcing his hands to relax, his jaw to unclench. She was still fragile from the rough handling she'd had the day before; now wasn't the time to force a confrontation, even if he had been sure of his control, which he wasn't. Later. He promised himself full satisfaction—later.

"We both need something to drink," he finally said. "Come on."

Unhesitatingly she got to her feet without any sign of her usual argumentativeness, which had to mean she was very thirsty.

They didn't have far to walk; Joe had already scouted the area and marked the most likely spot in a small arroyo, where the scrub grew profusely. He knelt on the sandy bottom and began scooping up the sand with his hands. It quickly grew damp. He slipped the knife from his boot and dug deeper, until muddy water began to gather in the hole.

His gag had been made from a handkerchief, and it came in handy now. He spread the square of cloth over the water to filter the liquid, then gestured for her. "Drink."

Caroline didn't take exception to his curt tone; he had produced water, and that was the important thing.

She didn't cavil about unsanitary conditions or the indignity of having to get on her hands and knees and lap liquid like a dog. It was water. She would gladly stand on her head to get it if it was required. She could feel the membranes of her mouth and throat absorbing the tepid moisture, and it was wonderful.

Still, she forced herself to stop long before her thirst was quenched and moved away from the tiny water hole. She gestured to him. "Your turn." She didn't know how much water there was; there might be only enough for both of them to have a few swallows each.

He stretched out full length on the sand to drink, which she considered and decided was a far more comfortable position. She should have thought of it herself, but then, she had never lapped water from a puddle before. She would know next time. Absently she studied his prone figure. As big as he was, it stood to reason that he had more blood in his body than she did, so he would probably require more water. Biology had never been one of her interests, but she would bet he had at least one more deciliter of blood than she did, perhaps two. An interesting little tidbit she needed to investigate...

She blinked and became aware that he had risen to his feet and was waiting, having evidently asked her something. "Do you want more water or don't you?" he repeated impatiently.

"Oh. Yes, thank you." This time she stretched out as he had done, which gave her better access to the small puddle of water. She sucked enthusiastically until she began to feel as if she'd had enough. She paused to ask, "Have you finished, or do you want more?"

"I've had enough," he said.

She soaked the handkerchief as best she could, then gingerly washed her face and hands, wincing when the water stung the scrapes. When she had finished, she offered the handkerchief to Joe, and he scrubbed the damp material over his own face and hands, and around the back of his neck. The moisture had a cooling effect, something he needed right then.

"We'll wait in the rocks until sundown," he said, and she nodded. Without another word she headed back to the protective niche.

Damn it, she was treating him like some stranger she'd been stranded with. No, even worse than that. She would have talked more to a stranger. She hadn't once looked him in the eye. Her gaze would slide past his face without connecting, as if he were someone she passed on the street. His hands clenched into hard fists as he strode after her. It was time to have it out, damn it.

She was sitting on the ground in the niche when he got there, her arms looped casually around her drawn-up knees. Joe deliberately walked so close that his boots nudged her feet, forcing her to either stand up and face him or tilt her head back as far as it would go. She continued to sit.

"Why the hell didn't you call me last night instead of tackling Gilchrist on your own?" he asked softly, so softly it would take a discerning ear to catch the quiet fury underlying the words.

Caroline heard it but didn't much care. She shrugged. "I didn't think of it. I wouldn't have, anyway. Why would I?"

"So I could take care of it. So you wouldn't nearly have gotten yourself killed."

"And you, too," she pointed out. "How *did* you get involved?"

"I was following you."

"Ah." She gave him a brittle smile. "Thought you'd catch me in the act, didn't you? What a surprise to find out it was someone else who got caught."

"And you knew it when you went there. Damn it, Caroline, for such a smart person, that was a stupid thing to do. You should have called me when you first suspected him."

"Yeah, sure. Why waste my breath?" she asked scornfully. "I'd already seen how much you believed me. I'd rather have called Adrian Pendley than you, and he hates my guts."

His breath hissed softly between his teeth as he leaned down and grasped her arms, jerking her unceremoniously to her feet. "If you ever need anything," he said, the words deliberately spaced as he forced them out, "you call *me*. My woman doesn't go to someone else."

She pulled sharply, trying to dislodge his grip on her arms, but he merely tightened his hands. "Interesting, I'm sure," she snapped. "When you find her, be sure to tell her that, but *I'm* not interested."

A red mist swam in front of his eyes. "Don't push me," he heard himself say hoarsely. "You're mine, damn it. Admit it."

Again she tried to pull away, her blue-green eyes spitting fire at him. If he thought he could just pick up again where they had left off, now that it had been proven to his satisfaction that she was worthy, he was in for a nasty surprise. She wanted to scream at him, but instead she limited herself to a scathing retort. "We had a hot weekend in bed, but that doesn't give you a deed to me. Boy, were my eyes opened. I knew you weren't madly in love with me or anything, but you really can't have much of an opinion of someone at all if you think they're capable of betraying their country. It was certainly a learning experience—"

"Shut up." His voice was guttural now.

"Don't tell me to shut up," she fired back. "The next time I go to bed with a man I'll make certain he—" *"You'll never go to bed with any man but me."* He began shaking her, the force of it whipping her head back and forth. The thought of her turning to another man was unbearable, shattering the last tenuous thread of his control and letting rage spew forth like lava, red-hot and molten. She was his, and he was never going to let her go.

Somehow his mouth was on hers, his hand locked in her hair at the back of her head, holding her still. He tasted blood, whether his or hers he didn't know, but the coppery taste called up a fiercely primitive instinct to brand her as his, sear his flesh into hers so she would never be free of him. His skin felt burning hot and too tight, as if it would burst from the force of his blood pounding beneath it. His manhood was iron hard with lust, straining against the front of his jeans.

He carried her to the ground, blind with the need to feel her soft body beneath him. He began jerking at her pants, tugging them down and off. Her underwear tore when it was subjected to the same treatment.

Caroline lay still, staring in mute fascination at his face. She had always sensed his control and resented it, but abruptly it had shattered, and the naked intensity of his expression was almost frightening. Almost, because in the deepest, most basic part of her, she trusted him not to hurt her. She saw the savagery of his eyes, felt the barely restrained strength of his hands as he stripped her clothing away, and his wildness called her own fierce spirit soaring up to meet him.

She heard herself give a wild cry; then her hands were buried in his thick black hair, pulling him down to her.

He tore at the fly of his jeans, grunting as he freed his rigid length. He entered her with a powerful, driving thrust that made her cry out again from the impact of it; then her legs came up to hold him in the cradle of her hips as her silky hot depths wrapped around him, yielding, caressing, demanding. The sensation made him feel as if his skull was going to explode.

He rode her hard, grinding her into the hard ground beneath them in his frenzy to irrevocably meld their flesh into one. He'd never felt so savage, so utterly dominant and primitive; he was out of control, reacting purely as a male animal who needed his mate more than anything else in the world.

Caroline lifted her hips to meet his heavy thrusts. She had been sucked up into the maw of a powerful storm, and she loved it, reveled in it, embraced it and wanted more. The pleasure exploded in her, hard and deep. She clutched his hair, her heels digging into the backs of his muscled thighs as her slim body arched in a powerful bow, lifting him with her. The rhythmic surge rolled through her like thunder, and she gave herself up to it with a cry.

Her completion called up his own, the exquisite milking sensation on his hard length sending him over the edge. He convulsed with a powerful jetting that emptied him but seemed to go on forever, longer and harder and deeper than he'd ever known before. He was barely conscious when it ended, barely able to move. He didn't have the strength to roll away from her, or even to support his weight on his arms. He sank down onto her with the dim wish that he would never have to move, that they could lie there entwined for the rest of their lives.

He *needed* her for the rest of his life. He'd always loved flying with a passion that had overshadowed what he'd felt for other women, but right from the start he'd found it impossible to put Caroline out of his mind as he'd always been able to do once he was in the cockpit. She would never make a comfortable wife, but hell, if comfort and placidity were what he wanted, he would never have become a fighter pilot. He'd never been in a fighter yet, not even Baby, that kept him on his toes the way Caroline did. She both delighted him and challenged him, and she met the strength of his sexual drive with matching strength. He was a warrior, and she was as fierce as he was, with more guts than brains, and that was saying a lot. In more ancient times she would have fought beside him, a sword in her own hand. His Valkyrie. He felt humbled by her spirit.

"I love you," he said. He hadn't known the words were there until they came out, but he wasn't surprised by them. Somehow he found enough strength to surge up onto his elbows, looking down at her with his savage, glittering eyes narrowed. "You're my woman. Don't ever forget it."

Caroline's eyes flared, the pupils expanding to huge black circles that almost completely swallowed the vivid color of her irises. "What did you say?" she demanded.

He thrust his hips against her, deepening the invasion of his still-firm male flesh. God, how could he still be aroused? He was almost dead from exhaustion, but the want, the need, was still there. "I said I love you. And you're mine, Caroline Evans. Forever and a day. 'Til death and beyond."

"In sickness and in health," she prompted; then suddenly tears welled and overflowed, trickling down her temples.

He cradled her head in his hands and caught the tears with his tongue, tenderly nuzzling against her.

His own chest felt tight. He'd never imagined his valiant little warrior crying, and it was almost more than he could bear. "Why the tears?" he murmured, pressing light kisses across her face and neck. "Did I hurt you?"

"You nearly killed me," she replied. "When you didn't believe me." And she balled up her fist and punched him on the side of the head, because it was the only place she could reach. It was an awkward punch, because of their closeness and her position, and didn't pack as much power as she would have liked, but he gave a very satisfying grunt. "Don't let it happen again."

He jerked his head back and glared down at her. "Why in hell did you do that?"

"Because you deserved it," she said, and blinked back another tear.

Joe's mouth twitched, and the glare turned into something tender. "I'm sorry," he breathed, feathering a kiss on each corner of her mouth. "I'm sorry. I was a blind, bull-headed ass. Just the suggestion that you might have betrayed me sent me into a flat spin, and I couldn't pull out of it. I was on my way over to see you when you came marching toward me, right down the middle of the base like you owned it, when you were supposed to be under guard." A quick frown knitted his brow, and he pulled back a little to scowl at her. "How *did* you get out?"

"I dismantled the glass slats in the bedroom window and crawled out."

He looked astounded. "You can't fit through there. It's too little."

"Hah. I got some scrapes from it and hurt my shoulder when I fell, because I had to go out headfirst, but it can be done." Then she judiciously added, "Though I don't think you would fit through even if you were greased from head to foot."

"Or any other man on base," he said dryly.

"Well, times have changed," she pointed out. "The security police should realize that women are a permanent part of the Air Force, even flying fighters into combat now, so they should adjust their thinking."

Typical of Caroline to point out the security police's errors in letting her escape. He would be sure to pass them on to Hodge. If he beat Caroline to it, that is.

She gave a delicate little cat yawn, and her dark sea-colored eyes looked sleepy. Still, Joe was reluctant to disengage their bodies, though she was lying naked with nothing beneath her but the hard ground. He solved the problem by anchoring her hips with a hard arm and rolling so he was on bottom. She made a soft sound of contentment, very like a purr, and nestled her head into the hollow where his neck and shoulder met.

He leisurely stroked her slim back for a minute, then abruptly his hands tightened, and he lifted her off his chest to give her a hard look. "What about you?" he demanded sharply. "Do you love me, Caroline? Say it."

"Yes, sir, Colonel," she murmured in response to the commanding tone. She supposed it was something he couldn't help. "I love you, Colonel, sir. Stupid of me, wasn't it, to fall in love when you were so determined to hold back, to not give me anything more than sex?"

Tension pulled the skin tight across his cheekbones, starkly revealing the chiseled bone structure. He felt the nausea of panic coiling in his stomach, because suddenly he saw that Caroline would never tolerate that rigid control, doling out passion and love in measured amounts. She wanted all of him. A cliff yawned at his feet, and if he stepped over the edge his life would never be the same, but if he didn't take that one step, he would lose her. He knew it all the way down to his bones, and just the thought of it was a hammer blow to the chest that told him he would never be able to survive the reality. His instincts were too sharp, too primal, for him to think he would be able to shrug it off. She was his mate; there was no other for him.

Somehow he forced his lips to move, though they felt numb. "I...I need to be in control."

He felt her hand on his hair, gently stroking, her soft fingertips trailing down to his cheek and then to his lips. "I noticed," she said, softly wry.

It was hard to explain, impossible with her lying on top of him, so close that she couldn't miss even the most minute change in his expression. He lifted her off him, though his body felt abruptly incomplete without the linkage to hers. She looked disoriented by the sudden shift, automatically crossing her arms over her bare breasts in response to her inner uncertainty. The gesture was so innately feminine that he grabbed her to him, holding her close and savoring the feel of her silky skin, gathering his strength. He brushed the dirt from her back, took off his shirt and slipped it on her. Her own clothes, he saw, were a tangled mess.

He kissed her, hard and quick, before tension drove him to his feet. He stood with his back to her, staring out over the stark, lovely desert.

"Dad was put in prison when I was six years old," he said. His voice was hoarse and raw. "He was innocent. The guy who had committed the crime was finally caught for something else, and he admitted everything. But Dad spent two years in prison, and for those two years I was in foster homes."

There was total silence behind him, but he sensed the intensity of her attention. "Maybe there was just something about me that the man in the first home hated. Maybe it was because I'm a half-breed. They kept other foster kids, but he singled me out. I was just a kid. I broke things, I'd lose my temper playing with the other kids, the way kids do. I was bigger and stronger than most kids my age, but I didn't know how to control that strength. If any of them said anything about Dad being a dirty half-breed jailbird, I went at them and did as much damage as I could. God, did I have a temper.

"And this man would beat me whenever I did something, even if it was stumble over an ashtray that he'd left on the floor. At first he used a belt, but it wasn't long before he was using his fists. I fought him, and he beat me that much worse. I missed more school than I attended, because he wouldn't let me go to school with my face bruised up.''

It got harder to say, the memories blacker as he dredged them up, and the worst was yet to come. He made himself continue. ''He kicked me down the steps once, broke a couple of my ribs. And still I kept fighting him. I guess you could say I didn't have stopping sense, but my temper flashed like black powder, and I couldn't control it. He started burning me with cigarettes if I sassed him, or twisting my fingers, just to see if he could make me cry.''

''I was in a nightmare and I couldn't get out,'' he said softly. ''Nobody seemed to care what happened to me. I was just a half-breed, worth less than a mongrel dog on the side of the road. Then one day he slapped me, and I really lost my temper. I went on a rampage. I kicked in the television set, threw all the little knicknacks against the wall, got in the kitchen and started breaking the dishes, and he was right behind me, hitting me with his fists, trying to kick my ribs in. I lost, of course. I was only six, even if I was big for my age. He dragged me down to the basement, stripped me naked and beat the bloody hell out of me.''

His heart was pounding now, just as it had been that day almost thirty years before. He'd never said it before, but it had to be said now. ''Then he raped me.''

He could hear the swift movement behind him, feel

the rush of air as Caroline surged to her feet. He kept his back turned.

"Looking back, I think it shocked him that he'd done it. He never touched me again, even in the slightest way. And I never lost control again," he said remotely. "He must have called the welfare people, or maybe his wife did. I was gone from that house within two weeks. I spent those two weeks in the basement, alone, silent. I stopped talking. The other foster homes were okay, I guess, but I didn't take any chances. I did exactly what I was told, never lost my temper, never lost control, never talked. Then one day, when I was eight, Dad showed up. He'd gotten out of prison and tracked me down. I don't know if he had authorization to get me or if no one was brave enough to tell him he couldn't, but he picked me up and held me so close it hurt, and it was the best hurt in the world. I was safe again."

"Did you tell him?" she asked, the first time she had spoken. He was a little startled at the harshness of her tone.

"No. I've never told anyone, until now. If you knew my dad, you'd know why. He would have gone after the guy and literally killed him with his bare hands, and I couldn't stand to lose Dad again." He steeled himself to turn and face her, braced for the pity he would see in her eyes, but what he saw was a long way from pity. She was standing with her fists clenched, her face savage with rage. If that long-ago man had been standing there right then, Caroline Evans would have killed him, too. She wasn't a half-breed Comanche warrior, but her spirit was just as swift and fierce, and her sea-colored eyes were blazing. Startled, he began to laugh.

"Don't laugh, don't you dare laugh!" she roared. "I'll *kill* him—"

"You don't have to, sweetheart," he soothed, jerking her into his arms when she evaded his more gentle attempts to embrace her. "He's dead. He died two years after the welfare people took me away. After I had graduated from the Academy I decided to check, just for the information. Hell, who am I kidding? There's no telling what I would have done if he'd still been alive."

He pushed her hair away from her face and kissed her. "Maybe I was tougher than most kids, but he didn't damage me permanently, except for always wanting to be in control. He didn't warp me sexually. Being around Dad was probably the best therapy I could have had, as far as sex is concerned. He was always totally open about it, treating it as just part of nature. And we had the horse ranch. A kid learns the basics damn fast on a ranch. I was okay within six months of getting back with Dad. There was a bedrock of love there that never let me down."

"Except you're still a control fanatic," she growled.

He had to laugh again. "You can't even lay all the blame for that on what happened. I'm a fighter pilot. My life depends on being in control. It's part of my training as well as my personality."

She nuzzled her face against his sweat-dampened

chest. "Well, you have a reason for it, but that doesn't mean I like it."

"No, I don't guess you would," he said in amusement. "That's why you continually push me, trying to make me lose control. Well, lady, you succeeded. Are you pleased with yourself?" His voice turned deep and serious. "I could have hurt you, sweetheart."

She looked like the cat who had had an entire gallon of cream, not just a measly saucerful. "It was *wonderful*," she purred. "And I wasn't frightened. You can't hurt me by loving me. The only way you'll ever hurt me is if you stop loving me."

His arms tightened around her. "Then you're safe for a lifetime." He held her close for a long, long time, and he felt something relax within him, something that he hadn't even known was tightly wound. She was inside his defenses now, and he no longer had to keep his guard up. Defeat had never been sweeter, because he'd come away with the grand prize.

At the moment his grand prize was bruised and half-naked, but still valiant. He released her with a little swat to her bare backside. "Get your clothes on, woman. It's sundown, and we have to get back to the base."

Chapter 14

It was almost anticlimactic. The danger the night before had been very real, but it wasn't long after dusk when they veered back close to the road and a car came by, cruising very slowly, shining a spotlight off to the side. Caroline gasped and started to hit the dirt, but Joe kept her upright with a firm grip on her arm. His eagle eyes had spotted something she couldn't make out in the darkness: the row of lights on top of the car. Literally dragging her in his wake, he strode out into the road.

The car stopped. The spotlight wavered, then settled on him. "I'm Colonel Joe Mackenzie, out of Nellis," he said. His deep voice carried that unmistakable note of command. "I need to get back to the base as soon as possible."

The state trooper switched off the spot and got out of the car. "We've been searching for you, sir," he said in a respectful tone. Military personnel or not, there was something about Joe Mackenzie that elicited that response. "Are you all right, injured in any way? A van was found—"

"We know about the van. We were in it," Joe said dryly.

"We were ordered by the governor to give every assistance to the military in finding you. A statewide search was started this morning."

Joe put his arm around Caroline and ushered her into the back seat; then he went around and took a seat up front. Caroline found herself staring at the back of his head through steel mesh.

"Hey," she said indignantly.

Joe glanced back and began to laugh. "Finally," he said, "I've found a way to control you."

"The sensor alarms went wild," Captain Hodge said. "Once when Ms. Evans entered the work area after she was already recorded as being inside, and again when you entered without your ID tag, Colonel. The first guard was there within two minutes, but the building was empty. They must have dragged both of you out immediately and then panicked. They loaded you in Mr. Gilchrist's van and bolted.

"Ms. Evans' quarters were checked and she was discovered missing. Amazing. I didn't know anyone could get out a window that small," he said, glancing at her.

"I'm not very thick," she replied coolly.

He cleared his throat at the look in her eyes. "I tried to notify you, Colonel, and found that you were missing, too, though there was no record of you leaving the base. Nor had Ms. Evans attempted to leave. There was a record, however, of Mr. Gilchrist leaving immediately after the alarm had sounded."

"The other guy must have been hidden in back with us," Joe said.

"Who was he?" she asked. "He looked familiar, but at the same time I didn't know him."

Hodge looked at his ever-present clipboard. "His name was Carl Mabry. You'd probably seen him in the control room. He was a civilian working with the radar."

"How did Gilchrist get involved with him?" Joe asked. "And there are others. Have you found out anything about them?"

They were sitting in his office. Both he and Caroline had been checked over by the medics and declared basically sound. Somewhere along the line, Caroline's clothes had vanished and the well-meaning nurses had tried to stuff her into one of the too-revealing backless, shapeless gowns that were standard for every hospital. Caroline's sense of style had been outraged, but the green surgicals had appealed to her. She was wearing a set now and somehow looked dashing in them.

"Evidently, Gilchrist was recruited after he began work here," Hodge said. "Mabry belonged to a radical group that opposed defense spending. You know

the type. They want the money for humanitarian pur-
poses, even if they have to kill to get it.''

"Then just how,'' Caroline asked in an awful tone,
"did he get security clearance?''

Hodge winced. "I—uh, we're still checking on
that. But he didn't have clearance into the laser building.''

"So how did he get in without triggering the
alarms?'' Joe asked impatiently.

Caroline snorted. "The program has a major weakness. The alarm is set off by a body entering or leaving without a card—but not a card entering or leaving
without a body.''

Hodge's hair was too short to pull, so he ran both
hands over his crew-cut head. "What?'' he almost
yelled.

"Well, it's obvious. I certainly didn't go into the
building with Cal when he was supposedly searching
for my tag, but the computer said that I did, which
means he must have had the tag with him and flashed
it so the sensors would pick it up, thereby destroying
any record that he had entered the building alone and
discrediting my story of having misplaced my tag.
There wasn't anything Cal didn't know about computers. He probably figured it out not long after he
started work on base, testing it by swinging the tag
through the doorway on a string, or something like
that. If he'd been caught, he wasn't doing anything
he would be arrested for, just playing with the computers like any hacker would. Evidently he picked up
my tag when I lost it, but left at the same time I did

that day so the sensors weren't set off. He carried it off base and had it duplicated, then returned the original to me the next morning so there wouldn't be a report on it. The night we caught them—'' She paused, looking confused. ''When was it? Just last night?''

''Seems longer, doesn't it?'' Joe commented, grinning at her.

''Anyway, he would have entered with the duplicate tag, then tossed it through the doorway to Mabry, who would also have used it to enter. If you check the logs, you'll probably find entry, exit, then reentry with just a few seconds between. *If* you had been on your toes, Captain Hodge, you would have made certain my code had been immediately deleted from the computer instead of waiting until morning, thinking you had me safely under guard.''

Hodge was crimson with embarrassment. ''Yes, ma'am,'' he mumbled.

''Likewise, instead of assuming you had the problem contained, the entire laser team should have been restricted to base until you were certain.''

''Yes, ma'am.''

''The sensor program needs to be rewritten. It's humiliating to think of a sophisticated security system being bypassed by two people tossing ID tags through a doorway like kids playing catch.''

''Yes, ma'am.''

Joe had covered his mouth with his hand to hide his grin, but his blue crystal eyes were shining. Poor Hodge, by-the-book person that he was, was no match

for Caroline at her most haughty, and his little hedgehog was most definitely feeling put upon. He decided
to intervene before the captain was reduced to a sense
of total inadequacy. "You used the past tense when
speaking of Mabry. Is he dead?"

"Suicide. Gilchrist, by the way, was doing it for
the money, not for any ideological reason, but Mabry
firmly believed that the Night Wing program should
be scrapped. They intended to cause so many problems with the tests that funding wouldn't be granted.
Good plan, considering the economic and political climate. Pressure is high in Washington to spend money
only on things that *work*. We've tied Mabry to a
group called Help Americans First. I don't know if
we'll be able to implicate any of them without his
testimony, but we might be able to turn up a paper
trail that ties them to it. We know they were willing
to kill both you and Ms. Evans to complete their sabotage of the lasers, so we aren't talking about innocent
do-gooders here."

"I want them nailed, Hodge," Joe said softly.

"Yes, sir. The FBI is working on it."

Caroline yawned. Despite sleeping all day, she was
tired; it had been an eventful twenty-four hours. Joe
leaned back in his chair and hooked his hands behind
his head, watching her. It gave him a deep sense of
contentment to watch her.

"You're the first to know, Hodge," he said lazily.
"Ms. Evans and I are going to be married."

To his amusement, a look of disbelief crossed the
captain's face. Hodge looked at Caroline the way he

would have looked at a wild animal that had suddenly been turned loose, as if he didn't know whether to run or freeze. She returned the look with a sort of warning indifference.

"Uh…good luck, Colonel," Hodge blurted out. "I mean—congratulations."

"Thank you. And I'll probably need that luck."

Two weeks later Caroline whirled in her husband's powerful arms to the strains of a waltz. Washington society glittered around them. The huge ballroom was resplendent with silks and satins, jewels both paste and real, bright chatter and serious dealing. Intermingled with the formal black, gray and midnight-blue tuxedos of the civilians were the gorgeous dress uniforms of the various branches of the military. Joe looked magnificent in his. Caroline saw more than one set of feminine eyes following him wherever he went, and she had been forced to glare several of the owners of those eyes into submission.

"We should have waited," she said.

"For what?" His arm tightened around her as he swung her around.

"To get married."

"For God's sake, why?"

"For your family."

He laughed aloud. "Dad understood. When he decided to marry Mary, he had the deed done within two days. It took me three."

"General Ramey seemed pleased," she commented.

"He is. The Air Force likes its officers to be married. It makes us more settled."

"Sure," she replied doubtfully. "If going Mach 3 is considered settled."

The funding for Night Wing had been granted by a wide margin in Congress the day before. Joe had had to testify before the committee, requiring his presence in Washington, and he had categorically refused to be separated from his wife, so Caroline's presence had also been required.

The federal investigation into Help Americans First was ongoing, as was the final phase of testing on the Night Wing project, but the aircraft and laser systems were all functioning perfectly. The damage Cal had done to the computer program had been rectified. And Caroline was slowly beginning to realize what it would mean to her life to be married to a career military officer. When the final testing was completed he would be taking over as wing commander of the 1st Tactical Fighter Wing at Langley AFB in Virginia. She had learned a lot about the military in the ten days they had been married and knew that Joe would be up for his first star after that posting. He was thirty-five years old and would probably make general before he was thirty-seven. She would never admit it to him, because she felt he needed someone who didn't jump every time he issued an order, but sometimes she was a little in awe of his abilities.

He pulled her closer, and the movement of the waltz brought her lower body into firm contact with his. Her gaze flew up to meet his, and she saw his arousal reflected in the glittering blue depths of his eyes.

"I like you in white," he murmured.

"That's good. I wear it a lot." She was wearing it now. Her ball gown was pure, snowy white.

"You look better on white sheets than anyone I know."

"Hmm. I'm going to take flying lessons, so maybe I'll need to have several jumpsuits made in white."

Incredibly, she felt his shoulder tense under her hand. "Flying lessons? Why? If you want to fly, I'll teach you."

She gave him a calm smile. "No. I'd turn you into a trembling wreck if you tried to teach me how to fly, and I'd be ready to kill you. But I need to know, so I'll know something of what it's like for you up there." She figured it was the best way to get over the fear she felt every time he went up. Rather than risk clipping his wings, out of his concern for her, she would grow her own wings.

He still looked uneasy. "Caroline..."

"Joe," she replied firmly, "I'm good at anything I decide to do. Physics, computers, sex. I'll be good at flying, too. And having babies."

He stopped dead in the middle of the dance floor. "Caroline!"

She lifted her brows, ignoring the smiling glances directed their way. "What?"

"Are you pregnant?"

"It's possible," she said serenely. "The timing wasn't right during our weekend in Vegas, but what about since then? Name one time when you used any protection. If I'm not now, the odds are good I will be before the end of the year.''

He couldn't seem to breathe. Hell, she probably was pregnant. As she had said, she was very good at anything she decided to do, and so was he.

"It'll be interesting," she said, "to find out if you make girl babies or boy babies.''

A slow grin moved his hard, beautiful mouth. "As long as I make you, I'm happy.''

"Oh, you do make me, Colonel Mackenzie. Very well indeed. When are we going to Wyoming?''

He adjusted to her lightning change of subject without a pause and resumed the dance. "Next month. I'll only have a week, but we'll get back for Christmas.''

"Good. I've talked to Boling-Wahl, and they'll try to keep me assigned to projects in your general vicinity, though of course I won't be working on any project for the Air Force. I may be working in Baltimore while you're at Langley, but the commute isn't bad.''

"Not bad," he said doubtfully, "but I don't really like the idea of you having to battle that traffic.''

She pulled back a little and her brows slowly rose. "Me?" she asked after a delicate pause.

He stifled a shout of laughter. "I have to be closer to the base than that," he explained, keeping his voice level with an effort.

"Oh." She considered the situation for a moment, then said, "Okay, I'll do it this time. But you owe me, big time, because I believe in being comfortable, and fighting the traffic violates that belief. I'll let you know when I think of some way you can make it up to me.''

He tugged her closer, still fighting laughter as he savored the feel of her in his arms. ''Mary's going to love you,'' he said under his breath.

Mary did love her.

The two women were immediate friends, sensing a basic likeness in each other. Caroline fell in love, not only with his family but with Ruth, Wyoming and the prosperous horse ranch on top of Mackenzie's Mountain. The place was beautiful, and the ranch house was one of the most cheerful places she'd ever been in her life.

Mary Mackenzie was a slight, delicately formed woman with soft blue-gray eyes, pale brown hair and the most exquisite complexion in the world. At first sight she struck Caroline as rather plain, but by day's end her gaze had accustomed itself to the glowing purity of Mary's features and she thought her mother-in-law incredibly beautiful. Certainly Wolf Mackenzie thought his wife was beautiful, if the obvious love and lust in his black eyes every time he looked at her were anything to go by.

She had never seen two men more alike than Joe and his father, the only real difference being that Wolf's eyes were as black as night while Joe's were that brilliant, diamond blue. And looking at Wolf, she could easily understand why Joe had thought his father would kill the man who had abused him, if he had known about it. Wolf Mackenzie protected his own. Like his son, he was pure warrior.

Mary was dwarfed by her sons, even thirteen-year-old Zane, the intense one. Michael was off at college; it would be Christmas before she would meet him. But Joshua, at sixteen, was almost as big as Wolf and Joe. Josh was as bright and lighthearted as Zane was dark and quiet, his gaze watchful. The same dangerous intensity that burned in both Joe and Wolf was evident in the boy.

Then there was Maris. At eleven, she was small for her age, with Mary's slight build and exquisitely translucent complexion. Her hair was pale, her eyes as black as Wolf's. She was her father's shadow, her small hands gentling and soothing the fractious horses as well as Wolf's strong ones did.

For the first time Caroline saw Joe with horses, and another element of his character fell into place. He was infinitely patient with them and rode as if he'd been born in the saddle, which he almost had.

She stood at the kitchen window watching him and Wolf and Maris in the corral with a tall black mare who was currently Maris's favorite. Mary came to stand beside her, knowing instinctively who Caroline was watching. "He's wonderful, isn't he?" Mary sighed. "I loved him the first moment I saw him, when he was sixteen. There aren't many men in this world like Joe. He was a man even then, and I mean it in the purest sense of the word. Of course, I'm prejudiced, but you are, too, aren't you?"

"Just looking at him gives me shivers," Caroline

admitted dreamily, then caught herself with a laugh. "But don't tell him that. Sometimes he can be very much the colonel. I try to keep him from being *too* commanding."

"Oh, he knows. The thing is, you give him shivers, too. Keeps things nice and balanced. I should know. His father has been giving me shivers for almost twenty years now. Do you suppose it's inherited?"

"It probably is. Look at Joshua and Zane."

"I know," Mary sighed. "I feel so sorry for all the girls in school. And all those poor girls in college with Michael haven't had time to get used to him, the way the girls he grew up with did. Not that it did them much good."

"Maris will balance it out with the boys."

Through the window she watched Joe lightly vault the fence and start toward the house. Wolf tousled Maris's hair and followed his son, while Maris remained with the mare.

Both men entered the house, their tall, broad-shouldered forms suddenly making the kitchen seem too small. They brought with them the earthy scents of the outdoors, horse and hay and clear fresh air mingled with their own male sweat.

"You two look guilty," Joe observed. "What have you been talking about?"

"Genetics," Caroline replied.

His brows lifted in that characteristic way. She shrugged. "Well, I can't help it. I'm probably going to be very interested in genetics for the next eight and

a half months. Do you want to lay odds on whether
it's a boy or a girl?''

"Oh, it's a boy," Mary said, her entire face lit with
delight. Joe had gone weak at the knees, and Wolf
was laughing at his son as he helped him to a chair.
"Joe's a Mackenzie, hardly a female sperm to be
found. Mackenzies have to work really hard to have
daughters. That's why they appreciate them so
much."

Epilogue

Mary was absolutely right. John Mackenzie, eight pounds and two ounces, made his debut right on time. His heritage was immediately apparent in the thick black hair, blue eyes and straight black brows of his father. After his birth Caroline slept, and Joe dozed in the chair by her bed, his son lying on his chest and making squeaky little grunting noises. Caroline awakened, her drowsy eyes moving around the room until her gaze lit on the pair by her side. She reached out, first touching her husband's hand and then the tiny hand that lay curled on his chest.

Joe's eyes opened. "Hi," he said softly.

"Hi, yourself." He looked wonderful, she thought. Kind of grubby and rumpled. He was still in uniform, having been summoned straight from the base. The nurses were probably all swooning at his feet. She grabbed his tie and pulled him closer. "Give me a kiss."

He did, his mouth lingering hungrily over hers. "In a few weeks I'll give you a lot more."

"Umm. I can't wait." He made a few lascivious promises to her that made her heart pound, and she laughed as she took the sleeping baby from him. "You shouldn't talk like that in front of him. He's too young."

"It's nothing new to him, sweetheart. He's been well acquainted with me from the very beginning."

She looked down at the tiny, serious face, and this time her heart swelled, blooming until it nearly filled her chest. It was incredible. This magnificent little creature was incredible. Her parents, having decided to stay in Greece for a couple of years, were on their way, but the flight was so long and the connections so horrible that it would be another ten hours before they arrived. John's other grandparents, however, had managed to get there before he was born, and he'd already been in their arms.

"Where are Wolf and Mary?" she asked sleepily.

"In the cafeteria. They said they were hungry, but I think they wanted to give us some time alone."

"I wish they'd brought Maris and the boys."

"They were taking final exams at school. They'll see him soon enough."

She looked back down at the baby, tracing the downy cheek with her fingertip. To her surprise, he abruptly turned his head toward the touch, the tiny mouth opening as he sought it.

Joe laughed and said, ''That isn't it, son. You need to fine-tune your targeting a little.''

The baby had begun fretting. Caroline opened her gown and gently guided the avid little mouth to her breast. He clamped down on it with a grunting noise.

''He's a typical Mackenzie,'' she murmured. ''Which means he isn't typical at all.''

She looked up and met Joe's eyes, brilliant and filled with more desire and love than she'd ever thought to see in her life. No, there was nothing typical about this man. He was on a fast track to the stars, and he was carrying her with him.

* * * * *

MACKENZIE'S PLEASURE

Mackenzie's Pleasure is dedicated to all the wonderful fans who fell as much in love with the Mackenzies as I did.

Prologue

Wolf Mackenzie slipped out of bed and restlessly paced over to the window, where he stood looking out at the stark, moonlit expanse of his land. A quick glance over his bare shoulder reassured him that Mary slept on undisturbed, though he knew it wouldn't be long before she sensed his absence and stirred, reaching out for him. When her hand didn't encounter his warmth, she would wake, sitting up in bed and drowsily pushing her silky hair out of her face. When she saw him by the window she would slide out of bed and come to him, nestling against his naked body, sleepily resting her head on his chest.

A slight smile touched his hard mouth. Like as not, if he stayed out of bed long enough for her to awaken, when they returned to the bed it wouldn't be to sleep but to make love. As he remembered, Maris had been conceived on just such an occasion, when he had been restless because Joe's fighter wing had just been deployed overseas

during some flare-up. It had been Joe's first action, and
Wolf had been as tense as he'd been during his own days
in Vietnam.

Luckily, he and Mary were past the days when spon-
taneous passion could result in a new baby. Nowadays
they had grandkids, not kids of their own. Ten at the last
count, as a matter of fact.

But he was restless tonight, and he knew why.

The wolf always slept better when all of his cubs were
accounted for.

Never mind that the cubs were adults, some of them
with children of their own. Never mind that they were,
one and all, supremely capable of taking care of themselves. They were *his*, and he was there if they needed
him. He also liked to know, within reason, where they
were bedding down for the night. It wasn't necessary for
him to be able to pinpoint their location—some things a
parent was better off not knowing—but if he knew what
state they were in, that was usually enough. Hell, sometimes he would have been glad just to know which *country* they were roaming.

His concern wasn't for Joe, this time. He knew where
Joe was—the Pentagon. Joe wore four stars now, and sat
on the Joint Chiefs of Staff.

Joe would still rather strap on a metal bird and fly at
twice the speed of sound, but those days were behind
him. If he had to fly a desk, then he would damn sure
fly it the best it could be flown. Besides, as he'd once
said, being married to Caroline was more challenging
than being in a dogfight and outnumbered four to one.

Wolf grinned when he thought of his daughter-in-law.
Genius IQ, doctorates in both physics and computer sciences, a bit arrogant, a bit quirky. She'd gotten her pilot's
license just after the birth of their first son, on the basis

that the wife of a fighter pilot should know something about flying. She had received her certification on small jet aircraft around the time the third son had made his appearance. After the birth of her fifth son, she had grumpily told Joe that she was calling it quits with that one, because she'd given him five chances and obviously he wasn't up to the job of fathering a daughter.

It had once been gently suggested to Joe that Caroline should quit her job. The company that employed her was heavily engaged in government contract work, and the appearance of any favoritism could hurt his career. Joe had turned his cool, blue laser gaze on his superiors and said, "Gentlemen, if I have to choose between my wife and my career, I'll give you my resignation immediately." That was *not* the answer that had been expected, and nothing else was said about Caroline's work in research and development.

Wolf wasn't worried about Michael, either. Mike was the most settled of all his children, though just as focused. He had decided at an early age that he wanted to be a rancher, and that's exactly what he was. He owned a sizable spread down toward Laramie, and he and his wife were happily raising cattle and two sons.

The only uproar Mike had ever caused was when he decided to marry Shea Colvin. Wolf and Mary had given him their blessing, but the problem was that Shea's mother was Pam Hearst Colvin, one of Joe's old girl-friends—and Pam's father, Ralph Hearst, was as adamantly opposed to his beloved granddaughter marrying Michael Mackenzie as he had been to his daughter dating Joe Mackenzie.

Michael, with his typical tunnel vision, had ignored the whole tempest. His only concern was marrying Shea, and to hell with the storm erupting in the Hearst family.

Quiet, gentle Shea had been torn, but she wanted Michael and refused to call off the wedding as her grandfather demanded. Pam herself had finally put an end to it, standing nose to nose with her father in the middle of his store.

"Shea *will* marry Michael," she'd stormed, when Ralph had threatened to take Shea out of his will if she married one of those damn breeds. "You didn't want me to date Joe, when he was one of the most decent men I've ever met. Now Shea wants Michael, and she's going to have him. Change your will, if you like. Hug your hate real close, because you won't be hugging your grand-daughter—or your great-grandchildren. Think about that!"

So Michael had married Shea, and despite his growling and grumping, old Hearst was nuts about his two great-grandsons. Shea's second pregnancy had been difficult, and both she and the baby had nearly died. The doctor had advised them not to have any more children, but they had already decided to have only two, anyway. The two boys were growing up immersed in cattle ranching and horses. Wolf was amused that Ralph Hearst's great-grandchildren bore the Mackenzie name. Who in hell ever would have thought?

Josh, his third son, lived in Seattle with his wife, Loren, and their three sons. Josh was as jet-mad as Joe, but he had opted for the Navy rather than the Air Force, perhaps because he wanted to succeed on his own, not because his older brother was a general.

Josh was cheerful and openhearted, the most outgoing of the bunch, but he, too, had that streak of iron determination. He'd barely survived the crash that left him with a stiffened right knee and ended his naval career, but in typical Josh fashion, he had put that behind him and concentrated on what was before him. At the time, that had been his doctor—Dr. Loren Page. Never one to dither around, Josh had taken one look at tall, lovely Loren and begun his courtship from his hospital bed. He'd still been on crutches when they married. Now, three sons later, he worked for an aeronautics firm, developing new fighter aircraft, and Loren practiced her orthopedic specialty at a Seattle hospital.

Wolf knew where Maris was, too. His only daughter was currently in Montana, working as a trainer for a horse rancher. She was considering taking a job in Kentucky, working with Thoroughbreds. From the time she'd been old enough to sit unaided on a horse, her ambitions had all centered around the big, elegant animals. She had his touch with horses, able to gentle even the most contrary or vicious beast. Privately Wolf thought that she probably surpassed his skill. What she could do with a horse was pure magic.

Wolf's hard mouth softened as he thought of Maris. She had wrapped his heart around her tiny finger the moment she had been placed in his arms, when she was mere minutes old, and had looked up at him with sleepy dark eyes. Of all his children, she was the only one who had his dark eyes. His sons all looked like him, except for their blue eyes, but Maris, who resembled Mary in every other way, had her father's eyes. His daughter had light, silvery brown hair, skin so fine it was almost translucent, and her mother's determination. She was all of five foot three and weighed about a hundred pounds, but Maris never paid any attention to her slightness; when she made up her mind to do something, she persisted with bulldog stubbornness until she succeeded. She could more than hold her own with her older, much larger and domineering brothers.

Her chosen career hadn't been easy for her. People

tended to think two things. One was that she was merely
trading on the Mackenzie name, and the other was that
she was too delicate for the job. They soon found out
how wrong they were on both counts, but it was a battle
Maris had fought over and over. She kept at it, though,
slowly winning respect for her individual talents.

The mental rundown of his kids next brought him to
Chance. Hell, he even knew where Chance was, and that
was saying something. Chance roamed the world, though
he always came back to Wyoming, to the mountain that
was his only home. He had happened to call earlier that
day, from Belize. He'd told Mary that he was going to
rest for a few days before moving on. When Wolf had
taken his turn on the phone, he had moved out of Mary's
hearing and quietly asked Chance how bad he was hurt.

"Not too bad," Chance had laconically replied. "A
few stitches and a couple of cracked ribs. This last job
went a little sour on me."

Wolf didn't ask what the last job had entailed. His
soldier-of-fortune son occasionally did some delicate
work for the government, so Chance seldom volunteered
details. The two men had an unspoken agreement to keep
Mary in the dark about the danger Chance faced on a
regular basis. Not only did they not want her to worry,
but if she knew he was wounded, she was likely to hop
on a plane and fetch him home.

When Wolf hung up the phone and turned, it was to
find Mary's slate blue gaze pinned on him. "How bad is
he hurt?" she demanded fiercely, hands planted on her
hips.

Wolf knew better than to try lying to her. Instead he
crossed the room to her and pulled her into his arms,
stroking her silky hair and cradling her slight body
against the solid muscularity of his. Sometimes the force

of his love for this woman almost drove him to his knees. He couldn't protect her from worry, though, so he gave her the respect of honesty. "Not too bad, to use his own words."

Her response was instant. "I want him here."

"I know, sweetheart. But he's okay. He doesn't lie to us. Besides, you know Chance."

She nodded, sighing, and turned her lips against his chest. Chance was like a sleek panther, wild and intolerant of fetters. They had brought him into their home and made him one of the family, binding him to them with love when no other restraint would have held him. And like a wild creature that had been only half-tamed, he accepted the boundaries of civilization, but lightly. He roamed far and wide, and yet he always came back to them.

From the first, though, he had been helpless against Mary. She had instantly surrounded him with so much love and care that he hadn't been able to resist her, even though his light hazel eyes had reflected his consternation, even embarrassment, at her attention. If Mary went down to fetch Chance, he would come home without protest, but he would walk into the house wearing a helpless, slightly panicked "Oh, God, get me out of this" expression. And then he would meekly let her tend his wounds, pamper him and generally smother him with motherly concern.

Watching Mary fuss over Chance was one of Wolf's greatest amusements. She fussed over all of her kids, but the others had grown up with it and took it as a matter of course. Chance, though…he had been fourteen and half wild when Mary had found him. If he'd ever had a home, he didn't remember it. If he had a name, he didn't know it. He'd evaded well-meaning social authorities by staying on the move, stealing whatever he needed, food, clothes, money. He was highly intelligent and had taught himself to read from newspapers and magazines that had been thrown away. Libraries had become a favorite place for him to hang out, maybe even spend the night if he could manage it, but never two nights in a row. From what he read and what little television he saw, he understood the concept of a family, but that was all it was to him—a concept. He trusted no one but himself.

He might have grown to adulthood that way if he hadn't contracted a monster case of influenza. While driving home from work, Mary had found him lying on the side of a road, incoherent and burning up with fever. Though he was half a foot taller than she and some fifty pounds heavier, somehow she had wrestled and bullied the boy into her truck and taken him to the local clinic, where Doc Nowacki discovered that the flu had progressed into pneumonia and quickly transferred Chance to the nearest hospital, eighty miles away.

Mary had driven home and insisted that Wolf take her to the hospital—immediately.

Chance was in intensive care when they arrived. At first the nursing staff hadn't wanted to let them see him, since they weren't family and in fact didn't know anything about him. Child services had been notified, and someone was on the way to take care of the paperwork. They had been reasonable, even kind, but they hadn't reckoned with Mary. She was relentless. She wanted to see the boy, and a bulldozer couldn't have budged her until she saw him. Eventually the nurses, overworked and outclassed by a will far stronger than their own, gave in and let Wolf and Mary into the small cubicle.

As soon as he saw the boy, Wolf knew why Mary was so taken with him. It wasn't just that he was deathly ill;

he was obviously part American Indian. He would have reminded Mary so forcibly of her own children that she could no more have forgotten about him than she could one of them.

Wolf's expert eye swept over the boy as he lay there so still and silent, his eyes closed, his breathing labored. The hectic color of fever stained his high cheekbones. Four different bags dripped an IV solution into his muscular right arm, which was taped to the bed. Another bag hung at the side of the bed, measuring the output of his kidneys.

Not a half-breed, Wolf had thought. A quarter, maybe. No more than that. But still, there was no doubting his heritage. His fingernails were light against the tanned skin of his fingers, where an Anglo's nails would have been pinker. His thick, dark brown hair, so long it brushed his shoulders, was straight. There were those high cheekbones, the clear-cut lips, the high-bridged nose. He was the most handsome boy Wolf had ever seen.

Mary went up to the bed, all her attention focused on the boy who lay so ill and helpless on the snowy sheets. She laid her cool hand lightly against his forehead, then stroked it over his hair. "You'll be all right," she murmured. "I'll make sure you are."

He had lifted his heavy lids, struggling with the effort. For the first time Wolf saw the light hazel eyes, almost golden, and circled with a brown rim so dark it was almost black. Confused, the boy had focused first on Mary; then his gaze had wandered to Wolf, and belated alarm flared in his eyes. He tried to heave himself up, but he was too weak even to tug his taped arm free.

Wolf moved to the boy's other side. "Don't be afraid," he said quietly. "You have pneumonia, and you're in a hospital." Then, guessing what lay at the bottom of the boy's panic, he added, "We won't let them take you."

Those light eyes had rested on his face, and perhaps Wolf's appearance had calmed him. Like a wild animal on guard, he slowly relaxed and drifted back to sleep.

Over the next week, the boy's condition improved, and Mary swung into action. She was determined that the boy, who still had not given them a name, not be taken into state custody for even one day. She pulled strings, harangued people, even called on Joe to use his influence, and her tenacity worked. When the boy was released from the hospital, he went home with Wolf and Mary.

He had gradually become accustomed to them, though by no stretch of the imagination had he been friendly, or even trustful. He would answer their questions, in one word if possible, but he never actually *talked* with them. Mary hadn't been discouraged. From the first, she simply treated the boy as if he was hers—and soon he was.

The boy who had always been alone was suddenly plunged into the middle of a large, volatile family. For the first time he had a roof over his head every night, a room all to himself, ample food in his belly. He had clothing hanging in the closet and new boots on his feet. He was still too weak to share in the chores everyone did, but Mary immediately began tutoring him to bring him up to Zane's level academically, since the two boys were the same age, as near as they could tell. Chance took to the books like a starving pup to its mother's teat, but in every other way he determinedly remained at arm's length. Those shrewd, guarded eyes took note of every nuance of their family relationships, weighing what he saw now against what he had known before.

Finally he unbent enough to tell them that he was called Sooner. He didn't have a real name.

Maris had looked at him blankly. "Sooner?"

His mouth had twisted, and he'd looked far too old for his fourteen years. "Yeah, like a mongrel dog."

"No," Wolf had said, because the name was a clue. "You know you're part Indian. More than likely you were called Sooner because you were originally from Oklahoma—and that means you're probably Cherokee."

The boy merely looked at him, his expression guarded, but still something about him had lightened at the possibility that he hadn't been likened to a dog of unknown heritage.

His relationships with everyone in the family were complicated. With Mary, he wanted to hold himself away, but he simply couldn't. She mothered him the way she did the rest of her brood, and it terrified him even though he delighted in it, soaking up her loving concern. He was wary of Wolf, as if he expected the big man to turn on him with fists and boots. Wise in the ways of wild things, Wolf gradually gentled the boy the same way he did horses, letting him get accustomed, letting him realize he had nothing to fear, then offering respect and friendship and, finally, love.

Michael had already been away at college, but when he did come home he simply made room in his family circle for the newcomer. Sooner was relaxed with Mike from the start, sensing that quiet acceptance.

He got along with Josh, too, but Josh was so cheerful it was impossible not to get along with him. Josh took it on himself to be the one who taught Sooner how to handle the multitude of chores on a horse ranch. Josh was the one who taught him how to ride, though Josh was unarguably the worst horseman in the family. That wasn't to say he wasn't good, but the others were better, especially Maris. Josh didn't care, because his heart was wrapped up in planes just the way Joe's had been, so perhaps he had been more patient with Sooner's mistakes than anyone else would have been.

Maris was like Mary. She had taken one look at the boy and immediately taken him under her fiercely protective wing, never mind that Sooner was easily twice her size. At twelve, Maris had been not quite five feet tall and weighed all of seventy-four pounds. It didn't matter to her; Sooner became hers the same way her older brothers were hers. She chattered to him, teased him, played jokes on him—in short, drove him crazy, the way little sisters were supposed to do. Sooner hadn't had any idea how to handle the way she treated him, any more than he had with Mary. Sometimes he had watched Maris as if she was a ticking time bomb, but it was Maris who won his first smile with her teasing. It was Maris who actually got him to enter the family conversations: slowly, at first, as he learned how families worked, how the give-and-take of talking melded them together, then with more ease. Maris could still tease him into a rage, or coax a laugh out of him, faster than anyone else. For a while Wolf had wondered if the two might become romantically interested in each other as they grew older, but it hadn't happened. It was a testament to how fully Sooner had become a part of their family; to both of them, they were simply brother and sister.

Things with Zane had been complicated, though.

Zane was, in his own way, as guarded as Sooner. Wolf knew warriors, having been one himself, and what he saw in his youngest son was almost frightening. Zane was quiet, intense, watchful. He moved like a cat, gracefully, soundlessly. Wolf had trained all his children, including

Maris, in self-defense, but with Zane it was something more. The boy took to it with the ease of someone putting on a well-worn shoe; it was as if it had been made for him. When it came to marksmanship, he had the eye of a sniper, and the deadly patience.

Zane had the instinct of a warrior: to protect. He was immediately on guard against this intruder into the sanctity of his family's home turf.

He hadn't been nasty to Sooner. He hadn't made fun of him or been overtly unfriendly, which wasn't in his nature. Rather, he had held himself away from the newcomer, not rejecting, but certainly not welcoming, either. But because they were the same age, Zane's acceptance was the most crucial, and Sooner had reacted to Zane's coolness by adopting the same tactics. They had ignored each other.

While the kids were working out their relationships, Wolf and Mary had been pushing hard to legally adopt Sooner. They had asked him if that was what he wanted and, typically, he had responded with a shrug and an expressionless, "Sure." Taking that for the impassioned plea it was, Mary redoubled her efforts to get the adoption pushed through.

As things worked out, they got the word that the adoption could go forward on the same day Zane and Sooner settled things between them.

The dust was what had caught Wolf's attention.

At first he hadn't thought anything of it, because when he glanced over he saw Maris sitting on the top rail of the fence, calmly watching the commotion. Figuring one of the horses was rolling in the dirt, Wolf went back to work. Two seconds later, however, his sharp ears caught the sound of grunts and what sounded suspiciously like blows.

He walked across the yard to the other corral. Zane and Sooner had gotten into the corner, where they couldn't be seen from the house, and were ferociously battering each other. Wolf saw at once that both boys, despite the force of their blows, were restraining themselves to the more conventional fisticuffs rather than the faster, nastier ways he'd also taught them. He leaned his arms on the top rail beside Maris. "What's this about?"

"They're fighting it out," she said matter-of-factly, without taking her eyes from the action.

Josh soon joined them at the fence, and they watched the battle. Zane and Sooner were both tall, muscular boys, very strong for their ages. They stood toe to toe, taking turns driving their fists into each other's faces. When one of them got knocked down, he got to his feet and waded back into the fray. They were almost eerily silent, except for the involuntary grunts and the sounds of hard fists hitting flesh.

Mary saw them standing at the fence and came out to investigate. She stood beside Wolf and slipped her small hand into his. He felt her flinch every time a blow landed, but when he looked at her, he saw that she was wearing her prim schoolteacher's expression, and he knew that Mary Elizabeth Mackenzie was about to call the class to order.

She gave it five minutes. Evidently deciding this could go on for hours, and that both boys were too stubborn to give in, she settled the matter herself. In her crisp, clear teaching voice she called out, "All right, boys, let's get this wrapped up. Supper will be on the table in ten minutes." Then she calmly walked back to the house, fully confident that she had brought detente to the corral.

She had, too. She had reduced the fight to the level of

a chore or a project, given them a time limit and a reason for ending it.

Both boys' eyes had flickered to that slight retreating figure with the ramrod spine. Then Zane had turned to Sooner, the coolness of his blue gaze somewhat marred by the swelling of his eyes. "One more," he said grimly, and slammed his fist into Sooner's face.

Sooner picked himself up off the dirt, squared up again and returned the favor.

Zane got up, slapped the dirt from his clothes and held out his hand. Sooner gripped it, though they had both winced at the pain in their knuckles. They shook hands, eyed each other as equals, then returned to the house to clean up. After all, supper was almost on the table.

At supper, Mary told Sooner that the adoption had been given the green light. His pale hazel eyes had glittered in his battered face, but he hadn't said anything.

"You're a Mackenzie now," Maris had pronounced with great satisfaction. "You'll have to have a real name, so choose one."

It hadn't occurred to her that choosing a name might require some thought, but as it happened, Sooner had looked around the table at the family that pure blind luck had sent him, and a wry little smile twisted up one side of his bruised, swollen mouth. "Chance," he said, and the unknown, unnamed boy became Chance Mackenzie.

Zane and Chance hadn't become immediate best friends after the fight. What they had found, instead, was mutual respect, but friendship grew out of it. Over the years, they became so close that they could well have been born twins. There were other fights between them, but it was well known around Ruth, Wyoming, that if anyone decided to take on either of the boys, he would find himself facing both of them. They could batter each other into the ground, but by God, no one else was going to.

They had entered the Navy together, Zane becoming a SEAL, while Chance had gone into Naval Intelligence. Chance had since left the Navy, though, and gone out on his own, while Zane was a SEAL team leader.

And that brought Wolf to the reason for his restlessness.

Zane.

There had been a lot of times in Zane's career when he had been out of touch, when they hadn't known where he was or what he was doing. Wolf hadn't slept well then, either. He knew too much about the SEALs, having seen them in action in Vietnam during his tours of duty. They were the most highly trained and skilled of the special forces, their stamina and teamwork proven by grueling tests that broke lesser men. Zane was particularly well-suited for the work, but in the final analysis, the SEALs were still human. They could be killed. And because of the nature of their work, they were often in dangerous situations.

The SEAL training had merely accentuated the already existing facets of Zane's nature. He had been honed to a perfect fighting machine, a warrior who was in top condition, but who used his brain more than his brawn. He was even more lethal and intense now, but he had learned to temper that deadliness with an easier manner, so that most people were unaware they were dealing with a man who could kill them in a dozen different ways with his bare hands. With that kind of knowledge and skill at his disposal, Zane had learned a calm control that kept him in command of himself. Of all Wolf's offspring, Zane was the most capable of taking care of himself, but he was also the one in the most danger.

Where in hell *was* he?

There was a whisper of movement from the bed, and Wolf looked around as Mary slipped from between the sheets and joined him at the window, looping her arms around his hard, trim waist and nestling her head on his bare chest.

"Zane?" she asked quietly, in the darkness.

"Yeah." No more explanation was needed.

"He's all right," she said with a mother's confidence. "I'd know if he wasn't."

Wolf tipped her head up and kissed her, lightly at first, then with growing intensity. He turned her slight body more fully into his embrace and felt her quiver as she pressed to him, pushing her hips against his, cradling the rise of his male flesh against her softness. There had been passion between them from their first meeting, all those years ago, and time hadn't taken it from them.

He lifted her in his arms and carried her back to bed, losing himself in the welcome and warmth of her soft body. Afterward, though, lying in the drowsy aftermath, he turned his face toward the window. Before sleep claimed him, the thought came again. Where was Zane?

Chapter 1

Zane Mackenzie wasn't happy.

No one aboard the aircraft carrier USS *Montgomery* was happy; well, maybe the cooks were, but even that was iffy, because the men they were serving were sullen and defensive. The seamen weren't happy, the radar men weren't happy, the gunners weren't happy, the Marines weren't happy, the wing commander wasn't happy, the pilots weren't happy, the air boss wasn't happy, the executive officer wasn't happy, and Captain Udaka sure as hell wasn't happy.

The combined unhappiness of the five thousand sailors on board the carrier didn't begin to approach Lieutenant-Commander Mackenzie's level of unhappiness.

The captain outranked him. The executive officer outranked him. Lieutenant-Commander Mackenzie addressed them with all the respect due their rank, but both men were uncomfortably aware that their asses were in a sling and their careers on the line. Actually, their careers were probably in the toilet. There wouldn't be any court-martials, but neither would be there any more promotions, and they would be given the unpopular commands from now until they either retired or resigned, their choice depending on how clearly they could read the writing on the wall.

Captain Udaka's broad, pleasant face was one that wore responsibility easily, but now his expression was set in lines of unhappy acceptance as he met the icy gaze of the lieutenant-commander. SEALs in general made the captain nervous; he didn't quite trust them or the way they operated outside normal regulations. This one in particular made him seriously want to be somewhere—anywhere—else.

He had met Mackenzie before, when both he and Boyd, the XO, had been briefed on the security exercise. The SEAL team under Mackenzie's command would try to breach the carrier's security, probing for weaknesses that could be exploited by any of the myriad terrorist groups so common these days. It was a version of the exercises once conducted by the SEAL Team Six Red Cell, which had been so notorious and so far outside the regulations that it had been disbanded after seven years of operation. The concept, however, had lived on, in a more controlled manner. SEAL Team Six was a covert, counterterrorism unit, and one of the best ways to counter terrorism was to prevent it from happening in the first place, rather than reacting to it after people were dead. To this end, the security of naval installations and carrier battle groups was tested by the SEALs, who then recommended changes to correct the weaknesses they had discovered. There were always weaknesses, soft spots— the SEALs had never yet been completely thwarted, even though the base commanders and ships' captains were always notified in advance.

At the briefing, Mackenzie had been remote but pleasant. Controlled. Most SEALs had a wild, hard edge to them, but Mackenzie had seemed more regular Navy, recruiting-poster perfect in his crisp whites and with his coolly courteous manner. Captain Udaka had felt comfortable with him, certain that Lieutenant-Commander Mackenzie was the administrational type rather than a true part of those wild-ass SEALs.

He'd been wrong.

The courtesy remained, and the control. The white uniform looked as perfect as it had before. But there was nothing at all pleasant in the deep voice, or in the cold fury that lit the pale blue gray eyes so they glittered like moonlight on a knife blade. The aura of danger surrounding him was so strong it was almost palpable, and Captain Udaka knew that he had been drastically wrong in his assessment of Mackenzie. This was no desk jockey; this was a man around whom others should walk very lightly indeed. The captain felt as if his skin was being flayed from his body, strip by strip, by that icy gaze. He had also never felt closer to death than he had the moment Mackenzie had entered his quarters after learning what had happened.

"Captain, you were briefed on the exercise," Zane said coldly. "Everyone on this ship was advised, as well as notified that my men wouldn't be carrying weapons of any sort. Explain, then, *why in hell two of my men were shot!*"

The XO, Mr. Boyd, looked at his hands. Captain Udaka's collar felt too tight, except that it was already unbuttoned, and the only thing choking him was the look in Mackenzie's eyes.

"There's no excuse," he said rawly. "Maybe the guards were startled and fired without thinking. Maybe it was a stupid, macho turf thing, wanting to show the big bad SEALs that they couldn't penetrate our security, after all. It doesn't matter. There's no excuse." Everything that happened on board his ship was, ultimately, his responsibility. The trigger-happy guards would pay for their mistake—and so would he.

"My men had *already* penetrated your security," Zane said softly, his tone making the hairs stand up on the back of the captain's neck.

"I'm aware of that." The breach of his ship's security was salt in the captain's wounds, but nothing at all compared to the enormous mistake that had been made when men under his command had opened fire on the unarmed SEALs. His men, his responsibility. Nor did it help his feelings that, when two of their team had gone down, the remainder of the SEAL team, *unarmed,* had swiftly taken control and secured the area. Translated, that meant the guards who had done the shooting had been roughly handled and were now in sick bay with the two men they had shot. In reality, the phrase "roughly handled" was a euphemism for the fact that the SEALS had beaten the hell out of his men.

The most seriously wounded SEAL was Lieutenant Higgins, who had taken a bullet in the chest and would be evacuated by air to Germany as soon as he was stabilized. The other SEAL, Warrant Officer Odessa, had been shot in the thigh; the bullet had broken his femur. He, too, would be taken to Germany, but his condition was stable, even if his temper was not. The ship's doctor had been forced to sedate him to keep him from wreaking vengeance on the battered guards, two of whom were still unconscious.

The five remaining members of the SEAL team were
in Mission Planning, prowling around like angry tigers
looking for someone to maul just to make themselves feel
better. They were restricted to the area by Mackenzie's
order, and the ship's crew was giving them a wide berth.
Captain Udaka wished he could do the same with Mackenzie. He had the impression of cold savagery lurking
just beneath the surface of the man's control. There
would be hell to pay for this night's fiasco.

The phone on his desk emitted a harsh *brr*. Though he
was relieved by the interruption, Captain Udaka snatched
up the receiver and barked, "I gave orders I wasn't to
be—" He stopped, listening, and his expression changed.
His gaze shifted to Mackenzie. "We'll be right there,"
he said, and hung up.

"There's a scrambled transmission coming in for
you," he said to Mackenzie, rising to his feet. "Urgent."
Whatever message the transmission contained, Captain
Udaka looked on it as a much-welcomed reprieve.

Zane listened intently to the secure satellite transmission, his mind racing as he began planning the logistics
of the mission. "My team is two men short, sir," he said.
"Higgins and Odessa were injured in the security exercise." He didn't say *how* they'd been injured; that would
be handled through other channels.

"Damn it," Admiral Lindley muttered. He was in an
office in the U.S. Embassy in Athens. He looked up at
the others in the office: Ambassador Lovejoy, tall and
spare, with the smoothness bequeathed by a lifetime of
privilege and wealth, though now there was a stark, panicked expression in his hazel eyes; the CIA station chief,
Art Sandefer, a nondescript man with short gray hair and
tired, intelligent eyes; and, finally, Mack Prewett, second

only to Sandefer in the local CIA hierarchy. Mack was
known in some circles as Mack the Knife; Admiral Lindley knew Mack was generally considered a man who got
things done, a man whom it was dangerous to cross. For
all his decisiveness, though, he wasn't a cowboy who was
likely to endanger people by going off half-cocked. He
was as thorough as he was decisive, and it was through
his contacts that they had obtained such good, prompt
information in this case.

The admiral had put Zane on the speakerphone, so the
other three in the room had heard the bad news about the
SEAL team on which they had all been pinning their
hopes. Ambassador Lovejoy looked even more haggard.

"We'll have to use another team," Art Sandefer said.

"That'll take too much time!" the ambassador said
with stifled violence. "My God, already she could be—"
He stopped, anguish twisting his face. He wasn't able to
complete the sentence.

"I'll take the team in," Zane said. His amplified voice
was clear in the soundproofed room. "We're the closest,
and we can be ready to go in an hour."

"You?" the admiral asked, startled. "Zane, you
haven't seen live action since—"

"My last promotion," Zane finished dryly. He hadn't
liked trading action for administration, and he was seriously considering resigning his commission. He was
thirty-one, and it was beginning to look as if his success
in his chosen field was going to prevent him from prac-
ticing it; the higher-ranking the officer, the less likely that
officer was to be in the thick of the action. He'd been
thinking about something in law enforcement, or maybe
even throwing in with Chance. There was nonstop action
there, for sure.

For now, though, a mission had been dumped in his lap, and he was going to take it.

"I train with my men, Admiral," he said. "I'm not rusty, or out of shape."

"I didn't think you were," Admiral Lindley replied, and sighed. He met the ambassador's anguished gaze, read the silent plea for help. "Can six men handle the mission?" he asked Zane.

"Sir, I wouldn't risk my men if I didn't think we could do the job."

This time the admiral looked at both Art Sandefer and Mack Prewett. Art's expression was noncommittal, the Company man refusing to stick his neck out, but Mack gave the admiral a tiny nod. Admiral Lindley swiftly weighed all the factors. Granted, the SEAL team would be two members short, and the leader would be an officer who hadn't been on an active mission in over a year, but that officer happened to be Zane Mackenzie. All things considered, the admiral couldn't think of any other man he would rather have on this mission. He'd known Zane for several years now, and there was no better warrior, no one he trusted more. If Zane said he was ready, then he was ready. "All right. Go in and get her out."

As the admiral hung up, Ambassador Lindley blurted, "Shouldn't you send in someone else? My daughter's life is at stake! This man hasn't been in the field, he's out of shape, out of practice—"

"Waiting until we could get another team into position would drastically lower our chances of finding her," the admiral pointed out as kindly as possible. Ambassador Lindley wasn't one of his favorite people. For the most part, he was a horse's ass and a snob, but there was no doubt he doted on his daughter. "And as far as Zane

Mackenzie is concerned, there's no better man for the job."

"The admiral's right," Mack Prewett said quietly, with the authority that came so naturally to him. "Mackenzie is so good at what he does it's almost eerie. I would feel comfortable sending him in alone. If you want your daughter back, don't throw obstacles in his way."

Ambassador Lindley shoved his hand through his hair, an uncharacteristic gesture for so fastidious a man; it was a measure of his agitation. "If anything goes wrong…"

It wasn't clear whether he was about to voice a threat or was simply worrying aloud, but he couldn't complete the sentence. Mack Prewett gave a thin smile. "Something always goes wrong. If anyone can handle it, Mackenzie can."

After Zane terminated the secure transmission he made his way through the network of corridors to Mission Planning. Already he could feel the rush of adrenaline pumping through his muscles as he began preparing, mentally and physically, for the job before him. When he entered the room with its maps and charts and communication systems, and the comfortable chairs grouped around a large table, five hostile faces turned immediately toward him, and he felt the surge of renewed energy and anger from his men.

Only one of them, Santos, was seated at the table, but Santos was the team medic, and he was usually the calmest of the bunch. Ensign Peter "Rocky" Greenberg, second in command of the team and a controlled, detail-oriented kind of guy, leaned against the bulkhead with his arms crossed and murder in his narrowed brown eyes. Antonio Withrock, nicknamed Bunny because he never ran out of energy, was prowling the confines of the room

like a mean, hungry cat, his dark skin pulled tight across
his high cheekbones. Paul Drexler, the team sniper, sat
cross-legged on top of the table while he wiped an oiled
cloth lovingly over the disassembled parts of his beloved
Remington bolt-action 7.62 rifle. Zane didn't even lift his
eyebrows at the sight. His men were supposed to be unarmed, and they had been during the security exercise
that had gone so damn sour, but *keeping* Drexler unarmed
was another story.

"Planning on taking over the ship?" Zane inquired
mildly of the sniper.

His blue eyes cold, Drexler cocked his head as if considering the idea. "I might."

Winstead "Spooky" Jones had been sitting on the
deck, his back resting against the bulkhead, but at Zane's
entrance he rose effortlessly to his feet. He didn't say
anything, but his gaze fastened on Zane's face, and a
spark of interest replaced some of the anger in his eyes.

Spook never missed much, and the other team members had gotten in the habit of watching him, picking up
cues from his body language. No more than three seconds
passed before all five men were watching Zane with complete concentration.

Greenberg was the one who finally spoke. "How's
Bobcat doing, boss?"

They had read Spooky's tension, but misread the
cause, Zane realized. They thought Higgins had died
from his wounds. Drexler began assembling his rifle with
sharp, economical motions. "He's stabilized," Zane reassured them. He knew his men, knew how tight they
were. A SEAL team had to be tight. Their trust in each
other had to be absolute, and if something happened to
one of them, they all felt it. "They're transferring him
now. It's touchy, but I'll put my money on Bobcat.

Odie's gonna be okay, too.'' He hitched one hip on the edge of the table, his pale eyes glittering with the intensity that had caught Spooky's attention. ''Listen up, children. An ambassador's daughter was snatched a few hours ago, and we're going into Libya to get her.''

Six black-clad figures slipped silently along the narrow, deserted street in Benghazi, Libya. They communicated by hand signals, or by whispers into the Motorola headsets they all wore under their black knit balaclava hoods. Zane was in his battle mode; he was utterly calm as they worked their way toward the four-story stone building where Barrie Lovejoy was being held on the top floor, if their intelligence was good, and if she hadn't been moved within the past few hours.

Action always affected him this way, as if every cell in his body had settled into its true purpose of existence. He had missed this, missed it to the point that he knew he wouldn't be able to stay in the Navy without it. On a mission, all his senses became more acute, even as a deep center of calm radiated outward. The more intense the action, the calmer he became, as time stretched out into slow motion. At those times he could see and hear every detail, analyze and predict the outcome, then make his decision and act—all within a split second that felt like minutes. Adrenaline would flood his body—he would feel the blood racing through his veins—but his mind would remain detached and calm. He had been told that the look on his face during those times was frighteningly remote, jarring in its total lack of expression.

The team moved forward in well-orchestrated silence. They each knew what to do, and what the others would do. That was the purpose of the trust and teamwork that had been drilled into them through the twenty-six weeks of hell that was formally known as BUD/S training. The bond between them enabled them to do more together than could be accomplished if each worked on his own. Teamwork wasn't just a word to the SEALs, it was their center.

Spooky Jones was point man. Zane preferred using the wiry Southerner for that job because he had unfrayable nerves and could ghost around like a lynx. Bunny Withrock, who almost reverberated with nervous energy, was bringing up the rear. No one sneaked up on Bunny—except the Spook. Zane was right behind Jones, with Drexler, Greenberg and Santos ranging between him and Bunny. Greenberg was quiet, steady, totally dependable. Drexler was uncanny with that rifle, and Santos, besides being a damn good SEAL, also had the skill to patch them up and keep them going, if they were patchable. Overall, Zane had never worked with a better group of men.

Their presence in Benghazi was pure luck, and Zane knew it. Good luck for them and, he hoped, for Miss Lovejoy, but bad luck for the terrorists who had snatched her off the street in Athens fifteen hours ago. If the *Montgomery* hadn't been just south of Crete and in perfect position for launching a rescue, if the SEALs hadn't been on the carrier to practice special insertions as well as the security exercise, then there would have been a delay of precious hours, perhaps even as long as a day, while another team got supplied and into position. As it was, the special insertion into hostile territory they had just accomplished had been the real thing instead of just a practice.

Miss Lovejoy was not only the ambassador's daughter, she was an employee at the embassy, as well. The ambassador was apparently very strict and obsessive about his daughter, having lost his wife and son in a terrorist attack in Rome fifteen years before, when Miss Lovejoy had been a child of ten. After that, he had kept her secluded in private schools, and since she had finished college, she had been acting as his hostess as well as performing her "work" at the embassy. Zane suspected her job was more window dressing than anything else, something to keep her busy. She had never really worked a day in her life, never been out from under her father's protection—until today.

She and a friend had left the embassy to do some shopping. Three men had grabbed her, shoved her into a car and driven off. The friend had immediately reported the abduction. Despite efforts to secure the airport and ports—cynically, Zane suspected deliberate foot-dragging by the Greek authorities—a private plane had taken off from Athens and flown straight to Benghazi.

Thanks to the friend's prompt action, sources on the ground in Benghazi had been alerted. It had been verified that a young woman of Miss Lovejoy's description had been taken off the plane and hustled into the city, into the very building Zane and his team were about to enter.

It had to be her; there weren't that many red-haired Western women in Benghazi. In fact, he would bet there was only one—Barrie Lovejoy.

They were betting her life on it.

Chapter 2

Barrie lay in almost total darkness, heavy curtains at the single window blocking out most of whatever light would have entered. She could tell that it was night; the level of street noise outside had slowly diminished, until now there was mostly silence. The men who had kidnapped her had finally gone away, probably to sleep. They had no worries about her being able to escape; she was naked, and tied tightly to the cot on which she lay. Her wrists were bound together, her arms drawn over her head and tied to the frame of the cot. Her ankles were also tied together, then secured to the frame. She could barely move; every muscle in her body ached, but those in her shoulders burned with agony. She would have screamed, she would have begged for someone to come and release the ropes that held her arms over her head, but she knew that the only people who would come would be the very ones who had tied her in this position, and she would do anything, give anything, to keep from ever seeing them again./

She was cold. They hadn't even bothered to throw a blanket over her naked body, and long, convulsive shivers kept shaking her, though she couldn't tell if she was chilled from the night air or from shock. She didn't suppose it mattered. Cold was cold.

She tried to think, tried to ignore the pain, tried not to give in to shock and terror. She didn't know where she was, didn't know how she could escape, but if the slightest opportunity presented itself, she would have to be ready to take it. She wouldn't be able to escape tonight; her bonds were too tight, her movements too restricted. But tomorrow—oh, God, tomorrow.

Terror tightened her throat, almost choking off her breath. Tomorrow they would be back, and there would be another one with them, the one for whom they waited. A violent shiver racked her as she thought of their rough hands on her bare body, the pinches and slaps and crude probings, and her stomach heaved. She would have vomited, if there had been anything to vomit, but they hadn't bothered to feed her.

She couldn't go through that again.

Somehow, she had to get away.

Desperately she fought down her panic. Her thoughts darted around like crazed squirrels as she tried to plan, to think of something, anything, that she could do to protect herself. But what *could* she do, lying there like a turkey all trussed up for Thanksgiving dinner?

Humiliation burned through her. They hadn't raped her, but they had done other things to her, things to shame and terrorize her and break her spirit. Tomorrow, when the leader arrived, she was sure her reprieve would be over. The threat of rape, and then the act of it, would shatter her and leave her malleable in their hands, desperate to do anything to avoid being violated again. At least that was what they planned, she thought. But she would be damned if she would go along with their plan.

She had been in a fog of terror and shock since they had grabbed her and thrown her into a car, but as she lay there in the darkness, cold and miserable and achingly vulnerable in her nakedness, she felt as if the fog was lifting, or maybe it was being burned away. No one who knew Barrie would ever have described her as hot-tempered, but then, what she felt building in her now wasn't as volatile and fleeting as mere temper. It was rage, as pure and forceful as lava forcing its way upward from the bowels of the earth until it exploded outward and swept away everything in its path.

Nothing in her life had prepared her for these past hours. After her mother and brother had died, she had been pampered and protected as few children ever were. She had seen some—most, actually—of her schoolmates as they struggled with the misery of broken parental promises, of rare, stressful visits, of being ignored and shunted out of the way, but she hadn't been like them. Her father adored her, and she knew it. He was intensely interested in her safety, her friends, her schoolwork. If he said he would call, then the call came exactly when he'd said it would. Every week had brought some small gift in the mail, inexpensive but thoughtful. She'd understood why he worried so much about her safety, why he wanted her to attend the exclusive girls' school in Switzerland, with its cloistered security, rather than a public school, with its attendant hurly-burly.

She was all he had left.

He was all she had left, too. When she'd been a child, after the incident that had halved the family, she had clung fearfully to her father for months, dogging his footsteps when she could, weeping inconsolably when his work took him away from her. Eventually the dread that he, too, would disappear from her life had faded, but the pattern of overprotectiveness had been set.

She was twenty-five now, a grown woman, and though in the past few years his protectiveness had begun to chafe, she had enjoyed the even tenor of her life too much to really protest. She liked her job at the embassy, so much that she was considering a full-time career in the foreign service. She enjoyed being her father's hostess. She had the duties and protocol down cold, and there were more and more female ambassadors on the international scene. It was a moneyed and insular community, but by both temperament and pedigree she was suited to the task. She was calm, even serene, and blessed with a considerate and tactful nature.

But now, lying naked and helpless on a cot, with bruises mottling her pale skin, the rage that consumed her was so deep and primal she felt as if it had altered something basic inside her, a sea change of her very nature. She would *not* endure what they—nameless, malevolent "they"—had planned for her. If they killed her, so be it. She was prepared for death; no matter what, she would not submit.

The heavy curtains fluttered.

The movement caught her eye, and she glanced at the window, but the action was automatic, without curiosity. She was already so cold that even a wind strong enough to move those heavy curtains couldn't chill her more.

The wind was black, and had a shape.

Her breath stopped in her chest.

Mutely she watched the big black shape, as silent as a shadow, slip through the window. It couldn't be human;

people made *some* sound when they moved. Surely, in the total silence of the room, she would have been able to hear the whisper of the curtains as the fabric moved, or the faint, rhythmic sigh of breathing. A shoe scraping on the floor, the rustle of clothing, anything—if it was human.

After the black shape had passed between them, the curtains didn't fall back into the perfect alignment that had blocked the light; there was a small opening in them, a slit that allowed a shaft of moonlight, starlight, street light—whatever it was—to relieve the thick darkness. Barrie strained to focus on the dark shape, her eyes burning as she watched it move silently across the floor. She didn't scream; whoever or whatever approached her, it couldn't be worse than the only men likely to come to her rescue.

Perhaps she was really asleep and this was only a dream. It certainly didn't feel real. But nothing in the long, horrible hours since she had been kidnapped had felt real, and she was too cold to be asleep. No, this was real, all right.

Noiselessly the black shape glided to a halt beside the cot. It towered over her, tall and powerful, and it seemed to be examining the naked feast she presented.

Then it moved once again, lifting its hand to its head, and it peeled off its face, pulling the dark skin up as if it was no more than the skin of a banana.

It was a mask. As exhausted as she was, it was a moment before she could find a logical explanation for the nightmarish image. She blinked up at him. A man wearing a mask. Neither an animal, nor a phantom, but a flesh-and-blood man. She could see the gleam of his eyes, make out the shape of his head and the relative paleness of his face, though there was an odd bulkiness to him that in no way affected the eerily silent grace of his movements.

Just another man.

She didn't panic. She had gone beyond fear, beyond everything but rage. She simply waited—waited to fight, waited to die. Her teeth were the only weapon she had, so she would use them, if she could. She would tear at her attacker's flesh, try to damage him as much as possible before she died. If she was lucky, she would be able to get him by the throat with her teeth and take at least one of these bastards with her into death.

He was taking his time, staring at her. Her bound hands clenched into fists. Damn him. Damn them all.

Then he squatted beside the cot and leaned forward, his head very close to hers. Startled, Barrie wondered if he meant to *kiss* her—odd that the notion struck her as so unbearable—and she braced herself, preparing to lunge upward when he got close enough that she had a good chance for his throat.

"Mackenzie, United States Navy," he said in a toneless whisper that barely reached her ear, only a few inches away.

He'd spoken in *English*, with a definitely American accent. She jerked, so stunned that it was a moment before the words made sense. *Navy. United States Navy.* She had been silent for hours, refusing to speak to her captors or respond in any way, but now a small, helpless sound spilled from her throat.

"Shh, don't make any noise," he cautioned, still in that toneless whisper. Even as he spoke he was reaching over her head, and the tension on her arms suddenly relaxed. The small movement sent agony screaming through her shoulder joints, and she sucked in her breath with a sharp, gasping cry.

She quickly choked off the sound, holding it inside as she ground her teeth against the pain. "Sorry," she whispered, when she was able to speak.

She hadn't seen the knife in his hand, but she felt the chill of the blade against her skin as he deftly inserted the blade under the cords and sliced upward, felt the slight tug that freed her hands. She tried to move her arms and found that she couldn't; they remained stretched above her head, unresponsive to her commands.

He knew, without being told. He slipped the knife into its scabbard and placed his gloved hands on her shoulders, firmly kneading for a moment before he clasped her forearms and gently drew her arms down. Fire burned in her joints; it felt as if her arms were being torn from her shoulders, even though he carefully drew them straight down, keeping them aligned with her body to lessen the pain. Barrie set her teeth again, refusing to let another sound break past the barrier. Cold sweat beaded her forehead, and nausea burned in her throat once more, but she rode the swell of pain in silence.

He dug his thumbs into the balls of her shoulders, massaging the sore, swollen ligaments and tendons, intensifying the agony. Her bare body drew into a taut, pale arch of suffering, lifting from the cot. He held her down, ruthlessly pushing her traumatized joints and muscles through the recovery process. She was so cold that the heat emanating from his hands, from the closeness of his body as he bent over her, was searingly hot on her bare skin. The pain rolled through her in great shudders, blurring her sight and thought, and through the haze she realized that now, when she definitely needed to stay conscious, she was finally going to faint.

She couldn't pass out. She refused to. Grimly she hung on, and in only a few moments, moments that felt much longer, the pain began to ebb. He continued the strong kneading, taking her through the agony and into relief. She went limp, relaxing on the cot as she breathed through her mouth in the long, deep drafts of someone who has just run a race.

"Good girl," he whispered as he released her. The brief praise felt like balm to her lacerated emotions. He straightened and drew the knife again, then bent over the foot of the cot. Again there was the chill of the blade, this time against her ankles, and another small tug, then her feet were free, and involuntarily she curled into a protective ball, her body moving without direction from her brain in a belated, useless effort at modesty and self-protection. Her thighs squeezed tightly together, her arms crossed over and hid her breasts, and she buried her face against the musty ticking of the bare mattress. She couldn't look up at him, she couldn't. Tears burned her eyes, clogged her throat.

"Have you been injured?" he asked, the ghostly whisper rasping over her bare skin like an actual touch. "Can you walk?"

Now wasn't the time to let her raw nerves take over. They still had to get out undetected, and a fit of hysteria would ruin everything. She gulped twice, fighting for control of her emotions as grimly as she had fought to control the pain. The tears spilled over, but she forced herself to straighten from the defensive curl, to swing her legs over the edge of the cot. Shakily she sat up and forced herself to look at him. She hadn't done anything to be ashamed of; she would get through this. "I'm okay," she replied, and was grateful that the obligatory whisper disguised the weakness of her voice.

He crouched in front of her and silently began removing the web gear that held and secured all his equipment.

The room was too dark for her to make out exactly what each item was, but she recognized the shape of an automatic weapon as he placed it on the floor between them. She watched him, uncomprehending, until he began shrugging out of his shirt. Sick terror hit her then, slamming into her like a sledgehammer. My God, surely *he* wasn't—

Gently he put the shirt around her, tucking her arms into the sleeves as if she was a child, then buttoning each button, taking care to hold the fabric away from her body so his fingers wouldn't brush against her breasts. The cloth still held his body heat; it wrapped around her like a blanket, warming her, covering her. The sudden feeling of security unnerved her almost as much as being stripped naked. Her heart lurched inside her chest, and the bottom dropped out of her stomach. Hesitantly she reached out her hand in an apology, and a plea. Tears dripped slowly down her face, leaving salty tracks in their wake. She had been the recipient of so much male brutality in the past day that his gentleness almost destroyed her control, where their blows and crudeness had only made her more determined to resist them. She had expected the same from him and instead had received a tender care that shattered her with its simplicity.

A second ticked past, two: then, with great care, he folded his gloved fingers around her hand.

His hand was much bigger than hers. She felt the size and heat of it engulf her cold fingers and sensed the control of a man who exactly knew his own strength. He squeezed gently, then released her.

She stared at him, trying to pierce the veil of darkness and see his features, but his face was barely distinguishable and blurred even more by her tears. She could make out some details, though, and discern his movements. He wore a black T-shirt, and as silently as he had removed his gear, he now put it on again. He peeled back a flap on his wrist, and she caught the faint gleam of a luminous watch. ''We have exactly two and a half minutes to get out of here,'' he murmured. ''Do *what* I say, *when* I say it.''

Before, she couldn't have done it, but that brief moment of understanding, of connection, had buoyed her. Barrie nodded and got to her feet. Her knees wobbled. She stiffened them and shoved her hair out of her face. ''I'm ready.''

She had taken exactly two steps when, below them, a staccato burst of gunfire shattered the night.

He spun instantly, silently, slipping away from her so fast that she blinked, unable to follow him. Behind her, the door opened. A harsh, piercing flood of light blinded her, and an ominous form loomed in the doorway. The guard—of course there was a guard. Then there was a blur of movement, a grunt, and the guard sagged into supporting arms. As silently as her rescuer seemed to do everything else, he dragged the guard inside and lowered him to the floor. Her rescuer stepped over the body, snagged her wrist in an unbreakable grip and towed her from the room.

The hallway was narrow, dirty and cluttered. The light that had seemed so bright came from a single naked bulb. More gunfire was erupting downstairs and out in the street. From the left came the sound of pounding feet. To the right was a closed door, and past it she could see the first step of an unlit stairway.

He closed the door of the room they had just left and lifted her off her feet, slinging her under his left arm as if she was no more than a sack of flour. Barrie clutched dizzily at his leg as he strode swiftly to the next room and slipped into the sheltering darkness. He had barely shut the door when a barrage of shouts and curses in the hallway made her bury her face against the black material of his pants leg.

He righted her and set her on her feet, pushing her behind him as he unslung the weapon from his shoulder. They stood at the door, unmoving, listening to the commotion just on the other side of the wooden panel. She could discern three different voices and recognized them all. There were more shouts and curses, in the language she had heard off and on all day long but couldn't understand. The curses turned vicious as the guard's body, and her absence, were discovered. Something thudded against the wall as one of her kidnappers gave vent to his temper.

"This is One. Go to B."

That toneless whisper startled her. Confused, she stared at him, trying to make sense of the words. She was so tired that it took her a moment to realize he must be speaking a coded message into a radio. Of course he wasn't alone; there would be an entire team of rescuers. All they had to do was get out of the building, and there would be a helicopter waiting somewhere, or a truck, or a ship. She didn't care if they'd infiltrated on bicycles; she would gladly walk out—barefoot, if necessary.

But first they had to get out of the building. Obviously the plan had been to spirit her out the window without her kidnappers being any the wiser until morning, but something had gone wrong, and the others had been spotted. Now they were trapped in this room, with no way of rejoining the rest of his team.

Her body began to revolt against the stress it had endured for so many long hours, the terror and pain, the hunger, the effort. With a sort of distant interest she felt each muscle begin quivering, the shudders working their way up her legs, her torso, until she was shaking uncontrollably.

She wanted to lean against him but was afraid she would hinder his movements. Her life—and his—depended completely on his expertise. She couldn't help him, so the least she could do was stay out of his way. But she was desperately in need of support, so she fumbled her way a couple of steps to the wall. She was careful not to make any noise, but he sensed her movement and half turned, reaching behind himself with his left hand and catching her. Without speaking he pulled her up against his back, keeping her within reach should he have to change locations in a hurry.

His closeness was oddly, fundamentally reassuring. Her captors had filled her with such fear and disgust that every feminine instinct had been outraged, and after they had finally left her alone in the cold and the dark, she had wondered with a sort of grief if she would ever again be able to trust a man. The answer, at least with *this* man, was yes.

She leaned gratefully against his back, so tired and weak that, just for a moment, she had to rest her head on him. The heat of his body penetrated the rough fabric of the web vest, warming her cheek. He even smelled hot, she noticed through a sort of haze; his scent was a mixture of clean, fresh sweat and musky maleness, exertion and tension heating it to an aroma as heady as that of the finest whiskey. *Mackenzie*. He'd said his name was Mackenzie, whispered it to her when he crouched to identify himself.

Oh, God, he was so warm, and she was still cold. The gritty stone floor beneath her bare feet seemed to be wafting cold waves of air up her legs. His shirt was so big it dwarfed her, hanging almost to her knees, but still she was naked beneath it. Her entire body was shaking.

They stood motionless in the silent darkness of the empty room for an eternity, listening to the gunfire as it tapered off in the distance, listening to the shouts and curses as they, too, diminished, listened for so long that Barrie drifted into a light doze, leaning against him with her head resting on his back. He was like a rock, unmoving, his patience beyond anything she had ever imagined. There were no nervous little adjustments of position, no hint that his muscles got tired. The slow, even rhythm of his breathing was the only movement she could discern, and resting against him as she was, the sensation was like being on a raft in a pool, gently rising, falling....

She woke when he reached back and lightly shook her. "They think we got away," he whispered. "Don't move or make any sound while I check things out."

Obediently she straightened away from him, though she almost cried at the loss of his body heat. He switched on a flashlight that gave off only a slender beam; black tape had been placed across most of the lens. He flicked the light around the room, revealing that it was empty except for some old boxes piled along one wall. Cobwebs festooned all of the corners, and the floor was covered with a thick layer of dust. She could make out a single window in the far wall, but he was careful not to let the thin beam of light get close to it and possibly betray their presence. The room seemed to have been unused for a very long time.

He leaned close and put his mouth against her ear. His warm breath washed across her flesh with every word. "We have to get out of this building. My men have made it look as if we escaped, but we probably won't be able to hook up with them again until tomorrow night. We need someplace safe to wait. What do you know about the interior layout?''

She shook her head and followed his example, lifting herself on tiptoe to put her lips to his ear. ''Nothing,'' she whispered. ''I was blindfolded when they brought me here.''

He gave a brief nod and straightened away from her. Once again Barrie felt bereft, abandoned, without his physical nearness. She knew it was just a temporary weakness, this urge to cling to him and the security he represented, but she needed him now with an urgency that was close to pain in its intensity. She wanted nothing more than to press close to him again, to feel the animal heat that told her she wasn't alone; she wanted to be in touch with the steely strength that stood between her and those bastards who had kidnapped her.

Temporary or not, Barrie hated this neediness on her part; it reminded her too sharply of the way she had clung to her father when her mother and brother had died. Granted, she had been just a child then, and the closeness that had developed between her and her father had, for the most part, been good. But she had seen how stifling it could be, too, and quietly, as was her way, she had begun placing increments of distance between them. Now this had happened, and her first instinct was to cling. Was she going to turn into a vine every time there was some trauma in her life? She didn't want to be like that, didn't want to be a weakling. This nightmare had shown her too vividly that all security, no matter how solid it seemed, had its weak points. Instead of depending on others, she would do better to develop her own strengths, strengths she knew were there but that had lain dormant for most of her life. From now on, though, things were going to change.

Perhaps they already had. The incandescent anger that had taken hold of her when she'd lain naked and trussed on that bare cot still burned within her, a small, white-hot core that even her mind-numbing fatigue couldn't extinguish. Because of it, she refused to give in to her weakness, refused to do anything that might hinder Mackenzie in any way. Instead she braced herself, forcing her knees to lock and her shoulders to square. ''What are we going to do?'' she whispered. ''What can I do to help?''

Because there were no heavy blackout curtains on this grimy window, she was able to see part of his features as he looked at her. Half his face was in shadow, but the scant light gleamed on the slant of one high, chiseled cheekbone, revealed the strong cut of his jaw, played along a mouth that was as clearly defined as that of an ancient Greek statue.

''I'll have to leave you here alone for a little while,'' he said. ''Will you be all right?''

Panic exploded in her stomach, her chest. She barely choked back the scream of protest that would have betrayed them. Grinding her teeth together and electing not to speak, because the scream would escape if she did, she nodded her head.

He hesitated, and Barrie could feel his attention focusing on her, as if he sensed her distress and was trying to decide whether or not it was safe to leave her. After a few moments he gave a curt nod that acknowledged her determination, or at least gave her the benefit of the doubt. ''I'll be back in half an hour,'' he said. ''I promise.''

He pulled something from a pocket on his vest. He unfolded it, revealing a thin blanket of sorts. Barrie stood

still as he snugly wrapped it around her. Though it was
very thin, the blanket immediately began reflecting her
meager body heat. When he let go of the edges they fell
open, and Barrie clutched frantically at them in an effort
to retain that fragile warmth. By the time she had managed to pull the blanket around her, he was gone, opening
the door a narrow crack and slipping through as silently
as he had come through the window in the room where
she had been held. Then the door closed, and once again
she was alone in the darkness.

Her nerves shrieked in protest, but she ignored them.
Instead she concentrated on being as quiet as she could,
listening for any sounds in the building that could tell
her what was going on. There was still some noise from
the street, the result of the gunfire that had alarmed the
nearby citizenry, but that, too, was fading. The thick
stone walls of the building dulled any sound, anyway.
From within the building, there was only silence. Had
her captors abandoned the site after her supposed escape?
Were they in pursuit of Mackenzie's team, thinking she
was with them?

She swayed on her feet, and only then did she realize
that she could sit down on the floor and wrap the blanket
around her, conserving even more warmth. Her feet and
legs were almost numb with cold. Carefully she eased
down onto the floor, terrified she would inadvertently
make some noise. She sat on the thin blanket and pulled
it around herself as best she could. Whatever fabric it
was made from, the blanket blocked the chill of the stone
floor. Drawing up her legs, Barrie hugged her knees and
rested her head on them. She was more comfortable now
than she had been in many long hours of terror and, inevitably, her eyelids began to droop heavily. Sitting there
alone in the dark, dirty, empty room, she went to sleep.

Chapter 3

Pistol in hand, Zane moved silently through the decrepit old building, avoiding the piles of debris and crumbled stone. They were already on the top floor, so, except for the roof, the only way he could go was down. He already knew where the exits were, but what he didn't know was the location of the bad guys. Had they chosen this building as only a temporary hiding place and abandoned it when their victim seemingly escaped? Or was this their regular meeting place? If so, how many were there, and *where* were they? He had to know all that before he risked moving Miss Lovejoy. There was only another hour or so until dawn; he had to get her to a secure location before then.

He stopped at a turn in the corridor, flattening himself against the wall and easing his head around the corner just enough that he could see. Empty. Noiselessly, he moved down the hallway, just as cautiously checking the few rooms that opened off it.

He had pulled the black balaclava into place and smeared dust over his bare arms to dull the sheen of his skin and decrease his visibility. Giving his shirt to Miss Lovejoy and leaving his arms bare had increased his visibility somewhat, but he judged that his darkly tanned arms weren't nearly as likely to be spotted as her naked body. Even in the darkness of the room where they had been keeping her, he had been able to clearly make out the pale shimmer of her skin. Since none of her clothes had been in evidence, giving her his shirt was the only thing he could have done. She'd been shaking with cold—evidence of shock because the night was warm—and she likely would have gone into hysterics if he'd tried to take her out of there while she was stark naked. He had been prepared, if necessary, to knock her out. But she'd been a little trooper so far, not even screaming when he had suddenly loomed over her in the darkness. With his senses so acute, though, Zane could feel how fragile her control was, how tightly she was strung.

It was understandable. She had likely been raped, not once but many times, since she had been kidnapped. She might fall apart when the crisis was over and she was safe, but for now she was holding together. Her gutsiness made his heart clench with a mixture of tenderness and a lethal determination to protect her. His first priority was to get her out of Libya, not wreak vengeance on her kidnappers—but if any of the bastards happened to get in his way, so be it.

The dark maw of a stairwell yawned before him. The darkness was reassuring; it not only signaled the absence of a guard, it would shield him. Humans still clung to the primitive instincts of cave dwellers. If they were awake, they wanted the comfort of light around them, so they could see the approach of any enemies. Darkness was a weapon that torturers used to break the spirit of their captives, because it emphasized their helplessness, grated on their nerves. But he was a SEAL, and darkness was merely a circumstance he could use. He stepped carefully into the stairwell, keeping his back to the wall to avoid any crumbling edges of the stone. He was fairly certain the stairs were safe, otherwise the kidnappers wouldn't have been using them, but he didn't take chances. Like idiots, people stacked things on stair steps, blocking their own escape routes.

A faint lessening of the darkness just ahead told him that he was nearing the bottom of the steps. He paused while he was still within the protective shadow, listening for the slightest sound. There. He heard what he'd been searching for, the distant sound of voices, angry voices tripping over each other with curses and excuses. Though Zane spoke Arabic, he was too far away to make out what they were saying. It didn't matter; he'd wanted to know their location, and now he did. Grimly he stifled the urge to exact revenge on Miss Lovejoy's behalf. His mission was to rescue her, not endanger her further.

There was a stairwell at each end of the building. Knowing now that the kidnappers were on the ground floor at the east end, Zane began making his way to the west staircase. He didn't meet up with any guards; as he had hoped, they thought the rescue had been effected, so they didn't see any point now in posting guards.

In his experience, perfect missions were few and far between, so rare that he could count on one hand the number of missions he'd been on where everything had gone like clockwork. He tried to be prepared for mechanical breakdowns, accidents, forces of nature, but there was no way to plan for the human factor. He didn't know how the kidnappers had been alerted to the SEALs' presence, but he had considered that possibility from the beginning and made an alternate plan in case something went wrong. Something had—exactly what, he would find out later: except for that brief communication with his men, telling them to withdraw and switch to the alternate plan, they had maintained radio silence.

Probably it was pure bad luck, some late-night citizen unexpectedly stumbling over one of his men. Things happened. So he had formulated Plan B, his just-in-case plan, because as they had worked their way toward the building, he'd had an uneasy feeling. When his gut told him something, Zane listened. Bunny Withrock had once given him a narrow-eyed look and said, ''Boss, you're even spookier than the Spook.'' But they trusted his instincts, to the point that mentally they had probably switched to Plan B as soon as he'd voiced it, before he had even gone into the building.

With Miss Lovejoy to consider, he'd opted for safety. That was why he had gone in alone, through the window, after Spook's reconnaissance had reported that the kidnappers had set guards at intervals throughout the first floor. There were no lights in any of the rooms on the fourth floor, where Miss Lovejoy was reportedly being held, so it was likely there was no guard actually in the room with her; a guard wouldn't want to sit in the darkness.

The kidnappers had inadvertently pinpointed the room for him: only one window had been covered with curtains. When Zane had reached that room, he had carefully parted the heavy curtains to make certain they hadn't shielded an interior light, but the room beyond had been totally dark. And Miss Lovejoy had been there, just as he had expected.

Now, ostensibly with nothing left to guard, the kidnappers all seemed to be grouped together. Zane cat-footed through the lower rooms until he reached the other staircase, then climbed silently upward. Thanks to Spooky, he knew of a fairly secure place to take Miss Lovejoy while they waited for another opportunity for extraction; all he had to do was get her there undetected. That meant he had to do it before dawn, because a half-naked, red-haired Western woman would definitely be noticeable in this Islamic country. He wouldn't exactly blend in himself, despite his black hair and tanned skin, because of his dark cammies, web gear and weaponry. Most people noticed a man with camouflage paint on his face and an automatic rifle slung over his shoulder.

He reached the room where he'd left Miss Lovejoy and entered as quietly as he'd left. The room was empty. Alarm roared through him, every muscle tightening, and then he saw the small, dark hump on the floor and realized that she had curled up with the thin survival blanket over her. She wasn't moving. Zane listened to the light, almost inaudible evenness of her breathing and realized she had gone to sleep. Again he felt that subtle inner clenching. She had been on edge and terrified for hours, obviously worn out but unable to sleep; the slight measure of security he'd been able to give her, consisting of his shirt, a blanket and a temporary, precarious hiding place, had been enough for her to rest. He hated to disturb her, but they had to move.

Gently he put his hand on her back, lightly rubbing, not shaking her awake but easing her into consciousness so she wouldn't be alarmed. After a moment she began stirring under his touch, and he felt the moment when she woke, felt her instant of panic, then her quietly determined reach for control.

"We're moving to someplace safer," he whispered,

removing his hand as soon as he saw she was alert. After what she had been through, she wouldn't want to endure a man's touch any more than necessary. The thought infuriated him, because his instinct was to comfort her; the women in his family, mother, sister and sisters-in-law, were adored and treasured by the men. He wanted to cradle Barrie Lovejoy against him, whisper promises to her that he would personally dismember every bastard who had hurt her, but he didn't want to do anything that would undermine her fragile control. They didn't have time for any comforting, anyway.

She clambered to her feet, still clutching the blanket around her. Zane reached for it, and her fingers tightened on the fabric, then slowly loosened. She didn't have to explain her reluctance to release the protective cloth. Zane knew she was still both extrasensitive to cold and painfully embarrassed by her near nudity.

"Wear it this way," he whispered, wrapping the blanket around her waist sarong-style so that it draped to her feet. He tied the ends securely over her left hipbone, then bent down to check that the fabric wasn't too tight around her feet, so she would have sufficient freedom of movement if they had to run.

When he straightened, she touched his arm, then swiftly lifted her hand away, as if even that brief touch had been too much. "Thank you," she whispered.

"Watch me closely," he instructed. "Obey my hand signals." He explained the most basic signals to her, the raised clenched fist that meant "Stop!" and the open hand that meant merely "halt," the signal to proceed and the signal to hide. Considering her state of mind, plus her obvious fatigue, he doubted she would be able to absorb more than those four simple commands. They didn't have far to go, anyway; if he needed more commands than that, they were in deep ca-ca.

She followed him out of the room and down the west staircase, though he felt her reluctance to step into the Stygian depths. He showed her how to keep her back to the wall, how to feel with her foot for the edge of the step. He felt her stumble once, heard her sharply indrawn breath. He whirled to steady her; his pistol was in his right hand, but his left arm snaked out, wrapping around her hips to steady her as she teetered two steps above him. The action lifted her off her feet, hauling her against his left side. She felt soft in his grip, her hips narrow but nicely curved, and his nostrils flared as he scented the warm sweetness of her skin.

She was all but sitting on his encircling arm, her hands braced on his shoulders. Reluctantly he bent and set her on her feet, and she immediately straightened away from him. "Sorry," she whispered in the darkness.

Zane's admiration for her grew. She hadn't squealed in alarm, despite nearly falling, despite the way he'd grabbed her. She was holding herself together, narrowing her focus to the achievement of one goal: freedom.

She was even more cautious in her movements after that one misstep, letting more distance grow between them than he liked. On the last flight of steps he stopped, waiting for her to catch up with him. Knowing that she couldn't see him, he said, "Here," when she was near, so she wouldn't bump into him.

He eased his way down the last couple of steps into the faint light. There was no one in sight. With a brief wave of his hand he signaled her forward, and she slipped out of the darkness of the stairwell to stand beside him.

There was a set of huge wooden double doors that opened onto the street, but Zane was aware of increased noise outside as dawn neared, and it was too risky to use that exit. From their left came a raised voice, shouting in Arabic, and he felt her tense. Quickly, before the sound of one of her kidnappers unnerved her, he shepherded her into a cluttered storage room, where a small, single window shone high on the wall. "We'll go out this window," he murmured. "There'll be a drop of about four feet to the ground, nothing drastic. I'll boost you up. When you hit the ground, move away from the street but stay against the side of the building. Crouch down so you'll present the smallest possible silhouette. Okay?"

She nodded her understanding, and they picked their way over the jumbled boxes and debris until they were standing under the window. Zane stretched to reach the sill, hooked his fingers on the plaster and boosted himself up until he was balanced with one knee on the sill and one booted foot braced against a rickety stack of boxes. The window evidently hadn't been used in a long time; the glass was opaque with dust, the hinges rusty and stiff. He wrestled it open, wincing at the scraping noise, even though he knew it wouldn't carry to where the kidnappers were. Fresh air poured into the musty room. Like a cat he dropped to the floor, then turned to her.

"You can put your foot in my hand, or you can climb on my shoulders. Which do you prefer?"

With the window open, more light was coming through. He could see her doubtful expression as she stared at the window, and for the first time he appreciated the evenness of her features. He already knew how sweetly her body was shaped, but now he knew that Miss Lovejoy didn't hurt his eyes at all.

"Can you get through there?" she whispered, ignoring his question as she eyed first the expanse of his shoulders and then the narrowness of the window.

Zane had already made those mental measurements.
"It'll be a tight fit, but I've been through tighter ones."

She gazed at his darkened face, then gave one of her
sturdy nods, the one that said she was ready to go on.
Now he could see her calculating the difficulty of maneuvering through the window with the blanket tied
around her waist, and he saw the exact moment when she
made her decision. Her shoulders squared and her chin
came up as she untied the blanket and draped it around
her like a long scarf, winding it around her neck and
tossing the ends over her shoulders to dangle rakishly
down her back.

"I think I'd better climb on your shoulders," she said.
"I'll have more leverage that way."

He knelt on the floor and held his hands up for her to
catch and brace herself. She went around behind him and
daintily placed her right foot on his right shoulder, then
lifted herself into a half crouch. As soon as her left foot
had settled into place and her hands were securely in his,
he rose steadily until he was standing erect. Her weight
was negligible compared to what he handled during training. He moved closer to the wall, and she released his
right hand to brace her hand against the sill. "Here I go,"
she whispered, and boosted herself through the window.

She went through it headfirst. It was the fastest way,
but not the easiest, because she had no way of breaking
her fall on the other side. He looked up and saw the
gleam of pale, bare legs and the naked curves of her
buttocks; then she vanished from sight, and there was a
thump as she hit the ground.

Quickly Zane boosted himself up again. "Are you all
right?" he whispered harshly.

There was silence for a moment, then a shaky, whispered answer. "I think so."

"Take the rifle." He handed the weapon to her, then dropped to the floor while he removed his web gear. That, too, went through the window. Then he followed, feet first, twisting his shoulders at an angle to fit through the narrow opening and landing in a crouch. Obediently, she had moved to the side and was sitting against the wall with the blanket once more clutched around her and his rifle cradled in her arms.

Dawn was coming fast, the remnants of darkness no more than a deep twilight. "Hurry," he said as he shrugged into the web vest and took the rifle from her. He slid it into position, then drew the pistol again. The heavy butt felt reassuring and infinitely familiar in his palm. With the weapon in his right hand and her hand clasped in his left, he pulled her into the nearest alley.

Benghazi was a modern city, fairly Westernized, and Libya's chief port. They were near the docks, and the smell of the sea was strong in his nostrils. Like the vast majority of waterfronts, it was one of the rougher areas of the city. From what he'd been able to tell, no authorities had shown up to investigate the gunfire, even supposing it had been reported. The Libyan government wasn't friendly—there were no diplomatic relations between the United States and Libya—but that didn't mean the government would necessarily turn a blind eye to the kidnapping of an ambassador's daughter. Of course, it was just as likely that it would, which was why diplomatic channels hadn't been considered. The best option had seemed to go in and get Miss Lovejoy out as quickly as possible.

There were plenty of ramshackle, abandoned buildings in the waterfront area. The rest of the team had withdrawn to one, drawing any pursuers away from Zane and Miss Lovejoy, while they holed up in another. They would rendezvous at oh-one-hundred hours the next morning.

Spooky had chosen the sites, so Zane trusted their relative safety. Now he and Miss Lovejoy wended their way through a rat's nest of alleyways. She made a stifled sound of disgust once, and he knew she'd stepped on something objectionable, but other than that she soldiered on in silence.

It took only a few minutes to reach the designated safe area. The building looked more down than up, but Spooky had investigated and reported an intact inner room. One outer wall was crumbled to little more than rubble. Zane straddled it, then caught Miss Lovejoy around the waist and effortlessly lifted her over the heap, twisting his torso to set her on the other side. Then he joined her, leading her under half-fallen timbers and around spiderwebs that he wanted left undisturbed. The fact that he could see those webs meant they had to get under cover, fast.

The door to the interior room hung haphazardly on one hinge, and the wood was rotting away at the top. He pulled her inside the protective walls. "Stay here while I take care of our tracks," he whispered, then dropped to a crouch and moved to where they had crossed the remnants of the outer wall. He worked backward from there, scattering dirt to hide the signs of their passage. There were dark, wet places on the broken pieces of stone that were all that remained of the floor. He frowned, knowing what those dark patches meant. Damn it, why hadn't she said something? Had she left a trail of blood straight to their hiding place?

Carefully he obliterated the marks. It wasn't completely her fault; he should have given more thought to her bare feet. The truth was, his mind had been more on her bare butt and the other details of her body that he'd already seen. He was far too aware of her sexually; the proof of it was heavy in his loins. After what she had been through that was the last thing she needed, so he would ignore his desire, but that didn't make it go away.

When he had worked his way to the room, he silently lifted the door and reset it in the frame, bracing it so it wouldn't sag again. Only then did he turn to face her. "Why didn't you tell me you'd cut your foot? When did it happen?" His voice was low and very even.

She was still standing where he'd left her, her face colorless in the half light coming through the open shutters of the window, her eyes so huge with fatigue and strain that she looked like a forlorn, bedraggled little owl. A puzzled frown knit her brows as she looked at her feet. "Oh," she said in dazed discovery as she examined the dark stains on her left foot. "I didn't realize it was cut. It must have happened when I stepped in that... whatever...in the alley. I remember that it hurt, but I thought there was just a sharp rock under the...stuff."

At least it hadn't happened any sooner than that. Their position should still be safe. He keyed the radio, giving the prearranged one click that told the team he was in the safe area and receiving two clicks in return, meaning his men were secure in their position, too. They would check in with each other at set intervals, but for the most part they would spend the day resting. Relieved, Zanc turned his mind to other matters.

"Sit down and let me see your foot," he ordered. The last thing he needed was for her to be hobbled, though from what he'd seen of her so far, she wouldn't breathe a word of complaint, merely limp along as fast as she could.

There was nothing to sit on except the broken stones of the floor, so that was where she sat, carefully keeping the blanket wrapped around her waist. Her feet were filthy, caked with the same mess that caked his boots. Blood oozed sullenly from a cut on the instep of her left foot.

Zane shucked off his black hood and headset, took off his web vest and removed his gloves; then he unpacked his survival gear, which included a small and very basic first-aid kit. He sat cross-legged in front of her and lifted her foot to rest on his thigh. After tearing open a small packet containing a premoistened antiseptic pad, he thoroughly cleaned the cut and the area around it, pretending not to notice her involuntary flinches of pain, which she quickly tried to control.

The cut was deep enough that it probably needed a couple of stitches. He took out another antiseptic pad and pressed it hard over the wound until the bleeding stopped. "How long has it been since your last tetanus vaccination?" he asked.

Barrie thought that she had never heard anything as calm as his voice. She could see him clearly now; it was probably a good thing she hadn't been able to do so before, because her nerves likely couldn't have stood the pressure. She cleared her throat and managed to say, "I don't remember. Years," but her mind wasn't on what she was saying.

His thick black hair was matted with sweat, and his face was streaked with black and green paint. The black T-shirt he wore was grimy with mingled dust and sweat, not that the shirt she had on was in much better shape. The material strained over shoulders that looked a yard wide, clung to a broad chest and flat stomach, stretched over powerful biceps. His arms were corded with long, steely muscles, his wrists almost twice as thick as hers; his long-fingered hands were well-shaped, callused, harder than any human hands should be—and immensely gentle as he cleansed the wound on her foot.

His head was bent over the task. She saw the dense black eyelashes, the bold sweep of his eyebrows, the thin and arrogantly high bridge of his nose, the chiseled plane of his cheekbones. She saw his mouth, so clear-cut and stern, as if he seldom smiled. Beard stubble darkened his jaw beneath the camouflage paint. Then his gaze flicked up to her for a moment, cool and assessing, as if he was gauging her reaction to the sting of the antiseptic, and she was stunned by the clear, pale beauty of his blue gray eyes. He had silently and efficiently killed that guard, then stepped over the body as if it didn't exist. A wicked, ten-inch black blade rode in a scabbard strapped to his thigh, and he handled both pistol and rifle with an ease that bespoke a familiarity that went far beyond the normal. He was the most savage, dangerous, lethal thing, man or beast, that she had ever seen—and she felt utterly safe with him.

He had given her the shirt off his back, treating her with a courtesy and tenderness that had eased her shock, calmed her fears. He had seen her naked; she had been able to ignore that while they were still trapped in the same building with her kidnappers, but now they were relatively safe, and alone, and she was burningly aware of both his intense masculinity and of her nakedness beneath his shirt. Her skin felt unusually sensitive, as if it was too hot and tight, and the rasp of the fabric against her nipples was almost painfully acute.

Her foot looked small and fragile in his big hands. He frowned in concentration as he applied an antibiotic ointment to the cut, then fashioned a butterfly bandage to close the wound. He worked with a swift, sure dexterity, and it was only a moment before the bandaging was complete. Gently he lifted her foot off his leg. "There. You should be able to walk with no problem, but as soon as we get you to the ship, get the doc to put in a couple of stitches and give you an injection for tetanus."

"Yes, sir," she said softly.

He looked up with a swift, faint smile. "I'm Navy. That's, 'Aye, aye, sir.'"

The smile nearly took her breath. If he ever truly smiled, she thought, she might have heart failure. To hide her reaction, she held out her hand to him. "Barrie Lovejoy. I'm pleased to make your acquaintance."

He folded his fingers around hers and solemnly shook hands. "Lieutenant-Commander Zane Mackenzie, United States Navy SEALs."

A SEAL. Her heart jumped in her chest. That explained it, then. SEALs were known as the most dangerous men alive, men so skilled in the arts of warfare that they were in a class by themselves. He didn't just look lethal; he *was* lethal.

"Thank you," she whispered.

"My pleasure, ma'am."

Hot color flooded her face as she looked at her blanket-covered lap. "Please, call me Barrie. After all, your shirt is the only thing I…" Her voice trailed off, and she bit her lip. "I mean, formality at this point is—"

"I understand," he said gently, breaking into her stumbling explanation. "I don't want you to be embarrassed, so the circumstances are strictly between us, if you prefer. But I advise you to tell the ship's surgeon, or your own doctor, for the sake of your health."

Barrie blinked at him in confusion, wondering what on earth her health had to do with the fact that he'd seen her naked. Then comprehension dawned; if she hadn't been so tired, she would have realized immediately what conclusion he had drawn from the situation.

"They didn't rape me," she whispered. Her face flushed even hotter. "They—they touched me, they hurt me and did some...other things, but they didn't actually rape me. They were saving that for today. Some important guy in their organization was supposed to arrive, and I suppose they were planning a sort of p-party."

Zane's expression remained calm and grave, and she knew he didn't believe her. Why should he? He'd found her tied up and naked, and she'd already been in the kidnappers' hands for most of a day. Chivalry wasn't part of their code; they had refrained from rape only on orders from their leader, because he wanted to be there to enjoy her himself before the others had their turn on her.

He didn't say anything, and Barrie busied herself with the used antiseptic pads, which were still damp enough to clean the rest of the disgusting muck from her feet. She longed for a bath, but that was so far out of the question that she didn't even voice the wish.

While she busied herself with tidying up, he explored the small room, which didn't take long, because there was nothing in it. He closed the broken shutters over the window; the wooden slats were rotted away at the top, allowing some light through but preventing any passersby from seeing inside.

With the room mostly dark once more, it was like being in a snug, private cave. Barrie smothered a yawn, fighting the fatigue that dragged on her like lead weights. The only sleep she'd had was that brief nap while Zane had been finding a way out of the building, and she was so tired that even her hunger paled in comparison.

He noticed, of course; he didn't miss anything. "Why

don't you go to sleep?'' he suggested. ''In a couple of hours, when more people are moving around and I won't be as noticeable, I'll go scrounge up something for us to eat and liberate some clothes for you.''

Barrie eyed the paint streaking his face. ''With makeup like that, I don't believe you're going to go unnoticed no matter how crowded the streets are.''

That faint smile touched his lips again, then was gone. ''I'll take it off first.''

The smile almost kept her awake. Almost. She felt her muscles slowly loosening, as if his permission to sleep was all her body needed to hear. Her eyelids were too heavy for her to hold open anymore; it was like a veil of darkness descending. With her last fraction of consciousness, she was aware of his arms around her, gently lowering her to the floor.

Chapter 4

She had gone to sleep like a baby, Zane thought, watching her. He'd seen it often enough in his ten nephews, the way little children had of dropping off so abruptly, their bodies looking almost boneless as they toppled over into waiting arms. His gaze drifted over her face. Now that dawn was here, even with the shutters closed, he could plainly see the exhaustion etched on her face; the wonder was that she had held up so well, rather than that she'd gone to sleep now.

He could use some rest himself. He stretched out beside her, keeping a slight distance between them; not touching, but close enough that he could reach her immediately if their hiding place was discovered. He was still wired, too full of adrenaline to sleep yet, but it felt good to relax and let himself wind down while he waited for the city to come completely awake.

Now he could also see the fire in her hair, the dark auburn shade that, when she stood in the sun, would glint with gold and bronze. Her eyes were a deep, soft green, her brows and lashes like brown mink. He wouldn't have been surprised by freckles, but her skin was clear and creamy, except for the bruise that mottled one cheek. There were bruises on her arms, and though he couldn't see them, he knew the shirt covered other marks left by brutal men. She'd insisted they hadn't raped her, but probably she was ashamed for anyone else to know, as if she'd had any choice in the matter. Maybe she wanted to keep it quiet for her father's sake. Zane didn't care about her reasons; he just hoped she would get the proper medical care.

He thought dispassionately about slipping to the building where they'd held her and killing any and all of the bastards who were still there. God knew they deserved it, and he wouldn't lose a minute's worth of sleep over any of them. But his mission was to rescue Miss Love-joy—Barrie—and he hadn't accomplished that yet. If he went back, there was the chance that he would be killed, and that would endanger her, as well as his men. He'd long ago learned how to divorce his emotions from the action so he could think clearly, and he wasn't about to compromise a mission now... But *damn,* he wanted to kill them.

He liked the way she looked. She wasn't drop-dead gorgeous or anything like that, but her features were regular, and asleep, with her woes put aside for the moment, her expression was sweetly serene. She was a pretty little thing, as finely made as an expensive porcelain figurine. Oh, he supposed she was probably of middle height for a woman, about five feet five, but he was six-three and outweighed her by at least a hundred pounds, so to him she was little. Not as little as his mother and sister, but they were truly slight, as delicate as fairies. Barrie Lovejoy, for all her aristocratic bloodlines, had the sturdiness of a pioneer. Most women, with good reason, would have broken down long before now.

He was surprised to feel himself getting a little drowsy. Despite their situation, there was something calming about lying here beside her, watching her sleep. Though he was solitary by nature and had always preferred sleeping alone after his sexual appetite had been satisfied, it felt elementally right, somehow, to guard her with his body as they slept. Had cavemen done this, putting themselves between the mouth of the cave and the sleeping forms of their women and children, drowsily watching the gentle movements of their breathing as the fires died down and night claimed the land? If it was an ancient instinct, Zane mused, he sure as hell hadn't felt it before now.

But he wanted to touch her, to feel the softness of her flesh beneath his hand. He wanted to fold her within the warm protection of his body, tuck her in close, curl around her and keep her there with an arm draped around her waist. Only the knowledge that the last thing in the world she would want now was a man's touch kept him from doing just that.

He wanted to hold her. He ached to hold her.

She was dwarfed by his shirt, but he'd seen the body hidden by the folds of cloth. His night vision was very good; he'd been able to discern her high, round breasts, not very big, but definitely mouth-watering, and tipped with small, tight nipples. She was curvy, womanly, with a small waist and rounded hips and a neat little triangle of pubic hair. He'd seen her buttocks. Just thinking about it made him feel hollowed out with desire; her butt was fine indeed. He would like to feel it snuggled up against his thighs.

He wasn't going to be able to sleep, after all. He was fully aroused, desire pulsing through his swollen and rigid flesh. Wincing, he turned onto his back and adjusted himself to a more comfortable position, but the comfort was relative. The only way he would truly find ease was within the soft, hot clasp of her body, and that wasn't likely to happen.

The small room grew brighter and warmer as dawn developed into full morning. The stone walls would protect them from most of the day's heat, but soon they would need water. Water, food, and clothes for her. A robe would be better than Western-style clothing, because the traditional Muslim attire would cover her hair, and there were enough traditionalists in Benghazi that a robe wouldn't draw a second glance.

The streets were noisy now, the waterfront humming with activity. Zane figured it was time for him to do some foraging. He wiped the camouflage paint from his skin as best he could and disguised what was left by smearing dirt on his face. He wasn't about to go unarmed, so he pulled the tail of his T-shirt free from his pants and tucked the pistol into the waistband at the small of his back, then let the shirt fall over it. Anyone who paid attention would know the bulge for what it was, but what the hell, it wasn't unusual for people to go armed in this part of the world. Thanks to his one-quarter Comanche heritage, his skin had a rich bronze hue, and in addition he was darkly tanned from countless hours of training in the sun and sea and wind. There was nothing about his appearance that would attract undue notice, not even his eyes, because there were plenty of Libyans with a European parent.

He checked Barrie, reassuring himself that she was still sleeping soundly. He'd told her that he would be slipping out for a while, so she shouldn't be alarmed if she woke while he was gone. He left their crumbling sanctuary as silently as he had entered it.

It was over two hours before he returned, almost time for the designated check-in time with his men. He had a definite talent for scavenging, he thought, though outright thievery would probably be a better term. He carried a woman's black robe and head covering, and wrapped up in it was a selection of fruit, cheese and bread, as well as a pair of slippers he hoped would fit Barrie. The water had been the hardest to come by, because he'd lacked a container. He'd solved that by stealing a stoppered gallon jug of wine, forbidden by the Koran but readily available anyway. He had poured out the cheap, sour wine and filled the jug with water. The water would have a definite wine taste to it, but it would be wet, and that was all they required.

While he had the opportunity, he disguised the entrance to their lair a bit, piling some stones in front of it, arranging a rotted timber so that it looked as if it blocked the door. The door was still visible, but looked much less accessible. He tested his handiwork to make certain they could still get out easily enough, then slipped inside and once again braced the door in its sagging frame.

He turned to check on Barrie. She was still asleep. The room was considerably warmer, and she had kicked the blanket aside. His shirt was up around her waist.

The kick of desire was like taking a blow to the chest. He almost staggered from it, his heart racing, his breath strangling in his throat. Sweat beaded on his forehead, ran down his temple. *God.*

He should turn away. He should put the blanket over her. He should put sex completely out of his mind. There were any number of things he should do, but instead he stared at her with a hunger so intense he ached with it, quivered with it. Greedily his gaze moved over every female inch of her. His sex was throbbing like a toothache. He wanted her more intensely than he'd ever wanted a woman before. His famous cool remoteness had failed him—there wasn't a cool inch on him, and his desire was so damn strong and immediate, he was shaking from the effort of resisting it.

Moving slowly, stiffly, he set his purloined goodies on the floor. His breath hissed between his clenched teeth. He hadn't known sexual frustration could be this painful. He'd never had any trouble getting a woman whenever he'd wanted one. This woman was off-limits, though, from even an attempt at seduction. She'd been through enough without having to fend off her rescuer, too.

As warm as the room was now, if he spread the blanket over her she would only kick it off again. Gingerly he went down on one knee beside her and with shaking hands pulled the shirt tail down to cover her. With slight disbelief he eyed the fine tremor of his fingers. He never trembled. He was rock steady during the most tense and dangerous situations, icily controlled in combat. He had parachuted out of a burning plane, swum with sharks and sewn up his own flesh. He had ridden unbroken horses and even bulls a time or two. He had killed. He had done all of that with perfect control, but this sleeping, redhaired woman made him shake.

Grimly he forced himself to turn aside and pick up the radio headset. Holding the earpiece in place, he clicked once and immediately heard two clicks in response. Everything was okay.

Maybe some water would cool him down. At least thinking about it was better than thinking about Barrie. He dropped a couple of purification tablets into the jug, in case the small amount of wine that had remained in it wasn't enough to kill all the invisible little critters. The tablets didn't improve the taste any—just the opposite—but they were better than a case of the runs.

He drank just enough to relieve his thirst, then settled down with his back to a wall. There was nothing to do but wait and contemplate the walls, because he sure as hell didn't trust himself to look at Barrie.

Voices woke her. They were loud, and close by. Barrie bolted upright, her eyes huge with alarm. Hard arms grabbed her, and an even harder hand clamped itself over her mouth, stifling any sound she might have made. Confused, disoriented, in sheer terror she began to fight as much as she could. Teeth. She should use her teeth. But his fingers were biting hard into her jaw, and she couldn't open her mouth. Desperately she tried to shake her head, and he merely gathered her in tighter, tucking her against him in a way that was oddly protective.

"Shh" came that toneless whisper, and the familiarity of it cut through the panic and fog of sleep. Zane.

Instantly she relaxed, weak with relief. Feeling the tension leave her muscles, he tilted her face, still keeping his hand over her mouth. Their eyes met in the shadowed light, and he gave a brief nod as he saw that she was awake now, and aware. He released her jaw, his hard fingers trailing briefly over her skin in apology for the tightness of his grip. The barely there caress went through her like lightning. She shivered as it seared a path along nerve endings throughout her body and instinctively turned her face into the warm hollow created by the curve of his shoulder.

The arm around her had loosened immediately when she shivered, but at her action she felt him hesitate a fraction of a second, then gather her snugly against him once more.

The voices were closer, and added to them were some thuds and the sound of crumbling rock. She listened to the rapid, rolling syllables of Arabic, straining to concentrate on the voices. Were they the same voices she had heard through yesterday's long nightmare? It was difficult to tell.

She didn't understand the language; hers had been a finishing-school education, suited to an ambassador's daughter. She spoke French and Italian fluently, Spanish a little less so. After her father's posting in Athens she had made it a point to study Greek, too, and had learned enough that she could carry on a simple conversation, though she understood more than she spoke.

Fiercely she wished she had insisted on lessons in Arabic, too. She had hated every moment she'd spent in the kidnappers' hands, but not speaking the language had made her feel even more helpless, more isolated.

She would rather die than let them get their hands on her again.

She must have tensed, because Zane gave her a light squeeze of reassurance. Swiftly she glanced at his face. He wasn't looking at her; instead he was concentrating on the fragile, half-rotted door that protected the entrance to their sanctuary, and on the voices beyond. His expression was utterly calm and distant. Abruptly she realized that he *did* understand Arabic, and whatever was being said by the people picking through the ruins of the building, he wasn't alarmed by it. He was alert, because their hiding place could be compromised at any moment, but evidently he felt confident of being able to handle that problem.

With reason, no doubt. From what she'd seen, she

thought he was capable of handling just about any situation. She would trust him with her life—and had.

The voices went on for a long time, sometimes coming so close to their hiding place that Zane palmed that big pistol and held it aimed unwaveringly at the door. Barrie stared at that hand, so lean and powerful and capable. There wasn't the slightest tremor visible; it was almost unreal, almost inhuman, for any man to be that calm and have such perfect control over his body.

They sat silently in the warm, shadowy little room, their breathing for the most part their only movements. Barrie noticed that the blanket no longer covered her legs, but the shirt, thank God, kept her reasonably decent. It was too hot to lie under the blanket, anyway.

Time crept by at a sloth's pace. The warmth and silence were hypnotic, lulling her into a half dream state of both awareness and distance. She was ferociously hungry, but unaffected by it, as if she was merely aware of someone else's hunger. After a while her muscles began to ache from being in one position for so long, but that didn't matter, either. Thirst, though, was different. In the increasing heat, her need for water began to gnaw at her. The kidnappers had given her some water a couple of times, but she'd had nothing to drink in hours—since she had learned they expected her to relieve herself in their presence, in fact. She had chosen to do without water rather than provide them with such amusement again.

Sweat streaked down Zane's face and dampened his shirt. She was perfectly content to remain where she was, nestled against his side. The arm around her made her feel safer than if their hiding place had been constructed of steel, rather than crumbling stone and plaster, and rotting wood.

She had never been exposed to a man like him before.

Her only contact with the military had been with the senior officers who attended functions at the embassy, colonels and generals, admirals, the upper brass; there were
also the Marine guards at the embassy, with their perfect
uniforms and perfect manners. Though she supposed the
Marine guards had to be exemplary soldiers or they
wouldn't have been chosen as embassy guards, still, they
were nothing like the man who held her so protectively.
They were soldiers; he was a warrior. He was as different
from them as the lethal, ten-inch black blade strapped to
his thigh was from a pocketknife. He was a finely honed
weapon.

For all that, he wasn't immortal, and they weren't safe.
Their hiding place could be discovered. He could be
killed; she could be recaptured. The hard reality of that
was something she couldn't ignore as she could hunger
and cramped muscles.

After a long, long time, the voices went away. Zane
released her and walked noiselessly to the door to look
out. She had never before seen anyone move with such
silent grace, like a big jungle cat on velvet paws instead
of a battle-hardened warrior in boots.

She didn't move until he turned around, the faint relaxation of his expression telling her the danger was past.
"What were they doing?" she asked, taking care to keep
her voice low.

"Scavenging building materials, picking up blocks,
any pieces of wood that hadn't rotted. If they'd had a
sledgehammer, they probably would have dismantled
these walls. They carted the stuff off in a wheelbarrow.
If they need more, they'll probably be back."

"What will we do?"

"The same thing we did this time—hunker down and
keep quiet."

"But if they come in here—"

"I'll handle it." He cut her worry short before she could completely voice it, but he did it with a tone of reassurance. "I brought some food and water. Interested?"

Barrie scrambled to her knees, eagerness in every line of her body. "Water! I'm so thirsty!" Then she halted, her recent experience fresh in her mind. "But if I drink anything, where will I go to…you know."

He regarded her with faint bemusement, and she blushed a little as she realized that wasn't a problem he normally encountered. When he and his men were on a mission, they would relieve themselves wherever and whenever they needed.

"I'll find a place for you to go," he finally said. "Don't let that stop you from drinking the water you need. I also found some clothes for you, but as hot as it's getting in here, you'll probably want to wait until night before you put them on."

He indicated the black bundle beside his gear, and she realized it was a robe. She thought of the modesty it would provide, and gratitude flooded her; at least she wouldn't have to face his men wearing nothing more than his shirt. But he was right; in the heat of day, and in the privacy of this small room, she would prefer wearing his shirt. They both knew she was bare beneath it; he'd already seen her stark naked, and demonstrated his decency by giving her the shirt and ignoring her nakedness, so there was no point now in swathing herself in an ankle-length robe.

He produced a big jug and unstoppered it. "It'll taste funny," he warned as he passed the jug to her. "Purification tablets."

It did taste funny—warm, with a chemical flavor. But

it was wonderful. She drank a few swallows, not wanting to make her stomach cramp after being empty for so long. While she was drinking, he unwrapped the bits of food he'd procured—a loaf of hard bread, a hunk of cheese and several oranges, plums and dates. It looked like a feast.

He straightened the blanket for her to sit on, then took out his knife and cut small portions of both the loaf and cheese and gave them to her. She started to protest that she was hungry enough to eat much more than that, but realized that what he had would have to last them all day, and perhaps longer than that. She wasn't about to complain about the amount of food she *did* have.

She had never been particularly fond of cheese, and she suspected that if she hadn't been so hungry she wouldn't have been fond of this cheese, either, but at the moment it was delicious. She nibbled at both bread and cheese, finding satisfaction in the simple act of chewing. As it happened, she had overestimated her appetite. The small portion he had given her was more than enough.

He ate more heartily, and polished off one of the oranges. He insisted that she eat a couple of the juicy slices and drink a bit more water. Feeling replete, Barrie yawned and refused the offer of another orange slice.

"No, thanks, I'm full."

"Would you like to freshen up now?"

Her head whipped around, sending her red hair flying. Amusement twinkled in his pale eyes at her eager, pleading expression. "There's enough water?"

"Enough to dampen a bandana."

She didn't have a bandana, of course, but he did. Carefully he poured just enough water from the jug to wet the square cloth, then politely turned his back and busied himself with his gear.

Slowly Barrie smoothed the wet cloth over her face, sighing in pleasure at the freshness of the sensation. She hadn't realized how grimy she felt until now, when she was able to rectify the situation. She found a sore place on her cheek, where one of the men had hit her, and other tender bruises on her arms. Glancing at Zane's broad back, she quickly unbuttoned the shirt just enough that she could slide the handkerchief inside and rub it over her torso and under her arms. After she fastened the garment, her dusty legs got the same attention. The dampness was wonderfully cooling, almost voluptuous in the sensual delight it gave her.

"I'm finished," she said, and returned the dark bandana to him when he turned around. "It felt wonderful. Thank you."

Then her heart leaped in her chest, because he evidently felt the same need to cool off as she had, but unlike her, he didn't keep his shirt on. He peeled the snug black T-shirt off over his head and dropped it on the blanket, then sat on his heels while he moistened the bandana and began scrubbing it over his face.

Oh, my. Helplessly she stared at the rippling muscles of his chest and stomach, the way they flexed and relaxed with the flow of his movements. The dim light caught the deep bronze of his skin, gleamed on the smooth, powerful curve of his shoulder. Her fascinated gaze wandered over the slant of his shoulder blades, the diamond of black hair that stretched from nipple to nipple on his chest. He twisted around to reach for something, and she found his back equally fascinating, with the deep furrow of his spine bisecting two muscular planes.

There was an inch-long scar on his left cheekbone. She hadn't noticed it before because his face had been so dirty, but now she could plainly see the silvery line of it.

It wasn't a disfiguring scar at all, just a straight little slash, as precise as a surgeon's cut. The scar along his rib cage was different, easily eight or nine inches in length, jagged, the scar tissue thick and ridged. Then there were the two round, puckered scars, one just above his waist, the other just below his right shoulder blade. Bullet wounds. She'd never seen one before, but she recognized them for what they were. There was another slash running along his right bicep, and God only knew how many other scars there were on the rest of his body. The warrior hadn't led a charmed life; his body bore the signs of battle.

He squatted half-naked, unconcernedly rubbing the damp handkerchief across his sweaty chest, lifting his arms to wash under them, exposing the smooth undersides and intriguing patches of hair. He was so fundamentally, elementally male, and so purely a warrior, that her breath strangled in her lungs as she watched him.

The rush of warmth through her body told her that she was more female than she'd ever imagined.

A little dazed, she sat back, resting against the wall. Absently she made certain the shirt tail preserved her modesty, but thoughts were tumbling through her mind, dizzyingly fast yet very clear.

They weren't out of danger yet.

During the past twenty-four horrific hours, she hadn't spent a lot of time wondering about the motive behind her kidnapping. She'd had too much to deal with as it was, the sheer terror, the confusion, the pain of the blows they'd given her.

She'd been blindfolded much of the time, and disoriented. She'd been humiliated, stripped naked and roughly fondled, taunted with the prospect of rape, and yet they had stopped short of rape—for a reason. Sheer psychological torture had undoubtedly played a role, but most of all they'd had orders to save her for the man who was to arrive today.

Who was he? He was the one behind her kidnapping; he had to be. But why?

Ransom? When she thought about it now, coolly and clearly, she didn't think so. Yes, her father was rich. Many a diplomat came from a moneyed background; it wasn't unusual. But if money had been the motive, there were others who were richer, though perhaps she had been chosen specifically because it was well known that her father would beggar himself to keep her safe. Perhaps.

But why would they have taken her out of the country? Wouldn't they have wanted to keep her close by, to make the exchange for money easier? No, the very fact that they'd taken her out of the country meant they'd kidnapped her for another reason. Maybe they would have asked for money anyway; since they already had her, why not? But money wasn't the primary object. So what was?

She didn't know, and since she didn't know who the leader was, she had no way of guessing what he truly wanted.

Not herself. She dismissed that notion out of hand. She wasn't the object of obsession, because no man so obsessed with a woman that he was driven to such lengths would let his men maul her. Nor was she the type to inspire obsession, she thought wryly. Certainly none of the men she'd dated had shown any signs of obsessive behavior.

So…there was something else, some piece of puzzle she was missing. Was it someone she knew? Something she'd read or seen?

Nothing came to mind. She wasn't involved in in-

trigue, though of course she knew which employees at
the embassy were employed by the CIA. That was standard, nothing unusual. Her father often spoke privately
with Art Sandefer and, lately, Mack Prewett, too. She'd
often thought that Art was more bureaucrat than spy,
though the intelligence in his tired gaze said he'd done
his time in the field, too. She didn't know about Mack
Prewett. There was something restless and hard about
him, something that made her uneasy.

Her father said Mack was a good man. She wasn't
certain about that, but neither did he seem like a villain.
Still, there had been that time a couple of weeks ago
when she hadn't known anyone was with her father and
had breezily walked in without knocking. Her father had
been handing a thick manila envelope to Mack; both of
them had looked startled and uncomfortable, but her father wasn't a diplomat for nothing. He'd efficiently
smoothed over the slight awkwardness, and Mack had
left the office almost immediately, taking the envelope
with him. Barrie hadn't asked any questions about it, because if it was CIA business, then it wasn't her business.

Now she wondered what had been in that envelope.

That small incident was the only thing the slightest bit
untoward that she could remember. Art Sandefer had
once said that there was no such thing as coincidence,
but could that moment be linked to her kidnapping?
Could it be the *cause* of it? That was a reach.

She didn't know what was in the envelope, hadn't
shown any interest in it. But she had seen her father giving it to Mack Prewett. That meant…what?

She felt as if she was feeling her way through a mental
maze, taking wrong turns, stumbling into dead ends, then
groping her way back to logic. Her father would never,
in any way, do anything that would harm her. Therefore,

that envelope had no significance—unless he was involved in something dangerous and wanted out. Her kidnapping made sense only if someone was using her as a
weapon to make her father do something he didn't want
to do.

She couldn't accept the idea of her father doing anything traitorous—at least, not voluntarily. She wasn't
blind to his weaknesses. He was a bit of a snob, he didn't
at all like even the idea that someday she might fall in
love and get married, he was protective to the point of
smothering her. But he was an honorable man, and a truly
patriotic man. It could be that the kidnappers were trying
to force her father to do something, give them some information, perhaps, and he had resisted; she could be the
means they were using to force him to do what they
wanted.

That felt logical. The envelope probably had nothing
at all to do with her kidnapping, and Art Sandefer was
wrong about coincidence.

But what if he wasn't?

Then, despite her instincts about him, her father was
involved in something he shouldn't be. The thought made
her sick to her stomach, but she had to face the possibility, had to think of every angle. She had to face it,
then put it aside, because there was nothing she could do
about it now.

If the kidnappers had been going to use her as a
weapon against her father, then they wouldn't give up. If
it had just been ransom, they would have thrown up their
hands at her supposed escape and said the Arabic equiv-
alent of, "Ah, to hell with it."

The leader hadn't been here. She didn't even know
where "here" was; she'd had too much on her mind to
ask questions about her geographic location.

"Where are we?" she murmured, thinking she really should know.

Zane lifted his eyebrows. He was sitting down, lounging against the wall at a right angle to her, having finished cleaning up, and she wondered how long she'd been lost in thought. "The waterfront district," he said. "It's a rough section of town."

"I meant, what town?" she clarified.

Realization dawned in his crystal clear eyes. "Benghazi," he said softly. "Libya."

Libya. Stunned, she absorbed the news, then went back to the mental path she'd been following.

The leader had been flying in today. From where? Athens? If he'd been in contact with his men, he would know she'd somehow escaped. But if he had access to the embassy, and to her father, then he would also know that she hadn't been returned to the embassy. Therefore, she would logically still be in Libya. Also logically, they would be actively searching for her.

She looked at Zane again. His eyes were half-closed, he looked almost asleep. Because of the heat, he hadn't put his T-shirt back on. But despite the drowsy look on his face, she sensed that he was vitally aware of everything going on around them, that he was merely letting his body rest while his mind remained on guard.

After the humiliation and pain her guards had dealt her, Zane's concern and consideration had been like a balm, soothing her, helping to heal her bruised emotions before she even had time to know how deep the damage went. Almost before she knew it, she had been responding to him as a woman does to a man, and somehow that was all right.

He was the exact opposite of the thugs who had so delighted in humiliating her. Those thugs were probably searching all over the city for her, and until she was out of this country, the possibility existed that they would recapture her. And if they did, this time there would be no respite.

No. It was intolerable. But if the unthinkable happened, she would be damned if she would give them the satisfaction they'd been anticipating. She would be damned if she would let them take her virginity.

She had never thought of her virginity as anything other than a lack of experience and inclination. At school in Switzerland there had been precious few opportunities for meeting boys, and she hadn't been particularly interested in those she had met. After she left school, her father's protective possessiveness, as well as her duties at the embassy, had restricted any social life she might have developed. The men she met hadn't seemed any more interesting than the few boys she had met while in school. With AIDS added in as a threat, it simply hadn't seemed worth the risk to have sex simply for the experience.

But she had dreamed. She had dreamed of meeting a man, growing to love him, making love with him. Simple, universal dreams.

The kidnappers had almost taken all that from her, almost wrecked her dream of loving a man by abusing her so severely that, if she had remained in their hands much longer, she knew she would have been so severely traumatized that she might never have been able to love a man or tolerate his touch. If Zane hadn't taken her out of there, her first sexual experience would have been one of rape.

No. A thousand times no.

Even if they managed to recapture her, she wouldn't let them murder that dream.

Scrambling to her feet, Barrie took the few steps to
where Zane lounged against the wall. She saw his muscled body come to alertness at her action, though he
didn't move. She stood over him, staring at him with
green eyes burning in the dim light. The look he gave
her was hooded, unreadable.

"Make love to me," she said in a raw voice.

Chapter 5

"**B**arrie..." he began, his tone kind, and she knew he was going to refuse.

"No!" she said fiercely. "Don't tell me I should think about it, or that I really don't want to do it. I know what I went through with those bastards. I know you don't believe it, but they *didn't* rape me. But they looked at me, they touched me, and I couldn't stop them." She stopped and drew a deep breath, steadying herself. "I'm not stupid. I know we're still in danger, that you and your men could be wounded or even killed trying to rescue me and that I could end up back in their hands anyway. I've never made love before, with anyone. I don't want my first time to be rape, do you understand? I don't want them to have that satisfaction. *I want the first time to be with you.*"

She had surprised him, she saw, and she had already noticed that Zane Mackenzie wasn't a man whose expression revealed much of what he was thinking. He sat up straight, his pale eyes narrowed as he examined her with a piercing gaze.

He was still going to refuse, and she didn't think she could bear it. "I promise," she blurted desperately. "They didn't do that to me. I can't have any disease, if that's what you're worried about."

"No," he said, his voice suddenly sounding strained. "That isn't what I'm worried about."

"Don't make me beg," she pleaded, wringing her hands together, aware that she was already doing exactly that.

Then the expression in those pale eyes softened, grew warmer. "I won't," he said softly, and rose to his feet with that powerful, feline grace of his. He towered over her, and for a moment Barrie felt the difference in their sizes so sharply that she wondered wildly what she thought she was doing. Then he moved past her to the blanket; he knelt and smoothed it, then dropped down on it, stretching out on his back, and watched her with a world of knowledge in his slightly remote, too-old eyes.

He knew. And until she read that knowledge in his eyes, she hadn't even been aware of what she really needed. But watching him lie down and put himself at her service, something inside her shattered. *He knew*. He understood the emotions roiling deep inside her, understood what had brought her to him with her fierce, startling demand. It wasn't just that she wanted her first time to be of her own volition, with the man of her choice; the kidnappers had taken something from her, and he was giving it back. They had tied her down, stripped her, humiliated her, and she had been helpless to stop them. Zane was giving control back to her, reassuring her and at the same time subtly letting her exact her vengeance against the male of the species.

She didn't want to lie helpless beneath him. She wanted to control this giving of her body, wanted things to move at her pace instead of his, wanted to be the one who decided how much, how far, how fast.

And he was going to let her do it.

He was giving control of his body to her.

She could barely breathe as she sank to her knees beside him. The warm, bare, richly tanned flesh lured her hands closer, closer, until the urge overcame her nervousness and her fingers lightly skimmed over his stomach, his chest. Her heart hammered wildly. It was like petting a tiger, knowing how dangerous the animal was but fascinated beyond resistance by the rich pelt. She wanted to feel all of that power under her hands. Carefully she flattened her hands along his ribs, molding his flesh beneath her palms, feeling the resilience of skin over the powerful bands of muscle and, beneath that, the strong solidity of bone. She could feel the rhythmic thud of his heartbeat, the expansion of his ribs as he breathed.

Both heartbeat and breathing seemed fast. Swiftly she glanced at his face and blushed at what she saw there, the heat in his heavy-lidded eyes, the deepened color of his lips. She knew what lust looked like; she'd seen the cruel side of it on the faces of her captors, and now she saw the pleasurable side of it in Zane. It startled her, because somehow she hadn't considered lust in the proposition she'd made to him, and her hands fell away from his body.

His lips parted in a curl of amusement that revealed the gleam of white teeth, and she felt her heart almost stop. His smile was even more potent than she'd expected. "Yeah, I'm turned on," he said softly. "I have to be, or this won't work."

He was right, of course, and her blush deepened. That

was the trouble with inexperience. Though she knew the mechanics of lovemaking, and once or twice her escort for the evening had kissed her with unexpected ardor and held her close enough for her to tell that he was aroused, still, she'd never had to deal directly with an erection— until now.

This particular one was there for her bidding. Furtively she glanced at the front of his pants, at the ridge pushing against the cloth.

"We don't have to do this," he offered once again, and Barrie flared from hesitance to determination.

"Yes, I do."

He moved his hands to his belt. "Then I'd better—"

Instantly she stopped him, pushing his hands up and away, forcing them down on each side of his head. "I'll do it," she said, more fiercely than she'd intended. This was her show.

"All right," he murmured, and again she knew that he understood. Her show, her control, every step of the way. He relaxed against the blanket, closing his eyes as if he was going to take a nap.

It was easier, knowing he wasn't watching her, which of course had been his intention. Barrie didn't want to fumble, didn't want to underline her inexperience any more than she already had, so before she reached for his belt she studied the release mechanism for a moment to make certain she understood it. She didn't give herself time to lose her nerve. She simply reached out, opened the belt and unfastened his pants. Under the pants were black swim trunks. Puzzled, Barrie stared at them. Swim trunks?

Then she understood. He was a SEAL; the acronym stood for SEa, Air and Land. He was at home in all three elements, capable of swimming for miles. Since Ben-

ghazi was a seaport, that was probably how his team had
infiltrated, from the sea. Maybe they'd used some sort of
boat to reach land, but it was possible they'd been
dropped off some distance from the port and had swum
the rest of the way.

He had risked his life to save her, was still doing so,
and now he was giving her his body. Everything inside
her squeezed tight, and she trembled from the rush of
emotion. Oh, God. She had learned more about herself
in the past twenty-four hours than in the entire past
twenty-five years of her life. Perhaps the experience had
changed her. Either way, something had happened inside
her, something momentous, and she was learning how to
deal with it.

She had let her father wrap her in a suffocating blanket
of protection for fifteen years; she couldn't blame him
for it, because she'd *needed* that blanket. But that time
was past. Fate had pitched her headlong into life, ripped
her out of her protective cocoon, and like a butterfly, she
couldn't draw the silken threads back around her. All she
could do was reach out for the unknown.

She slipped her hands under the waistband of the swim
trunks and began working them, and his pants, down his
hips. He levered his pelvis off the ground to aid her.
"Don't take them all the way off," he murmured, still
keeping his eyes closed and his hands resting beside his
head. "I can handle things if I get caught with my pants
down, but if they're completely off, it would slow me
down some."

Despite her nervousness, Barrie smiled at that supreme
self-confidence, the wry humor. If he wasn't so controlled, he could be described as cocky. He had no doubt
whatsoever about his fighting ability.

Her hands stroked down his buttocks as she slipped

her hands inside his garments. An unexpected frisson of pleasure rippled through her at the feel of his butt, cool and smooth, hard with muscle. Tush connoisseurs would envy her the moment, and she wished she had the nerve to linger, to fully appreciate this male perfection. Instead she tugged at his clothes, pulling them down to the middle of his thighs. He relaxed, letting his hips settle on the blanket again, and Barrie studied the startling reality of a naked man. She'd read books that described sexual arousal, but seeing it firsthand, and at close range, was far more impressive and wondrous.

Blindly she reached out, her hand drawn as if by a magnet. She touched him, stroking one fingertip down the length of his swollen sex. It pulsed and jerked upward, as if following the caress. He inhaled sharply. His reaction warmed her, and the tightness in her chest, her body, clenched once more, then began to loosen with that rush of warmth. Bolder now, she folded her fingers around him, gently sighing with pleasure as she felt the heat beneath the coolness, iron beneath silk, the urgent throbbing.

And she felt her own desire, rushing like a heated river through her flesh, turning angry determination into love-making. *This is how it should be,* she thought with relief; they should come together in pleasure, not in anger. And she didn't want to wait, didn't want to give herself time to reconsider, or she would lose her nerve.

Swiftly she straddled him, mounted him. No longer in anger at other men, no longer in desperation. *Pleasure,* warm and sweet. With her knees clasping his hips, acting on instinct, she held the thick shaft in position and slowly sank down on him, guiding their bodies together.

The first brush of his flesh against hers was hot, startling, and she instinctively jerked herself upright, away from the alien touch. Zane quivered, the barest ripple of reaction, then once more lay motionless between her legs, his eyes still closed, letting her proceed at her own pace.

Her chest was so constricted she could barely breathe; she sucked in air in quick little gasps. That contact, brief as it had been, had touched off an insistent throbbing between her legs, as if her body, after its initial startled rejection, had paused in instinctive recognition of female for male. Her breasts felt tight and feverish beneath the black fabric of his shirt. Alien, yes...but infinitely exciting. Desire wound through her, the river rising.

She told herself that she was prepared for the sudden acute sense of vulnerability, for her body's panic at the threat of penetration, even though desire was urging her on to that very conclusion. More gingerly, she settled onto him again, holding herself steady as she placed him against the entrance to her body and let her weight begin to impale her on the throbbing column of flesh.

The discomfort began immediately and was worse than she'd expected. She halted her movement, gulping as she tried to control her instinctive flinching away from the source of pain. He was breathing deeply, too, she noticed, though that was the only motion he made. She pushed harder, gritting her teeth against the burning sensation of being stretched, and then she couldn't bear any more and jerked herself off him. This time the discomfort between her legs didn't go away but continued to burn.

It wasn't going to get any better, she told herself. She might as well go ahead and do it. Breathing raggedly, once more she lowered herself onto him. Tears burned in her eyes as she struggled to complete the act. Why wouldn't it just go *in?* The pressure between her legs was enormous, intolerable, and a sob caught in her throat as she surged upward.

"Help me," she begged, her voice almost inaudible.

Slowly his eyes opened, and she almost flinched at the pale fire that burned there. He moved just one hand, the right one. Gently he touched her cheek, his callused fingertips rough and infinitely tender; then he trailed them down her throat and lightly over the shirt to her left breast, where they lingered for a heart-stopping moment at her nipple, then finally down to the juncture of her legs.

The caress was as light as a whisper. It lingered between her legs, teasing, brushing, stroking. She went very still, her body poised as she concentrated on this new sensation. Her eyes closed as all her senses focused on his hand and what it was doing, the way he was touching her. It was delicious, but not…quite… enough. He tantalized her with the promise of something more, something that was richer, more powerful, and yet that lightly stroking finger never quite touched her where she wanted. Barrie inhaled deeply, her nipples rising in response. Her entire body hung in suspense. She waited, waited for the gentle touch to brush her with ecstasy, waited…. Her hips moved, her body instinctively seeking, following his finger.

Ah. There. Just for a moment, *there.* A low moan bubbled up in her throat as pleasure shot through her. She waited for him to repeat the caress, but instead his fingers moved maddeningly close, teasing and retreating. Again her hips followed, and again she was rewarded by that lightning flash of pure sensation.

A subtle, sensual dance began. He led, and she followed. The just-right touches came more often, the pleasure became more shattering as the intensity built with each repetition. Between her legs, his male shaft still probed for entrance, and somehow each movement of her hips seemed to ease him a bit closer to that goal. Her body rocked, swaying in the ancient rhythm of desire, surging and retreating like the tides. She could feel him stretching her, feel the discomfort sharpened by her movements…and yet the desire lured her onward like a Lorelei, and somehow she began to need him inside her, need him to the point that the pain no longer mattered. She braced her hands on his chest, and her movements changed, lifting and falling rather than swaying side to side. His touch changed, too, suddenly pressing directly on the place where she most wanted it.

She bit her lip to keep from crying out. His thumb rubbed insistently, releasing a torrent, turning the warm river into something wild and totally beyond her control. She was so hot that she was burning up with desire, aching with emptiness. The pain no longer mattered; she had to have what his body promised, what hers needed. With a low moan she pressed downward, forcing her soft flesh to admit the intruder. She felt the resistance, the inner giving; then suddenly his hot, swollen sex pushed up inside her.

It hurt. It hurt a lot. She froze in place, and her eyes flew open, huge with distress. Their gazes locked, hers dark with pain, his burning with ruthlessly restrained desire. Suddenly she became aware of how taut the muscled body beneath her was, how much his control was costing him. But he had promised to let her set the pace, and he had kept that promise, moving only when she had asked for help.

Part of her wanted to stop, but a deeper, more powerful instinct kept her astride him. She could feel him throbbing inside her, feel the answering tightening of her body, as if the flesh knew more than the mind, and perhaps it did. He tensed even more. His skin gleamed with sweat, his heartbeat hammered beneath her palm. She felt a jolt of excitement at having this supremely male, incredibly dangerous warrior as hers to command, just for this time suspended from reality. They had met only hours ago; they had only hours left before they would likely never see each other again. But for now he was hers, embedded inside her, and she wasn't going to forgo a moment of the experience.

"What do I do now?" she whispered.

"Just keep moving," he whispered in return, and she did.

Rising. Falling. Lifting herself almost off him, then sinking down. Over and over, until she forgot about the pain and lost herself in the primeval joy. His hand remained between her legs, continuing the caress that urged her onward, even though she no longer needed to be urged. She moved on him, faster and faster, taking him deeper and deeper. His powerful body flexed between her thighs, arching, and a growl rumbled in his throat. Immediately he forced himself to lie flat again, chained by his promise.

Up. Down. Again. And again, the crescendo building inside her, the heat rising to an unbearable fever, the tension coiling tighter and tighter, until she felt as if she would shatter if she moved another muscle. She froze in place over him, whimpering, unable to push herself over the final hurdle.

The growl rumbled in his throat again. No, deeper than a growl; it was the sound of a human volcano exploding from the forces pent up inside. His control broke, and he moved, fiercely clamping both hands on her hips and pulling her down hard even as he arched once more and thrust himself in her to the hilt. He hadn't gone so deep before; she hadn't taken that much of him. The sensation was electric. She stifled a scream as he convulsed beneath her, heaving upward between her thighs, lifting her so that her knees left the ground. His head was thrown back, his neck corded with the force of his release, his teeth bared. Barrie felt the hot spurting of his release, felt him so deep inside her that he was touching the very center of her being, and it was enough to push her over the edge.

Pure lightning speared through her. She heard herself cry out, a thin cry of ecstasy that nothing could stifle. All her inner muscles contracted around him, relaxed, squeezed again, over and over, as if her body was drinking from his.

Finally the storm subsided, leaving her weak and shaking. Her bones had turned to jelly, and she could no longer sit upright. Helplessly she collapsed forward, folding on him like a house of cards caught in an earthquake. He caught her, easing her down so that she lay on his chest, and he wrapped his arms around her as she lay there gasping and sobbing. She hadn't meant to cry, didn't understand why the tears kept streaming down her face. "Zane," she whispered, and couldn't say anything more.

His big, hard hands stroked soothingly up and down her back. "Are you okay?" he murmured, and there was something infinitely male and intimate in his deep voice, an undertone of satisfaction and possessiveness.

Barrie gulped back the tears, forcing herself to coherency. "Yes," she said in a thin, waterlogged tone. "I didn't know it would hurt so much. Or feel so good," she added, because she was crying for both reasons. Odd, that she should have been as unprepared for the pleasure as she had been for the pain. She felt overwhelmed, unbalanced. Had she truly been so foolish as to think she could perform such an intimate act and remain untouched emotionally? If she had been capable of that kind of mental distance she wouldn't have remained a virgin until now. She would have found a way around her father's obsessive protectiveness if she had wanted to, if any man had ever elicited one-tenth the response in her this warrior had aroused within two minutes of their meeting. If her rescuer had been any other man, she wouldn't have asked such an intimate favor of him.

Their lovemaking had forged a link between them, a bond of the flesh that was far stronger and went far deeper than she'd imagined. Despite her chastity, had she believed the modern, permissive notion that making love could have no more lasting meaning than simple fun, like riding a roller coaster? Maybe, for some people, *sex* could be as trivial as a carnival ride, but she would never again think of lovemaking as anything that shallow. True lovemaking was deep and elemental, and she knew she would never be the same. She hadn't been from the moment he had given her his shirt and she had fallen in love with him. Without even seeing his face, she had fallen in love with the essence of the man, his strength and decency. It wouldn't have mattered if, when morning came, his features had been ugly or twisted with scars. In the darkness of that barren room, and the darkness of her heart, she had already seen beneath whatever lay on the surface, and she had loved him. It was that simple, and that difficult.

Just because she felt that way didn't mean he did. Barrie knew what a psychologist would say. It was the white-knight syndrome, the projection of larger-than-life characteristics onto a person because of the circumstances. Patients fell in love with their doctors and nurses all the time. Zane had simply been doing his job in rescuing her, while to her it had meant her life, because she hadn't for a moment supposed that her captors would let her live. She owed him her life, would have been grateful to him for the rest of that life—but she didn't think she would have loved just any man who had crawled through that window. She loved *Zane.*

She lay silently on him, her head nestled against his throat, their bodies still linked. She could feel the strong rhythm of his heartbeat thudding against her breasts, could feel his chest expand with each breath. His hot, musky scent excited her more than the most expensive cologne. She felt more at home here, lying with him on a blanket in the midst of a shattered building, than she ever had in the most luxurious and protected environment.

She knew none of the details of his life. She didn't know how old he was, where he was from, what he liked to eat or read or what programs he watched on television. She didn't know if he'd ever been married.

Married. My God, she hadn't even asked. She felt suddenly sick to her stomach. If he was married, then he wouldn't be the man she had thought he was, and she had just made the biggest mistake of her life.

But neither would the fault be entirely his. She had begged him, and he had given her more than one chance to change her mind. She didn't think she could bear it if he'd made love to her out of pity.

She drew a deep breath, knowing she had to ask. Ignorance might be bliss, but she couldn't allow herself that comfort. If she had done something so monumentally wrong, she wanted to know.

"Are you married?" she blurted.

He didn't even tense but lay utterly relaxed beneath her. One hand slid up her back and curled itself around her neck. "No," he said in that low voice of his. "You

can take your claws out of me now.'' The words were
lazily amused.

She realized she was digging her fingernails into his
chest and hastily relaxed her fingers. Distressed, she said,
''I'm sorry, I didn't mean to hurt you.''

''There's pain, and there's pain,'' he said comfortably.
''Bullets and knives hurt like hell. In comparison, a little
she-cat's scratching doesn't do much damage.''

''*She-cat?*'' Barrie didn't know if she should be af-
fronted or amused. After a brief struggle, amusement
won. None of her friends or associates would ever have
described her in such terms. She'd heard herself described as ladylike, calm, circumspect, conscientious, but
certainly never as a she-cat.

''Mmm.'' The sound was almost like a purr in his
throat. His hard fingers lazily massaged her neck, while
his other hand slipped down her back to burrow under
the shirt and curl possessively over her bottom. His palm
burned her flesh like a brand. ''Dainty. And you like
being stroked.''

She couldn't deny that, not when he was the one doing
the stroking. The feel of his hand on her bottom was
startlingly erotic. She couldn't help wiggling a little, and
then gasped as she felt the surge of his flesh inside her.
His breath caught, too, and his fingers dug into the cleft
of her buttocks.

''I need to ask you a couple of questions,'' he said,
and his voice sounded strained.

Barrie closed her eyes, once again feeling the warm
loosening deep inside that signaled the return of desire.
That had been a remarkable sensation, when his sex had
expanded inside her, both lengthening and getting
thicker. Oh, dear. She wanted to do it again, but she
didn't think she had the strength. ''What?'' she mur-

mured, distracted by what was happening between her legs.

"Did you get rid of the ghosts?"

Ghosts. He meant her lingering horror at the way those men had touched her. She thought about it and realized, with some surprise, that she had. She was still angry at the way she'd been treated, and she would dearly love to have Zane's pistol in her hands and those men in her sights, even though she'd never held a pistol before in her life. But the wounded, feminine part of her had triumphed by finding pleasure in making love with Zane, and in doing so she had healed herself. Pleasure… somehow the word fell far short of what she had experienced. Even ecstasy didn't quite describe the intensity, the sensation of imploding, melting, becoming utterly lost in her physical self.

"Yes," she whispered. "The ghosts are gone."

"Okay." His voice still sounded strained. "Second question. Will that damn shirt have to be surgically removed?"

She was startled into sitting upright. The action drove him deeper inside her and wrenched a sharp gasp from her, a groan from him. Panting, she stared at him. They had just made love—were, in fact, *still* making love— but the shirt she wore was what had kept her from going to pieces when he'd first found her, had given her the nerve to run barefoot down dark alleys, had become the symbol of a lot more than just modesty. Maybe she wasn't as recovered as she'd thought. The kidnappers had stripped her, forced her to be naked in front of them, and when Zane had first entered the room and seen her that way, she had been mortified. She didn't know if she could be naked with him now, if she could let him see the body that had been pinched and bruised by other men.

His crystal clear gaze was calm, patient. Again he understood. He knew what he was asking of her. He could have left things as they were, but he wanted more. He wanted her trust, her openness, with no dark secrets between them.

He wanted them to become lovers.

The realization was sharp, almost painful. They had loved each other physically, but with restraint like a wall between them. He had done what she had asked of him, had held himself back until the last moment, when his climax had shattered his control. Now he was asking something of her, asking her to give as he had given.

Almost desperately she clutched the front of the shirt. "I—they left marks on me."

"I've seen bruises before." He reached up and gently touched her cheek. "You have one right here, as a matter of fact."

Instinctively she reached up to the cheek he'd touched, feeling the tenderness. As soon as she released the front of the shirt, he moved his hands to the buttons and slowly began unfastening them, giving her time to protest. She bit her lip, fighting the urge to grab the widening edges of the cloth and hold them together.

When the garment was open all the way down, he slid his hands inside and cupped her breasts, his palms hot as they covered the cool mounds. Her nipples tingled as they hardened, reaching out for the contact. "The bruises shame *them*," he murmured. "Not you."

She closed her eyes as she sat astride him, feeling him hard and hot inside her, his hands just as hard and hot on her breasts. She didn't protest when his hands left her breasts, left them feeling oddly tight and aching, while he pushed the black shirt off her shoulders. The fabric puddled around her arms, and he lifted each in turn, slipping them free.

She was naked. The warm air brushed against her bare skin with the lightest of touches, and then she felt his fingertips doing the same, trailing so gently over each of the dark marks on her shoulders, her arms and breasts, her stomach, that she barely felt him. "Lean down," he said.

Slowly she obeyed, guided by his hands, down, down—and he lifted his head, meeting her mouth with his.

Their first kiss...and they'd already made love. Barrie was shocked at how she could have been so foolish as to forgo the pleasure of his kisses. His lips were firm, warm, hungry. She sank against him with a little sound of mingled surprise and delight humming in her throat. Her breasts flattened against him, the crisp hair on his chest rasping her ultrasensitive nipples, another joy she had unknowingly skipped.

Oh, this was delicious. His tongue probed for entrance, and she immediately gave it.

Several minutes later he let his head drop to the blanket. He was panting slightly, his eyes heavy-lidded. "I have another question."

"What?" She didn't want to give up the delights of his mouth. She'd never enjoyed kissing so much before, but he was diabolically good at it. She followed him down, nipping at his lower lip, depositing hot little kisses.

He chuckled beneath her mouth. The deep, rusty sound charmed her. She sensed that his laughter was even rarer than his smiles, therefore doubly precious.

"Will you let me be on top this time?"

The question surprised her into laughter. She stifled it as best she could, burying her head against his neck, but her body shook with giggles. He slipped out of her, making her laugh even harder. She was still laughing when he wrapped one strong arm around her and rolled, lifting her so they didn't roll off the blanket, efficiently tucking her beneath him and settling between her legs. Her laughter caught on a gasp as he surged heavily into her.

Her senses swam as she was bombarded by new feelings, when she had already experienced so much. She'd known he was a big man, but lying beneath him sharply brought home the difference in their sizes. Though he propped his weight on his forearms to keep from crushing her, she still felt the heaviness of that iron-muscled body. His shoulders were so broad that he dwarfed her, wrapped around her, shielded her. When she had been on top, she had controlled the depth of his penetration. The control was his now, her thighs spread wide by his hips. He felt bigger, harder than he had before.

He waited a moment to see how she would accept the vulnerability of her position. But she didn't feel vulnerable, she realized. She felt utterly secure, buffered by his strength. Tremulously she smiled at him and lifted her arms to wind them around his neck.

He smiled in return. And then Zane Mackenzie made love to her.

Chapter 6

There seemed to be scarcely a moment for the rest of the day when they weren't making love, resting from making love or about to make love. The sounds of the waterfront surrounded them, the low bellow of ships, truck horns, the sounds of chains and cranes, but inside that small, dim room there seemed to be nothing else in the world but each other. Barrie lost herself in the force of his unbridled sensuality and discovered within herself a passion that matched his. The need to be quiet only added to the intensity.

He kissed the bruises on her breasts and sucked her nipples until they throbbed with pleasure. His beard-stubbled chin rasped against her breasts, her belly, but he was always careful not to cause her pain as he searched for all the other bruises on her body and paid them the same tender homage.

"Tell me how they hurt you," he murmured, "and I'll make it better."

At first Barrie shied away from divulging the details, even to him, but as the hot afternoon wore on and he pleasured her so often she was drunk with the overload on her senses, it began to seem pointless to keep anything from him. Haltingly she began to whisper things to him.

"Like this?" he asked, repeating the action that had so upset her—except it wasn't the same. What had been meant to punish at the hands of the kidnappers became purest pleasure in Zane Mackenzie's hands. He caressed her until her body forgot those other touches, until it remembered only him.

She whispered another detail, and he wiped out that memory, too, replacing the bad with caresses that lifted her to peak after sensual peak. She couldn't imagine being handled more tenderly than he handled her, or with such delight. He didn't try to hide how much he enjoyed looking at her, touching her, making love to her. He reveled in her body, in the contrast between her soft curves and his hard muscularity. It aroused her to be the focus of such intense masculine pleasure, to feel his absorption with the texture of her skin, the curve of her breast, the snug sheathing between her legs. He explored her; he petted her, he drowned her in sexuality. The area around them was still so busy they didn't dare converse much, so they communicated with their bodies.

Three times, while they were lying drowsily in the aftermath of loving, he checked his watch and reached for the headset radio. He would click it once, listen, then put it aside.

"Your men?" she asked, after the first time.

He nodded. "They're hiding out, waiting until it's safe to rendezvous."

Then the chatter of voices outside became louder as some people approached, and they fell silent.

The afternoon wore on, and the light began to dim. She wasn't particularly hungry, but Zane insisted that she eat. He pulled up his pants; she once more donned his shirt. More formally attired now, they sat close together on the blanket and finished off the bread and fruit, but neither of them wanted any of the cheese. The water was warm and still tasted of chemicals. Barrie sat within the curve of his arm and dreaded leaving.

She wanted to be safe and comfortable again, but she hated to lose this closeness with Zane, this utter reliance and companionship and intimacy. She wouldn't push him to continue their relationship; under the circumstances, he might feel responsible and think he would have to let her down gradually, and she didn't want to put him in that position. If he indicated that he wanted to see her afterward, then…why, then her heart would fly.

But even if he did, it would be difficult for them to see each other regularly. He was more than just a military man; he was a SEAL. Much of what he did couldn't be discussed. He would have a home base, duties, missions. If they escaped safely, the danger to him didn't end there. A chill settled around her heart when she thought of the times in the future when, because it was his job, he would calmly and deliberately walk into a deadly situation. While they were hidden in this small room might be the only time she could ever be certain he was safe and unharmed.

The fear and uncertainty would almost drive her mad, but she would endure them, she would endure anything, for the opportunity to see him, to grow closer to him. Their relationship, if there was to be one, would have to grow in reverse. Usually people came to know each other, grew to trust and care, and then became lovers; they had become lovers almost immediately, and now they would have to get to know each other, find out all the quirks and personal history and tastes that made them individuals.

When she got back, she would have to deal with her father. He must be frantic, and once she was safely home, he would be even more paranoid and obsessive. But if Zane wanted her, she would have to deliberately hurt her father's feelings for the first time in her life; he would be supplanted as number one in her life. Most parents handled the change in their offsprings' lives with happiness, assuming the chosen mate was decent, but Barrie knew it wouldn't matter who she fell in love with, her father would be opposed to him. No man, to him, was good enough for her. Even more, he would bitterly resent anything that would take her out of his protection. She was all he had left of his family, and it didn't help that she greatly resembled her mother. As ambassador, her father had a very active social life, but he'd only ever loved one woman, and that was her mother.

She would never turn her back on her father, because she loved him dearly, but if the chance for a relationship, possibly a lifetime, with Zane was in the balance, she would put as much distance between herself and her father as necessary until he accepted the situation.

She was planning her life around dreams, she thought wryly as she brushed the bread crumbs from the blanket. She would do better to let the future take care of itself and concern herself with how they were going to get out of Benghazi.

"What time do we leave?"

"After midnight. We'll give most people time to get settled down for the night." He turned to her with the heavy-lidded gaze she had already learned signaled arousal and, reaching out, he began to unbutton her shirt. "Hours," he whispered.

Afterward they lay close together, despite the heat, and dozed. She didn't know how long it was before she woke, but when she did it was to almost total darkness. Unlike the night before, though, when she had lain in cold, lonely terror, now she was pressed against Zane's side, and his arms securely held her. Her head was pillowed on his shoulder, one bare leg was hooked over his hips. She stretched a bit and yawned, and his arms tightened, letting her know that he was awake. Perhaps he had never slept at all, but had held her and safeguarded her. The noise beyond the ruined building had died down; even the sounds from the docks were muted, as if the darkness smothered them.

"How much longer?" she asked, sitting up to fumble for the jug of water. She found it and drank; the taste wasn't too bad, she decided. Maybe she was becoming used to the chemicals, whatever they were.

He peeled the cover from his watch so he could see the luminous dial. "Another few hours. I need to check in with the guys in a couple of minutes."

She passed the water jug to him, and he drank. They lay back down, and she cuddled close. She put her right hand on his chest and felt the strong, healthy thudding of his heart. Idly she twirled her fingers in the crisp hairs, delighting in the textures of his body.

"What happens then? When we leave, I mean."

"We get out of the city, make our rendezvous point just at sunrise, and we're picked up."

He made it sound so simple, so easy. She remembered the swim trunks he wore and lifted her head to frown at him, even though she knew he couldn't see her. "Is our rendezvous point on dry land?"

"Not exactly."

"I see. I hope you have a boat?" It was a question, not a statement.

"Not exactly."

She caught his chest hairs and gave them a tug. "*Exactly* what *do* you have?"

"Ouch!" Snagging her hand, he disentangled it and lifted it to his mouth, lightly brushing his lips across her knuckles. "*Exactly,* we have a Zodiac, a seven-man, motorized inflatable craft. My team came in short two men, so there are only six of us. We'll be able to fit you in."

"I'm so glad." She yawned and snuggled her head more securely into the hollow of his shoulder. "Did you leave someone behind so there would be room for me?"

"No," he said shortly. "We're undermanned because of a problem I'll have to take care of when we get back. If there had been any other team available, we wouldn't be here, but we were the closest, and we needed to get you out in a hurry, before they moved you."

His tone dissuaded her from asking about the problem that put him in such a black mood, but she'd seen him in action; she knew she wouldn't want to be on the receiving end of his anger when he got back. She waited while he picked up the headset and checked in with his men, then returned to her questions.

"Where do we go in the Zodiac?"

"Out to sea," he said simply. "We radio ahead, and we'll be picked up by a helicopter from the *Montgomery,* an aircraft carrier. You'll be flown home from the carrier."

"What about you?" she whispered. "Where will you go?" That was as close as she would allow herself to get to asking him about his future plans.

"I don't know. My team was performing exercises on

the *Montgomery*, but that's blown to hell now, with two of them injured. I'll have to clean up that mess, and I don't know how long it will take."

He didn't know where he would be, or if he did, he wasn't saying. Neither was he saying that he would call her, though he *did* know where *she* would be. Barrie closed her eyes and listened painfully to all that he wasn't saying. The hurt was worse than she'd anticipated, but she closed it off in a place deep inside. Later it would come out, but if she only had a few hours left with him, she didn't intend to waste them crying about what might have been. Few women would have a chance to even know a man like Zane Mackenzie, much less love him. She was greedy; she wanted it all, wanted everything, but even this little bit was more than a lot of people experienced, and she would have to be grateful for that.

Whatever happened, she could never return to the safe little cocoon her father had fashioned for her. She couldn't let herself forget the kidnapping and the unknown *why* of it. Of course, her father would know why; the kidnapper would already have made his demands. But Barrie wanted to know the reason, too; after all, she had been more directly affected than anyone else.

Lightly Zane touched her nipple, circling it with his callused fingertips and bringing it erect. "I know you have to be sore," he said, sliding his hand down her belly to nestle it between her legs. "But can you take me again?" With the utmost care he eased one long finger into her; Barrie winced, but didn't flinch away from him. Yes, she was sore; she had been sore since the first time. She had discovered that the discomfort was easily discounted when the rewards were so great.

"I could be persuaded," she whispered, sliding her hand down his belly to measure his immediate seriousness. She found that he was very serious. Granted, she had no experience against which to compare this, but she had read magazine articles and knew that usually only teenage boys and very young men could maintain this pace. Maybe it was because he was in such superb physical condition. Maybe she was just lucky, though twenty-four hours before she hadn't thought so. But circumstances had changed, and so had she.

Fate had given her this man for now, and for a few more hours, she thought as he leaned over her and his mouth captured hers. She would make the most of it.

Once more he led her through the maze of alleys, but this time she was clad in the enveloping black robe, and a chador covered her hair. Her feet were protected by slippers, which were a little too big and kept slipping up and down on her heels, but at least she wasn't barefoot. It felt strange to have on clothes, especially so many, even though she was bare underneath the robe.

Zane was once more rigged out with his gear and weaponry, and with the donning of those things he had become subtly more remote, almost icily controlled, the way he'd been the night before when he'd first found her. Barrie sensed his acute alertness and guessed that he was concentrating totally on the job at hand. She silently followed him, keeping her head a little bowed as a traditional Muslim woman would do.

He halted at the corner of a building and sank to his haunches, motioning for her to do the same. Barrie copied him and took the extra precaution of drawing the chador across her face.

"Two, this is One. How's it looking?" Once more he was speaking in that toneless whisper that barely carried to her, though she was right behind him. After a moment he said, "See you in ten."

He glanced around at Barrie. "It's a go. We don't have to shift to Plan C."

"What was Plan C?" she whispered.

"Run like hell for Egypt," he said calmly. "It's about two hundred miles due east."

He would do it, too, she realized. He would steal some kind of vehicle and go for it. His nerves must be made of solid iron. Hers weren't; she was shaking inside with nervousness, but she was holding up. Or maybe it wasn't nervousness; maybe it was exhilaration at the danger and excitement of action, of *escaping*. As long as they were still in Benghazi, in Libya, they hadn't really gotten free.

Ten minutes later he stopped in the shadow of a dilapidated warehouse. Perhaps he clicked his radio; in the dark, she couldn't tell. But suddenly five black shapes materialized out of the darkness, and they were surrounded before she could blink.

"Gentlemen, this is Miss Lovejoy," Zane said. "Now let's get the hell out of Dodge."

"With pleasure, boss." One of the men bowed to Barrie and held out his hand. "This way, Miss Lovejoy."

There was a certain rough élan about them that she found charming, though they didn't let it interfere with the business at hand. The six men immediately began moving out in choreographed order, and Barrie smiled at the man who'd spoken as she took the place he had indicated in line. She was behind Zane, who was second in line behind a man who moved so silently, and blended so well into the shadows, that even knowing he was there, sometimes she couldn't see him. The other four men ranged behind her at varying distances, and she realized that she couldn't hear them, either. In fact, she was the only one of the group who was making any noise, and she tried to place her slippered feet more carefully.

They wound their way through the alleys and finally stopped beside a battered minibus. Even in the darkness Barrie could see the huge dents and dark patches of rust that decorated the vehicle. They stopped beside it, and Zane opened the sliding side door for her. "Your chariot," he murmured.

Barrie almost laughed as he handed her into the little bus: if she hadn't had experience navigating long evening gowns, she would have found the ankle-length robe awkward, but she managed it as if she was a nineteenth-century lady being handed into a carriage. The men climbed in around her. There were only two bench seats; if there had ever been a third one in the back, it had long since been removed, perhaps to make room for cargo. A wiry young black man got behind the steering wheel, and Zane took the other seat in front. The eerily silent man who had been on point squeezed in on her left side, and another SEAL sat on her right, carefully placing her in a human security box. The other two SEALs knelt on the floorboard behind them, their muscular bodies and their gear filling the limited space.

"Let's go, Bunny Rabbit," Zane said, and the young black man grinned as he started the engine. The minibus looked as though it was on its last wheels, but the motor purred.

"You shoulda been there last night," the black guy said. "It was tight for a minute, real tight." He sounded as enthusiastic as if he was describing the best party he'd ever attended.

"What happened?" Zane asked.

"Just one of those things, boss," the man on Barrie's right said with a shrug evident in his voice. "A bad guy stepped on Spook, and the situation went straight into fubar.''

Barrie had been around enough military men to know what fubar meant. She sat very still and didn't comment.

''Stepped right *on* me,'' the SEAL on her left said in an aggrieved tone. ''He started squalling like a scalded cat, shooting at everything that moved and most things that didn't. Aggravated me some.'' He paused. ''I'm not staying for the funeral.''

''When we got your signal we pulled back and ran like hell,'' the man on her right continued. ''You must've already had her out, because they came after us like hound dogs. We laid low, but a couple of times I thought we were going to have to fight our way out. Man, they were walking all over us, and they kept hunting all night long.''

''No, we were still inside,'' Zane said calmly. ''We just stepped into the next room. They never thought to check it.''

The men snorted with mirth; even the eerie guy on her left managed a chuckle, though it didn't sound as if he did it often enough to be good at it.

Zane turned around in the seat and gave Barrie that brief twitch of a smile. ''Would you like some introductions, or would you rather not know these raunchy-smelling bums?''

The atmosphere in the bus *did* smell like a locker room, only worse. ''The introductions, please,'' she said, and her smile was plain in her voice.

He indicated the driver. ''Antonio Withrock, Seaman Second Class. He's driving because he grew up wrecking cars on dirt tracks down South, so we figure he can handle any situation.''

''Ma'am,'' said Seaman Withrock politely.

"On your right is Ensign Rocky Greenberg, second in command."

"Ma'am," said Ensign Greenberg.

"On your left is Seaman Second Class Winstead Jones."

Seaman Winstead Jones growled something unintelligible. "Call him Spooky or Spook, not Winstead," Zane added.

"Ma'am," said Seaman Jones.

"Behind you are Seamen First Class Eddie Santos, our medic, and Paul Drexler, the team sniper."

"Ma'am," said two voices behind her.

"I'm glad to meet you all," Barrie said, her sincerity plain. She had trained her memory at countless official functions, so she had their names down cold. She hadn't yet put a face to Santos or Drexler, but from his name she figured Santos would be Hispanic, so that would be an easy distinction to make.

Greenberg began to tell Zane the details of everything that had happened. Barrie listened and didn't intrude. The fact was, this midnight drive through Benghazi felt a little surreal. She was surrounded by men armed to their eye-teeth, but they were traveling through an area that was still fairly active for so late at night. There were other vehicles in the streets, pedestrians on the sidewalks. They even stopped at a traffic light, with other vehicles around them. The driver, Withrock, hummed under his breath. No one else seemed concerned. The traffic light changed, the battered little minibus moved forward, and no one paid them any attention at all.

Several minutes later they left the city. Occasionally she could see the gleam of the Mediterranean on their right, which meant they were traveling west, toward the center of Libya's coast. As the lights faded behind them, she began to feel lightheaded with fatigue. The sleep she had gotten during the day, between bouts of lovemaking, hadn't been enough to offset the toll stress had taken on her. She couldn't see herself leaning on either of the men beside her, however, so she forced herself to sit upright and keep her eyes open.

She suspected that she was more than a little punch-drunk.

After a while Zane said, "Red goggles."

She was tired enough that she wondered if that was some kind of code, or if she'd misunderstood him. Neither, evidently. Each man took a pair of goggles from his pack and donned them. Zane glanced at her and said in explanation, "Red protects your night vision. We're going to let our vision adjust now, before Bunny kills the headlights."

She nodded, and closed her eyes to help her own vision adjust. She realized at once that, if she wanted to stay awake, closing her eyes for whatever reason wasn't the smartest thing to do, but her eyelids were so heavy that she couldn't manage to open them again. The next thing she knew, the minibus was lurching heavily from side to side, throwing her against first Greenberg, then Spooky. Dazed with sleep, she tried to hold herself erect, but she couldn't seem to find her balance or anything to hold on to. She was about to slide to the floorboard when Spooky's forearm shot out in front of her like an iron bar, anchoring her in the seat.

"Thank you," she said groggily.

"Anytime, ma'am."

Sometime while she had been asleep, Bunny had indeed killed the headlights, and they were plunging down an embankment in the dark. She blinked at something shiny looming in front of them; she had a split second of panic and confusion before she recognized the sea, gleaming in the starlight.

The minibus lurched to a halt. "End of the line," Bunny cheerfully announced. "We have now reached the hidey-hole for one IBS. That's military talk for inflatable boat, small," he said over his shoulder to Barrie. "These things are too fancy to be called plain old rafts."

Zane snorted. Barrie remembered that he'd described it as exactly that, a raft.

Watching them exit the minibus was like watching quicksilver slip through cracks. If there had been a working overhead light when the SEALs had commandeered the vehicle, they had taken care of that detail, because no light came on when the doors were cracked open. Spooky slipped past her, no mean feat given the equipment he was carrying, and when Greenberg slid the side door open a few inches, Spooky wiggled on his stomach through the small opening. One second he was there, the next he was gone. Barrie stared at the door with widened eyes in full appreciation of how he'd acquired his nickname. He was definitely spooky.

The others exited the minibus in the same manner; it was as if they were made of water, and when the doors opened they simply leaked out. They were that fluid, that silent. Only Bunny, the driver, remained behind with Barrie. He sat in absolute silence, pistol in hand, as he methodically surveyed the night-shrouded coast. Because he was silent, she was too. The best way not to be any trouble to them, she thought, was to follow their example.

There was one quick little tap on the window, and Bunny whispered, "It's clear. Let's go, Miss Lovejoy."

She scooted over the seat to the door while Bunny eeled out on the driver's side. Zane was there, opening the door wider, reaching in to steady her as she slid out onto the ground. "Are you holding up okay?" he asked quietly.

She nodded, not trusting herself to speak, because she was so tired her speech was bound to be slurred.

As usual, he seemed to understand without being told. "Just hold on for another hour or so, and we'll have you safe on board the carrier. You can sleep then."

Without him, though; that fact didn't need stating. Even if he intended to continue their relationship, and he hadn't given any indication of it, he wouldn't do so on board the ship. She would put off sleeping forever if it would postpone the moment when she had to admit, once and for all, that their relationship had been a temporary thing for him, prompted by both the hothouse of intimacy in which they'd spent the day, and her own demands.

She wouldn't cry; she wouldn't even protest, she told herself. She'd had him for a day, for one incredibly sensual day.

He led her down to the small, rocky strip of beach, where the dark bulk of the IBS had been positioned. The other five men were gathered around it in specific positions, each standing with his back to the raft while he held his weapon at the ready, edgily surveying the surroundings.

Zane lifted her into the IBS and showed her where to sit. The IBS bobbed in the water as the men eased it away from the shore. When the water was chest deep on Santos, the shortest one, they all swung aboard in a maneuver they had practiced so many times it looked effortless. Spooky started the almost soundless motor and aimed the IBS for the open sea.

Then a roar erupted behind them, and all hell broke loose.

She recognized the sharp *rat-tat-tat* of automatic weap-

ons and half turned to look behind them. Zane put his
hand on her head and shoved her down to the bottom of
the boat, whirling, already bringing his automatic rifle
around as he did so. The IBS shot forward as Spooky
gave it full throttle. The SEALs returned fire, lightning
flashing from the weapons, spent cartridges splattering
down on her as she curled into a ball and drew the chador
over her face to keep the hot brass from burning her.

"Drexler!" Zane roared. "Hit those bastards with ex-
plosives!"

"Got it, boss!"

Barrie heard a grunt, and something heavy and human
fell across her. One of the men had been hit. Desperately
she tried to wriggle out from under the crushing weight
so she could help him, but she was effectively pinned,
and he groaned every time she moved.

She knew that groan.

Terror such as she had never felt before raced through
her veins. With a hoarse cry she heaved at the heavy
weight, managing to roll him to the side. She fought her
way free of the enveloping chador and didn't even notice
the hot cartridge shell that immediately skimmed her
right cheek.

An explosion shattered the night, lighting up the sea
like fireworks, the percussion knocking her to the bottom
of the boat again. She scrambled to her knees, reaching
for Zane. "No," she said hoarsely. "No!"

The light from the explosion had sharply delineated
every detail in stark white. Zane lay sprawled half on his
side, writhing in pain as he pressed his hands to his abdomen. His face was a colorless blur, his eyes closed, his
teeth exposed in a grimace. A huge wet patch glistened
on the left side of his black shirt, and more blood was
pooling beneath him.

Barrie grabbed the chador and wadded it up, pressing it hard to the wound. A low animal howl rattled in his throat, and he arched in pain. "Santos!" she screamed, trying to hold him down while still holding the chador in place. *"Santos!"*

With a muttered curse the stocky medic shouldered her aside. He lifted the chador for a second, then quickly pressed it into place and grabbed her hand, guiding it into position. "Hold it," he rapped out. "Press down—hard."

There was no more gunfire, only the hum of the motor. Salt spray lashed her face as the boat shot through the waves. The team maintained their discipline, holding their assigned positions. "How bad is it?" Greenberg yelled.

Santos was working feverishly. "I need light!"

Almost instantly Greenberg had a flashlight shining down on them. Barrie bit her lip as she saw how much blood had puddled around them. Zane's face was pasty white, his eyes half-shut as he gasped for breath.

"He's losing blood fast," Santos said. "Looks like the bullet got a kidney, or maybe his spleen. Get that damn helicopter on the way. We don't have time to get into international waters." He popped the cap off a syringe, straightened Zane's arm and deftly jabbed the needle into a vein. "Hang on, boss. We're gonna get you airlifted outta here."

Zane didn't reply. He was breathing noisily through his clenched teeth, but when Barrie glanced at him she could see the gleam of his eyes. His hand lifted briefly, touched her arm, then fell heavily to his side.

"Damn you, Zane Mackenzie," she said fiercely. "Don't you *dare*—" She broke off. She couldn't say the word, couldn't even admit to the possibility that he might die.

Santos was checking Zane's pulse. His eyes met hers, and she knew it was too fast, too weak. Zane was going into shock, despite the injection Santos had given him.

"I don't give a damn how close in we still are!" Greenberg was yelling into the radio. "We need a helo *now*. Just get the boss out of here and we'll wait for another ride!"

Despite the pitching of the boat, Santos got an IV line started and began squeezing a bag of clear plasma into Zane's veins. "Don't let up on the pressure," he muttered to Barrie.

"I won't." She didn't take her gaze off Zane's face. He was still aware, still looking at her. As long as that connection was maintained, he would be all right. He had to be.

The nightmare ride in the speeding boat seemed to take forever. Santos emptied the first bag of plasma and connected a second one to the IV. He was cursing under his breath, his invectives varied and explicit.

Zane lay quietly, though she knew he was in terrible pain. His eyes were dull with pain and shock, but she could sense his concentration, his determination. Perhaps the only way he could remain conscious was by focusing so intently on her face, but he managed it.

But if that helicopter didn't get there soon, not even his superhuman determination would be able to hold out against continued blood loss. She wanted to curse, too, wanted to glare at the night sky as if she could conjure a helicopter out of thin air, but she didn't dare look away from Zane. As long as their gazes held, he would hold on.

She heard the distinctive *whap-whap-whap* only a mo-

ment before the Sea King helicopter roared over them,
blinding lights picking them out. Spooky throttled back,
and the boat settled gently onto the water. The helicopter
circled to them and hovered directly overhead, the powerful rotors whipping the sea into a frenzy. A basket
dropped almost on their heads. Working swiftly, Santos
and Greenberg lifted Zane into the basket and strapped
him in, maneuvering around Barrie as she maintained
pressure on the wound.

Santos hesitated, then indicated for her to let go and
move back. Reluctantly she did. He lifted the chador,
then immediately jammed it back into place. Without a
word he straddled the basket, leaning hard on the wound.
''Let's go!'' he yelled. Greenberg stepped back and gave
the thumbs-up to the winch operator in the helicopter.
The basket rose toward the hovering monster, with Santos perched precariously on top of Zane. As the basket
drew even with the open bay, several pairs of hands
reached out and drew them inward. The helicopter immediately lifted away, banking hard, roaring toward the
carrier.

There was an eerie silence left behind. Barrie slumped
against one of the seats, her face rigid with the effort of
maintaining control. No one said a word. Spooky started
the motor again, and the little craft shot through the darkness, following the rapidly disappearing lights of the helicopter.

It was over an hour before the second helicopter settled
onto the deck of the huge carrier. The remaining four
members of the team leaped to the deck almost before
the helicopter had touched down. Barrie clambered after
them, ran with them. Greenberg had one hand clamped
on her arm to make certain she didn't get left behind.

Someone in a uniform stepped in front of them. "Miss Lovejoy, are you all right?"

Barrie gave him a distracted glance and dodged around him. Another uniform popped up, but this one was subtly different, as if the wearer belonged on board this gigantic ship. The first man had worn a dress uniform, marking him as a non-crew member. Greenberg skidded to a halt. "Captain—"

"Lieutenant-Commander Mackenzie is in surgery," the captain said. "Doc didn't think he'd make it to a base with such a high rate of blood loss. If they can't get the bleeding stopped, they'll have to remove his spleen."

The first uniformed officer had reached them. "Miss Lovejoy," he said firmly, taking her arm. "I'm Major Hodson. I'll escort you home."

The military moved at its own pace, to its own rules. She was to be taken home immediately; the ambassador wanted his daughter back. Barrie protested. She yelled, she cried, she even swore at the harried major. None of it did any good. She was hustled aboard another aircraft, this time a cargo transport plane. Her last glimpse of the *Montgomery* was as the sun's first rays glistened on the blue waters of the Mediterranean, and the sight was blurred by her tears.

Chapter 7

By the time the transport touched down in Athens, Barrie had cried so hard and for so long that her eyes were swollen almost shut. Major Hodson had tried everything to pacify her, then to console her; he assured her that he was just following orders, and that she would be able to find out how the SEAL was doing later. It was understandable that she was upset. She'd been through a lot, but she would have the best medical care—

At that, Barrie shot out of the uncomfortable web seat, which was all the transport plane afforded. "*I'm* not the one who was shot!" she yelled furiously. "I don't need medical care, best, worst or mediocre! I want to be taken to wherever Zane Mackenzie is taken. I don't care what your orders are!"

Major Hodson looked acutely uncomfortable. He tugged at the collar of his uniform. "Miss Lovejoy, I'm sorry. I can't do anything about this situation. After we're

on the ground and your father is satisfied that you're
okay, then where you go is up to you.''

His expression plainly said that as far as he was concerned, she could go to hell. Barrie sat down, breathing
hard and wiping away tears. She'd never acted like that
before in her life. She'd always been such a lady, a perfect hostess for her father.

She didn't feel at all ladylike now; she felt like a ferocious tigress, ready to shred anyone who got in her
way. Zane was severely wounded, perhaps dying, and
these *fools* wouldn't let her be with him. Damn military
procedure, and damn her father's influence, for they had
both wrenched her away from him.

As much as she loved her father, she knew she would
never forgive him if Zane died and she wasn't there. It
didn't matter that he didn't know about Zane; nothing
mattered compared to the enormous horror that loomed
before her. *God, don't let him die!* She couldn't bear it.
She would rather have died herself at her kidnappers'
hands than for Zane to be killed while rescuing her.

The flight took less than an hour and a half. The transport landed with a hard thump that jerked her in the web
seat, then taxied for what seemed like an interminable
length of time. Finally it rolled to a stop, and Major Hodson stood, plainly relieved to be free of his unpleasant
burden.

A door was slid open, and a flight of steps rolled up
to it. Clutching the black robe around her, Barrie stepped
out into the bright Athens sunlight. It was full morning
now, the heat already building. She blinked and lifted a
hand to shield her eyes. It felt like forever since she'd
been in the sunshine.

A gray limousine with darkly tinted windows was
waiting on the tarmac. The door was shoved open, and

her father bounded out, dignity forgotten as he ran forward. "Barrie!" Two days of worry and fear lined his face, but there was an almost desperate relief in his expression as he hurried up the steps to fold her in his arms.

She started crying again, or maybe she had never stopped. She buried her face against his suit, clutching him with desperate hands. "I've got to go back," she sobbed, the words barely intelligible.

He tightened his arms around her. "There, there, baby," he breathed. "You're safe now, and I won't let anything else happen to you, I swear. I'll take you home—"

Wildly she shook her head, trying to pull away from him. "No," she choked out. "I've got to get back to the *Montgomery*. Zane—he was shot. He might die. Oh, God, I've got to go back *now!*"

"Everything will be all right," he crooned, hustling her down the steps with an arm locked around her shoulders. "I have a doctor waiting—"

"I don't need a doctor!" she said fiercely, jerking away from him. She'd never done that before, and his face went blank with shock. She shoved her hair out of her face. The tangled mass hadn't been combed in two days, and it was matted with sweat and sea spray. "Listen to me! The man who rescued me was shot. *He might die.* He was still in surgery when Major Hodson forced me on board this plane. I want to go back to the ship. I want to make sure Zane is okay."

William Lovejoy firmly took hold of his daughter's shoulders again, leading her across the tarmac to the waiting limo. "You don't have to go back to the ship, sweetheart," he said soothingly. "I'll ask Admiral Lindley to find out how his man is doing. He *is* one of the SEAL team, I presume?"

Numbly she nodded.

"There wouldn't be any point in going back to the ship, I'm sure you can see that. If he survived surgery, he'll be airlifted to a military hospital."

If he survived surgery. The words were like a knife, hot and slicing, going through her. She balled her hands into fists, every cell in her body screaming for her to ignore logic, ignore the attempts to soothe her. She needed to get to Zane.

Three days later, she stood in her father's office with her chin high and her eyes colder than he'd ever seen them. "You told Admiral Lindley to block my requests," she accused.

The ambassador sighed. He removed his reading glasses and carefully placed them on the inlaid walnut desk. "Barrie, you know I've denied you very little that you've asked for, but you're being unreasonable about this man. You know that he's recovering, and that's all you need to know. What point would there be in rushing to his bedside? Some tabloid might find out about it, and then your ordeal would be plastered in sleazy newspapers all over the world. Is that what you want?"

"My ordeal?" she echoed. "*My* ordeal? What about his? He nearly died! That's assuming Admiral Lindley told me the truth, and he really is still alive!"

"Of course he is. I only asked Joshua to block any inquiries you made about his location." He unfolded his tall form from the chair and came around to lean against the desk and take her resistant hands in his. "Barrie, give yourself time to get over the trauma. I know you've invested this...this guerrilla fighter with all sorts of heroic characteristics, and that's only normal. After a while, when you've regained your perspective, you'll be glad you didn't embarrass yourself by chasing after him.''

It was almost impossible to contain the volcanic fury rising in her. Nobody was listening; no one wanted to listen. They kept going on and on about her ordeal, how she would heal in time, until she wanted to pull her hair out. She had insisted over and over that she hadn't been raped, but she had fiercely refused to be examined by a doctor, which of course had only fueled speculation that the kidnappers had indeed raped her. But she'd known her body bore the marks of Zane's lovemaking, marks and traces that were precious and private, for no one else's eyes. Everyone was treating her as if she was made of crystal, carefully not mentioning the kidnapping, until she thought she would go mad.

She wanted to see Zane. That was all. Just see him, assure herself that he would be all right. But when she'd asked one of the Marine officers stationed at the embassy to make some inquiries about Zane, it was Admiral Lindley who had gotten back to her instead of the captain.

The dignified, distinguished admiral had come to the ambassador's private quarters less than an hour before. Barrie hadn't yet returned to her minor job in the embassy, feeling that she couldn't keep her mind on paperwork, so she had received the admiral in the beautifully appointed parlor.

After polite conversation about her health and the weather, the admiral came to the point of his visit. ''You've been making some inquiries about Zane Mackenzie,'' he said kindly. ''I've kept abreast of his condition, and I can tell you now with complete confidence that he'll fully recover. The ship's surgeon was able to stop the bleeding, and it wasn't necessary to remove his spleen. His condition was stabilized, and he was trans-

ferred to a hospital. When he's able, he'll be sent State-
side for the remainder of his convalescence.''

"Where is he?'' Barrie had demanded, her eyes burning. She'd scarcely slept in three days. Though she was
once more impeccably clothed and coifed, the strain
she'd been under had left huge dark circles under her
eyes, and she was losing weight fast, because her nerves
wouldn't let her eat.

Admiral Lindley sighed. "William asked me to keep
that information from you, Barrie, and I have to say, I
think he's right. I've known Zane a long time. He's an
extraordinary warrior. But SEALs are a breed apart, and
the characteristics that make them such great warriors
don't, as a whole, make them model citizens. They're
trained weapons, to put it bluntly. They don't keep high
profiles, and most information about them is restricted.''

"I don't want to know about his training,'' she said,
her voice strained. "I don't want to know about his missions. I just want to see him.''

The admiral shook his head. "I'm sorry.''

Nothing she said budged him. He refused to give her
even one more iota of information. Still, Zane was alive;
he would be all right. Just knowing that made her feel
weak inside, as the unbearable tension finally relaxed.

That didn't mean she would forgive her father for interfering.

"I love him,'' she now said deliberately. "You have
no right to keep me from seeing him.''

"Love?'' Her father gave her a pitying look. "Barrie,
what you feel isn't love, it's hero-worship. It will fade, I
promise you.''

"Do you think I haven't considered that?'' she fired
back. "I'm not a teenager with a crush on a rock star.
Yes, I met him under dangerous, stressful circumstances.

Yes, he saved my life—and he nearly died doing it. I know what infatuation is, and I know what love is, but even if I didn't, the decision isn't yours to make.''

"You've always been reasonable," he argued. "At least concede that your judgment may not be at its sharpest right now. What if you acted impulsively, married this man—I'm sure he'd jump at the chance—and then realized that you really didn't love him? Think what a mess it would be. I know it sounds snobbish, but he isn't our kind. He's a sailor, and a trained killer. You've dined with kings and danced with princes. What could the two of you have in common?''

"First, that doesn't just *sound* snobbish, it *is* snobbish. Second, you must not think much of me as a person if you consider your money my only attraction.''

"You know that isn't what I meant," he said, genuinely shocked. "You're a wonderful person. But how could someone like that appreciate the life you live? How do you know he wouldn't have his eye on the main chance?''

"Because I know him," she declared. "I know him in a way I never would have if I'd met him at an embassy party. According to you, a SEAL couldn't be kind and considerate, but he was. They all were, for that matter. Dad, I've told you over and over that I wasn't raped. I know you don't believe me, and I know you've suffered, worrying about me. But I swear to you—I *swear*—that I wasn't. They were planning to, the next day, but they were waiting for someone. So, though I was terrified and upset, I haven't been through the trauma of a gang rape the way you keep thinking. Seeing Zane lying in a pool of blood was a hell of a lot more traumatic than anything those kidnappers did!''

"Barrie!" It was the first time her father had ever

heard her curse. Come to think of it, she had never cursed at all, until rough men had grabbed her off the street and subjected her to hours of terror. She had cursed them, and meant it. She had cursed Major Hodson, and meant that, too.

With an effort, she regulated her tone. "You know that the first attempt to get me out didn't quite work."

He gave an abrupt nod. He'd suffered agonies, thinking their only hope of rescuing her had failed and imagining what she must be suffering. That was when he'd given up hope of ever seeing her alive again. Admiral Lindley hadn't been as pessimistic; the SEALs hadn't checked in, and though there were reports of gunfire in Benghazi, if a team of SEALs had been killed or captured, the Libyan government would have trumpeted it all over the world. That meant they were still there, still working to free her. Until they heard from the team that the rescue had failed, there was still hope.

"Well, it did work, in a way. Zane came in alone to get me, while the rest of the team was a diversion, I guess, in case things went wrong. He had a backup plan, what to do if they were spotted, because you can't control the human factor." She realized she was repeating things Zane had said to her during those long hours when they had lain drowsily together, and she missed him so much that pain knotted her insides. "The team was so well-hidden that one of the guards didn't see Spooky until he actually stepped on him. That's what gave the alarm and started the shooting. A guard had been posted in the corridor outside the room where they had me tied up, and he ran in. Zane killed him," she said simply. "Then, while the others were chasing the team, he got me out of the building. We were separated from the team and had to hide for a day, but I was safe."

The ambassador listened gravely, soaking up these details of how she had been returned to him. They hadn't talked before, not about the actual rescue. She had been too distraught about Zane, almost violent in her despair. Now that she knew he was alive, even though she was still so angry she could barely contain it, she was able to tell her father how she had been returned to him alive.

"While I stayed in our hiding place, Zane risked his life by going out and stealing food and water for us, as well as the robe and chador for me. He took care of the cut on my foot. When scavengers were practically dismantling the place around us, he kept himself between me and any danger. That's the man I fell in love with, that's the man you say isn't 'our kind.' He may not be yours, but he's definitely mine!"

The expression in her father's eyes was stunned, almost panicked. Too late, Barrie saw that she had chosen the wrong tack in her argument. If she had presented her concern for Zane as merely for someone who had done so much for her, if she had insisted that it was only right she thank him in person, her father could have been convinced. He was very big on preserving the niceties, on behaving properly. Instead, she had convinced him that she truly loved Zane Mackenzie, and too late she saw how much he had feared exactly that. He didn't want to lose her, and now Zane presented a far bigger threat than before.

"Barrie, I..." He fumbled to a stop, her urbane, sophisticated father who was never at a loss for words. He swallowed hard. It was true that he'd seldom denied her anything, and those times he had refused had been because he thought the activity she planned or the object she wanted—once it had been a motorcycle—wasn't safe. Keeping her safe was his obsession, that and holding tightly to his only remaining family, his beloved child, who so closely resembled the wife he'd lost.

She saw it in his eyes as his instinct to pamper her with anything she desired warred with the knowledge that this time, if he did, he would probably lose her from his life. He didn't want occasional visits from her; they had both endured that kind of separation during her school years. He wanted her *there,* in his everyday life. She knew part of his obsession was selfish, because she made domestic matters very easy for him, but she had never doubted his love for her.

Pure panic flashed in his expression. He said stiffly, "I still think you need to give yourself time for your emotions to calm. And surely you realize that the conditions you describe are what that man is *used* to. How could he ever fit into your life?"

"That's a moot question, since marriage or even a relationship was never discussed. I want to see him. I don't want him to think that I didn't care enough even to check on his condition."

"If any sort of relationship was never discussed, why would he expect you to visit him? It was a mission for him, nothing more."

Barrie's shoulders were military straight, her jaw set, her green eyes dark with emotion. "It was more," she said flatly, and that was as much of what had happened between her and Zane as she was willing to discuss. She took a deep breath and pulled out the heavy artillery. "You owe it to me," she said, her gaze locked with his. "I haven't asked any details about what happened here, but I'm an intelligent, logical person—"

"Of course you are," he interrupted, "but I don't see—"

"Was there a ransom demanded?" She cut across his interruption.

He was a trained diplomat; he seldom lost control of his expression. But now, startled, the look he gave her was blank with puzzlement. "A ransom?" he echoed.

A new despair knotted itself in her stomach, etched itself in her face. "Yes, ransom," she said softly. "There wasn't one, was there? Because money wasn't what *he* wanted. He wants something from you, doesn't he? Information. He's either trying to force you to give it to him, or you're already in it up to your eyebrows and you've had a falling out with him. Which is it?"

Again his training failed him; for a split second his face revealed panicked guilt and consternation before his expression smoothed into diplomatic blandness. "What a ridiculous charge," he said calmly.

She stood there, sick with knowledge. If the kidnapper had been using her as a weapon to force her father into betraying his country, the ambassador most likely would have denied it, because he wouldn't want her to be worried, but that wasn't what she'd read in his face. It was guilt.

She didn't bother responding to his denial. "You owe me," she repeated. "You owe Zane."

He flinched at the condemnation in her eyes. "I don't see it that way at all."

"You're the reason I was kidnapped."

"You know there are things I can't tell you," he said, releasing her hands and walking around the desk to resume his seat, symbolically leaving the role of father and entering that of ambassador. "But your supposition is wrong, and, of course, an indication of how off-balance you still are."

She started to ask if Art Sandefer would think her supposition was so wrong, but she couldn't bring herself to threaten her father. Feeling sick, she wondered if that made her a traitor, too. She loved her country; living in Europe as much as she had, she had seen and appreciated the dramatic differences between the United States and every other country on earth. Though she liked Europe and had a fondness for French wine, German architecture, English orderliness, Spanish music and Italy in general, whenever she set foot in the States she was struck by the energy, the richness of life where even people who were considered poor lived well compared to everywhere else. The United States wasn't perfect, far from it, but it had something special, and she loved it.

By her silence, she could be betraying it.

By staying here, she remained in danger. Kidnapping her had failed once, but that didn't mean *he,* the unknown, faceless enemy, wouldn't try again. Her father knew who *he* was, she was certain of it. Immediately she saw how it would be. She would be confined to the embassy grounds, or allowed out only with an armed escort. She would be a prisoner of her father's fear.

There was really no place she would be entirely safe, but remaining here only made the danger more acute. And once she was away from the enclave of the embassy, she would have a better chance of locating Zane, because Admiral Lindley's influence couldn't cover every nook and cranny of the globe. The farther away from Athens she was, the thinner that influence would be.

She faced her father, knowing that she was deliberately breaking the close ties that had bound them together for the past fifteen years. "I'm going home," she said calmly. "To Virginia."

*   *   *

Two weeks later, Zane sat on the front porch of his parents' house, perched on top of Mackenzie's Mountain, just outside Ruth, Wyoming. The view was breathtaking, an endless vista of majestic mountains and green valleys. Everything here was as familiar to him as his own hands. Saddles, boots, some cattle but mostly horses. Books in every room of the sprawling house, cats prowling through the barns and stables, his mother's sweet, bossy coddling, his father's concern and understanding.

He'd been shot before; he'd been sliced up in a knife fight. He'd had his collarbone broken, ribs cracked, a lung punctured. He had been seriously injured before, but this was the closest he'd ever come to dying. He'd been bleeding to death, lying there in the bottom of the raft with Barrie crouched over him, pressing the chador over the wound with every ounce of her weight. Her quickness, her determination, had made the difference. Santos squeezing the plasma from the bags into his veins had made the difference. He had been so close that he could pick out a dozen details that had made the difference; if any one of them hadn't happened, he would have died.

He'd been unusually quiet since leaving the naval hospital and returning home for convalescence. It wasn't that he was in low spirits, but rather that he had a lot of thinking to do, something that hadn't been easy when practically the entire family had felt compelled to visit and reassure themselves of his relative well-being. Joe had flown in from Washington for a quick check on his baby brother; Michael and Shea had visited several times, bringing their two rapscallion sons with them; Josh and Loren and their three had descended for a weekend visit, which was all the time Loren's job at the hospital in Seattle had allowed. Maris had driven all night to be there when he was brought home. At least he'd been able to walk on his own by then, even if very slowly, or likely

she would still be here. She had pulled up a chair directly
in front of him and sat for hours, her black eyes locked
on his face as if she was willing vitality from her body
into his. Maybe she had been. His little sister was fey,
magical; she operated on a different level than other people did.

Hell, even Chance had shown up. He'd done so warily,
eyeing their mother and sister as if they were bombs that
might go off in his face, but he was here, sitting beside
Zane on the porch.

"You're thinking of resigning."

Zane didn't have to wonder how Chance had known
what was on his mind. After nearly battering each other
to death when they were fourteen, they had reached an
unusual communion. Maybe it was because they'd shared
so much, from classes to girls to military training. Even
after all this time, Chance was as wary as a wounded
wolf and didn't like people to get close to him, but even
though he resisted, he was helpless against family.
Chance had never in his life been loved until Mary had
brought him home with her and the sprawling, brawling
Mackenzies had knocked him flat. It was fun to watch
him still struggle against the family intimacy each time
he was drawn into the circle, because within an hour he
always surrendered. Mary wouldn't let him do anything
else; nor would Maris. After accepting him as a brother,
Zane had never even acknowledged Chance's wariness.
Only Wolf was willing to give his adopted son time to
adjust—but there was still a limit on how much time he
would allow.

"Yeah," he finally said.

"Because you nearly bought it this time?"

Zane snorted. "When has that ever made any difference to either of us?" He alone of the family knew the

exact details of Chance's work. It was a toss-up which of them was in the most danger.

"Then it's this last promotion that did it."

"It took me out of the field," Zane said quietly. Carefully he leaned back in the chair and propped his booted feet on the porch railing. Though he was a fast healer, two and a half weeks wasn't quite long enough to let him ignore the wound. "If two of my men hadn't been wounded in that screwup on the *Montgomery,* I wouldn't have been able to go on this last mission."

Chance knew about the screwup. Zane had told him about it, and screwup was the most polite description he'd used. As soon as he'd regained consciousness in the naval hospital, he'd been on the phone, starting and directing the investigation. Though Odessa would fully recover, it was likely Higgins would have to retire on disability. The guards who had shot the two SEALs might escape court-martial if their counsel was really slick, but at the very least they would be cashiered out of the service. The extent of the damage to the careers of Captain Udaka and Executive Officer Boyd remained to be seen; Zane had targeted the shooters, but the ripple effect would go all the way up to the captain.

"I'm thirty-one," Zane said. "That's just about the upper limit for active missions. I'm too damn good at my job, too. The Navy keeps promoting me for it, then they say I'm too highly ranked to go on missions."

"You want to throw in with me?" Chance asked casually.

He'd considered it. Very seriously. But something kept nagging at him, something he couldn't quite bring into focus.

"I want to. If things were different, I would, but..."

"What things?"

Zane shrugged. At least part of his uneasy feeling could be nailed down. "A woman," he said.

"Oh, hell." Chance kicked back and surveyed the world over the toes of his boots. "If it's a woman, you won't be able to concentrate on anything until you've gotten her out of your system. Damn their sweet little hides," he said fondly. Chance generally had women crawling all over him. It didn't hurt that he was drop-dead handsome, but he had a raffish, daredevil quality to him that brought them out of the woodwork.

Zane wasn't certain he could get Barrie out of his system. He wasn't certain he wanted to. He didn't wonder why she had disappeared without even saying goodbye, hope you're feeling better. Bunny and Spook had told him how she'd been dragged, kicking and yelling and swearing, aboard a plane and taken back to Athens. He figured her father, combined with the Navy's policy of secrecy concerning the SEALs, had prevented her from finding out to which hospital they'd taken him.

He missed her. He missed her courage, her sturdy willingness to do whatever needed doing. He missed the serenity of her expression, and the heat of her lovemaking.

God, yes.

The one memory, more than any of the others, that was branded in his brain was the moment when she had reached for his belt and said in that fierce whisper, "I'll do it!"

He'd understood. Not just why she needed to be in control, but the courage it took her to wipe out the bad memories and replace them with good ones. She'd been a virgin; she had told the truth about that. She hadn't known what to do, and she hadn't expected the pain. But she had taken him anyway, sweetly, hotly, sliding her tight little body down on him and shattering his control the way no other woman had ever done.

She could have been a spoiled, helpless little socialite; she *should* have been exactly that. Instead she had made the best of a tense, dangerous situation, done what she could to help and hadn't voiced a single complaint.

He liked being with her, liked talking to her. He was too much of a loner to easily accept the word love in connection with anyone other than family, but with Barrie…maybe. He wanted to spend more time with her, get to know her better, let whatever would develop get to developing.

He wanted her.

First things first, though. He had to get his strength back; right now he could walk from room to room without aid, but he would think twice about heading down to the stables by himself. He had to decide whether or not he was going to stay in the Navy; it felt like time to be moving on, since the reason he'd joined in the first place was being taken away from him as he moved up the ranks. If he wasn't going to remain a SEAL, then what would he do for a living? He had to decide, had to get his life settled.

Barrie might not be interested in any kind of relationship with him, though from the way Spook and Bunny had described her departure, he didn't think that was the case. The day of lovemaking they had shared had been more than propinquity for both of them.

Getting in touch with her could take some doing, though. That morning he had placed a call to the embassy in Athens. He'd given his name and asked to speak to Barrie Lovejoy. It had been Ambassador William Lovejoy who had come on the line, however, and the conversation hadn't been cordial.

"It isn't that Barrie doesn't appreciate what you did, but I'm sure you understand that she wants to put all of that behind her. Talking with you would bring it all back and needlessly upset her," the ambassador had said in a cool, well-bred voice, his diction the best money could buy.

"Is that her opinion, or yours?" Zane had asked, his tone arctic.

"I don't see that it matters," the ambassador had replied, and hung up.

Zane decided he would let it rest for now. He wasn't in any shape to do much about it, so he would wait. When he had his mind made up about what he was going to do, there would be plenty of time to get in touch with Barrie, and now that he knew the ambassador had given orders for his calls not to be routed to her, the next time he would be prepared to do an end run around her father.

"Zane," his mother called from inside the house, pulling his thoughts to the present. "Are you getting tired?"

"I feel fine," he called back. It was an exaggeration, but he wasn't unduly tired. He glanced at Chance and saw the smirk on his brother's face.

"With all the worry about you, she forgot about my cracked ribs," Chance whispered.

"Glad to be of service," Zane drawled. "Just don't expect me to get shot every time you bang yourself up a little." The entire family thought it was hilarious the way Chance reacted to Mary's coddling and fussing, as if the attention terrified him, even though he was never able to resist her. Chance was putty in Mary's hands, but then, they all were. They'd grown up with the fine example of their father to emulate, and Wolf Mackenzie might growl and stomp, but Mary usually got her way.

"Chance?"

Zane controlled a grin as Chance stiffened, the smirk disappearing from his face as if it had never been.

"Ma'am?" he answered cautiously.

"Are you still keeping a pressure wrap on your ribs?"

That familiar panicked expression was in his eyes now. "Ah...no, ma'am." He could have lied; Mary would have believed him. But none of them ever lied to her, even when it was in their best interests. It would hurt the little tyrant's feelings too much if she ever discovered any of her kids had lied to her.

"You know you're supposed to wrap them for another week," said the voice from inside the house. It was almost like hearing God speak, except this voice was light and sweet and liquidly Southern.

"Yes, ma'am."

"Come inside and let me take care of that."

"Yes, ma'am," Chance said again, resignation in his voice. He got up from his rocking chair and went into the house. As he passed Zane, he muttered, "Getting shot didn't work. Try something else."

Chapter 8

Two months later, Sheriff Zane Mackenzie stood naked at the window of the pleasant two-bedroom Spanish-style house he had bought in southern Arizona. He was staring out over the moonlit desert, something wild and hot running through him at the sight. His SEAL training had taught him how to adapt to any environment, and the hot, dry climate didn't bother him.

Once he'd made up his mind to resign his commission, things had rapidly fallen into place. Upon hearing that he was leaving the Navy, a former SEAL team member who was now on the governor's staff in Phoenix had called and asked if he would be interested in serving the remaining two years of the term of a sheriff who had died in office.

At first Zane had been taken aback; he'd never considered going into law enforcement. Moreover, he didn't know anything about Arizona state laws.

''Don't worry about it,'' his friend had said breezily.

"Sheriff is a political position, and most of the time it's more administrative than anything else. The situation you'd be going into is more hands-on, though. A couple of the deputies have quit, so you'd be shorthanded until some more can be hired, and the ones still there will resent the hell out of you because one of them wasn't appointed to finish out the sheriff's term."

"Why not?" Zane asked bluntly. "What's wrong with the chief deputy?"

"She's one of the ones who quit. She left a couple of months before the sheriff died, took a job on the force in Prescott."

"None of the others are qualified?"

"I wouldn't say that."

"Then what would you say?"

"You gotta understand, there's not a lot of selection here. A couple of the young deputies are good, real good, but they're *too* young, not enough experience. The one twenty-year guy isn't interested. A fifteen-year guy is a jerk, and the rest of the deputies hate his guts."

Sheriff. Zane thought about it, growing more intrigued with the idea. He had no illusions about it being a cakewalk. He would have difficulties with the fifteen-year veteran, at least, and likely all the other deputies would have some reservations and resistance about someone from the outside being brought in. Hell, he liked it better that way. Cakewalks didn't interest him. He'd rather have a challenging job any day. "Okay, I'm interested. What does it involve?"

"A lot of headache, mostly. The pay's decent, the hours are lousy. A reservation sits on part of the county, so you'll have to deal with the BIA. There's a big problem with illegal immigrants, but that's for the INS to worry about. Generally, this isn't a high crime area. Not enough people.''

So here he was, his strength back, the owner of a house and a hundred acres of land, newly sworn in as sheriff. He'd brought in a few of his horses from his parents' place in Wyoming. It was a hell of a change from the Navy.

It was time to see about Barrie. He'd thought about her a lot over the past few months, but lately he couldn't think about anything else. The uneasy feeling was persisting, growing stronger. He'd put his resources to work, and to his surprise found that she'd left Athens within a week of being returned there. She was currently living at the Lovejoy private residence in Arlington, Virginia. Moreover, last month the ambassador had abruptly asked to be replaced, and he, too, had returned to Virginia. Zane wished Mr. Lovejoy had remained in Athens, but his presence was a problem that could be handled.

No matter what her father did or said, Zane was determined to see Barrie. There was unfinished business between them, a connection that had been abruptly cut when he'd been shot and she had been forced aboard a flight to Athens. He knew the hot intimacy of those long hours together could have been a product of stress and propinquity, but at this point, he didn't give a damn. There were other considerations, ones he couldn't ignore. That was why he had a flight out of Tucson to Washington in the morning. He needed to be sleeping, but one thought kept going around and around in his head. She was pregnant.

He couldn't say why he was so convinced of it. It was a gut feeling, an intuition, even a logical conclusion. There hadn't been any means of birth control available; they had made love several times. Put the two facts together, and the possibility of pregnancy existed. He didn't think it was a mere possibility, though; he thought it was a fact.

Barrie was going to have his baby.

The rush of fierce possessiveness he felt was like a tidal wave, sweeping away all his cautious plans. There wouldn't be any gradual getting-to-know-each-other stage, no easing into the idea of a serious relationship. If she was pregnant, they would get married immediately. If she didn't like the idea, he would convince her. It was as simple as that.

She was pregnant. Barrie hugged the precious knowledge to herself, not ready yet to let anyone else know, certainly not her father. The kidnapping and the aftermath had driven a wedge between them that neither of them could remove. He was desperate to restore their former relationship; nothing else could have induced him to resign from a post, an action that could have had serious repercussions for his career if it hadn't generally been thought that he had resigned because she had been so traumatized by the kidnapping that she couldn't remain in Athens and he wanted to be with her.

She tried not to think about whatever he might be involved in, because it hurt. It hurt horribly that he might be a traitor. Part of her simply couldn't believe it; he was an old-fashioned man, a man to whom honor wasn't just a word but a way of life. She had no proof, only logic and her own deductions…that, and the expression he hadn't quite been able to hide when she had asked him directly if he was involved in anything that might have resulted in her being kidnapped.

It also hurt horribly that he had kept her from Zane. She had made inquiries once she reached Virginia, but once again she had collided with a stone wall. No one would give her any information at all about him. She had even contacted SEAL headquarters and been politely stonewalled again. At least with the SEALs it was probably policy to safeguard the team members' identities and location, given the sensitive nature of the antiterrorism unit.

She was having his baby. She wanted him to know about it. She wouldn't expect anything of him that he didn't want to give, but she wanted him to know about his child. And she desperately wanted to see him again. She was adrift and lonely and frightened, her emotions in turmoil, and she needed some security in that part of her life, at least. He wasn't the kind of man who would blithely walk away from his offspring and ignore their existence. This baby would be a permanent link between them, something she could count on.

She doubted her father would relent concerning Zane even if he knew about the baby; his possessiveness would probably extend to a grandchild, even an illegitimate one. He would take steps to keep her pregnancy quiet, and even when the news got around, as it inevitably would, people would assume it was a child of rape, and they would look at her pityingly and talk about how brave she was.

She thought she would go mad. She had escaped to Virginia only to have her father follow. He panicked if she went anywhere unescorted. She had her own car, but he didn't want her driving it; he wanted his driver to take her wherever she wanted to go. She had had to sneak to a pharmacy to buy a home pregnancy test, though she had been sure fairly early on that she was pregnant. The test had merely confirmed what her body had already told her.

Barrie knew she should be worried and upset about this unplanned pregnancy, but it was the only thing in her life right now that made her happy. She was intensely lonely; the kidnapping and the long hours alone with Zane had set her apart from the other people in her life. She had memories they couldn't share, thoughts and needs no one could understand. Zane had been there with her; he would have understood her occasional pensiveness, her reticence in talking about it. It wasn't that she was secretive, for she would have liked to talk to someone who understood. But what she had shared with Zane was like a combat experience, forming a unique bond between the people who had lived it.

She wouldn't be able to keep her pregnancy secret much longer; she had to arrange prenatal care, and all telephone calls were now recorded. She supposed she could sneak out again and set up a doctor's appointment from a pay phone, but she would be damned if she would.

Enough was enough. She was an adult, and soon to be a mother. She hated the fact that her relationship with her father had deteriorated to the point where they barely spoke, but she couldn't find a way to mend it. As long as the possibility of his involvement in treasonous activities remained, she was helpless. She wanted him to explain, to give her a plausible reason why she had been kidnapped. She wanted to stop looking over her shoulder every time she went out; she didn't want to feel as if she truly *needed* to be guarded. She wanted to live a normal life. She didn't want to raise her baby in an atmosphere of fear.

But that was exactly the atmosphere that permeated the house. It was stifling her. She had to get away, had to remove herself from the haunting fear that, as long as her father was involved in whatever had given him such a guilty expression, she could be kidnapped again. The very thought made her want to vomit, and she didn't have just herself to worry about now. She had her baby to protect.

The fatigue of early pregnancy had gotten her into the habit of sleeping late, but one morning she woke early, disturbed by a pair of raucous birds fighting for territory in the tree outside her window. Once she was awake, nausea soon followed, and she made her usual morning dash to the bathroom. Also as usual, when the bout of morning sickness had passed, she felt fine. She looked out the window at the bright morning and realized she was inordinately hungry, the first time in weeks that the idea of food was appealing.

It was barely six o'clock, too early for Adele, the cook, to have arrived. Breakfast was normally at eight, and she had been sleeping past that. Her stomach growled. She couldn't wait another two hours for something to eat.

She put on her robe and slippers and quietly left her room; her father's bedroom was at the top of the stairs, and she didn't want to disturb him. Even more, she didn't want him to join her for an awkward tête-à-tête. He tried so hard to carry on as if nothing had happened, and she couldn't respond as she had before.

He should still be asleep, she thought, but when she reached the top of the stairs she heard him saying something she couldn't understand. She paused, wondering if he'd heard her after all and had been calling out to her. Then she heard him say *Mack* in a sharp tone, and she froze.

A chill roughened her entire body, and the bottom dropped out of her stomach. The only Mack she knew was Mack Prewett, but why would her father be talking to him? Mack Prewett was still stationed in Athens, as far as she knew, and since her father had resigned, he shouldn't have had any reason to be talking to him.

Then her heart leaped wildly as another possibility occurred to her. Perhaps he had been saying *Mackenzie* and she'd heard only the first syllable. Maybe he was talking about Zane. If she listened, she might find out where he was, or at least *how* he was. With no additional information about his condition, it had been hard to believe Admiral Lindley's assurance that he would fully recover. Belief required trust, and she no longer trusted the admiral, or her father.

She crept closer to his door and put her ear against it.

"—finished soon," he was saying sharply, then he was silent for a moment. "I didn't bargain on this. Barrie wasn't supposed to be involved. Get it wrapped up, Mack."

Barrie closed her eyes in despair. The chill was back, even colder than before. She shook with it, and swallowed hard against the return of nausea. So he *was* involved, he and Mack Prewett both. Mack was CIA. Was he a double agent, and if so, for whom? The world situation wasn't like it had been back in the old days of the Cold War, when the lines had been clearly drawn. Nations had died since then, and new ones taken their place. Religion or money seemed to be the driving force behind most differences these days; how would her father and Mack Prewett fit into that? What information would her father have that Mack wouldn't?

The answer eluded her. It could be anything. Her father had friends in every country in Europe, and any variety of confidential information could come his way. What didn't make sense was why he would sell that information; he was already a wealthy man. But money, to some people, was as addictive as a narcotic. No amount was ever enough; they had to have more, then still more, always looking for the next hit in the form of cash and the power that went with it.

Could she have been so wrong in her judgment of him? Had she still been looking at him with a child's eyes, seeing only her father, the man who had been the security in her life, instead of a man whose ambitions had tainted his honor?

Blindly she stumbled to her bedroom, not caring if he heard her. He must still have been engrossed in his conversation, though, or she didn't make as much noise as she thought she had, because his door remained closed.

She curled up on the bed, protectively folding herself around the tiny embryo in her womb.

What was it he hadn't bargained on? The kidnapping? That was over two months in the past. Had there been a new threat to use her as a means of ensuring he did something?

She was helplessly fumbling around in the dark with these wild conjectures, and she hated it. It was like being in alien territory, with no signs to guide her. What was she supposed to do? Take her suspicions to the FBI? She had nothing concrete to go on, and over the years her father had made a lot of contacts in the FBI; who could she trust there?

Even more important, if she stayed here, was she in danger? Maybe her wild conjectures weren't wild at all. She had seen a lot during her father's years in foreign service and noticed even more when she had started working at the embassy. Things happened, skulduggery went on, dangerous situations developed. Given the kidnapping, her father's reaction and now his unreasonable attitude about her safety, she didn't think she could afford to assume everything would be okay.

She had to leave.

Feverishly she began trying to think of someplace she could go where it wouldn't be easy to find her, and how she could get there without leaving a paper trail that would lead a halfway competent terrorist straight to her. Meanwhile, Mack Prewett wasn't a halfway competent bureaucrat, he was frighteningly efficient; he was like a spider, with webs of contacts spreading out in all directions. If she booked a flight using her real name, or paid for it with a credit card, he would know.

To truly hide, she had to have cash, a lot of it. That meant emptying her bank account, but how could she get there without her father knowing? It had reached the point where she would have to climb out the window and walk to the nearest pay phone to call a cab.

Maybe the house was already being watched.

She moaned and covered her face with her hands. Oh, God, this was making her paranoid, but did she dare *not* suspect anything? As some wit had observed, even paranoids had enemies.

She had to think of the baby. No matter how paranoid an action seemed, she had to err on the side of safety. If she had to dress in dark clothing, slither out a window in the wee hours of the morning and crawl across the ground until she was well away from this house...as ridiculous as it sounded, she would do it. Tonight? The sooner she got away, the better.

Tonight.

That decision made, she took a deep breath and tried to think of the details. She would have to carry some clothing. She would take her checkbook and bank book, so she could close out both her checking and savings accounts. She would take her credit cards and get as much cash as she could on them; everything together would give her a hefty amount, close to half a million dollars. How would she carry that much money? She would need an empty bag.

This was beginning to sound ludicrous, even to her. How was she supposed to crawl across the lawn in the darkness, dragging two suitcases behind her?

Think! she fiercely admonished herself. Okay, she wouldn't have to carry either clothes or suitcases with her. All she would need to carry was her available cash, which was several hundred dollars, her checkbook and savings account book, and her credit cards, which she would destroy after they had served their purpose. She could buy new clothes and makeup, as well as what luggage she would immediately need, as soon as a discount store opened. She could buy do-it-yourself hair coloring and dye her red hair brown, though not until after she had been to the bank. She didn't want the teller to be able to describe her disguise.

With cash in her possession, she would have several options. She could hop on Amtrak and go in any direction, then get off the train before her ticketed destination. Then she could buy a cheap used car, pay cash for it, and no one would know where she went from there. To be on the safe side, she would drive that car for only one day, then trade it in on a better car, again paying cash.

These were drastic measures, but doable. She still wasn't certain she wasn't being ridiculous, but did she dare bet that way, when her life, and that of her child, could hang in the balance? *Desperate times call for desperate measures.* Who had said that? Perhaps an eighteenth-century revolutionary; if so, she knew how he had felt. She had to disappear as completely as possible. She would mail her father a postcard before she left town, letting him know that she was all right but that she thought it would be better to get away for a while, otherwise he would think she had indeed been kidnapped again, and he would go mad with grief and terror. She couldn't do that to him. She still loved him very much, even after all he had done. Again a wave of disbelief and uncertainty hit her. It seemed so impossible that he would sell information to terrorists, so opposite to the man she had always known him to be. She was aware that he wasn't universally well liked, but the worst accusation she had ever heard leveled against him was that he was a snob, which even she admitted was accurate. He was very effective as a diplomat and ambassador, working with the CIA, which was of course set up in every embassy, using his social standing and contacts to smooth the way whenever a problem cropped up. He had personally been acquainted with the last six presidents, and prime ministers called him a friend. This man was a traitor?

It couldn't be. If she had only herself to consider, she would give him the benefit of the doubt.

But there was the baby, the tiny presence undetectable to any but herself. She could feel it in her breasts, which had become so tender she was always aware of them, and in the increased sensitivity and pressure low down in her abdomen, as her womb began to swell with amniotic fluid and increased blood flow. It was almost a hot feeling, as if the new life forming within her was generating heat with the effort of development.

Zane's baby.

She would do anything, no matter how Draconian, to keep it safe. She had to find some secure place where she could get the prenatal care she needed. She would have to change her name, get a new driver's license and a new social security card; she didn't know how these last two would be accomplished, but she would find out. There were always shady characters who could tell her. The driver's license could be forged, but the social security card would have to come through the regular administration. Even though social security was being phased out, until it was completely gone, everyone still had to have a number in order to get a legitimate job.

There was something else to consider. It would be stupid of her to live off her cash until it was all gone. She would need a job, anything that paid enough to keep a roof over their heads and food in their stomachs. She had degrees in art and history, but she wouldn't be able to use her own name, so she wouldn't be able to use those degrees to get a teaching job.

She didn't know what the job situation would be wherever she settled; she would simply have to wait and see. It didn't matter what she did, waiting tables or office work, she would take whatever was available.

She glanced at the clock: seven-thirty. Nerves notwithstanding, she was acutely hungry now, to the point of being sick with it. Her pregnant body had its own agenda, ignoring upset emotions and concentrating only on the business at hand.

The thought brought a smile to her face. It was almost as if the baby was already stomping a tiny foot and demanding what it wanted.

Tenderly she pressed her hand over her belly, feeling a slight firmness that surely hadn't been there before. "All right," she whispered to it. "I'll feed you."

She showered and dressed, mentally preparing herself to face her father without giving anything away. When she entered the breakfast room, he looked up with an expression of delight, quickly tempered by caution. "Well, it's a pleasure to have your company," he said, folding the newspaper and laying it aside.

"Some birds woke me up," she said, going to the buffet to help herself to toast and eggs. She fought a brief spell of nausea at the sight of sausage and changed her mind about the eggs, settling on toast and fruit. She hoped that would be enough to satisfy the demanding little creature.

"Coffee?" her father asked as she sat down. He already had the silver carafe in his hand, poised to pour.

"No, not today," she said hastily, as her stomach again clenched warningly. "I've been drinking too much caffeine lately, so I'm trying to cut down." That was a direct lie. She had stopped drinking anything with caffeine in it as soon as she suspected she might be pregnant, but it was as if her system was still warning her against it. "I'll drink orange juice." So far, that hadn't turned her stomach.

She applied herself to her food, replying civilly to his conversational gambits, but she couldn't bring herself to wholeheartedly enter into a discussion with him the way she once would have done. She could barely look at him, afraid her feelings would be plain on her face. She didn't want him any more alert than he already was.

"I'm having lunch with Congressman Garth," he told her. "What are your plans for the day?"

"None," she replied. Her plans were all for the night.

He looked relieved. "I'll see you this afternoon, then. I'll drive myself, so Poole will be available to drive you if you do decide to go anywhere."

"All right," she said, agreeing with him because she wasn't going anywhere.

Once he'd left the house, she spent the day reading and occasionally napping. Now that she had made up her mind to go, she felt more peaceful. Tomorrow would be an exhausting day, so she needed to rest while she could.

Her father returned in the middle of the afternoon. Barrie was sitting in the living room, curled up with a book. She looked up as he entered and immediately noticed how the drawn look of worry eased when he saw her. "Did you have a nice lunch?" she asked, because that was what she would have done before.

"You know how these political things are," he said. Once he would have sat down and told her all about it, but this time he smoothly evaded talking specifics. Senator Garth was on several important committees concerning national security and foreign affairs. Before she could ask any more questions, he went into his study, closing the door behind him. Before, he had always kept it open as an invitation to her to visit whenever she wanted. Sadly Barrie looked at the closed door, then returned to her book.

The doorbell startled her. She put the book aside and went to answer it, cautiously looking through the peephole before opening the door. A tall, black-haired man was standing there.

Her heart jumped wildly, and a wave of dizziness swept over her. Behind her, she heard her father coming out of his study. "Who is it?" he asked sharply. "Let me get it."

Barrie didn't reply. She jerked the door open and

stared up into Zane's cool, blue gray eyes. Her heart was pounding so hard she could barely breathe.

That sharp gaze swept down her body, then came up to her face. "Are you pregnant?" he asked quietly, his voice pitched low so her father couldn't hear, even though he was rapidly approaching.

"Yes," she whispered.

He nodded, a terse movement of his head as if that settled that. "Then we'll get married."

Chapter 9

Her father reached them then, and shouldered Barrie aside. "Who are you?" he demanded, still in that sharp tone.

Zane coolly surveyed the man who would be his father-in-law. "Zane Mackenzie," he finally replied, when he had finished his appraisal. His darkly tanned face was impassive, but there was a piercing quality to his pale eyes that made Barrie suddenly aware of how dangerous this man could be. It didn't frighten her; under the circumstances, this quality was exactly what she needed.

William Lovejoy had been alarmed, but now his complexion turned pasty, and his expression froze. He said stiffly, "I'm sure you realize it isn't good for Barrie to see you again. She's trying to put that episode behind her—"

Zane looked past Lovejoy to where Barrie stood, visibly trembling as she stared at him with pleading green eyes. He hadn't realized how green her eyes were, a deep forest green, or how expressive. He got the impression that she wasn't pleading for him to be nice to her father, but rather that she was asking for help in some way, with some thing. His battle instincts stirred, his senses lifting to the next level of acuity. He didn't know exactly what she was asking of him, but he would find out, as soon as he dealt with the present situation. It was time to let the former ambassador know exactly where he stood.

"We're getting married," he said, still looking at Barrie, as he cut through the ambassador's continuing explanation on why it would be best if he left immediately. His steely voice, which had instantly commanded the attention of the deadliest guerrilla fighters in the world, cut through Lovejoy's stuffy, patronizing explanation.

The ambassador broke off, and a look of panic flashed across his face. Then he said, "Don't be ridiculous," in a strained tone. "Barrie isn't going to marry a sailor who thinks he's something special because he's a trained assassin."

Zane's cool gaze switched from Barrie to her father and went arctic cold, the blue fading to a gray that glinted like shards of ice. Lovejoy took an involuntary step back, his complexion going from pasty to white.

"Barrie, will you marry me?" Zane asked deliberately, keeping his gaze focused on Lovejoy.

She glanced from him to her father, who tensed as he waited for her answer.

"Yes," she said, her mind racing. Zane. She wouldn't question the miracle that had brought him here, but she was so desperate that she would have married him even if she hadn't loved him. Zane was a SEAL; if anyone could keep her safe from the unknown enemy who had her father so on edge, he could. She was carrying his child, and evidently that possibility was what had brought him to Virginia in search of her. He was a man who took his responsibilities seriously. She would have preferred that he cared for her as deeply as she did for him, but she would take what she could get. She knew he was attracted to her; if he wasn't, she wouldn't be pregnant.

She would marry him, and perhaps with time he would come to love her.

Her father flinched at her answer. Half turning to her, he said imploringly, "Baby, you don't want to marry someone like him. You've always had the best, and he can't give it to you."

Squaring her shoulders, she said, "I'm going to marry him—as soon as possible."

Seeing the intractability in her expression, her father looked at Zane. "You won't get a penny of her inheritance," he said with real venom.

"Dad!" she cried, shocked. She had her own money, inheritances from her mother and grandparents, so she wasn't worried about being destitute even if he carried through on his threat; it was the fact that he'd made the threat at all, that he would try to sabotage her future with Zane in such a blatant, hurtful manner, that hurt.

Zane shrugged. "Fine," he said with deceptive mildness. Barrie heard the pure iron underlying the calm, even tone. "Do what you want with your money, I don't give a damn. But you're a fool if you thought you could keep her with you for the rest of your life. You can act like an ass and cheat yourself out of your grandchildren if you want, but nothing you say is going to change a damn thing."

Lovejoy hung there, his face drawn with pain. Anguish darkened his eyes as he looked at his daughter. "Don't do it," he pleaded, his voice shaking.

Now it was her turn to wince, because in spite of everything, she hated to hurt him. "I'm pregnant," she whispered, straightening her shoulders against any other hurtful thing he might say. "And we're getting married."

He swayed on his feet, stunned by her announcement. She hadn't thought it possible he could turn any whiter, but he did. "What?" he croaked. "But—but you said you weren't raped!"

"She wasn't," Zane said. There was a soft, drawling, very masculine undertone in his voice.

Their eyes met. Barrie gave him a soft, wry smile. "I wasn't," she verified, and despite everything, a sudden, subtle glow lit her face.

Her father couldn't think of anything else to say. He gaped at them for a moment, unable to handle this turn of events. Then a red tide of anger ran up his face, chasing away the pallor. "You bastard!" he choked out. "You took advantage of her when she was vulnerable—"

Barrie grabbed his arm and jerked him around. "Stop it!" she yelled, her slender body tense with fury. Her nerves had been shredded since that morning, and this confrontation was only making them worse. Zane's sudden appearance, though it made her almost giddy with happiness, was another shock to her system, and she'd had enough. "If anyone took advantage, *I* did. If you want the details I'll give them to you, but I don't think you really want to know!"

It was on the tip of her tongue to ask him if he'd thought he could keep her a virgin forever, but she bit the bitter words off unspoken. That would be too hurtful, and once said, she would never be able to take the words back. He loved her, perhaps too much; his fear of losing her was why he was lashing out. And, despite everything, she loved him, too. Pain congealed inside her as she stared starkly at him, all pretense gone. "I know," she whispered. "Do you understand? I *know*. I know why you've been so paranoid every time I've left the house. *I have to leave.*"

He inhaled sharply, shock ripping away his last vestige of control. He couldn't sustain her burning gaze, and he looked away. "Keep her safe," he said to Zane in a stifled voice, then walked stiffly toward his study.

"I intend to." That difficulty solved, he spared no more than a glance for his departing foe. His gaze switched to Barrie, and a slow, heart-stopping smile touched his lips. "Go get packed," he said.

They were on their way within the hour.

She hurried up to her bedroom and filled her suitcases, bypassing the evening gowns and designer suits in favor of more practical clothing. The ankle-length cotton skirt she was already wearing was comfortable enough for travel; she pulled on a silk shirt over the sleeveless blouse she wore and let it go at that. Every instinct she had was screaming at her to hurry.

She dragged the bags to the top of the stairs. It didn't require a lot of effort, they all had wheeled bottoms, but when Zane saw her, he left his post by the door and took the stairs two at a time. "Don't lift those," he ordered, taking the bags from her hands. "You should have called me."

His tone was the same one he had used in commanding his men, but Barrie was too nervous to fight that battle with him right now. He lifted all three cases with an ease that made her blink and started down the stairs with them. She rushed after him. "Where are we going? Are we flying or driving?"

"Las Vegas. Flying."

"You already have the tickets?" she asked in surprise.

He paused and glanced over his shoulder at her, the dark wings of his eyebrows lifting fractionally. "Of course," he said, and resumed his trip down the stairs.

Such certainty and self-assurance were daunting. Briefly she wondered what on earth she was getting herself into. More and more she was becoming aware of just how much in control Zane Mackenzie was, of himself and everything around him. She might never be able to break through that barrier. *Except in bed.* The memory zinged through her, bringing a flush to her cheeks that wasn't caused by rushing around. He had lost control there, and it had been…breathtaking.

"What time is the flight?" Once more she hurried to catch up to him. "Will we have time to go to my bank? I need to close out my accounts—"

"You can transfer them to a local bank when we get home."

While he carried her bags out to the rental car he was driving, Barrie went to the study and knocked softly on the door. There was no answer; after a moment she opened the door anyway. Her father was sitting at the desk, his elbows propped on top of it and his face buried in his hands.

"Bye, Dad," she said softly.

He didn't answer, but she saw his Adam's apple bob as he swallowed.

"I'll let you know where I am."

"No," he said, his voice strangled. "Don't." He lifted his head. His eyes were anguished. "Not yet. Wait…wait a while."

"All right," she whispered, understanding slicing through her. It was safer for her that way. He must suspect the phone line was tapped.

"Baby, I—" He broke off and swallowed hard again. "I only want you to be happy—and safe."

"I know." She felt dampness on her cheeks and wiped away the tears that were wetting them.

"He isn't the kind of man I wanted for you. The SEALs are—well, never mind." He sighed. "Maybe he *can* keep you safe. I hope so. I love you, baby. You've been the center of my life. You know I never meant—" He halted, unable to go on.

"I know," she said again. "I love you, too."

She quietly closed the door and stood with her head bowed. She didn't hear him approach, but suddenly Zane was there, his arm hard around her waist as he drew her with him out to the car. He didn't ask any questions, just opened the door for her and helped her inside, then closed the door with a finality that was unmistakable.

She sat tensely during the drive to the airport, watching the traffic buzz around them.

"This is the most privacy we'll have for a while," Zane said as he competently threaded the car through the insanity of rush hour. "Why don't you tell me what's going on?" He had slipped on a pair of sunglasses, and his eyes were hidden from her view, but she didn't have to see them to know how cool and remote the expression in them was.

She lifted her chin and stared straight ahead, considering the way his suggestions sounded like orders. This wasn't going to be easy, but he had to know everything. She needed his protection, at least while she still carried his child. He wouldn't be on guard unless he knew there was a threat. She had to be honest with him. "I want you to know—one of the reasons I agreed to marry you is that I need protection, and you're a SEAL. If anything… dangerous…happens, you'll know how to handle it."

"Dangerous, how?" He sounded very matter-of-fact, almost disinterested. She supposed that, given his job, danger was so common to him that it was more the rule than the exception.

"I think the kidnappers may try again. And now I have more than just myself to worry about." Briefly, unconsciously, her hand moved to her lower belly in the instinctive way a pregnant woman touched the growing child within, as if reassuring it of its safety.

He glanced in the rearview mirror, calmly studying the traffic behind and around them. After a moment of consideration, he went straight to the heart of the matter. "Have you notified the FBI? The police?"

"No."

"Why not?"

"Because I think Dad may be involved," she said, almost strangling on the words.

Once again he checked the rearview mirror. "In what way?"

He sounded so damn remote. She clenched her hands into fists, determined to hold on to her control. If he could be self-contained, then so could she. She forced her voice to evenness. "The reason for the kidnapping wasn't ransom, so they must want information from him. I can't think of anything else it *could* be."

He was silent for a moment, deftly weaving in and out of the tangle of vehicles. She could almost hear that cool, logical brain sorting through the ramifications. Finally he said, "Your father must be in it up to his neck, or he'd have gone to the FBI himself. You would have been taken to a safe place and surrounded by a wall of agents."

He'd reached exactly the same conclusion she had.

That didn't make her feel any better. "Since we've been back in Virginia, he's been impossible. He doesn't want me to leave the house by myself, and he's monitoring all telephone calls. He was always protective, but not like this. At first I thought he was overreacting because of what happened in Athens, but when I thought it through, I realized the threat still existed." She swallowed. "I'd made up my mind to sneak out tonight and disappear for a while."

If Zane had waited another day, she would have been gone. He wouldn't have had any idea where to find her, and she had no way of contacting him. Tears burned her eyes at the thought. Dear God, it had been so close.

"Hold on," he said, then jerked the steering wheel to the right, cutting across a lane of traffic and throwing the car into a sharp turn into another street. The tires squealed, and horns blared. Even with his warning, she barely had time to brace herself, and the seat belt tightened with a jerk.

"What's wrong?" she cried, struggling to right herself and ease the strangling grip of the seat belt.

"There's a possibility we had company. I didn't want to take any chances."

Alarmed, Barrie twisted around in the seat, staring at the cars passing through the intersection behind them, vainly trying to see anyone who looked familiar or any vehicle making an obvious effort to cut across traffic and follow them. The traffic pattern looked normal.

"Two Caucasian men, in their thirties or forties, both wearing sunglasses," Zane said with no more emphasis than if he'd been observing the clouds in the sky. She remembered this almost supernatural calmness from before. In Benghazi, the more tense the situation, the cooler he had become, totally devoid of emotion. For him to take the action he had, he'd been certain they were being followed. The bottom dropped out of her stomach, and she fought a sudden rise of nausea. To suspect she was in danger was one thing, having it confirmed was something else entirely.

Then what he'd said registered in her brain. "Caucasian?" she echoed. "But—" She stopped, because of course it made sense. While she had subconsciously been looking for Libyans, she had to remember that this Gordian knot of intrigue involved both Libyans and Mack Prewett's cohorts; given his resources, she had to be suspicious of everyone, not just Middle Easterners. Black, white or Oriental, she couldn't trust anyone—except Zane.

"Since they know what I'm driving, we're going to ditch the car." Zane took another turn, this time without the dramatics, but also without signaling or slowing down more than was necessary. "I'll make a phone call and have the car taken care of. We'll get a ride to the airport."

She didn't ask who he would call; the area was crawling with military personnel from all the branches of service. Someone in dress whites would collect the car and return it to the rental company, and that would be that. By then, she and Zane would be on their way to Las Vegas.

"They'll be able to find me anyway," she said suddenly, thinking of the airline ticket in her name.

"Eventually. It'll take a while, though. We have a substantial grace period."

"Maybe not." She bit her lip. "I overheard Dad talking to Mack Prewett this morning. Mack's CIA, deputy station chief in Athens. Dad told him that he wanted this finished, that he never meant for me to be involved."

Zane lifted his eyebrows. "I see."

She supposed he did. If her father was working with the CIA in anything legitimate, he would have been able to protect her through legal channels. Mack Prewett's involvement changed the rules. He would have access to records that ordinary people wouldn't have. Even though the CIA didn't operate within the United States, the tentacles of influence were far-reaching. If Mack wanted to know if she'd taken a flight out of either of the major area airports, he would have that information within minutes.

"If they were sharp enough to get the license plate number on the car, they'll have my name very shortly," he said. "If they didn't get the number, then they won't have a clue about my identity. Either way, it's too late to worry about it now. They either have it or they don't, and there's no need to change our immediate plans. We'll take the flight to Las Vegas and lose them there, at least for a while."

"How will we lose them? If Mack can get access to your records..."

"I resigned my commission. I'm not a SEAL anymore."

"Oh," she said blankly. She struggled to adjust to yet another change. She had already been imagining and mentally preparing for life as the wife of a military officer, with the frequent moves, the politics of rank. It wouldn't have been much different from life in the embassy, just on a different level. Now she realized she had no idea what kind of life they would have.

"What will we do, then?" she asked.

"I've taken the job of sheriff in a county in southern Arizona. The sheriff died in office, so the governor appointed me to complete his term. There are two years left until new elections, so we'll be in Arizona for at least two years, maybe more.''

A sheriff! That was a definite surprise, and the offhand manner with which he had announced it only deepened her sense of unreality. She struggled to focus on the important things. ''What your job is doesn't matter,'' she said as evenly as possible. ''It's your training that counts.''

He shrugged and wheeled the car into the entrance of a parking garage. ''I understand.'' His voice was flat, emotionless. ''You agreed to marry me because you think I'll be able to protect you.'' He let down the window and leaned out to get the ticket from the automatic dispenser. The red barrier lifted, and he drove through.

Barrie wound her fingers together. Her initial flush of happiness had given way to worry. Zane had come after her, yes, and asked her to marry him, but perhaps she'd been wrong about the attraction between them. She felt uprooted and off-balance. Zane didn't seem particularly happy to see her, but then, she had certainly tossed a huge problem into his lap. He would become a husband and a father in very short order, and on top of that, he had to protect them from an unknown enemy. He hadn't even kissed her, she thought, feeling close to tears, and she was a little surprised at herself for even thinking of such a thing right now. If he was right and someone had been following them, then the danger had been more immediate than she had feared. How could she worry about his reasons for marrying her? After all, the baby's safety was one of the reasons she was marrying *him*. ''I want you to protect our baby,'' she said quietly. ''There are other reasons, but that's the main one.'' Her feelings for him were something she could have handled on her own; she wouldn't take that chance with her baby's safety.

"A damn important one. You're right, too." He gave
her a brief glance as he pulled the car into a parking slot
on the third level. "I won't let anything hurt you or the
baby."

He pulled off his sunglasses and got out of the car with
a brief "Wait here," and strode off toward a pay phone.
When he reached it, he punched in a series of numbers,
then turned so he could watch her and the car while he
talked.

Barrie felt her nerves jolt and her stomach muscles
tighten as she stared across the parking deck at him. She
was actually marrying this man. He looked taller than she
remembered, a little leaner, though his shoulders were so
wide they strained the seams of his white cotton shirt.
His black hair was a bit longer, she thought, but his tan
was just as dark. Except for the slight weight loss, he
didn't show any sign of having been shot only a little
over two months earlier. His physical toughness was intimidating; *he* was intimidating. How could she have forgotten? She had remembered only his consideration, his
passion, the tender care he'd given her, but he'd used no
weapon other than his bare hands to kill that guard. While
she had remembered his lethal competency and planned
to use it on her own behalf, she had somehow forgotten
that it was a prominent part of him, not a quality she
could call up when she needed it and tuck away into a
corner when the need was over. She would have to deal
with this part of him on a regular basis and accept the
man he was. He wasn't, and never would be, a tame
house cat.

She liked house cats, but she didn't want him to be
one, she realized.

She felt another jolt, this time of self-discovery. She
needed to be safe now, because of the baby, but she

didn't want to be permanently cossetted and protected. The grueling episode in Benghazi had taught her that she was tougher and more competent than she'd ever thought, in ways she hadn't realized. Her father would have approved if she'd married some up-and-coming ambassador-to-be, but that wasn't what she wanted. She wanted some wildness in her life, and Zane Mackenzie was it. For all that maddening control of his, he was fierce and untamed. He didn't have a streak of wildness; he had a core of it.

The strain between them unnerved her. She had dreamed of him finding her and holding out his arms, of falling into them, and when she had opened the door to him today she had expected, like a fool, for her dream to be enacted. Reality was much more complicated than dreams.

The truth was, they had known each other for about twenty-four hours total, and most of those hours had been over two months earlier. In those hours they had made love with raw, scorching passion, and he had made her pregnant, but the amount of time remained the same.

Perhaps he had been involved with someone else, but a sense of responsibility had driven him to locate her and find out if their lovemaking had had any consequences. He would do that, she thought; he would turn his back on a girlfriend, perhaps even a fiancée, to assume the responsibility for his child.

Again she was crashing into the brick wall of ignorance; she didn't know anything about his personal life. If she had known anything about his family, where he was from, she would have been able to find him. Instead, he must think she hadn't cared enough even to ask about his condition, to find out if he had lived or died.

He was coming back to the car now, his stride as

smooth and effortlessly powerful as she remembered, the silent walk of a predator. His dark face was as impassive as before, defying her efforts to read his expression.

He opened the door and slid behind the wheel. "Transport will be here in a few minutes."

She nodded, but her mind was still occupied with their personal tangle. Before she lost her nerve, she said evenly, "I tried to find you. They took me back to Athens immediately, while you were still in surgery. I tried to get in touch with you, find out if you were still alive, how you were doing, what hospital you were in—anything. Dad had Admiral Lindley block every inquiry I made. He did tell me you were going to be okay, but that's all I was able to find out."

"I guessed as much. I tried to call you at the embassy a couple of weeks after the mission. The call was routed to your father."

"He didn't tell me you'd called," she said, the familiar anger and pain twisting her insides. Since she'd been forced off the *Montgomery,* those had been her two main emotions. So he *had* tried to contact her. Her heart lifted a little. "After I came home, I tried again to find you, but the Navy wouldn't tell me anything."

"The antiterrorism unit is classified." His tone was absent; he was watching in the mirrors as another car drove slowly past them, looking for an empty slot.

She sat quietly, nerves quivering, until the car had disappeared up the ramp to the next level.

"I'm sorry," she said, after several minutes of silence. "I know this is a lot to dump in your lap."

He gave her an unreadable glance, his eyes very clear and blue. "I wouldn't be here if I didn't want to be."

"Do you have a girlfriend?"

This time the look he gave her was so long that she

blushed and concentrated her attention on her hands, which were twisting together in her lap.

"If I did, I wouldn't have made love to you," he finally said.

Oh, dear. She bit her lip. This was going from bad to worse. He was getting more and more remote, as if the fleeting moment of silent communication between them when he'd asked her to marry him had never existed. Her stomach clenched, and suddenly a familiar sensation of being too hot washed over her.

She swallowed hard, praying that the nausea that had so far confined itself to the mornings wasn't about to put in an unexpected appearance. A second later she was scrambling out of the car and frantically looking around for a bathroom. God, did parking decks *have* bathrooms?

"Barrie!" Zane was out of the car, striding toward her, his dark face alert. She had the impression that he intended to head her off, though she hadn't yet chosen a direction in which to dash.

The stairwell? The elevator? She thought of the people who would use them and discarded both options. The most sensible place was right there on the concrete, and everything fastidious in her rebelled at the idea. Her stomach had different ideas, however, and she clamped a desperate hand over her mouth just as Zane reached her.

Those sharp, pale eyes softened with comprehension. "Here," he said, putting a supporting arm around her. The outside barriers of the parking deck were waist-high concrete walls, and that was where he swiftly guided her. She resisted momentarily, appalled at the possibility of throwing up on some unsuspecting passerby below, but his grip was inexorable, and her stomach wasn't waiting any longer. He held her as she leaned over the wall and helplessly gave in to the spasm of nausea.

She was shaking when it was over. The only comfort she could find was that, when she opened her eyes, she saw there was nothing three stories below but an alley. Zane held her, leaning her against his supporting body while he blotted her perspiring face with his handkerchief, then gave it to her so she could wipe her mouth. She felt scorched with humiliation. The strict teachings of her school in Switzerland hadn't covered what a lady should do after vomiting in public.

And then she realized he was crooning to her, his deep voice an almost inaudible murmur as he brushed his lips against her temple, her hair. One strong hand was splayed over her lower belly, spanning her from hipbone to hipbone, covering his child. Her knees felt like noodles, so she let herself continue leaning against him, let her head fall into the curve of his shoulder.

"Easy, sweetheart," he whispered, once again pressing his lips to her temple. "Can you make it back to the car, or do you want me to carry you?"

She couldn't gather her thoughts enough to give him a coherent answer. After no more than a second, he evidently thought he'd given her enough time to decide, so he made the decision for her by scooping her up into his arms. A few quick strides brought them to the car. He bent down and carefully placed her on the seat, lifting her legs into the car, arranging her skirt over them. "Do you want something to drink? A soft drink?"

Something cold and tart sounded wonderful. "No caffeine," she managed to say.

"You won't be out of my sight for more than twenty seconds, but keep an eye out for passing cars, and blow the horn if anything scares you."

She nodded, and he hit the door lock, then closed the door, shutting her inside a cocoon of silence. She preferred the fresh air but understood why she shouldn't be standing outside the car, exposed to view—and an easy target. She leaned her head against the headrest and closed her eyes. The nausea was gone as swiftly as it had come, though her insides felt like jelly. She was weak, and sleepy, and a bit bemused by his sudden tenderness.

Though she shouldn't be surprised, she thought. She was pregnant with his child, and the possibility of exactly that was what had brought him in search of her. As soon as he'd realized she was nauseated, a condition directly related to her condition, so to speak, he'd shown nothing but tender concern and demonstrated once again his ability to make snap decisions in urgent situations.

His tap on the window startled her, because in her sleepy state she hadn't thought he'd been gone nearly long enough to accomplish his mission. But a green can, frosty with condensation, was in his hand, and suddenly she ferociously wanted that drink. She unlocked the door and all but snatched the can from him before he could slide into the seat. She had it popped open and was drinking greedily by the time he closed the door.

When the can was empty, she leaned back with a sigh of contentment. She heard a low, strained laugh and turned her head to find Zane looking at her with both amusement and something hot and feral mingled in his gaze. "That's the first time watching a woman drink a soft drink has made me hard. Do you want another? I'll try to control myself, but a second one might be more than I can stand."

Barrie's eyes widened. A blush warmed her cheeks, but that didn't stop her from looking at his lap. He was telling the truth. Good heavens, was he ever telling the truth! Her hand clenched with the sudden need to reach out and stroke him. "I'm not thirsty now," she said, her voice huskier than usual. "But I'm willing to go for a second one if you are."

The amusement faded out of his eyes, leaving only the heat behind. He was reaching out for her when his head suddenly snapped around, his attention caught by an approaching vehicle. "Here's our ride," he said, and once again his voice was cool and emotionless.

Chapter 10

She was marrying him because she wanted his protection. The thought gnawed at Zane during the long flight to Las Vegas. She sat quietly beside him, sometimes dozing, talking only if he asked her a question. She had the drained look of someone who had been under a lot of pressure, and now that it had eased, her body was giving in to fatigue. Finally she fell soundly asleep, her head resting against his shoulder.

The pregnancy would be taking a toll on her, too. He couldn't see any physical change in her yet, but his three older brothers had produced enough children that he knew how tired women always got the first few months — at least, how tired Shea and Loren had been. Nothing ever slowed Caroline down, not even five sons.

At the thought of the baby, fierce possessiveness jolted through him again. His baby was inside her. He wanted to scoop her onto his lap and hold her, but a crowded plane wasn't the place for what he had in mind. That would have to wait until after the marriage ceremony, when they were in a private hotel room.

He wanted her even more than he had before.

When she had opened the door and he'd looked down into her stunned green eyes, his arousal had been so strong and immediate that he'd had to restrain himself from reaching for her. Only the sight of her father bearing down on them had held him back.

He shouldn't have waited as long as he had. As soon as he'd been able to get around okay, he should have come after her. She had been living in fear, and handling it the same way she had in Benghazi, with calm determination.

He didn't want her ever to be afraid again.

Bunny's and Spooky's arrival at the parking deck, in Bunny's personally customized 1969 Oldsmobile 442, had been like a reunion. Barrie had tumbled out of the rental car with a happy cry and been enthusiastically hugged and twirled around by both SEALs. They were both discreetly armed, he'd noticed approvingly. They were wearing civilian clothes, with their shirts left loose outside their pants to conceal the firepower tucked under their arms and in the smalls of their backs. Normally, when they were off-duty, they didn't carry firearms, but Zane had explained the situation to them and left their preparations to their own discretion, since he wasn't their commanding officer any longer. In typical fashion, they had prepared for anything. His own weapon was still resting in a holster under his left armpit, covered by a light-weight summer jacket.

"Don't you worry none, ma'am," Spooky had reassuringly told Barrie. "We'll get you and the boss to the airport safe and sound. There's nothing outside of NASCAR that can keep up with Bunny's wheels."

"I'm sure there isn't," she'd replied, eyeing the car. It looked unremarkable enough; Bunny had painted it a light gray, and there wasn't any more chrome than would be on a factory job. But the deep-throated rumble from the idling engine didn't sound like any sound a factory engine would make, and the tires were wide, with a soft-looking tread.

"Bulletproof glass, reinforced metal," Bunny said proudly as he helped Zane transfer her luggage to the trunk of his car. "Plate steel would be too heavy for the speed I want, so I went with the new generation of body armor material, lighter and stronger than Kevlar. I'm still working on the fireproofing."

"I'll feel perfectly safe," she assured him.

As she and Zane crawled into the back seat of the two-door car, she whispered to him, "Where's Nascar?"

Spooky could hear a pin drop at forty paces. Slowly he turned around in the front seat, his face mirroring his incredulity. "Not where, ma'am," he said, struggling with shock. "*What.* NASCAR. Stock car racing." A good Southerner, he'd grown up with stock car racing and was always stunned when he encountered someone who hadn't enjoyed the same contact with the sport.

"Oh," Barrie said, giving him an apologetic smile. "I've spent a lot of time in Europe. I don't know anything about racing except for the Grand Prix races."

Bunny snorted in derision. "Play cars," he said dismissively. "You can't run them on the streets. Stock car racing, now that's real racing." As he was speaking, he was wheeling his deceptive monster out of the parking deck, his restless gaze touching on every surrounding detail.

"I've been to horse races," Barrie offered, evidently in an attempt to redeem herself.

Zane controlled a smile at the earnestness of her tone. "Do you ride?" he asked.

Her attention swung to him. "Why, yes. I love horses."

"You'll make a good Mackenzie, then," Spooky drawled. "Boss raises horses in his spare time." There was a bit of irony in his tone, because SEALs had about as much spare time as albinos had color.

"Do you really?" Barrie asked, her eyes shining.

"I own a few. Thirty or so."

"Thirty!" She sat back, a slight look of confusion on her face. He knew what she was thinking: one horse was expensive to own and keep, let alone thirty. Horses needed a lot of land and care, not something she associated with an ex-Naval officer who had been a member of an elite antiterrorism group.

"It's a family business," he explained, swiveling his head to examine the traffic around them.

"Everything's clear, boss," Bunny said. "Unless they've tagged us with a relay, but I don't see how that's possible."

Zane didn't, either, so he relaxed. A moving relay surveillance took a lot of time and coordination to set up, and the route had to be known. Bunny was taking such a circuitous route to the airport that any tail would long since have been revealed or shaken. Things were under control—for now.

They made it to National without incident, though to be on the safe side Bunny and Spooky had escorted them as far as the security check. While Zane quietly handled his own armed passage through security, his two former team members had taken themselves off to collect the rental car and turn it in, though to the agency office at

Dulles, not National, where he had rented it. Just another little twist to delay anyone who was looking for them.

Now that they were safely on the plane, he began planning what he would do to put an end to the situation.

The first part of it was easy. He would put Chance on the job of finding out what kind of mess her father was involved in; for her sake, he hoped it wasn't anything treasonous, but whatever was going on, he intended to put a stop to it. Chance had access to information that put national security agencies to shame. If William Lovejoy was selling out his country, then he would go down. There was no other option. Zane had spent his adult years offering his life in protection of his country, and now he was a peace officer sworn to uphold the law; it was impossible for him to look the other way, even for Barrie. He didn't want her to be hurt, but he damn sure wanted her to be safe.

Barrie slept until the airliner's wheels bounced on the pavement. She sat upright, pushing her hair away from her face, looking about with a slight sense of disorientation. She had never before been able to sleep on a plane; this sleepiness was just one more of the many changes her pregnancy was making in her body, and her lack of control over the process was disconcerting, even frightening.

On the other hand, the rest had given her additional energy, something she needed to face the immense change she was about to make in her life. This change was deliberate, but no less frightening.

"I want to shower and change clothes first," she said firmly. This marriage might be hasty, without any resemblance to the type of wedding ceremony she had always envisioned for herself, but while she was willing to forgo

the pomp and expensive trappings, she wasn't willing—
outside of a life-and-death situation—to get married
wearing wrinkled clothes and still blinking sleep from her
eyes.

"Okay. We'll check in to a hotel first." He rubbed his
jaw, his callused fingers rasping over his beard stubble.
"I need to have a shave anyway."

He had needed to shave that day in Benghazi, too. In
a flash of memory she felt again the scrape of his rough
chin against her naked breasts, and a wave of heat
washed over her, leaving her weak and flushed. The cool
air blowing from the tiny vent overhead was suddenly
not cool enough.

She hoped he wouldn't notice, but it was a faint hope,
because he was trained to take note of every detail around
him. She imagined he could describe every passenger
within ten rows of them in either direction, and when
she'd been awake she had noticed that he'd shown an
uncanny awareness of anyone approaching them from the
rear on the way to the lavatories.

"Are you feeling sick?" he asked, eyeing the color in
her cheeks.

"No, I'm just a little warm," she said with perfect
truth, while her blush deepened.

He continued to watch her, and the concern in his eyes
changed to a heated awareness. She couldn't even hide
that from him, damn it. From the beginning it had been
as if he could see beneath her skin; he sensed her reactions almost as soon as she felt them.

Slowly his heavy-lidded gaze moved down to her
breasts, studying the slope and thrust of them. She inhaled sharply as her nipples tightened in response to his
blatant interest, a response that shot all the way to her
loins.

"Are they more sensitive?" he murmured.

Oh, God, he shouldn't do this to her, she thought wildly. They were in the middle of a plane full of people, taxiing toward an empty gate, and he was asking questions about her breasts and looking as if he would start undressing her any minute now.

"Are they?"

"Yes," she whispered. Her entire body felt more sensitive, from both her pregnancy and her acute awareness of him. Soon he would be her husband, and once again she would be lying in his arms.

"Ceremony first," he said, his thoughts echoing hers in that eerie way he had. "Otherwise we won't get out of the hotel until tomorrow."

"Are you psychic?" she accused under her breath.

A slow smile curved his beautiful mouth. "It doesn't take a psychic to know what those puckered nipples mean."

She glanced down and saw her nipples plainly beaded under the lace and silk of her bra and blouse. Her face red, she hastily drew her shirt over the betraying little nubs, and he gave a low laugh. At least no one else was likely to have heard him, she thought with scant comfort. He'd pitched his voice low, and the noise on board made it difficult to overhear conversations, anyway.

The flight attendants were telling them to remain in their seats until the plane was secured and the doors opened, and as usual the instructions were ignored as passengers surged into the aisles, opening the overhead bins and dragging down their carry-on luggage or hauling it out from under the seats. Zane stepped deftly into the aisle, and the movement briefly pulled his jacket open. She saw the holster under his left arm and the polished metal butt of the pistol tucked snugly inside it. Then he automatically shrugged one shoulder, and the jacket fell into place, a movement he'd performed so many times he didn't have to think about it.

She'd known he was armed, of course, because he'd informed the airport and airline security before they'd boarded the plane. During the boredom and enforced in-activity of the flight, however, she had managed to push the recent events from her mind, but the sight of that big automatic brought them all back.

He extended his hand to steady her as she stepped into the aisle ahead of him. Standing pressed like sardines in the line, she felt him like a warm and solid wall at her back, his arms slightly extended so that his hands rested on the seat backs, enveloping her in security. His breath stirred the hair on top of her head, making her realize anew exactly how big he was. She was of average height, but if she leaned back, her head would fit perfectly into the curve of his shoulder.

The man in front of her shifted, forcing her backward, and Zane curved one arm around her as he gathered her against his body, his big hand settling protectively over her lower belly. Barrie bit her lip as her mind bounced from worry to the pleasure of his touch. This couldn't go on much longer—either this exquisite frustration or the sharp darts of terror—or she would lose her mind.

The line of passengers began to shuffle forward as the doors were opened and they were released from the plane. Zane's hand dropped from her belly. As she began to move forward, Barrie caught the eye of an older woman who had chosen to remain in her seat until the stampede was over, and the woman gave her a knowing smile, her gaze flicking to Zane.

"Ma'am," Zane said smoothly in acknowledgment, and Barrie knew he'd caught the little byplay. His acute awareness of his surroundings was beginning to spook her. What if she didn't want him to notice everything? Most women would be thrilled to death with a husband who actually took note of details, but probably not to the extent that Zane Mackenzie did.

On the other hand, if the alternative was living without him, she would learn how to cope, she thought wryly. She'd spent over two months pining for him, and now that she had him, she wasn't about to get cold feet because he was alert. He was a trained warrior—an assassin, her father had called him. He wouldn't have survived if he hadn't been aware of everything going on around him, and neither would she.

That alertness was evident as they followed the signs to the baggage claim area. The airport was a shifting, flowing beehive, and Zane's cool gaze was constantly assessing the people around them. As he had more than once before, he kept himself between her and everybody else, steering her close to the wall and protecting her other side with his body. He'd already taken one bullet while doing that, she thought, and had to fight the sudden terrified impulse to grab him and shove *him* against the wall.

Before they reached the baggage claim, however, he pulled her to a halt. "Let's wait here a minute," he said.

She strove for calm, for mastery over the butterflies that suddenly took flight in her stomach. "Did you see anything suspicious?" she asked.

"No, we're waiting for someone." He looked at her, his cool gaze warming as he studied her face. "You're a gutsy little broad, Miss Lovejoy. No matter what, you hold it together and try to do the best you can. Not bad for a pampered society babe."

Barrie was taken aback. She'd never been called a

broad before, or a society babe. If it hadn't been for the teasing glint in his eyes, she might have taken exception to the terms. Instead, she considered them for a moment, then gave a brief nod of agreement. "You're right," she said serenely. "I *am* gutsy for a pampered society babe."

He was surprised into a chuckle, a deliciously rich sound that was cut short when they were approached by a middle-aged man who wore a suit and carried a radio set in his hand. "Sheriff Mackenzie?" he asked.

"Yes."

"Travis Hulsey, airport security." Mr. Hulsey flashed his identification. "We have your luggage waiting for you in a secure area, as requested. This way, please."

So he'd even thought of that, Barrie marveled as they followed Mr. Hulsey through an unmarked door. An attempt to grab her inside the airport would be tricky, given the security, so the most logical thing to do would be to wait at the ground transportation area, where everyone went after collecting luggage, then follow them to their destination and wait for a better opportunity. Zane had thwarted that; he must have made the arrangements when he'd gone forward to the lavatory.

The dry desert heat slapped them in the face as soon as they stepped through the door. Her three suitcases and his one garment bag, which he had collected from a locker at National, were waiting for them at a discreet entrance well away from the main ground transportation area. Also waiting for them was a car, beside which stood a young man with the distinctive austere military haircut, even though he wore civilian clothes.

The young man all but snapped to attention. "Sir," he said. "Airman Zaharias at your service, sir."

Zane's dark face lit with amusement. "At ease," he said. "I'm not my brother."

Airman Zaharias relaxed with a grin. "When I first saw you, sir, I wasn't sure."

"If he pulled rank and this is messing up your leave time, I'll get other transport."

"I volunteered, sir. The general did me a personal favor when I was fresh out of basic. Giving his brother a ride downtown is the least I can do."

Brother? *General?* Barrie raised some mental eyebrows. First horses, now this. She realized she didn't know anything about her soon-to-be husband's background, but the details she'd gleaned so far were startling, to say the least.

Zane introduced her with grave courtesy. "Barrie, Airman Zaharias is our safe transport, and he has donated his personal vehicle and time off for the service. Airman Zaharias, my fiancée, Barrie Lovejoy."

She solemnly shook hands with the young airman, who was almost beside himself in his eagerness to please.

"Glad to meet you, ma'am." He unlocked the trunk and swiftly began loading their luggage, protesting when Zane lifted two of the bags and stowed them himself. "Let me do that, sir!"

"I'm a civilian now," Zane said, amusement still bright in his eyes. "And I was Navy, anyway."

Airman Zaharias shrugged. "Yes, sir, but you're still the general's brother." He paused, then asked, "Were you really a SEAL?"

"Guilty."

"Damn," Airman Zaharias breathed.

They climbed into the air-conditioned relief of the airman's Chevrolet and were off. Their young driver evidently knew Las Vegas well, and without asking for instructions he ignored the main routes. Instead he circled around and took Paradise Road north out of the airport.

He chattered cheerfully the entire time, but Barrie noticed that he didn't mention the exact nature of the favor Zane's general brother had done for him, nor did he venture into personal realms. He talked about the weather, the traffic, the tourists, the hotels. Zane directed him to a hotel off the main drag, and soon Airman Zaharias was on his way and they were checking in to the hotel.

Barrie bided her time, standing quietly to one side while Zane arranged for them to be listed in the hotel's computer as Glen and Alice Temple—how he arrived at those names she had no idea—and ignoring the clerk's knowing smirk. He probably thought they were adulterous lovers on a tryst, which suited her just fine; it would keep him from being curious about them.

They weren't alone in the elevator, so she held her tongue then, too. She held it until they were in the suite Zane had booked, and the bellman had been properly tipped and dismissed. The suite was as luxurious as any she had stayed in in Europe. A few hours before, she might have worried that the cost was more than Zane could afford, that he'd chosen it because he thought she would expect it. Now, however, she had no such illusion. As soon as he had closed and locked the door behind the bellman, she crossed her arms and stared levelly at him. "Horses?" she inquired politely. "Family business? A brother who happens to be an Air Force general?"

He shrugged out of his jacket, then his shoulder holster. "All of that," he said.

"I don't know you at all, do I?" She was calm, even a little bemused, as she watched him wrap the straps around the holster and deposit the weapon on the bedside table.

He unzipped his garment bag and removed a suit from it, then began unpacking other items. His pale glance flashed briefly at her. "You know *me*," he said. "You just don't know all the details of my family yet, but we haven't had much time for casual chatting. I'm not deliberately hiding anything from you. Ask any question you want."

"I don't want to conduct a catechism," she said, though she needed to do exactly that. "It's just..." She spread her hands in frustration, because she was marrying him and she didn't already know all this.

He began unbuttoning his shirt. "I promise I'll give you a complete briefing when we have time. Right now, sweetheart, I'd rather you got your sweet little butt in one shower while I get in the other, so we can get married and into this bed as fast as possible. About an hour after *that*, we'll talk."

She looked at the bed, a bigger-than-king-size. Priorities, priorities, she mused. "Are we safe here?"

"Safe enough for me to concentrate on other things."

She didn't have to ask what those other things were. She looked at the bed again and took a deep breath. "We could rearrange the order of these things," she proposed. "What do you think about bed, talk and then wedding? Say, tomorrow morning?"

He froze in the act of removing his shirt. She saw his eyes darken, saw the sexual tension harden his face. After a moment he pulled the garment free and dropped it to the floor, his movements deliberate. "I haven't kissed you yet," he said.

She swallowed. "I noticed. I've wondered—"

"Don't," he said harshly. "Don't wonder. The reason I haven't kissed you is that, once I start, I won't stop. I know we're doing things out of order—hell, everything's been out of order from the beginning, when you were naked the first time I saw you. I wanted you then, sweetheart, and I want you now, so damn bad I'm aching with it. But trouble is still following you around, and my job is to make damn sure it doesn't get close to you and our baby. I might get killed—''

She made a choked sound of protest, but he cut her off. ''It's a possibility, one I accept. I've accepted it for years. I want us married as soon as possible, because I don't know what might happen tomorrow. In case I miscalculate or get unlucky, I want our baby to be legitimate, to be born with the Mackenzie name. A certain amount of protection goes with that name, and I want you to have it. Now.''

Tears swam in her eyes as she stared at him, at this man who had already taken one bullet for her and was prepared to take another. He was right—she knew *him,* knew the man he was, even if she didn't know what his favorite color was or what kind of grades he'd made in school. She knew the basics, and it was the basics she had so swiftly and fiercely learned to love. So he wasn't as forthcoming as she might have wished; she would deal with it. So what if he was so controlled it was scary, and so what if those uncanny eyes noticed everything, which would make it difficult to surprise him on Christmas and his birthday? She would deal with that, too, very happily.

If he was willing to die for her, the least she could do was be completely honest with him.

''There's another reason I agreed to marry you,'' she said.

His dark brows lifted in silent question.

''I love you.''

Chapter 11

He wore a dark gray suit with black boots and a black hat. Barrie wore white. It was a simple dress, ankle length and sleeveless, classic in its lines and lack of adornment. She loosely twisted up her dark auburn hair, leaving a few wisps hanging about her face to soften the effect. Her only jewelry was a pair of pearl studs in her ears. She got ready in the bath off the bedroom, he showered in the bath off the parlor. They met at the door between the two rooms, ready to take the step that would make them husband and wife.

At her blunt declaration of love, an equally blunt expression of satisfaction had crossed his face, and for once he didn't hide anything he was feeling. "I don't know about love," he'd said, his voice so even she wanted to shake him. "But I do know I've never wanted another woman the way I want you. I know this marriage is forever. I'll take care of you and our children, I'll come home to you every night, and I'll try my damnedest to make you happy.''

It wasn't a declaration of love, but it was certainly one of devotion, and the tears that came so easily to her these days swam in her eyes. Her self-contained warrior *would* love her, when he lowered his guard enough to let himself. He had spent years with his emotions locked down, while he operated in tense, life-and-death situations that demanded cool, precise thoughts and decisions. Love was neither cool nor concise; it was turbulent, unpredictable, and it left one vulnerable. He would approach love as cautiously as if it was a bomb.

''Don't cry,'' he said softly. ''I swear I'll be a good husband.''

''I know,'' she replied, and then they had both gone to their separate bathrooms to prepare for their wedding.

They took a taxi to a chapel, one of the smaller ones that didn't get as much business and didn't have a drive-through service. Getting married in Las Vegas didn't take a great deal of effort, though Zane took steps to make it special. He bought her a small bouquet of flowers and gave her a bracelet of dainty gold links, which he fastened around her right wrist. Her heart beat heavily as they stood before the justice of the peace, and the bracelet seemed to burn around her wrist. Zane held her left hand securely in his right, his grip warm and gentle, but unbreakable.

Outwardly it was all very civilized, but from the first moment they'd met, Barrie had been acutely attuned to him, and she sensed the primal possessiveness of his actions. He had already claimed her physically, and now he was doing it legally. She already carried his child inside her. His air of masculine satisfaction was almost visible, it was so strong. She felt it, too, as she calmly spoke her vows, this linkage of their lives. During a long, hot day in Benghazi they had forged a bond that still held, despite the events that had forced them apart.

He had one more surprise for her. She hadn't expected a ring, not on such short notice, but at the proper moment he reached into the inside pocket of his jacket and produced two plain gold bands, one for her and one for him. Hers was a little loose when he slipped it over her knuckle, but their eyes met in a moment of perfect understanding. She would be gaining weight, and soon the ring would fit. She took the bigger, wider band and slid it onto the ring finger of his left hand, and she felt her own thrill of primal satisfaction. He was hers, by God!

Their marriage duly registered, the certificate signed and witnessed, they took another taxi to the hotel. "Supper," he said, steering her toward one of the hotel's dining rooms. "You didn't eat anything on the plane, and it's after midnight eastern time."

"We could order room service," she suggested.

His eyes took on that heavy-lidded look. "No, we couldn't." His tone was definite, a little strained. His hand was warm and heavy on the small of her back. "You need to eat, and I don't trust my self-control to last that long unless we're in a public place."

Perhaps feeding her was his only concern, or perhaps he knew more about seduction than most men, she thought as they watched each other over a progression of courses. Knowing that he was going to make love to her as soon as they reached the suite, anticipating the heaviness of his weight on her, the hard thrust of his turgid length into her…the frustration readied her for him as surely as if he was stroking her flesh. Her breasts lifted hard and swollen against the bodice of her dress. Her insides tightened with desire, so that she had to press her legs together to ease the throbbing. His gaze kept dropping to her breasts, and as before, she couldn't temper her response. She could feel her own moisture, feel the heaviness in her womb.

She was scarcely aware of what she ate—something bland, to reduce the chances of early-pregnancy nausea. She drank only water. But turnabout was fair play, so she lingered over each bite while she stared at his mouth, or in the direction of his lap. She delicately licked her lips, shivering with delight as his face darkened and his jaw set. She stroked the rim of her water glass with one fingertip, drawing his gaze, making his breath come harder and faster. Beneath the table, she rubbed her foot against the muscled calf of his leg.

He turned to snare their waiter with a laser glare. ''Check!'' he barked, and the waiter hurried to obey that voice of command. Zane scribbled their room number and his fictitious name on the check, and Barrie stared at him in amazement. It was hard to believe he could remember something like that when she could barely manage to walk.

For revenge, when he pulled her chair back so she could stand, she allowed the knuckles of one hand to brush, oh, so very lightly, against his crotch. He went absolutely rigid for a moment, and his breath hissed out between his teeth. All innocence, Barrie turned to give him a sweetly inquiring What's-wrong? look.

His darkly tanned face was even darker with the flush running under the browned skin. His expression was set, giving away little, but his eyes were glittering like shards of diamond. His big hand closed firmly around her elbow. ''Let's go,'' he said in the soundless whisper she'd first heard in a dark room in Benghazi. ''And don't do that again, or I swear I'll have you in the elevator.''

"Really." She smiled at him over her shoulder. "How…uplifting."

A faint but visible shudder racked him, and the look he gave her promised retribution. "Here I've been thinking you were so sweet."

"I am sweet," she declared as they marched toward the elevator. "But I'm not a pushover."

"We'll see about that. I'm going to push you over." They reached the bank of elevators, and he jabbed the call button with more force than necessary.

"You won't have to push hard. As a matter of fact, you can just blow me over." She gave him another sweet smile and pursed her lips, blowing a tiny puff of air against his chest to demonstrate.

The bell chimed, the doors opened, and they stood back to allow the car's passengers to exit. They stepped inside alone, and even though people were hurrying toward them to catch that car, Zane ruthlessly punched their floor number and then the door close button. When the car began to rise, he turned on her like a tiger on fresh meat.

She stepped gracefully out of his reach, staring at the numbers flashing on the digital display. "We're almost there."

"You're damn right about that," he growled, coming after her. In the small confines of the elevator she didn't have a chance of evading him, not that she wanted to. What she wanted was to drive him as crazy as he was driving her. His hard hands closed around her waist and lifted her; his muscled body pinned her to the wall. His hips pushed insistently at hers, and she gasped at how hard he was. Automatically her legs opened, allowing him access to the tender recesses of her body. He thrust against her, his hips moving rhythmically, and his mouth came down on hers, smothering, fiercely hungry.

The bell chimed softly, and the elevator gave a slight lurch as it stopped. Zane didn't release her. He simply turned with her still in his grasp and left the elevator, striding rapidly down the hall to their suite. Barrie twined her arms around his neck and her legs around his hips, biting back little moans as each stride he took rubbed his swollen sex against the aching softness of her loins. Pleasure arced through her like lightning with every step, and helplessly she felt her hips undulate against him in a mindless search for a deeper pleasure. A low curse hissed out from between his clenched teeth.

She didn't know if they passed anyone in the hall. She buried her face against his neck and gave in to the soaring hunger. She had needed him for so long, missed him, worried herself sick about him. Now he was here, vitally alive, about to take her with the same uncomplicated fierceness as before, and she didn't care about anything else.

He pushed her against a wall, and for one terrified, delirious moment she thought she had tempted him too much. Instead he unhooked her legs from around his waist and let her slide to the floor. He was breathing hard, his eyes dilated with a sexual hunger that wouldn't be denied much longer, but on one level he was still very much in control. Lifting one finger to his lips to indicate silence, he slipped his right hand inside his jacket. When his hand emerged, it was filled with the butt of that big automatic. He thumbed off the safety, dealt with the electronic lock on the door to their suite, depressed the door handle and slipped noiselessly inside. The door closed as silently as it had opened.

Barrie stood frozen in the hallway, sudden terror chasing away her desire as she waited with her eyes closed and her hands clenched into fists, all her concentration focused on trying to hear anything from inside the suite. She heard nothing. Absolutely nothing. Zane moved like a cat, but so did other men, men like him, men who worked best under cover of night and who could kill as silently as he had dispatched that guard in Benghazi. Her kidnappers hadn't possessed the same expertise, but whoever was behind her abduction wouldn't use Middle Eastern men here in the middle of the glitter and flash of Las Vegas. Perhaps this time he would hire someone more deadly, someone more interested in getting the job done than in terrifying a bound and helpless woman. Any thump, any whisper, might signal the end of Zane's life, and she thought she would shatter under the strain.

She didn't hear the door open again. All she heard was Zane saying, "All clear," in a calm, normal tone, and then she was in his arms again. She didn't think she moved; she thought he simply gathered her in, pulling her into the security of his embrace.

"I'm sorry," he murmured against her hair as he carried her inside. He paused to lock and chain the door. "But I won't take chances with your safety."

Fury roared through her like a brushfire. She lifted her head from the sanctuary of his shoulder and glared at him. "What about yours?" she demanded violently. "Do you have any idea what it does to me when you do things like that? Do you think I don't notice when you put yourself between me and other people, so if anyone shoots at me, you'll be the one with the bullet hole?" She hit him on the chest with a clenched fist, amazing even herself; she had never struck anyone before. She hit him again. "Damn it, I want you healthy and whole! I want our baby to have its daddy! I want to have more of your babies, so that means you have to stay alive, do you hear me?''

''I hear,'' he rumbled, his tone soothing as he caught her pounding fists and pressed them against his chest, stilling them. ''I'd like the same things myself. That means I have to do whatever's necessary to keep you and Junior safe.''

She relaxed against him, her lips trembling as she fought back tears. She wasn't a weepy person; it was just the hormonal roller coaster of pregnancy that was making her so, but still, she didn't want to cry all over him. He had enough to handle without having to deal with a sobbing wife every time he turned around.

When she could manage a steady tone, she said in a small voice, ''Junior, is it?''

She saw the flash of his grin as he lifted her in his arms. ''I'm afraid so,'' he said as he carried her to the bed. ''My sister Maris is the only female the Mackenzies have managed to produce, and that was twenty-nine years and ten boys ago.''

He bent and gently placed her on the bed and sat down beside her. His dark face was intent as he reached beneath her for the zipper of her dress. ''Now let's see if I can get you back to where you were before you got scared, and we'll introduce Junior to his daddy,'' he whispered.

Barrie was seized by a mixture of shyness and uneasiness as he stripped the dress down her hips and legs, then tossed it aside. Since her kidnappers had stripped her in a deliberate attempt to terrorize her, to break her spirit, she hadn't been comfortable with being naked. Except for those hours hidden in the ruins in Benghazi, when Zane had finally coaxed her out of his shirt and she had lost herself in his lovemaking, she had hurried through any times of necessary nudity, such as when she showered, pulling on clothes or a robe as soon as possible. Once upon a time she had lingered after her bath, enjoying the wash of air over her damp skin as she pampered herself with perfumed oils and lotions, but for the past two months that luxury had fallen beneath her urgent need to be covered.

Zane wanted her naked.

Her dress was already gone, and the silk and lace of her matching bra and underpants weren't much protection. Deftly he thumbed open the front fastening of her bra, and the cups loosened, sliding apart to reveal the inner curves of her breasts. Barrie couldn't help herself; she protectively crossed her arms over her breasts, holding the bra in place.

Zane paused, his face still as his pale gaze lifted to her face, examining the helpless, embarrassed expression she wore. She didn't have to explain. He'd been there; he knew. "Still having problems with that shirt?" he asked gently, referring to the way she'd clung so desperately to his garment.

He'd switched on a single lamp. She lay exposed in the small circle of light, while his face was shadowed. She moistened her lips and nodded once, a slight acknowledgment that was all he needed.

"We can't undo things," he said, his face and tone serious. Using one finger, he lightly stroked the upper curves of her breasts, where they plumped above the protection of her crossed arms. "We can put them behind us and move on, but we can't undo them. They stay part of us, they change us inside, but as other things happen, we change still more. I remember the face of the first man I killed. I don't regret doing it, because he was a bomb-happy piece of scum who had left his calling card

on a cruise ship, killing nine old people who were just
trying to enjoy their retirement. Right then he was trying
like hell to kill *me*...but I always carry his face with me,
deep inside.''

He paused, thinking, remembering. ''He's a part of me
now, because killing him changed me. He made me
stronger. I know that I can do whatever has to be done,
and I know how to go on. I've killed others,'' he said,
as calmly as if he was discussing the weather, ''but I
don't remember their faces. Only his. And I'm glad I
won.''

Barrie stared at him, the shadows emphasizing the
planes and hollows of his somber face, deepening the
oldness in his eyes. Deep inside she understood, the realization going past thought into the center of instinct.
Being kidnapped had changed her; she'd faced that before Zane had rescued her. She *was* stronger, more decisive, more willing to take action. When he'd shown up
that afternoon, she had been preparing to take extraordinary measures to protect herself and the child she carried by disappearing from the comfortable life she'd always known. She'd been naked with Zane before—and
enjoyed it. She would again.

Slowly she lifted one hand and stroked the precise line
of the small scar on his left cheekbone. He turned his
head a little, rubbing his cheek against her fingers.

''Take off *your* clothes,'' she suggested softly. Balance. If her nudity was balanced by his, she would be
more comfortable.

His eyebrows quirked upward. ''All right.''

She didn't have to explain, but then, she'd known she
wouldn't. She lay on the bed and watched him peel out
of his jacket, then remove the shoulder holster, which
once more carried its lethal cargo. This last was carefully

placed on the bedside table, where it would be within reach. Then his shirt came off, and he dropped it on the floor, along with her dress and his jacket.

The new scar on his upper abdomen was red and puckered, and bisected by a long surgical scar where the ship's surgeon had sliced into him to stop the bleeding and save his life. She had seen the scar before, when he had removed his shirt before showering, but she had been under orders not to touch him then lest she make him forget his priorities. There was no such restriction now.

Her fingers moved over the scar, feeling the heat and vitality of the man, and she thought how easily all of that could have been snuffed out. She had come so close to losing him....

"Don't think about it," he murmured, catching her hand and lifting it to his lips. "It didn't happen."

"It could have."

"It didn't." His tone was final as he bent over to tug off his boots. They dropped to the floor with twin thuds, then he stood to unfasten his pants.

He was right. It hadn't happened. Pick yourself up, learn something, and go on. It was in the past. The future was their marriage, their child. The present was *now,* and as Zane swiftly stripped off his remaining clothes, a lot more urgent.

He sat beside her again, comfortable in his own skin. It was such wonderful skin, she thought a little dreamily, reaching out to stroke his gleaming shoulders and furry chest and rub the tiny nipples hidden among the hair until they stood stiffly erect. She knew she was inviting him to reciprocate, and her breath caught in her chest as she waited for him to accept.

He wasn't slow about it. His hands went to the parted

cups of her bra, and his gaze lifted to hers. "Ready?" he asked with a slight smile.

She didn't reply, just shrugged one shoulder so that her breast slid free of the cup, and that was answer enough.

He glanced downward as he pushed the other cup aside, and she saw his pupils flare with arousal as he looked at her. His breath hissed out through parted lips. "I see our baby here," he whispered, gently touching one nipple with a single fingertip. "You haven't gained any weight, your stomach's still flat, but he's changed you here. Your nipples are darker, and swollen." Ever so lightly, his touch circled the aureola, making it pucker and stand upright. Barrie whimpered with the rush of desire, the familiar lightning strike from breast to loin.

He rubbed his thumb over the tip, then gently curved his hand beneath her breast, lifting it so that it plumped in his palm. "How much more sensitive are they?" he asked, never looking up from his absorption with these new details in her body.

"Some—sometimes I can't bear the touch of my bra." she breathed.

"Your veins are bluer, too," he murmured. "They look like rivers running under a layer of white satin." He leaned down and kissed her, taking possession of her mouth while he continued to fondle her breasts with exquisite care. She melted with a purring little hum of pleasure, lifting herself so she could taste him more deeply. His lips were as hot and forceful as she remembered, as delicious. He took his time; the kiss was slow and deep, his tongue probing. Her pregnancy-sensitive breasts hardened into almost painful arousal, her loins becoming warm and liquid.

He bore her down onto the pillows, his hands slipping

over her body, completely removing the bra and then disposing of her underpants. His eyes glittered hotly as he leaned over her. "I'm going to do everything to you I couldn't do before," he whispered. "We don't have to worry about being on guard, or making noise, or what time it is. I'm going to eat you up, Little Red."

She should have been alarmed, because his expression was so fierce and hungry she could almost take him literally. Instead, she reached out for him, almost frantic with the need to feel him covering her, taking her.

He had other ideas. He caught her hands and pressed them to the bed, as she had once done to him. He had trusted her with control, and now she returned the gift, arching her body up for whatever was his pleasure.

His pleasure was her breasts, with their fascinating changes. He took one distended nipple into his mouth, carefully, lightly. That was enough to make her moan, though not with pain; the prickles of sensation were incredibly intense. His tongue batted at her nipple, swirled around it, then pushed it hard against the roof of his mouth as he began suckling.

Her cry was thin, wild. Her breath exploded out of her lungs, and she couldn't seem to draw in any replacement air. Oh, God, she hadn't realized her breasts were *that* sensitive, or that he would so abruptly push her past both pleasure and pain into a realm so raw and powerful she couldn't bear it. She surged upward, and he controlled the motion, holding her down, transferring his mouth to her other nipple, which received the same tender care and enticement, then the sudden, deliberate pressure that made her cry out again.

He wouldn't stop. She screamed for him to, begged him, but he wouldn't stop. She heard her voice, frantic, pleading: "Zane—please. Oh, God, please. Don't—more.

More." And then, sobbing, *"Harder!"* And she realized she wasn't begging him to stop, but to continue. She writhed in his arms as he pushed her higher and higher, harder and harder, his mouth voracious on her breasts, and suddenly all her senses coalesced into a huge single throb that centered in her loins, and she came apart with pleasure.

When she could breathe again, think again, her limbs were weak and useless in the aftermath. She lay limply on the bed, her eyes closed, and wondered how she had survived the implosion.

"Just from sucking your breasts?" he murmured incredulously as he kissed his way down her stomach. "Oh, damn, are we going to have fun for the next seven months!"

"Zane…wait," she whispered, lifting one hand to his head. It was the only movement she had enough energy to make. "I can't—I need to rest."

He slid down between her legs and lifted her thighs onto his shoulders. "You don't have to move," he promised her in a deep, rich voice. "All you have to do is lie there." Then he kissed her, slowly, deeply, and her body arched as it began all over again, and he showed her all the things he hadn't been able to do to her before.

He brought her to completion once more before finally crawling forward and settling his hips between her thighs. She moaned when he filled her with a smooth, powerful thrust. She quivered beneath him, shocked by the thickness and depth of his penetration. How could she have forgotten? The discomfort took her by surprise, and she clung to him as she tried to adjust, to accept. He soothed her, whispering hot, soft words in her ear, stroking her flesh, which was already so sensitive that even the smooth sheet beneath her felt abrasive.

But, oh, how she had wanted this. *This*. Not just plea-sure, but the sense of being joined together, the deep and intimate linkage of their bodies. This fed a craving within her that the climaxes he'd given her hadn't begun to touch. Her hips lifted. She wanted all of him, wanted him so deep that he touched her womb, ripening with his seed. He tried to moderate the thrusts that were rapidly pushing her toward yet another climax, but she dug her nails into his back, insisting without words on everything he had to give.

He shuddered, and with a deep-throated groan, gave her what she asked.

She slept then. It was long after midnight on the east coast, and she was exhausted. She was disturbed by the presence of the big, muscled man beside her in the bed, though, his body radiating heat like a furnace, and she kept waking from a restless doze.

He must sleep like a cat, she thought, because every time she woke and changed positions, he woke up, too. Finally he pulled her on top of him, settling her with her face tucked against his neck and her legs straddling his hips. "Maybe now you can rest," he murmured, kissing her hair. "You slept this way in Benghazi."

She remembered that, remembered the long day of making love, how he had sometimes been on top when they dozed, and sometimes she had. Or perhaps she had been the only one who dozed while he had remained alert.

"I've never slept with a man before," she murmured in sleepy explanation, nestling against him. "*Slept* slept, that is."

"I know. I'm your first in both cases."

The room was dark; at some time he had turned off the lamp, though she didn't remember when. The heavy curtains were drawn against the neon of the Las Vegas night, with only thin strips of light penetrating around the edges. It reminded her briefly of that horrible room in Benghazi, before Zane had taken her away, but then she shut out the memory. That no longer had the power to frighten her. Zane was her husband now, and the pleasant ache in her body told her that the marriage had been well and truly consummated.

"Tell me about your family," she said, and yawned against his neck.

"Now?"

"Mmm. We're both awake, so you might as well."

There was a twitch of flesh against her inner thigh. "I can think of other things to do," he muttered.

"I'm not ruling anything out." She wriggled her hips and was rewarded by a more insistent movement. "But you can talk, too. Tell me about the Mackenzie clan."

She could feel his slight shrug. "My dad is a half-breed American Indian, my mom is a schoolteacher. They live on a mountain just outside Ruth, Wyoming. Dad raises and trains horses. He's the best I've ever seen, except for my sister. Maris is magic with horses."

"So the horses really are a family business."

"Yep. We were all raised on horseback, but Maris is the only one who went into the training aspect. Joe went to the Air Force Academy and became a jet jockey, Mike became a cattle rancher, Josh rode jets for the Navy, and Chance and I went to the Naval Academy and got our water wings. We can both fly various types of aircraft, but flying is just a means of getting us to where we're needed, nothing else. Chance got out of Naval Intelligence a couple of years ago."

Barrie's talent with names kicked in. She lifted her head, all sleepiness gone as she ran that list of names through her head. She settled on one, put the details together and gasped. "Your brother is General Joe Mackenzie on the Joint Chiefs of Staff?" Of course. How many Joe Mackenzies were Air Force generals?

"The one and only."

"Why, I've met him and his wife. I think it was the year before last, at a charity function in Washington. Her name is Caroline."

"You're right on target." He shifted a little, and she felt a nudging between her legs. She inhaled as he slipped inside her. Talk about right on target.

"Joe and Caroline have five sons, Michael and Shea have two boys, and Josh and Loren have three," Zane murmured, gently thrusting. "Junior will be the eleventh grandchild."

Barrie sank against him, her attention splintered by the pleasure building with each movement of his hips. "Don't talk," she said, and heard his quiet laughter as he rolled over and placed her beneath him…just where she wanted to be.

Chapter 12

Barrie awoke to nausea, sharp and urgent. She bolted out of bed and into the bathroom, barely reaching it in time. When the bout of vomiting was over, she sank weakly to the floor and closed her eyes, unable to work up enough energy to care that she was curled naked on the floor of a hotel bathroom, or that her husband of less than twelve hours was witness to it all. She heard Zane running water; then a wonderfully cool, wet washcloth was placed on her heated forehead. He flushed the toilet, something she hadn't been able to manage, and said, "I'll be right back."

As usual, she rapidly began to feel better after she had thrown up. Embarrassed, she got up and washed out her mouth and was standing in front of the mirror surveying her tousled appearance with some astonishment when Zane appeared with a familiar green can in his hand.

He had already popped the top. She snatched the can from him and began greedily drinking, tilting the can up like some college freshman guzzling beer. When it was empty, she sighed with repletion and slammed the can down on the countertop as if it was indeed an empty soldier of spirits. Then she looked at Zane, and her eyes widened.

"I hope you didn't go out to the drink machine like that," she said faintly. He was still naked. Wonderfully, impressively naked. And very aroused.

He looked amused. "I got it out of the minibar in the parlor." He glanced down at himself, and the amusement deepened. "There's another can. Want to go for it?"

Barrie drew herself up and folded a bold hand around his thrusting sex. "I'm not the kind of woman who loses her inhibitions after a couple of Seven-Ups," she informed him with careful dignity. She paused, then winked at him. "One will do."

Somehow she had expected they would make it back to the bed. They didn't. His hunger was particularly strong in the mornings, and after a tempestuous few moments she found herself on her knees, half bent over the edge of the bathtub while he crouched behind her. Their lovemaking was raw and fast and powerful, and left her once again lying weakly on the floor. She found some satisfaction in the fact that he was sprawled beside her, his long legs stretched under the vanity top.

After a long time he said lazily, "I'd thought I could wait until we were in the shower. I underestimated the effect of a soft drink on you, sweetheart…and what watching you drink it does to me."

"I think we're on to something," she reflected, curling nakedly against him and ignoring the chill of the floor. "We need to buy stock in the company."

"Good idea." He turned his head and began kissing her, and for a moment she wondered if the bathroom floor was going to get another workout. But he released her and rose lithely to his feet, then helped her up. "Do you want to have room service, or go down to a restaurant for breakfast?"

"Room service." She was already hungry, and with room service their breakfast should be there by the time she showered and dressed. She gave Zane her order, then, while he called it in, she selected the clothes she wanted. The silk dress was badly wrinkled, so she carried it into the bathroom with her to let the steam from her shower repair the damage.

She took her time in the shower, but even so, some wrinkles remained in the dress by the time she finished. She left the water running and turned it on hot to increase the amount of steam. On a hook behind the door hung a thick terry-cloth bathrobe with the hotel's logo stitched on the breast pocket. She pulled it on and belted it around her, smiling at the weight and size of the garment, and went out to see how long it would be before their breakfast arrived.

Zane wasn't in the bedroom; she could hear him talking in the parlor, and wondered if room service had been unusually quick. But she heard only his voice as she walked to the open door.

He was on the phone, half-turned away from her as he sat on the arm of the couch. She had the impression that he was listening to the shower running even as he carried on his conversation.

"Keep the tail on her father, as well as on *his* tail," he was saying. "I want to catch them all at one time, so I don't have to worry about any loose ends. When the dust settles, Justice and State can sort it out between them."

Barrie gasped, all the color washing out of her face.

Zane's head jerked around, and he stared at her, the blue mostly gone from his eyes, leaving them as sharp and gray as frost.

"Yeah," he said into the receiver, his gaze never wavering from hers. "Everything's under control here. Keep the pressure on." He hung up and turned fully to face her.

He hadn't showered yet, she noticed dully. His hair wasn't wet; there was no betraying dampness to his skin. He must have gotten on the phone as soon as she had begun her shower, setting in motion the betrayal that could send her father to jail.

"What have you done?" she whispered, barely holding herself together against the pain that racked her. "Zane, *what have you done?*"

Coolly he stood and came toward her. Barrie backed up, clutching the lapels of the thick robe as if it could protect her.

He flicked a curious glance toward the bathroom, where billows of steam were escaping from the half-open door. "Why is the shower still running?"

"I'm steaming the wrinkles out of my dress," she answered automatically.

His eyebrows lifted wryly. Though she didn't find the pun amusing, she had the thought that this was evidently a wrinkle he hadn't anticipated.

"Who were you talking to?" she asked, her voice stiff with hurt and betrayal and the strain of holding it all under control.

"My brother Chance."

"What does he have to do with my father?"

Zane watched her steadily. "Chance does intelligence work for a government agency; not the FBI or CIA."

Barrie swallowed against the constriction in her throat.

Maybe Zane hadn't betrayed her father; maybe he'd already been under surveillance. "How long has he been following my father?"

"Chance is directing the tails, not doing them himself," Zane corrected.

"How long?"

"Since last night. I called him while you were showering then, too."

At least he didn't try to lie or evade. "How could you?" she whispered, her eyes wide and stark.

"Very easily," he replied, his voice sharp. "I'm an officer of the law. Before that, I was an officer in the Navy, in service to this country. Did you think I would ignore a traitor, even if it's your father? You asked me to protect you and our baby, and that's exactly what I'm doing. When you clean out a nest of snakes, you don't pick out a few of them to kill and leave the others. You wipe them out."

The edges of her vision blurred, and she felt herself sway. Oh, God, how could she ever forgive him if her father went to prison? How could she ever forgive herself? She was the cause of this. She had known the kind of man Zane was, but she had allowed herself to ignore it because she'd wanted him so desperately. Of course he'd turned her father in; if she'd been thinking clearly, instead of with her emotions, her hormones, she would have known exactly what he would do, what he had done. It didn't take a genius to predict the actions of a man who had spent his life upholding the laws of his country, and only a fool would ignore the obvious conclusion.

She hadn't even thought about it, so she guessed that made her the biggest fool alive.

She heard him say her name, his tone insistent, and

then her vision was blocked by his big body as he gripped her arms.

Desperately she hung on to consciousness, gulping in air and refusing to let herself faint. ''Let go of me,'' she protested, and was shocked at how far away her voice sounded.

''Like hell I will.'' Instead he swung her off her feet and carried her to the bed, then bent to place her on the tumbled sheets.

As he had the night before, he sat beside her. Now that she was lying down, her head cleared rapidly. He was leaning over her, one arm braced on the other side of her hip, enclosing her in the iron circle of his embrace. His gaze never left her face.

Barrie wished she could find refuge in anger, but there was none. She understood Zane's motives, and his actions. All she could feel was a huge whirlpool of pain, sucking her down. Her father! As much as she loved Zane, she didn't know if she could bear it if he caused her father to be arrested. This wasn't anything like theft or drunken driving. Treason was heinous, unthinkable. No matter what conclusion her logic drew, she simply couldn't see her father doing anything like that, unless he was somehow being forced to do it. She knew *she* wasn't the weapon being used against him, although she had been drawn into it, probably when he had balked at something. No, she and Zane had both realized immediately that if she was being threatened and her father had nothing to hide, he would have had her whisked away by the FBI before she knew what was happening.

''Please,'' she begged, clutching his arm. ''Can't you warn him somehow, get him out of it? I know you didn't like him, but you don't know him the way I do. He's always done what he thought was best for me. He was always there when I needed him, and b-before I left he gave me his blessing.'' Her voice broke on a sob, and she quickly controlled it. ''I know he's a snob, but he isn't a bad person! If he's gotten involved in something he shouldn't, it was by accident, and now he doesn't know how to get out without endangering me! That *has* to be it. Zane, please!''

He caught her hand, folding it warmly within his. ''I can't do that,'' he said quietly. ''If he hasn't done anything wrong, he'll be all right. If he's a traitor—'' He shrugged, indicating the lack of options. He wouldn't lift a finger to help a traitor, period. ''I didn't want you to know anything about it because I didn't want you to be upset any more than necessary. I knew I wouldn't be able to protect you from worry if he's arrested, but I didn't want you to find out about it beforehand. You've had enough to deal with these past couple of months. My first priority is keeping you and the baby safe, and I'll do that, Barrie, no matter what.''

She stared at him through tear-blurred eyes, knowing she had collided with the steel wall of his convictions. Honor wasn't just a concept to him, but a way of life. Still, there was one way she might reach him. ''What if it was *your* father?'' she asked.

A brief spasm touched his face, telling her that she'd struck a nerve. ''I don't know,'' he admitted. ''I hope I'd be able to do what's right...but I don't know.''

There was nothing more she could say.

The only thing she could do was warn her father herself.

She moved away from him, sliding off the bed. He lifted his arm and let her go, though he watched her closely, as if waiting for her to faint or throw up or slap him in the face. Considering her pregnancy and her state of mind, she realized, all three were possible, if she relaxed her control just a fraction. But she wasn't going to do any of them, because she couldn't afford to waste the time.

She hugged the oversize robe about her, as she had once hugged his shirt. "What exactly is your brother doing?" She needed as much information as possible if she was going to help her father. Maybe it was wrong, but she would worry about that, and face the consequences, later. She knew she was operating on love and blind trust, but that was all she had to go on. When she thought of her father as the man she knew him to be, she knew she had to trust both that knowledge and his honor. Despite their enormous differences, in that respect he was very like Zane, the man he'd scorned as a son-in-law: honor was a part of his code, his life, his very being.

Zane stood. "You don't need to know, exactly."

For the first time she felt the flush of anger redden her cheeks. "Don't throw my words back at me," she snapped. "You can say no without being sarcastic."

He studied her, then gave a curt nod. "You're right. I'm sorry."

She stalked into the bathroom and slammed the door. The small room was hot and damp with steam, the air thick with it. Barrie turned off the shower and turned on the exhaust fan. There wasn't a wrinkle left in the silk dress. Hurriedly she shed the robe and pulled on the underwear she'd carried into the bathroom, then pulled the dress on over her head. The silk stuck to her damp skin; she had to jerk the fabric to get it into place. The need to hurry beat through her like wings. How much time did she have before room service arrived with their breakfast?

The mirror was fogged over. She grabbed a towel and

rubbed a clear spot on the glass, then swiftly combed her hair and began applying a minimum of makeup. The air was so steamy that it would be a wasted effort to apply very much, but she wanted to appear as normal as possible.

Oh, God, the exhaust fan was making so much noise she might not have heard their breakfast arriving. Hastily she cut it off. Zane would have knocked if their food was here, she assured herself. It hadn't arrived yet.

She tried to remember where her purse was, and think how she could get it and get out the door without Zane knowing. His hearing was acute, and he would be watching for her. But the room service waiter would bring their breakfast to the parlor, and Zane, being as cautious as he was, would watch the man's every move. That was the only time he would be distracted, and the only chance she would have to get out of the room undetected. Her window of opportunity would be brief, because he would call her as soon as the waiter left. If she had to wait for an elevator, she was sunk. She could always try the stairs, but all Zane would have to do was take the elevator down to the lobby and wait for her there. With his hearing, he probably heard the elevator every time it chimed, and that would give him an idea of whether she had been able to get one of the cars or had taken the stairs.

She opened the bathroom door a little, so he wouldn't be able to catch the click of the latch.

''What are you doing?'' he called. It sounded as if he was standing just inside the double doors that connected the bedroom to the parlor, waiting for her.

''Putting on makeup,'' she snapped, with perfect truth. She blotted the sweat off her forehead and began again with the powder. Her brief flash of anger was over, but she didn't want him to know it. Let him think she was furious; a woman who was both pregnant and angry deserved a lot of space.

There was a brief knock on the parlor door, and a Spanish-accented voice called out, "Room service."

Quickly Barrie switched on the faucet, so the sound of running water would once again mask her movements. Peering through the small opening by the door, she saw Zane cross her field of vision, going to answer the knock. He was wearing his shoulder holster, which meant, as she had hoped, that he was on guard.

She slipped out of the bathroom, carefully pulled the door back to leave the same small opening, then darted to the other side of the bedroom, out of his line of sight if he glanced inside when he passed by the double doors. Her purse was lying on one of the chairs, and she snatched it up, then slipped her feet into her shoes.

The room service cart clattered as it was rolled into the room. Through the open parlor doors she could hear the waiter casually chatting as he set up the table. Zane's pistol made the waiter nervous; she could hear it in his voice. And his nervousness made Zane that much more wary of him. Zane was probably watching him like a hawk, those pale eyes remote and glacier-cold.

Now was the tricky part. She eased up to the open double doors, peeking through the crack to locate her husband. Relief made her knees wobble; he was standing with his back to the doors while he watched the waiter. The running faucet was doing its job; he was listening to it, rather than positioning himself on the other side of the table so he could watch both the waiter and the bathroom door. He probably did it deliberately, dividing his senses rather than diluting the visual attention he was paying to the waiter.

Her husband was not an ordinary man. Escaping him, even for five minutes, wouldn't be easy.

Taking a deep breath, she silently crossed the open expanse, every nerve in her body drawn tight as she waited for his hard hand to clamp down on her shoulder. She reached the bedroom door to the hallway and held the chain so it wouldn't clink when she slipped it free. That done, her next obstacle was the lock. She moved her body as close to the door as possible, using her flesh to muffle the sound, and slowly turned the latch. The dead bolt slid open with smooth precision and a snick that was barely audible even to her.

She closed her eyes and turned the handle then, concentrating on keeping the movement smooth and silent. If it made any noise, she was caught. If anyone was walking by in the hallway and talking, the change in noise level would alert Zane, and she was caught. If the elevator was slow, she was caught. Everything had to be perfect, or she didn't have a chance.

How much longer did she have? It felt as if she had already taken ten minutes, but it was probably no more than one. Crockery was still rattling in the parlor as the waiter arranged their plates and saucers and water glasses. The door opened, and she slipped through, then spent the same agonizing amount of time making sure it closed as silently as it opened. She released the handle and ran.

She reached the elevators without hearing him shout her name and jabbed the down button. It obediently lit, and remained lit. There was no welcoming chime to signal the arrival of the elevator. Barrie restrained herself from punching the button over and over again in a futile attempt to convey her urgency to a piece of machinery.

"Please," she whispered under her breath. *"Hurry."*

She would have tried calling her father from the hotel room, but she knew Zane would stop her if he heard her on the phone. She also knew her father's phone was tapped, which meant that incoming calls were automatically recorded. She would try to protect her father, but she refused to do anything that might endanger either Zane or their baby by leading the kidnappers straight to the hotel. She would have to call her father from a pay phone on the street, and a different street, at that.

Down the hall, she heard the room service cart clatter again as the waiter left their suite. Her heart pounding, she stared at the closed elevator doors, willing them to open. Her time was down to mere seconds.

The melodic chime sounded overhead.

The doors slid open.

She looked back as she stepped inside, and her heart nearly stopped. Zane hadn't yelled, hadn't called her name. He was running full speed down the hall, his motion as fluid and powerful as a linebacker's, and pure fury was blazing in his eyes.

He was almost there.

Panicked, she simultaneously pushed the buttons for the lobby and for the door to close. She stepped back from the closing gap as Zane lunged forward, trying to get his hand in the door, which would trigger the automatic opening sensor.

He didn't quite make it. The doors slid shut, and the box began to move downward. "God *damn* it," he roared in frustration, and Barrie flinched as his fist thudded against the doors.

Weakly she leaned against the wall and covered her face with her hands while she shook with reaction. Dear God, she'd never imagined anyone could be so angry.

He'd been almost incandescent with it, his eyes all but glowing.

He was probably racing down the stairs, but he had twenty-one floors to cover, and he was no match for the elevator—unless it stopped to pick up passengers on other floors. This possibility nearly brought her to her knees. She watched the numbers change, unable to breathe. If it stopped even once, he might catch her in the street. If it stopped twice, he would catch her in the lobby. Three times, and he would be waiting for her at the elevator.

She would have to face that rage, and she'd never dreaded anything more. Leaving Zane had never been her intention. After she'd warned her father, she would go back to the suite. She didn't fear Zane physically; she knew instinctively that he would never hit her, but somehow that wasn't much comfort.

She had wanted to see him lose control, outside of that final moment in lovemaking when his body took charge and he gave himself over to orgasm. Nausea roiled in her stomach, and she shuddered. Why had she ever wished for such a stupid thing? Oh, God, she never wanted to see him lose his temper again.

He might never forgive her. She might be forsaking forever any chance that he could love her. The full knowledge of what she was risking to warn her father rode her shoulders all the way to the lobby, one long, smooth descent, without any stops.

The rattle and clink of the slot machines never stopped, no matter how early or how late. The din surrounded her as she hurried through the lobby and out to the street. The desert sun was blindingly white, the temperature already edging past ninety, though the morning was only half gone. Barrie joined the tourists thronging the sidewalk, walking quickly despite the heat. She reached the corner, crossed the street and kept walking, not daring to look back. Her red hair would be fairly easy to spot at a distance, even in a crowd, unless she was hidden by someone taller. Zane would have reached the lobby by now. He would quickly scan the slot machine crowd, then erupt onto the street.

Her chest ached, and she realized she was holding her breath again. She gulped in air and hurried to put a building between herself and the hotel entrance. She was afraid to look back, afraid she would see her big, black-haired husband bearing down on her like a thunderstorm, and she knew she would never be able to outrun him.

She crossed one more street and began looking for a pay phone. They were easy to find, but getting an available one was something else again. Why were so many tourists using pay phones at this time of the morning? Barrie stood patiently, the hot sun beating down on her head, while a blue-haired elderly lady in support stockings gave detailed instructions to someone on when to feed her cat, when to feed her fish and when to feed her plants. Finally she hung up with a cheerful, ''Bye-bye, dearie,'' and she gave Barrie a sweet smile as she hobbled past. The smile was so unexpected that Barrie almost burst into tears. Instead she managed a smile of her own and stepped up to the phone before anyone could squeeze ahead of her.

She used her calling card number because it was faster, and since she was calling from a pay phone, it didn't matter how she placed the call. *Please, God, let him be there*, she silently prayed as she listened to the tones, then the ringing. It was lunchtime on the east coast; he could be having lunch with someone, or playing golf—he could be anywhere. She tried to remember his schedule, but nothing came to mind. Their relationship had been so strained for the past two months that she had disassociated herself from his social and political appointments.

"Hello?"

The answer was so cautious, so wary sounding, that at first she didn't recognize her father's voice.

"Hello?" he said again, sounding even more wary, if possible.

Barrie pressed the handset hard to her ear, trying to keep her hand from shaking. "Daddy," she said, her voice strangled. She hadn't called him Daddy in years, but the old name slipped out past the barrier of her adulthood.

"Barrie? Sweetheart?" Life zinged into his voice, and she could picture him in her mind, sitting up straighter at his desk.

"Daddy, I can't say much." She fought to keep her voice even, so he would be able to understand her. "You have to be careful. You have to protect yourself. People *know*. Do you hear me?"

He was silent a moment, then he said with a calmness that was beyond her, "I understand. Are you safe?"

"Yes," she said, though she wasn't sure. She still had to face her husband.

"Then take care, sweetheart, and I'll talk to you soon."

"Bye," she whispered, then carefully hung the receiver in its cradle and turned to go to the hotel. She had taken about ten steps when she was captured in the hard grip she had been dreading. She didn't see him coming, so she couldn't brace herself. One second he wasn't there, the next second he was, surfacing out of the crowd like a shark.

Despite everything, she was glad to see him, glad to

get it over with instead of dreading the first meeting during every dragging step to the hotel. The tension and effort had drained her. She leaned weakly against him, and he clamped his arm around her waist to support her. "You shouldn't be out in the sun without something on your head," was all he said. "Especially since you haven't eaten anything today."

He was in control, that incandescent fury cooled and conquered. She wasn't foolish enough to believe it was gone, however. "I had to warn him," she said tiredly. "And I didn't want the call traced to the hotel."

"I know." The words were brief to the point of curtness. "It might not make any difference. Las Vegas is crawling with a certain group of people this morning, and you may have been spotted. Your hair." Those two words were enough. Redheads were always distinctive, because there were so few of them. She felt like apologizing for the deep, rich luster of her hair.

"They're here?" she asked in a small voice. "The kidnappers?"

"Not the original ones. There's a deep game going on, baby, and I'm afraid you just jumped into the middle of it."

The sun beat down on her unprotected head, the heat increasing by the minute. Every step seemed more and more of an effort. Her thoughts scattered. She might have plunged Zane and herself into the very danger she'd wanted to avoid. "Maybe I *am* a pampered society babe with more hair than brains," she said aloud. "I didn't mean—"

"I know," he said again, and unbelievably, he squeezed her waist. "And I never said you have more hair than brains. If anything, you're too damn smart, and it seems you have a natural talent for sneaking around.

Not many people could have gotten out of that suite without me hearing them. Spook, maybe. And Chance. No one else.''

Barrie leaned more of her weight against him. She was on his left side, and she felt the hard lump of the holster beneath his jacket. When he'd grabbed her, he'd instinctively kept his right hand free, in case he needed his pistol. What he *didn't* need, she thought tiredly, was having to support her weight and keep his balance in a firefight. She forced herself to straighten away from him, despite the way his arm tightened around her waist. He gave her a questioning look.

''I don't want to impede you,'' she explained.

His mouth curved wryly. ''See what I mean? Now you're thinking of combat stuff. If you weren't so sweet, Mrs. Mackenzie, you'd be a dangerous woman.''

Why wasn't he lambasting her? She couldn't imagine he'd gotten over his fury so fast; Zane struck her as the type of man who seldom lost his temper, but when he did, it was undoubtedly a memorable occasion—one that could last for years. Maybe he was saving it for when they were in the privacy of the suite, remaining on guard while they were in the street. He could do that, compartmentalize his anger, shove it aside until it was safe to bring it out.

She found herself studying the surging, milling, strolling crowd of tourists that surrounded them, looking for any betraying sign of interest. It helped take her mind off how incredibly weak she felt. This pregnancy was making itself felt with increasing force; though it had been foolish of her to come out into the sun without eating breakfast, and without a hat, normally she wouldn't have had any problem with the heat in this short amount of time.

How much farther was it to the hotel? She concentrated on her steps, on the faces around her. Zane maintained a slow, steady pace, and when he could, he put himself between her and the sun. The human shade helped, marginally.

"Here we are," he said, ushering her into the cool, dim cavern of the lobby. She closed her eyes to help them adjust from the bright sunlight and sighed with relief as the blast of air-conditioning washed over her.

The elevator was crowded on the ride up. Zane pulled her against the back wall, so he would have one less side to protect, and also to set up a human wall of protection between them and the open doors. She felt a faint spurt of surprise as she realized she knew what he was thinking, the motives behind his actions. He would do what he could to keep anything from happening, and to protect these people, but if push came to shove, he would ruthlessly sacrifice the other people in this elevator to keep her safe.

They got off on the twenty-first floor, the ride uneventful. A man and woman got off at the same time, a middle-aged couple with Rochester accents. They turned down the hallway leading away from the suite. Zane guided Barrie after them, following the couple until they reached their room around the corner. As they walked past, Barrie glanced inside the room as the couple entered it; it was untidy, piled with shopping bags and the dirty clothes they'd worn the day before.

"Safe," Zane murmured as they wound their way to the suite.

"They wouldn't have had all the tourist stuff if they'd just arrived?"

He slanted an unreadable look at her. "Yeah."

The suite was blessedly cool. She stumbled inside, and

Zane locked and chained the door. Their breakfast still sat on the table, untouched and cold. He all but pushed her into a chair anyway. "Eat," he ordered. "Just the toast, if nothing else. Put jelly on it. And drink all the water." He sat down on the arm of the couch, picked up the phone and began dialing.

Just to be safe, she ate half a slice of dry toast first, eschewing the balls of butter, which wouldn't melt on the cold toast anyway. Her stomach was peaceful at the moment, but she didn't want to do anything to upset it. She smeared the second half slice with jelly.

As she methodically ate and drank, she began to feel better. Zane was making no effort to keep her from hearing his conversation, and she gathered he was talking to his brother Chance again.

"If she was spotted, we have maybe half an hour," he was saying. "Get everyone on alert." He listened a moment, then said, "Yeah, I know. I'm slipping." He said goodbye with a cryptic, "Keep it cool."

"Keep what cool?" Barrie asked, turning in her chair to face him.

A flicker of amusement lightened his remote eyes. "Chance has a habit of sticking his nose, along with another part of his anatomy, into hot spots. He gets burned occasionally."

"And you don't, I suppose?"

He shrugged. "Occasionally," he admitted.

He was very calm, unusually so, even for him. It was like waiting for a storm to break. Barrie took a deep breath and braced herself. "All right, I'm feeling better," she said, more evenly than she felt. "Let me have it."

He regarded her for a moment, then shook his head—regretfully, she thought. "It'll have to wait. Chance said there's a lot of activity going on all of a sudden. It's all about to hit the fan."

Chapter 13

They didn't have even the half hour Zane had hoped for.

The phone rang, and he picked it up. "Roger," he said, and placed the receiver into its cradle. He stood and strode over to Barrie. "They're moving in," he said, lifting her from the chair with an implacable hand. "And you're going to a different floor."

He was shoving her out of harm's way. She stiffened against the pressure of his hand, digging in her heels. He stopped and turned to face her, then placed his hand over her belly. "You have to go," he said, without a flicker of emotion. He was in combat mode, his face impassive, his eyes cold and distant.

He was right. Because of the baby, she had to go. She put her hand over his. "All right. But do you have an extra pistol I could have—just in case?"

He hesitated briefly, then strode into the bedroom to

his garment bag. The weapon he removed was a compact, five-shot revolver. "Do you know how to use it?"

She folded her hand around the butt, feeling the smoothness of the wood. "I've shot skeet, but I've never used a handgun. I'll manage."

"There's no empty chamber, and no safety," he said as he escorted her out the door. "You can pull the hammer back before you fire, or you can use a little more effort and just pull the trigger. Nothing to it but aiming and firing. It's a thirty-eight caliber, so it has stopping power." He was walking swiftly toward the stairs as he talked. He opened the stairwell door and began pushing her up the stairs, their steps echoing in the concrete silo. "I'm going to put you in an empty room on the twenty-third floor, and I want you to stay there until either Chance or I come for you. If anyone else opens the door, shoot them."

"I don't know what Chance looks like," she blurted.

"Black hair, hazel eyes. Tall. So good-looking you start drooling when you see him. That's what he says women do, anyway."

They reached the twenty-third floor. Barrie was only slightly winded, Zane not at all. As they stepped into the carpeted silence of the hallway, she asked, "How do you know which rooms are empty?"

He produced one of the electronic cards from his pocket. "Because one of Chance's people booked the room last night and slipped me the key card while we were eating supper. Just in case."

He always had an alternate plan—just in case. She should have guessed.

He opened the door to room 2334 and ushered her inside, but he didn't enter himself. "Lock and chain the door, and stay put," he said, then turned and walked swiftly toward the stairwell. Barrie stood in the doorway and watched him. He stopped and looked at her over his shoulder. "I'm waiting to hear the door being locked," he said softly.

She stepped back, turned the lock and slid the chain into place.

Then she stood in the middle of the neat, silent room and quietly went to pieces.

She couldn't stand it. Zane was deliberately walking into danger—*on her account*—and she couldn't join him. She couldn't be there with him, couldn't guard his back. Because of the baby growing inside her, she was relegated to this safe niche while the man she loved faced bullets for her.

She sat on the floor and rocked back and forth, her arms folded over her stomach, keening softly as tears rolled down her face. This terror for Zane's safety was worse than anything she'd ever felt before, far worse than what she'd known at the hands of her kidnappers, worse even than when he'd been shot. At least she'd *been* there then. She'd been able to help, able to touch him.

She couldn't do anything now.

A sharp, deep report that sounded like thunder made her jump. Except it wasn't thunder; the desert sky was bright and cloudless. She buried her face against her knees, weeping harder. More shots. Some lighter, flatter in tone. A peculiar cough. Another deep thundering, then several in quick succession.

Then silence.

She pulled herself together and scrambled to the far corner of the room, behind the bed. She sat with her back against the wall and her arms braced on her knees, the pistol steady as she held it trained on the door. She didn't see how anyone other than Zane or Chance could know where she was, but she wouldn't gamble on it. She didn't know what any of this was about, or who her enemies were, except for Mack Prewett, probably.

Time crawled past. She didn't have her wristwatch on, and the clock radio on the bedside table was turned away from her. She didn't get up to check the time. She simply sat there with the pistol in her hand and waited, and died a little more with each passing minute of Zane's absence.

He didn't come. She felt the coldness of despair grow in her heart, spreading until it filled her chest, the pressure of it almost stopping her lungs. Her heartbeat slowed to a heavy, painful rhythm. *Zane.* He would have come, if he'd been able. He'd been shot again. Wounded. She wouldn't let herself even think the word *dead,* but it was there, in her heart, her chest, and she didn't know how she could go on.

There was a brief knock on the door. "Barrie?" came a soft call, a voice that sounded tired and familiar. "It's Art Sandefer. It's over. Mack's in custody, and you can come out now."

Only Zane and Chance were supposed to know where she was. Zane had said that if anyone else opened the door, to shoot them. But she'd known Art Sandefer for years, known and respected both the man and the job he did. If Mack Prewett had been dirty, Art would have been on top of it. His presence here made sense.

"Barrie?" The door handle rattled.

She started to get up and let him in, then sank back to the floor. No. He wasn't Zane and he wasn't Chance. If she had lost Zane, the least she could do was follow his last instructions to the letter. His objective had been her safety, and she trusted him more than she had ever trusted anyone else in her life, including her father. She definitely trusted him more than she did Art Sandefer.

She was unprepared for the peculiar little coughing sound. Then the lock on the door exploded, and Art Sandefer pushed the door open and stepped inside. In his hand was a pistol with a thick silencer fitted onto the end of the barrel. Their eyes met across the room, his weary and cynical and acutely intelligent. And she knew.

Barrie pulled the trigger.

Zane was there only moments, seconds, later. Art had slumped to a sitting position against the open door, his hand pressed to the hole in his chest as his eyes glazed with shock. Zane kicked the weapon from Art's outstretched hand, but that was all the attention he paid to the wounded man. He stepped over him as if he wasn't there, rapidly crossing the room to where Barrie sat huddled in the corner, her face drawn and gray. Her gaze was oddly distant and unfocused. Panic roared through him, but a swift inspection didn't reveal any blood. She looked unharmed.

He hunkered down beside her, gently brushing her hair from her face. "Sweetheart?" he asked in a soft tone. "It's over now. Are you all right?"

She didn't answer. He sat down on the floor beside her and pulled her onto his lap, holding her close and tight against the warmth of his body. He kept up a reassuring murmur, a gentle sound of reassurance. He could feel the thud of her heartbeat against him, the rhythm hard and alarmingly slow. He held her tighter, his face buried against the richness of her hair.

"Is she all right?" Chance asked as he, too, stepped over Art Sandefer and approached his brother and new sister-in-law. Other people were coming into the room, people who tended to the wounded man. Mack Prewett was one of them, his eyes sharp and hard as he watched his former superior.

"She'll be fine," Zane murmured, lifting his head. "She shot Sandefer."

The brothers' eyes met in a moment of understanding. The first one was tough. With luck and good care, Sandefer would survive, but Barrie would always be one of those who knew what it was like to pull that trigger.

"How did he know which room?" Zane asked, keeping his voice calm.

Chance sat down on the bed and leaned forward, his forearms braced on his knees. His expression was pleasant enough, his eyes cool and thoughtful. "I must have a leak in my group," he said matter-of-factly. "And I know who it is, because only one person knew this room number. I'll take care of it."

"You do that."

Barrie stirred in Zane's grip, her arms lifting to twine around his neck. "Zane," she said, her voice faint and choked, shaking.

Because he'd felt the same way, he heard the panic in her voice, the despair. "I'm okay," he whispered, kissing her temple. "I'm okay."

A sob shook her, then was quickly controlled. She was soldiering on. Emotion swelled in his chest, a huge golden bubble of such force that it threatened to stop his breathing, his heartbeat. He closed his eyes to hold back the tears that burned his lids. "Oh, God," he said shakily. "I thought I was too late. I saw Sandefer walk in before I could get off a round at him, and then I heard the shot."

Her arms tightened convulsively around his neck, but she didn't say anything.

Zane put his hand on her belly, gulping in air as he fought for control. He was trembling, he noticed with distant surprise. Only Barrie could make mincemeat of his nerves. "I want the baby," he said, his voice still shaking. "But I didn't even think about it then. All I could think was that if I lost you—" He broke off, unable to continue.

"Baby?" Chance asked, politely inquiring.

Barrie nodded, her head moving against Zane's chest. Her face was still buried against him, and she didn't look up.

"Barrie, this is my brother Chance," Zane said. His tone was still rough, uneven.

Blindly Barrie held out her hand. Amused, Chance gently shook it, then returned it to Zane's neck. He had yet to see her face. "Glad to meet you," he said. "I'm happy about the baby, too. That should deflect Mom's attention for a while."

The room was filled to overflowing: hotel security, Las Vegas police, medics, not to mention Mack Prewett and the FBI, who were quietly controlling everything. Chance's people had pulled back, melting into the shadows where they belonged, where they operated best. Chance picked up the phone, made one brief call, then said to Zane, "It's taken care of."

Mack Prewett came over and sat down on the bed beside Chance. His face was troubled as he looked at Barrie, clutched so tightly in Zane's arms. "Is she all right?"

"Yes," she said, answering for herself.

"Art's critical, but he might make it. It would save us a lot of trouble if he didn't." Mack's voice was flat, emotionless.

Barrie shuddered.

"You were never meant to be involved, Barrie," Mack said. "I began to think Art was playing both sides, so I asked your father to help me set him up. The information had to be legitimate, and the ambassador knows more people, has access to more inside information, than can be believed. Art went for the bait like a hungry carp. But then he asked for something really critical, the ambassador stalled, and the next thing we knew, you'd been snatched. Your dad nearly came unglued.''

''Then those bastards in Benghazi knew we were coming in,'' Zane said, his eyes going cold.

''Yeah. I managed to shuffle the time frame a little when I gave the information to Art, but that was the most I could do to help. They weren't expecting you as early as you got there.''

''I couldn't believe it of him. Art Sandefer, of all people,'' Barrie said, lifting her head to look at Mack. ''Until I saw his eyes. I thought *you* were the dirty one.''

Mack smiled crookedly. ''It rocked me that you figured out anything was going on at all.''

''Dad tipped me off. He acted so frightened every time I left the house.''

''Art wanted you,'' Mack explained. ''He was playing it cool for a while, or we would have had this wrapped up weeks ago. But it wasn't just the information. Art wanted *you*.''

Barrie was stunned by what Mack was saying. She glanced at Zane and saw his jaw tighten. So that was why she hadn't been raped in Benghazi; Art had been saving her for himself. He could never have released her, of course, if she had seen his face. Perhaps he would have drugged her, but more likely he would simply have raped her, kept her for himself for a while, then killed her. She shuddered, turning her face once more against Zane's throat. She was still having trouble believing he was safe and unharmed; it was difficult to drag herself out of the black pit of despair, even though she knew the worst hadn't happened. She felt numb, sick.

But then a thought occurred to her, one she would have had sooner if concern for Zane hadn't wiped everything else from her mind. She looked at Mack again. "Then my father's in the clear."

"Absolutely. He was working with me from the get-go." He met her gaze and shrugged. "Your dad can be a pain in the rear, but his loyalty was never in question."

"When I called him this morning—"

Mack grimaced. "He was relieved to know you loved him enough to call, despite the evidence against him. Your leaving the hotel stirred up a hornet's nest, though. I thought we had everything under control."

"How?"

"Me," Chance interjected, and for the first time Barrie looked at her brother-in-law. She didn't drool, but she had to admit that his good looks were startling. Viewed objectively, he was the most handsome man she'd ever seen. However, she far preferred Zane's scarred, somber face, with its ancient eyes.

"I checked into another hotel under Zane's name," Chance explained. "You weren't listed at all, but Art knew you were with Zane, because he'd checked the license plate on that rental car and traced the rental to Zane's credit card. We didn't want to make it too obvious for him, we wanted him to have to work to find us, so he wouldn't be suspicious. When he found out you'd married Zane, though, he stopped being so cautious." Chance grinned. "Then you went for a walk this morning, and fubar happened. The pay phone you chose was right across the street from the hotel where I'd checked in, and Art's people spotted you immediately."

Across the room, the medics finally had Art Sandefer

ready for transport to a hospital. Zane watched the man being carried out, then cut his narrowed gaze to Mack. "If I'd known about you a little sooner, most of this could have been avoided."

Mack didn't back down from that glacial stare. "As far as that goes, Commander, I didn't expect you to have the contacts you have—" he glanced at Chance "—or to move as fast as you did. I'd been working on Art for months. You made things happen in one day."

Zane stood, effortlessly lifting Barrie in his arms as he did so. "It's over now," he said with finality. "If you gentlemen will excuse me, I need to take care of my wife."

Taking care of her involved getting a third room, because the suite was in bad shape and he didn't want her to see it. He placed her on the bed, locked the door, then stripped both her and himself and got into bed with her, holding their naked bodies as close together as possible. They both needed the reassurance of bare skin, no barriers between them. He got hard immediately, but now wasn't the time for lovemaking.

Barrie couldn't seem to stop trembling, and, to her astonishment, neither could Zane. They clung together, touching each other's faces, absorbing the smell and feel of each other in an effort to dispel the terror.

"I love you," he whispered, holding her so close her ribs ached from the pressure. "God, I was so scared! I can't keep it together where you're concerned, sweetheart. For the sake of my sanity, I hope the rest of our lives are as dull as dishwater."

"They will be," she promised, kissing his chest. "We'll work on it." And tears blurred her eyes, because she hadn't expected so much, so fast.

Then, finally, it was time for more. Gently he entered her, and they lay entwined, not moving, as if their nerves couldn't stand a sharp assault now, even one of pleasure. That, too, came in its own time…her pleasure, and his.

Epilogue

"Twins," Barrie said, her voice still full of stunned bewilderment as she and Zane drove along the road that wound up the side of Mackenzie's Mountain. "Boys."

"I told you how it would be," Zane said, glancing at the mound of her stomach, which was much too big for five months of pregnancy. "Boys."

She gave him a glassy stare of shock. "You didn't," she said carefully, "say they would come in pairs."

"There haven't been twins in our family before," Zane said, just as carefully. In truth, he felt as shaky as Barrie did. "This is a first."

She stared out the window, her gaze passing blindly over the breathtaking vista of craggy blue mountains. They lived in Wyoming now; with Zane's two-year tenure as sheriff in Arizona over, he had declined to run for election, and they had moved closer to the rest of the family. Chance had been after him for those two years to join his organization—though Barrie still wasn't certain exactly what that organization *was*—and Zane had finally relented. He wouldn't be doing fieldwork, because he didn't want to risk the life he had with Barrie and Nick and now these two new babies who were growing inside her, but he had a rare knack for planning for the unexpected, and that was the talent he was using.

The entire family, including her father, was gathered on the mountain to celebrate the Fourth of July, which was the next day. Zane, Barrie and Nick had driven up two days before for an extended visit, but today had been her scheduled checkup, and he'd driven her into town to the doctor's office. Given the way her waistline had been expanding, they should have expected the news, but Zane had simply figured she was further along in her pregnancy than they'd thought. Seeing those two little fetuses on the ultrasound had been quite a shock, but there hadn't been any doubt about it. Two heads, two tails, four arms and hands, four legs and feet—and both babies definitely male. Very definitely.

"I can't think of two names," Barrie said, sounding very near tears.

Zane reached over to pat her knee. "We have four more months to think of names."

She sniffed. "There's no way," she said, "that I can carry them for four more months. We'll have to come up with names before then."

They *were* big babies, both of them, much bigger than Nick had been at this stage.

"After Nick, it took a lot of courage just to think of having another baby," she continued. "I'd geared myself up for one. *One.* Zane, what if *they're both like Nick?*"

He blanched. Nick was a hellion. Nick had a good shot at turning the entire family gray-haired within another year. For a very short person with a limited vocabulary, their offspring could cause an unbelievable uproar in a remarkably short period of time.

They reached the crest of the mountain, and Zane slowed the car as they neared the large, sprawling ranch house. A variety of vehicles were parked around the yard—Wolf's truck, Mary's car, Mike and Shea's Suburban, Josh and Loren's rental, Ambassador Lovejoy's rental, Maris's snazzy truck, Chance's motorcycle. Joe and Caroline and their five hooligans had arrived by helicopter. Boys seemed to be everywhere, from Josh's youngest, age five, to John, who was Joe's oldest and was now in college and here with his current girlfriend.

They were adding two more to the gang.

They got out and walked up the steps to the porch. Zane put his arm around her and hugged her close, tilting her face up for a kiss that quickly grew heated. Barrie glowed with a special sexuality when she was pregnant, and the plain truth was he couldn't resist her. Their love play was often extended these days, now that pregnancy had once again made her breasts as sensitive as they had been when she'd carried Nick.

''Stop that!'' Josh called cheerfully from inside the house. ''That's what got her in that condition in the first place!''

Reluctantly Zane released his wife, and together they went into the house. ''That isn't exactly right,'' he told Josh, who laughed.

The big television was on, and Maris, Josh and Chance were watching some show-jumping event. Wolf and Joe were discussing cattle with Mike. Caroline was arguing politics with the ambassador. Mary and Shea were organizing a game for the younger kids. Loren, who was often an oasis of calm in the middle of the Mackenzie hurricane, gave Barrie's rounded stomach a knowing look. "How did the checkup go?" she asked.

"Twins," Barrie said, still in that numb tone. She gave Zane a helpless, how-did-this-happen look.

The whirlwind of activity came to a sudden stop. Heads lifted and turned. Her father gasped. Mary's face suddenly glowed with radiance.

"Both boys," Zane announced, before anyone could ask.

A sigh almost of relief went around the room. "Thank God," Josh said weakly. "What if it was another one— or *two*—like Nick!"

Barrie's head swiveled around as she began searching for a particular little head. "Where *is* Nick?" she asked.

Chance bolted upright from his sprawled position on the couch. The adults looked around with growing panic. "She was right here," Chance said. "She was dragging one of Dad's boots around."

Zane and Barrie both began a rapid search of the house. "How long ago?" Barrie called.

"Two minutes, no more. Just before you drove up." Maris was on her knees, peering under beds.

"Two minutes!" Barrie almost moaned. In two minutes, Nick could almost single-handedly wreck the house. It was amazing how such a tiny little girl with such an angelic face could be such a demon. "Nick!" she called. "Mary Nicole, come out, come out, wherever you are!" Sometimes that worked. Most times it didn't.

Everyone joined in the search, but their black-haired little terror was nowhere to be found. The entire family had been ecstatic at her birth, and she had been utterly doted on, with even the rough-and-tumble cousins fascinated by the daintiness and beauty of the newest Mackenzie. She really did look angelic, like Pebbles on the old *Flintstones* cartoons. She was adorable. She had Zane's black hair; slanted, deceptively innocent blue eyes; and dimples on each side of her rosebud mouth. She had sat up by herself at four months, crawled at six, walked at eight, and the entire family had been on guard ever since.

They found Wolf's boot beneath Mary's glassed-in collection of angels. From the scuff marks on the wall, Zane deduced his little darling had been trying to knock the collection down by heaving the boot at it. Luckily the boot had been too heavy for her to handle. Her throwing arm wasn't well developed yet, thank God.

She had a frightful temper for such a little thing, and an outsize will, too. Keeping her from doing something she was determined to do was like trying to hold back the tide with a bucket. She had also inherited her father's knack for planning, something that was eerie in a two-year-old. Nick was capable of plotting the downfall of anyone who crossed her.

Once, when Alex, Joe's second oldest, had seen her with a knife in her hand and swiftly snatched it away before she could harm anyone or anything, Nick had thrown a howling temper tantrum that had been halted only when Zane swatted her rear end. Discipline from her adored daddy made her sob so heartbrokenly that everyone else got a lump in their throats. That, and making her sit down in her punishment chair, were so far the only two things they'd discovered that could reduce her to tears.

When she had stopped sobbing, she had pouted in a corner for a while, all the time giving Alex threatening looks over one tiny shoulder. Then she had gone to Barrie for comfort, crawling into her mother's lap to be rocked.

Her next stop had been Zane's lap, to show him that she forgave him. She'd wound her little arms around his neck and rubbed her chubby little cheek against his rough one. She'd even taken a brief nap, lying limply against his broad shoulder. She'd woken, climbed down and darted off to the kitchen, where she'd implored Mary, whom she called Gamma, for a "dink." She was allowed to have soft drinks without caffeine, so Mary had given her one of the green bottles they always kept in store especially for Nick. Zane and Barrie always shared a look of intimate amusement at their daughter's love for Seven-Up, but there was nothing unusual about seeing her clutching the familiar bottle in her tiny hands. She would take a few sips, then with great concentration screw the top onto the bottle and lug it around with her until it was finally empty, which usually took a couple of hours.

On this occasion, Zane had happened to be watching her, smiling at her blissful expression as her little hands closed on the bottle. She had strutted out of the kitchen without letting Mary open the bottle for her and stopped in the hallway, where she vigorously shook the bottle with so much vigor that her entire little body had been bouncing up and down. Then, with a meltingly sweet smile on her face, she had all but danced into the living room and handed the bottle to Alex with a flirtatious tilt of her head. "Ope' it, pees," she'd said in her adorable small voice...and then she'd backed up a few steps.

"No!" Zane had yelled, leaping up from his chair, but it was too late. Alex had already twisted the cap and broken the seal. The bottle spewed and spurted, the sticky liquid spraying the wall, the floor, the chair. It hit Alex full blast in the face. By the time he'd managed to get the cap securely back on the bottle, he was soaked.

Nick had clapped her hands and said, "Hee, hee, hee,"

and Zane wasn't certain if it was a laugh or a taunt. It didn't matter. He had collapsed on the floor in laughter, and there was an unbreakable law written in stone somewhere that you couldn't punish youngsters if you'd laughed at what they'd done.

"Nick!" he called now. "Do you want a Popsicle?" Next to Seven-Ups, Popsicles were her favorite treat.

There was no answer.

Sam tore into the house. He was ten, Josh and Loren's middle son. His blue eyes were wide. "Uncle Zane!" he cried. "Nick's on top of the house!"

"Oh, my God," Barrie gasped, and rushed out of the house as fast as she could. Zane tore past her, his heart in his throat, every instinct screaming for him to get to his child as fast as possible.

Everyone spilled into the yard, their faces pale with alarm, and looked up. Nick was sitting cross-legged on the edge of the roof, her little face blissful as she stared down at them. "Hi," she chirped.

Barrie's knees wobbled, and Mary put a supporting, protective arm around her.

It was no mystery how Nick had gotten on the roof—a ladder was leaning against the house, and Nick was as agile as a young goat. The ladder shouldn't have been there; in fact, Zane would have sworn it hadn't been when he and Barrie had arrived, no more than five minutes earlier.

He started up the ladder, his gaze glued on his daughter. A scowl screwed her small features together, and she scrambled to her feet, perilously close to the edge of the roof. "No!" she shrieked. "No, Daddy!"

He froze in place. She didn't want to come down, and she was absolutely fearless. She paid no more heed to her danger than if she'd been in her bed.

"Zane," Barrie whispered, her voice choked.

He was shaking. Nick stomped one little foot and pointed a dimpled finger at him. "Daddy down," she demanded.

He couldn't get to her in time. No matter how fast he moved, his baby was going to fall. There was only one thing to do. "Chance!" he barked.

Chance knew immediately. He ambled forward, not making any swift movements that would startle her. When he was directly below her, he grinned at his cherubic niece, and she grinned at him. He was her favorite uncle.

"Dance," she crowed, showing all her tiny white teeth.

"You little Antichrist," he said fondly. "I'm really going to miss you when you're in prison. I give you…oh, maybe to the age of six."

Benjy, Josh's youngest, piped up behind them, "Why did Uncle Chance call her Dannychrist? Her name's Nick."

Nick spread her arms wide, bouncing up and down on her tiptoes. Chance held up his arms. "Come on, cupcake," he said, and laughed. "Jump!"

She did.

He deftly snagged her in midair, and hugged the precious little body to his chest. Barrie burst into tears of relief. Then Zane was there, taking his daughter in his arms, pressing his lips to her round little head, and Barrie rushed over to be enveloped in his embrace, too.

Caroline looked at Joe. "I forgive you for not having any female sperm," she announced, and Joe laughed.

Josh was frowning sternly at Sam. "How did the ladder get there?" he demanded.

Sam looked at his feet.

Mike and Joe began to frown at their boys.

"Whose bright idea was it to play on top of the house?" Mike asked of the seven boys who hadn't been inside, and thus absolved of blame.

Seven boys scuffed their shoes on the ground, unable to look up at the three fathers confronting them.

Josh took down the ladder, which was supposed to be in the barn. He pointed to the structure in question. "March," he said sternly, and two boys began their reluctant walk to the barn—and their retribution. Benjy clung to Loren's leg, blinking at his two older brothers.

Mike pointed to the barn. His two boys went.

Joe raised an eyebrow at his three youngest. They went.

The three tall, broad-shouldered brothers followed their sons to the barn.

Nick patted Barrie's face. "Mommy cwy?" she asked, and her lower lip quivered as she looked at Zane. "Fix, Daddy."

"I'll fix, all right," he muttered. "I'll fix some glue to your little butt and stick you on a chair."

Barrie giggled through her tears. "Everyone wished for a girl," she said, hiccuping as she laughed and cried at the same time. "Well, we got our wish!"

Wolf reached out and plucked his only granddaughter from his son's brawny arms. She beamed at him, and he said ruefully, "With luck, it'll be thirty years before there's another one. Unless..." His dark eyes narrowed as he looked at Chance.

"No way," Chance said firmly. "You can turn that look on Maris. I'm not getting married. I'm not reproducing. They're starting to come by the bunches now, so it's time to call a halt. I'm not getting into this daddy business.''

Mary gave him her sweet smile. ''We'll see,'' she said.

Escape into

Just a few pages into any Silhouette® novel and you'll find yourself escaping into a world of desire and intrigue, sensation and passion.

Silhouette